Curio's Carnival

(The Curio Chronicles)

Robin John Morgan

First published (Paperback) in the UK in 2024 by Violet Circle Publishing.

Manchester, England, UK.

Print ISBN: 978-1-910299-46-3
Digital ISBN: 978-1-910299-47-0

Text Copyright © Robin John Morgan 2020.

Cover Illustration 'A Curious Carnival' © Rin Zara Morgan 2024.
Cover background, digital images, and design. © Rin Zara Morgan 2024

British Library Cataloguing in Publication Data.
A catalogue record for this book is available from the British Library.

All paper used in the production of this book are sourced only from wood grown in sustainable forests.

www.violetcirclepublishing.co.uk

Also by Robin John Morgan.

Heirs to the Kingdom.

Book One, The Bowman of Loxley.
Book Two, The Lost Sword of Carnac.
Book Three, The Darkness of Dunnottar.
Book Four, Queen of the Violet Isle.
Book Five, Crystals of the Mirrored Waters.
Book Six, Last Arrow of the Woodland Realm.
Book Seven, Bridge Of Sequana.
Book Eight, The Circle of Darkness.

The Curio Chronicles.

Part One, Abigail's Summer.
Part Two, Curio's Summer.
Part Three, Curio's Christmas.
Part Four, Abigail's Wedding
Part Five, Curio' Carnival

Of The Ravens of Berengar Trilogy

Rise of the Raven.
The Countess of Darkness
Violet Stone

Other works.

Han's Cottage

The most powerful feeling in the world, is acceptance.
Be you, and you will find a tribe that accepts you.

You are not alone.

It was strange, we have fought so hard against name calling, bullying, and intimidation, even sexual discrimination and homophobia. We have faced so much, and gone through the fires several times, and how times have changed. There have been so many bumps in the road for us, and it has been tough at times to overcome them.

I will never forget that day, at the bottom of Manor Road, as I buried my face in Birch's shoulder and wept out of fear, because I was so afraid to face my mum, and the village. Those years were rough, they almost broke me, I almost did something so stupid, that I cannot believe it now.

(Abigail Jennifer Watson)

Chapter 1

Normality Almost?

Oh, two weeks of sun, love, and just relaxing with my wild and wonderful girlfriend... oops!!! Nope, scratch that, I mean my WIFE, oh my God, I am still not use to it. Although, I am so happy, I won't deny, I am going to miss the hot sun and sand, as back to dear old Blighty we come, and there is drizzle and dark skies... Although, it is good to be home.

Birch slept most of the flight back, and I sat back, put on some Avril, and just relived all the memories of the last few weeks of my life. We had a private dwelling all to ourselves, with two staff who appeared daily to care for the place. We also had a car in the garage we could use, and I have had candle lit dinners in quiet restaurants, long walks on the beach, and oh boy have we talked? I think it is the one thing I will remember the most, the long close intimate conversations.

We get time at home together, but it was nothing like this, in many ways it was like being at Sunny Bank, only hotter with blue seas, and white beaches, and palm trees, lots and lots of palm trees. I have never been anywhere quite like it. We sat out most nights with a glass of wine, and just watched the sky turn red, in what can only be described, as the most amazing sunsets I have ever seen. I have ten memory cards absolutely filled with photos and video, and yes, we even have a few really sexy and naughty ones.

We spent a lot of time in bed, just lounging around, talking, making love, or sleeping, we hardly used the rest of the house, apart from the pool. When it got too hot, and boy did it get hot, we dived in and chilled out in the warm water. I feel so relaxed and chilled out, it is unbelievable, although, I wish I had worn thicker clothing to return to the UK in, it feels freezing here compared to our villa, and my jumper is in my case.

We landed, disembarked, and headed for our luggage, it felt bitter sweet for me, because although it was nice to be home, I will have to go back to sharing Birch with everyone else. I feel a little sad about that, because if the truth be told, I could have spent the rest of my life in that villa alone with her, I feel so amazingly happy. Birch grabbed my arm, and leaned in close.

"Sweetie we are home... We have pressies at home."

She gave an excited chuckle, I had to smile, and she was right. We had left our wedding towards the end, and flown out to the sea and sun of the Bahamas, and so at home, we had all our wedding gifts still to open.

We grabbed our cases, and walked up to the gates happy and giggling, when a man in a uniform loomed up in front of us. I stopped with a slight shock, and looked at him, he looked really stern. His face was completely devoid of emotion, and he was tall, I mean, massive. I felt instantly intimidated, his voice was crisp and precise.

"Mrs, and Mrs Dixon, would you please come with me?"

He pointed to a room, I swallowed hard, and looked at Birch, her smile had gone, she looked at the Customs Official.

"Is there a problem?" He stared blankly at her.

"Just come this way please." Feeling utterly intimidated, we turned and followed.

It is at times like this when I panic like mad, I mean, I have not done anything wrong, but they look at you with that hard stare, and for no reason at all, I feel guilty, I know, it's insane. Customs officials have a sort of head teacher malice about them, I am sure they are very nice people really, but I find them pretty bloody scary, and even though I am completely sure that I am innocent, I still feel terrified, and my heart starts to race.

I felt a cold shiver run down my back, as we turned and followed him, as the scariest thought ever slid into my mind, and I really regretted watching all those airport shows now. I looked at Birch as we followed the officer, and I lowered my voice, to almost a whisper, she appeared completely unaffected, and walked with a smile.

"Birch, please tell me you are not carrying anything someone gave you?" She frowned at me, and gave me an odd sort of look.

"No... Why would I do that?"

I know her, as smart as she is, at times she is too soft for her own good. If you want proof, tell her there is a puppy trapped somewhere, and she will sob the house down.

"Baby, I know how you love to help people, no one came up to you in the airport, and asked for help did they?" She shook her head.

"Sweetie relax, he probably just wants to frisk us, so shove your bum out, and let him have a good feel." I stared at her as we headed towards a door, and panicked.

"WHAT!?" She gave me a sweet smile.

"You are famous, and I love your cute round little bum, I am sure he does too."

I could not believe her, why was she so bloody calm, I was panicking, shouldn't she be wondering, why were we being detained? He opened a door.

"In here please."

I felt my heart beating inside my chest, as we approached the door, Birch smiled at him, my legs were shaking, as a million possibilities went through my head. We walked into the room; it was much bigger than I thought. He did not come in, he just closed the door behind us, and I felt my heart pounding in my ears, my hands trembled as I let go of my pull along case, and put my laptop bag down, as I looked around.

The room was almost empty, it had a table, three chairs and a wall filled with posters about illegal contraband. I knew she did not have the knife, knowing we were alone, I turned to Birch as she looked round, and started to read the posters.

"Birch, what the hell do they want, we have not done anything wrong, why are we here... Please Baby, please tell me that you have nothing on you that you bought in those weird open market shops?" Birch shook her head.

"Sweetie, I told you, we have nothing." I felt like I was going to suffocate.

"Birch, I have heard all sorts of horror stories about this, you know they might want to do a body cavity search?" Birch, snapped her head round.

"What!?" Finally, I had her attention, I could tell by her

forehead lines she was slightly freaked out.

"A lot of famous people have had a rectal examination, for no other reason than they are famous, they get off on it and take pictures." She shuddered.

"Sweetie, please stop, you are unsettling me, I don't want man fingers there."

I swallowed hard, as I felt my tiny little rose bud tighten inside my jeans. I wiped my head on my sleeve, it felt really hot in here, why the hell do I say this shit, now I am ten times more freaked out?

The door opened, and I jumped out of my skin, Birch jumped more as a reaction to me. A tall stern looking man with greying hair, in an officer uniform walked in, and looked right at me. His eyes were piercing, and I felt terror surge through me, I was right, this was my celebrity search, my bum hole instantly tightened more.

"Mrs Dixon... Watson?"

I was freaking the hell out, what did he want me for, I was too small and pretty to be violated by his large fat finger? I looked at his hands, Jesus, they were massive, I swallowed really hard as my legs trembled, and squeaked out a dry and somewhat feeble.

"Yes... That is me."

Crap, I sound like Micky Mouse, Birch put her head down and smirked, the twisted bitch was relieved, she would probably ask to watch, and film it as I was bent over the table? He smiled at me.

"Would you sign this for me please? I have been trying to get to all your signings, and the lines are so long by the time I get in, it is over. My daughter would die for a signed copy of your book, for her birthday next week." I momentarily felt slightly wrong footed.

"Huh?" Birch sniggered.

He pulled a new copy of Sanctuary Arch out of his back pocket, and handed me a pen. The sudden realisation of what he was asking bamboozled me, it took a few seconds for my panic to die.

"You do not want to search me?"

He smiled, and his whole facial features changed, he looked quite jolly, as he suddenly realised what I was thinking, and gave a happy chuckle.

"No, not at all, I have been promising her I would get a signed copy. I am so sorry; did you think I was going to…"

He gave a mighty roar of a laugh, as I relaxed and breathed out in relief, although, my bum hole was still really tight, and not slackening anytime soon. I took the book as Birch gripped my arm and snuggled in.

"Sweetie, your cute little hole is safe."

I looked at her bright green dancing eyes, I am actually sure she would have loved to watch, I looked back to the officer.

"What is your daughter's name?" He swelled up with pride, it was actually nice to see.

"She is called Hazel."

I smiled as I wrote happy birthday in her book, and then signed it, I looked at him, and knowing my little butt hole was safe, I thought I would show my gratitude.

"If you have a phone, could you call her, and put her on speaker?"

He looked really excited, and took his phone out, and dialled, Birch gave a giggle, as she hugged my arm.

"That is sweet Deads." The phone rang, and it was picked up.

"Dad I am a little busy, what do you want, I with Kirsten and the girls?" I leaned over, and spoke into the phone.

"Hi Hazel… This is Abigail Jennifer Watson, and I am here with your dad at the airport, and just wanted to say, Happy Birthday for next week." The phone was quiet, Birch giggled.

"Hazel Sweetie, I am Doctor Jemima Dixon…SURPRISE!!" The officer giggled.

"Are you still there darling?" Her voice was really quiet.

"Dad it's her… Dad it is really her, isn't it?" I gave a giggle.

"Hazel your dad has you on speaker phone and yes, it is me, I just flew back into the UK, I am sure when I walk out of this airport the press will prove that tomorrow, by filling tomorrow's papers. Have a really happy birthday, and thank you for reading my books." I could hear faint giggles; I think she also had me on speaker phone, so her friends could hear.

"Miss Watson, I am so happy, I am crying and my friends are laughing, I love your books, I really do, I think you are wonderful." Birch gave my arm a squeeze.

"Thank you, Hazel, I love all my readers too, thank you so

much." The officer lifted his phone, and took it off speaker.

"See, I told you I would see her today. I have to go now because I have work, but I will tell you all about it later." He gave a lovely smile.

There are days when being well known is wonderful, and today was one of them. Greatly relieved and happy, the officer who was called Mike thanked me, and I posed for some pictures with him, to show his daughter. Finally feeling greatly relieved, and unviolated, we headed out towards the arrival gate, and in the direction of home.

Birch squealed as we saw the line of gnome looking figures, that looked like they were off to a gay pride for little people, all holding signs with, 'lesbo wives, nymphomaniac's, slut wives, sex addicts, and dirty bitches on them.

Oh God it was nice to be home, although the last two weeks of my life had been gloriously wonderful, but it was back to reality, and normality, with a bang.

"Abigail… Abigail.. Abigail how was the honeymoon?" Yep, the press were also here to meet us?

The cameras flashed, and I lowered my head and looked at the floor, I had not got my glasses on. With a squeal, Chloe and Deb's ducked under the barrier and came running at us, I smiled as Deb's bright happy face launched herself round my neck.

"I missed you; did you have an amazing time?"

Chloe ran up and dragged us both into a tight hug, and it felt so nice, it was good to be home, and back with these very special people. Anthony and Edwina joined in the hugs with Izzy, and together they all surrounded us, and blocked out the cameras of the press, God, I love these guys so much.

Leaving the airport was loud and noisy and filled with excitement, and the thing about that was, they were louder than the reporters, who raced down in front of us trying to get shots. I just smiled with Birch hugging my arm, and feeling the warmth of my Curio family.

It felt so strange to be home, and it was even stranger to find that whilst we were away, Edwina and Chloe moved all of Birch's things into my room, they even moved her forever tree onto my balcony. Her clothes were in a new even bigger wardrobe, and her room was empty. It felt surreal and unsettling, even the door had both our little door pictures together on it.

Birch had arranged it all before leaving, although, I was not completely unhappy about it at first. I sat on my bed, and gave a long sigh as Birch took my hand.

"Sweetie, everywhere we go, we are together, except here, I want us to be together here, just us in one room, sharing every aspect of our life." I nodded.

"I do too, but I liked the idea of having two rooms, and two beds." She smiled and kissed the side of my cheek.

"I am going to ask Deb's to move into my room, you two are really close, and she was also a huge part of our life in the guest house, so it will still be familiar, but different at the same time." I relaxed, it made sense, and it was better than an empty room.

"I think walking through and seeing it empty was just so shocking, I was not ready to see that. I guess, I just always thought we would have two rooms." She smiled.

"If it is bothering you that much, I will move everything back Sweetie?" I shook my head.

"No... I want this, I really do Birch, it was just a shock, I had not expected it so soon. I actually love the idea, we have a really cool wardrobe with all our clothes combined, I don't have to secretly nick your stuff anymore." She giggled and leaned in and kissed my cheek.

"I love you Deads." I pulled her close.

"Yeah, I love you too, welcome home Mrs Dixon." She giggled, and raised her eyebrows.

"You know Sweetie, we are married, and yet we have not had wifey sex in this house, since?" I looked at her bright dancing eyes.

"I do believe you may be right, whatever can we do to remedy that?" She gave that wonderful happy giggle, pushed me back on the bed.

"I have been thinking about that Mrs Dixon."

Edwina looked up at the ceiling as she peeled the potatoes and smiled.

"It is nice to have everything back to normal again, I have really missed those two." Chloe smiled, and sipped her coffee.

"I feel happier, I missed Abby each morning, I missed our chats." Edwina smiled.

"You have grown really close to Abby, you know, I worry a lot less about you these days, because I know you have her, and Deb's. It is so weird Chloe to think that you all once saw each other as enemies. I watched you during the wedding, as she stood there with Birch, and you were so there for her, so happy for her, I was really proud of you." Chloe frowned and put down her cup.

"Why?" Edwina put down the potato and picked up another unpeeled one.

"Chloe, I remember Stephanie Johnson, and Vanessa Slater, and how they influenced you. I hated them you know? They were fake shallow bitches that used you for their own purposes. I hated the way you plastered makeup all over yourself, and had those ridiculous eyebrows, and those stupid false nails just to fit in with them. The clothes you bought cost a fortune, and to be honest, they made you look cheap." Chloe gave a gasp.

"Wow, don't hold back much Weena." Edwina gave a chuckle.

"I am really proud of you Chloe, I admire you more now than I ever have, I am thrilled you are my little sister." Chloe stared at her and swallowed hard, as she watched her, Edwina smiled.

"I watched you walk on stage at the Curio event, and you were just you. Not what your friends thought you should be, you were the girl I knew so well. No posh nails, no painted on eyebrows and layers of foundation, and you were stood there in paint splattered dungarees and a bikini top, and the thing I loved most, was you were simply being you. God, I was so proud to have you as my sister." Chloe teared up, and stared at her.

"Don't... You are getting me going Weena." She put down the peeler, and wiped her hands.

"I mean every word of it Chloe, I really do. Abby and Birch have been great for you, they never told you how to be, they just loved you so you would be just you. I can never repay them for what they have done, and I will always be grateful to them. You know, when Luke proposed, that was not the happiest day of my life?" Chloe wiped her eyes and looked shocked.

"It wasn't?" She came around the island and sat at her side, and took Chloe by the hand, and her voice was soft and caring.

"No... It should have been, but honestly it was not. The happiest day of my life was watching Abby and Birch walk you into that empty studio, with a new easel stood in it, and watching as they told you it was yours. I bawled my brains out, knowing you were out of that shit hole, and soon to leave that dead end job, and you finally had the chance to be you, a painter, an artist of great talent. I will always remember feeling so relieved and grateful to them, because I could not save you, but they could, and they did. I love you Chloe, I always will, you are my special little sister."

Chloe gave a huge sniffle and wiped her eyes again.

"Fuck Weena, what brought all this on, you are really intense?" She leaned forward and kissed Chloe on the cheek.

"I just felt it was time to tell you, I wanted you to know. You know, they are back now, and you have watched a lot of movies in the last two weeks. Abby and Birch are here, you can paint again." Chloe smiled.

"You spotted that then?" Edwina got up.

"Chloe, you feed off their creative energy, we all do, even me, that is why we all live here, go on, go paint."

I lay back gasping looking at the ceiling, Birch gave a giggle and leaned on my shoulder, her cheeks were red as she panted a little.

"So does it feel like home yet, my little beastie?" My eyes moved to look at her, I was too knackered to move. I gave a breathless gasp.

"Yeah... Now it does." I chuckled, she snuggled in to me, and gave a happy sigh.

"I love this, I have missed it." I gave a laugh.

"Birch, we just spent two weeks in the Bahamas, screwing each other's brains out, how could you miss it?" She breathed out a long contented breath.

"I mean this Sweetie, this bed, this room, the scents of us in it, and all our stuff. This is my true comfy place; I have always preferred your bed to mine." I looked up at the wall as it reached up from the head board.

While we were away on our honeymoon, Chloe had hung Birch's pictures in my room. I have always had Hatty's picture above my bed, and now on either side we had the pictures done by Chloe, one of us kissing at Deb's wedding, and the one she did of me back when I was only nineteen. It looked good, and we both loved the paintings so much, I glanced at Birch, her eyes were closed, and she was breathing softly.

"Christ, you are worse than a bloke, just seconds after sex, and you are out cold?"

I did not blame her, we were jet lagged, and on a different time zone still, and we had pretty much worn ourselves out for two weeks having endless sex. I looked around the room, and although it was different, I kind of liked it. Before we were married, I had moved my desk closer to the window, so I could see my arch, Edwina had pushed the sofa up, and in the space, slid in Birch's little desk.

I smiled, I actually loved the idea of that, I could work with her as she worked in a room that was not the library, and it felt a little bit like our dorm from Uni. I have had some really happy times sat in the dorm with her working beside me, and watching her write her papers. I lay back and drifted, my head filled with happy memories, and as I listened to Birch breathe, I felt that sense of calmness I always have around her, and suddenly I was really tired.

While we lay sleeping, Wotton was wide awake and busy, as the afternoon rolled onwards, Deb's who had taken the morning off to help collect us from the airport, was back in the shop with Denise. Ellen had baby Jenny over at the gallery, to give her a break, as Deb's had been feeling tired, and Jimmy was in the studio with the band. Although, in between sessions, and especially at night, Jimmy had been really involved, and was loving being a dad.

The bell to the shop, which was a new edition, pinged, and Denise looked up from the till, to Sophia, dolled up to the eyeballs wearing designer clothing, and strutting like she owned the place. She walked up to the till, flicked back her bleached blonde hair, and looked round the book shop.

"Is Deborah here, I need to talk to her, yar?"

Denise leaned out from the till to locate Deb's. She was unpacking the latest copies of Ann Packers new erotic sex novel, and Denise called.

"Deb's, you are wanted."

Deb's looked up, and noticed Sophia, she got up and walked to the front of the shop, she smiled at Sophia, even though she could not really stand her.

"Hi Sophia, I am surprised to see you here, what can I do for you?"

Sophia looked her up and down, taking note of her clothes, which were her pregnancy dungarees, and a tight fitting long sleeve top, she smirked.

"I am running for the Vice Chair, and Primula and myself are asking businesses to support our traditional community campaign, yar?" Deb's nodded.

"Sophia, you are aware that I am running for the position of officer, and backing Abby, and Jemi, but if you are trying to do something to help the village, I am listening?"

Deb's noted the scowling rat face of Prim outside the window, and was not surprised, she did not have the guts to come in to the shop. Sophia gave a sigh.

"Yeah, about that... We want you to know, we are supporting you... Well, we are if they lose, look yar, we want to stop Andrew from expanding his car park, and are trying to build a children's play space yar!" She looked at Denise.

"When Primula wins, he won't need it will he?" Deb's shrugged.

"The playground has been suggested a lot in the past, but it always failed because of the cost, and the fact it is right on a dangerous corner." Deb's gave a sigh.

"You know Sophia, it is not a cheap project, and it is expensive to build." She nodded.

"I know yar... But Primula is paying, well Nigel is, so it is free for the village, and we will be putting in traffic lights, and one of them stripy road things, yar?" She gave another long sigh.

"So will you support us and put a flyer up, in the window, yar?"

Sophia pulled a flyer out of her bag, and handed it her. Deb's looked down at it, with a huge picture of Prim on it, she looked up at Sophia, who was looking around the shop.

"Can I read it, and then decide, would that be alright?" She shrugged.

"Yar... We are funding a lot of new stuff, parking meters and pay and display at the station, to make the village quieter and safer, so I will keep you up to speed, yar?" Deb's nodded, Sophia turned and strutted her way out of the shop, she turned at the door, as Deb's watched, and she looked back.

"Do people actually buy these, yar?" Deb's frowned, Denise smiled.

"Yar, they do." Deb's smirked, Sophia looked surprised.

"Why... There is no time, all I read is Insta comments." Deb's gave a nod.

"It shows." Sophia smiled, and opened the door, Denise gave a gasp.

"Please tell me she did not think that was a compliment?" Deb's gave a snigger.

"Now let's not use long words Denise, yar!?"

They both giggled. Debs looked at the flyer, and it bothered her a lot. It looked like Prim was going too far, parking meters were the kiss of death to tourists, and Wotton needed them. She looked at the long list, and it was pretty clear who was behind this, and surprisingly enough, it was not Marjorie. She folded it up and put it in her pocket.

Felicity sat with Hatty in the back of the Tea Rooms. Hatty gave a sigh as she put down the leaflet.

"This has Parkinson's grubby little finger prints all over it, that shit has wanted meters and pay and display for years, and as for painting the shop fronts, and whatever this Dursley Woods Project is, all this costs money, money the council has always refused to pay out." Felicity sat back in her seat and thought about it.

"You know Hatty, the thing that I do not understand, is Madge has always been against parking meters, and pay and display. It was one of the things we always fought side by side on in complete agreement, parking fees kill tourists. The only reason we have parking permits is because Parkinson got it through Oxendale Council, we both opposed that and lost, as he slipped it through." Hatty lifted her cup.

"The front of the shops painted, and the children's play space are a bribe, Primula must be worried, because it looks like she is prepared to spend Nigel's money to buy votes, I cannot deny, it is clever Flick." She frowned.

"Why is it clever, I am not sure I understand?" Hatty gave a grin.

"Look even you missed it... If you keep everyone happy with a paint job, and make a huge deal about a kid's play park, no one will notice when you revoke the old licencing law, and remove Andrew's need for extra space. The only reason he wants to take it over is because his extended hours have led to an overspill of vehicles. I mean, the car park is already too small because he has to allow deliveries access to the back of the shops. If Prim kills that space and revokes the old law, everyone will lose out. She is buying them off with paint." It made perfect sense, and Felicity, understood her plan.

"Abby will need to know about this, and we will need to find out what this Dursley Woods Project is all about, because if Parkinson really is behind Primula, then you can pretty much be sure, there is a land deal through Oxendale Council involved." Hatty gave a nod.

"Leave that to me, if there is a plan on the table, I will find out about it. I know someone who will definitely know about it." Felicity gave her a shrewd look.

"You do... Oh, pray, do tell?" Hatty smiled.

"It is not for your ears Flick, trust me on that." She gave a little smile, and Felicity's eyes opened wide.

"Oh my god, are you actually blushing?" Hatty giggled, and stood up.

"Come on you have to get back to the gallery, Deb's little shit bucket will be bawling its brains out, and need to go back to its mum for a feed." She turned, and Felicity chuckled as she followed her out of the placc.

Chloe smiled as she sat on the bed, and shook me.

"Abby... Abby, come on, you need to eat." I opened my eyes and blinked, and looked at her smiling at me.

"Abby... Edwina has worked really hard making you a welcome home meal, I know you both are tired, but we sort of want to see you guys back at the table with us, we have all missed it." I yawned and looked down.

"Eww, I really wish she would not do that?"

Birch had drooled all over my boob, Chloe sniggered, and reached for a tissue, and handed it to me, I started to wipe as she stood up.

"You know all your things are still in the office, if you want, I will give you a lift after we have eaten, you guys got shit loads of presents." Birch sat up straight with her eyes closed.

"I love presents." She turned to me as I wiped my boob dry and opened her eyes.

"Hi Sweetie." She looked at my boob, and wrinkled her nose.

"Yuk! Where are our presents, I love presents?" I nodded and shook my head.

"Food first, and make sure you chew it properly, no rushing just because you are excited, it makes you fart way too much." She turned and saw Chloe, and pointed upwards.

"Chloe Sweetie, see, we hung your pictures." Chloe stood back and looked at them, and gave a wide smile.

"They look really cool there, thanks guys."

I smiled and turned to look up, yeah, they did look good, I think I am really starting to like this room more, and actually, it is nice being back home.

Chapter 2

Future Plans.

The greatest thing about Sundays... Bed!

It was one in the afternoon when I sat up, I was tired, jet lag really gets to me, Birch was sat at her desk, working on her laptop, I rubbed my eyes.

"Hey... What are you doing?"

She turned in her chair, and smiled, her eyes sparkled like emeralds.

"Hi Sweetie... I was reading the last chapter again, I really got into Karen, she is a great character. It is such a shame this is the last book in the series. I loved the way she helped save Willis, and then helped free Gabrielle, and reunite them. I will not lie; I wept a little. But I am still a little sad it is the end, and why did Karen change her name and leave? Oh God Deads, when she walked off into the darkness, and renamed herself Krisandra, I almost bawled my brains out, it was a really great ending. I am just sad it is over; I have been reading it since Uni."

I loved her excitement, I slid my legs out of bed, I felt a lot more alive than I did yesterday.

"Do you want a spoiler?" She looked really excited, and started to get giddy, I regretted it the moment it left my lips.

"Oh, Deads, tell me, tell me, I want to know?" She looked like a kid, I walked over to her, and leaned down and kissed her on the lips.

"I need coffee." She pulled her lip, as I walked towards the door.

"That is not a spoiler, everyone knows that." I giggled, as I grabbed the door handle.

"I am writing a whole new series about Krisandra, it is going to be called, the Cursed Books of Krisandra."

I walked through the door, and down the hall towards the stairs, I smiled as I heard her squeal with happiness, and as I headed down the stairs. Birch came flying out of the room and ran after me.

"Deads wait, you cannot just say that and leave, I need to know more. Sweetie wait, tell me, tell me." I laughed as I walked into the kitchen, Birch came hammering down the stairs, Edwina smiled as she put down a cup of fresh coffee.

"It is nice to have us all back to normal." Birch came gasping into the kitchen, her eyes were wide and bright green.

"I need more, Sweetie that is not enough, please, just a bit more." I sipped my coffee and smiled.

"Birch I am ten chapters in, even I do not know the whole story yet." She slid on the stool at the side of me and hugged my arm.

"Please Sweetie, just a little bit more?" I chuckled.

"Birch it will spoil the story if I tell you it all now." She giggled, and hugged me harder.

"Just a bit more, please, where do the cursed books come from?" Chloe popped her head around the studio door, and stared at us, I turned and looked at Birch.

"How the hell did you pass a doctorate on clinical psychology? Look at you, honestly you are like a crazy person." Edwina sat down with her cup.

"And that is how they pass, because that is how they understand it all, they are all equally as bonkers as their patient's." Birch stared at me with big eyes. I gave a sigh.

"Okay... Karen's father is the priest, who wants to rid the world of vampires, and he dedicated his life to the study of it, and Karen has spent twenty six years living with him. So, she too knows all about his research, which is how she got the resurrection sword for Willis, yes?" She nodded rapidly.

"Well, there are seven books, which when brought together, can be used to enhance, or destroy the vampire race. Well, considering her father is now dead, her uncle is the only other person who also knows about the books, so that is why she changes her name to Krisandra, as he is already seeking them. This series will be her race in Cognito, to find them before he does, and save all the vampires... Is that enough to keep you happy until I have actually written them?" She smiled and kissed my cheek.

"I am excited, I cannot wait to read them, I really like Karen, I think she is your best ever character." Edwina frowned.

"Wow Birch, girl crush much or what?" I giggled.

"I am going to read the last chapter again." Birch got up and hurtled off back upstairs, I smiled at Edwina.

"Maybe I should have told her they are all marked in a circle of white. There is one in that chapter, she stands in it at the very end of the book?" Edwina chuckled.

"You are so mean." Chloe leaned back around the door.

"What the fuck is wrong with you Abby?" I turned to look at her.

"What?" Chloe looked freaked.

"Cursed books in white circles, are you deliberately trying to kill off everyone?" I gave a smirk.

"To be honest Chloe, it is your obsession with the book that gave me the idea. I was thinking, one makes you cry, one makes you laugh, and one makes you kill, and the last one, you will love it, it makes you want to screw." Chloe stared at me.

"Holy shit, you will have readers killing each other, and fucking each other, and those who cannot will cry, or piss themselves laughing. I think I have it wrong, I should put a ring of salt around you when you are writing."

Edwina and me started to laugh, I lifted my cup and took another big swig, oh it was nice to be home again, as much as I absolutely loved every second of my time away with Birch, I had also missed everyone here.

The problem with being a full time writer is, if you are not writing, you are promoting, or blogging, and if you are not doing those, you are either researching and brain storming, or sleeping, it really is a twenty four, seven occupation, and you never take a break.

Fashion Voice Magazine, had done an amazing feature on our wedding. From the messages I had received from Anita, they were really happy, so I was now free to post pictures. My job for today was to add to the blog, and over the honeymoon, I had done a little writing, and pretty much had most of the content ready.

Birch and I had picked out some pictures, which were more private and special to us, and did not clash with the magazine, and we also had some from the honeymoon, and I put together a special feature, and uploaded it to my website, all the pictures were tagged and watermarked, to keep the papers from using them without consent.

By far one of the most wonderful things about my life are my readers. My site had hundreds of comments, and messages, all from readers of my books, wishing both Birch and myself congratulations on our wedding. It was just mind blowing to get pictures sent of us outside as we left for the airport, with the most lovely little messages attached.

The love I have been shown is simply the best part of my writing life, and there have been days when I was down and struggling with the suffocating press, and yet within minutes of arriving at an event, and meeting fans, I was lifted up, and felt like a million dollars, there simply is nothing like it.

I slid back in my chair and looked at Birch, she was sat smiling and reading the last chapter for yet another time, I was thrilled she loved it so much.

"Birch, you know we have to deal with all the presents?" And those were the magic words, she sat up straight in her chair.

"I love presents."

I chuckled at her, she did indeed. The next hour was spent emptying Edwina's office, which she was overjoyed about, and we moved them all into Birch's empty room. I sat cross legged on the floor, set my camera on its tripod, and sat back and watched, as Birch shredded the gift wrap, with wild excited abandon, and opened everything we had got. It was actually great fun, and I just sat laughing.

Her eyes were huge, and she had crazy infectious giggles, as she would rip something open, and then her eyes just danced as the gift was revealed. We got all sorts of things, and the strange thing was, because we already had a house, very few gifts were house related, although we did get a toaster. We got black and white bathrobes with our names on, matching jewellery, sexy underwear, these people had no idea we were commando 99% of the time. Bev, true to her word, bought us a strap on, and Deb's bought us both gold pens, and mine had little bats engraved on it.

We had enough bath accessories and wine glasses to supply the nation, but to be honest, no one can ever have enough bath products, and the good thing was that Bradley had sent a crew to

Sunny Bank to do some improvements, and put in a bigger bath, so we could take half of what we got there.

I sat there thinking of bathing, and looked at Birch as she sat giddy, surrounded by gift wrap, she was opening and reading some of the cards we had not got around to, and smiling.

"Birch, do we have to share our bathroom?" She looked up at me.

"What Sweetie... Look isn't this a beautiful card, I am going to save everyone?"

"Birch, this is really important to me, please listen?" She turned and looked at me, she put the card down.

"Sorry Sweetie, what is wrong, tell me?" She sat cross legged, and looked at me, her eyes were bright and sparkling, I looked right at her.

"I was saying, if we have to let someone else use this room, can we block the door off, because that bathroom is a special place to me. I know it sounds mad, and pathetic, but it has always been a sacred space where we talk in the bath privately. Am I being selfish by not wanting to share it?" Birch smiled, and turned her head to one side.

"Oh Sweetie, does that really bother you so much?" I looked down at the paper covered carpet.

"Birch, I have told you more times than I can count, how much I love you curled in that tub more than anywhere else. You told me about May in there, and the day you proposed we sat in that bath having wine and being so wonderfully happy. I find it hard to explain, but I just do not want to share it with others, even Deb's who I love to bits, I get it, I sound like a little princess..."

"Don't call yourself that... You are not!" I looked up at her, she looked angry. I gave a sigh.

"It's alright, just forget I said anything... Read your cards, I need a drink."

I got up off the floor and headed to my room for my mug, as I walked past her, she stood up and grabbed my wrist.

"Deads, Sweetie, wait... Please Sweetie, I am sorry, I just hate you calling yourself that." I turned and looked at her, she looked upset.

"She calls you that and I hate it. Sweetie, if this is that important to you, it is not a problem, I can have Bradley fit a new bath in this room in the alcove, honestly, I love the idea. I want you to be happy, and if you do not want to share with anyone but me, I totally get it, and we will do it." I turned back to her.

"Are you sure... I am sorry, but it is a special place for me, I love how when we jump in the bath together, people leave us alone, and it is just me and you, and it feels so very special, and precious." She smiled, and pulled me to her.

"Sweetie, you are right, it is special, and I agree with you, I have such happy memories of us together bathing, from your mum's and here. I will get hold of Bradley in the morning and talk to him, and we will fit another suite in here for guests." I felt a huge sense of relief, and hugged her hard.

"Thanks... I know it sounds silly, but it really matters to me." She slid out of my arms.

"I tell you what..., Go grab a bottle of wine, we have bath products, and new glasses, and sexy bathrobes, let's try them out. I will run the bath." I smiled, and gave a nod.

"Yeah, I would love that, I really would, my first bath with my wife in this house." She gave a giggle.

"My Mrs Sweetie in my bath, oh that sounds so nice, and I am excited." I leaned in and kissed her softly.

"Thanks Baby... I am really happy."

Thirty minutes later, I lay in a hot bath up to my neck, with my eyes closed, as I leaned against Birch, and I relaxed happily in her arms. I gave a long happy sigh.

"This is nice, life will be back to normal tomorrow, and all that time we have had alone will end, I think I am going to feel quite lonely tomorrow without you." She pulled her arms tighter round my waist.

"Life goes on, but this time the bond is stronger, the love is far more, and we will take every second we can, to keep the precious memories building." I leaned back my head.

"Back to village life, I wonder what I have coming next?" She gave a chuckle.

"Well Sweetie, you need to decide what you are going to do for the presentation at the end of the month, and then you need to campaign to fight Prim." I gave a sigh, she smirked.

"Deads, if she is trying to buy off the voters, we will need to come up with something far better to show all the skills we have." I turned around and looked at her.

"How do you mean, something far better, Birch, I have no intention of buying votes?" She smiled.

"Sweetie, I know that, I did a lot of thinking on the beach, especially about the D&D thing, I think you have a great idea, and a first great project, but I am wondering if there is a way to maximise on the idea."

Dixon and Dixon came from making the advertising posters for the village, which got me thinking, because I have done book fairs and conventions. None of those were Dixon Group events, but because Katie was in charge of that aspect of the Dixon Group she was always involved. Anita is my publicist, and is currently looking at ways to get me extra exposure, so technically, she can also promote me outside of the Group. When I thought about it, her job is to get the exposure that gets sales.

After the Katie fiasco, I wanted to stay as far away from her as possible, and it was whilst looking at Chloe's sketches I had an idea, and talked to Anita about doing something special for Chloe. When I talked to Birch before we got married, she loved the idea, and offered to help me, and D&D Events was born as a concept, which would be a private venture for Birch and myself to organise things for others.

I have borrowed all Chloe sketches, which with the help of Edwina, have been digitally scanned, and currently, although she has no idea, I am having a lot of frames made for her sketches. One way or the other, she is going to get the exposure she needs, and Birch and myself will make sure of it. I stood up in the bath, and turned to face Birch, she smiled and raised her eyebrows.

"Oh Sweetie, hot, wet soapy full frontal, yes, I like it." She grinned at me, and winked.

"Birch be serious... How does the D&D thing involve the parish council?" She leaned forward and licked up my vagina, and I shuddered, she giggled.

"Yummy... Is it weird I like the taste of soapy you?" She looked up with bright green eyes, and I felt butterflies and smiled.

"Will you please be serious just for a minute?" She giggled.

"I seriously want to screw you about now, is that good enough?"

I stepped out of the bath and grabbed my new robe, with little bats on it, she pouted.

"Sweetie, it's not cold yet."

I walked into the bedroom and sat on the bed, and started to rub myself dry. I heard her get out of the bath, and she walked in, she looked disappointed.

"Sweetie, I am sorry." She gave another pout.

"I wanted us to make love in the bath." I sighed.

"I am sorry… But you just dropped half a thought on me and then went off on a perv, Birch, Prim could seriously win, she has only just started, so what else is she planning, and if she is in partnership with that MP, our life is going to get really hard?" I looked at her and softened my voice.

"Birch I am so happy, they are not as hard on me as they were, and honestly, I do not think I can go back through all that hell like I did nine years ago. So yes, if you have an idea that could help, please, don't piss about, talk to me about it." She stood wrapped in her white robe and gave a nod.

"I am sorry Sweetie, look we are going to do this thing for Chloe, so we will be creating an events business, and as I told you on the beach, we potentially have a chance to do something really good for the village. The way I see it, we should play to our strengths, and use it to our advantage."

Okay so that made some sense, the problem was I had no idea which strengths she was talking about.

"So how do we do that, actually?" She smiled.

"Deads, you are a gothic fantasy writer, and I am a sex therapist, and let's be honest Prim and her brood are always throwing God in our faces. They are always calling us whores, Satanists, and immoral and weird, so why don't we play to their expectations, and give this village exactly what they expect?" I frowned.

"What, you want to open up some sort of deviant gothic themed brothel?" She gave a loud cackle, and clapped her hands together.

"Oh Sweetie, I really want to do that now." She giggled and shook her head.

"Deads the Parish Council organise all this villages events, so whoever wins, has to prove they can do that well, and we already know we can. Be honest, we have been involved with pretty much all of it, and we organised all the Curio Event long before mum and Katie got involved, so why don't we do that?" She smiled.

"There is an opening this village has never catered to; can you think of what it is?" I wasn't sure what she meant.

"The council does a lot of seasonal events, they do Christmas, Easter, May Day, Harvest, and the Summer Fete, there really is nothing else left." Birch shook her head and smiled.

"Sweetie that is if you only follow the Church, but we have access to more, we also have witchcraft." She wiggled her eyebrows up and down and smiled, I stared at her.

"Birch are you insane, they would love to burn us at the stake?" She sat on the floor and gave a chuckle.

"Sweetie you are missing it, we have the greatest seasonal event that everyone loves, especially the kids. We could really bring pagan life out and lay it out in front of them and everyone would love it." Suddenly I understood, God, she was a genius.

"Oh Christ, yeah... You are talking about Halloween?" She smiled, and her bright eyes lit up with mischief.

"Deads, it is perfectly us.... Slutty, satanic, and crazy as hell, especially if you throw in something really big, like a circus. We could have a full scale Wotton Carnival, and it would be a D&D event, and nothing at all to do with the Parish Council. If we make it big, bold and brash, and get everyone involved, we would prove hands down we were the best there is, and no matter how much money Prim spends. A full scale village wide event literally days before the vote, well, they will not be thinking of Prim when they tick those boxes."

I got off the bed, and crawled across the carpet towards her, and she giggled.

"You are bloody brilliant; do you know that? I am so hot for you right now; I am having you there on the floor."

She gave a happy squeal, and her eyes danced with delight. I pushed her backwards and pulled opened her robe, and she giggled wildly.

"Take me my dark little beastie, take me and devour me." I came down on her stomach and started to rub my tongue around her belly button, and she squealed out in laughter, kicking her feet up and down on the floor.

"SWEETIE NO, IT TICKLES... HA, HA, HA, HA, HA, HA!"

Chloe looked up at the ceiling, and smiled.

"Those two have more sex than me." Anthony gave a smirk and rolled his eyes, sat at the island.

"Oh, Chloe darling, if there was a medal for fornicating couples, trust me, you and Percy would win it hands down. Grief girl, your perversion knows no bounds." Chloe gave a big smile and turned to Anthony.

"Aw Anthony, that is so sweet, thanks." Upstairs, Birch squealed in laughter.

Anthony and Chloe were making the meal tonight, so as we sat around the table, Birch and myself filled everyone in on what we had in mind, as we needed to brain storm more to see what was possible. Anthony put his fork down.

"It is probably just me, but why do we have to call it Wotton Carnival, after all it is not them doing it, it will be us, and we will be doing it for them? Wotton Carnival sounds just like the Parish Council organised it." Birch nodded, and looked at me.

"He has a point Deads, this must look like we did it." Chloe shrugged.

"If all of us are going to be involved, then it's a Curio event, why not call it Curio Carnival Wotton? If you think about it, that will pull people here from all over, and we can collect more donations for the centre, because to be honest looking at the renovations of the centre, it will be mid to late November, before it opens." I agreed with her.

"Yeah, and it will bring a lot of publicity for the centre if we do it right." Chloe looked at me.

"That red haired bitch is not involved is she, because if she is, I am sorry Abby, but count me out?" Birch shook her head.

"Thanks Chloe, that is sweet, and we appreciate it... No, she is nothing to do with this, this is all Deads and me, it is something we are playing with, as we want to do things outside of the Dixon Group. This will be all of us, we will bring in outside contractors if we need to." I looked at Luke.

"We want G5 in on this, and maybe the band if they are free, they are recording their album at the moment, so if they are not on tour, we can use the extra hands." He smiled.

"Guys you know us, if it involves you lot and mischief, we are on board, and to be honest, we all loved the wedding, it was something completely different for us, so yeah, count us in." Edwina smiled, and kissed his cheek.

"What about villagers, because we know there are some who can keep a secret, because not a word of the Hen night has slipped out. So, there are some we can rely on for total secrecy, especially if you want to keep this quiet until after the Fete?" Chloe chewed her veg and nodded.

"You should announce it at the Fete, it would be stupid not to, be honest, it is the biggest event of the summer, get all those visitors informed of another huge event, and they will mark it in their diaries." It was a good point, Birch agreed.

"It does make sense, we will be eight weeks away at that point, and well into the planning. Prim will be pushed to do anything at that point to compete, no matter what she does at the moment, by then, we will have the upper hand from that point on."

Anthony leaned back in his chair and lifted his glass of wine.

"This will still need council approval, and we will need Gail on board, but I am sure she won't object, her and Moon have become good friends. Peter Saxon can be trusted we are in the naturist club together; our problem will be Philip Morrison. He cannot keep anything to himself, he is going to be the weakest link, he cannot know until the Fete which could be a problem." Birch shook her head.

"Not really, this is not a village event, it is a private venture, all we need is Chair and Vice approval, Flick will back us and so will Celia, both of them will vote for us. Celia is delighted Abby is running, she texted me to tell me she had two posters up in the Tea Rooms. What we need to do is find out what we can do, plan it, and then get on with it so that when we announce it, everything else is already in play, one committee member, even with Madge behind them, cannot out vote the rest."

Chloe frowned and looked at Birch.

"I think this is a great idea, but the one thing I want to know is, how do we pay for this, guys this will cost a lot of cash to pull off?" Birch smiled, and her eyes twinkled as she looked at me.

"Cash is not a problem Chloe, D&D Events have all the funds they need, let us take care of all that, remember, this is our gift to the community. It just so happens that it should bring tourists flocking in, and they spend money, everyone will benefit from our generosity at a time when people are in a lull before Christmas. I say, if we do this right, every business in Wotton will thank us. Let's be honest here, happy business owners talk to their customers."

I smiled at her, it was a really good point, I loved how her brain worked and was ten steps ahead of all of us in her thinking. I actually felt a real surge of excitement flow up into me, if we could pull this off, it would be spectacular.

Chapter 3

Understanding Home.

Suddenly, the honeymoon is over, and I am sat at the kitchen island, sipping coffee, and not speaking, as everyone races around getting ready for work, and Chloe watches on with sleepy eyes.

Lay on a beach, or in our room in the Bahamas, life had ticked by slowly at a gentle pace, and now we were home, it was back to work. Birch had a lot of catching up to do with the Curio centre project, I was busy working with Anita on the release of my new book 'Resurrection Sword' which was the final book of the 'Hands of Death' series, and writing the new 'Cursed Books of Krisandra' series, as well as organising something very special for Chloe, and preparing my speech for the presentation at the Parish Council, which would officially launch my bid for Chair Person.

If that was not enough, we also were starting our secret event for the village, and I was actually getting very excited about it. I loved that this would be a full Curio participation project, and unlike the live event, there was no Katie, so we would all be free to just be us, and enjoy the project fully.

Birch brought in Bradley, and began plans of creating a new on suite in her old room, and suddenly, her door disappeared, and our bathroom became private. It took a week to get all the new walls and fittings done, and soon we had a second spare room once again, albeit a little smaller. Deb's did not want it, she wanted to stay in the room she was in, which she had since first moving in, and had everything she needed for little Raisin in it.

Birch began her sessions again with Nigel, in private away from the practice at my mum's, his black eyes had healed a great deal, so obviously the two weeks we had been away, had seen Prim calm down a little. Birch reported that he was a lot more talkative and calmer, I put that down to the fact that Moon had decided to stay on for a while, and had moved further up the canal, and was tied up in the canal basin below the locks.

Summer was on the horizon, and Anthony and Edwina had a lot on their plate, it is strange as things appear to go round in circles, as suddenly, our kitchen table filled with piles of paperwork, and long evenings were spent assembling packs to send out.

The best thing about it all, was all of us mucked in, and when you have the full Curio crew, plus G5 helping, the work became much less daunting and stressful. I watched Edwina many nights running, and she was really good at this stuff, and in a way, I did not understand why she had not put herself up as Chair? I think she would be amazing at it.

It was two nights to go, before the large Parish Council meeting, for the summer program, and I sat in the library relaxing at my desk and gave a sigh. Birch and Edwina were sat at their desks, with Deb's, who was visiting, and her and Chloe, were both sat on the long table eating biscuits.

"What the hell is this bloody Dursley Woods Project, I cannot find any information on it? Prim is supporting it, but I have no idea at all what it is, does anyone know why it is so secret?" Edwina sat back on her chair, and shook her head.

"I have searched everywhere to find out, and it is like it does not exist, which to be honest bothers me more than you realise, because no one on the Parish Council has a clue about it." Birch shrugged.

"I have asked around, and no one knows anything, what bothers me is Derek Sutton, and Geoff Pilkington know nothing about it at all, and they are two of the biggest landowners around here. If they do not know, there is definitely something fishy going on." I agreed, Deb's crunched on her biscuit.

"I asked my dad, and he has no idea, it bothered me that he said he had never heard of it. What I don't get, is if there is anything planned, firstly the Parish Council are normally informed, then public notices are put up, and plans are displayed at the town hall in Oxendale, and none of those have happened. My dad actually asked, if this was real or just a bluff by Prim to look good?"

The front door banged, and there were giggles as Anthony and Luke arrived home, Luke walked in looking tired, he bent down and kissed Edwina on the lips.

"Hey, how are things going, read this?" He dropped a paper on her desk, she looked at it and frowned at him.

"God, why do you read this rag?" He shook his head.

"I don't, Morty gave it me, look at page eight... I am grabbing a sandwich, and will put the kettle on." Edwina opened the paper and looked at page eight, and gave a big sigh.

"Wow, this girl really takes the cake."

She turned the paper so we all could see, there was a full page spread, and a picture of Prim, and under it was a voucher that gave a discount to all customers, up to the value of ten pounds, at selected village shops, and businesses. Edwina read down the list.

"Hardware Shop, The Dress Shop, Gift Shop, Butcher, Sweet Shop, and the Craft Shop. There is also a discount of ten pounds off an MOT at Wilks Garage, and HOLY SHIT!" She looked up.

"There is even a discount voucher for a meal at dads place." Chloe slid off the table, and walked over to take a look.

"What the fuck, why is dad kissing her ass?" Edwina shook her head.

"Free bloody money, come on you know dad, he will mark every meal up a few quid, and then get Prim to pay him with the discount money, he never turns down a chance to make cash." Chloe smiled, and took the paper out of her hand.

"Cool, I am booking a table, cutting this out, and we are all going out for a meal tonight." Edwina looked at me.

"See... Just like dad, if its discount or you can make a few extra quid, she is in." I giggled with Birch; Chloe looked scandalised.

"I am buying you a free meal, you rancid bitch, you should be grateful." Edwina sniggered.

"Really, Chloe we are their daughters, we get free meals." She smirked.

"Okay, Luke gets a free meal as well, paid for by me. I will ring up now."

At eight o'clock we arrived on Station Road in two cars, and parked on the station car park. Obviously, we were not in Chloe's, that thing is a death trap, and to be honest, it has been sat in the garage rusting for almost a year, it is a hunk of complete junk. Eight of us walked up Station Road, Birch was happy and hanging on my arm.

"Sweetie this is like a date, do you remember the first time we came here, it was such a lovely night?" I looked at her in disbelief.

"Birch, you tripped Chloe and covered her in curry, then took her in the toilets and almost beat the shit out of her, how the hell was that lovely?" She smiled, and her eyes danced.

"I was protecting the love of my life, of course it was lovely." Chloe turned, and gave her a strange look.

"That curry burned my tits, and then you terrified the living shit out of me, and threatened to have me raped by a ferocious lesbian, who I have since met. I have never forgotten that night, you were scary as fuck." Birch smiled.

"Chloe, I was defending Dead's, I would never have harmed you, I just wanted to make you understand that I loved her." She gave a smile.

"I get that now, but honestly, you can be really scary when you want to be." Birch gave my arm a squeeze, and looked at me and grinned.

"I will always protect you Deads."

It was kind of nice to know, although I do prefer her none violent. The eight of us arrived and walked in, the place was half full, and to my surprise Fidelity was a waitress, she came up with a smile.

"Hi guys, it's a table for eight, yes?"

Chloe viewed her with suspicion, in her mind she was Prude Party. Edwina took over and we headed towards the back. The table we had sat at way back when I first brought Birch here was gone, it had been taken out to free up the door space, and prevent accidents.

We sat as far back as possible, Fidelity looked a little nervous, knowing two of her customers, were in fact not only the daughters of her boss, but also probably the best that had ever worked here. Chloe especially was watching every move she made.

We looked at the menus as Martin Seddon, the other waiter, appeared to see what we would like to drink, Birch leaned into me.

"Sweetie what would your dad buy?" I chuckled.

"I am not sure they serve anything here he would buy." She kissed my cheek.

"Good, that means everything here is drinkable... Seriously

Deads, what the hell was that horrible stuff he gave us for our wedding... Yuk!?”

Edwina ordered the house white, and assured us it was the same level of piss we drank at home, and that was good enough for me. It was nice being out as a group, and it was not long before we all started to get the giggles. We looked at the menu, and Chloe guided us.

“The chicken is great mum cooks it, avoid the lamb, my dad never does it enough. Mum does the veggie menu and it’s great, I love the pasta, my mum does that, and that is what I will be having.” Izzy looked at her.

“What about the beef.” Chloe shook her head; Izzy gave a sigh.

“Dad again?” Chloe gave a nod, Birch laughed.

“Sweetie your dad can cook, yes?” Chloe smirked.

“He thinks he can, me and mum disagree.”

Everyone started to laugh, and Edwina nodded in agreement. Fidelity appeared with her pad, Izzy, Anthony, Luke, Michael, and Edwina all looked at her and said ‘Chicken’ and then we all laughed. Birch and myself went veggie, and Chloe was pasta. She gave a smile and wrote it all down, and then headed into the kitchen, Chloe gave an evil smile, she pulled out her token, and placed it on the table in full view. I frowned at her.

“Are you seriously going to use that?” Chloe lifted her wine, and took a sip and winked.

“How enraged do you think Prim will be to find out she paid for your discounted meal?” Birch giggled, as she looked at me, and leaned on my shoulder.

“I think we finally trained the girl properly.”

I giggled and looked up the restaurant, and noticed we were being watched, a lot of the customers were watching and whispering, some things never change. Our meal arrived, and Fidelity spotted the voucher and smiled, I looked up at her, as she placed my food down.

“How does that work?” She looked a little nervous, as she looked at me.

“Abigail, please, I don’t want to be in the middle of you two, I have always liked you, and I really admire what all of you have done. I grew up with Molly and Sophia, I have known them all my life, and to be honest, who else can I hang out with?” Birch looked up at her.

"Have you actually looked?" She sighed, and glanced up the restaurant.

"You know what, I would love to talk to you guys, honestly, I would, but to be honest look at you, all of you are so close, it's intimidating. Primula is critical, it costs a fortune being around her, but I know Molly and Sophia." Chloe looked up at her.

"You know me well enough, we hung out for a while at school, I have let on to you loads of times. I did not know you were working for mum and dad though, and we all have sites connected to the main village site, why didn't you message us?" Birch leaned around me and looked at her.

"I don't know you, but I will never accept that we are more intimidating than Primula. I have seen you around the place with your Gucci and makeup, trying to look the part. As a therapist I can tell you now, changing to fit in will never make you happy, why don't you just try being yourself, and see who stays around, which is all we did?" She gave a sigh, and nodded.

"I have a customer; will you excuse me?" She turned and walked up the room, as a group finished off their meal and waved for the bill. Izzy cut into her chicken.

"That one is confused to fuck, talk about torn between two fires?"

We carried on eating, and as is always the case with us, sex ended up on the menu, as we all giggled, whilst Izzy eyed up those who were staring at us, and gave us the low down on their sexual fetishes or persuasion. It still freaked Chloe out how she could tell, I loved it, and laughed like crazy as she described the people sat around us. Even Anthony had complete belief, especially when she pointed out Philip Darnten sat with his wife, and commented.

"So in the closet." Both Chloe and myself were shocked, and shook our heads.

"No freaking way?" Anthony chuckled.

"Oh you poor dear girls, it is as clear as day." Michael nodded in agreement.

"Oh yeah, look how he wipes his face with his napkin, so lost in the closet."

Chloe turned and stared, I looked twice, Phil was a pretty good looking guy, and had a really ripped body for a forty year old, I knew I would defo sleep with him, Chloe turned and stared at me.

"Shit Abby, I once wanked thinking of him." Birch gave a giggle and looked at me, and she lifted her eye brows, I felt my cheeks burn. She smiled.

"Okay, YES... I have played around with myself too thinking about him in the past, I kind of feel let down now." Birch giggled and put her arms round me.

"Sweetie, we have each other, we don't need a man, Bev bought us a strap on."

Michael coughed as he choked on his food, and Anthony gave him a slap. Just talk of Bev went into the many stories Birch had of her, and we all sat laughing and joking, and the night slowly slipped by in a fun, noisy way.

By midnight we were ready to go, and Chloe's parents came out, and we hugged them and told them how great our night and the food was. Birch took Derek on one side, and asked the question we had wanted to answer. He looked at her and smiled.

"I don't know about the others, but we take a double receipt from the till, clip it to the token, and Sophia collects them, and three days later we get a cheque. I mean, we will still be voting for you and Abby, but I add a few extra quid to the bill and she pays me back a percentage, so I am not complaining. But I will say this Birch, we have had a lot of those tokens in, people are using them, and you should take her seriously, she means to win."

We finally made our way to the door, having consumed a lot of white wine, and giggling like idiots, as Anthony opened the door, like a real gent. I heard Fidelity call out my name, and turned to see her walk towards me, she smiled.

"Thanks for the tip, you know you didn't have to tip that high, but I appreciate it. Look, watch your backs, all of you." She pushed a small piece of folded paper into my hand.

"Abby she is not a nice person, and she is dangerous, especially some of her new friends." I closed my hand on the paper.

"Thanks... I appreciate the heads up, watch yourself, and you know what, just be yourself, I do remember school, and you were a cool kid." She smiled.

"It was so long ago; some days I wish I was still there." I didn't,

I hated it, I was happier at Uni, but I had Birch with me now, so I still had something similar. I nodded at her.

"You should call round someday; I am always home." She gave me a smile.

"Actually, I would really love that."

I slipped the paper in my pocket, and gave her a nod, turned and left. She stood at the door and watched, as Birch slipped her arm around my waist, and we crossed the road, Chloe was on the other side, staring at a car in Mr Wilks compound.

"Oh, guys she is adorable, I want her."

Birch and myself caught up, and I looked at the beat up van, Chloe turned around and looked at us with bright shining eyes.

"Isn't she beautiful, I really want her?" Birch looked through the railings.

"It is about 1979, and in pretty good condition, but it will not be cheap Chloe, those things go for at least twelve to twenty thousand." I looked at Birch and pointed at the orange van looking thing.

"For that piece of shit, what is it with you lot, is it like a thing, buy the biggest piece of shit on wheels you can? Chloe it's a hunk of junk." She shook her head and smiled.

"Abby, that is a VW camper van, it's beautiful, it's artisan, and I am going to buy it." I was stunned.

"You are all insane, do you know that?" Birch giggled and squeezed my arm.

"Deads, it is a collector's piece, keep it in good condition, and it just increases in value, honestly she should buy it." I looked at Chloe, who had gone as doe eyed, as she always does when she sees Phileas.

"The only good thing about it, is there is less rust on it than the one you have now, and if it runs, that is two for two."

We headed towards Petal and Edwina's estate, which were the only cars left on the parking spots, and we jumped in, Anthony sat in the passenger seat and Michael drove us home.

I like the village at night, I like how quiet and still it is. When I was younger, I would sneak out at night, just to walk around with no one else there. I have always loved this village, it is beautiful, and has a charm that seeps into your bones. I do feel a connection to it, maybe that is because this is where I call home, I am not sure, but I do love it. It is special at night, the air is fresh with the smell of the country, and it has a feel of the ancient past to it. I used to fantasise that all my ancestors watched over me, or I was a vampire walking in my night time world, either way, I knew my heart would always have a place here.

I just wish the people could see and understand that, they are the ones that have spoiled the place, with their inner ugliness, and their hypocrisy, and their endless crusade to put down those they deemed did not belong. I think it is why I really do love Norman and Daisy, not just because they are kind, but because like me, they have been ridiculed and shamed since the day they took over. I often wonder how they have coped with it, behind the scenes there must have been a lot of quiet tears shed, especially by Daisy?

It was nice to be home, and I was a little tipsy, as was Birch, she held my hand and we walked up the stairs together, to our room. I was sort of use to it now, I suppose it had felt like a huge change, but now we were settled and with her door gone from the bathroom, I was actually loving sharing with her again. I sat on the bed and gave a happy sigh, as I watched Birch slip off her top, showing her beautifully round breasts, she dropped it on the floor, and began to undo her buttons on her black pants, she looked towards me, and her eyes twinkled.

"So, what was on the note?"

I had to laugh, I thought no one had seen it, I leaned back and slipped my hand into my pocket, and located it. I pulled it out, and opened it up to read. Birch dropped her pants, stepped out of them, and climbed on the bed behind me, as I looked down to read.

'Abby, Primula is doing everything she can to beat you, and in doing so, is doing deals that will threaten the village. The child's play space is a bluff, she needs to stop Andrew expanding, because that area has been designated for an access road into Dursley Woods. The Dursley Wood Project, is not a green policy, it is actually a full scale housing project being backed by Walter Parkinson. He needs Primula to win, because she is going to grant the planning consent for Oxendale Council. If she finds out I told you, I am fried, but be aware, those are the stakes you are playing for. Consent will be granted in mid November, so for now, play it down, but you must get elected to stop it.' Below that was her mobile number, I looked up at Birch.

"We need to win Birch; I cannot let this happen." She nodded and slid back up the bed, and leaned against our pillows.

"I think we need to meet Fidelity somewhere safe and talk to her. Deads, we need to keep a lid on this for now, I think we need to get all the facts first." I slipped off my jeans and pulled up my top.

"Birch, I have to give my presentation on Friday, what do I tell the villagers?" She sighed as I slid up to her side.

"For now, say nothing, stick with what you have, Nigel was more talkative tonight, I think he is starting to trust me, I will ask him a few questions and see if I can get him to slip up. Although, if I am honest, I think they pretty much live separate lives in that house."

I nodded, I wanted to ask, but I knew she would not say anything. I turned and could see her looking at me, she smiled, she knew me so well, she took my hand in hers.

"I am happy he has no more black eyes. Moon is up by the locks, is he still... You know... With her?" Birch's eyes twinkled.

"He has not talked about it, but I have talked to Moon, she is getting much better with texting. Deads, are you jealous?" I blurted out a laugh, and looked at her, she smiled.

"CHRIST NO...! To be honest, in a crazy way, I am actually happy for him. Birch I could not sleep with him, you know, there was a time when I honestly thought of going on one date with him. I thought I would have a drink, maybe let him kiss me on the cheek, but I knew, my skin would crawl. I don't hate him, if anything I have always felt indifferent towards him, but I also do not want to see him beaten up." She nodded at me.

"Yeah, I get that, I have met guys like that too. Look Sweetie, I am helping him, you need to focus on beating Prim, in what is looking like a rigged fight. If you want my opinion, she is more dangerous than Madge, and if she is involved with other forces, then we need to be really careful and plan discreetly, because otherwise, this village could really suffer." I really understood that

"I should have known that bloody MP would be up to no good, Madge is no longer useful to him, so he has targeted Prim, and she is so power hungry she will fall for everything he offers. I wonder if she thinks she will profit from it, you know, like a share or a payoff, we need more intel, but how do we get it?" Birch shook her head.

"You know this place better than I do, I am still pretty new to the background of this place, but I am telling you Deads, one way or the other, I aim to find out."

Dursley Woods was a special place to me. As teenagers it is where we would hang out after school with our friends, which in my case was Deb's and Ben. There are parts of it that are quite dense, and out of sight of anyone walking their dogs. I first got drunk in those woods, and dare I say it, it was the place I let a boy feel my boobs for the first time. Okay, so that is a weird reason to love the place, and probably not one I should share with the community.

But it is special, and very beautiful, which again adds to the charm and beauty of the place. I cannot believe that Walter Parkinson would bulldoze it to make money, scratch that, actually I can, that is all he cares about, like so many other members of this community, cash counts for everything.

Living with Birch has really opened my eyes. I remember that day when she told me that she had just given me half of a four million pound house; to her it was nothing, it was just like giving me a bunch of flowers or a box of chocolates. Money is just a tool to her, it is not something she desires, if anything, the fact that interest piles up on her money, giving her even more, makes her miserable.

Through Birch, I have seen another side to wealth, to her it has nothing to do with currency, wealth to her is a happy life and health for all those she loves. Birch has no need of this big house, she would happily live in our guest house, but this house has provided a safe haven for Chloe, Edwina, and Anthony, and that means more to her than any amount of cash ever could. I remember her sitting on my bed a few days after we moved in here, and telling me.

'Sweetie, if I was broke, I would still be a very rich woman, because, I have you, our friends and our parents, and there is no monetary value I can place on that.'

She was so right, seeing Chloe hum as she paints, or that faint smile on Edwina's face as she codes, or hearing Anthony laugh and giggle as he games with the guys, that is the true currency of life. I came out of my thoughts as Birch gave a quiet giggle, I blinked, and my eyes moved to look at her, she was sat watching me, her eyes twinkling, wearing a huge smile on her face.

"What?" She gave a smirk.

"I love to watch you when you ponder, your eyes just drift off and stare into space, and they sparkle like sapphires. God Deads, it is so attractive, I could stare at you like that all day. So, tell me, what is that scheming little brain of yours up to?" I shook my head.

"I was just thinking... Well, more remembering, you know that day we walked together through the woods, and also some of the things Deb's and me got up to as young teenagers there?"

Birch smiled at me, I knew it, I had opened the door, and walked right into her trap, there are days I hate therapists. She pulled up the duvet, pulled it over us, and snuggled up to me, her eyes dancing with excitement.

"Oh, young Abby stories, really, do tell?" I giggled.

"Birch it was a long time ago." Her eyes danced.

"So, you were that naughty then?" I started to laugh.

"Not so sure about naughty, compared to the stuff we have done, although!"

She gave a squeak, and snuggled into my arm, I smiled, I loved her like this, I looked at her bright excited face.

"Deb's got fingered for the first time there, by Russel Pritchard." Birch erupted with a high pitched squeaky laugh.

"Oh my god, this is seriously sexy stuff, did she cum?" I exploded into laughter.

"I don't know, I was over in the bushes with Harry." I suddenly realised, shit, I had walked right into her trap again, Birch let out a squeal, and her eyes danced.

"Tell me everything, I want to know all about Harry?"

I gave a sigh, shit, there was no going back now. I slid down a little in the bed, and she got really excited. I had no choice, so I looked her right in the eyes, as she giggled.

"I let him touch my boobs, if he showed me his willy."

Birch squealed with laughter, and I went beetroot, and I have no idea why, she has after all, watched me screw a guy. She rolled back in the bed with hysterics, I started to giggle with her, she was so funny. She calmed down a little and rolled back to me, she looked so happy, her bright green eyes locked into mine.

"So, did he get hard?" I sniggered.

"Jesus Birch, I was only fourteen... It moved in my hand so I dropped it, and ran away completely freaked out. Honestly, I have never touched rubbery doughy play stuff since, because that is what it felt like."

Birch exploded into laughter as I laughed, she kicked her legs into the air, and roared out with joy, I lay there watching, thinking she was quite insane, but loving her reaction. I giggled at her.

"Honestly it is not funny, it was all soft and warm, just like the doughy stuff, and then it just sort of pulsed, and I freaked the hell out." She screamed with laughter.

It took her quite a while to calm down, and we lay facing each other, smirking and giggling, she stroked my hair back from my face. Her eyes were so full of happiness and life.

"I love hearing about your life, I really do, you know, some days I look at you, and that girl who knocked on my door is still there, sort of shy, awkward, and innocent. I really love that you still have that, I have seen it so often, especially when you talk to your readers, it is such a beautiful thing Deads."

And there it is, that part of her no one sees, the soft caring quiet Birch. I saw so much of this side of her at Sunny Bank, or on the honeymoon. We walked along the beach, holding hands, and she would softly talk, in that caring reflective gentle manner, and it is impossible to not be captivated by her.

There is such deep hidden depths to her, it is something I have never seen in anyone else. It is a rich layer just filled with such love, and such intelligence, and somehow, she just looks at you, and you are engulfed and surrounded by her presence. I find it so alluring, I am like a moth to a flame, caught in the dazzling brightness of its beauty, and I have no will at all to fight it, all I want is to surrender to it, and bask in its brilliance.

We snuggled down, it was getting late and she had work tomorrow. It was not long before her soft breathing signalled, she was fast asleep, and I lay in bed warm and toasty, my mind lost in thought of memories of the past. Wotton had not really changed much, behind closed doors, there were still as many secrets and hidden skeletons, the difference being, some of the players were changing.

How it looks on the outside is far more important than it is on the inside, echoed in my brain. Marjorie once ruled with an iron grip, and I lived in fear, and yet I always felt I brought change back from Uni with me, but had I really?

They say one dictator is always replaced by another, and it was looking like Primula was heading for her new seat in control of everything. I thought back to my meeting with Marjorie, before Birch's and my wedding, and how she had struggled to see her son hurt, and the emotion that had risen up inside her.

It is crazy to think it, but she is a mum, as hard as her exterior is, she still cares about her son. Hadn't Milton told me, she was not always like this, she once was fun? I guess after all she is just human, her son and grandchild mean something, and that made me ponder. If we really did help Nigel, which in turn improved his life, was there a way I could win her allegiance, and actually get her to vote against her own daughter in law?

That was a really interesting question, and I had a speech to write, and only one day left to get it perfect.

Chapter 4

Preparing For Politics.

Birch sat bolt upright in bed.

"CRAP, I AM LATE!"

I opened my eyes, as the bed moved, and there was a thump, and she headed for the bathroom, I yawned and sat up and rubbed my eyes. I blinked as she came hurtling into the bedroom, she still had her toothbrush in her mouth, as she lifted her blouse off the chair and gave it a sniff.

"YUK!" She dropped it, and headed for the wardrobe, and yanked opened the doors, I was still sleepy.

"Wear the green one, it matches your eyes." She looked back and smiled.

"Hi Sweetie... I am late."

She grabbed her green blouse and pulled it on, then headed back into the bathroom, I heard her spit, then the tap run. Moments later, she appeared buttoning up her blouse and grabbed her pants. I blinked at her.

"If you smell the crotch, I will be repulsed." She giggled, as she slipped them on.

"Oh Sweetie, I thought you like my scent?" I tried to smile, and failed, not enough coffee was in my system.

"Me smelling them may be one thing, smelling your own is unsettling."

She giggled, as I slid out of bed, and padded softly on the warm floor towards the door, she followed me out grabbing her shoes on route. I made it to the stairs as she hurried down to my side.

"So do you?" I was not really awake enough yet for long words.

"Do what?" She gave a smirk.

"You know, smell them?" I shuddered, and screwed up my face.

"God no...." I stopped and looked at her.

"Please tell me you do not smell mine?" She gave a smirk, and kissed my cheek.

"I did once in the guest house." I gave another shudder.

"Okay, I am not talking now until I have had at least three coffees', you are messed up."

In the kitchen I sat down, Chloe stared into space holding her mug. I like Chloe, she understands how to wake up. Edwina put my coffee in front of me, I like Edwina too. Anthony and Michael sorted out their things, and Birch raced round, stuffing papers in her case and slurping coffee. She stuck a piece of toast in her mouth, and munched hands free as she gathered together her things, I smiled, and Chloe understanding why, shuddered. Finally, she raced up to me and kissed me softly, she slid round to my ear, and whispered.

"They smelt sweet... Bye Sweetie."

I shuddered, and felt a cold trickle run down my back. Samantha walked in, and smiled as she headed for the coffee machine, and poured out a coffee, Chloe stared at me, I frowned.

"What?" She put her cup down.

"Did I just hear that right?" I gave a giggle.

"Is it weird Birch smelt my used panties once?" Samantha slurped her coffee, coughed and choked, Edwina patted her back, and she gave a violent gasp, and breathed in.

"Christ, trigger warnings guys!" I could see Chloe considering the question, she looked at me and smiled.

"I once had a guy in the restaurant ask me if he could buy my knickers." Edwina gasped, and looked at her with absolute horror.

"Christ Chloe, when?" She giggled and winked at me, Samantha gasped in the background, Chloe looked at her sister.

"It was a good few years back, when we had that long hot summer, and I was really hot and horny. Do you remember, I told you how wet I was, and he giggled?" She thought for a second, and then looked at her with absolute horror in her eyes.

"You don't mean that vicar who was visiting from South Wales?" Chloe shrugged.

"He had a Welsh accent; I didn't know he was a vicar though." Edwina looked even more horrified, Samantha and myself watched on, eagerly awaiting the result.

"Hell Chloe, what did he say to you?" She turned and looked at me.

"He was about forty, he had this really sexy voice, I got to say, just hearing him made me even wetter. He just asked what kind of panties I was wearing, I told him when we are serving, mum made us wear panties, although, I usually wore thongs."

Edwina was looking even more horrified, I was actually really interested, and by the look of it so was Samantha.

"So, what did he say?" She gave a really naughty smile.

"He told me he had overheard me, and asked if I would care to sell my panties to him, I figured why not, so asked how much. He asked how long I had been wearing them, and I told him two days, as I was working the weekend. He just smiled back, and told me he would give me two hundred quid cash for them." I gasped out in surprise.

"Holy shit!" She giggled, and Edwina stood frozen looking at her sister in absolute shock, Chloe shrugged.

"He gave me the cash, inside his menu, so I went into the toilet, gave myself a little fingering, pushing them up into me a little. They were soaked I am telling you, and then slipped them off, put them in a freezer bag from the kitchen, and went and gave them to him." Edwina sat down with the thump.

"Jesus Chloe, and he gave you two hundred quid just like that?" She nodded quite unphased.

"Yeah, he went to the toilet a little after to sniff them I think, he was happy, and I made two hundred, so I was chuffed, I put it towards my new laptop."

My mind was blown, and I think Edwina's was too, she looked like she did not know if she should be repulsed or admire her sister? Chloe did not seem to mind at all, I was a little impressed, she looked at me.

"You know Abby, your panties on Ebay would make thousands, people are really into it, especially celebrities. I have done it a few times for extra cash, you can make some good money, and if you put a video up of you playing in them, holy fuck, the price rockets." Edwina took a deep breath, as she stared at her sister.

"Please tell me you have not uploaded a video of you doing that?" She shook her head.

"No, it is really hard to film, I got too excited and dropped the camera." I thought Edwina was going to pass out, she gave a gasp.

"I am so glad your paintings are selling, please Chloe, don't do it again." She shrugged.

"I am okay for cash, but if I ever get strapped, I know where I can make money."

I had to chuckle, I actually thought she was brave, I could never ever do that, just the thought that some perverted vicar had my panties would freak me the hell out, and that would be with just clean ones!

Today there was a lot on my mind, and so I headed to the library to work. I checked my emails, and as always, I had one from Anita. She loved the wedding pictures on my website and gushed about how beautiful we looked together; it made me really happy. She also told me she was going to come to the meeting tomorrow, as she wanted to get a feel for the village, and understand the lifestyle here.

My next big job was to think deeply, and write my speech for tomorrow, I had thought about it last night in the darkness, and it was all there in my thoughts. All I had to do was get it out, in a way that made sense to me, and so I set to work, and let all my thoughts flow out of me, in the very same way I would writing a book.

Coffee's arrived care of Chloe, who I had not even been aware was behind me reading what I was writing, and the morning moved on as I edited, and then edited again, until I was satisfied, I actually had something worth saying. Pleased with my final draft, I saved it, and sent it to print out, in my room upstairs. I slid out of my seat, and picked up my cup and drained it, and headed to the kitchen.

The day was overcast, but it was warm, so with a refilled cup, I headed out for some fresh air, and to sit under my arch. The afternoon passed lost in thought, with my back to the wall in the corner, and the sun finally came out, and shone down on my face. I discovered, sun warmed brick, and stone, is really nice for naturists to sit on. I just drifted away in my thoughts, trying to visualise how the meeting would go, so much so, I hadn't really taken the time into account. I realised when I felt my legs stung, and looked down.

My legs were red with sunburn, I got up, and headed back to the house, and up to my room. I walked in and found Birch sat on the bed reading my presentation, she smiled, then saw my legs.

"Oh, Sweetie, that looks painful." I nodded, and hobbled over to the bed, she ran into the bathroom, and shortly reappeared.

"Oh, Sweetie, this is wonderful, I can play nurse." I was not so sure, she looked way too excited for my liking, and I was in pain. She held up a can of shaving foam, I frowned.

"Hell Birch, I am in pain with sunburn, I don't need my legs shaving."

She sprayed a big blob into the palm of her hand, and smeared it on my legs, and I felt it cool instantly, she watched me as she slowly massaged my thighs with the foam, I started to chuckle.

"Forget it pervert, this is painful." She giggled.

"I like being the nurse, I have a strong urge to take your temperature."

I needed to change the subject; I had no idea what method of temperature taking she wanted. I just figured, I didn't, and I was sat on the bed covered in foam, looking at a pervert.

"What do you think of the presentation, do you think it will win people over?" She looked up at me and her eyes sparkled.

"I think it is good, but would you mind if I made some suggestions?" I shook my head.

"Birch you are going to be Vice Chair, I want to know what you think, you know, this is us, not me, us, I want this to be a team effort all the way."

And so began hours of talk and rewriting, as I sat at my desk, and she pulled her desk chair over. The serious side of Birch came out, as we discussed each and every point in detail, and slowly we formulated an idea of what we felt, was the direction of the village's future.

Food appeared in the shape of battered fish, with chips and peas, and we sat on the sofa, with our feet up, facing each other as we ate, and the conversation continued, and suddenly out of nowhere as we spoke, I felt a huge burst of joy.

I was loving this, if this was the future, if this was what being on the council was going to be like with her, then I was really excited to win and do it? I really wanted us to both get up on the stage and present this to the whole village, and let them see how serious we were. I got back at my desk and hammered out our presentation, and finally we both sat back and sipped our gin... I stopped and looked at Birch.

"Where did this come from?" She looked at her glass and shrugged.

"I just saw it and picked it up, didn't you get them?" I shook my head.

"No, I have not left the room since you came home."

Birch turned and gave a smile, Chloe was flat out on the bed, her dinner plate at her side, a bottle of gin and a bottle of lemon was on the bedside unit with her empty glass. I looked at her and gave a chuckle.

"How long has she been there?" Birch shrugged.

"No idea, I think she handed me my dinner, but that was three hours ago, has she been there all along?"

Looking at her plate I assumed so, she must have given us our meal, and then sat listening, it was the only real explanation. I got out of my chair and walked over to the bed and lifted her plate.

"I will take these down and wash them for her."

I grabbed ours, and headed for the kitchen, and when I returned, Birch had put her in our bed, she was fast asleep and it seemed a shame to wake her. It is funny how we attract guests to our bed; it has been a trend since we first came home from Uni. I cannot say I have ever understood it, but it is kind of nice, to know that if any of the others feel insecure, it is usually our room they head to. We really are the parent figures in this house. We finally crashed out, the three of us, and feeling confident, I fell straight to sleep.

The day of the meeting seemed to fly past, as I sat at my desk and went over my speech, and tried to learn as much of it as possible. I knew I would deviate from the script a little, but I felt very confident, and prepared. Feeling as ready as ever, I hit the wardrobe and went through Birch's clothes, as I was determined to look the part.

When Birch arrived at home, I was walking down the stairs in one of her business suits, and a white shirt, she stopped and looked up at me, her eyes were really wide.

"Oh Sweetie, how long do we have before we have to go, because honestly, I am feeling very hot about now?"

I gave a giggle, she really looked very excited, I walked down, and she pulled me into her arms and kissed me passionately. Wow, she took my breath away, I pulled out of her kiss with a smile, feeling my insides flutter a little, and turned to see Chloe stood with her eyes wide open watching us. I looked at her, and she blinked.

"Wow Abby, I got to say, your ass looks awesome in those pants, and I noticed, and I am so fucking straight it's unbelievable, but I got to say... Wow, love the pony tail."

I walked up to her with a smile, and softly stroked her chin and kissed her on the cheek, and lowered my voice.

"You know Chloe, if you ever want to flip, I would so do you in the naughtiest ways possible." She gave a shudder and swallowed hard.

"I need to go to my room."

Birch laughed, as Chloe ran up the stairs to her room, and her ever ready Percy. I walked down the hall towards the kitchen feeling very happy.

At seven o'clock, we all entered the hall, and it was as always packed. Anita was waiting inside wearing her suit, she was impressed when she saw me. The three of us sat at the back, and watched, as the hall rumbled to the many conversations. Izzy appeared and slapped a paper down in front of us.

"You really need to read this before you go up there."

I looked at the paper as Birch and Anita leaned in from either side, the article was written by Ben Shepard, and featuring Primula, and her vision for a traditional village, we all read it with utter surprise, I looked at Birch.

"Have you seen this?"

Primula was spouting on about how the village was steeped in a history of tradition, and how under my mother those traditions had been watered down, and have lessened the value of the village. What really hit hard, was when she added, it has got so bad, that we were now faced with a couple of immoral and sacrilegious, sinners, challenging her in the election. She questioned how could anyone trust such a position of responsibility to two Godless deviant lesbians? Now the village faced the onslaught of complete moral decay, and she had to make a stand for morality and God. I was so angry; God, I was so pissed off I wanted to punch the bitch.

"Birch how the hell can she say that, we have done nothing wrong? We really love and care for each other, hell, we have a more honest and loving relationship than most of this village." Birch took my hand, and her soft green eyes looked at me, her voice was soft and caring.

"Deads, she is desperate, listen to me, stick to the script, we know what we want to say, and we know what we have planned. We knew she was going to rise up to replace Madge, and we knew she would be worse. Let her empty Nigel's bank account in her desperate bid to try and fool the villagers, Sweetie, stay calm and stay focused on the job at hand."

I sat back and silently seethed. The paper passed to the others, Edwina was clearly enraged, Chloe smirked and leaned forward.

"Wow Abby, she is really afraid you will win."

I did not care, personal attacks had never been a part of the council elections, mum and Madge had sparred, but there was always a respectful rivalry between them. It was never lowered to the level of public name calling. Stacy and Louise arrived, they saw us at the back and headed our way, and sat in the row in front of us, as did G5, Denise, Megan and Alex, it was nice to see, as I remembered my first summer home from Uni, where it was just the five of us.

Others sat further back from the rest close by, and I felt their solidarity, the Wheelers, Clive, Peter and Mary, and the Jessops, even Andrew Boswell, smiled, and sat down three rows in front, although we had given him enough business in one night to pay for his pub for three months, and got him laid. Lillian arrived and waved, she leaned over with a big smile.

"Abigail good luck, you already have our vote." Birch's eyes twinkled.

"Looking smoking hot tonight, Lilly."

She flustered and giggled, as she made her way to the front. The good news was, we were surrounded by youth, and they were the future, and they also had grateful parents, because they remained in the village. The doors opened and I glanced up and took a breath in, and stood up.

"DAD!" He smiled as he saw me. I moved quickly along the line to him.

"Dad, what are you doing here?"

He pulled me into a hug, and gave me a squeeze, Angela smiled at his side. I pulled back and looked at him as I smiled, is it weird that I felt so happy seeing him here? He looked good, so much better than before the wedding.

"Abby, your mother and I always hoped you would take this step. I may no longer be anything to do with this village, but I was born here, and I was never going to miss this moment. I know how hard it has been coming back here for you, and that makes what you are doing tonight even more impressive. I wanted to make sure you knew that you were supported." I was all smiles and really touched.

"Thanks Dad, it really means a lot to me, it is not going to be an easy win, my competition is going out of their way to smear me already." He winked.

"She is that worried about losing to a superior force then?" I looked down.

"I am not sure about that Dad, but we are going to try." His hand softly touched my chin and lifted my face.

"Abigail, you have everything and more than your mother has. Trust me when I tell you, I have waited a long time for this day, because I have always known, that the day you stood up there on that stage, this village would prosper in a far better way than it has in the past. Abigail, you have grown up around committee business, it is in your blood, now you tell me, what would a girl from Millington know after only a few years here? You have been involved one way or another for twenty eight years, trust me, you have far more than what it takes." I could not believe what he was saying, but I really needed to hear it.

"Thanks Dad, that is something I really need to hear tonight." He smiled, I looked at Angela.

"Thanks for coming tonight." She pulled me into a hug.

"He would not have missed it for the world, he has been talking about it all week." Birch came up and pulled my dad into a hug.

"Thanks Ed, it will really help having you here for her." He smiled as she hugged him, although she had amazing boobs, and he could probably feel them pressed into his shirt?

It was not long before other people realised who it was with me, and he was drawn to familiar faces, who were pleased to see him, and shook his hand, Angela followed, and my father introduced her to everyone. It was another sign of the times, Patrick was here tonight for my mum, and Angela for my dad. Life was still going on, even though the familiar patterns of the past were different. Birch slid her arm around my waist.

"It was really good of him to come and show his support." She turned and looked at me, her eyes were bright and sparkled.

"Deads, Sweetie... Have you any idea how much I want to screw you at this moment, that business suit is driving me wild?" I gave a smile.

"You want to play boardrooms later, and have me boss you around, and dock your wage if you don't please me?" Her eyes widened as much as her smile, and she jumped on the spot.

"Sweetie I so want to do that, oh God, I am so excited." Giggling, we made our way back to our seats, Marion was stood by the doors smiling at us, I am sure she overheard us. Mum stood below the stage steps holding the paper, and looked at Hatty.

"If that little shit comes within ten feet of me, I will slap the bitch, how could she write this, we have never attacked on a personal level?" Hatty smiled.

"Listen Flick, those two have faced a lot worse, just sit back and let Abby deal with this, have some faith in her. I know her, she will be polite and respectful, and she will get her point across, and if not, I will look forward to watching Birch deal with her." Flick looked bothered.

"That is what I am worried about Hatty, she once threatened to batter Angela with an ash tray." Hatty sniggered.

"Speak of the devil, make way for Eddy Stark and the Pepper Shaker. Wow he came to see her, hey, now he has that thing in his chest, do you think she plugs him in at night to recharge his batteries?" Felicity sniggered.

"He is not that modern; she probably has a big key in the wardrobe." Hatty and Felicity both burst into fits of giggles, and Felicity slapped Hatty's arm playfully.

"Stop it now, he is coming towards us." Hatty sniggered.

"Hey do you think it buzzes when he is... You know, doing it, and it reminds her of all those nights she spent alone, when he was with you?" Felicity gave a snort, and covered her mouth.

"Stop it, I mean it Hatty... He is here for Abby and that is nice."
Hatty tittered at her side as Edwin walked up all smiles.

"Felicity, Harriet, how are you?" Hatty smiled.

"Simply buzzing Edwin, and you?" Felicity put her head down,
as Hatty beamed a big bright smile.

Birch sat with a pad on her knee, and watched the room, I could
see she had an idea, she turned, and smiled at me, and her eyes
twinkled.

"Sweetie, I will be back in a minute." I gave her that 'what are
you up to now, look?' She giggled, and blew a kiss. Anita leaned
into me.

"Christ Abby, how awful is this woman you are up against, that
article is pretty offensive, which one is she?"

I pointed down the room, to where Primula stood wearing a
large rosette on her jersey, even smiling she was unattractive. She
was surrounded by Sophia and Molly and a few others she had
gathered to her cause.

Nigel sat alone on his chair, as Prim smiled and talked, and it
was pretty clear, she was very happy with her article. She had a
large stack of the newspapers on a chair at the side of her, which
she was handing out to everyone, my God, she was a smug bitch.
Anita sized her up.

"Wow she is not pretty is she, she has got power and control
stamped all over her?" I nodded, watching her smug face.

"Her and her little Prude Party swan around the village like they
think they own the place, and all they do is call us for our lack of
morality and sinful ways, she is a complete homophobe."

"I take it the drip sat alone is her husband, don't you think it
is weird that he is not at her side supporting her like the dutiful
husband?"

I had not thought of that, and as I looked back, I remembered
how Milton would always be at Madge's side. My dad was the
same too, he was always beside mum, hell, even Lillian was
always at the side of Celia supporting her for the vice position. It
dawned on me Nigel was not supporting her, I turned and looked
at Anita.

"You are far more insightful than I thought, I knew working
with you would be a good thing, I did not even spot that, but yes,

why is he not at her side supporting her?"

Birch climbed over the seat and slid down next to Bradley, he smiled.

"Hello... What trouble are you up to now, and will I go to prison if I help?" She giggled.

"Deb's has a big mouth, I have no secrets left these days." Ellen chuckled at his side.

"Oh, Birch, she loves you and Abby so much, but yes, she never stops talking about you guys. By the way, your wedding was wonderful, I cried buckets, but you two looked stunning, and I see Abby is looking so much better on her return home?" Birch glanced back, and looked at me and smiled.

"She is beautiful, she has no idea how stunning she is, and we had such a lovely time away, I think we came back stronger than ever." Bradley smiled, and nodded his head.

"You know Jemi, that is probably a good thing, I think Primula will sling a lot of mud at you before this is over, this is not going to be easy for either of you, but if we can help, you know we are on board and we will do everything we can to help you?" She smiled a sweet smile.

"Yeah, about that?" He started to chuckle.

"I knew it... Oh shit, what am I getting into?" Birch grabbed his arm and hugged it.

"Sweetie... If I wanted to tear somewhere up and fill it with houses, but I did not want anyone to know, until all my bribes had stitched up all the loose ends, how would I do that exactly?" His eyes narrowed.

"Jemi, you are not getting into real estate are you, because if you are, what you are suggesting is illegal, I would have nothing to do with it?" She smiled.

"But it can be done... You know, quietly without anyone finding out?" He nodded.

"Jemi, please tell me you and Abby are not involved with anything like that? If you want to get into that market, I am happy to make introductions that are safe and legal." She sat back in her seat.

"It is not Deads or me, and if I ever want to buy more, we will always deal through you. If I was to say that I had heard of such a scheme though, where would I look to find the actual plans?" He stared at her.

"Do you know of such a plan?" She smiled at him.

"Bradley, for now I cannot say anything, we want to keep a lid on it, call it our big guns for later, it is really important, that no one finds out yet." He gave her a nod.

"Jemi if what I think you are suggesting is true, well that does not take a huge amount of brain space to work out who is behind it. Jemi you will not even get close to this, please trust me, and I will find out very quietly. Let me help you on this, as I possibly am the only one with enough clout to get close to this." Birch leaned over and winked at Ellen.

"Has he always been this easy to win over?" She chuckled, and slipped her arm in his with a smile.

"Oh yes, especially if she has big bright hazel eyes, and a long brown bushy ponytail, he is a big softy really Jemi." He patted her arm and smiled, and turned to Birch.

"Call me tomorrow, and we will talk, and I will jump on this for you, Jemi if what you say is true, you may have less time than you realise."

"Thanks Bradley, listen carefully to Deads tonight, I am sure her hints will give you a very good idea."

She kissed his cheek and stood up, and then climbed back over the chair. Birch winked as she approached me, and considering the intensity of Bradley, it was clear what she had been up to. She sat at my side and leaned on my shoulder.

"That was so easy, God, he is such a big softy, he took the bait straight away. I was right, none of us will even get close enough to get any details, but he will."

The committee headed up the steps onto the stage, and sat in their seats. Edwina winked at us, I saw Prim turn around and scowl at me, I smiled. Mum banged the gavel, and the meeting began with the minutes and all the current business. I sat back, as they introduced their Summer Events program, and all the large scale events that would lead up to the Summer Fete, which was being planned to be bigger than ever before.

I have sat through these all my life, and they take a long time. Birch snuggled into me, we all made quips and sniggered at private jokes, and for over an hour each committee member laid out the plans in turn. Towards the end, I picked up my notes and gave them one last read through. Mum walked up to the mic and faced everyone.

"Ladies and gentlemen, we will take a short break of fifteen minutes, and there will be one final presentation." A lot of people turned round, and looked our way, where I was sat going over my notes.

Deb's and Jimmy appeared with a tray filled with coffees for us all, and she sat down in front of me.

"Are you nervous?" I shook my head.

"Surprisingly enough no, if anything I am angry, and resisting the urge to walk over to her, and beat the shit out of her with a chair." She giggled and her hazel eyes twinkled at me.

"Dad hit the roof when he saw it, and then he showed Jimmy, and he got real steamed up. They both stood at the barbeque ranting at what a snivelling ugly bitch she was, me and mum laughed our asses off." Birch chuckled.

"Sweetie, you had a barbeque and did not invite us, a hot slab of meat about now would be good?" She looked at me.

"Well, you dressed like that and would not screw me, and a girl needs her desires met." Deb's laughed.

"You do look really lovely, I will not deny I had a perv at your ass, when you were talking to your dad." I smiled.

"I bet Chloe did too, she was scoping me out in the hallway earlier." She leaned forward and nodded.

"So... Well okay, yeah, I did, but I am so fucking straight it's unbelievable." I looked at her.

"Yeah, so straight you got so hot looking, you had to jump Percy straight away." She smirked.

"Percy knows all my weak spots." Deb's looked at her.

"Wow, does he have a sponge too?" We giggled, and Chloe blushed, and sat back.

Mum banged the gavel, and people started making their way back to their seats, the room slowly came to order, and she walked to the mic, and looked at me at the back of the room.

"Ladies and gentlemen, Mrs Abigail Dixon will now make a presentation to start off her campaign for the coming November

4th election." The room burst into applause, and Birch leaned in and kissed my cheek.

"Go get 'em Sweetie."

I stood up with my paperwork, and walked towards the stage, and suddenly I felt a little nervous and wished my legs were not sunburned. I glanced back to see Birch and Deb's leaning over the end of the row of seats, looking at my ass, I smiled, wiggled my hips, and walked onto the steps up to the stage as applause surrounded me.

Chapter 5

The Presentation.

I stood on the stage looking out at the villagers of Wotton, and smiled as I arranged my papers on the podium. I took a deep breath, and tried to get into the mental head space I needed, Birch gave a tiny wave at the back and I smiled.

"Good evening, Parish Council members, ladies and gentlemen of Wotton, and guests. I am delighted to be here tonight to present my arguments, on why I feel, that myself, and Doctor Jemima Dixon, would be better candidates, for the position of Chair, and Vice Chair, of this village's Parish Council." Anita slid up to the side of Birch.

"She looks good up there; she commands a lot more respect than I realised." Birch smiled.

"She honestly has no idea." I took a deep breath.

"I would like to start tonight by firstly, expressing my admiration and respect for the current council. I feel over the last few years, they have done an amazing job, and have set a very high bar for whichever candidate wins to work to, especially in the development of the summer events list, and the continuing additions to the Christmas lights and festivities. It is also very noticeable, how the e commerce of this village has found a greater audience, due to their technical skills and additions to our online presence. It is indeed remarkable how this village has moved forward, and yet remains as beautiful and as highly maintained, as the traditional village it has always been, whilst embracing such modern technologies." I took another breath, and lifted Prim's leaflet off the podium.

"I think it is important to embrace tradition, as my opposition candidate made very clear, in her presentation last month. I would like to thank G5 who filmed it for me, so I could watch it, to gain a full understanding of my rival, and I have also a copy of her flyer, which is one of many circulating the village currently."

I looked up at the audience, who were all quietly listening. I looked right at them.

"However, considering all her points, I find them more sentimental, ill informed, not factual, and actually very dangerous for the future of this village." The was a sudden low hum of muttering, I smiled.

"I can understand such mistakes from someone who has only been a resident of this village for such a short span of a matter of years, whereas, I was born here. As was pointed out to me earlier, I have grown up in a house with serving members of previous councils, and have been an active volunteer for pretty much most events, for twenty eight years, it is, as they say, in my blood." I noticed the smiles on many faces.

"It is important we do honour the traditions of this village, and it is vitally important we look back to the past, and honour the fights for this village to maintain it to the high standards it has attained. I must admit, the thought of rows of steel parking meters popping up from our pavements, appals me. I cannot think of an uglier way to soil the beauty of this place we call home, and if my candidate wins, I will strongly oppose it, and fight with all I have to prevent it, as I did at the side of Marjorie Wallace and my mother and father ten years ago." I looked right at Prim, and she was fuming, as she stared at me with hate.

"Pay and display kills tourism, it has been proven on all four surveys of this village, but my candidate would not know that, she was not resident when they were done, whereas, I was." Titters rose up in the hall, Birch sat back and smiled.

"God I am so hot for her right now." Anita giggled. I smiled.

"I am happy to give my opponent my full support for a paint the village program, although, I feel it should be extended beyond the retail aspects of this village. Should I take office, I will start a campaign to raise extra funds to help, to ensure every building contained within the area of the Village Green gets support, including the backs of the residential buildings that overlook the green." That was greeted with great enthusiasm. I was feeling a little less nervous, and took a breath.

"I see on this list, a proposed Dursley Woods Project Proposal, but it appears that there is absolutely no information available on this so called project. I have looked very hard, and yet I find no one I have spoken to, including council members have any idea of this. So could I please ask my opposition to provide a presentation before the vote, so all of us can have a greater understanding. Dursley Woodlands is a place of great natural beauty for all of us in our life here, I personally have some very precious memories of it. It is an idyllic and beautiful area that enhances this village, and I am keen to learn what will be done to enhance it." Birch leaned forward in her seat and whispered into Deb's ear.

"I am going to finger Deads in those woods, so you can both have special memories of it, and if you want, I will grope your boobs so you will be even?" Deb's went beetroot.

"Abby has a big bloody mouth, screw you Birch." She sniggered and kissed the top of her ear, Deb's shuddered.

"I bloody hate you two." I looked at my notes.

"I think a playground for children again is a wonderful idea, but I cannot support it in that location. As in previous discussions raised, it was made clear, the area is dangerous for children, and it has also been noted, that it is not really a good example to have young children playing next to a busy public house? I have made a few phone calls, as I could support this plan, and I am happy tonight to inform you, that I have had talks with Mr Norman Merryweather, who has six acres of meadow on his property. Should I be elected, I will work with him to co fund a full sized play park for children on his property, in a very safe environment, which I feel, will be to the greater benefit of every parent and child within the boundaries of this village." I lifted the glass of water, and took a sip, I breathed slowly and placed the glass down, and then looked up. I was feeling calmer and more relaxed.

"I am against restrictions being placed on the two public houses of this village, some traditions are worth keeping, but not the outdated licencing restrictions. I am an avid supporter of all business in this village, and I feel that both public houses should have the same rights as all other business to their full trading hours." That was well received with big smiles.

"I would like to publicly commend Mrs Primula Wallace for some of her more recent endeavours to garner support. My friends and myself had the most wonderful subsidised meal the other night at Pemberton's, and I would like to publicly thank her for reducing my bill, although, I will not be voting for her obviously. I will say, the vegetarian option I chose was beautiful, and the high standards of Pemberton's food, impressed me greatly." Primula fumed; she was irate, and a little louder than she intended, as others looked at her.

"It was not meant for that whore." I smiled, and a lot of people turned and scowled at her.

"I read her recent interview, in the paper, I have it here in front of me, and I agree, tradition is massively important, so important that even in my immoral life, in my sinful relationship, even I am aware of its importance. But could I just please point out for the record, that my beautiful wife, and myself, do not identify as lesbians, we prefer the term Curio, I feel that is a fact that she should correct. Tradition is greatly important, and I fully intend to follow in the footsteps of two people who I feel understand tradition in this village better than any of us. All my life I have watched as Marjorie Wallace and my mother Felicity Watson, fought side by side to protect the heritage of this village, and I was always a hundred percent behind them, and fully intend to continue on their work into the future, as they are both role models I feel should be followed."

From the audience, there were many nods and words of 'here, here,' I smiled, and looked at Marjorie and she gave me a nod, and smirked.

"Mrs Wallace, we have sparred on many occasions, but I will always admire your dedication to this community, and I will maintain what you have built." There were a lot of approving nods, I turned back to the audience.

"Tradition is important, but there is room for additions that will enhance the lives of all of us. Just a few weeks ago I had the honour and the privilege, of becoming Mrs Dixon, and I understand that not all of you fully understand that. Primula calls me a sinner and immoral, I am saddened by that, because I have every intention of following my predecessors and keeping this campaign cordial and free of personal attacks. Even though many of you may not understand my partnership, I saw something in this village which was so traditional, it was inspiring. I watched Priestess Moon, join with Rev Gail Watkins Linley, to jointly share my wedding service. The pagan church was around thousands of years before Christianity, but they came together as friends, and nothing could be more traditional."

I lifted my glass and took a big swig, my mouth was dry, the audience was as still as stone, listening carefully to every word I spoke.

"So, what does Abigail Dixon stand for, what can you expect from me? Well, just look at your sons and daughters who are in this village today. I hope you are happy to have them close to home, because it was Doctor Dixon, supported by the group who go under the name of the Curio's who introduced The Adult Recognition, Training Support program? To date, through that program, we have managed to keep eighty three young adults employed here in their home village, and we are still adding more, with each passing generation. I do not think I need to remind anyone that the program was not a Parish Council program, that was a private program run by us. I hope that alone shows how dedicated Dr Dixon and myself are, and how loyal we are to this village?"

Mumbles broke out again, in a low hum all around the village hall, Primula looked even more enraged. I raised my tone a little higher.

"The youth of today are the most important asset of this village and we need them. Every year I have heard the Chair ask for volunteers, and every year it has been the same. Chloe Pemberton, Anthony Parker, Edwina Pemberton, Debbie Battersby, Nigel Wallace, Sophia Banbury, Molly St Vincent, myself, and a few assorted others. I have never once seen the name of Primula Wallace on any of those lists, and I should know, I have stewarded volunteers every year for well over a decade. So, I have to ask the question, is she even qualified to handle the role of Chair? I know I am; I have grown up with it, and whilst she was learning her A-B-C's, I was learning the constitution of this village's council. I am sure there are quite a few who remember a few years back, where I quoted it paragraph for paragraph in the post office?" I stood back and smiled.

"If you want to know if I am capable with the help of Doctor Dixon, of organising this village, just cast your memory back a few months to the Curio Live event, which was planned and executed by Doctor Dixon, and the Curio group. For over a year we worked on that at home, and then we took it to the world on live stream. In just a few months we will open the first of several centres, which will be a first of their kind, and trust me, a village fete after that, will be child's play for us. If you are still not convinced, before the vote, we will show you the full power of our abilities, in something special we are currently planning for this village."

I gave a satisfied smirk, as I saw the looks of approval on the faces of the room. I waited a few moments and waited for them to quieten.

"If you want parking meters, out of date licensing laws, and an unsafe playground, but pretty shops, then vote for Primula. If you want organisation on a competent scale, in a pair of safe hands, and a dedication to this village unrivalled by any young person, with no vote purchased and decent honest, open transparent council workings, you know my name, so put a tick next to it. Ladies and gentlemen, thank you for hearing me out, and be sure to vote for Dixon and Dixon."

I stepped back, and the applause started, screams and whistles echoed at the back, and I smiled, as I turned, and saw Hatty, she gave me a thumbs up, and I walked to the steps. People were smiling and applauding, and it was very loud, they grabbed my hand and shook it, and patted my shoulder. I nodded and said thank you, who the hell would ever have believed this could happen? Birch flung herself into my arms and squeezed me to death.

"My pants are so frigging wet right now, that is the sexiest thing you have ever done. Oh Sweetie, I am so going to keep you up late tonight." I giggled into her.

"I am trembling, they really liked it." She almost crushed me.

"They loved it Deads, it was honest, sincere, and factual, you did a perfect job of it. I am so proud of you, you really looked like a Council Chair, you came across as a leader, and they lapped it up." I hoped so, Prim would destroy this place.

Deb's and the others all pulled me into hugs, it felt wild, and my mum banged the gavel for quiet, everyone settled down, as I sat next to Birch and Anita, who patted my hand and whispered.

"I know you hate it, but shit Abby, you should be on a stage talking about your books."

I was not sure about that; my mum approached the mic.

"Thank you, Mrs Abigail Dixon, for a very informative and enlightening presentation. You have all seen both candidates, and I am sure we will see both of them at all future events to talk to you and consider your views, and also present their own ideas to you all before voting. I think considering the Parish Council still has no details, that the suggestion of Mrs Dixon, is valid, and we will work with Mrs Primula Wallace to ascertain all the details of this new Dursley Wood Project. As you know, drinks are available, and so I would like to thank all of you for attending, please feel free to mingle and discuss the candidates."

I leaned back in my seat as everyone got up, and walked around, I really needed a drink, and by that I meant alcohol. Sadly, that time was not close, Birch and myself were candidates, and we got swamped with people who asked a million questions. We stood side by side and talked until we were so dry; we could hardly speak.

As the crowd thinned, my dad came up and gave me a massive hug.

"My God you were brilliant, Angela filmed it, and I am going to watch it again when I get home. Abigail, I am so proud of you, you were perfect, and spoke with great authority. I have to say, you were forceful in just the right places. I was blown away by it, I really was, I am so proud of you Abigail." He was all smiles, it was weird as hell, but it was nice.

"Thanks Dad, but I learned from the best, both of you were great role models." He nodded, and just smiled.

"I am at a loss for words, and just so proud, so many have told me tonight how amazing you were, I cannot wait to see you win this." I shrugged.

"That is a way off, and she will not fight fair, so we will see." He patted my cheek.

"You got this in the bag Abigail."

I hugged him and Angela goodbye, as the hall emptied, leaving just a few of us.

Mum was all smiles, Hatty was bouncing on her heels with delight, Primula was nowhere to be seen, she had stormed out before anyone got a chance to talk to her, I hugged mum.

"Was that alright, did I come across dignified, I really don't want to let you down?"

"You acted with great knowledge and skill, you were very dignified and a shining example of what is expected of this village, in fact Mrs Dixon, I was very impressed." I turned to see Madge, and swallowed hard, she held out her hand, and I took it, she had a grip like a vice.

"I wanted to thank you Abigail, you showed me great honour and respect, and I do believe you will continue the legacy of your mother and I; it is a shame I cannot say the same for my own daughter in law. Your presentation was flawless, and credit should be given where it is deserved." I smiled.

"Coming from you Mrs Wallace, that is really a huge compliment, thank you." She smiled a grizzly smile.

"I look forward to seeing what else you have up your sleeve, this is going to be an interesting summer, but again, well done." Wow, I was lost for words, Milton grabbed my hand, I think he smiled, because his teeth moved.

"Yes, yes, Abigail, wonderful presentation, I thoroughly enjoyed it, very sophisticated and eloquent, most enjoyable, good for you." I smiled again.

"Thank you, Reverend Wallace."

All around me G5 and the rest of the Curio's were putting the chairs away, I noticed Fidelity had hung back and was helping. Mum hugged me and oozed praise and adoration on me, she stood back and gripped my shoulders and smiled at me.

"I was so proud of you tonight, Abby, you are the most remarkable of women, you presented your case with dignity and style. I just sat there filled with unbelievable pride." Hatty gave a nod.

"You fucking rocked it Abby, and you stuck it to that bitch, in such a way, you proved you were up to the job, and they all noticed. Well done you."

"I really need a drink; my knees are still shaking a little." She smiled.

"Go home and have the biggest one, you earned it."

I mucked in and helped with the chairs, and with such a large crew, it was done in no time. We prepared to go, and Fidelity came up.

"You were really good, but be careful Abby, she is really angry, she is not a nice person, and she will find a way to hurt you." I already understood that.

"It is expected, we know what we are doing, what you up to?" She shrugged.

"Home to bed, not much else happening, it's Wotton." Birch smiled as she walked up.

"It's Friday night and still early, so that means Uni rules apply." Fidelity frowned.

"What are Uni rules?" Chloe walked past carrying the last chair.

"All girls should end up pissed and naked, it's the law." I chuckled as she looked a little shocked.

"We are heading back to our place for a drink, do you want to come, you are welcome to?" She looked a little nervous.

"If it is alright with everyone else, I would love to." Birch linked her arm.

"Follow us, into our den of immorality, do you fear losing your soul young lady, for we collect them?" Deb's chuckled as she walked up.

"Are you and Jimmy coming too?" She looked at me, and looked a little down.

"I would love to, but Jenny is asleep, we really should get her home." I shrugged.

"Deb's, you have a room with a crib and a double bed, we have cameras with sound, the house is pretty sound proof, and let's be honest, Aunty Birch is a psychotic clothing junkie. You have more clothes for Jenny than she will ever wear. Come on, have some fun with us, we miss you, stay the night and celebrate with me." She gave me that huge familiar smile.

"Yeah, I would love to."

I linked her arm, and we walked towards Jimmy stood holding Jenny in his arms. Anita tagged on and left her car, and we all headed back to our place to chill with a drink, it was Friday, and Uni rules applied.

We arrived home, and headed for the kitchen, drinks came out from under the island, and we all dived in, white wine was poured, gin and vodka, and within minutes Chloe and Birch were naked." Fidelity was a little shocked, I smiled at her.

"If you hang out with us, you will have to get used to it, pretty much all of us are naturists, we only wear clothes when we go outdoors, well not in the garden or the pool obviously. On the street, we dress, well Birch does most of the time, we do try to keep her on this side of the wall naked. Fidelity was intrigued.

"So you all hang out with no clothes at all on... Guys and girls?" Anita appeared as interested. I nodded at her; it is funny how it just boggles people's minds.

"It is not sexual, it is body freedom, comfort and body confidence, nothing more. Despite Prim, I am in a relationship with Birch, Deb's is with Jimmy, Edwina with Luke, and Anthony and Michael are together. It is true we have sex, but only with our partners, everyone else is single, although Chloe and Terry do have a FWB thing going on. Look, we are liberated, open minded, but we are nowhere near as deviant as we are painted, we believe in live and let live with no judgement, nothing more. Actually, you would be surprised how many naturists actually live around here, there are a lot more than you realise." Fidelity gave a sly smile.

"I have never really thought of it, although I do not wear much in my flat, I usually only wear my knickers at home." Anita nodded.

"Yeah, me too, although when I was with Katie, it was pretty hard staying dressed." I lifted my glass.

"The rule here is, when you want to be naked be that, and when you want to be dressed, be that too."

We headed into the living room where everyone was excited and chatting. It was warm and snug, and soon layers were shedding, I curled into my corner and Birch slid up to me, she was excited and happy, and she nuzzled in to me, and very horny as she started to unbutton my blouse.

Izzy walked in wearing suspenders and black lace panties but no top, Anita was already half undressed and Fidelity looked around amazed to see everyone just chilled out and laughing and joking. Chloe as always was sprawled out on the floor, eating biscuits and drinking gin, she looked at Fidelity.

"Just do it Deli, try it, if you hate it don't do it again, but you will love it, we all do, it is liberating and the ultimate sense of freedom. I hardly wear clothes these days, and I always paint naked."

Fidelity looked at us, Birch had my blouse off, and was already looking for ways to get my pants off. I smiled.

"It is your body, and your call, there is no judgement here, and also no pressure."

There was noise and excitement and the talk began, Fidelity who had decided, sod it, stripped, folded her clothes neatly and sat with Chloe. She was a little embarrassed at first, but we treated her as we do each other, and very soon she was relaxed and happy.

"Guys, Prim is really scary, she wants this more than you realise, and tonight you blew her out of the water, her weakness is her big mouth." Birch sat up interested.

"How so?" Fidelity looked at her.

"The Dursley Woods Project, for one thing, she boasted how she had done a deal that would give her more power than even Madge had, and how she would become rich for pushing it through quietly. They are going to build all over that area, the houses will come up right to the church." Birch gave a nod.

"That much we know, or have guessed, but there are rules and laws, how does she think this will get passed?" Fidelity sat cross legged, at the side of Chloe, and sipped her drink.

"Wow this is way more fun than her place." She smiled.

"The plans will be on display in the council offices, the only problem is, they will be on the top floor, where no public go. It is still legal, as people walk past them, so technically, they are publicly displayed." Birch understood.

"I really want to see those plans, I knew Deads calling her out would panic her, and she did look worried." Fidelity gave a smirk.

"It scared the hell out of her, it is why she left early, she wanted to ring that bent MP, and find out what could be done about it, it really rattled her." I could see that from the stage, her stares of anger at me, were intense.

"If she is in deep with Parkinson, he will tell her he will protect her, but he won't, that shit bag will hang her out to dry if word gets out. No doubt Nigel will have another black eye tomorrow."

Fidelity looked at me.

"You know about that then?" I nodded; she gave a sigh.

"I really feel sorry for him Abby." Chloe frowned and looked at her.

"Yeah, but you don't fancy him, do you?" Fidelity looked horrified.

"Christ Chloe, NO! I saw the live stream; he has nothing I want anywhere near me." She gave a violent shudder, and we all giggled, she looked down at the floor, and her voice lowered.

"I do feel sorry for him though, you know once you get to know him, he is a gentle lad, and he is actually really soft and kind. I hate the way she humiliates him in front of everyone, she treats him terribly, and she spends his money like water."

Birch was watching her closely, I sat back to observe, I cannot deny, I love it when she is like this, it really turns me on.

"What is her relationship with Madge like?" I smiled; she was not wasting time. Fidelity looked up.

"She hates Madge, she is constantly saying that Madge is trying to tell her how to live and rule her life, you know Madge told her about the parking meters, but she would not listen? I think Madge is a bit afraid of her, I mean, she is getting old, and Prim is really violent."

It made perfect sense, we had thought it, but having it confirmed helped. I leaned forward in my seat, and watched Fidelity carefully.

"I must admit, as soon as I heard about the meters, I knew Madge was not behind her, she fought like hell last time to prevent them. She argued that the only reason Oxendale Council wanted them was to boost their own revenues, none of that money went to the village." Things were starting to make more sense, and Birch was figuring it all out, she relaxed back on the sofa.

"I think Madge suggested the council to give Prim a focus, so she would stop abusing Nigel, and Prim got power hungry, and cut her out completely, she has gone rogue with the MP." Fidelity gave a nod.

"Even Molly thinks she is out of control, and she is the biggest ass kisser I have ever known, and Sophia is too innocent to know anything different, she does exactly what she is told, that girl lives for Insta likes." Deb's smiled.

"We know Yar!" Everyone started giggling, I got up to go and refill my glass, and Birch dived and grabbed my pants and pulled.

"Got ya!" I looked down and stepped out, I did not even know the buttons were open. I walked into the kitchen to refill my glass; Anita followed me in.

"Abby that shipment will arrive tomorrow afternoon, will you be here?" I gave her a big smile.

"She is going to be blown away, I gave her sketches back, I have measured them all and the frames are almost ready." Anita sat down, I offered her the bottle, she shook her head.

"As much as I would love to, if I have another, I will not be able to drive home." I poured a measure into her glass.

"So stay here, we have two spare rooms, and that way you will be here when they arrive. Come on, you have worked hard on this for her, you should share a little of the joy. I can tell you worked with Katie, she drove you hard and you got few breaks, you are working with me now. Look at you all naked, smiling and chilled out, just stay over, you can get your car tomorrow after they arrive. Go on tell me, when was the last time you actually socialised?" She picked up her drink.

"Not since Katie, Abby, I really cared about her, I know you don't see it, but I thought I could have what you and Jemi have with her. It really hurt when I found out I was just a lure for you, I was heartbroken, and she was so cold. You know after what she did at the book fair, she came to see me and asked if we could get back together?" I sat down in front of her.

"I did not know, that must have been a tough one?" She smiled a sad smile.

"It was really hard because a part of me really wanted her back, when I told I didn't think so, she really went off on one, it was yet another act. To be honest Abby, I was glad you had the contract, at the moment I am steering clear of relationships, I am not ready to get back out there, I just want to work and be happy with me for a while."

"I can understand that, I felt the same way after I left Birch at Uni and came home. I went two years before I dated again, and I caught him snorting coke off another girls' boobs, and looking at the powder marks, it was obvious where she had snorted from. I quit on everything for a while, and then Birch came back, and as they say, this happened." She smiled.

"She is right for you, I watched her tonight as you spoke, she did not take her eyes off you for a second, and she had a small happy smile for the whole time. She was really proud of you tonight, the love you guys have is like a beacon, we all see it. I will also say, you look a lot happier now than you did at the Curio event."

I loved that people saw it, I have always worried people would not understand me, it made me happy to know that it was so obvious. I looked at my ring on my finger.

"I always swore I would never marry, but when she asked me, honestly Anita, my heart exploded with joy. I could hardly speak I was so shocked; I think I have always known I would be beside her always. Since the day I met her, I was attracted to her, which was weird because I thought I was straight." She smiled.

"Been there, I beat myself up for ages coming to terms with my bi side, and then a friend just sat down and said to me, why sweat it, everyone is fluid to a degree, and once I accepted that, I was fine."

We sipped our drinks and talked, and slowly the group appeared and joined in, and we all sat in the kitchen chatting. Fidelity was told to stay, she took the single bed, and Anita got Birch's old room, and around two in the morning, I staggered into my room with Birch. She spun me round and kissed me softly, and I gazed into her eyes and smiled, I giggled as I looked at her.

"You do know pulling your bosses pants off is a sackable offence, explain to me just how you intend to prevent me firing you?" Birch gave a happy squeal, and threw me on the bed.

"Please don't sack me boss, I have a girlfriend with expensive tastes, if I get fired, she will leave me." I lay there and eyed her up and down slowly.

"Well then, if you want to stay in my employ, earn it." I snapped my legs wide open really quickly and she blinked.

"Now get back to work."

She gave a squeal of delight, she was way too excited, but there again, so was I.

Chapter 6

Surprises.

"It's coming, it's coming!"

I blinked open my eyes and turned over, Birch looked sleepy, she smiled, and dreamily spoke quietly.

"Hi Sweetie... If that is Chloe shouting about Percy, she is more screwed up than we thought?" The bedroom door burst open, and Chloe came flying in, and launched herself at the bed.

"Guys wake up, it's coming." Birch groaned.

"If it's the apocalypse, tell it I am busy sleeping." Chloe frowned.

"Huh?" I sat up, and her face went right back to a smile.

"Abby, it's coming today." I nodded and yawned.

"Chloe you are always coming, honestly, you should get a Noble Prize for it."

"Huh?" She grinned.

"Oh yeah, funny Abby. Guys, Mr Wilks, is dropping it off, and grabbing Myrtle." I frowned at her.

"Huh?" She gave a sigh.

"You know Myrtle... My car?" I blinked, and then rubbed my eyes, I had not had anywhere near enough coffee.

"Your car is called Myrtle?" She nodded.

"Yeah, I thought you knew that? Whenever I went above thirty it used to make this weird sound, and it was just like Moaning Myrtle, so I named it that." I looked at Birch who was watching me struggle with my coffee deprived brain.

"Please help me?" She giggled, and sat up.

"Chloe Sweetie, it's early, and Deads needs caffeine, explain to us in basic English using full sentences instead of it's coming, we have no idea what you are talking about." She smiled and nodded.

"Yeah sorry, I am really excited, because I bought the VW, and Mr Wilks, is going to deliver her to me soon, and he is taking my old car as part trade. I am really chuffed, it only cost me seven grand." My eyes snapped open, and suddenly I was wide awake.

"You paid seven grand for that pile of shit, Petal was in better condition, and she only cost two?"

"One and a half Sweetie, but actually you got it for a good price, it is a 1979, and the cheapest I could find was twelve, so yeah, well done Sweetie." Chloe beamed with delight.

"Guys I am really excited, I can go to Sunny Bank in it, and sleep in my own van, and I can have tons of sex in it, which means I can drive out to meet people." I sniggered.

"Well, you have pretty much road tested most of the male population of this area, so why not cast your net wider?" I slid my legs over the edge of the bed.

"Where is everyone?" Chloe jumped off the bed.

"Deb's, Raisin and Jimmy are downstairs with Deli and Edwina, Anthony is at work, Anita is still in bed, Izzy went out, and you guys are here." I nodded and headed for the door, Birch sat up and rubbed her eyes, slipped out of bed, and followed on behind.

I made it to the kitchen in relative peace, and Edwina put a cup down in front of me, Deb's was feeding Jenny. Birch arrived yawning and sat at my side, Fidelity was still naked, and eating muesli, I smiled and sipped my coffee. Birch looked at Deb's and then nudged me.

"I did that to you last night." She giggled.

"Yep, that is why you still have a job." Her eyes twinkled, as she smiled, Deb's looked at us strangely.

"Please tell me you were not playing mummies and babies, because you are both freaking me the hell out?" Birch sniggered, I stared at her blankly.

"Have you not tried it with Jimmy, it's fun?" She cringed.

"Jesus you two are weird since you were married." Fidelity sniggered.

I sat sipping my coffee slowly, and feeling life slowly return to my body, I noticed Fidelity watching me.

"What?" She smiled a big smile.

"You guys, this house, the way you live, it's so close and bonded, you are all pretty cool, I love the way you are all so open and honest with each other. I had such a great night last night, I just wanted to thank all of you, I am blown away by your kindness, I truly am." I smiled.

"We are a pretty unique group, not everyone gets us, but we don't mind." Birch nodded as she took her bowl off Edwina.

"None of us have secrets, we live an open life, we know pretty much every aspect of everyone, and if there is a problem, we all chip in to solve it. The Kitchen and living rooms are free forums, we debate and discuss everything, and every major decision, is a group activity, it really is the only way to live." She nodded.

"It probably sounds weird, but I love how normal you are with each other, at Prim's, you have to hide everything, just in case it pisses her off, that girl loses her shit over everything." Birch looked up at her as she chewed.

"If you don't mind me asking, you don't come across like Molly or Sophia, why do you put up with them, or even hang out with them, I get the feeling you just don't fit?" She nodded her head, and gave a sigh.

"All my friends from school have left the area, the only people I know from school now are Molly and Sophia. I knew of Abby, and I was mates with Chloe in year eight, and I knew Deb's a little bit, but to be honest I was intimidated by you all. I have been on the Curio site, and you guys are rock solid." Birch nodded.

"We are a family, but we have a lot of friends in the village, at least now you know you have an alternative, don't suffer and pretend to be someone you are not to fit in Fidelity, just be you, and see who still wants you around, because those are your people."

Anita staggered into the kitchen, with her eyes half closed, and her hair sticking out everywhere.

"Christ your house mate is loud, my head is banging." She flopped down at the end of the island, Edwina chuckled as she put down a cup of coffee and two pain killers. Anita tried to smile. Birch looked at her.

"Ooh Sweetie, you look really rough, are you alright?" Anita tried to nod and regretted it immediately.

"I have not really drunk anything for a while, honestly, I had a wonderful night, but at the moment, the less I move the better." We all giggled, this was normal when first meeting us, we left her to quietly awaken.

It took around an hour for all of us to wake up fully, I went up to my room and sat at my desk, and was checking my email, when Anita knocked on the door. I smiled and waved her in.

"It probably sounds cheeky, but would you by any chance have any spare knickers I could borrow?" I swung round in my seat.

"I have not worn any in ten years, but I think I have a pair my mum bought me for under my wedding dress." I smiled.

"I didn't wear any that day either." She walked in and looked around the room.

"Wow I love that picture." She was looking up at the picture of me at nineteen, I pulled open my drawer and lifted out a pair of small flowery panties, still in a plastic bag.

"Will these do?" I lifted them up and she smiled.

"Yeah thanks, I will wash them and let you have them back." I scoffed.

"Keep them, I won't be wearing them... If you want to borrow some jeans and a top, help yourself, it is better than wearing your work clothes on a Saturday, Birch has a slightly longer leg than me, so they should fit."

I grabbed my black dungarees and a long sleeved top, then got some socks out of the drawer, I threw Anita a new pair, she was looking at my computer.

"Is that the sunset on your honeymoon?"

I walked over and pulled Birch's chair over, and sat in my chair, she pulled on some jeans and came over, she sat on the chair, as she pulled on her socks. I had the photos on slide show, so they changed every few seconds, Anita smiled at the pictures of the beach.

"I really admire you two you know?" I swung round in my seat.

"Why, we are just another couple?" She shook her head.

"No, you are not, I have a lot of lesbian friends, but to be honest, their relationships never last long. They become volatile so easily, it is the one thing I fear about being in a relationship with another woman, I do not want to get too attached, and end up losing her." I could understand that.

"You are forgetting, we are not really lesbians, to be honest both of us still think we are straight, and yet we have a very deep love, and we are sexual with just each other. The thing is, I am not attracted to other women, and neither is Birch, it took us years to really figure it all out. I don't think I really did until Katie tried to destroy us, that was when I really knew, seeing Birch completely break down, and tell me how she was now too soiled for me, broke my heart. I knew in that moment; I would never leave her side." She looked really sad, and I smiled.

"You are not responsible for that Anita; it was nothing to do with you. Katie crossed a line, it was her choice, and in doing so, she undid everything. Anita, that week I learned that we have to trust and finally let go, and I did. I let go of everything and just lived in the wonder of the moment, and there inside, I found a whole other side to Birch, and I fell in love with her all over again." She sat back in her chair and smiled.

"I understand, I put too much pressure on myself, and maybe I do need to let go a little. I sat and watched Fidelity last night, and her reaction to you both, and I watched how she just let go and embraced something completely new. I think you guys changed her forever, just by being normal." I chuckled as I sat back.

"I am not convinced we are normal, but we are true to ourselves, and that makes a difference."

The screams outside our door, announced the fact that Chloe had been sat at her bedroom window waiting, and her new vehicle had arrived. We wandered out of our room and headed downstairs, the front door was wide open, so we headed out, and down the drive to the gates. Mr Wilks was at the back of his trailer, holding the control as it slowly tipped, and then he let the winch move slowly, and Chloe's new vehicle rolled backwards carefully on to the road.

Chloe bounced up and down with excitement, as Mr Wilks stopped the winch, and then opened the door, and pulled on the handbrake, before uncoupling the winch off the front of the van. Everyone stood in a line and watched, Birch appeared very excited, and again, maybe it is me, but who else buys this junk? I do not understand why people do not buy something up to date and modern.

The next job was to collect Chloe's car out of the garage. The thing was dead, which meant it had to be pushed onto the drive. We all gathered behind it, and grunted, gasped, and heaved, how the hell can something with so many holes in it, be so hard to move?

Breathing hard, and feeling like the weak and feeble women we were, the car was finally lined up on the drive, and after a swapping of documents, Mr Wilks, winched it up onto the trailer, secured it and then drove off, and Chloe stood beaming with delight. She opened the side door, to reveal the small kitchen and back seat/bed. Birch revelled in it and climbed in to look, I stood outside with Anita and watched, and it was quite cool.

Chloe climbed in the driver's seat; it did look pretty basic. Deb's who appeared equally as delighted, jumped in the front passenger seat and looked around.

"It really is a pretty sweet little van; I think it suits you, Chloe." She was all smiles as she wound down the window.

"I love it, as soon as I saw her, I knew I wanted it, I think I am going to call it Bess, as in short for bestie, because this is the best car I have ever owned."

Birch who was sat in the back looking at the little cupboards and kitchen stove, with great enthusiasm, turned to look at the front.

"I still have decals in the garage of flowers, and I think a rainbow, with the orange paintwork, and some decals, it will look really retro." I smiled.

"Yeah, make love not war, and when the flowers are a bobbing, don't come knocking, it's perfect." I giggled with Anita; Deb's turned to Chloe.

"What was that?" Chloe eyed her suspiciously.

"Why would you say that?" She shrugged.

"Didn't you hear it?" Chloe shook her head.

"No, and I don't want to, fuck off Deb's, every time you say that, something fucked up happens. So just shut the fuck up, I love this van, don't spoil it." Anita pointed to Birch, or at least behind her on the unit.

"Guys, is that what I think it is?" Birch turned to look as my blood ran cold, and how do I put it exactly?

There was this deafeningly loud and ear piercing scream of terror, and a flash of a fast moving white mass, as Birch exited the van, and ran off up the lane shrieking like a maniac. The driver's door and passenger door both flew open rapidly, to more terror filled screams. One paint splattered artist ran across the road, and Deb's appeared behind me, in a flash, and cowered, gripping my shirt behind me shaking violently, I looked at Anita.

"Yep, that is definitely a frigging huge rat." Birch bobbed up and down fifty feet away.

"Sweetie, I don't like it, get rid of it." I had absolutely no idea why she thought I would, I shook my head.

"Screw you Birch, it's Chloe's van, it's her job." She peered round, from behind the tree across the lane, and shook her head vigorously.

"I don't like mice." Deb's muttered into my shirt behind me.

"That is not a mouse, it is a bloody huge rat. Please Abby, do something, I am afraid of rats."

The rat was a big fat brown thing, the size of a medium sized cat. It sat on top of the small polished wooden cabinet eating what looked like a nut, I shuddered, I looked at Anita, and she shook her head, and pointed across the road.

"Get screwed, it's her van." She gave a violent shudder. Fidelity had come to look at the van, she was now stood behind the gate post, peeping around it, I smiled at her.

"Come and have a closer look." She shook her head and slid back behind the post. Birch was still up the street dithering on the spot, and looking very alarmed.

"Sweetie, I don't like it, please make it go away."

I didn't want to laugh, I really didn't, but I could not help it. I was freaked the hell out, but it was funny watching them all be more freaked out, Chloe peered out from behind the tree.

"Has it gone yet?" I shook my head.

"Nope, it is just sat there enjoying staring at you, and eating something." She shuddered violently.

"Erghhhh!" Deb's mumbled.

"We need Jimmy." I looked towards Fidelity, and she nodded and disappeared.

It took a few more minutes of Birch's dithering dance fifty feet away, Chloe playing peek a boo behind the tree, and Deb's mumbles into my back, before Jimmy appeared with a tire iron, I looked at him.

"What the hell is that for?" He looked at me, and held it up.

"You know Doll... To bash it's fucking head in with." All of us shivered together. Birch dithered even faster.

"Erghhhhhh!" I stepped back, as Jimmy marched up to the side of the van, Birch covered her eyes, with a squeal.

"Please don't hurt it." I felt my jaw drop.

"WHAT THE HELL, MAKE YOUR MIND UP?" She shook her head.

"I don't like death Sweetie." Jimmy looked over the van at her.

"Don't worry Doll, one good whack and we are good." Everyone shuddered again.

"Erghhhh!"

Anita gripped my arm, as Jimmy climbed into the van slowly, I felt a strong desire to close my eyes. They made it to squint, and morbid curiosity kicked in. He lifted the tire iron up really slowly, Chloe disappeared back behind the tree with a whimper, and Birch danced in the middle of the road with her hands on her eyes. Deb's head appeared on my shoulder.

Moving very slowly, Jimmy positioned himself, and quicker than lightening, he swept the thing down, and missed.

Anita squealed like a pig, I screamed the loudest I ever have, as the rat jumped on the floor of the van. Deb's legged it, the rat jumped out of the van onto the path, and I fled screaming with Anita towards Birch.

Birch pulled her hands off her face, saw us hurtling, and screaming towards her, with a big fat rat running behind us along the gutter, she went into melt down, squealed, ran on the spot, then turned and legged it leaving us.

Anita grabbed my wrist, and dragged me over to the other side of the road, as the rat ran past us, and Birch squealed with abject terror, as it chased her down the lane.

"Sweetie, I don't like it, tell it to go home."

I stopped, gasping for air, my heart thumping in my chest, and turned round, Jimmy was up the lane standing behind Deb's looking white faced. My heart was pounding in my ears. Chloe came out from behind the tree, and looked at him.

"I thought you were going to fucking kill it?" He looked a little panicked.

"It was bigger than it looked Doll." Deb's shuddered violently, and Jimmy swallowed hard.

"What do you want, it's fucking gone now?" Chloe looked nervously at her van.

"Do you think that was it, or are there any more?" I was bent double getting my breath back, and looked up at her.

"It's your van, go have a look." She looked at Deb's and Jimmy.

"Will you come with me?" Deb's shook her head.

"Screw you, Chloe, I am going nowhere near that, until you double check it is rodent free."

We all returned to the house, and Luke went into the van and opened every cupboard, and lifted up the seat pads, to make sure the van, or 'Bess' was completely vermin free. Chloe rang Mr Wilks who did apologise, and told her rats sometimes come up from the railway and hang around the cars. He explained it must have jumped in when one of his boys had all the doors open checking out the electrics.

Birch finally staggered in, bright red in the face and exhausted. She had run all the way down the lane, and then along the canal, up the embankment, and in through my mums back gate, and come through mum's side gate. and over the road home.

With the final seal of safety given by a smiling Luke, Chloe transferred her insurance over from her old car to her new one, on the phone, and took Edwina and Luke for a drive, delighted with her new car. Having had a stiff gin, or two, I felt much better when the large truck pulled up, and a guy with a pallet truck full of boxes knocked on the door.

This was what I had been waiting for, and I asked him nicely if he would pull them into the garage for me, and the pallets were dropped where Chloe's old car had been parked. I tore off the shrink wrap, and grabbed the top box, addressed to me, and carried it into the library, where feeling very excited, Anita and myself, surrounded by the others, opened the box, and gasped with delight.

I lifted out the large heavy book, it was a faux leather in deep red, and on it in bold golden letters, it read, 'Sanctuary Art, Sketches for the Hand of Death book series, illustrated by Chloe Pemberton.' I smiled as I placed it carefully on the table, Anita smiled, and ran her hand softly across the cover, Deb's eyes were huge.

"Oh, I am defo having a copy of that." I looked at her.

"It is a limited edition, there are 2000 copies only, and they are for sale at £140.00 each. Chloe has no idea we have done this; it is part of a big surprise for her. This book will go on sale for her to signed each numbered copy at her first major art exhibition in London, on August seventeenth, and it will run for four weeks. All the frames have been made, and her sketches will be framed this week, and then we will ship them to the gallery, and Chloe will get her first public event." They all smiled.

"We are using D&D Events to promote her, and obviously because it is art from my books, we have been quietly putting the word out, that I will be there at her side for the launch. Guys, Chloe needs to see how good she is, and so does the rest of the world. We have done her a load of prints and posters to sell on the day as well, so hopefully, she will finally understand her true value as an artist."

Anita opened the cover to the title page and read it out loud.

"Sanctuary Art, Sketches for the Hands of Death, book series, illustrated by Chloe Pemberton. Commentary by Abigail Jennifer Watson." She turned the page and everyone gasped as they saw the arch from the canal, and now in the garden, drawn in graphic detail.

"Wow Abby, she is so talented."

On each page, was a high resolution image she had sketched for me, and underneath was a short commentary I had written about the sketch, and why I loved it. It was a thrill for me, but I knew this would mean to world the her. Birch was all smiles.

"Chloe is so lovely, she deserves this. Guys, when we post this to the D&D web site, spam the shit out of it. Let's all plaster social media with it, and make sure everyone knows about it." In the bottom of the box was a stack of posters for the event, Deb's grabbed a hand full.

"I have to go to the shop soon, I will get these all over Wotton today." I stepped back and let all of them inspect the book, Birch slipped her arm round me, and leaned on my shoulder.

"I love living here, I love our family." I smiled.

"What even with a rat infested Bess?" Everyone shuddered.

"Erghhhh!"

Deb's had to go to the book shop, and Anita walked with her, so she could pick up her car, which was still parked on Church Rise.

I took the boxed books upstairs so I could have a proper look at it. This book was number one, and everyone was numbered up until 2000, but this one was her copy, it was special and on the inside of the cover, I picked up my golden pen, and wrote the inscription.

'To my most beautiful friend, Chloe. I am inspired, as I see my words come alive in the drawings you have done, and I will be forever grateful, to have shared such wonderful moments of my life with you. I love you dearly... Abigail Jennifer Watson.'

I smiled, as I put the pen down, and turned the page to once again see the beautiful sketch of my arch. When Birch came in, I was lost in thought, sat with my legs crossed on my office chair, the book in my lap, as I turned each page and marvelled at Chloe's work. Birch leaned over my shoulder and kissed my cheek, and I blinked, and looked up, she smiled.

"She really has no idea at all how good she is." I shook my head softly as I looked at the sketch of Gabriella and Willis, there was such depth and richness to the picture.

"I love these pictures Birch, I love that I created these in my head, and I gave them life with my words, but Chloe gave them their souls."

Birch sat in her chair and her eyes shone and sparkled, as sunlight streamed in through the window on to her face, and her hair shone white.

"I have spoken to Bradley today Deads, and told him what we know. He said we should keep quiet and say nothing, and let him look into it, and when he knows something, he will let us know."

Last night had gone well for me, but today I did not want to think about it, all I wanted was to open up the world for Chloe. I feel I owe her so much, she has illustrated my covers, done designs for posters, given me countless images for my website, and always refused when I wanted to pay her, and always told me she did it because I was her friend and she loved me.

She has no idea how good she is, and also how important she has become to me. Our shared painful experiences together, have at times been a life line, from sitting with her legs in my pool with me after Nigel, to cuddling up to me the night that Birch was in hospital, and I was falling apart with worry. She fought to protect me when Martin fired shots into the Tea Room, and she has been there every morning to sit with me and keep me grounded as we drank coffee.

Friends like Chloe are so rare, we have laughed and cried together, and had such crazy moments together, and yet she has never asked anything of me, and she has always been there at my side. After a huge amount of planning with Birch and Anita, we have managed to find a way to set up our own little promotion's vehicle, and Chloe will be our first venture into the promotional world, outside of the Dixon Group. Honestly, I am really excited about today, and I cannot wait to hand her this book.

Chloe was wild with excitement when she arrived back. She parked Bess on the large paved raft at the side of the garage, so it was close to her studio, and she could paint some detail on it. We were all in the living room, Fidelity had said she was leaving, but I convinced her to stay a while longer, and enjoy our own special little way of celebrating each other.

We all grabbed drinks and sat waiting, and Chloe bounced into the room with a huge smile. She crashed down on the sofa opposite me with her drink, she was almost breathless from talking so much. I slid forward on my seat, and Birch slid up at my side, she was excited and gave a giggle. I looked down, where the box was on the floor out of her sight. Chloe relaxed with her drink and looked around the room.

"So, what have you guys been up to?" I smiled at her, as she sat watching us, waiting for a response.

"Chloe, as you know Birch and I with the help of Anita, have set up a new small company D&D, to promote outside the Dixon Group. It is so we will have no involvement with Katie, and we have all been sat here talking about what we should do next. A little while back, Birch said something that really hit a chord with me, and it really made me think, because you know, you have done so much for me in the last nine years, especially in the art department for my covers. I wanted to say thanks to you, because your pictures are so special to me, so I want to give you something as a token of my gratitude." She shrugged.

"Abby, you don't have to, I love drawing for your books, it is great practice for me." I nodded my head.

"Yeah, I love your stuff, I really do, and so I want to give you this." I lifted the box off the floor and put it on the table, and slid it across to her. Birch got giddy.

"I love presents." Chloe slid forward on her seat.

"What is it?" I pointed at the box.

"Open it, and see."

I sat back and watched, and she edged across towards the table. She pulled the box close, and Birch gripped my arm and gave a quiet giggle. Chloe looked up as she opened up the box and looked inside, and I smiled as I saw her eyes fill with tears, she looked up at me.

"What is this?" I smiled.

"The biggest thank you I can think of... Lift it out and look at it."

Chloe picked it up and pulled it to her lap, she wiped her eyes, and ran her fingers over it. I was holding my breath as I watched, she looked up and smiled.

"It's a book, and has my name on it, what is this Abby, I do not understand, you are the writer?" I smiled; I could feel the lump in my throat as I watched her.

"Chloe, just open it."

She looked up and sniffed up, and then lifted the cover and opened it, and read the title page and my inscription, and she shook, Birch smiled at her as she clung to my arm.

"Chloe you are a brilliant artist, that is book one of two thousand limited editions, and we bought all of them for you. We want you to sign them, and they will provide you with more income to fund more art."

She gave a sharp intake of breath, as she opened the cover and saw the huge high resolution page of her picture. Edwina leaned into her and handed her a tissue.

"It is time we showed the world who you are, all of us have taken giant steps forward with what we do, and it is now time for you to follow us." She looked at me as the tears ran down her face.

"Abby this is too much... It is so beautiful; I do not know what to say." I wiped my eyes.

"You say nothing, this is my thanks to you. Chloe, you deserve this, I cannot paint you a picture, and I am sure if I wrote you a story like I did for Birch, you would probably hide it in a crypt." She gave a giggle, and wiped her eyes as she turned the pages.

"It is beautiful, I love it, I really do, but I am not sure I will sell many." Deb's patted her shoulder.

"I am buying one, so is Birch, Abby, Edwina and Anita, I mean at one hundred and forty quid it's a steal." Chloe's head snapped round.

"Fuck off, no book sells for that much." Deb's shrugged.

"Put it in the right environment and it will." Chloe turned, and looked at me sat with Birch and Anita.

"What does she mean?" Anita leaned forward and lifted the flyer out of the box.

"Well considering our first event as D&D will be an art exhibition, and we happened to mention to all Abby's fans that you and her would be the stars of the show, we thought the 2000 books we have stashed in your garage will sell there."

Chloe took the poster and stared at it, she looked up and her face went white.

"Abby this is the Winchester Gallery?" I nodded.

"We figured you are that good, well you better had be. We have all the frames made at mums gallery, and all you have to do is mount them, then ship them to the gallery for four weeks, and at ten quid to get in, we think you will have art supplies for about ten years worth of paint."

It was a little weird watching her as the colour drained from her face, and suddenly without warning, she sort of exploded, burst into tears, and dived across the table at me and pulled me into a hug, mumbling something I really could not understand. I fell back on the sofa and wrapped my arms round her, and spoke softly to her.

"Chloe, you have suffered for your art enough, it is time you got what you deserve. You are so talented, you really have no idea, and we all want you to see your own art, through the eyes of others. It is time you walked into the spotlight, Chloe, I love you, I want this so much for you, can you understand that?"

She just clung to me and wept, and Birch and Anita were sat wiping their eyes, I held her tight, and stroked her hair, until she started to settle down.

"Abby, guys, I really love you too." Birch wiped her eyes.

"Enough to screw us all Chloe?" She started to giggle, she sat up and wiped her eyes.

"Oh God Birch, I really love you, but honestly, I am so fucking straight it's unbelievable."

Chloe finally calmed down, and we all sat round drinking and laughing. She disappeared and I went looking for her, and found her in her studio, sat on the floor with her book, touching each page as she stroked them, and smiling quietly to herself. I left her to it, happy to know that finally, the last of the original Curio's would have her time to shine.

Chapter 7

Self Doubt.

By the time we curled up into bed, we had spent most of the night working on websites. Anita stayed another night, Fidelity had to go home, and Deb's headed off, so as Anthony, Michael, and Luke chilled out gaming, the four of us updated all the sites, and launched the D&D site, and linked it everywhere, with all the Art Exhibition information. Edwina took some great shots of the books, and the launch of Sanctuary Art, was set.

Sunday came, and the talk of the village was Nigel's face, which was cut and swollen, he looked like he had been brutalised, with both his eyes blackened. To make things worse, in church. right in the middle of the church service. he got up and walked out, much to the surprise of everyone.

The gossips were rife outside the church, which played to my benefit, as most of the talk over the last few days had been about the presentation at the Parish Council meeting. Comparisons were being made about how different we both were, and obviously right in the thick of it was Celia and Lillian singing our praises.

Birch's phone going off woke me, around twelve fifteen, she held it to her ear looking tired, and rubbing her eyes, as she listened. I sat up feeling groggy, we had worked late on the sites, and I was not ready to get up, but now I knew I was awake, there was no going back. I looked at Birch, she gave a smile and waved at me, I flopped back in the pillow and rubbed my eyes. Birch nodded into the phone.

"Okay Sweetie, call me when you are ready, and I will be there." She ended the call and gave a sigh.

"That was Moon, Nigel is with her, and in a right state, she says he is black and blue, and has cuts on his face." I sat up feeling really guilty.

"This is all my fault Birch, she is obsessed with him liking me, and two nights ago, I stood up there, and called her out in front of the whole village. Primula is lashing out at the easiest target. If I was not running for Chair..." Birch turned quickly, and stared at me.

"She would still be hitting him. Deads, she was beating the hell out of him, long before you chose to run." Her eyes looked really fiery, and I actually felt a little intimidated by them. I slid back on the bed.

"Birch, calm down, okay, I get it, honestly I was just thinking out loud, I didn't mean to piss you off." She blinked.

"Sweetie, did I scare you?" I nodded at her.

"Yeah... You did a bit." She softened and gave a sigh.

"Deads, I am sorry, I just thought you were going to quit, and I don't think you should. Sweetie, stepping up in this village has taken a long time, I really think you have taken the right bold move, and you must follow this through no matter what happens. Look Deads, this has been in your mind since you were small, and now it is your time to step up. If it was not Prim, it would have been someone else, just stand fast, this village needs you, even if they do not know it yet." I nodded at her, and slid out of bed; my stomach felt like it was twisting into knots.

"I cannot help how I feel Birch, and I do feel some responsibility, it is just how I am feeling." She gave a small smile.

"Okay Sweetie, I am really sorry I got carried away, I never intended to scare you." I gave her a smile and I nodded.

"I know Baby, it's just me."

I headed downstairs, I needed to really wake up, and I was hungry. I thought food may settle my swirling insides, so I sought out something to eat. I sat in the kitchen, alone, Chloe was in her studio looking at her book, I noticed she had pinned the poster on her wall, Edwina was in her office working on yet more promotion, and also looking at the formats of what was possible for the carnival.

Two hours later, we were on the canal climbing up onto Moon's narrow boat, yes, I have been corrected, it was not called a barge. Inside, Nigel sat at the table looking miserable, as Moon explained how Prim had been calling him in the church, and he just got sick of it, so he left. To be honest I was a little proud of him, he had finally made a stand for himself, although, I was also aware, he would pay for it.

I sat at the table and looked at him, he looked sad and dejected, like he had done several brutal rounds with a boxer. I gave a long sigh.

"Christ Nigel, why do you let her do this to you? It is just like school all over again. You should not have to put up with this at home as well." He looked down at the table, and shrugged.

"She is scary Abby. None of you have seen her when she loses her temper, she just goes insane, she frightens Rupert, and I just want to keep him calm." I understood him.

"You try to protect your son?" He nodded.

"I don't want her near him Abby when she is like that, it scares me she will hurt him." I gave a sigh; he made perfect sense.

"Honestly Nigel, I get it, I do, but at this rate, you will not survive another year with her. She is going too far now, if you do not make a stand, she will just get worse. I mean, look at you, why is your face so cut up?" He looked back at the table.

"Abby, I don't like you seeing me like this, I know you mean well, I do, you were always nice to me in school, but she hits me because I liked you. When you stood for the chair, she got really mad and hit me in the face with a pot statue and smashed it. Abby, she wants to win, but you are making it hard for her."

I sat back and could see Birch watching me biting her lip, she knew what I was thinking, and she slowly shook her head as if to say don't, but what choice did I have?

"Okay, I will pull out of the vote, and I will let her win."

"NO!" I jumped, Nigel stared at me with wide eyes, he shook his head.

"Abby no, you must not let her win, she is not right for this village, and she will hurt you and your friends even more. Abby, you must win, you must." For the first time in my life, I actually saw something in Nigel, something in his eyes, he was angry at me for even suggesting it.

"Nigel, if I win, it will make things even worse for you, how can I allow that? If she was attacking me, I would have the chance to fight back, but she is not, and what about your son, what about him? If you get badly hurt who will care for him, your parents are not exactly young, it will be hard for them?" He nodded at me, and tried to smile, his face hurt and he winced.

"Abby, I have to do this, I have to find a way, promise me you will not pull out?"

I felt horrible inside, how could I? If I am absolutely honest, I did not think he had what it took. I looked at Birch and she smiled; she knew full well how much this was getting to me. I think she was relieved that even Nigel wanted me to stay in the race. I felt caught in a trap, whatever I did, people would suffer. I looked at him looking miserable and desperate.

"Nigel can you honestly stand up to her, and take what will come if I win?"

There was a sadness in his eyes I knew, I had seen it in the mirror many times. He stared at me, and I felt something inside him was trying so desperately to hang on. Was that my problem, was I identifying with a part of him I knew in myself? It is so easy to forget the pain we have carried when times improve, and try to brush aside the dark feelings forever, and not truly understand them? Was this what was happening to me, was the wedding and all the joy I now felt in my life wiping away my memory of those dark and terrible times?

It felt like an important moment, was Nigel taking me back in time, to a time I had buried behind happiness and joy, to remind me what my life had been about? Or was he showing me his pain, because he knew, only I would really understand it? I did not know, I just know that what I felt, the guilt, inner darkness, the pain was real, and most importantly very familiar. He licked his lips almost as if he understood my thoughts.

"Abby, I am going to try, I really am." I have no idea why, but I felt the tears fill my eyes, as I looked at him.

"You must Nigel, you must not let her win, no matter how hard it gets, never let her break your spirit. Care about yourself enough to stand tall, and be who you are meant to be, be you, be gloriously and wonderfully you... Do you understand me?" Birch gave a huge sob, and I turned, and saw her tears, and I smiled at her.

"It helped when you told me, it got me through Birch."

For in that moment looking into his eyes, all I could do was repeat word for word what Birch told me on my darkest day, and it was the only reason I made it through, and suddenly I understood exactly where Nigel was in life. I stood up, and wiped my eyes.

"Nigel, I have to go, so spend some time with Moon and talk, and dig deep, and find the strength to move forward."

I smiled at him, as he stared blankly at me, but I knew I could not be here, something inside me was stirring deeply, and I felt afraid of it. Was it a memory, a feeling, I really was not sure, I just knew I needed to get out and in the fresh air? I walked towards the door, and up the two steps to the deck, and breathed in the fresh air, as the huge wave of emotion washed over me. I jumped onto the canal path, feeling lost, almost as if I had to find my way back to my own reality, and my life today. I walked up the path a little way, and saw the bench, for Hatty's mum, and I sat on it, and just breathed in the air around me and closed my eyes.

"You understand don't you, it is not guilt, it is understanding, you know more than anyone else, where he is?"

I opened my eyes and she was squatting in front of me, her beautiful green eyes, that long flowing white hair, illuminated by sun, and a smile of love and kindness. I stared at her, and she reached out and touched my knee.

"You would make an incredible therapist, today you saw what I have in my sessions with him, and in recognising it, he connected with you. Oh Sweetie, you have such a powerful gift, you just reached right into him and touched his soul, and I think made a big difference." I breathed in and just let the air fill my lungs.

"Birch, I don't want to go back there, it was four years ago, and it was a horrible place to be. I found my way out, and I have been so happy recently, remembering scares me." She smiled and softly rubbed my leg.

"The gift of empathy is a very harsh one, to be able to honestly stand in someone else's shoes is hard. But for those of us who can, to actually stand there and fully understand, it is a frightening place to be at times. Deads, to witness another with such clarity can be terrifying, but it is also a great skill, for it allows you to help without hindering. Now you know his pain Deads." I shook my head, and felt a huge surge flow up inside me, and I felt the tears run onto my cheeks.

"Birch, I do not want to, I have done that, and it almost

destroyed me, I don't want to go back there."

"Oh Sweetie, you won't, I will never allow it." She leaned forward and put her head against mine.

"It is good you saw it, but I will never let you suffer alone like that again. I put a ring on your finger and swore my devotion to you, and I will never stray from that path... Come on, let's go home, Moon will help him, she understands him very well." She took my hands in hers, and pulled me forward.

Holding hands, we walked slowly along the canal path under the trees of green, and I felt her calmness wash into me. I glanced at her as we walked.

"How do you do that every day Birch; does it not grind you down?" She smiled.

"Some days it is not easy, and so I come home, and put my arms round you, hold you close, and I feel it leave me. You see, just like you, it is the joy we share that heals me too."

Life is so strange, we are taught that out there is a person who is our ideal, but we are never told how to recognise them. We have to flounder in hope that we will one day find them. It is such a ridiculous notion, for years in my youth I believed this idea, and I fantasied about who they would be, and in the midst of all this idealisation, the most unexpected person walked into my life and changed it forever.

If only I could go back to meet me at sixteen, I would say to myself, stop that now, you are being stupid, stop romanticising everything, it will only lead to bitterness and pain. How I wish someone had said to me that there are no rules, and the odds are you will never find the right perfect person for you by looking and selecting from a list. You just have to believe that a person out there, will one day complete you, and sweep the darkness from your soul, and they will be nothing like you expect.

Life would be much simpler if we taught this to our children, because then every person you meet, will have the potential to make your future happier, and we will not dismiss them, looking for our idealised idea of right.

At home Chloe was excited, people on her site were commenting they wanted copies of her book, and she really was happy, and it was so nice to see. We all sat in the living room talking. Anita had to go home soon, so we grabbed coffees and had one last discussion, and it was decided we would divide up to focus on projects. Now Chloe was aware of what was going on, she joined with Anita and me to organise the art show. Birch was going to focus on the carnival with Edwina and Luke, and Birch would also continue with Edwina and Aden, on the Curio Centre.

Anthony would be involved in all the projects as a floater, helping out where needed, and overall it seemed like a great plan? Anita finally hugged us all and said her goodbyes, I think it had done her a lot of good to just take some time out, and really get to know us, she now had a better idea of who we all were, and how we interacted, which would serve her well in the future organising events. She left with a smile, and a signed copy of Chloe's book.

I headed up to my room, sat on the bed, and opened my copy of the book. We had set up an order form for pre booked editions of the book on Chloe's site, to collect from the exhibition, and spammed all our social media for her. I opened my copy, it was numbered two, and I smiled as I looked at her inscription. 'Not good with words like you are, so I've done this.' She had drawn a picture of herself holding her heart, and she was smiling, it was such a lovely picture and felt very special.

I slowly turned the pages, enjoying the pictures, and I think I will never get tired of seeing them. My arch, the old church, the graveyard, Willis, and Gabrielle, all my words were alive, it felt so strange, and yet so amazing. I have spent so many days in the past, reading my words over and over, and questioning why the books were not selling at the time. So many dark nights in the guest house alone, feeling like I was the biggest failure on the planet, because these words, and these stories I loved so much, were ignored by everyone, when all I had wanted was others to get the same joy I did writing them.

It is the hardest thing about being a writer, there is such joy in writing, such happy explosions of excitement writing, and yet when you see nothing has sold, you question everything about your own ability. It has never been about the money, what I wanted was for people to curl up, and live in my world for a while. To share the spaces of my mind that I commit to paper, and when they don't, it really is soul destroying.

Alone in my room of self doubt, I suffered a lot back then, I would look at my mum, or Katie and I got to see it in their eyes. I had not lived up to their expectations, it was so hard to deal with. I remembered having to look Birch in the eyes, and admit I had failed as a writer, and that was one of the worse moments of my life. Looking and feeling less in front of her was the vilest punishment ever, trust me, no writer ever wants to see that in a loved one's eyes.

I guess I am one of the lucky ones, I finally made it, I am a recognised face in writing today, my books sell. Well for now they do, but that can end anytime, which is the risk we all take. My hand of death series has ended, and I have something new, and for all I know, my established fans might hate it, that is the risk I take with every word, and my life could drift back into that darkness, and that is scary.

By the time Birch finished working with Edwina, I was already asleep, she undressed me, and put me into bed. I slept long and deep and missed breakfast, when I woke up the bed was empty and the house was quiet. I wandered downstairs and headed for coffee.

At the far end of Lilac Street, in the two story residential flats, as Wotton came alive and the day began, Fidelity was fast asleep in her bed, having stayed late at her parents talking the night before. She was snuggled up, hugging her pillow lost to the world, when, BANG... BANG... BANG! Made her jolt in her sleep.

She opened her eyes, it could not be her place, no one ever came here, she wriggled under her duvet, and closed her eyes again. BANG... BANG... BANG! Her eyes snapped open.

"Who the hell is that?"

She sat up in bed and reached for her waitress blouse, and slipped it on, she had on red lace panties, which admittedly did show, but she was covered, as she staggered towards the door, feeling a little annoyed.

"Hold on, I am bloody coming!"

She felt tired, and still sleepy, who the hell bangs at this time in the morning? It was ten, so maybe not so uncommon, she pulled open the door and froze.

"Primula?" Prim barged past her, pushing her back out of the way.

"Where is he?" Still not fully awake she looked at Molly. who was still stood in the doorway, looking awkward?

"What is going on?"

Primula walked around the two bedroom flat, looking into the bedroom, Fidelity turned and looked at her, as she came out of her room.

"You know Primula it is a little rude to just barge in like this, if you wanted to visit, why didn't you just text?"

Primula stood in the centre of her kitchen come living room, with her arms folded.

"I did, and you ignored it." Fidelity looked at Molly.

"Do you want to come in so I can close my door?" Molly stepped in, and the door closed, Fidelity turned to face Prim again, she was scowling at her not unsimilar to Madge.

"I am sorry, I was at my mums last night, I must have forgotten to turn it back on... So, what can I do for you?"

She walked the few paces to her kettle, lifted it and shook it, to see how much water was in it, put it down and switched it on. Prim stared at her.

"Nigel did not come home last night; I want to know where he is?" Fidelity turned.

"He didn't, well where is he, has he had an accident?" Prim gritted her teeth.

"Don't play innocent with me missy, he is obviously having an affair, and it is not hard to work out who with is it now, after all, out of all of us, your morals are most lapsed?" The kettle started to rumble, and Fidelity looked at her.

"Hold on a bloody minute, are you saying I have been sleeping with Nigel, Jesus Prim, how mad are you? Firstly, I have not been laid in over six months, and secondly, no offence, but he is not really my type, I only date guys with a spine." Prim watched her with her dark malicious eyes.

"Well, if it is not you, then it must be her, so you tell me which?" Fidelity was nowhere near awake enough for this, she rubbed her eyes, and sighed.

"Primula, I am really tired, I have a lot on my mind at the moment, and I did not sleep well. Look if your husband is sleeping with someone else, I can assure you it is not me, and as for Abby, whom I assume you are referring to, I hate to point this out, but she married a woman." Primula shook her head.

"Don't play innocent with me, you know something, I know it, do not think for one moment I do not know what you are up to. You are not as good at hiding your tracks as you think, I know you were with those whores." Fidelity closed her eyes for a second, the kettle behind her clicked off.

"Primula are you spying on me now?"

"I know everything about you, and yes, I have been watching, I have not trusted you since you said hello to that tramp at the café." Fidelity gave a sigh.

"Well then, you know I have not touched your husband then, so why are you really here?" Primula walked right up to her and leaned into her.

"I know you spent the night with those whores, is that where Nigel is, in her bed?" Fidelity felt her legs tremble.

"Okay yes, I know Abby, Chloe and Deb's from school, they asked me if I would like to join them, they were having a few people round for drinks, and so I went. You do not own me Primula, I am free to live as I choose. I have few friends around here, and it was nice to catch up with Chloe, we were good friends at school, even Molly will tell you that. It is none of your business what I do or where I go." Primula leaned in even further.

"Well then, we know where we stand, don't we? You like those whores so much, let's see just how good a friend they really are?" Fidelity swallowed hard.

"What do you mean by that?" Primula stepped back, and opened her handbag.

"You have your friends and I have mine, I warned you not to cross me, well missy, you have crossed a line, and there is no return now."

She pulled a long envelope out of her bag and slammed it into Fidelity's ribs, it hurt and she winced, and felt the shock ripples from it.

"TAKE IT!"

Fidelity jumped, and lifted her hand and took it, Primula smiled a twisted smile.

"We reap what we sow."

She turned and marched to the door, yanked it open and walked out, Molly stood staring at Fidelity, her face as white as snow. She blinked, turned, and ran after Primula, leaving the door open. Fidelity stood with her back still pressed into the kitchen unit trembling, holding the envelope, she was terrified.

It took several minutes to calm down, and stop trembling. She finally took a breath and walked to the door and closed it, she dropped the envelope on the small table, and made a coffee, then sat down and just breathed in and out, as she sipped her coffee and tried to fully calm down. As she sipped and slowly came to life, she stared at the envelope, what had she meant, I have my friends and she has hers?

She reached down and picked up the envelope, there was nothing written on it, she placed her cup on the mat on the table, and opened it up, and slid out the papers, unfolded them, and her heart almost stopped as she read the top heading.

'Notice of Eviction.'

She read on, the owner of the property Walter Parkinson was evicting her, and no valid reason was stated. Fidelity stared at it unable to comprehend this, all she had done was hang out with Abby and her friends, it is not like she had broken any laws. She dropped it onto the table, and burst into tears.

Finally feeling awake, I had to head into the village to deliver Chloe's sketches, to be mounted and framed. Chloe had been prepping Bess for a little decoration, she washed it, rinsed it off, and then wiped it down with spirit, then threw a huge tarp over it. Once done, and ready, she joined me, and helped me pack her A1 sized sketches in the large wallet, and we set off, laughing and talking towards the village.

Today is the first day of the summer program, as the village gears up for the big summer fete, it is something Chloe and I have grown up with, as events and activities are planned all summer. It was around noon, but the village was quite busy. The weather was overcast but quite warm, but there were plenty of kids running around, as today was a fun activities day, and mum was out with Edwina organising.

Ellen was running the gallery, and Gavin was in the back. We walked through the main shop, towards his workshop area, and there were all the frames. Chloe looked really excited, as she saw all thirty five frames neatly lined up on his rack, all glazed and ready for her pictures. He lifted one off the rack and lay it on the blanket covered bench.

"I hope you like them." She looked at him, and then back at the frames, and ran her hand along it.

"They are beautiful Gav." I lifted up the large wallet.

"These are the pictures; how long will this take?" He smiled, as he saw one of her pictures through the clear vinyl.

"Give me a couple of days, I am not going to rush this. I need to know what colour board you want to use for the mounts, everything I use is acid free, so your art will be nice and safe. I have got to say Chloe, I actually feel really honoured to have this job, you have inspired me a great deal since I had my first drawing lesson with you."

She gave him a smile, she was nowhere near as cocky as she normally was, I think she was a little overwhelmed by it all, her voice was quite soft and low key.

"I hope you are still drawing Gav, this is a good trade, but you are at heart a good artist with a lot of potential?" He gave a nod as he turned, and lifted up his card swatches.

"I have a few pieces in the shop, not much interest yet, but hey, that is the artisan life. When it gets slow, I sit out back and sketch, and at home I do more graphic stuff." He laid out the swatches on the bench.

"It is up to you, but looking at the tone of the paper and the stroke of your pencil, I think this is perfect." He handed her a deep red card.

"With the pale frames and the depth of the images, and considering these are for a gothic novel, I think this would be perfect, but it is up to you?" Chloe took it and looked at it, she held it against the frame.

"Yeah, I think you are right, go with that." I left them to talk art, and wandered over to Ellen, she smiled and looked at Chloe behind me talking with Gavin.

"He is really excited to be doing this job, I think there is a little bit of fan boy going on with him, he inspects every picture she sends in." I looked back and chuckled.

"She was his first, I am not so much sure he lost his virginity, more than she robbed him of it." Ellen giggled.

"She looks a little overwhelmed, she is not as bubbly as normal when she is in here. We have made up a feature for her, we have not unveiled it yet, I thought she might like the honours?" I looked back at her, she was talking, and running her finger along the frame.

"She is so talented Ellen, and the thing I love is she has no idea at all of how good she is. I watch her every day, sat on the floor painting, humming to her music, it is her little world, and once they are dry, she just stacks them up, throws a cloth over them, and starts another. You really should come round and see her backstock, she has a lot."

"I may just do that, her stuff is getting a lot of interest, maybe we should do a feature of her to coincide with her gallery appearance, and put some more on the website? I really hope it goes well for her; she deserves it."

Gavin walked around the back room showing Chloe the few pieces he had in the shop, she would stop and look at the picture, and then step back, and get a wider view of it, and then talk to him, and point aspects out. He stood with his eyes glued to her, like she was his teacher, and yes, Ellen was right, he was a complete fan boy.

Ellen walked into the main gallery, and I followed her. At the far end close to the window, there was a large white cloth on the wall, she looked back to check where they were, and smiled at me.

"Edwina has made an extra large advertisement for her, as you can see, it is big, but it will feature her heavily in the gallery."

The cloth on the wall was at least five feet high, and a good six wide, I smiled as I looked at it. I loved how much support she was getting, the door behind me opened and the tiny electronic buzzer bleeped. I felt a hand softly rub my bum, gave a jump, and spun round quickly ready to slap, Birch stood smiling, her voice was soft and sultry.

"Well, hey sexy, if you like pictures, I have some I just know you will love?"

I giggled, she did slutty well, Ellen smirked. I looked her up and down, in her suit, and as I browsed her middle, she opened her jacket, showing her soft breasts and nipples through her pale lemon blouse, and winked at me.

"Sorry love I am married." Ellen burst out laughing, and Birch giggled.

"So am I Sweetie, but there are times when a little unseen naughty can work wonders, especially with the right gal." I sniggered.

"That's it, that is your best line?" Birch giggled.

"Okay, so what would you say?" I leaned right into her, and got close to her wide green eyes, and in my best northern deep accent I said.

"Well, you are a right fit bird, wanna bang?" Ellen fell about laughing, as Birch squealed with delight, and jumped on the spot and clapped.

"I do, I do!" She pulled me into a hug with the giggles.

"I love it when you do Bev."

When Chloe came into the gallery end of the shop, she was smiling.

"You know, he is getting better all the time Mrs W; you have some nice pieces of his?" Ellen looked through to the back, he was already busy taking out the pictures and admiring them before framing them, she looked at Chloe.

"It is very exciting, isn't it?" Chloe nodded.

"To be honest Mrs W, I am still trying to get used to the idea, I mean, I am really excited, but I am also a bit scared." Ellen nodded.

"Chloe you are so talented, relax, you are going to do fine, although could you please do me a little favour?" She nodded.

"Yeah, what?" Ellen pointed.

"Pull that string."

Chloe turned and looked at it, she reached out and gave it a soft pull, and the cloth fell down. Even I gasped at the large printed poster, half of which was a picture of Chloe on stage at the Curio event, and the other was a massive blow up of her exhibition poster.

"A bit of local advertising never hurt." She smiled as Chloe stared at it in shock. Birch put her arm round her waist and looked up at it.

"Love the dungarees, very artisan." Chloe looked at her.

"Do my boobs look really big in that, or is it me?" Birch chuckled.

"You have great tits Chloe, I would play with them, but you are just so straight it's unbelievable." Chloe sniggered.

"Oh Birch, you have no idea?"

There were a few tears, and a lot of saying thank you before we left. Birch gave me a long passionate kiss, which made my heart flutter, and skipped off across the road back to work, and I walked with Chloe over towards the Tea Rooms, I was buying today, my treat.

Chapter 8

True Colours.

The Tea Rooms, had large posters up, and Celia and Lillian made such a fuss of Chloe, and even gave her a free cream bun. As we sat at the table, having passed Madge who said nothing. Chloe looked back at Celia and Lillian, who waved with big smiles

"Abby, they do know I am straight, right?" I chuckled as I sipped my coffee, she leaned in to me.

"Abby, it feels weird seeing my face everywhere, do they have to put up so many?" I glanced at the wall where four large posters advertised her event.

"Chloe, to them, they are showing support for a local, I think it's wonderful that finally, the people around here are starting to see us as we should be seen. Although, if this puts you off, stay out of your dad's place, he has seven up." She looked terrified.

"Oh God, I knew he would go overboard, it is why I did not tell him."

"Nope, your very proud big sister did, who do you think gave them to him?" She sighed.

"Is this what it is like for you?" I chuckled at the look on her face.

"Chloe relax, you have not made the papers yet." She looked up from her cup.

"Oh fuck, do they know?" I smiled.

"Sorry, my bad, I asked Anita to pull a few strings, and get you some added publicity." She groaned into her cup.

Outside on the green under the cover of the small marquee, Felicity was organising a mum's and tots painting afternoon, and Hatty wandered round, ensuring everyone was well supplied. The shops were busy as new summer lines appeared, and at the bottom of the green, a small string quartet played on a small stage. The atmosphere was fun and happy, and the village felt very much alive.

We were sat with our back to the door talking, when in walked Primula with Sophia and Molly, she spotted my hair, and came marching down the Tea Rooms, a look of anger on her face. She shrieked at the top of her voice, and the whole place went silent, Marjorie turned to look at her.

"ABIGAIL WATSON, WHERE IS MY HUSBAND?"

I closed my eyes; was it not bad enough with the Shrew Crew? I turned in my seat and looked up at her, stood in her tweed, with her hands on her hips. Her brown hair was in a tight knotted bun, and her mousey eyes were staring at me from under her furrowed brow. I looked her up and down, Christ she was only twenty five, and yet she looked forty.

"How the hell would I know, he is your husband?" Her face screwed up, as she stared at me with hate.

"I think he is having an affair, I found one of those protection things in our room, and let's be honest, if anyone would be sleeping with him, it would obviously be the village slut." Chloe stood up and turned on her, as her chair slid back with a screech.

"Why you fucking dried up..." I stood up and grabbed her arm, Chloe's eyes were blazing, and she looked really angry, Primula looked a little wary.

"Leave it Chloe, she deserves it, but we should not lower ourselves." Chloe stepped back, but her hatred of Prim was clearly visible. I took a pace closer; I was slightly taller than her, and aimed to use it to my advantage.

"Primula, firstly, I am not a slut as you say, I hate that word, but also do not put down a fellow female because she enjoys the pleasure of a loved one. Secondly, I am married, and the only person I have slept with is my wife, she has incredible passions, and I have to confess, she does wear me out somewhat. So honestly, even if I did have the chance or felt the slightest inclination to do so, which I don't, I am just too sexed up and tired from my wife's veracious appetites. As to his whereabouts, I cannot deny, he is highly educated, and from where I am standing, anywhere you are not, seems like the best place to be, and who could blame him for that?"

Madge put her head down and bit her lip, Primula's face screwed up with her anger.

"YOU'RE A LIAR, I KNOW YOU WANT HIM?" Chloe snorted.

"Yeah, about as much as syphilis!" I leaned into her, and she leaned back, I will not deny, I could feel my anger rising.

"Looking at his face, I cannot deny, if the rumours are true, then I would not blame him for not being around you. To be honest, if he did come to me, which he won't, I would probably drive him to the tip of Scotland to give the poor sod a break, and time to heal from you."

She pushed me in the chest and stepped back. The whole room and gone completely silent, and I could see everyone sat still watching me, Lillian dithered behind the counter looking frightened.

"I am not afraid of you Abigail Watson, you think you are tough, just because you have your friends around you, but we all know you are not. We all heard how you cried in here that day." She smirked.

"Not so tough then, were you?" It caught my breath and I faltered for a second, Madge turned sharply.

"Primula, that is enough, you are embarrassing this family. Apologise."

She spun on her heels and lifted her hand, she was about to say something horrible to Madge, I suddenly realised, and as her arm came up, I caught it, and held her firmly by her wrist. Her head snapped around, as she looked at me with hate, her temper was clearly visible. I gritted my teeth and swallowed back my anger, but it did show, as I spoke through gritted teeth.

"That is enough, in this village we show respect to our elders, you need to leave and leave now. I mean it Primula, I don't want to, but if I have to, I will toss you out of here." Her eyes burned at me with anger and hate, and she pointed at Madge, with her free hand.

"She hates you; she has made your life a misery, and you have the nerve to defend her?" I held her arm firm.

"As I said, we respect our elders, no matter who they are, or what they have done, it is called being decent. Now you need to leave, and leave now before I do something I will regret."

She spat at me, and Chloe nudged up at my shoulder ready to pummel her, I could feel Chloe's anger behind me. Primula smirked as she saw the spit on my top.

"You have no right to throw me out, you do not own this place."

"No but I do... GET OUT!"

Her head snapped around, to see Celia pointing at the door, I let go of her wrist. Prim spun round, and stormed towards the door.

"You have not heard the last of this Abigail Watson, just you wait and see."

Celia looked at me and I nodded, she smiled and nodded back, I was trembling I was so angry. Madge looked up at me and gave a slight nod, I gave her one back, and took a deep breath to swallow my anger, leaned over Madge and whispered.

"Do not worry, he is safe and well cared for, where no one will find him." She looked relieved and smiled, I stood back up and looked at Chloe. She nodded.

"I wanted to punch the bitch." I smiled at her, once again she had my back.

"Me too, but that would have made things far worse. Out on the green, I would have knocked her the hell out, but not here Chloe, this is Celia's and Lillian's place." She nodded and we sat down.

I am sure I have told you before, around here, the gossip network is faster than email, and within ten minutes Birch came rushing in, saw me, and hurried down the room towards me.

"Are you alright Sweetie?" Chloe smiled up at her.

"She is banging, she faced the bitch out nice and calm, and got her booted out." Birch bit her lip.

"The message said you had hold of her, I had a panic that you would look like a panda, and came straight here." I chuckled.

"Birch, I can handle myself if I need to, ask Chloe?" She nodded vigorously and rubbed her cheek.

"Yeah, she packs a good punch, trust me on that." Birch gave a sigh of relief.

"I just needed to see you were fine, it scared me Dead's." I patted the seat at my side.

"Have you got the time to have a coffee with me?" She looked back at Celia and Lillian who gave a smile and a nod, she turned back to me and smiled.

"I shouldn't really, but more time with you, yes, I can do that." She sat down and took my hand.

"You are sure you are fine... Okay, tell me what happened?" I lifted my serviette and wiped my shoulder.

"The filthy cow spat at me." Birch stood bolt upright, and her chair fell over, as she looked out of the window, her eyes instantly fiery.

"She did what, I will rip her fucking head off." Chloe sniggered, as I grabbed her hand and Chloe lifted her chair back up, then I pulled her back down.

"Birch it was sorted, leave it." Celia appeared with three coffees, and a plate of buns.

"These are on us, our token of thanks." Birch winked a saucy wink.

"There are lots of ways to show gratitude Celia." She smirked.

"Oh God you have no idea of the pictures I have had in my dreams girls." She looked at Chloe and winked.

"You too." Chloe looked panicked, and yet blushed.

"Oh Celia, I am so straight it's unbelievable." I sniggered.

"Then why blush?" Celia chuckled, as she walked away, Birch leaned over the table and looked Chloe right in the eye.

"She just got so wet looking at you Chloe, I could smell it." Chloe looked horrified, and shivered, her voice rose several octaves higher.

"Oh fuck!"

We finished our coffee, and walked back with Birch to the practice, then called in to see Deb's, and again the window had another large poster supporting Chloe. I explained what had happened, they too had been sent alerts, and Denise and Deb's leaned on the counter as I filled them in. Shortly after Mum arrived, Hatty had seen me and tipped her off, and I had to go over the whole story again.

"Oh darling, do try and stay away from her, this is not good publicity for a village leader."

"Mum, I was sat minding my own business, she was the one who came at me. I am happy to ignore her, honestly, nobody wanted that." She gave a sigh.

"Alright darling, just be careful, I worry about you, she is dangerous Abby, do not underestimate her. Hatty heard her ranting at Molly, and told her to watch out, or she would end up like Fidelity, this girl is not to be underestimated." I frowned, and looked at Chloe.

"What has happened to Deli?" She shrugged, and shook her head.

"No idea, I have not heard from her, have you guys?" Deb's shook her head.

"I hope she does not have a black eye as well." I looked at my phone and swiped up and went to messages, I typed a quick message.

'Are you alright, if you need me, call?'

I waited until closing, and then walked with Birch and Chloe, back to the house, Chloe was once again becoming excited as she told Birch all about the frames, and how cool they looked, and how good Gavin was with wood. Birch just smiled as she listened, and I cannot deny, I loved seeing that sparkle in her eye, as she excitedly rambled on and on about it all.

It was nice to sit in the kitchen and drink coffee, Birch sat at my side and leaned on my shoulder, and hugged my arm, whilst Chloe went into her studio to collect up her paints, and the new decals of flowers Birch had given her. It looked like tonight; Bess was getting a makeover. I picked up my phone and looked at it, Birch noticed.

"Are you alright, you have looked at your phone four times in the last half an hour?" I was unsure what to do, and leaned on her.

"I messaged Fidelity, and I have not heard back, when I tried to ring, her phone was off. After today, I am just worried, Birch people are getting hurt. Prim is out of control, ignore me, I am worried, I will be fine when I hear from her." She squeezed my arm.

"Would you like me to run a bath, and give you a good rub down?" I smiled, and glanced sideways at her, she had that cheeky glint in her eyes.

"How good a rub down?" She giggled, and leaned into my ear and spoke slow and sexy, in a deep husky voice.

"It will be long, soft, and very attentive to all your important little places, and oh so hot it will be unbearable." I giggled.

"Wow, you are a proper mint bitch, you know that, you wanna be my bird?" Birch gave an excited squeal.

"Oh God Dead's, why does it turn me on so much when you talk like Bev, am I messed up?" Edwina walked in, in her white blouse and black pants.

"You guys are looking at messed up in the rear view mirror, can you make your own dinner tonight?" I looked up at her and frowned.

"Why are you wearing those clothes?" She looked down and smiled.

"It's been a while, Fidelity has not shown up, and Mum cannot get hold of her, so I said I would cover for her. Chloe wants to do her painting on Bess, so I thought I would leave her. Plus, weirdly enough, this stuff gets Luke hot, so tonight he will be getting served on a more personal level." She giggled and raised her eye brows.

"Okay, I will see you all later, Anthony will be late, so do not cook straight away." I looked at Birch.

"Something is wrong, Deli was telling me how grateful she is that she got the job at Pemberton's, so she can stay in the village. Birch, she would not risk that job, she really needs the cash." Birch stood up.

"Alright Sweetie, let me change, and then if you want, we will go and see if she is at home, do you know where she lives?" I shook my head.

"No, I never thought to ask, I will ask Chloe." Birch nodded.

"Alright give me a few minutes, and we will go and see what we can do."

It took almost two hours to find out where she lived. Chloe had no idea, when she knew her before, she lived with her parents on Garden Street, but they moved just after she finished college to Tethering Dibley, and Fidelity got a flat.

I rang Edwina who asked her mum, but she was busy in the kitchen, and the restaurant was full tonight, so it took a little time to find out, we eventually got her address, and jumped into Petal, and at ten minutes past nine, we pulled up outside the flats on Lilac Street.

She was in flat seven, and I pushed the buzzer, I noticed the names on the numbers, and both Molly and Sophia lived here as well. There was no response, Birch stood back and looked up, all the lights were on in all the rooms. I pressed again and held it in.

I looked back at Birch, she looked worried, I hated thinking it, but I was hoping and praying she had not done something stupid, I pressed again. The speaker gave a hiss then crackled.

"If that is you again Prim, bugger off and leave me alone." I leaned in to the speaker.

"Deli, it is Abby, can I come in please?" There was silence, and then a sniffle.

"Oh Abby, I am a mess." She started to cry.

"Deli, press the buzzer, and let me in." The buzzer sounded, and I grabbed the door handle and pulled it open, Birch followed me in, and pointed.

"She is upstairs Dead's."

She pulled open the stairwell door and I followed, as we hurried up the stairs to the second floor. We entered the hallway and I counted down the doors, until we came to number seven, I knocked on the door, and she opened it, she looked in a right state.

Fidelity stood there in a white shirt, red knickers, and her makeup had streaked all down her face, she looked at us both, and burst into tears, I put my arms around her and pulled her close, and held her.

I could not really understand her, Birch closed the door and looked at the flat, there was a sofa bed, a coffee table, and a rug, that was it. She walked to the small kitchen, which was part of the room, and filled the kettle, and clicked it on. Fidelity wept in my arms, and Birch saw the letter on the coffee table, with the bold words printed in red on it, she picked it up and gave a sigh.

"Looks like Prim has struck again." She turned, and showed me the letter, I gave a sigh, and pulled her closer. It took a while to calm her down, I sat her on the sofa, and handed her a coffee.

"So, she found out you had been to our house, and got the owner to evict you, what a bitch?" Fidelity sniffled, and wiped her nose.

"I am sorry, this is not your problem, I turned my phone off, because she sent me so many horrible messages, I couldn't take anymore." Birch sat on the small table and took her hands in hers.

"Sweetie, don't apologise, she is just nasty, and vindictive, trust me she is a hateful bitch." Fidelity nodded, I looked at her.

"Deli, what are you going to do, you know they cannot just evict you, there are laws that protect you too?" She looked at me and wiped her eyes.

"Do you honestly think Prim or Parkinson care?" Birch frowned.

"What has he got to do with it?" She wiped her nose.

"Who do you think owns the building, seriously do you think the law applies to him, he has wriggled out of more than just booting an unemployed girl out of her flat?" I patted her leg.

"You are not unemployed, your job is safe, Edwina is covering for you, and once Chloe talks to her mum, trust me, you will still be employed." She gave a sniffle.

"I have worked so hard since leaving college, I had two jobs at one point just to stay afloat, but this was mine, my little safe place. There is no work in Tethering, which is why I stayed here, it was closer to Oxendale, and I could take the train, and now she is going to take it all away." She started to weep, and I looked at Birch, she read my mind and smiled.

"Yes, we have two spare, it is not a problem." I smiled at her, and looked at Fidelity.

"Okay pack your stuff, you are moving out tonight, let me make a few calls." She looked at me.

"Where can I go, Abby there is nowhere around here, all the flats are taken, and twice the price of this one. I only earn just over a grand a month, and it cost eight hundred to live here, and that is only because Prim knows him, and Molly got me a discount?" I smiled.

"You are moving in with us, we have space and spare rooms, so get dressed, or stay like that, Deli I have more shit in my room than you have in this whole flat. Screw Prim, come live with us." She shook her head.

"Abby your house is huge, it must cost a fortune, I would love to, but I cannot afford it." Birch smiled.

"Yeah, about that, we have a system, it is called the all girls together system of management, trust us, you can afford it. Look, we will talk about all that later, first, let's get you packed, and then get you out." She looked lost for words, and started crying again.

"You guys are so amazing, I really do not know why they hate you, all I have seen is kindness, and I am so desperate and grateful, I cannot do anything but cry. I am so sorry I am; I am so sorry." I looked around the room, it was so empty.

"I will grab the crates and phone Chloe; you get her stuff ready to go."

Birch gave a chuckle. I dialled as I ran down the stairs, I don't really know why, there is a lift. I opened up Petal and pulled out all our plastic crates. I wedged my hoodie under the door to keep it open, and then ran back and forth stacking the crates next to the lift. When I had them all in and gasping for air, I spoke to Chloe and explained what had happened, she was on board with it, and told me she was going to call Terry to see if he was free, he only lived two streets up.

I got all the crates into the lift, and came up to the top floor, and then slid them all out on the smooth floor as a stack. I had left the door a jar, so it was easy to take them in stacked in a more manageable stack of threes. Birch was in her bedroom stripping her bed, I came panting in, she looked at me.

"The bed is hers, so we are taking that, crate her clothes up."

I looked round, the closet was built in, so that was good, she had hardly anything, just a bed, sofa, a small table, and few other bits and pieces. I pulled her clothes out and folded them as a wad, and placed them into the crates, and she had little baskets with her underwear in, so I just grabbed them and dropped them into the crates.

Birch unpacked her kitchen cupboards into more crates, again, she had just what she needed, which was two of everything, except mugs, she had six. The buzzer went off and Chloe and Terry arrived, he had the works van, and after an hour of frantic packing, we started shipping things downstairs and out of the door, Petal and Bess were filled with crates and small items, like the table and two lamps.

The bed was two bases on wheels, that were bolted together with four nuts, and Terry quickly took it apart and unscrewed the legs, and then carried it all down to his van. Everything else, which was not much, went into bin bags, and by eleven forty five, her flat was empty, and we were pulling on to the drive outside our house, hot sweating and knackered. Talk about fast work, although, there were five of us, and she did not have much, the sofa bed was the biggest thing she owned.

We parked up and headed for the kitchen, and talked to Anthony and Michael and explained the situation, they were on board. With the help of Luke, and after Chloe insisted, the room next to hers on the landing was allocated to Fidelity. Luke and Terry shipped out the two singles, and moved them up to the attic, and Anthony and Michael helped hoover, and get her double bed, and bed side unit in and set up. Next came the sofa, followed by her tables, there was already a wardrobe and chest of drawers in there.

Deli and Chloe sorted out the room and unpacked, and we all carried up the last of her stuff, and by one am, thoroughly exhausted we all sat in the kitchen pretty much hot, sweating, and naked, and had a very big drink. Fidelity was calmer and emotionally drained, although, she still had what Birch remarked as, 'Halloween eyes.' We sat round the island, and Birch went down the house rules.

"The house is shared, and we have a special account for that, and it is based on what each person can pay, so do not worry, I will talk privately about that in a while. The dress code is comfort, and as you know that includes nudity. We all share cooking, cleaning, and chores, we are a team, a family, and if something is upsetting you, we have a house meet and talk it out. Guests of a romantic nature can stay over, but a polite heads up helps. Apart from that, be you, be happy." We all nodded, that was pretty much how we lived, she was lost for words.

"I want to say so much, but I have no idea where to begin." I smiled at her.

"Look, we are not the villains we have been painted, four of us know of you from school, so we know we can trust you. We do have parties, and we can get wild, all we ask is what happens in the house stays in the house, taking those details outside, will get you booted. Deli just live your life your way and enjoy it, we are all girls together, I am sure you have seen the back of Petal?" She smiled.

"Yeah, I have seen the painting of you all, thanks... All of you, I owe every one of you, and I will find a way to show how appreciative I am."

There were nods all around, and Birch stood up and took her hand, and guided her to the library, and showed her how things in the house worked, and talked her through the financial arrangements. It was getting late, and we were all tired, Birch went ahead to run a bath for us, and I leaned on Deli's door and tapped. Deli was stood surrounded by the crates, she was folding her clothes and putting things away, she smiled and I walked in, and sat on her bed.

"It will feel strange for a few days, this house is huge, it took me ages to get used to it. We have a heated pool, use it anytime you like, you have your own on suite with a shower, but the spare room does have a bath if you want to use it. The walls are soundproof, but that does not always filter out Chloe, if she gets too rowdy, bang on the door, we do. Are you going to be alright now?" She stood still holding her folded top, and looked at me.

"I am blown away at the kindness of you all, and I am struggling for words, but I am really grateful, and happy. I rang my mum and dad and told them where I am, and that I am safe, and they are relieved. My dad does not like Prim, and I did get a lot of I told you so off him. Abby, thanks for this, you did not need to do this, which is actually what makes it so special." I leaned over and patted her shoulder.

"I have a hot wife waiting for me, so sleep well, there is no set routine, just follow whatever pattern suits you. Your parents by the way are always welcome to visit, just give us a heads up so we can dress if needed." She gave a big smile and nodded.

"Yeah, I will, sleep well Abby, thanks."

Chapter 9

Fidelity, And Friendship.

I wandered downstairs, as Birch zoomed round the house, she was late again, Izzy sighed, as Birch looked for her bag. Michael and Luke had already left with Terry, and Anthony tutted, as he looked at his watch. I sat quietly sipping coffee; Chloe had already briefed Deli on the morning routine.

The happy squeal announced she had found her bag, and she arrived at high speed, leaned down and snogged me to death, and took my breath away, she pulled away and smiled.

"Back later Sweetie, have fun." The door banged, and silence descended, as I sipped my third coffee. Deli smiled.

"Is every morning this mental?" I nodded at her.

"Pretty much... How did you sleep?" She lifted her cup.

"I was pretty exhausted which helped, I don't really remember getting into bed I was so tired. It was a little strange waking up, but I was warm and snug, and I felt happy." I smiled.

"Good, it will take a while to get used to everything, but you will get there." She looked around the kitchen.

"This house is so beautiful, I feel really lucky, although you know when Prim finds out, it could bring trouble on you all." I gave a chuckle.

"Deli, we have had shit thrown at us for the last four years, we will handle whatever comes our way. After my confrontation with her yesterday, we were going to get it anyway. If you look at it for now, no one really needs to know, your mum knows and your boss knows, you do not have to publicly advertise it." She put her cup down.

"You lot are all so cool about it, honestly, she really scares me, I have seen her explode, and she can be terrifying." Chloe nodded.

"Everyone can, until you smack them in the mouth, that is what she needs, someone to beat the shit out of her, and to be honest, I would not mind the job, I hate her."

At Meadow Cottage, Primula fumed.

"WELL, WERE IS SHE, SHE IS SUPPOSED TO SUFFER, NOT LEAVE?" She walked around the room; Sophia looked at Molly.

"The guy next door said he saw guys taking her stuff out, yar. I am sad, she was a good neighbour, she did my nails for me, and now I have to go to Oxendale, it sucks yar?" Primula snapped her head round.

"She was a traitor, she went to them, do you not understand that you idiot? My God, are you really that stupid, we cannot have her telling them everything we do?" Sophia pouted.

"What is the point, everyone is leaving, if there is no one left it's dull, I want Nigel and Fidelity to just be friends again, I miss them Primula?" Primula stared at her and Molly, she gave a snort, and looked at Molly.

"Has she any idea of the power we will have in the village, we will get new friends, tell her, when we run the council, they will have no choice but to be friends." Molly nodded at her, but she did not seem convinced.

"It bothers me Primula, because from what we can tell, everything has gone, she handed the keys to the caretaker, I mean, where did she go?" Primula gave a shrug.

"Who cares, she will not get anything around here, Walter has made sure of that, there is not a flat in ten miles she can afford, so she must have gone home." Sophia looked at her phone.

"I messaged her on Insta, and it says it was not delivered, she is not friends with me, I think she hates me, and I feel sad, she was my friend and she is not anymore, yar." She started to cry, and Molly gave a sigh.

"Sophia, we have lots of friends, it is only one, you still have us." She wiped her eyes.

"Yar, I know, but I used to go and sit and drink tea with her, and she did my nails. She was kind to me, and used to tell me everything would be alright, she was my friend, yar?" She started to cry again, and Molly gave a sigh, and put her arm round her. Primula tutted, showing her impatience.

"All that over a cup of tea, my God it is ridiculous, the way I see it, she is gone, and good riddance, we have things to do, and a summer to plan, so pull yourself together Sophia. We need to refocus on that whore, and find ways to stop her, and to be honest Sophia, if you are so sad that Fidelity has gone, then blame that whore and get focused, because she is the reason she has gone."

We finished breakfast and Chloe offered to show Deli around the house properly, which included the cellar and the attic, I had work to do, so I headed up to my room, my job for today was organising prints and posters. All the files had been sent to the printers, and I had to check we had everything in production, ready to be delivered here, so we could ship some to the gallery.

The good news was, the post card packs had been shipped and were on their way, as well as the key rings and bamboo travel mugs, all of which had the arch printed on them. Two hundred of each would be sent to the gallery for the VIP guest bags, and a further thousand of each would be delivered later for their gallery shop. This event had cost a great deal, but with merchandise D&D should make most of it back, but this was for Chloe, and so making a profit was not our priority.

I had an email from Simone, who was the gallery manager, and she had sent the specs for the large vinyl banner that would hang from the gallery, it was huge and featured a large picture of Chloe, taken by Edwina, and a massive picture of the Sanctuary Arch, which unbeknown to Chloe had already been reserved by me. There was no way I was letting that picture out of this house. Everything was going to plan, and Anita emailed me with her ideas for the press conference, which would take place in a different room.

I sat back and sipped my now cold coffee, and there was a tap on the door, it was Deli, I smiled and nodded her in, she came through the door.

"I am not disturbing you, am I?" I shook my head.

"Not really I am working on Chloe's event, it is sort of lots of little things, it is not like when I am writing, normally people just walk in, and I don't even notice them." She sat in Birch's chair.

"The house is quiet." I smiled at her.

"It can be, for Chloe and myself that is a bonus, but evenings and weekends, it can be pretty noisy when we are all at home, you will get used to it. It just takes a little time; give it a week and it will just feel like home. The thing is, if you get bored, Chloe is always in her studio, I sit with her a lot and talk while she paints, I love watching her paint. Deli we all wander from room to room chatting, you will always be welcome, you are one of us now." She nodded.

"You are all so busy during the day, and I work evenings until late, so there is not much to do for me during the day, I usually sleep till about eleven, and then potter around the flat, I would do that here, but this house is so clean, there is nothing to do." I gave a chuckle.

"Wait till it gets warmer, we all rush round in the mornings getting stuff done, and then hang out in the garden all day, it is really nice out back in summer. If you really need something to do during the day, then what else do you do, I know you went off to college, what did you do there?"

"I did my health, social care, in children's and young people's settings and workforce levels, I also have some office level I.T. quals. I used to temp in Oxendale in offices, but there are so many young people in the market trying to stay in the area, it is hard." I was impressed.

"So, you are a nanny that can run an office, that is pretty cool?" She sighed.

"Not as cool as you would think, it is almost impossible to get work at the moment. I have been on every agency there is, and they don't half take a cut of the wage, it is why I applied at the restaurant. I worked at the Hunters, when I was at college, and Derek and Margret remembered me, which is how I got the job, I worked with Chloe for a while there." I looked at my screen, and thought about it for a few moments.

"The way I see it, Edwina might be able to throw you some part time work, I know Birch and I probably will with the D&D thing, and it might be a long shot, but have you thought of talking to Deb's?" She frowned.

"What in the bookshop?" I nodded.

"Well not in the shop, in child care. Jimmy is always in the studio and she has little Jenny with her in the shop all day, have a chat and see if she needs help. Even if it is a few hours a day, it will get you out, and give you a little extra cash. Deli, I know you talked to Birch, but I do not want you worrying about money here. Trust me, there are many ways to pay your way, and not all of them involve cash, when Chloe moved in, she had no income at all. She worked hard cooking and helping in the garden, and was always there when we needed a shoulder to cry on, something as simple as making us brews when we are busy on a project counts here as payment." She smiled.

"Yeah, I kind of see that, you know for a large group, you all get on really well, it's nice." I finished my coffee.

"Moon calls us a tribe of misfits, we sort of look at each other as family, give it a few months and you will get it, although I will warn you, Chloe will definitely want to paint you naked, she has done all of us... Right, next job, we still have boxes in the garage of yours to sort out, I think we have food and pots?" She nodded, and I got up.

"Come on then, I am pretty much done for now, we can do it together. See you are already making a donation, you brought food." She smiled.

"How does that work actually?" We walked out of the door and down the stairs.

"We have a card for our bills account, we usually shop in pairs, and take the card, we bulk buy a lot of stuff, no one likes shopping. If you want sweets and treats for yourself, you buy those yourself, Chloe stashes her orange creams in the back of her wardrobe, she does not know we know." She giggled as we made our way towards the left hand door in the kitchen, that led down the passage to the garage.

We spent the afternoon moving things around the garage, we still had huge pallets of Chloe's new books to sort out, so we cleared all Fidelity's stuff that she wanted in the house, and then what was left, we boxed in spare boxes, and I placed them on the top shelves in the store room for safety.

In the kitchen we put the food away, and as is tradition, Chloe watched as I sent her to the end top cupboard. She gave a squeal, and Chloe and myself laughed, as she looked at all the vibrators and dildos. I explained how it was our little secret house joke, and we pranked everyone with it at some point. She saw the joke, and laughed along with us which was a good sign.

As we put the last few things away, I opened the draw and took out the set of keys Rodney had made when he was here, and slid them across the counter towards her.

"Welcome to the neighbourhood, you will need those, the one with a red sleeve is the front door, and the black thing, is the gate release." She smiled as she lifted them up, it was such a nice smile, I winked.

"You are no longer a guest now; you are resident in the Wotton Mental Institution for wild girls." She giggled and dropped the keys in her pocket.

"Thanks for today, Abby, I was feeling a little insecure." I passed her a coffee.

"I know, I was the same my first day, although, I spent it naked writing in the library, so the distraction helped." I smiled.

"That was the day I wrote the last chapter of Seeds of Summer, I forgot I was naked and walked in here for a coffee, poured it out, smiled at the workers fitting the fridge, and offered them a coffee. Deb's pointed out I was naked, and they were not smiling because I was polite, but because they could see everything." She giggled at me, and I shrugged.

"It happens, we have all flashed someone by accident at some point." She sat back and stared into space.

"Abby you guys really have it all together, I mean, look at you all, you are like this huge famous writer, and yet you are naked in the kitchen. Hell, I am sat here in my knickers, Chloe is a brilliant artist, those pictures in your room are mind blowing. Edwina runs her own business, Anthony is just mind blowing at hair, and Birch, she is this mega talented therapist. My life is a bloody mess, I have no direction at all, I work my ass off to struggle." I shrugged.

"Been there, it got so bad I sat on my bed drunk, and looked at the sleeping pills, and if I had not passed out, I would have died that night." She looked shocked.

"How, shit Abby, when was that?"

"Just four years ago, if Birch had not come back to Wotton, I probably would be dead now. Deli, all of us have been there, even Birch, why do you think we did Curio Live? Deli we probably look like we have all the answers, but we don't, what we have is what Birch taught us." She shook her head.

"I do not understand, what has she taught you all." I smiled at her.

"Be yourself, live as you choose peacefully, and look out for each other." She frowned at me.

"What that is it?" I nodded, and gave her a smile.

"Simple isn't it, and yet Primula is incapable, pretty much most people are incapable, but honestly, Deli if you just accept that, and stop putting pressure on yourself, you will see it and get it. And I will add, fit right in here, just go with the flow. Deli, you have a good job, and the Pemberton's are nice people, with us you have support, you are not alone, so just relax and breathe, and start to live as you have always wanted to, live as yourself." She smiled.

"I love the way you see the world, Abby; I find you inspiring." I stood up and reached for the coffee pot.

"So, try looking at the world our way for a while and see what you think of it, if it works, go with it. That is all I am doing, none of us are perfect, we screw up and have to take stock, but we have so much support, we know we are safe to do that."

The delivery truck arrived, and pallets were unloaded, and moved into the garage, or placed just outside. Chloe joined in and slowly we filled the shelves in the store room, and marked each box so we knew what it was, and after a very long day of sorting posters, prints, travel cups, post cards and books, we finally had the garage empty, and our large store room was looking fuller than it ever had.

We were hot and sweaty, and covered in dust, as we headed back into the kitchen. I grabbed three cans of cold drink out of the fridge, and passed them round, and we sat together and drank, and cooled down. Finally feeling uncomfortable with my sweaty body, I headed for a shower, Deli came up with me and we separated at the top of the stairs, I stopped and looked at her, as she wiped her neck.

"So, today was busy?" She turned and smiled.

"It was really fun, hot, but fun." I gave a smile.

"Not quite as quiet as we thought, but that is this place, you really never know what will happen?" She gave a chuckle, and nodded at me.

"Yep, I did not expect that, but again, it was really fun." I turned.

"It was a good contribution, and it has helped, so thanks for that." I headed towards my room and heard her chuckle to herself, as she made her way towards her own room.

Fidelity came out of the shower feeling clean and refreshed, and sat on her bed wrapped in a towel, she brushed her long wet hair, and picked up her dryer, and started to dry her hair. She smiled to herself as she thought of her day, and even though unexpected, she had loved mucking in. her phone lit up as it rang, and she switched off her dryer and answered it, and put it on speaker phone.

"Hi Mum."

"Deli, sweetheart how are you settling in?" She smiled as she looked at the phone.

"I am doing really well Mum, I helped Abby today and we talked a lot."

"That is good, I have known Felicity for years, and Abby is very like her, very likeable." Fidelity smiled, and nodded at her phone, she slid back and sat cross legged on her bed.

"She is, to be honest Mum she is the same as she was in school, she is clever, witty, and funny, and so kind. Mum, you have no idea how kind these people are, it is weird, they want nothing from me." Her mum gave a chuckle.

"Not the den of deviance the papers painted it then?" She smiled.

"No... They are just down to earth and normal, they are nothing like the papers say, it is so different from being around Primula and her friends, I really like it here."

"To be honest Deli, I am actually very relieved, if you want my honest opinion, I think they are a better crowd than that other lot of stuck up little madams. Just from what you were telling me the other night about them, I think you are in a better company, and you are certainly a lot more secure there. I told you then, you do not get to their level of achievement by not working hard for it, learn from them Deli." She smiled at her phone.

"I will Mum, they are really interesting people, they said you can visit whenever you want, so you will have to come and meet them all."

"I Intend to, I want to see your new home, and I really would like to meet them all, especially that Birch girl. I saw her mum talk a few years back in the village, if this Birch is anything like her mother, she will be a good influence for you."

"Mum, I am just happy being me, I don't want to copy, I think just being me here is a good thing." Her mum gave a chuckle.

"Deli, you will have to get ready for work soon, is your uniform pressed and neat?"

"Yes Mum... It always is."

"Good, the Pemberton's are nice people, don't let them down." She gave a long sigh.

"Mum, I won't."

"Alright Sweetheart, I will call you tomorrow." She smiled.

"Okay Mum, talk soon."

She touched her screen, and ended the call, sat on her bed, and looked round her room. This room alone was almost as big as her flat, and then there was the rest of the house to roam, it was massively better for her, and most importantly, it was the one place Prim could not get at her.

It took a few days for Deli to settle, and get into a routine that suited her, I kept my eye on her, and made sure everyone knew that for now, no one was to mention she was living here. To make sure she was alright at work, Birch, Edwina, and myself took it in turns picking her up from work when she finished. We used Edwina's black estate, as Petal and Bess were too recognisable.

Our days were busy, I was working full time on Chloe's exhibition, Birch was making headway planning our Halloween event, and Bradley gave us regular updates on the building and modernisation process of the Curio Centre.

Jimmy and the boys had been busy in the studio, and had pretty much laid down all the tracks for their next album, and their management arranged for them to fly to New York, to do the final mixing, so that meant only one thing, Deb's would be back for about four weeks.

Nigel had been staying with Moon for a week, he had taken a few weeks off work, he had not taken a holiday in two years, and with a little careful planning, we showed him the path to our back gate, which he appeared very familiar with, much to my disturbance, after all he did get a picture of me topless in my bedroom some years ago.

Using the back gate, he was able to come to my mum's house, where he met both Birch and Marjorie, she brought him clean clothes and his bank cards, she had a spare set of keys, so went in when Primula was out.

Primula decided to go to her mother's for a break, and so drove Nigel's car to Millington, and the village calmed down. Molly went to stay with friends, which gave Deli the space to get used to her new life. Knowing everything was safe, she decided she was going to walk to work, but Edwina leant her the car keys for her estate, none of us wanted her walking home alone after one in the morning, even though Wotton's greatest aspect was there was hardly any crime.

Things were moving fast, the summer events program was in full swing, and in the kitchen, papers were starting to pile up as Anthony and Edwina moved into Summer Fete mode. It felt strange one afternoon to see Anthony stood at our table with a large plan laid out.

I had seen my dad do this for years, and had often helped him. I instantly noticed Anthony's errors, and took charge, with a strong.

"Look, if you put your piles of paperwork like this, and then mark the plan like this, you will find as you use each sheet and mark it on the plan, then pile it here, you will avoid confusion."

He looked at it, and gave a chuckle as he understood, and he did not argue or comment, and just got on with it, all the others smiled, and suddenly I was being treated as Chair, it felt really weird.

This year we were going big, the Fete was our launch for the Halloween Event, and also D&D, in Wotton, so we rented a trader marquee to present our ideas to the village. Mum and Celia had loved the idea, and given it their approval, the fact there were no costs involved for the village made them more than keen, and another first for the event, would be book sales and merchandise from the D&D tent, in support of Chloe and myself.

Preparations were busy, I sewed large tablecloths, Birch arranged folding stands for our large display boards, and Chloe painted a sign, for D&D Events. Edwina and Luke set up a mobile stand linked to a large monitor, and had a loop running explaining who D&D were, and what was to come, which covered the Art Exhibition, Merchandise, and the large village wide Halloween event.

It was Friday the 10th of August and it was getting really hot, and the excitement level was building. In one week, we would be putting on Chloe's art exhibition, and this weekend we were going to drive to London, to get our first walk round the gallery. Deli did not work weekends, so we included her in the plans, she had done a surprising amount of work for all of us during the day, and we all felt she should be a part of it, we had rooms booked for Saturday night in London, and we were all excited.

It was a slow night at the restaurant, people were away on holiday, and the days had started to get really hot, and most people were at home having barbeques, so around ten Derek told Deli she could call it a night. She was hot and red in the face when she came out, the sun was just lowering in the sky, but there was a nice breeze as she walked down the ramp to the station car park, and she unbuttoned the top of her blouse and pulled it out of her skirt. She walked past the ticket office, and a figure stepped out, she jumped back and gave a startled scream. Just for a moment she had been terrified, until she realised who it was.

"Soph… You scared me, what are you doing here?"

She looked a mess, her hair was unkempt, she had no makeup on, and her nails were chipped, she stared at her blankly, and then her eyes filled with tears, and she whimpered.

"I miss you, you were my friend, you unfriended me, and I really miss you, I am so lonely with you gone." She burst into tears, and sobbed.

Deli felt a deep pang inside her, as Sophia stood sobbing and shaking. She stepped forward and pulled her into a hug, and held her tight, she stunk of alcohol. Mr Pemberton stood at his door and watched, as he had every night to make sure she got to her car safe, and watched as Deli embraced Sophia, he lifted his phone, and dialled. Fidelity held her tight.

"I am sorry, I should have known better than to leave you alone with them, I really am so sorry Soph, can you forgive me?" She wept bitterly into Fidelity's shoulder.

"I don't want them hurting you Deli, and when they did, I had no one to talk to. Prim is nasty and I don't like her, I don't want a stupid Vice, I just want my friends to be nice." She sobbed really hard, and Deli had no idea what to do. Sophia sobbed even harder.

"Why did you not tell me, I would have come with you, you are my friend?" Deli sobbed with her.

"Sophia, I did not realise, honestly, I really did not. I didn't mean to leave you, they kicked me out of the building, I had no choice I had to go." She sobbed again.

"I looked for you, I looked everywhere, and Prim said you had left town, yar? Deli, I missed you so much, I missed sitting and talking, and drinking tea, and all your friends on Insta have stopped following me." She gave a huge sob, and howled into her shoulder.

"I only have five thousand followers now!" She wailed even louder. Deli gave a sigh.

"God Soph, you really need to mix more with real people."

I sat at my desk in the library, and looked at Edwina.

"My dad said it is Sophia and she is crying, and Deli is holding her, and talking to her. He says she looks like shit."

I smiled, the look of horror and happiness on Edwina's face was funny as hell. I looked at Birch, sat at her desk.

"What do we do?" Birch sat back.

"It was bound to come out sooner or later, eventually people will know she is living with us, and this is her home too." I nodded and picked up my phone, and opened my messages, found Deli, and typed. 'Bring her here, she will be fine,' and then pressed send.

Deli lifted her off her shoulder, she looked awful, and her eyes were blotchy, she looked at her.

"Soph, we cannot stay here, come on get in the car." She gave a sniffle.

"My tissue ran out, yar." Deli's phone pinged, and she pulled it out, and tapped the message, she gave a smile.

"Come on, come back to my place and we will have some tea." Sophia blinked, and then smiled.

"You will drink tea with me?" Deli smiled, and nodded and took her hand.

"Yes, we can drink tea again." Soph gave a sniffle and smiled again.

"Can I be your friend again, I promise, I will be better so you don't run away again, yar?" Deli nodded and gave her a smile.

"Yes, we can be friends again, come on." She pulled her hand, and walked her to the car.

"I chipped a nail, yar." Deli smiled.

"I will fix it, don't worry." She smiled as she opened the door, and Sophia slipped in.

"No offence, yar, but don't put a picture of this on Insta, if people see this, you will lose tons of followers." Deli gave a chuckle as she shut the door, and walked around to the driver's side, some things never change.

Chapter 10

Sophia's Secret.

Fidelity pulled into the drive, and the gates swung closed behind her. She got out of the car as Sophia looked up at the house.

"Your house is big, baby sitting pays better than brows, yar? If I lived here, I would put it on Insta." Deli smiled as she put the key in the door, she stopped and looked at her, as she got out.

"Soph... Do you know who else lives here?" She shook her head.

"No... Should I, have I forgotten again, I am sorry, yar?" Deli smiled, and turned the key and the door opened.

"Guys, I am home, where are you?" Sophia looked around the hall.

"I would definitely post this on Insta, yar?"

"IN THE KITCHEN!" She took a deep breath, took hold of Sophia's hand, and walked down the hall, as Sophia pointed things out.

"Those stairs, that plant, this pot woman... Insta yar?"

We were mainly sat at the island, Anthony and the boys were sat at the table, when Deli walked in with Sophia. Sophia stared, and then turned round and tried to leave.

"Deli, they hate me, please leave with me, it's dangerous, yar." Birch got up, and walked towards Sophia, she looked really scared, and shied away from her.

"Don't hurt me, it was not me, yar." Birch smiled, and lowered her voice.

"Hi Sweetie... No one here wants to hurt you. Sweetie, do not be scared, we do not hate you, Sophia." She looked really nervous; Deli looked at her.

"Sophia, these are my housemates, and I live with them, they are my friends, and they are nothing like Prim says they are." She shook her head.

"Prim told me Deli; they want to hurt me, yar?" I shrugged as I looked at her, I must admit, I have never ever seen her looking this rough.

"I don't Sophia, I knew you at school, same with Deb's and Anthony, we never fell out ever, Primula has lied to you a lot." She nervously looked around the room and then back at me.

"Deli is my friend, I miss her, all I want is tea with my friend, please don't hate me for it." I smiled.

"I will put the kettle on then, so she can make your tea for you." Sophia looked at Deli.

"Is that alright, yar? Can she do that, because I always boil the water?" Deli nodded at her and smiled.

"When you are not here, we all take it in turns to boil the water." She nodded.

"Alright, Deli, I feel scared, they are cool people, but Prim will go mad if she knows, yar." Birch looked at her.

"So don't tell her Sweetie, if you don't, we won't, is that a deal?" She looked at Birch, and nodded.

"I am called Sophia, I don't know a Sweetie, cool hair though, you should definitely put that on Insta, yar." Chloe and Deb's sniggered, Birch looked puzzled, Edwina leaned in, and whispered.

"Whoa, she totally wrong footed Birch, I like this girl." I looked at Sophia, and tried not to smirk, I failed.

"I have Insta Sophia, we all do." She looked interested, and took a step forward.

"I have five thousand followers yar, I do brows for people and they pay me, I also give fashion tips, yar." Deb's held up her phone.

"I have ten thousand followers." Anthony gave a sigh.

"Oh, please darling, I am at one ninety K." Sophia's eyes widened; Birch sniggered.

"Beginner, I have two hundred and seventy thousand." Sophia gasped with amazement. I laughed as I opened my phone.

"Oh, you sad people, I have just over two million and a verified account." Sophia gasped out really loud, walked right up to me, and held out her hand looking star struck.

"O.M.G You are an influencer; I am honoured to meet you, yar." Everyone giggled as I looked on, not quite knowing what to do.

Edwina leaned into Chloe.

"And that is Abby's mind completely blown, I am frigging loving this girl."

Deli made tea for her and Sophia, and put it in a little tea pot, on a tray, with a bowl of sugar lumps, and a small jug of milk, and carried it into the living room. We all poured gins and followed and sat down, as Deli explained how Sophia would come round and have tea with her, and this had become a little ritual they had. Sophia looked quite emotional as Deli added two sugar lumps, and some milk and poured the tea.

She pulled out her phone and took a picture of it, and posted it to Insta, with the hashtag #teaagainhappy.

I felt sad for her as I watched, but it made her so happy, and finally Deli got her to take her thick coat off, she did not look good, to be honest she was hardly recognisable without makeup, and I felt it was a shame, because she was actually quite pretty without it.

We all talked Insta, which is not as easy as you would think, but Sophia relaxed and started to smile more. She held up her bone China tea cup and sipped at it, just like Deli did, and it really cheered her up. Deb's being Deb's, and naturally chatty tried having a conversation with her, when suddenly Sophia realised who she was.

"You have that shop, yar, it has those books in it yar?" Deb's nodded.

"Yes, I love it, I can spend all day reading books, it's awesome." Sophia stared at her.

"They have no pictures, yar?" I watched Edwina lean forward next to Chloe, with a fixed gaze, Deb's smiled.

"Well, no, they are meant to be stories, you have to imagine the pictures as you read." Sophia frowned, and lifted her phone to show Deb's her Insta.

"Why... I have all the pictures and the story to go with it, you should read more Insta, yar?" Deb's looked stunned, and Edwina gave a small side fist punch, and turned to Chloe.

"Three out of frigging three, she is a genius, I absolutely bloody love her."

I sniggered, Deli gave a giggle, Deb's really wanted to say something, but could not quite find the words, and sat back looking puzzled. Sophia sipped her tea and we tried to restart the conversation again, Anthony stepped up to the plate and Edwina's eyes lit up with joy. I did not know which one to watch, Anthony or Edwina, I noticed Birch was paying extra attention.

Anthony who was sat on the edge of the table looked at her, and flicked his long blonde fringe out of his eyes.

"You know Sophia, if you would like me to look at that hair, I would be very happy to, it has somewhat lost its volume and style?" Sophia shook her head, and Edwina leaned further forward.

"Prim says that if you thatched a roof, the way you thatch hair, we would all drown in our beds, yar?"

Anthony stood up really fast, with a gasp, and gripped his heart, Edwina grabbed a cushion and stuffed it into her mouth, and fell back shaking, as Anthony took two steps back as he stared at Sophia with horror, he opened his mouth, and gave a weak squeak.

Edwina thrashed around on the end of the sofa, holding up four fingers, I had to put my head down, Birch's stomach was wobbling like crazy as she bit her lip, and hid under her hair, and what sounded like air flow, rushed out of Anthony's mouth.

His lip trembled, he turned, and ran out of the room, Edwina pulled the cushion off her mouth and breathed in deeply, she looked at Deli.

"Hell, bring her here whenever you want." Birch grunted, and put her hand on her mouth.

I had to go and make a new drink, I walked slowly out of the room down the hall, and saw Anthony in the kitchen pouring a double gin, he looked flustered to hell, he waved his hand across his chest as I approached.

"Just don't, words darling fail me, just why exactly did she go to school?" I giggled as I poured a fresh drink.

"Don't be hard on her Anthony, she does not know any different, and Prim has clearly poisoned her mind against us all. Did you see how scared she was when she first saw us?" He gave a nod.

"It boggles the mind, when you find out what is really said and done behind our backs. She is very clearly a scheming bitch, although it is not like we do not know that already?" I shook my head.

"Deli actually looks happy we have been nice to her; I think it is important we help her to help Sophia." Anthony took a deep breath.

"I must admit, when she first walked in Abby, I was mortified to see her. I mean, she is no model, but I always credited the girl for her clothing style, where has she been sleeping, the park?"

I shrugged, I honestly did not know, she just looked really rough. Deli came down the hallway with the tray, Sophia followed. I sat down in my usual spot at the island, and watched as Sophia handed each thing from the tray to Deli and she washed it. They clearly had a routine, and Sophia followed it, paying attention to every detail, it fascinated me to watch. She dried them and stacked them neatly, back on the tray, they emptied the sugar lumps back into the box, and wiped the little bowl and put it back. Birch slipped in at my side and leaned onto me. Her voice was really low so only I could hear her.

"Fascinating, isn't it, she has a perfect routine for everything, I think it is her safety net, she uses it to hide her insecurities, as long as the routine is fine, she is fine. If you take the routine away or change it, she falls apart, watch this, I have an idea." I looked at her and frowned, she smiled.

"Sophia Swe... Sophia, when did you last go home?" She turned and frowned, and looked a little sheepish.

"I went out when Molly left, yar, I wanted to look for my friend Deli." Birch nodded and smiled.

"When did Molly leave?" She stood and thought about it.

"She went on holiday on Saturday, for three weeks, because Prim has gone home, yar?" I suddenly began to realise where Birch was going with this, Birch smiled.

"Sophia, that was six days ago." Deli stopped wiping the tea pot, and went white, she stood frozen. Sophia nodded.

"Yar!" I swallowed hard as I understood, and could not help myself.

"Sophia, are you telling me you have not been home since?" She nodded.

"I was lonely, I wanted to find Deli, she is my friend, but she left, and I did not like it at home without her, so I looked for her." Deli realising, put her hand to her mouth, Birch smiled.

"Where did you look Sophia?" She shrugged.

"I walked... And looked, and then I saw her." She smiled, and looked at Deli who was stood frozen, with her eyes full of tears, Sophia smiled.

"I found you, yar.? Birch smiled at her.

"Sophia... Where are your tablets?" She looked amused, as if she was playing a game.

"At home, they are always at home, I keep them next to the bed." Birch gave a nod as Deli tried to make sense of it all.

"Sophia, who is your contact support worker?" She smiled.

"Ruth, she is my friend too, I like Ruth, she helps me." Deli stared at Birch, and Birch smiled.

"Sophia, have you seen Chloe's artwork; she is a really good painter?" Chloe shook her head looking panicked; she noticed the smile on Edwina's face. Sophia looked at Chloe.

"Do you have pictures too, yar?" Chloe gave a sigh, and got up, and smiled.

"Yeah, I love to paint, well it is all I do, well except have sex too." Sophia giggled, as she followed Chloe to the studio.

"I love sex too, when I kissed Nigel, Prim got angry, and hit me. I told her his stick was up and that is what it is for, she did not understand." Chloe blinked, and her mouth fell open, Edwina hurried to follow them, so did Deb's. Deli looked at Birch.

"How did you know?" Birch gave her a smile.

"Sweetie, it is what I do for a living, I have a few of Ruth's patients come to the practice, is it Asperger's?" Deli gave a nod and reached for the gin.

"I think so, I know she is on the scale. I feel awful, she would have got frightened and gone for some booze, it really messes her up. Honestly, when she is on her meds her mind is clear and she is fine, oh God guys, she has been walking around because Molly went away, and I was not there, I feel so horrible now." Birch understood it all now.

"The tea ritual was your way of making sure she was fine each day; I get it now. Look Deli, you cannot blame yourself for this, you got evicted, that was not your fault. I am going to go and call Ruth, I think it is better if she stays here tonight, Dead's and me will go and get her meds, and I will get Ruth to come here tomorrow." Deli gave a sigh of relief, and wiped her eyes.

"Thanks', you guys have been so good with her; I really appreciate it." I smiled at her as she poured herself a gin.

In the studio, Deb's and Edwina watched from the door, as Chloe showed her a picture, Sophia looked at it.

"You sell these, why?"

Chloe frowned, she was acutely aware of Edwina, and watching her every word, as she chose them very carefully.

"People want them, so they buy them." She smirked at Edwina, Sophia pulled out her phone and 'CLICK' she looked at her phone, and then turned it to Chloe.

"I got one now, and didn't have to buy it, yar?" Edwina fell back on the kitchen floor as Chloe's jaw hit the floor, Deb's sniggered as Edwina screeched.

"FIVE OUT OF FRIGGING FIVE, I BLOODY LOVE HER!" She rolled round holding her tummy, pissing her sides laughing. Sophia looked at Chloe.

"Is your sister like me, broken, yar?" Edwina sat up, and stopped laughing, she stared at Sophia.

"Sophia, you are not broken, I think you are wonderful. I actually think the way you see the world is lovely, I have friends like you." Debs looked shocked, as she saw tears in Edwina's eyes. Sophia smiled at her.

"We are friends, yar?" Edwina swallowed, and nodded then smiled at her.

"Yeah, I am your friend." Sophia lifted out her phone.

"I will add you on Insta yar?"

Chloe watched the speed she shot through the menu, found Edwina, added her, and wrote her a message with one hand, she gave a gasp, never had she seen anyone work a phone with such skill. Edwina smiled as she looked at her phone, she turned it to show the screen.

"Look, I accepted you on Insta." She smiled.

"Well yar, we are friends."

I sat in the library with Birch, as she talked to Ruth on the phone, she was concerned as Sophia had missed her appointment, but she was glad to know she was fine. Birch nodded as they spoke.

"I will keep her here with Fidelity tonight, and you can come and see her in the morning if that is alright?"

"That is really wonderful, I am grateful to you Doctor Dixon, I was worried about her, she is such a sweet girl, and I am very fond of her. I am so relieved, she has done so well for years, and then out of the blue, she just went off the rails and disappeared. I will see you in the morning. Good night." Birch sat back and looked at Deli.

"I am keeping her here, and Ruth wants to pick her up for evaluation tomorrow." Deli nodded, and looked down.

"I feel terrible, if I had known Molly had gone away, I would have visited her, I have her spare key, just in case, I will get it for you, it is flat nine."

Deli told Sophia she could stay with her tonight, she made me giggle, when Deli told her they would have to share the bed, she appeared okay with it. She needed to get a wash, so Deli took her upstairs for a shower, and to show her where she now slept. Birch and I jumped in Petal, and headed once again to Lilac Street, we already knew the door code, and used the lift.

Her flat was immaculate, I was really surprised. Birch warned me to touch nothing, everything was laid out and had its place, she opened a draw to reveal all matching knickers and bra sets, it looked like the lowest pile was blue, so she lifted the black ones from the next pile. I was starting to understand the routine she used to do everything, including dress.

Birch opened her wardrobe, and all her clothing were matched, where there was a gap, Birch took the next item, it was one hanger, and everything was on it, this girl had a level of organisation beyond anything I had ever heard of.

We picked up her tablets, one of which was her contraception, and packed them, and then headed back to the door. Birch drove, as I had drunk three gins. Back home, Sophia was in the shower, which was set to not touch her face.

We left Deli to handle her, and dry her hair, and when I checked on them a little later, they were both curled up together asleep, I smiled to myself, as I pulled the door too. They looked cute, and I wondered if that was what Birch and I looked like?

A little later, I curled up with Birch, and relaxed.

"How did you know?" Birch pulled me closer.

"Insecurity, lack of eye contact, the way she studied everything, like a photographer would, and her simple logic, her Insta obsession. Her use of my friend gave her away, I have a few clients at the practice and they always mention people as their friends, but when she did not call Prim her friend, I knew for sure." I looked back at her in the lamp light, her eyes were bright and sparkled at me.

"So she does not see Prim as a friend at all?" Birch shook her head.

"She is afraid of Prim, which is why she does everything she is told to do, she mentioned Prim has hit her, that was when I knew for sure. Prim wants her on the council because if you sit Sophia in front of a computer, you will see a whole different side of her, I would imagine her ability is as good as Edwina's. I would also think she is brilliant at maths. Prim wants her to do all the work, whilst she gets all the glory. Think about it Deads, she will never argue with Prim, I would think if you ask, Sophia has no interest in being on the committee at all."

It felt strange to know that Sophia has difficulties, and yet she was on her own, living in a flat, I looked into Birch's bright green eyes, she understood so much more than I realised.

"Birch is it alright letting her live alone, what if she had been hurt?" Birch smiled; her eyes were so intense.

"Sweetie, we cannot save everyone, look, Sophia has medication that helps her, and she is actually a lot brighter than she appears. She can function in a relatively normal way, and live her life on her terms. Socially she is hampered, which is how people like Prim can exploit her, but she does have support systems like Ruth in place, so she has some normality in life. I would also say her friendship with Deli is vastly important, if you want to be a part of that, do so, after all, it can only benefit her." I was impressed.

"Wow it blows my mind how you watch, and got all that from just observing her, what else do you know?" She gave a small smirk.

"I know you have not broken eye contact, which means staring into my eyes is making you ever so wet."

I started to giggle, and she smiled, and leaned down to me and kissed me softly, and then I felt her hand slowly slide down my tummy, I relaxed my legs a little and gave her access, she was so right, I was as horny as hell.

I was groggy when I came down the stairs, and wandered down the hall, into the kitchen. I walked in and Chloe was sat next to Sophia, who was eating scrambled eggs, she pointed at me with her fork and looked at Chloe.
"See... You have to go for the right ascetic with nudity, look at her proportions, she is perfect, just like Deli, her boobs balance out with her waist, if the top is too heavy, it throws out all proportion, Abby has perfect balance, yar?"
I looked down at my orange sized boobs, and then looked at Deli's, we were about the same. I looked at Chloe and smiled. Never again would I worry about small boobs, I was perfectly proportioned. Sophia leaned over the island and looked at Deb's phone, she pointed with her fork.
"No, swipe left... There ya go, now tap the arrow, see the dots, tap them, and there you are, now just edit it, yar?" Deb's gave a gasp.
"Wow, that is how it's done, I have been trying for weeks to edit it." Sophia smiled, and filled her fork with more eggs.
I was amazed at how well she had just fitted in with everyone, and how different she was. Her hair and makeup were done, and she was dressed in clean clothes, and completely different to last night, and more like the Sophia I knew. Edwina handed me a coffee, and I sat down, and Sophia smiled at me.
"You know, I never told you yar, but I love the hair Abby, always have, I get the blonde Avril look, but seriously, as an influencer, the black and red is much better yar?"
I smiled and sipped my coffee, I was not awake enough to talk, and two compliments in one minute, that was enough for me.

Birch walked down the hallway with Ruth, the support worker.
"I washed and dried her things last night; Fidelity has packed them in her bag. She stunk of booze, and looked like she has hardly slept, but after a shower and good night's sleep, she does appear much better."
"I appreciate your care of her Doctor Dixon, I will take her back to the centre, and we will give her a full medical and check her over. Give her a few days, and she will be right as rain, and back

around her friends." They walked into the kitchen, and Sophia smiled as she saw Ruth.

"Sophia it is check up time again, you missed last week, come on, we will go and meet up with Arthur." She smiled and looked at Fidelity.

"I have to go; I will message you, yar?" Fidelity gave a nod.

"Yeah, let me know how you are doing, go with Ruth, and when you come back, we will have tea again." She got up and looked around the room, she was obviously a lot more aware now.

"Look... You are all nice people, I like you, you are kind yar... Thanks." I smiled.

"You are welcome, Sophia, if you get lonely, just don't go walking around, you could get hurt." She nodded.

"Check you out on Insta, yar?" I gave a small chuckle.

"Yar. Check you out on Insta too." She waved as she took Ruth's hand, and walked down the hall, I heard her say.

"Abby is my friend, and she is an influencer, she is cool, yar?" Fidelity gave a big sigh and I looked at her.

"You did a good thing Deli, now do you understand who we are?" She nodded, and smiled.

"Yeah, I really do, thanks for letting her stay guys, we talked a lot last night, I told her to write a letter and remove herself as Vice. Primula is taking advantage of her, and I am going to stop it." Chloe lifted her cup and looked over it.

"If you need any back up, I will be there, I would love to punch that bitch." Edwina walked past with her phone.

"Oh... Look... Art..." Click, she looked at her phone.

"It's mine now, yar?" Chloe narrowed her eyes.

"Fuck you, Weena." We all started to giggle.

As Birch waved Ruth and Sophia off, a large truck pulled up outside, Morty leaned out of the window.

"I hope this is big enough, it is the only one they had, I got all the pictures in, and there is a good amount of room?"

The garage door opened, and Luke pulled out a pallet on a truck, loaded up with boxes. Morty jumped out, and walked round the back of the truck. He lifted the roller shutter and dropped the tail lift, Birch walked round to see all the pictures on a large wooden rack, wrapped up in thick fabric, Morty handed her a wallet and a small box.

"That guy Gavin gave me these, they are, er... Certificates of prominence, and the stamp?" She smiled.

"Providence, they are provided to prove they are the authentic pictures done by Chloe." He smiled.

"What would I know, I am just the hired beef?" He laughed.

Today was a big day for us, and especially for Chloe, it was the start of two days of hanging and organising, ready for next Friday's VIP event, and a four week run of her art relating to the Hand of Death series of books. I was nervous, and she was terrified, so much so, Edwina drove her and Deb's, with baby Jenny, in Bess, and I drove Birch and Fidelity with me in Petal, with most of the luggage.

I won't deny, I hate driving in London. As we got close to the Winchester Gallery, looking for the road to the rear loading dock, Birch pulled an envelope out of her back pocket of her jeans, and handed it to Fidelity in the back.

"Here you go Sweetie, I almost forgot." Fidelity took it and looked at it.

"What is it?" Birch turned and smiled.

"Your pay packet, Edwina submitted the work you had done, so did Deads, and I added the hours you did for me. The cash was transferred to you last night." She opened it and pulled out the pay slip, she looked up and I smiled in the mirror.

"Guys there is three hundred quid?" I nodded as I looked out of the window and spotted the street and indicated.

"We know all Pemberton's employees are self employed, so keep the slip, you will need it for tax, but you did thirty hours work for us, and we pay ten per hour, so that is three hundred, is that a problem?" She shook her head.

"I was just helping out to say thanks." Birch smiled at her.

"Sweetie, hoovering and cooking is helping us out, computer work, is working for us. If you want to drive that scary lawnmower, that would be helping, it runs off with me and crashes into things, we don't pay for that, driving it is a life choice." She sat back and smiled.

"This will really help, thanks."

I smiled as I saw the big truck with Morty and Luke stood next to it, and pulled in at the side of it. Edwina was not far behind us, and Bess came chugging around the corner, Chloe leaned her head out of the side window, and looked wildly excited.

"Did you see the banner, it is massive?" I smiled as she jumped out and threw her arms around me.

"Abby, it is huge, and it has the arch on it." I smiled, her eyes were huge and bright and happy.

"Chloe, Birch and me designed it for them." She kissed my cheek.

"Do you think they will let me have it for my bedroom wall when this is done?" Birch leaned in.

"Sweetie, it is over thirty feet long, and ten foot high, you could wrap the whole house in it." I giggled, as Birch walked over to the back doors and pressed the bell. A voice came out of the speaker.

"Hello, who is it?" Birch leaned in.

"It is the team from D&D with the Artwork for the Chloe Pemberton exhibition."

"One moment please..." The Buzzer went off.

"Come on in please, Simone will be with you in a moment." Edwina gripped Chloe's arm.

"Jesus Chloe, I am shaking like a leaf, you know, I am so proud of you, and I am so excited for you. Really savour this, because your first one will always mean the most, and enjoy it. You were there in our bedroom the night I launched my business, and it was just us together. After everything I have done since, that is the night I remember the most, just you and me and cheap wine." She pulled her into a hug, and Chloe squeezed her tight.

"It wasn't cheap, I nicked it from dad's stash."

The door opened into a large loading bay, there was a woman of about fifty stood decked out in gold and designer clothing, and at her side was...

"Mum, what are you doing here?" Roni smiled at Birch.

"Hello sweetheart, I decided to join the rebellion against Katie, and considering Chloe is practically a daughter to me, and Simone and I go way back, I thought I would sneak in and pitch in." I started to giggle, as Birch looked completely wrong footed, she shrugged and smiled at us.

"I have already bought one, you know me darling, I never buy on the day, I always order up front." I felt my heart beat increase.

"Which one did you buy?" Roni smiled.

"Relax... It is so obvious which one you will buy, so I bought the resurrection sword cover, I knew you would want the arch." I gave a huge sigh of relief.

"Girls always buy before the show, when this exhibit opens, certain collectors like to see those little red dots to show they have sold. If they don't, they will not buy anything, and I want this one a sell out." Birch looked at me, and shook her head.

"I should have known, there are no secrets when your mum and dad are both psychologists." I giggled at her.

"Or wife."

Chapter 11

The Business of Art.

It is pretty interesting seeing how a gallery works. The room was huge, and had dark smoked glass windows, and several little side rooms. Chloe and myself were given white gloves by Birch, to handle each picture, and small markers had been placed on the floor where each picture was to be hung.

The good news was, because of insurance purposes, we did not have to hang them, their own people did that. While I helped Chloe unwrap her art, as this was her first time seeing them framed, and Gavin had done a great job, I went through the glossy catalogue to work out the viewing order, that Chloe had picked. Chloe kept sniffling and wiping her eyes.

Roni and Simone oversaw us, and gave us hints and tips, which really helped. Birch was in charge of the book table, and worked with Luke. He was a strong guy and could carry the boxes easily, and in a side room, Edwina worked with Deb's and Fidelity, packing two hundred VIP gift bags.

Chloe had picked fifty guests, and the gallery picked the other one hundred and fifty, who were all interested parties, they had all received tickets for Friday night's preview. Morty walked round with the camera, and filmed every aspect of what we did, Edwina was going to make a small feature video of the whole event for the D&D site.

This was also going to be the official launch of Chloe's Art Book, and related merchandise, we had done a deal with the gallery, which was sale or return. They would put everything out, it would be logged and catalogued by Birch, and a gallery assistant called Fiona. At the end of the event, which was four weeks, whatever was left in stock we would collect. The gallery would pay for what they had sold, less their commission.

We were not really that concerned about making a profit on this one, we were more concerned about being able to pay Chloe a good share to boost her income. Waterside Galleries were selling her stuff, but we hoped with this exposure, more people would be driven towards her paintings, because they made serious money for everyone. The official souvenir program, which would be available for sale through the gallery was fifteen pounds, and at the back, there was the online sales advert for Waterside featuring Chloe's painted artwork.

There were posters and prints for sale, bamboo travel mugs, post card packs, keyrings, note books, and even a selection of fridge magnets, and all of them were displayed in a long glass case in the gallery shop. Chloe had been given all two thousand copies of the books, and we had boxed them up with their number sequence on the front of the box, written in thick black pen. The shop store was equally as big, and we had a whole section dedicated to the event, and neatly stacked all the excess.

A long table was set up, on which all the VIP bags would be placed, and handed out as people arrived. It felt like a long day, and at five o'clock feeling hot and tired, the room was locked, as other aspects of the gallery were still open to the public, and we headed out back, and off to the hotel to meet Anita, who had just checked in, and texted us.

The hotel was not a five star, but I did not care, it had a bed and a bath, and a restaurant, so I was good. Our rooms were all on the same floor, Deb's with baby in a travel cot had her own room, but it had a partition door, which the twin room was being shared by Chloe and Fidelity. Morty was a few doors down in a single, he was also personal security with Luke for this event. Anita was across the hall from us, with Roni next door to her, and Edwina and Luke were at the side of us. I felt happy but tired as I sat on the bed.

Birch ran a bath, and opened a bottle of wine, we had to be back at the gallery for eleven the following day, so tonight was ours to do as we pleased, although a large table had been booked at eight for our meal. I slipped into the water and leaned back into Birch, and relaxed with my eyes closed.

"Oh, this is heaven, I am exhausted." I felt her hands slide around me, and she gave a soft chuckle.

"Deads, we are in a hotel, and alone, and we have not been here before?" I started to giggle as her hands explored me.

"Mm, mm… That feels so nice."

I slipped my hands onto her legs either side and rubbed them softly up and down, and just let her explore, feeling all those wonderful feelings. She started to softly kiss my neck and I smiled.

"Oh baby, yes that is so nice." I lifted my legs slightly and spread them, and her hands wandered down.

"Oh God… Oh yes baby." I stiffened in the water, and lifted my legs to the side of the bath.

"OOH! Oh yes baby."

At seven thirty we came out of our room happy, and met Roni, as we headed towards the lift, she glanced at us.

"Girls, tomorrow, do not rush off, I have a meeting I want you to attend, I have booked a room here for six, it will not take long, but it involves the Dixon Group and I want you there, is that alright?" I was okay with it, and Birch nodded.

"We can do that if you need us." Roni smiled at us.

"As shareholders, it is important you are there, it will be casual, no need to dress up."

This experience was so different from my last. We all sat around the table talking and laughing, as we do at home, there were sly clicks from other guest's mobiles as we were recognised. All in all, it was just great fun, as we ate and drank, and giggled. I sat between Roni and Fidelity, as they asked me all about the honeymoon, and I smiled with joy, as I told them all about it, well most of it, after all, there were some things I would never openly tell.

It was nice to watch Chloe, as she smiled and talked, she was so excited and happy, sat at the side of Edwina, and then something really wonderful happened, a young girl walked up with a copy of Resurrection Sword in her hand, and stood next to her looking nervous.

"Excuse me, Miss Pemberton?" I sat still and smiled, as the whole table went instantly quiet, Chloe turned and saw the book, the girl smiled.

"I love your artwork, Miss Pemberton, would you please sign the cover for me?"

Chloe looked at me and swallowed hard, she looked at the girl, it was so strange to be the spectator, as I watched her go very quietly spoken.

"You would like me to sign it?" She nodded.

"Yes please, you are an amazing artist, I am an art student, and so excited about your exhibition, my dad is bringing me to see it next week?" Chloe looked completely wrong footed, as the girl handed her a pen.

"Actually, on the cover if that is alright, I am sure Miss Watson will not mind." I smiled across the table; I had not realised; she had not seen me.

"Not at all, I think the art is as magic as you do."

The young girl looked at me and froze on the spot, her eyes went huge. Chloe signed the book and passed it across to me, Chloe looked so thrilled, I looked at the girl as I opened the cover.

"What is your name?" She swallowed hard.

"Miss Watson, I am so sorry, I did not see you there, my name is Johanna." I smiled as I wrote in her book.

"Well, it is your lucky day Johanna, thank you for showing such respect to my best friends art. I agree with you, she is an amazing artist, we are here today setting up the exhibition, so it will be nice to see you again next weekend."

I slid the pen back in the book and handed it across the table to Chloe, she took it with a smile and handed it to her.

"That is my very first autograph, I am a little blown away right now, but honestly, thanks." Johanna smiled a huge smile.

"I want to be an illustrator one day." Chloe smiled at her.

"If you ever need a few tips, message me at my website, and I will help you out."

She looked so blown away, her eyes were just so huge, and Chloe was so natural with her, I saw Edwina wipe her eye, and smile. Johanna said thank you and went back to her table, and I winked at Chloe.

"Get used to it, you are in the big league now." She smiled and looked back where the girl was showing her parents, and telling them all about it. Roni leaned into me.

"She really has no idea what is coming does she?"

"Nope, none at all, just like Curio Live, she will be blown away by it all." Deli smiled as she watched Chloe, who was smiling a lot more than she was, if that is even possible?

I will not deny, I was a little drunk when we got to our room, and Birch was holding me up slightly, I staggered in, and pushed her onto the bed, and then jumped on her and tore her clothes off, whilst she squealed with laughter.

Sunday was not good; I had a major headache, as we checked out, and loaded our baggage into Petal. We arrived at the gallery and began the job of making all those final preparations. The pictures were half up, and in the back room with Birch, Deb's and myself, we wrote the cheques and purchased our pictures, which would be available to us after the event. Roni was not with us today; she was preparing whatever it was she wanted us for.

In a side room, just off the gallery room we were using, Birch put up huge posters of Me, Chloe, and the art exhibition poster, and a long Dixon and Dixon Events banner. In front of it, a table was set up with another long vinyl banner hanging from the front of it. This week it would serve as an advertisement, and at six o'clock next Friday evening, it would host a press conference, and the press would be allowed in to see the exhibition for thirty minutes to photograph it for the papers. By four thirty we were done, and had one last walk around.

Most of the pictures were in place, with cards on the wall below them, with the title of each picture, four of the pictures had small red dots on the cards to show them as sold. Golden stands with red ropes through, created a barrier to keep people at a respectful distance. From the end of the room a huge banner of Chloe hung, as well as several other banners to advertise the event, which were in each room. It looked perfect.

Morty filmed Chloe and Edwina, as they walked around for the first time, seeing it competed, and Chloe wept as she looked at it. I had tears too, she was so lovely and so humbled by it all, it reminded me very much of my first ever book event, and meeting the fans. Birch linked my arm as we followed them, it looked so amazing.

"We did good Birch, this looks so professional and high class, she really deserves this, I am thrilled at how it all turned out, I cannot deny, I am getting really excited for next weekend."

"You did a really good job Sweetie, it is stylish, and professional, and makes Chloe look very credible, I really love it, so does mum." I looked at her.

"This was not all me, you, Edwina and Chloe did a lot." Birch stopped and turned to me.

"Deads, Sweetie, I deliberately did as little as possible, because you needed to do something to show you have the talent. Be honest, you were always going to pull out all the stops for Chloe, and look what you did, mum was right, you are ready to do more." I gave her a shrewd look.

"What do you mean, mum was right?" She smirked and her eyes danced, and shone bright emerald green.

"Sweetie, who's idea do you think it was to do this? We both knew if we laid out Chloe's pictures so you could see them, you would go straight into Abby mode, and plan something special for your friend. All I did was tell Chloe to sort them in the library, the light was better. I showed you one great picture, and you did all the rest." She leaned in and kissed my cheek.

"It is why I love you, you are resourceful, and last night, wow Sweetie, you were really resourceful." She giggled.

I could not believe I had been hoodwinked, the crafty, devious, sneaky, bitches!

Chloe sat on the step of Bess, and waited for all of us to get ready, Deb's and Jenny were in the back belted in, Edwina was talking to Luke. Morty and him were driving north with the truck to grab some kit she needed, and Fidelity was sat in Petal. I walked over towards her; she looked worn out emotionally.

"We have a little Dixon Group business to attend to, and then we will be right behind you. How are you feeling, it must feel weird for you tonight having seen it done?" She looked up at me.

"I want to cry, but I have run out of tears, Abby I know this was all you, I love you so much, you know that right, but this, how do I beat this?" I looked at Birch talking to Fidelity in Petal.

"Chloe, this is not about keeping score, it is about being there for each other always. You know, I almost lost Birch four years ago, and you stepped in and schooled me on it. I got a black eye for it, and not long ago you stood at my side as I put that ring on her finger. You tell me Chloe, how do I repay you for that, because she is my world?" She smiled, and gave a sigh.

"Never argue with a writer, because the odds are, they have already seen this coming, and got a come back prepared. I get it, I do, so thanks, what you have done means the world to me too." I winked.

"Looks pretty even to me then, we will see you at home, drive safely, I need you alive Friday, there is no bleeding way I am doing this alone." She giggled as I walked off, and jumped in Petal.

Nigel picked up the unwashed cups, and looked around the room with a sigh, the door opened and Marjorie stood there, he smiled.

"I told you I would come back; I wanted time to think."

She nodded and walked in, he lifted another cup, she watched as he tried to clean up the mess Prim had left. Marjorie gave a sigh.

"What are you going to do Nigel, things clearly cannot go on as they are?" She lifted a dirty plate off the table.

He walked through to the kitchen, and put the pots in the sink, she followed with the plate. The kitchen was just as big a mess, he turned on the taps and turned to her. He looked a little lost, but she felt there was also another quality to him. He filled the kettle and flicked it on, Marjorie sat down at the table watching, this was the quietest she had ever been with him, he turned and looked at her.

"You are wrong Mother." It surprised her.

"I am... Would you like to elaborate?"

He turned the tap off, and let the pots soak, and leaned against the sink as he looked at her, his face still had the yellow patterns from his healing bruises, he was still a little awkward, his eyes looked at her and then looked away.

"I talked to Doctor Dixon, and it helps, she is a really nice person. I also talked to Abby, she is not like you said, she is kind Mother, and she is clever. Not like me, clever with people, she listens, and she talks honestly. I felt ashamed of myself in front of her, because she told me I am worth more, and should be proud of myself. Abby told me I need to stand tall, and stand up for myself, and she is right."

Marjorie gave a smile, she had told him the same so many times and he had not heard her, and yet once again Abigail Watson pops up, and finds a way right through all his barriers, she looked him in the eye.

"I agree with you Nigel, and what may I ask, will you do as a result?" He looked at her.

"I married Primula because I was told to, and that was wrong. Primula does not love me; she loves my money. I am married and I love my son, he is my son Mother, and it means a lot to me, but Primula is not a wife. I want things, and she ignores them. I am going to keep talking to Doctor Dixon, but I want Primula to talk to one of her therapists, and if she does that, we can try to sort something out. If she refuses to talk to a therapist..." He took a deep breath.

"I will ask her for a divorce, and will work hard to provide for Rupert."

Marjorie took a long intake of breath, he knew her views on divorce, especially in this family.

"That is a big step Nigel, I am sure your father will want to talk to you about it." He looked very nervous but gave a nod.

"I will talk to him, Mother, I want to stay here, and I want to live here, I like this house, but I have to make the decisions. It is hard for me and I struggle, but I have to do it, I have to stand on my own feet." She gave a smile; he was finally growing up.

"Alright Nigel, just promise me you will talk to us more, we do want to help." He nodded.

"She frightens me Mother, I will not deny it, she says and does horrible things, and I never know what to do, but I want to be better, I want Abby to see that." Marjorie gave a sigh.

"Nigel she is a married woman, she lives with a woman, I do not agree with those unions as you know, but you must understand, there is no future for you with her?" He nodded at her.

"I know that Mother, but you are wrong, there is a future, because she showed me that she is my friend, and I want to be friends with her. I don't want to marry her, I don't want to marry anyone, I don't want to be married to Primula, but I am, and I have to work that out. Abby is a nice person, and I think you should understand that. She cares about people, and this village, you have been wrong about her."

He turned to the kettle and lifted up two cups.

"I drink herbal tea now; it is good for my chi." Marjorie frowned.

"Excuse me?"

Nigel pulled a bag of hessian tea bags out of his pocket, and put one in his cup, he made his mother a regular tea. Marjorie watched not quite sure what to think of it all.

"Nigel, where have you been, you still have not told me?" He turned with the tea, and sat down, and handed her a cup, he smiled.

"I have been sailing with a friend, they taught me the ropes. It did me a lot of good, and showed me things I have never considered, I really enjoyed it." He gave a snigger, and Marjorie looked confused.

For Nigel it was possibly the most rebellious he had ever been in his life, but he had liked the feeling it had given him. Moon was twelve years his senior, but maybe that is what he needed, a woman who understood life and its joys. Not only had he discovered a whole new world of sexual desires, she had told him of people, the goodness of souls, and their connection to everything, and in a very strange way, he understood everything she told him.

She had no idea that as she talked about the function and connection of people, in a strange twist, Nigel saw it the same way he had researched and studied genes, and he had noted how the connections were the same. In doing so, Moon had given him a deeper understanding of people, and their interactions. For the very first time in his life, he realised his connection to Abby and everyone else, and suddenly everything about people that had confused him all his life, made complete sense.

As I drove out of the gallery, through the streets and the horrendous one way system back to the hotel to meet Roni, Marjorie sat with her son in his kitchen, and probably had the first ever adult conversation with him. In just one week he had changed, he was still a little awkward, but not as much. To her, he had just a little more confidence, a little more assertion, she was not sure how, but she was pleased to see it.

We parked up and Deli looked at me.

"What do I do, wait here?" I shook my head as I looked at her.

"No, you are one of us, we will hit the bar, and then do the meeting, you may have to wait for a minute or two, but no, Deli you are one of us now, where we go you come too." I smiled at her and she nodded.

"Okay, although it is a bit early in the day for me and alcohol... You know if you want to have a drink, I can drive back... Actually, I would love to, Petal is pretty cool you know?" Birch swung round in her seat.

"She is Sweetie, we are having coffee, but if you really want to drive her, you can do, I have multi driver insurance." Fidelity's eyes sparkled.

"Really... Yeah, I want to drive." Birch gave a giggle and opened her door.

"Everyone loves Petal, honestly Sweetie, I hardly get to drive her." She climbed out, and I turned to Deli.

"It's not love, it's survival, she drives like a maniac." Deli giggled, as she headed toward the back door.

We climbed out and locked Petal up, and headed back into the hotel through the rear doors, Roni and Will were sat drinking coffee in the lounge bar, I was surprised to see Anita was still there, she smiled.

"Witness." I frowned; Roni looked up.

"We have some papers to sign, Anita and Fidelity, if she would like to can act as witnesses?" She shrugged.

"It is better than being alone with a load of creepy business men, that one over there is weird, he keeps smiling at me." She gave a shudder, Birch noted him, smiled and turned to Fidelity.

"Sweetie if you want to get rid of a guy, pull the L card."

Fidelity looked confused, Birch leaned into her and gave her a gentle kiss on the lips, Deli looked shocked as hell when Birch pulled away, I giggled at her as her face turned beetroot. Birch smiled.

"Is he looking now?" She looked, and turned back to Birch.

"No, but... But... Jesus Birch don't do that in front of your wife, it is wrong." She turned to me.

"Abby, I am s..." I gave her a soft peck on the lips, and smiled, she looked stunned, Roni burst into laughter.

"There, all is equal." She gave a gasp.

"Stop bloody kissing me, both of you." I winked at her.

"Admit it, you are wet?" She turned a deeper scarlet.

"Knew it." Birch sniggered, and behind her back lifted her arm,

I high fived her, as Roni and Will giggled, Deli gave a sigh.

"I am not sure I am safe living with you two." Birch chuckled.

"We are harmless, but there again, you do sleep next door to Percy." Deli frowned and turned to Birch.

"Who the hell is Percy, I thought I was next door to Chloe?" Roni gave a loud gasp.

"Has she not met Percy yet?" Birch shook her head. Deli looked at Roni.

"Have you met Percy, who is he, and why do I feel freaked out?" Roni sat back with a big smile on her face.

"Fidelity dear, meeting Percy is something that needs to be experienced in its whole, it is sort of a right of passage." Birch and I sniggered, she looked at me and then turned to Birch.

"Why am I freaking out about meeting Percy?" Roni lifted her cup of coffee.

"Good instincts in this one, she will fit right in at your place." Fidelity looked very alarmed.

A waitress brought us much needed coffee, and our attention turned back to the exhibition, Roni talked of how well we had done, and how proud she was of all of us, I went over the specs and the numbers with Roni, and she listened carefully. She put down her cup.

"I realise this is a thank you for Chloe, and she does deserve it, but if you are serious about D&D as a side outlet, you need to be more on the ball with profit." I sat back drinking my coffee feeling very relaxed.

"We will make money on this, the merchandise will be profitable, but you are missing the obvious Roni." She looked at me.

"I am, please update me?" I leaned forward in my seat.

"Our two biggest aces are Anita, and the four week running time. I trust Anita to work her ass off to impress me, because she is recently new to working with me. If she does half of what I think she can do, over the next four weeks that exhibition will be packed. Simone will ask to extend, because I know she has few bookings for the end of summer, and into the autumn, it is why I picked that gallery. The bigger galleries have out competed her; she needs more people."

Roni smiled and looked at Will, he nodded his head, and she turned back to me.

"That is very clever, I did not see it, I take it you can top up the merchandise?" I nodded.

"Everything except the books, the fact they are limited editions pretty much guarantees we will clear the lot, but everything else, can be ordered and delivered right to the gallery, it is why we negotiated a percentage of the door price, if she extends, it keeps the cash flowing and the royalties to Chloe will increase, as will our cut."

Birch smiled as she looked at her mum, and Roni winked at her, she was impressed, which is not the easiest of tasks. A portly figure in a suit walked up to the table.

"Mrs Dixon?" Three of us turned and looked at him.

"Yes?" Roni giggled, as did Will, Roni looked up at him.

"Is the room ready now?" He gave a nod.

"It is, if you would like to all follow me?"

We got up, and Roni lifted her case off the floor, and we all followed him down the hall to a conference room, which was the obligatory large long table, blinds on the windows and leather seats. Roni directed us to our seats, which were all down one side. Fidelity and Anita sat a little further down, there was a knock on the door as I slid into my leather seat, it opened and my heart skipped a beat, Roni smiled.

"Margret, you made it?" The Shredder smiled, and I felt my little rose bud tighten, Birch took my hand and leaned into me.

"Relax, I saw her in the restaurant, she has eaten today, she ate two judges and a court clerk raw."

I sniggered and leaned on to Birch. The Shredder rubbed her hands together, saw me and smiled, I wish I had not drunk my coffee now, I was not sure, but I thought I felt a little leakage.

"Lovely wedding girls, hope the honeymoon was a busy one?" She gave a gravel like chuckle, and as I nodded and smiled, my eyes moved upwards to check the ceiling for cracks. Birch squeezed my hand tighter, and whispered.

"Sweetie, I want to pee."

Roni put her case on the table and lifted out a stack of blue hard backed document books, she placed them on the table, and being nosey I had a quick peep. The top one had gold letters on it that read, 'Dr William Dixon.' I assumed there was one each. She sat down and relaxed, as she leaned in and spoke quietly to Will, we sat holding hands unsure of what exactly we were doing here.

It was warm in here, and Anita walked along the table, and placed small bottles of water in front of us. I felt that she was taunting me, my mouth was dry, but with the Shredder in the room, I was not sure it was safe to drink anymore. I licked my lips as I looked at it, feeling caught in a trap.

Anita sat down at the side of Fidelity and talked quietly to her, she nodded and whispered something back. It felt oppressive, we had no idea what was going on, I felt I should ask, and as I turned to Roni, there was a tap at the door. My attention moved back as the door opened, and Roni stood up, and I felt the air run out of my lungs. Birch stood up and looked at her mum, she looked really angry, as she pointed.

"What the hell is she doing here?" Roni turned casually.

"Sit down Jemi, and you will find out... Come on in Katie, and take a seat, I assume this is your legal representation?"

I glanced to the right and at the bottom of the table, Anita looked shocked and upset. Birch dropped into her seat with a thump, I could almost feel the anger surrounding her. Katie looked around the room, and gave a knowing nod.

"I might have known; you would fucking ambush me Roni." Roni was calm and matter of fact.

"Sit down or leave, make your mind up Katie, we are all busy people?

Chapter 12

Dixon Business.

Katie shook her head as she sat down, she was clearly not happy, but honestly, I did not care, Roni smiled, as she looked at her.

"You wanted a meeting, and you wanted a chance to get back your shares, and this is it. I am not messing around here Katie, this is strictly business, what you did was reprehensible, and I have not forgotten it. The fact you are here is a miracle, but I got some very good advice from a colleague that made sense, and so on her advice, I have arranged this meeting." Katie glared at me with hatred in her eyes.

"Why is she here, come to gloat have we?" Roni sat down.

"No, she is the colleague who advised me." Katie looked at Roni.

"What... She is the one you went to; wow, talk about a crooked deal?" I looked at her and felt nothing but anger.

"I actually told Roni I felt you were the best one for the job. There was a time I thought of us as friends, and I have always acknowledged your skilful ability to run the productions side of things. in that respect I have no objection to you, but as a person, I feel you are not to be trusted. Katie, it never needed to be like this, if you had just listened to me, all of this would have been avoided. Now do you want back in, or are you going to sit and whine for much longer?" Birch squeezed my hand, as Katie looked at Roni, and nodded.

"So, do I get my controlling shares or not?"

I cannot deny, her attitude to me looked like it had not changed at all, and I was not in a rush to work with her. In truth, I hated her for what she did to Birch, and I want to be a good person, but I will never forgive her for it. Roni handed round the blue hard backed books, I opened mine and read it, Birch did the same. Katie opened it up and read the top page, she frowned and looked up.

"What the fuck is this, that only gives me forty five percent, how the fuck is that a controlling interest if you still have fifty?" Birch gave a sigh.

"She doesn't Miss O'Reilly, she only has thirty percent, the other shares are now in the possession, of Deads and myself, they were a wedding gift and a means of ensuring you have control, as long as it is for business purposes and interests only. Call it our equivalent of Tony."

I had to look down, Birch was so calm, and yet there was just a tinge of enjoyment to her words, Katie shook her head.

"Fuck you too, Jemi, we were supposed to be friends, okay, so I stepped out of line, but this, is this how it is going to be? We go back a long way; it was supposed to mean something Jemi." Birch took a deep breath.

"Katie, I notice you are not bleeding, that is my homage to our friendship. I will not deny when I saw you, my first instinct was to beat the living shit out of you, but this is business. Deads is right, you are the best at what you do, and you have enhanced this business, but when it comes to friendship, we are done. I will never forgive you for almost costing me the love of my life. Now I hope you finally understand, she is everything, and the only thing that could ever make me happy. Do your job, be polite, and make sure you put forward a dammed good business proposal, because if you don't, I will be voting against it." Roni looked at her across the table.

"What a shame it had to come to this Katie, you had a really good number going for you. I hope you now realise that yes, we arc a family, and you were a part of that, and it is up to you now, to prove you should be a part of us again."

She looked at her solicitor, and he gave a nod; she gave a sigh.

"Fuck you lot are cold bitches, but we have a deal, and don't worry little princess, I will be staying well clear of you." Her eyes glared as she looked at me, I nodded back at her.

"Suits me perfectly, stay away from my wife, sign the frigging papers, and get the hell out of my sight." Margret walked around the table, and placed the papers in front of her.

"Sign here, and here on each document." Katie lifted her pen, clicked it and signed each document, in front of her solicitor, he looked up at Roni.

"The payment will be authorised as soon as the papers are signed, it will be a direct payment into the Dixon Group Account." She smiled.

"Thank you, Kevin."

Katie signed, the Shredder grabbed the papers and carried them around to Birch, she placed them down in front of her. Birch signed, and passed it on to me, I signed and passed it Roni, and as each one was signed, it passed down to the Shredder at the bottom of the table. The Shredder walked down the table and placed them in front of Anita.

"Sign here, and here, you too Miss Hannigan."

Wow, the Shredder was good, she knew her name already, although why does that also freak me out, what else does she know? With the papers all signed she walked back around the table, and we all got a copy each for our file, Roni looked at Katie.

"HR have already been informed, and I would like to see you on Tuesday at 10am at my home office, there have been a lot of changes, so I will bring you back up to speed." She gave a nod, and slipped her papers in the folder.

"The art exhibition?" Roni shook her head.

"That is not a Dixon Group event." Katie frowned at her.

"It is a Dixon and Dixon promotion, that features Abby, how is it not part of the group?" Roni watched her carefully.

"Dixon and Dixon Events is nothing to do with us, Abby is a guest at the event. It has been organised by D&D yes, but that is a private venture outside the group, and is actually the responsibility of Abby, Jemi is working on another unrelated event. Jemi and Abby have their own small scale promotions company, for a few things they want to do outside publishing and therapies." Kate looked at me and smiled.

"Fuck... You are also a rival, hell, this just gets better and better." I stared at her blankly.

"I am not in competition with K.O. I wanted to stretch my legs outside writing, so I teamed up with Birch and Anita for a little extra fun, nothing more." She shook her head and lifted her hands.

"You know what, I wanted to screw you, and fuck, did I get screwed, I just thought it would be a little bit more romantic than this. I will not deny, I am actually impressed, I did tell you that you were capable of bigger things, maybe I should have kept my big mouth shut?" I shook my head.

"I have no problem with your big mouth Katie, I do however have a problem with you putting it on my passed out wife." Anita looked down and sniggered. Katie picked up her file.

"I take it we are done?" Roni gave a nod.

"We are, thank you for coming today, and I will see you Tuesday."

We all stood up with her, and she lifted her document book off the table, she looked at all of us stood in a row, and then walked around the table, and held out her hand to Birch.

"No hard feelings?" Birch looked at her, and lifted her hand.

SLAP! I blinked in shock, Katie recoiled as a red mark rose on her cheek, Birch took her hand and shook it.

"No hard feelings now Sweetie, we are even." Katie rubbed her cheek, it looked really red.

"Yeah, I owed you that, I am sorry Jemi." Birch nodded, and Katie looked at me.

"You have impressed me today, although, there is no way I am shaking your hand, but I wouldn't mind a truce?" I nodded.

"Keep it business only and we will be fine, I meant what I said, you are the best at your job." She nodded.

"From you, that actually means something. Congratulations on your wedding, I hope both of you will be happy." Katie turned and headed for the door, I watched her feeling nothing at all, I was just glad when she left the room. Roni picked up her file.

"Not how I expected it, but I think she fully understands her situation now." Birch shook her hand and turned to me.

"Sweetie, that really hurt, why didn't you stop me? Ow, ow, ow, ow, Sweetie, it hurts!"

I looked at Roni and she rolled her eyes, I burst out laughing, Birch frowned, as she shook her hand.

"Dad it really hurts... Tell them to stop laughing." He looked down at the floor and smirked.

Katie sat at the bar and lifted her double scotch, she looked at Kevin, and gave a long sigh.

"Fuck that was awful, God, I am so fucking stupid?" He nodded at her as he sipped his drink.

"You picked a fight with three psychologists and a writer, who have probably one of the most terrifying solicitors on the London court circuit and lived. Trust me, you came out of this better than I thought you would, they were actually pretty lenient, that could have been a bloodbath." Katie looked at him like he was mad.

"What, that wasn't?" He sat back, and looked at her.

"Katie, they have D&D, they could have transferred all the assets of K.O. over to it and handed you back an empty warehouse. Trust me, you have done the best deal possible today, they could have destroyed you completely, yet they didn't. Painful as it may be, you need to show some gratitude." Katie looked at him and nodded.

"You are right, I knew Abby had what it took, you know, she is quite the little powerhouse when she needs to be, but that is the problem. I am so fucking attracted to her, I would happily let her walk all over me, the same goes for Jemi, I am messed up, I need to get my head straight." He lifted his glass.

"We all do, I will certainly drink to that."

We all hugged and said goodbye, Anita walked out to the car park with us.

"You did really good today, it was hard for me being there, I have no idea how hard that must have been for you, but to be honest, you handled it like a pro."

"I do not trust her Anita, just when you think her teeth have been pulled, she twists around and comes at you from a whole other angle. Please, try and keep her away from me, I know it is a lot to ask of you, but the way I see it, if we stick together and avoid her, we will be fine." She gave me a big smile.

"I have to say Abby, my job has never been as much fun as it has in this last month, I really do love working with you, and your house full of insane friends. I love what you did for Fidelity, she really is a nice girl, oh God, I wish she was gay, I would so go for her, she really is my type. I am looking forward to Friday, I still have calls to be made, but will give it everything I have this week, as I am working from home, any problems or you need stuff, call me." She gave me a polite hug, which made me smile.

"Relax a little if you can, as I said, you can drop by for the pool anytime, we are always around somewhere." She waved to Birch and Deli, and opened her car door.

"I might hold you to that, I love your pool." I smiled as she slid into her seat and I stood back. She gave a wave and drove off, I walked over to Birch, and she smiled as I slipped into her arms.

"Hi Sweetie, are you alright?"

"I am now, take me home sexy lady." She leaned in and gave me a soft kiss.

"Oh God, my life is sad and pathetic compared to you two." We giggled, and we turned round, I tossed the keys at her.

"The hot seat is yours Miss Hannigan, take us home." She gave a big excited smile, and unlocked the door.

"I am so looking forward to this, I love this jeep." Birch glanced at me.

"That bothers me, more than you would think it would, it's a Land Rover."

I let go of her hand, and walked around to the back, and opened the door and climbed in. Fidelity clicked on her belt and started up Petal, and with a big beaming smile, she drove off, and we headed home.

It was nice to lie back in Petal as we drove home. My mind was filled with hundreds of thoughts as I processed the last few days of my life, Deli, Sophia, the exhibition, and Katie, so much had happened. Deli had settled in, and was getting used to the strange life we lived, and I cannot deny, she has actually been a huge help. Her secretarial skills are really advanced, and she has no fear of jumping in the deep end, she has also been very hands on with the exhibition.

I do feel excited about the exhibition, and I am really proud of the way it has all come together. I have learned a lot from Birch working at her side for the Curio event, and I think it has rubbed off. She pretty much dumped me in the deep end, and I had to make it work, and as a result I have done the exhibition, and knowing that, I know I can run the village as leader of the Parish Council.

Katie for me is a different story, the images of Birch hurting herself and sobbing in the shower still haunt my dreams. I cannot forgive her, even if I have to work with her. In my mind, Birch is a rare and highly beautiful flower, and what Katie did, is the equivalent of pulling her petals off, and I will never trust her again. I came out of my thoughts to hear Birch talking to Deli. Birch was sat with her feet up on the dash and her shoes off.

"There is only one truth Deli, and that is yourself. Look we have an internet full of facts from so called reliable sources, but we really have no idea, so many pages on the internet are fake or hacked, there really is no definite way of telling. What you are, how you feel, what your instincts say, that is your truth, and the only thing you can depend on. We all have to understand who we truly are, and what we are truly capable of, and once we know that and accept it, we move forward. We must look with our eyes, and trust only our hearts." She was looking out of the window focused on the road, but she was nodding.

"So, what you are saying is that no matter what anyone says, even you, I should trust only myself?" Birch looked at her.

"Okay, I never lie to people, and in time you will see that, but yes, trust only your instincts. Look at the other month, you sat outside the Tea Rooms with Molly and Prim, and I gave a quote from known facts about the bible. You questioned it, and wanted me to clarify it was a true fact. All the others immediately assumed it was a lie, because they believed Prim's accusations that Deads and me, are sluts and whores, yet you did not, your instincts told you to question it, that is your truth."

She leaned back and saw me sat watching.

"Hi Sweetie, we are not far from home." I smiled, and leaned over the low partition, and took her hand in mine.

"Good, I think I am going to have a long swim, and I actually think a good drink, I think we have earned it." Deli indicated as she saw the slip road.

"Just a few more minutes, and we will be home."

I sat back and watched out of the window, within minutes we were driving down Pilkington's, heading towards Station Road. It was hot in the back, even with the windows open, the sun was high in the sky, and even though it was almost seven thirty in the evening, I was so hot, I was cooking.

We arrived home, unloaded Petal and dumped everyone's luggage in the hall, and then headed into the kitchen, I grabbed an ice cold beer, all the doors were open, and I walked out into the garden, and over to the pool where Edwina was already swimming.

I pulled off my clothes, tossed them onto the sun lounger, and dived in, and it felt divine. Deli followed me and stripped down to her knickers, I watched as she looked around to see pretty much everyone was naked, and she bit her lip, slid them down, and then dived in, she swam over to where I was sipping my cold beer, and gave a gasp.

"I have never swum naked before." I lifted my can to my lips.

"It is the only way I can swim; I haven't owned a swim suit in ten years, I love the freedom I feel in the water." She smiled and gave a slight giggle.

"Honestly, I never thought I would do anything like this, and it is so weird, because I actually love it."

She looked around the garden where everyone was chilling out, either on the grass or patio naked. Chloe was at the side of the house, sat naked and cross legged as she painted Bess, with an intricate design around the big flower decals. Edwina came up in front of me, smiling.

"Abby, Chloe is so happy tonight, and she is inspired, thanks, what you and Birch have done, is wonderful for her. I sent my mum pictures and she is so excited to see it, they are actually closing the restaurant next Friday."

The whole atmosphere of the house was one of happiness and excitement, as we sat out in the garden. I wandered down to my arch with a blanket and some cushions and camped out in my corner relaxed with my eyes closed, and it was not long before Birch appeared and curled up with me. Then came Deb's with a monitor, as baby was asleep in her crib, then Deli, and so on, and we sat around under the shadow of the arch and talked with our drinks, and enjoyed each others company, this was how life was meant to be.

Monday morning arrived with a groan from everyone, I sat and ate breakfast looking at my darkened coffee, Chloe gave a sigh.

"We need to shop; this milk is shit for coffee."

I looked up, as everyone was dashing around, getting ready, I was on my third cup, and I had to admit it did taste strange. I had just thought it was because of the booze last night. I had been really drunk, as was evident from my banging head. Deli took a sip and smacked her lips.

"This does taste a bit funky." She licked her lips.

"Although, as daft as it sounds, it tastes familiar." Something was not right; I took another sip, and agreed.

"Yeah, it is familiar, and yet weird, why is that?" Chloe shrugged.

"I told you; it is that weird stuff, you know the milk in the little bottles?"

Silence descended instantly on the kitchen, and everyone stopped and stared at Chloe. Anthony looked like his head was going to explode, as he fought with his emotions, and twitched and jerked.

"Chloe… Darling… Are you talking about the row of small bottles in the top shelf of the fridge?" She nodded.

"Yeah, it's weird, but alright I suppose for coffee."

I stared into my cup feeling horror rise up inside me, Anthony dithered as he tried to control his emotions, and then failed, and his ticks kicked in big time.

"YOU GAVE US BREAST MILK, WHAT THE HELL WERE YOU THINKING?"

He looked like he was going to have a break down, as tick after tick overtook him, as he stared with horror at Chloe, she looked around.

"Oh, is that what it is? I thought maybe the carton was leaking again, so one of you poured it into little glasses." Suddenly the penny dropped and she stared at me.

"Oh fuck, Abby, I just drank from Deb's tit, holy fuck, am I a lesbian now for liking it?"

Birch picked up her cup and emptied it, she smacked her lips, and looked at me.

"Your tits are sweeter… YUK!" Anthony dithered, and flapped his hands around.

"O. M. G. I feel like a rapist, whatever will Deb's think when she finds out we all have partaken of her bosom?" He gave a squeal.

"Mouth wash!" Chloe shrugged.

"Cow tit, Deb's tit, it's pretty much the same either way, and hey, look on the bright side, it is really healthy." Deli shuddered.

"Well, I have had it puked on me, and spilled on me, never had it in my coffee before though." Birch leaned and kissed me.

"I am off now Sweetie... Yuk, milk breath!" She gave a cackle as she ran down the hall.

"Anthony, I am going, get your tonsils out of the sink." He came pounding down the stairs, and then the front door banged, and I sat staring at Chloe.

"Petal or Bess?" She smiled.

"Petal, I am not finished yet, I will grab the card... Are you coming Deli?" She nodded.

"Yeah, I want to see how you guys do this."

I got up and put my cup in the sink, and opened the cupboard door, she saw the list hanging on the clip, and smiled as I pulled it off and went through it. Chloe arrived holding the card, and showed it Deli.

"The draw under Birch's computer in the library, we use the green one for shopping." She noted it.

We all piled into Petal, and headed for the road to Oxendale, Deli looked around with a frown.

"Guys, you do know there is a really large Mesco supermarket near Millington, it is a lot closer?" I smirked.

"Hmm, we have a slight issue with that one, or at least Chloe does. Let me just say, she is not as welcome as she used to be." Deli frowned, as Chloe sniggered in the back. Twenty minutes later we arrived, locked Petal and grabbed a trolley.

Shopping is always fun with Chloe, although Deli was new to our games, and gasped with shock and horror, as we pissed about writing rude words in the spices, and putting tubes of thrush cream in the condom display. At the fresh veg section, Chloe picked a good sized cucumber, and waved it in front of Deli.

"Do you want this one, or longer?" She looked at it and frowned.

"What does it matter, they all taste the same?" Chloe winked.

"This is not for eating; it is for you... Are you going to sneak it out, or will you be paying for it?" Deli looked horrified as Chloe started to undo her jeans, Deli turned purple and panicked, as she fell apart.

"Jesus Chloe, you cannot do that, not here, holy shit, please stop, you will get us arrested." I laughed my ass off, and she smiled and winked at me.

"This one is too easy Abby, but she is fun." A grumpy looking, very well dressed woman stopped, and looked at Chloe.

"I hope young lady you are going to eat that?" Chloe shook her head.

"Nope, I am going to do bad things to myself with it, why, do you want it when I am finished?"

She took two steps back looking at Chloe with horror, she looked at me as if she was going to say something, I just nodded.

"She is a pervert, it's an illness."

Deli snorted, and turned her back, the woman turned, and hurried off with her trolly, constantly looking back at us. We headed out with a full trolly towards Petal, laughing and giggling, and filled the black crates in the back, Deli was laughing and wiping her eyes.

"You two are insane, but that is the most fun I have had shopping ever." Chloe took the trolly back, and I jumped in the driver seat, and looked in the back at Deli's smiling face, as she pulled the back door shut.

"This is what we do, we make the mundane fun, and live every second we can." She nodded.

"I can really see that, I really can." I turned the key and Petal started up; Chloe jumped in. It was time to head home for a decent coffee, I checked the road was clear, and pulled out, and noted Deli sat smiling in the back.

Once home, we unpacked Petal, put the shopping away, washed the pots, and then cleaned the house, and then we hit the computers, and once again promoted the upcoming art event. The day was long and busy, and soon they all blended into one, as we hurtled towards Friday, and I was walking back inside the back door of the hotel, from the underground car park, with my case, followed by Chloe and Birch.

Back in Wotton, the rest of the group were organising for the day's events. Luke had hired a mini bus, having arrived back in the early hours of the morning, and unloaded the truck of everything they had collected for Edwina. The hire company were going to pick up the truck, and drop off the mini bus.

In the village, Izzy had arranged for a coach, to take everyone to the event, and there was a lot of excitement, mum and Patrick, along with Hatty and Clive were driving up early and staying overnight, as were most of the Curio's. Anthony had Sunday duties, with the committee, and so he was going on the coach with Michael, and returning the following morning.

At the hotel we had adjoining rooms, with a partition door, so Chloe would not feel isolated, she was becoming very nervous. Birch had the answer, in the form of her survival kit, and so we sat and had a good stiff rum and coke. At two o'clock, Ella arrived with her two girls, and gave us all big smiles, as they carried in their dress bags, she gave us all huge hugs.

"Abby, you look amazing, I love the tan, wow you look so happy and healthy, I do believe marriage is very good for you." She was very excited, as Alice hung the bag up on the bathroom door.

"Right Abby, you gave me the usual gothic, but this is a business endeavour, and a partnership, so I have this jacket." April unzipped the bag and slipped out a black fitted velvet jacket with slightly fluted cuffs, and matching boot cut hipster pants.

"This is all tailored to your figure, it will fit where it touches, and with your black wedged heel boots, it will be perfect, elegant, and chic. The blouse as you can see is red, with lace cuffs that will extend out of the jacket cuffs, and it has a very sexy plunge if you leave open the top buttons, to show just a hint, of your lovely little breasts."

I looked at it and smiled, it was gorgeous, Chloe gave it a nod of appreciation, Ella turned.

"Jemi, you are partners, D&D, so you have similar but in a dark bottle green, except, your blouse is silk, and more of a medium green. Stood side by side you match and complement each other perfectly. Your blouse does not have the lace cuffs, but let's be honest, your slightly larger breasts will give you a good cleavage reveal, and really talk sex appeal. I brought you some green suede boots to match, so you will both be the same height proportion as normal." Birch felt the fabric and smiled.

"Ella Sweetie, you know us so well, I really like this, it feels so soft, although, I have always loved silk." Ella smiled.

"I love working with you two, your figures will enhance anything I make, and if I can ask you a huge favour... Would all three of you model these tonight, and let me shoot you in them, a gallery is such a perfect arena for photography? I am making up a catalogue to hand out, I have some amazing shots from the wedding, and with these plus my other models, I will have a really wide range to show." I smiled; how could we refuse.

"We would love to, we are doing a press conference at six to launch the show, and so we are going in at four just to prepare, so if you want, you can shoot then, we will meet you in the foyer around three thirty?" She gave a big smile and looked at Chloe, who was looking terrified.

"Right, the star of the night, we are talking formal artisan chic, not too conventional, and hey you are the star, so I want you to stand out, but look pure classy sexy." Chloe gave a chuckle.

"I do not feel very sexy, I am so nervous I am afraid I will puke." Ella looked at her.

"I love the hair; I love the way the colours blend into each other and change as they fall down your back. So, with that in mind, I have this for you." Alice and Carol undid the bag and revealed her dress, and she gave a gasp, I was really impressed. It was hard to describe it, Ella looked at it.

"This is a formal gown, with open sides, which as you can see form a web across the back, and are encrusted with beads. There is a lot of skin on view here, so it is really comfortable for you. The fabric is silk, so it is high class and chic, the long dress splits, so use it to show off your lovely long tanned legs."

I moved closer to look at it, the dress was white with yellow streaks, but as it reached the bottom, it had a mix of colour, almost the same as Chloe's hair that bled upwards into the white and yellow.

"Wow Ella, this is really sumptuous and classy." Chloe nodded at her.

"I really love it; and it is way posher than I am. I grew up on the council estate in Oxendale." Ella winked.

"Tonight, Chloe, you are the top of the pyramid, all these VIP's are there for one reason, your talent, so wear this and walk with your head up. The best thing about this is you won't need underwear." Chloe smiled.

"Yep, that is me." Ella giggled.

"I think this is very boho chic artisan, I really enjoyed creating it for you."

Ella pulled a bottle of white wine out of her bag, and some

plastic glasses, and poured it out, and all six of us toasted Chloe, she looked a little shy and awkward, which just made her even more beautiful.

For the next hour, Ella and the girls helped with hair and makeup, and then we dressed ready for the day's events. I looked in the mirror, and twisted and turned my hips, with the hair down, and dark eyes, plus the clothing, I was very dark little business beastie, and Birch loved it.

She stood at my side, and I felt her hand explore my bum as she smiled, she looked gorgeous with her long white hair, which she had pulled up at the side and clipped it back, into a deep emerald pin, God, she looked sexy as hell. I turned and Chloe stood in the door, and wow, I was lost for words. The dress was perfect, she looked at her breasts, which formed two nice full mounds, in the bra like top section.

"What do you think, does my bum look big or is it me?" She turned, and we all smiled, I was struggling for words, but Birch found them.

"Chloe Sweetie, if you do not get laid in that, there is no hope left for women." She smiled a huge smile.

"You think so?" I winked.

"I would do you in it…. Even though you are oh so bloody straight." There was a knock on the door and Carol answered it, Anita walked in and looked at Chloe.

"Shit… Why are all the straight girls the ones I want to screw?" She wafted herself.

"Wow Chloe, if I get drunk, please forgive me in advance if I hit on you." She looked at Birch and myself stood side by side.

"I would tell you what I am really thinking, but my contract forbids it." She gave a little giggle.

"So, are we ready, let's go and show this gorgeous sexy woman to the world of art?" Chloe took a huge deep breath.

"Guys I am shitting myself." I smiled at her.

"Good, that proves you are human."

Chapter 13

Red Carpet Arrival.

We all met downstairs in the foyer, and made our way to the underground car park. The long black limo stood waiting, and Markus gave a bow, I had booked him especially, as he was really special, and on the ball. He opened the door and Chloe slipped in, we followed with Ella, and Anita, her girls were waiting back at the hotel, and preparing all the clothing for Anita, Ella, and themselves.

Ella would do the shoot, and Markus would drive her back, we had the press conference to do, and then Anita would drive back and get ready, and be one of the first guests to arrive, as she worked with Simone and her team to meet and greet all the guests. We would wait in a back room, and at the given moment, Markus would drive us around London, and we would make our entrance across the front plaza, and into the gallery.

As we drove to the back of the event, Luke and G5 were already there organising the security teams, as they erected barriers up the plaza, and laid out the long red carpet. Fans were already gathering, and stood waiting behind a taped off line until the fences were up.

Chloe was sat in the back loving the limo ride, she had seen us so often drive off in one, but today it was her turn, and Birch poured her a soft drink, and she sat back with a huge smile, honestly, she was like a little child. Markus pulled up at the rear, and we stepped out, and Simone's assistant let us in. Ella gasped as she saw the exhibition, she walked slowly round trying to take it in, she saw the huge pictures on the wall of Chloe and myself, and she smiled.

"I want you guys here, with that in the background."

She dropped to her knees, opened her bag, and lifted out her tripod, and started to set up her camera. I loved she was a full one man team, designer, seamstress and photographer, she knew what she wanted, and how she wanted it. She set up quickly and then posed us as she wanted us, her face was a constant smile.

"Wow, this is such a perfect setting, you all look stunning, Chloe, just turn to your left about a few inches."

Chloe knew this role well, she had posed enough models to draw their junk, and she moved just enough, Ella started to shoot and give us direction, as she rattled off pictures. Then we posed alone, and she took a few dozen more, Birch turned and looked at her.

"Does that have an auto shoot setting?" Ella gave a nod.

"Yes why?" Birch looked at her.

"You should pose with us, and Anita, you should join us for a full team picture."

Ella set up the camera, and we gathered together, and the camera flashed, she smiled as she walked back to the camera.

"I will send you a copy of that, guys you are such a pleasure to work with, I cannot thank you enough."

We looked awesome, we should be thanking her, because it was her clothes making us look amazing. Is it weird that although I love to live mainly naked, I actually do love wearing Ella's clothing?

Anita was watching the clock, and soon we had to move to our position for the press conference, Ella thanked us, and headed off to Markus, and we gathered behind the door, waiting for our signal, as we heard the press on the other side as they set up their equipment. Luke appeared, dressed in a black suit.

"I have G5 on the other side waiting, so just relax and enjoy this moment, Anita is in there talking now." Chloe took a deep breath and I took her hand.

"Remember, tonight is your night, this is your event, so head up, and speak slowly and clearly, and just be you. Try not to swear."

She nodded, I squeezed her hand, and Luke listened to his head set, and when the moment arrived, he gave us the nod, he walked to the door, and smiled.

"Birch first, then Chloe, then you Abby."

We all took a deep breath, he opened the door, and Birch led the way, and we followed. I slipped on my glasses, and entered the room as a thousand flashes went off and cameras rattled, Anita guided us to our seats, and sat down at my side. Chloe looked tense, but she smiled for the cameras, as Birch whispered tips and hints to her, under the table, we both held her hands.

Anita sat down and we relaxed in front of the microphones on the table, she smiled at the press.

"Good afternoon ladies and gentlemen, you all know the procedure, I point, you name yourself, and then ask your question, and be civil, this is a big occasion for Miss Pemberton." I glanced at Chloe, and she noticed and smiled. Anita pointed; a male reporter leaned forward in his seat.

"Robert Smithers, Classic Arts Magazine. Miss Pemberton, I believe you are more a painter than a sketch artist, although, I cannot deny, your line work is quite incredible, could you tell me why you did not paint the covers of Miss Watson's books. Do you not think they would have been a better introduction to the art world?"

Chloe looked at me, and I gave her a smile and nodded, she looked at him.

"Abby asked me to provide sketches, so I read her manuscript, and drew what I thought would work for her. I was just out of college on the first cover, I think I have improved a great deal since." I could feel her leg slightly trembling under the table, I looked at Smithers.

"They were commissioned that way Mr Smithers, I had an idea in my head of what I wanted, and I expressed that to Miss Pemberton. As you know, this is not a Dixon Group event, it is a private new venture, for my wife and I, and when considering the Art Book, we knew the sketches would work better, and so we coupled the book launch with the exhibition. D&D will be considering a future exhibition of Miss Pemberton's painted works." He smiled and gave a nod.

"I will look forward to it, please do not misunderstand me Miss Pemberton, I find your work thrilling." She gave a huge smile and the cameras flashed, he winked at her. Anita pointed.

"Amy Walker, River Cable TV News. Miss Pemberton, Chloe, it is so nice to see you stepping out to finally showcase your art. I think all of us remember well your stage appearance at Curio Live, this must be a little daunting for you. Would you tell my audience how it feels for you today?" She gave Chloe a huge smile, Chloe leaned into the mic.

"Honestly, I am terrified, I have watched Abby do this, and I have followed her on TV, and at all her interviews. I have never done anything like this before, and it feels strange and scary, but it has made me very happy. I cried a lot when we hung everything up, I am so grateful to Abby and Birch, I could not have done this without them." Birch leaned forward.

"She has no idea Amy how talented she is, and I hope everyone of Abby's fans, and all the Curio fans will come down and see how amazing her art is." Anita smiled, and pointed, I saw the reporter and felt a pang in my stomach.

"Mary Wilkinson, The Mail Today. Doctor Dixon, firstly congratulations on your marriage. Your mother is well known for her stage work, and the Dixon Group, owns the lion's share of K.O. productions, is there any special reason why Katie O' Reilly is not involved, and you felt the need to team up with your wife to set up a rival company?" Birch looked at her and smiled.

"I remember you, nice hair. Firstly Miss Wilkinson, Miss O' Reilly is the major shareholder of K.O. not Dixon Group, and I should know, I am share holder in both companies. This is not a rival company, Dixon Group deals with Therapy, and Publishing, and this is neither, it is arts. My wife and I, wanted to express a little creative independent freedom, and that is what D&D is all about, it is us two larking around, and stepping into small scale events for fun. We are no threat to K.O, and as you are aware, they handle other contracts, such as band tours, which has nothing to do with my mother's company."

"Didn't you beat her up in a hotel earlier this year?" Anita stepped in.

"Only one question each, we have a lot to get through, and Miss Wilkinson, you are out of line, and amazingly misinformed. I would have thought after Curio Live, and your treatment of Miss Watson, you would have learned to be a little more respectful?" She pointed across the room.

"Wendy Patterson: Devonshire Chronicle. Miss Watson, or should I say Dixon? Congratulations on your marriage. I have travelled up from Devon with a two coach party, who will be visiting this weekend, such is your appeal in my region. Could you tell us out of the thirty five pictures to be on exhibition, which one is your absolute favourite?" I gave a wide smile.

"The people of Devon are close to my heart, they showed me such warmth earlier this year. I will look forward to seeing them hopefully tomorrow, as I will be here all day. I cannot really say I have a favourite, because Chloe is so talented, but I will say this. When I write my story, the characters come alive, and my readers love that, but when Chloe sketches them, she gives them their souls, and for myself as the author, it feels like a huge honour, and it inspires me. I have purchased one of the exhibits in advance, but I will not say which, but honestly, I want all of them, but I do have a full set of prints at home as well." Chloe leaned forward.

"Miss Patterson, you have to understand, that Abby writes them in such a way, they are easy to bring alive on paper. I have read her books hundreds of times, and so when I sketch, I feel like I am sketching friends, as I do at home with my housemates." She gave a nod and smiled, she clearly understood that. Anita pointed.

"John Tucker. Abigail Jennifer Watson Fan Blog...." I turned and looked at him.

"I have a fan blog?" Chloe giggled, he looked at me, and smiled, there were titters all around the room.

"Yes Miss Watson, we have about four million subscribers worldwide. Could I ask all three of you what the Hands of Death, means to you all personally?" Birch smiled and leaned forward.

"When Abby left Uni, I really missed her, because we had shared a dorm for two years, and I still had four to go. It felt so strange not having her there with me. I would lie in bed at night and read her first book over and over, and imagine she was reading it to me, and she will never know how much that helped me in my loneliness."

That caught my breath, she had never told me that, and I felt the emotions run up inside me, Chloe gave my hand a squeeze under the table.

"The first time I read the Handed Death, I was sat in a crummy flat in Oxendale, and I cried, because I missed her. I sat at the window, with a big street light outside, and I sketched pictures, and one of them was a painting of her from memory, she has it hung up in her room at home. Her words have always inspired me." My eyes teared up.

"Pack it in guys, you know I hate crying in front of cameras." Chloe smiled; Anita handed me a tissue. I looked at the guy, I had forgotten his name.

"What does it mean to be the writer of this series? All I can say is that when I write, I find an inner peace nothing else gives me. I think I spend so much time thinking of these stories, that I fill my head to the point of being overloaded, and then out it all comes, and with it is a sense of inner calm like nothing I have ever felt, and it is euphoric. I do not think now I could live without it. Chloe's pictures have enhanced that feeling for me, and I often sit alone and simply look at them, she is an amazing talent. My books are my world, and they are filled with secret moments of my life, so for me, her pictures are a very personal collection of feelings and emotions that match my words." He gave a big smile.

"You should contact me, and we should talk, if I have a fan blog, I should appear on it." He looked really happy and gave me a huge smile, Anita pointed.

"Jess Taylor, Daily Informer. Miss Pemberton, with sketches for sale at twelve thousand, and a book for one hundred and forty pounds, you are going to clean up and make a tidy profit if this all goes well, will you be buying new dungarees?" Birch leaned into the mic.

"Miss Pemberton has no dealings with price setting, that is all negotiated with the gallery, and D&D. Is this a business event, yes, it is, and therefore are we aware of a return on the capital invested, yes, we are. The gallery and Miss Pemberton are not here to offer a free service, they are both tax paying members of the community, and frankly sir I find your comment offensive to Miss Pemberton. When Miss Pemberton first started out, she was broke, I actually purchased her first ever painting to ensure she could actually afford paint and canvasses, she has every right to sell her work, and to imply that is improper is grossly out of order." Chloe leaned forward.

"If it is a free picture you want, give me a pad and pencil, I will happily sketch your ridiculous face for you, and sign it, so you can sell it on Ebay." The rest of the journalist giggled, and Anita smirked, and pointed.

"John Barlow, Book Readers Digest. Miss Pemberton, Miss

Watson has ended her series with Resurrection Sword, has she now put you out of a job?" I giggled, and Chloe leaned forward.

"I am banned from giving spoilers, but I can assure you, I will have plenty of work in the future. I know Abby very well, and writing, like my art, is her life, she is already working on new material, and honestly, I think your readers will love it, I cannot wait for the first manuscript." Birch leaned forward.

"D&D have a lot of plans for the future like this one. We are looking forward to seeing the response to tonight and tomorrow, and so hopefully if we get a good turn out, we will be back with more from Miss Pemberton in the future. I would like to add what an amazing gallery the Winchester is, they have been so accommodating and made this whole event so much easier than we thought. I find it odd other artists do not approach it, as it really is a first class gallery." I saw Simone at the back of the room smile, that for her was a good plug in front of the TV cameras.

We answered many more questions, but time was moving on, and Anita stood up and looked at all the journalists.

"Ladies and Gentlemen, we have run over a little, but you have free reign over the exhibition for the next thirty minutes to take pictures. Again, should any of you wish further questions with our guests today, you have my cards, and feel free to contact me. The exhibition as advertised will open tomorrow at ten o' clock and Miss Pemberton and Mrs Dixon, will be here from eleven onwards. Thank you for your time and respect."

Luke opened the door and we trooped out, I felt relieved and slid down my glasses, Chloe gave a sigh.

"Fuck Abby, how do you do that all the time?" I shrugged.

"It is part of life now Chloe, we keep them happy, and hopefully we get to talk to our fans out there."

Anita had to leave to change, and we were guided to a room at the rear to relax in, there was coffee, fruit juice and some eats, and a much to our joy, a toilet, which Chloe shot off to. I sat back, and Birch took my hand.

"How are you feeling?"

"Is it mad that I am really nervous for Chloe?" She smiled.

"She handled it all really well Sweetie, I think Anita is far better than Katie, she briefed them well, and jumped in when needed, I was glad to see that."

Back at the hotel, everyone was arriving in the bar, to meet up. Edwina was on the phone to Luke checking to see how things went, as Felicity, Patrick, Hatty, and Clive all sat with a scotch. Deb's and Deli arrived out of the lift, Roni and William were on route towards the lift, with Bradley and Ellen. Time was moving on, and Luke walked into the exhibition with the rest of G5, he stood at the far end, and looked at the reporters all taking shots.

"Ladies and gentlemen, will you please exit the event, so we can prepare for tonight's VIP event, we need the floor clear, and all none gallery personnel, out of the building?" Anita had two river reporters on standby to cover the VIP evening, so all the others had to leave.

Creamy looked imposing all dressed in black, and the reporters all turned, and headed for the door. Doors at the back opened, and tables were carried in, for the gift bags and also the catering, the final pieces were falling into place, it would not be long before the first VIP guests arrived.

Anita was looking rushed, but was back in the foyer dressed in a tight figure hugging black dress, Edwina looked her up and down and smiled.

"Wow, that fits exactly what it touches, and commando I do believe." Anita looked nervous.

"If there is a god, there will be just one lesbian there tonight, who just wants something tasteless and meaningless with a horny woman." Edwina smiled.

"I hope there is, Deli will not flip, she is in the straight wing of the house, next door to Chloe." Anita smiled.

"I will not deny, I find her highly attractive, she really is my type." Edwina looked back at her.

"Pray for a bent Deli then." Anita giggled, and looked nervous. Edwina's phone pinged, and she looked at it.

"G5 are on the carpet ready to escort us all, we are good to go." She turned and clapped her hands.

"Everyone, we are good to go, the cars will be arriving shortly, will you gather at the doors please."

Luke walked into the rest room and smiled at the three of us.

"Guests will be arriving shortly, Anita has just left the hotel, Simone is at the doors with her staff, and Edwina is right on schedule. Get yourselves organised; Markus is outside waiting."

Anita arrived at the back doors in a cab, and entered, she smiled as we walked towards her, she looked at Chloe.

"Have fun tonight, this is your exhibition, so just enjoy it. I will be at the door waiting when you arrive out front, you know the routine, just smile, and Luke and G5, will be with you, listen to their advice."

Chloe took a deep breath and nodded, Anita gave me a nod, and then headed to the front of the gallery, and we walked outside, to Markus, and jumped in the limo.

At the front of the gallery, the red carpet ran up from the curb, right to the doors, it was about twelve feet wide, and on either side, there were masses of people. To the right were mainly fans, and to the left, TV and press, Anita had pulled out all the stops, and she had everyone from the press and TV, outside waiting.

Markus pulled off, as we were to have a small drive around London before heading to the gallery, everything had been arranged to show off Chloe to the maximum. She looked pale, and I smiled.

"Relax, when you get out, it will be nerve racking. If you feel intimidated, talk to the fans, because I know they will want to talk to you." She nodded.

"Chloe I will be a few feet behind you, it will be just like the gala at Curio Live."

Outside there was a lot of anticipation, cars were starting to arrive, and as people got out, all cameras were pointing their way. Alison Williams and her husband arrived; her career had taken an upsurge since she did the Curio Live event. Gordon Stimes and his wife got a lot of press attention, as did Ann Packer, erotica author, and Juliet Samson fantasy Author as they arrived. The press screamed for attention, and they got it.

The coach pulled in, and the residents of Wotton disembarked, Izzy, Celia and Lillian looked very show business, Colin from Sweetie's retreat smiled a huge smile, as did the other therapists. Peter and Mary Saxon, Norman and Daisy, Gail and Moon Raven, Gill and Aden, and the tea room girls with Meg and Alex, even Denise was there with John. Michael and Anthony stepped off to a blitz of cameras, as the Curio fans screamed their lungs out. Anthony smiled dressed in his best suit, and looked as immaculate and dashing as he always did.

Bongo stood by the coach door, and awaited the last ones off, which was of course Derek and Margret Pemberton, they were blown away when they looked up, and saw the huge banner with their daughter on it. Margret was already close to tears; she was so happy. Bongo escorted them, and much to their surprise, the press shouted out to them, asking how proud they were. Derek smiled and waved, and shouted back.

"You have no idea how happy, and how so incredibly proud of her we are."

Bongo guided them carefully, and swung them to Amy Walker, with River Cable TV News, to talk, and Margret was so close to tears she could hardly say a word, Derek did all the talking.

Anthony was posing for pictures, then turning to the fans, it took him a long time to arrive at the door. Felicity arrived with Patrick, and the press again shouted out, she found it all a little overwhelming, but stopped to talk. Hatty was very popular, she was a well known artist, and quite famous, as was Roni, and both of them stopped to be questioned. So far, the night was going really well, art critics, art buyers, celebrities were all pouring in, and a long black car pulled up, to be met by Luke, and the door opened and Deli with Deb's got out.

Baby Jenny was with a registered child minder, linked to the hotel, and Deli approved. One look at Deb's and the fans erupted, and then right behind her Edwina got out, and linked Luke's arm, the press and fans went crazy. Deli had been added to the Curio's as an official member and house mate, so she was really shocked when Curio fans started asking her questions, as she stood next to Deb's, smiling and doing her best to answer everyone.

Inside everyone was being met by Anita and Simone, and staff handed out gift bags, and the large gallery was filled with the very cream of the crop, of art lovers and celebrities. The air was filled with discussions. Outside Edwina pulled back as she talked to Amy, she really wanted to see Chloe arrive, she got the ping on her phone from Birch, and she stepped back, and looked right down the carpet. I smiled at Chloe.

"Are you ready to do this?"

She breathed in and swallowed, she was shaking a little, the gin she had been sipping had helped, the car pulled up, and it was already pretty noisy. I watched her face as she realised the size of the crowd. Terry stood waiting for her, she looked at me.

"Fuck Abby, there are millions." I patted her leg.

"Take Terry's arm, and let him guide you, we will be right behind you. Chloe those are Curio supporters and they want to see you and talk to you." She looked out of the window.

"Oh Fuck!"

I giggled; I knew that feeling. Ella was out on red carpet with her camera, this was the moment she had been waiting for, she crouched down and focused on the car door, waiting for Chloe in her design step out. The door opened, and the screams were deafening, Edwina watched as Chloe stepped out and it took Edwina's breath away, she held her hands to her mouth, the crowd went wild. Amy William's pointed the camera at Edwina, and smiled, as she saw her tears fill her eyes. Chloe looked almost dazed, and yet was smiling such a beautiful smile.

Terry walked very slowly, he turned to face the press and stepped back, and the flashes bombarded her, and she smiled. He took her arm and guided her to the fans, and they all held out pens and books and pictures, and she happily chatted and signed autographs. Birch and myself watched from inside the limo, as she walked slowly towards the gallery. Birch took my hand.

"Are you ready for this Mrs Dixon?"

Birch as always slid out first, tonight there was no parasol, although, there was mirrored glasses. The crowd went wild yet again, as I stood up, and waved, the press attacked us with cameras. Birch linked my arm, and we stepped forward, smiling for the cameras and waving at the fans. Chloe was stood signing autographs, and we moved slowly towards her, she looked back, and her face was so happy, she looked stunning in that dress, and the press loved it.

Abby fans were everywhere, and soon I was in the thick of it, signing and talking as I moved slowly up. Luke watched carefully a few feet behind me, as I stepped back, he guided me to press selected by Anita. Terry was doing the same with Chloe, and it felt like forever before I saw Amy and stopped to chat for a few minutes.

"Abby, you look stunning, as does your gorgeous wife, how are you both feeling now you are married?" I smiled at the camera.

"We are delightfully happy, but tonight is Chloe's night, and we are going to sit back and let her stand in a spotlight that has been a long time coming for her. Curio fans, if you are out there, you must come and see how amazing she is, you all have four weeks." Amy gave a huge smile.

"Doctor Dixon, you see Chloe paint every day, what is it like having such a great talent at home?" Birch leaned forward, it really was loud and noisy.

"Most of the time you do not know she is there; she sits in her studio from dawn till dusk painting. She has done some wonderful pictures of us, we have them up in our room. We may one day loan them to a gallery."

Luke urged us on, we waved goodbye, and we finally made it to the door, where Chloe stood happily waving, Anita ensured all three of us gave one last wave, and the press lapped it up, and then we stepped back, turned, and entered the gallery.

Chloe was breathless, Edwina and her mum were in tears, as they hugged her, Derek was so proud, and he pulled her into his arms. I looked at them all.

"Guys, it is time to launch a book, will you all go in, and Chloe will be in shortly."

It took a while, but eventually they headed inside, and I looked at Chloe, she was wiping her eyes, but so happy. Terry took her arm; he looked really smart in his suit.

"Okay Terry, you know what to do?" He nodded.

I took Birch's arm, and with Anita, the three of us walked in, to tremendous applause, we smiled as we walked up the gallery, and up to a small stage, and up the steps on to it. Anita stepped up to the microphone.

"Ladies and gentlemen, your hosts for tonight, Dixon and Dixon." There was more applause, and we stood smiling as we waited, nodding our appreciation, and waited for it to die down, Birch leaned into the mic.

"Our deepest thanks, to you specially selected two hundred special VIP's. Tonight, we are here to honour the talent, and a new artist, and to present her for the first time to the world. Not only is she an amazing painter, she is a wonderfully talented illustrator, who has as you know, created the stunning covers of my wife's books. Here to tell you a little about it, is the Author of the hand of death series, Abigail Jennifer Watson." Birch smiled with utter delight, as she stepped back, and I moved closer to the mic, I took a breath and smiled.

"Ladies and gentlemen, almost eight years ago, as I finished the first manuscript, I had no cover, and it was during a meeting of my friends Debbie and Anthony, in the Tea Rooms at my local village, that they suggested I text Chloe, and ask for drawings. I did, and I sent her a copy of the unpublished manuscript, and two weeks later, I got several drawings back via email. Chloe at that time had just finished her degree, and had moved out of the village to chase her dream of becoming a full time artist, she worked in an art shop during the day, and sketched at night. Most of you do not realise, she sketched, because pads were cheap, and she could not afford the paint and canvass. I offered to pay her, and she refused point blank to take a penny, all she wanted was an illustrator's credit inside the book. The rest as they say is history."

I looked down at Deb's and smiled.

"It was great advice, thanks Deb's. Chloe has produced far more sketches than you see here, but these are my favourites, which is why I wanted to present them in such a way, that everyone could see them, in an exhibition, and the limited edition book Sanctuary Art. Tonight is my way of saying thanks, and actually getting her to see how loved her work is. Not only is she a remarkably talented artist, she is an unbelievable friend, Ladies and gentlemen, please show your appreciation, for Illustrator and Artist, Miss Chloe Pemberton."

I held out my arm, and she entered through the door, and everyone turned around and applauded, she looked shy and awkward, but smiled with happiness. Terry guided her through the crowd, as everyone shook her hand, and congratulated her, and slowly she headed to the stage. I clapped as hard as I could, and her parents who were stood close to the stage smiled with immense pride.

Finally, I had done it, I got her in front of everyone, and showcased her talent, and I was delighted for her. She was guided up the steps, and came to my side, she had tears in her eyes, I stepped back and held out my hand.

"It is all yours Chloe, this is your night."

Chapter 14

The Artisan.

Chloe stood up in front of the assembled guests, and took a huge breath, this was not like the Curio event, tonight she could see everyone.

"Hi... Thank you. I am not very good at this, I prefer to sit quietly and paint, this is all so big and new to me, and I am a little terrified at the moment. I love Abby's books, I see everything so clearly when I read them, so I pick up my pad and sketch. I am so happy you came to look at my pictures, and the book is mind blowing, I never expected it, and I don't know what else to say really, I am just really so very happy." She stepped back, and Anita walked back to the mic, as the guests gave her another huge round of applause.

"Ladies and Gentlemen, isn't she delightful, Dixon and Dixon Events, are proud to officially launch the release of Sanctuary Art, the illustrations of Chloe Pemberton. Please remember this is a numbered collector's edition, limited to just two thousand copies, so grab it while you can, as demand is higher than even we expected. If you are interested in a purchase of artwork, please consult the Gallery Curator, Miss Simone Vanderstat. We really would like to thank such a prodigious gallery, for hosting Miss Pemberton, and thank them for all they have done for her. Enjoy your evening, and thank you for supporting Miss Pemberton tonight."

With that, we knew we had done all we could, and we came down off the stage to mingle. I stood back and watched the crowd, it was not long before Gordon Stimes and his wife approached me, he was carrying a copy of the book, I gave him a huge grin.

"Thanks for supporting Chloe." He smiled.

"I have bought a painting as well, she is talented, I suppose you bought the arch?"

I gave a giggle, he had researched me far better than I realised for his show, I gave him a nod.

"How could I not, it is my arch?" He chuckled.

"I noted the real one has been saved by your wife, and now lives in your garden, you could have saved me the picture." I gave a smirk.

"What can I say, I am a collector of arches?" He held up the book.

"I would be honoured if you would sign this for me Abby."

I was delighted to, and pulled out my golden pen. He held it open as I wrote. 'To my favourite TV host, from a collector of arches, Abigail Jenifer Watson.' He chuckled as he read it.

"Perfect."

Chloe was wandering around looking at her pictures lost to the world, people she did not know, stopped her, and praised her work, or asked her questions, and she smiled and was happy. She looked beautiful, almost as if she was floating, Ella came up at my side.

"She really is quite a beautiful woman, she has not got a clue who all these people are, to her, they like art, and that is enough for her. I do like that about her, she is a true artisan, all that matters is the work."

I agreed, she was a simple creature at heart, oblivious to the rich and powerful, she was only capable of being Chloe, and to me that was very special indeed.

As the night moved on, and we drank white wine, and ate luxury finger food, of which I will not deny, I ate a lot as I was starving, I noticed the red dots appearing, and counted seventeen towards the end. It was a really good start to the event, and Simone was very happy. Tomorrow was the first day of opening to the public, and once again we would be on full display, but as Birch appeared having spent time with her parents, and slipped her arm around my waist, I was really tired.

The crowd started to thin around eleven o'clock, and by eleven thirty, there was just a few of us. Mrs Pemberton was still emotional as she hugged me, and thanked me over and over, as she did Birch. I was just happy that they got to see her here today. The coach arrived to drive them all to the hotel, and finally we thanked Simone, and climbed into the limo outside, Chloe looked worn out but very happy, the fleet of black cars headed for the hotel, and all I cared about was bed.

We arrived back to a few photographers, all sober and decent, and headed to our rooms. Chloe lay back on her bed and was flat out in minutes. I helped Birch undress her, hung up her dress, and we slid her under the duvet, then went through the door into our room, and climbed into bed. Birch snuggled round me, I was happy but exhausted, and just enjoyed being cuddled.

I don't know how many pictures we had taken together, or how many strangers introduced themselves, and spoke to me. I signed posters, prints and books, I even signed a couple of fridge magnets, it was fun, but this was not about me, I was just the means to get people to come. It had always been Chloe's night, and seeing her so happy, made me feel really good inside, and I drifted with that thought into sleep.

Birch sat on my waist as I opened my eyes, she was bright, happy and giggling, and way too cheery for before coffee.

"Hi Sweetie, I made coffee, we need to get up."

She grabbed my arms and pulled at me, and I groaned as I sat up, and she pulled me into a cuddle.

"Do I have to; Birch I am tired?" I leaned my head on her shoulder, and she pulled me close, it felt nice, her body was soft and warm.

"We have to awaken our star Deads, she has a big day, we are supposed to be the organisers, and need to be on the ball."

I gave a sigh, and turned my head, and burrowed into her neck, and nibbled. Birch gave a loud giggle, and hunched her shoulders.

"Deads, no it tickles... Ha... Ha... Ha, no stop!"

Chloe walked in rubbing her eyes, her hair was stuck out everywhere.

"Guys, it's too early." I flopped back in the bed with a smile.

"Good she is up, now let me sleep." Birch jumped off the bed, and looked at Chloe, she handed her a coffee.

"Oh, Sweetie, you look rough, here drink this."

Waking was not an easy process this morning, but I was awake and knew I would not be going back to sleep. Birch supplied coffee, while Chloe and myself sat on the bed slowly coming to life. Today was the opening to the public, and we would be in the specially roped off area to meet and greet. I was going to wear the black suit again, Ella had supplied a matching white blouse, and Birch had a similar white blouse.

Chloe, was back to a more festival, boho look, with a long, floral patterned wide flared silk pants, and a crop top, with a long crochet, sleeveless colourful over jacket, she looked elegant, and feminine, and with her hair pulled back at the sides, and her make up done, she looked absolutely lovely.

The restaurant was rowdy, the coach party were all sat talking and smiling, and having the time of their lives. Apparently quite a few of them had stayed up late to party in the bar, and there were various stories of Hatty, and Celia bouncing around the room to giggles.

Chloe went over and sat with her parents, Birch and I joined Roni and Will, who were sat with mum and Patrick, Hatty was still passed out with Clive. It was nice to sit and drink coffee and eat toast, as Birch devoured a full English breakfast, honestly how the hell does she stay so thin, when she eats like an Amazon warrior?

The group from the village had to leave after breakfast, and the coach pulled up outside, as Anthony and Izzy organised everyone. There were still barriers outside which was probably a good thing, as there were some journalists but also fans. As soon as we stepped out there were wild screams, as we walked to the coach, and said goodbye and thank you. Gail was delighted as she hugged Chloe, and last came her parents.

I grabbed Chloe and pulled her over to some of the fans, and as her parents came out, they could see their daughter laughing and smiling at my side, as we signed pictures and books. For them this was an amazing experience. I gently pulled Chloe back, she was so excited as she turned to face her mum and dad. I stood back and smiled, as cameras all around us went off. She pulled them both into a massive hug, and I could see by their faces, the joy they felt, it felt like such an amazing moment.

As the coach pulled away, everyone could see us talking to fans and signing autographs, and I knew, the gossip network at home would be on fire, as the word spread across the village. We slowly made our way back inside waving to everyone, Chloe was on cloud nine, Anita was waiting with a smile, it was now time to head to the gallery, which would be in our limo, with my favourite driver.

"Good morning, Markus."

He gave a big smile as he held the door, I pulled out an envelope and handed it to him.

"Just a little something, because you an amazing human being, it will be mad busy later and we do not want to forget." He gave a sigh.

"I do not need this; I get paid very well." I winked.

"It is either this, or I will jam the screen open, and make Birch sing Pat Benatar at the top of her lungs there and back, and trust me, nobody wants that." He slid the envelope in his pocket with a smile.

"I trust you, so no, please don't..." I giggled as I climbed in.

There were still barriers, the gallery had never had a line like it, and Simone was over the moon, although it would have to be controlled, as the gallery was not made for such numbers. This time we had to walk straight in, we could not go down the line which ran along the side of the smoked glass windows, to keep the plaza clear.

As we drove up, even I was blown away. It was eleven in the morning, the line went all the way down the road, it was massive. Chloe stared in disbelief, as Markus pulled in, and Luke and Creamy were stood waiting, wearing head sets.

Edwina was by the doors; she too was security today, dressed in all black. Anita exited first, and stood back, and then we let Chloe step out, the crowd screamed wildly, as Birch and myself hung back, to let her walk with Luke and Anita to the main doors. Finally, as she was almost there and looked back with a smile, Birch stepped out, and I followed to flashes and yet more screams, it was insane.

Birch linked my arm, and we walked towards the doors, escorted by Creamy, as we smiled and waved to everyone. The noise was deafening, and I just wanted to laugh and scream with them, it was amazing even for me, and I had been greeted like this at every public event for a few years.

I spotted the River Cable van, and waved to them as we walked up, they were filming from a distance, so I stopped and smiled and blew them a kiss. Amy waved with Mark and Brett, I knew she would love that, and just knew, Brett had me on zoom. We made it to the door, and once again prepared, Simone was over the moon, she smiled.

"Never have we had such attention; I am overwhelmed, this is possibly the best thing to ever happen to this gallery." I smiled, even her assistant was quite overwhelmed, although the poor girl looked like she could use a good holiday.

"Simone, we are so delighted, we are really happy, that firstly you took the gamble for Chloe, and that it has been such a success so far, we hope you will have many more busy days like this over the next four weeks."

Luke and Creamy opened the doors, and suddenly I understood why the gap between the pictures, which was roped off was so wide. The gallery was packed, and we got to walk between the rope and the walls. Chloe went first to masses of applause, Anita and Luke walked just behind her, as everyone stopped and clapped, Birch smiled as she leaned into my shoulder.

"Look at her, she looks lost, I am so happy Sweetie, even I did not think she would have this big of a reception." I just watched her looking so stunned and so happy, as she smiled and nodded to everyone, she was just so polite, as she thanked them all.

"She more than any deserves this Birch, she went through hell to get here, I never want her going back there." Creamy tapped my shoulder.

"You are up Abby."

Chloe had made the stage and was being seated, and so with a deep breath, I walked in with Birch, and we smiled and nodded, as again we were applauded, and I began to realise, that actually, smiling really makes your face ache.

People settled back into their routine, as we sat at the long table. Creamy and Luke returned outside, there were still some VIP visitors that had arranged to visit, and their job was to escort them in avoiding the lines. For us it was business as usual, and the shop was packed with people looking at the items for sale. We had taken the biggest gamble to date on numbers, and really stocked up. Back at home there was still a lot available should we need it.

A small ornamental barrier had been placed along the front of the staged area, where we sat at a long table with ample pens and drinks, and very quickly a line grew. The first of many meetings today started, as people came up one at a time, supervised by Anita and Edwina, and we began to sign our hearts out, watched over by Terry, Bongo, and Morty. Anita had been shrewd, having us there signing, meant the shop was busier, as visitors wanted something connected to the event to be autographed.

We had small conversations, smiled, and I wrote my name a million times, and drank gallons of water and cola. I hardly lifted my head, I was so busy looking down, as Birch slid item after item across the table to me, which Deli would lift, and pass on to Chloe as the line moved.

I signed a travel mug in sharpie, and it moved as I was thanked, next came a copy of Sanctuary Art, I opened it up.

"Would you make it out to Edwin and Angela." Birch sniggered and leaned in.

"SURPRISE!" I laughed as I looked up.

"Dad, why didn't you say, I would have had one signed and sent it to you?" He smiled.

"I wanted to see this, I wanted to be a part of the atmosphere."

The line had come to a standstill, I smiled, I understood that and signed the book, and added a love heart to it, Angela smiled with pride. Chloe looked really surprised as he moved to her.

"Mr W, I would have had one delivered, but thanks for coming, it is kind of mad here today." He gave her a big smile.

"You have an exceptional talent, and you stood by my daughter, and I appreciate that. I am delighted to say, I will go home today and clear a spot in my study, for the new picture I purchased today. Keep up the good work." Chloe looked stunned, and I grinned at her, I have never seen her this happy. She smiled a beautiful smile.

"Thanks Mr W, that really means a lot to me."

He moved on, and I started to frantically sign again. At one o'clock we had a break, which was much needed, as my hand ached like hell. We were escorted out to a small room, where we had a light lunch, which in my case was a salad. We were not due back until two, so after a glass of wine, we walked back into the gallery, and stayed behind the ropes.

This was great fun, as we stopped and talked to those in the gallery. They took pictures on their phones, and told us how amazing the pictures were, and Birch and myself stood side by side and talked of our wedding, and I talked about which ever picture was behind me, and of course the book.

I have never had this kind of controlled access to readers before, and I really loved it. Meeting people and talking and sharing my thoughts of the books and artwork, was the best part of the day for me. The crazy thing was, I talked to all age groups, and I had always thought my books would be read by mainly younger people, but I was wrong, it was right across the board.

I was delighted to see Mable and Seth, who were accompanied by Cissy Benson, I thanked them for coming, and even posed for a few shots, which Birch took for us, much to Mable's delight. I somehow felt, that over the next few days, the message apps in Devon would be very hot with gossip.

I looked across and watched as Chloe stood back against the wall, and people took pictures of her, I somehow thought, today, her Insta would explode with new followers. Mum and Hatty waved, it was nice to see those who understood art, make a sudden swoop at her, I think Hatty was having as good a time as Chloe. Simone was rushed off her feet, but smiling away, she was clearly grateful for the business.

We returned to the table, the crowd outside was still there waiting in line, and I wondered if we would have to stay open all night, just to get through them all? We went back to signing, talking, and smiling, and finally by five o'clock, we were done in every way possible. My throat was dry, and my hand hurt like hell, Anita arrived with three tall glasses of ice cold gin, and it felt glorious. The line outside had finally tapered off, as the few remaining people in the gallery wandered round having one last look, I smiled at Birch.

"We did it Baby." She nodded and relaxed in her chair.

"It was wonderful Sweetie; I don't think I have ever seen you two so happy." Chloe gave a long relieved sigh.

"I want a burger, and a Percy." We all started to chuckle, here she was the star of the day, and she could only be Chloe, she is lovely.

The gallery finally cleared, and we had one last look around, as

Simone talked to her assistants and staff. They were open again tomorrow, but it would be a lot less crazy for her, she smiled as we gave her our thanks, and prepared to leave. She was very happy.

"We have never had such a busy or fun day; this will be one for the record books for this place. You two are really surprising, and I will not deny, I thought a four week run would be a little longer than needed, but we had the space free, so I went with it. I am sure we may be talking of extending, if this goes anything like we think it might." Chloe was thrilled.

"I am glad it has been good for your gallery; I will always remember you gave me a chance at my first show, it has meant the world to me." Simone gave her a big smile.

"My dear, this is just the first, trust me, having seen this, and the catalogue on your website, I think we will be talking at some point of a return with your acrylics, those I really want to see up close." Chloe gave a big smile.

"I do have a lot at home." She smiled and took her hand.

"We want to see them, you have an amazing talent young lady, and a very bright future, I will see to it."

For me, that was a perfect end, to a perfect day, just standing back and seeing her face, made all the hours and weeks of work worth it. I felt we had done all we could, and now we could sit back, and let her talent do the talking.

After a lot of organising, and one more last good look around, we jumped into the cars at the rear, and headed back to the hotel, and up to our room to relax. Within seconds we were all naked and lay on the beds feeling cooler. Birch decided to run a bath, I must admit the bath here was huge, and as we slipped in, holding yet another glass of gin, and lemon, I gave a massive sigh of relief. Chloe wandered in and sat on the toilet.

"Guys, this weekend has been mind blowing for me, I am not used to all this hype and stuff, but I just want you to know, I have never felt as happy as I do now, you two are amazing."

I smiled, up to my neck in hot fragrant bubbles, leaning against Birch.

"Shut the hell up you soppy bitch, and jump in." She giggled and her eyes danced. I pointed at the taps.

"That's the straight end."

Birch chuckled as Chloe climbed in, and all three of us sat in the bath, laughing and talking and relaxing, oh God, I really needed this. Birch gave a moan of happiness.

"Oh Sweeties, this is the life, booze and hot water." Chloe smiled.

"Some fucking would be nice." I winked at her.

"How do you know we are not?" She sat up fast.

"What... Holy fuck is she fiddling with you?" I laughed out loud.

"Your face... ha, ha, ha!" She slipped back down in the water.

"Bitch!" Birch giggled, and I felt her free hand wander under the bubbles.

Fresh, clean, and in ordinary casual clothes, we headed down to the bar in search of food, and the rest of our party. We were finished, all that was left was payments and paperwork, and that all happened on Monday. It was Saturday night and we were ready to relax, which could only mean one thing, burgers, beer, and a lot of messing around, and so we walked into the bar, and prepared to enjoy ourselves.

The night started with a group of tables, which we took over and dominated, and we began with shots, followed by whatever we fancied. It was loud and wild, of which Hatty and Roni were the loudest, and we celebrated Chloe with many toasts, and slowly slid down in our seats.

The night ended with me hanging over Luke's shoulder, Birch over Will's, Chloe over Creamy's, and Fidelity over Morty's. They carried us back to our rooms, where Deb's and Edwina stripped us, and tucked us up in bed safe, although they did dump Deli in with Chloe, who in her drunken stupor, curled around Deli, cupped her boob, and slept happily.

Sunday morning was a startling surprise, as St Pauls struck up its bells half a mile away, and Birch went from sleeping to standing in one swift move, and grabbed her head.

"YOU HAVE GOT TO BE FUCKING JOKING, IS THERE NO FUCKING SANCTUARY ANY WHERE FROM THOSE TWATS!?" She staggered over to the patio doors, yanked them open, poked her head out and screamed.

"WILL YOU PLEASE SHUT THE FUCK UP, US SINNERS HAVE A HANGOVER!"

I sat up, groaned, and whispered.

"Birch for the love of whatever gods you sacrifice chickens to, shut the hell up." She turned and slammed the door, and I jumped in the bed, and grabbed my head.

"Hi Sweetie, those fucking twats, are asserting their fucking power over us again, it's a fucking liberty, that's what it is you know, a fucking liberty." She looked at me, and sat ddown on the bed.

"Oh Sweetie, do you have a headache?" I glared at her through lidded eyes, and spoke with gritted teeth.

"Yes!" She smiled.

"I have painkillers, and I will make coffee."

She got up grabbed her bag and pulled out a packet of paracetamol, she then lifted out a jar of coffee. I did wonder if she also had the kettle in there too. A few minutes later, she handed me a cup, and sat on the bed, and smiled.

"We need bacon." I sipped slowly.

"What, you don't have any in your bag?" She giggled at me.

"You are grumpy on Sunday mornings." I sipped again, holding the cup with both hands, I just moved my eyes, it was easier and less painful.

"Maybe that is because I live with a bonkers person, who leans out of windows, and yells at cathedrals half a mile away?" Her lip curled.

"Fucking Bell Twats, they think they rule Sundays. We should start a petition to tell the church of England to shut the fuck up on Sundays."

Birch kept the coffee coming, and I eventually got up, and went for a pee, then stood at the door and looked at Chloe and Deli curled together, I frowned.

"Did those two get up to something last night?" Birch looked around the door.

"I don't think so, but looking at Chloe's grip on her boob, I am not sure." She looked at me weird.

"I thought they were straight?" I shrugged.

"Me too, but hey who am I to judge?" I grabbed their cups, and made them coffee, then sat on the bed and gave Deli a nudge.

"Deli... Deli, hey come on, it will be breakfast soon." She opened her eyes, and smiled.

"Hey Abby." I smiled.

"I hate to wake you up, you look so comfy, but we will have to go eat soon, then check out. You have a coffee here." She smiled, and then yawned.

"I slept really well, how about you?" Birch leaned in through the door.

"Not so good, the two straight girls next door made a hell of a din screwing each other for half the night."

It took a moment, and then Deli realised someone was clasping her boob, she looked back and saw Chloe flat out with a smile on her face. She sat bolt upright in bed.

"Holy shit... Did I shag Chloe?" She gave a groan, and clasped her hands to her skull. Birch gave her a grin.

"We heard what we heard." Deli stared at her in horror.

"Shit!" Chloe sat up and groaned at her side, Deli turned and looked at her.

"Chloe, did we really shag each other?" Chloe blinked.

"Huh." Deli swallowed hard.

"Birch said we kept them up half the night shagging each other." Chloe slipped her hand under the covers.

"How wet are you?" Deli looked appalled, but slid her hand below the covers, and felt herself, she looked at me terrified.

"Oh Christ, I shagged Chloe." Birch collapsed in hysterics, as she pointed at Deli.

"Sweetie, you look so funny." Chloe looked at Deli.

"They are bitches, I did warn you." Deli frowned.

"Hang on, why aren't you bothered, holy shit Chloe, would you shag me?" Chloe blinked.

"Deli, you are really pretty, and you have half decent boobs, but I am so fucking straight it is unbelievable." She did not look convinced.

"I had a dream I was being fingered, and when I woke up you were holding my tit, are you sure?" Birch was on the bed laughing her ass off, I smiled and sipped my coffee.

"That is easily proven, just smell her fingers." They both looked appalled, Chloe shuddered.

"You are so fucked up Abby." Deli lifted the duvet, and sniffed the air.

Breakfast was very quiet, Birch ate bacon, lots of bacon, I stuck to toast. Birch appeared very happy, I looked at her as she smiled.

"I am baking cakes today when we get home." I felt the familiar cold shiver of Flickness run down my spine.

"Oh god, it is next weekend, is there no end to my hell?"

The truth was, we had been so busy with the event, I had forgotten, next weekend was the Summer Fete, which meant cakes, jams and flowers, and days of stewarding. It was that time of year when the whole village went mad, and produced enough cakes, and jam to feed the starving in Africa.

Hidden out of sight in our cellar, was the box pile of hell, that contained jam jars, cake boxes, and a wide range of assorted strange objects to arrange flowers in. It was the curse of my existence, and every house in Wotton had them.

Finally awake, and with calmer headaches, the three of us, packed our things, loaded Petal and checked out. Luke filled the mini bus, Deli and Deb's with Jenny, jumped in with us, and I drove, and just for a last look, I drove past the gallery, and again there was a good sized line.

The banner looked brilliant, and Chloe snapped a picture on her phone. I smiled as we left the gallery behind, and drove on to the motorway, and headed for Wotton. The village was busy as we drove through, and a lot of people smiled and waved, after all, it was hard to miss Petal, and finally the gates swung open, and we pulled up in front of the house.

Luke was already in action with a clip board, as he supervised Morty and Bongo, who were loading boxes into the mini bus, they were heading back to the gallery with more stock, which was a great thing to see.

After yet more coffee, and unloading all our things, I crashed onto the bed, and sprawled out, I was exhausted, and soon was out cold.

As Wotton filled with tourists, and they flocked to the arranged events, at three Waterside Lane, the house was silent, except for the bubbling of pans. Every room was filled with its sleeping inhabitants, exhausted from weeks of hard graft, emails, and phone calls. Over the hill in Millington, Anita sat naked on her bed, relaxing as she talked to her mum on speaker phone.

"Mum I am so happy at the moment, I love working with them, they are crazy, but in the nicest of ways, and my God mum, the way they work is hard, but so creative. I have never known anyone quite like them. Honestly, I felt out of my depths a few times, I was struggling to keep up with them, working for Abby is the best decision I ever made. I literally have no idea what they will do next, I love it."

"Nita, I am so happy for you, and I must admit when your dad saw you on the TV, he was over the moon. You sound so much better than you have in a long time, I have told you, getting away from that Katie is the best thing you have ever done. I think by what you are saying, you work for much more honest and decent people now?"

"I do Mum, but to be honest, I am so glad I have a day off today and tomorrow, all I want to do is sleep." Her mum chuckled on the other end of the phone.

"Get your head down Nita and sleep, and recharge, you do sound tired. I will ring you on Tuesday."

"Okay Mum, I will talk then, bye."

Anita slid down the duvet and slid into bed, she grabbed her pillow, and hugged it with a smile, and closed her eyes.

"I am so tired; I think those two are going to kill me."

Chapter 15

New Curio.

I opened my eyes and sniffed the air.

"Oh shit, she has started!"

The smell of cake wafted around the house, I rolled over and rubbed my eyes, the clock read seven thirty pm. I sat up and slid off the bed, and took off my pants, my legs were red hot, and I pulled my top over my head and threw it on the floor. It was time to face my demons, and headed for the kitchen, where I knew my insane wife, had turned full on Felicity, and was destroying the kitchen.

Chloe appeared as I came out of my room, she looked as rough as I felt, she looked at me with bleary eyes.

"She has fucking started, hasn't she?"

I nodded; the apocalypse was upon us. We headed downstairs together, and walked cautiously to the kitchen. Birch was stood with her hair in a bun, naked, apart from her red apron. Her face was red, and had white smears of flower on her cheeks, she smiled a big smile as she stirred the huge pan, it smelt really weird.

"Hi Sweetie... I am cooking jam."

I cautiously edged towards her, as Fidelity sweated running around in just her knickers, wiping flour off everything. I peered into the pan; it was a really weird colour.

"Ergh... What the hell are you making?" I stepped back, it had infected my nose, and I was not keen. Birch beamed with delight.

"Sweetie, this year I thought I would do something really different." Chloe sat at the island.

"No offence Birch, but in order to do that, you have to start at normal, and you have never actually been there."

Deli sniggered as she wiped the white dust off the floor. I hated asking, but I was curious as to the contents, which looked a milky green, and had orange spots in it, I went for delicate investigation.

"Birch, what the frigging hell is in it?" She looked at me surprised.

"What... You cannot tell?" We all shook our heads; she looked over the pan with pride.

"I started with plums, and a few apples, then I put loads of tangerines in, and it lacked something." Chloe smirked.

"Digestibility and a health warning perhaps?" Deli giggled. Birch gave her a glance, and looked back at me.

"I wanted a better texture, so I put five avocados' in as well." I shuddered and stepped back.

"Birch it's a jam contest." She nodded.

"I know Sweetie." I hated to be the bearer of bad news, but someone had to be.

"Birch Baby, you put oranges in it, they make marmalade?" She gave a frown.

"Yeah, about that... I thought about it, and I just figured I would list it as, 'Jarmalade,' you know, half jam, half marmalade?"

There was utter silence, as the three of us stared at the mad lady stirring the pan. She looked at me and smiled.

"Deads, I have told you; a good jam should not require a label, you should know it the moment you taste it." Chloe sniggered.

"Toxic might be a good label, we could put a skull and cross bones on it, and give it to kids on Halloween." Birch smiled, and then jumped on the spot, with excitement, she ran to the fridge.

"I did this as well." She opened the fridge door and pulled out a jar of a weird green substance, and unscrewed the lid.

"I call it Cumberlade." Chloe stared at her.

"Did you use my cucumber; I was using that?" Deli dropped her dust pan, and stared at Chloe, looking impressed, repulsed, and horrified all at the same time.

"Please tell me you are joking?" Chloe shook her head, and Deli sort of gasped a little. Chloe smiled.

"I was going to use it in Tuesday's art still life class, on the green." Deli gave a gasp of utter relief.

"Thank god for that, honestly for a moment I thought you had been playing hide the cucumber whilst shopping with it." Birch smirked.

"We have all seen that act, but it was not cucumber." Chloe

shook her head, as Deli picked up her dust pan.

"No, it's alright, I left that one in my room, it has gone a bit soft now." Deli dropped the dustpan again, and stared at Chloe in horror, I smirked.

"You can say it Deli... Yep, she is a slut, and hey, she is in the room right next door to you." Chloe suddenly realised.

"Oh, I get it... Deli, I was going to eat it while I sketched, but I got distracted and left it on my bed side table, and it is a bit soft now, I prefer them hard." Edwina walked in.

"Ain't that the fucking truth, and I will add as often as possible. God you are such a slut Chloe." Edwina looked at Birch's hand.

"What the hell have you done now?" Birch held it out with pride, as her eyes sparkled.

"It's Cumberlade." Edwina poked her finger in it and we all screamed.

"DON'T FUCKING EAT IT!" She sucked her finger, and smiled.

"Actually Birch, that is bloody delicious, can I have this?" Birch swelled up with pride.

"Of course you can Sweetie, I have another twenty eight jars."

Yeah, that is the other thing about Birch, all her recipes come in bulk. Edwina took it as we all stared, as she picked up a pack of crackers.

"Cheers Birch, this really is lovely, I am going to let Luke try it." Birch was elated, Chloe turned, and watched her sister walk out of the kitchen.

"She is really weird these days, she hasn't half been eating some strange shit." There was a sudden moment of awakening amongst us, and pennies dropped all around us, I stared at Chloe.

"Oh Christ. You don't think she is... You know... Up it?" Chloe stared at me; Deli watched us. Chloe whispered.

"We need expert advice." We all looked at each other, and then it hit us and we all said it together.

"DEB'S!"

The stampede began, Birch dithered, torn between stirring the pan, and coming along with us. We charged upstairs, well three of us did, and Deli was not even sure why? We legged it down the hallway towards her door. Birch stirred the spoon really fast in the pan, then let go and ran to the stairs, two seconds later she came running back.

"Nope, nope, nope, nope, I cannot burn you Sweetie." She jigged on the spot.

"Oh, this is not fair, I want to play too."

The three of us burst into Deb's room and skidded to a halt.

Note to the readers: There are some things that you really do not want to know about your friends. Case in point was in front of us, as Deb's writhed around shoving a huge black dildo up herself, and such was her enjoyment, she had not noticed her three terror laden naked friends, who were rooted to the spot in shock.

"Oh Creamy!" And that was me done, I looked at Chloe.

"I am out, it can wait."

My voice alerted her to our presence, and she sat up fast, and gave a wild moan and her eyes opened really wide. Suddenly, Deb's had joined the how to lose your virginity Birch style club. Deb's turned scarlet, as she stared at us with horror.

"WHAT THE HELL GUYS?" Her legs started to spasm, and her face went really weird.

"OooooooooooooOOOOH!" Chloe nodded.

"Well yeah, that just about covers it, should we clap now or later, because I for one am fucking impressed?"

I backed out slowly, holding Deli by the arm, I figured now she understood why we needed the kitchen cupboard. Chloe realised we had gone, and she was alone watching Deb's orgasm. She panicked, turned and ran out of the room and caught us up, Deli was having trouble forming sentences, poor girl, I think she was traumatised.

"Guys... It was... It was..." She stopped and stared at me, I smiled.

"Frigging huge?" She nodded.

"Yeah... Holy shit did you see it, how the hell did it fit?" Chloe patted her back, and looked at me with a wry smile.

"See... Told you hers was bigger than mine?" We headed back into the kitchen, and Birch looked at me and frowned.

"Is everything alright Sweetie?" I sat down on my seat, and gave a long flow of breath out of my lungs.

"I need vodka... Really bloody strong vodka, we just watched Deb's screwing herself with a dildo bigger than Creamy." Deli nodded.

"I feel I should bleach my eyes; I will never get that image out of my head." Birch smiled.

"Oh Sweetie, you look pale, here see this."

She picked up her phone, and flicked through the pictures, turned it around, and showed it to Deli. She squealed, jumped back, and pointed at the phone.

"IS THAT THE FRIGGING VICAR?" I giggled; I seem to remember I did exactly that too.

"Welcome to the insane hell that is Fete Week, trust me, it gets a lot worse from here on in."

Chloe poured strong drinks, and we all gratefully accepted them, as we watched, Birch pour her weird green slop into jars. My stomach, appeared alerted to the fact that at some point, it knew that I really loved my insane wife, and when she offered me a taste, I was too weak to rebel, and it violently lurched, in protest.

She smiled, she was happy, and I loved that, she looked so angelic, and beautiful, even innocent, but no one knew of the demons, that lurked inside her head, hell bent on killing all the judges at the fete, with her poison. God, she is scary at times.

We sipped our cold drinks and relaxed, Deb's had not appeared, I figured she was either embarrassed or fantasising about Creamy again. Chloe looked uncomfortable and kept squirming in her seat. My theory of that is, if she knows someone within a hundred miles is screwing, she has to as well, which pretty much explains Percy. I looked at her.

"For God's sake Chloe, go see bloody Percy and sort it out, seriously, you take one look at the thing in Deb's, and you cannot control it?" She looked at me.

"It's not my fault, I am really wet now, I keep thinking of a big one." I gave a sigh.

"Just go to Percy and deal with it." Deli frowned and looked at us.

"Who the hell is Percy, everyone talks about him, but I have never met him?" Birch looked at me.

"Oh, Sweetie, should we let her, I mean, it took you a month to get over him?" Chloe smiled at Deli, she looked way too excited for my comfort.

"You want to meet him?" I looked at Deli.

"Just be aware, you need to think really carefully before you answer that." She did look a little worried.

"Well, who is he exactly?" Birch gave an evil grin.

"Sweetie, Percy is Chloe's best friend who lives in her bedroom." I sniggered, and Deli looked a little puzzled.

"I can see him right; I mean, he is not a figment of her imagination or anything?" I smirked, and Birch giggled.

"Oh Sweetie, a day will come when you really wish he was."

Chloe got up out of her seat, Birch reached up to the cupboard, and pulled a giant purple dildo out, and then offered it Deli, she smiled.

"Just in case... You know.... For self defence, or omelettes?"

She looked freaked out as Birch pushed it into her hand. I put my head down, and tried to hold in the laughter. I grabbed my phone and sent out a text to Edwina and Deb's, it read, 'Deli on route to meet Percy, get ready'.

Chloe took her hand, and Birch and me giggled as we walked behind them, Deli followed along holding a bright purple dildo in her hand, looking nervous, as she walked up the stairs, she looked at the dildo, and then Chloe.

"Percy won't hurt me, will he?" Birch smirked.

"Not physically, the jury is still out on mentally." Chloe shook her head.

"Percy is not like that, he is sweet and nice, and very loving." She looked relieved, talk about a lamb to the slaughter, the poor girl had no idea of what was coming.

At the top of the stairs, stood Edwina, Deb's and Luke, who had a semi, which shows you the power of Percy, Luke and Edwina actually stopped mid coitus to see this. Chloe turned holding Deli by the hand, and led her to her bedroom, she looked like a delicate little fly, about to be devoured by the weirdest frigging spider she will ever meet.

We walked behind them like a group of jailers following the convicted to the gas chamber, I sort of felt a little sorry for her, but this was after all a part of living here, and we had all been through it. In a way, it was the initiation of living in this house.

Chloe opened the door and they stepped in. We all waited silently in the hallway, holding our breath. The was a loud terrified squeal.

"HOLY SHIT!" Birch smiled.

"She met him then?"

The door opened at high speed, and Deli came flying out, she slammed her back into the wall, and panted as she held her heart. I looked at Deb's.

"Yep, that is pretty much how I reacted!"

Deli looked at us, her eyes were really huge, and her face was as white as snow, as she pointed behind her.

"Percy is a frigging teddy, with a really frigging huge...." We all nodded. Birch smiled.

"We know Sweetie, it was time you met him." Deli breathed really hard, to regulate her breathing.

"I really want to say something normal, like hey what a guy, or no that is not messed up at all, but honestly, I am freaking the hell out. Just knowing he is in the next room, scares the crap out of me." None of us wanted to giggle, but...

Chloe gave a long moan, the door was not quite shut, and Deli gave a huge shudder, and moved away from the wall.

"Now I know why everyone here drinks so frigging much, I really need a pint of vodka to calm the hell down." She took a deep breath.

"Is anyone in this house actually normal?" Birch smiled.

"Deads and me are very normal." Deli glanced at her, and then looked at me.

"She does know that is not true, doesn't she?" I gave a chuckle, and took her hand.

"You needed to meet him, and now you know why no one ever wants to meet in her room." She nodded her head.

"Jesus Abby my heart is pounding, she just opened her wardrobe, and it sprung right out at me, Christ, I almost fainted with shock. I was concerned, when she told me she kept him in her wardrobe, I thought hell, is she a sadist, now I just want him staying in there forever?"

I sat in the garden with Deli, at the edge of the pool whilst Birch swam.

"Now I hope you see where our bond comes from? Look Deli, we believe in liberty, and everyone has a right to be sexual, even with a screwed up teddy. There is a long story behind why she uses him as comfort, but she does also have a huge sex drive, and Percy keeps her calm whilst men are scarce." She took a deep breath and sipped her drink.

"I get it, honestly, I do, I was just not prepared for what I saw. You know, if someone had said, hey you know our messed up mate, well she actually has a life sized teddy with a frigging huge rubber dick that she screws, I would have been half prepared at least?" I shook my head.

"Trust me, no amount of preparation helps. I avoided her room for two years, and I knew about him, it made no bloody difference when I saw him, it freaked me the hell out." She nodded her head, and took another sip of her drink.

"Just do me a favour, never let Sophia go in her room, Christ, no one wants to see that on Insta?" I couldn't help but giggle, she started to laugh with me.

"Honestly, that is the most terrified I have ever been." She started to laugh again.

"Deli, I tell you what, I will go through it all with you. Okay, Edwina is a bisexual, but is madly in love with Luke. Debbie and Jimmy did have an open relationship, because he was sleeping with groupies, until she slept with Creamy, and Jimmy walked in on him posing for Chloe, took one look at his junk, and has left the groupies alone since." I lifted my glass, and took a swig.

"Chloe is a pervert with Percy and men, she collects a picture of everyman she has had sex with erect, and she has a lot of pictures. She paints and screws, that is her whole life. Izzy is into some pretty extreme BDSM, there is a special club in the village that is very secret where she goes, and Birch and myself are sort of the odd ones, because we are technically straight, we just want to be sexual with each other, not other women, they just don't appeal to us." She nodded and looked at me.

"So, Luke is straight, and Anthony and Michael are a gay couple?" I nodded.

"Yep, that about sums it up, although, I should just probably warn you about Bev."

"GUARD YOUR VAGINA'S." I giggled, as I looked round at the

others lay on the grass.

"She is now bisexual apparently, but up in Uppermill where she lives, she is known as the legend of the lesbians, and trust me, she is well known for her abilities with her mouth and tongue. She is one of Birch's best friends, and she is really sweet, but she does look terrifying when you first meet her." Deli was starting to understand.

"Seeds of Summer really was based on real life then, you do live naked, even though that is not sexual, some of you are friends with benefits, and you are all completely open and honest with each other. I hate asking but who have you had sex with apart from Birch?" I smiled.

"None of these." She turned and looked at me.

"So you really are the real deal, she is the love of your life." I nodded.

"We have had some threesomes, at an occasional party, we have partnered up with guys for an hour or two, but mainly we only want each other. I am not fussed about guys these days, Birch is special." She giggled and looked at me.

"She most certainly is unique, but you know what Abby, I think she is the kindest person I have ever met; she really loves you, that is for sure."

We stood up and walked around the garden, and for several hours I sat at my arch, and talked with Deli, and filled her in on a lot of detail of our life and our struggles. She sat and listened, as she got what was basically the story of all our lives, and she really started to understand why we had such a powerful bond. Birch came down and sat with us, as she snuggled into me, she listened without interrupting, but smiling, as I painted the picture of Curio life at number three Waterside Lane.

By the time the sun started to fall, she felt happy and reassured, she was not living in an insane asylum. She fitted in here, that was clear, I had watched her all week, and seen how she just jumped in and got involved, and as we walked slowly up the lawn back to the house, she smiled to herself.

"I guess I am on my own journey of self discovery Abby. I have never really fitted in anywhere, and yet I do feel really at home here. I am very grateful you let me live here, you know at first, I thought you all saw me as a snitch for Prim, but I really am not. Knowing what I know about all of you, I will never tell a soul anything about life here. I was super blown away by the way you treated Sophia, you could have hung her out to dry, but you didn't, that really made me see how much you have been wrongly accused of so much." Birch looked at her.

"We are all girls together Deli, and we protect each other, and look out for each other. Everything we do, we do as a group, and if one of us is attacked, the rest of us come out fighting, you are a part of that now, you are a Curio, if you do not believe me, go look at Curio Life, Edwina has added you to the house members group." She looked really surprised.

"She has, honestly, I am a Curio?" Birch smiled.

"Yeah, about that, be ready for it, because it involves a lot, and it is time you made a video, and introduce yourself." She looked really excited, and then stopped.

"What will I say?" I shrugged.

"How about telling the story of how a landlord illegally evicted you, on the request of someone for no other reason, than you hung out for one night with us." Birch agreed.

"Just do not mention any names, we keep everything we say nameless to avoid legal action, which as you know, is why Madge is known as the Shrew?"

Thirty minutes later, Fidelity sat on her bed, and looked into the camera on a tripod, and took a huge breath, and breathed out slowly.

"Hi everyone, my name is Fidelity, and as you know, I am the new house mate living with the Curio's. As I have found out since coming to this house, life here is pretty amazing, and so today I sat with Deadly and Birch, and listened to the story of their journey, and it was pretty mind blowing." She took a deep breath and looked at the camera.

"This is a lot harder than it looks, anyhow, Deadly and Birch wanted me to introduce myself, and tell you my story, so as the new house mate, they all call me Deli, I am going to tell you how I ended up here."

I sat back and smiled as Deli began her story, and I sat silently listening to her, as she described being confronted and threatened, and then served with the eviction order. She talked of how she sat all day falling apart, getting hate texts, and how heart breaking it was. She shed some tears and wiped her eyes, and carried on, and suddenly I felt I was back to four years ago, and making my own video.

Deli talked of how we found out, and came straight over, and within seconds had a plan to give her a new home. She smiled and wiped her eyes, as she talked of the speed we worked at, and how within a matter of hours, she found herself lay on this very bed she was sat on, feeling insecure, but safe. Deli smiled as she looked at the camera.

"I have been on this site many times, and I watched every second of Curio Live, but guys, honestly, you have no idea how amazing and caring, and kind the Curio's are. I watched Chloe this weekend, host her first art exhibition, and even though I only did a tiny bit to help, I was delighted to see how happy she was. I have really got to know Chloe in the last few weeks, I did know her at school, but she has changed so much, and she is as lovely and adorable as you all think she is. I was so proud of her in London." Deli smiled and took a deep breath.

"I am hoping to help with the new Curio Centre, which I am told is coming along really well, and I hope at some point we can all meet and swap stories, I will definitely be on the site talking to all of you. I hope, I can help you all as much as the rest of the Curio family have, I am certainly going to try."

I pressed the button and the file started to save; Birch gave a smile.

"See Edwina and she will give you the log in details for your new profile. Welcome home little Curio, you are one of us now for sure." She gave a huge smile.

"I meant what I said, you guys are the nicest and kindest people I have ever met, albeit totally bonkers, but I can deal with that." Birch chuckled.

"I think you have to Sweetie; we are too far gone to change." She lifted the camera, and headed out of the door to find Edwina, the video would go live tonight. I patted her leg.

"Nice job little sister, I am off for coffee, it is going to be a busy week, we have a fete to muck in with, and this year we have stalls to attend as well."

I came down the stairs, where Birch was in the library with Edwina and Luke, as they uploaded Deli's video to the site. I leaned on the doorframe and watched.

"That is a good video, she will be a good addition to the group." Edwina turned in her seat, and looked at me.

"We think she fits well, she just needs to find her madness, but yeah, I have to say, she is good on a keyboard, and she is a good researcher. She wants extra work, and I am happy to pay her. I was going to look for a new staff member, but I actually think I will give her the work, she is certainly keen and able." Luke agreed.

"I watched her at the gallery, she is not afraid to muck in that is for sure, I think she has adjusted to the house well, and I know how hard that can be, even I felt it when I first started dating Weena. I know Michael did, and she has settled a lot faster."

It was nice to see them all accepting her, I had worried when I first saw her falling apart in her flat. I don't know why though, I knew then she would fit, and I knew the whole household would accept her, that is the best thing about living here, the people. Edwina sat back in her seat.

"Okay, Fidelity is now official, I just sent her all the details she needs, and she can log in and start talking."

The Curio site came up on her screen, and there was a ping, and just below her video, it read, 'one comment.' I smiled before Edwina opened it, I knew exactly who that was from, and sure enough, it was Chloe. I gave a laugh.

"She is definitely official now, Chloe just marked her with a welcome. She never ceases to amaze me. I am making coffee; if anyone wants one, I will be in the kitchen."

I walked down the hall, as the sun fell in the sky, darkness was descending. I filled the kettle, and switched it on, and stood by the doors watching my arch, with the sun slowly fading behind it, I felt happy inside, because once again, everyone here had reached out in acts of kindness, and embraced Deli.

It had been a strange sort of day, as I looked back at my life, and could see how far I come from those days before Uni. I had been isolated and afraid of everything back then, and it was clear, some of it had been due to the control placed on my life, and some was simply a lack of understanding of the world.

I was so sheltered and lacked the knowledge of what life could be, and through that, I did not have the means, to really understand who I was, who I wanted to be, and what I could achieve. Most importantly, I really had no understanding of who Abby was, I simply did not know myself. It amazes me to understand how lonely and how sad my life had been before Birch, and yet so much had changed, and now I was surrounded by very creative people who cared, supported and encouraged me.

Maybe that was what I saw in Deli, and even Nigel to a degree, was Birch right, was that how I had been able empathise with them both, had I looked at them, and seen a former shadow of myself? In a way I thought I did, and as I stand here lost in thought staring out into the darkness of the garden, maybe only now I am starting to understand what Birch really has done for me, and in doing so, I have done the same for Deli.

I was leaning on the door lost in thought, when everyone started to appear, Deb's looked at me and frowned.

"Why does Edwina want us all to assemble in the garden?" I turned and looked at her as my phone pinged.

"No idea, I was with her not that long ago, and she said nothing." Chloe appeared followed by Deli. Birch looked around, there was no sign of her.

"Oh God, what is she up to now?"

She slipped through the open door, and we all walked out behind Birch, across the patio and onto the lawn. Whatever it was, none of us had any idea at all, and to be honest, I was starting to feel a little nervous, and I had no idea why.

Chapter 16

Fete Frolics.

It was pretty dark in the garden, but with the flood lamps on, it was bright as day, we walked out onto the grass, and looked around, there was nothing to see. I turned and looked at Birch.

"Why do we have to meet out here, where is she?"

The garden lights went out, and Deb's grabbed Chloe's arm, Chloe turned to her in the dark.

"Just so you know, if you dare to even say what is that, I am decking you Debs." I stood still, and looked around. Deli stood behind us and shivered, I had a strange feeling inside me.

"Hell Birch, I never realised it was this black out here at night." There was a creaking noise, like a rusty hinge, and Deb's turned to Chloe, she shook her head at her.

"Don't you even dare fucking say it Deb's." Deb's dithered behind us, there was a flash, I turned and looked at my arch.

Out of the floor, a skeleton rose up. Birch shrieked, and gripped my arm like a vice. It glowed in the dark, and Chloe who was stood a few feet behind me gave a slight moan.

"Oh fuck Birch, who's grave did you dig up, because you lifted some twat, and they are really pissed off about it?" Birch whimpered.

"Sweetie, I don't like it, send it back."

The skeleton turned, and looked at me, it had red eyes. Okay, I was really freaked out. It took a step towards me, and Birch wailed at me.

"Sweetie run, it wants a body and you are it."

I stepped back and felt my heart thump in my chest, my brain kept telling me it was not possible, but the impossible took another step towards me, and I was starting to panic. It gave a hiss, and took another step towards me, a cold haunting whisper echoed across the grass.

"Deadly."

"Oh fuck guys, I am so sorry."

Chloe looked down at her wet legs and grass, Deb's was nowhere to be seen, Deli stood rooted to the spot, her eyes wide open.

"Please tell me you are all seeing this guys, because I really do not want to admit I am?" She took two steps back. I did not want admit it, because I knew it could not be real, and yet it took another step forward.

Birch clung to my arm and dithered. I turned to head back, and was preparing to run, and gave a huge gasp, as a massive pirate ship rose out of the lawn, filled with Skeletons in pirate hats, and Birch squealed.

The flood lights came on, and Edwina stood on the balcony, outside the spare room, and everything disappeared.

"How bloody awesome was that?" I looked up at her.

"What the hell did you do?" She gave a big smile.

"It is a seven D holographic projection; they use them in Japan. It is why Luke went north last week, I needed to get the stuff I needed, this stuff is cutting edge kit, and I thought we could really make Wotton come to life with this on Halloween."

I could not deny, I was impressed, and a little freaked out, it looked so real, and really creepy. Birch still had her face buried in my shoulder; Deb's crawled out from under a sun lounger.

"You mean that was not real?" Edwina laughed.

"Deb's, you wuss, when was the last time you believed a skeleton could rise from the dead?" Deb's pointed down the garden.

"I never have until ten minutes ago, I frigging shit myself Edwina." I gave a giggle.

"Yeah, but you didn't piss your legs." Chloe snapped round.

"I was fucking fine until it talked, I thought it was fucking Gwenda." Edwina laughed up on the balcony, I looked up at her.

"How can we use this in the village?" She looked down and smiled.

"Abby, I am still working on the program, there is a hell of a lot to do, but if I can blow this stuff up larger, and get the projection angles right, I can haunt the whole village from the roof of the Church Hall. You know, put on a show, like no one has ever seen before. I can also have things flying all over the place." Birch slipped out of my shoulder.

"Sweetie, I don't like skeletons, they really freak me out, and talking without a voice box, is just too bloody creepy for me." I pulled her close.

"It's alright Baby, I will get them all to talk like Bev, and have them run round the village saying. Hey Bird, you wanna fuck?" She gave a squeal, and her eyes exploded with joy.

"Can we do that, oh Deads, I really want to see that now?" I shook my head; she can be really weird at times.

It was getting chilly, and most of us were naked, so we headed inside, and Edwina came down with a big smile. It was true, we wanted something different and unique, something to really make people sit up and think, and what better way, than to bring the village to life from the past, with ghouls and ghosts, but not skeletons, Birch was terrified of skeletons.

The talk was loud and filled with excitement, and ideas exploded out of everyone, as we sat in the living room and imagined all the possibilities of what Edwina could do. Ideas popped out of nowhere, and suddenly our Curio Carnival was looking to be really big and busy.

When we finally made it into bed, it had felt like a long very strange day, we had woken up in the hotel, yelled at Bell Twats, headed home, and Birch had been able to bake eight cakes, and make forty three jars of jam. We had recorded a new video from Deli, and had skeletons rise up from the floor, my life is so strange at times.

As my thoughts drifted, and Birch climbed into bed behind me and pulled me close, I felt the exhaustion kick in again, and as much as I would love to sit up and talk, I could not, my eyes closed and I was dead to the world, warm, cosy and relaxed.

Monday for me started late, I had an inbox full of emails, Birch had been on and paid all the invoices, so I printed out all the receipts, and filed them, then set too answering all the other enquiries. Deli appeared, and I showed her the spare computer, Birch had set her up an account, so she logged into the Curio site, and began her first day online as a Curio, and she was pretty excited as she typed away.

In the village, talk was rife, as Celia, Lillian and Hatty went to work, and the gossip networks were in full swing, singing the praises of the Art Exhibition, which for Birch and myself was a big bonus. We had organised it, and our skills had been showcased to their fullest potential. There were critics, namely the Shrew Crew, and a few others, but the vibe for us was very positive. Waterside Galleries got a lot more visitors; to view the work of the village's second resident artist, Ellen had filled the whole shop with Chloe's art.

Chloe was busy getting serious about her sketching classes, which would run on the Village Green, through Tuesday and Wednesday. She was back to normal, almost as if the weekend had not happened, only she had a fixed smile no matter what she was doing.

The Summer Fete was Wotton's crowning glory, and Anthony and Edwina were busy, Samantha was mucking in, and the kitchen table was its usual big map, and stacks of papers, and Anthony had the day off to pack it, and move it all to the Church Hall.

Michael had borrowed the works van, and had moved most of it last night, and today, Lillian was alone with the two girls in the Tea Rooms, as Celia helped Anthony organise and set up the tables with mum.

Fete fever was in town, and the shops were making the most of it with extra stands and racks of gifts, and behind closed doors, debate of jam recipes and sponge cake recipes were a heated topic. It was infectious, Izzy had joined in, and created, as she held it up with pride, 'Scotch Pear Jam.' It was about 40% proof, and we loved it. Although a word of caution, stay out of the kitchen when she is cooking, the fumes alone get you pissed.

Monday night we all gathered in the kitchen, and made jam, Birch had made hers, which were now in the cellar out of sight, and Chloe had stuck a 'Toxic' sign above them. I made apple and seedless blackberry, Deli made an insane cherry jam, Chloe made what she called an artisan jam, which basically meant, she took all the left over fruit, bunged it in a pan and boiled it up with sugar, but I must admit, it tasted wonderful.

Between handling the exhibition stock levels, and ordering more items and helping with the fete, the days went too fast, all of us were spending every moment we had mucking in, because we also had the Curio tent to organise. Morty edited the art event footage like crazy in the loft, with spare beds up there, he would work then crash out, and then work again, as he made a short documentary of the whole thing, it was long hours of work for him, but he was enjoying it.

New posters arrived Tuesday afternoon, as we had some of Chloe's signed posters available on the Curio stand, with my books, and the last of the Curio Live merchandise, as well as a big advert for the Halloween event, billed as a gift for Wotton. Wednesday morning arrived, and I headed to the gallery, and the village was really busy, today was really hot, as a heat wave moved in, and everyone gave a sigh of relief, the last thing we needed was rain for the fete.

I smiled to myself as I left the gallery, in tiny shorts and a vest, with my sunglasses on, my dad always panicked if it even looked cloudy, and somehow, I had ended up being the same. Who would of thought it, and who would of thought how important this village had become to me? I sat on the wall of the Hunters, at one time in my life, this had been somewhere I would often sit, lost in grief and missing Birch, how different my life was now.

The Village Green, was really busy, Chloe had packed the marquee out for her first ever solo art classes, and Deli had been drafted in to help. Sophia was back, looking healthier, and was a little more coherent when she spoke, it was almost as if she had never suffered, and she had planned to step down when she next saw Prim.

Vehicles trundled around the green delivering to the fete site, and the marquee trucks were arriving to set up. Everything was going as normal, just like it had for all of my life, the players had changed, but it was business as usual. The only real change was it was my mum and Anthony in hard hats and yellow bibs, organising at the show field gate. I sat lost in thought when out of the blue, he appeared.

"Hi Abby." I came out of my dream state and looked at him, he looked different.

"Hey Nigel, love the jeans and sweatshirt, it looks good on you, how are you?" For the first time in my life, rather than stand in front of me, looking love sick, he leaned against the wall at the side of me, and watched the village.

"James had a few days off, so I went shopping with him, and did a lot of talking to him, he made me realise a lot."

I nodded and smirked a little, I was hard on James in the supermarket, probably harder than I had needed to be, which was probably why he never called me back.

"That is good to hear, you should get out more, and update your wardrobe, we are living in modern times now Nigel, this village has been stuck in the past for too long." He still fidgeted, but not as much, and maybe it is a horrible thing to say, but I was glad he was a lot less nerdy.

"Abby, there is something bothering me, and I need to talk to you." Oh dear, that did not bode well, I nervously looked at him.

"Okay, should I be worried?" He turned slightly, and looked a little afraid, and very nervous. He was clearly picking his words with care.

"Abby, I did a horrible thing to you, and yet you have still been very kind to me. I am trying to be braver like you told me, and so I want to say, that I am sorry for what I did." And, I did not see that coming, talk about out of left field? I smiled at him.

"Nigel we were kids, that is all in the past, leave it there." He shook his head, and looked at the floor.

"Abby it was wrong, I should not have done what I did... To myself, you know?"

I did, but honestly, I really did not want to think about it, he took a deep breath. He looked a little ashamed, and I felt this has to be really hard for him, I watched him as he looked for the right words.

"I talked to Doctor Dixon about it, and she agreed, I should make some gesture, and she is right. I need to apologise, as a proper gentleman should."

Bless him, this was killing him, but he was trying, and actually, it did mean something. I smiled.

"That is very noble and honourable of you Nigel, and I will accept that in the spirit it is given. That means a lot to me Nigel, and yes, it is the mark of a true gent, so thank you for that." He smiled; it was still weird to look at him.

"The truth is, I do think you are very pretty, but I only wanted to date you, because I thought you would sleep with me, and

I wanted that. I got carried away, and I am sorry for that." I nodded and understood.

"You have apologised with great sincerity, so let us leave it in the past, and not let it have an effect on our friendship." He gave another weird smile; his teeth actually moved a lot more than his fathers.

"Primula has decided to stay with her mother until after the fete, so I have gone home now, I will still see Doctor Dixon, it has helped me a lot." I gave a nod and looked across the green.

"Nigel, what are you going to do about Primula, you know she cannot treat you like she has been doing?" He nodded and swallowed hard; his voice softened a little.

"I know… She does scare me Abby, but she is also my wife, and I have a son. I want to be a good dad to Rupert. Doctor Dixon has helped me, and she also met my mother. They helped me set up a new bank account, I am going to give Primula an allowance from now on, my father has helped me with that as well. I talked to her last night on the phone, she is very angry with me at the moment. I told her she has to have therapy, and I want more sex."

I coughed, as I pulled my drink away from my mouth, I was not expecting that. You see this is why I never dated him, he actually wants sex with Prim, that messes with my head on so many levels it is unbelievable. I coughed and cleared my throat.

"Nigel, Primula is strong willed, and trust me, she can be very vindictive, you know, she may not do any of those things?" He smiled.

"I know Abby, but those are my terms, because I cannot live like I have been, I learned that from you. Abby, I do not understand you marrying a woman, I don't, but in a strange way, I am jealous that Doctor Dixon loves you so much. I want someone to love me that way, I think that would be nice."

And just when you think you have seen it all, BOOM, Nigel blows your mind. I smiled a soft smile and lowered my voice a little.

"It is wonderful to be loved so deeply Nigel, I hope one day you have that, I really do, but I have to ask you, do you honestly think Prim can love you like that?" He gave a sigh.

"Abby, I did not want to marry her, but I did, I talked a lot with Moon about it, and she made a lot of sense, it is not all her fault, she did the same, and so we must try to see if it can work, and if not... I know what to do."

Wow, he was really surprising me, God, Birch is bloody good at her job. Maybe she has helped him grow up a little, I know Moon did, holy shit, I saw her hip action silhouetted in the curtain.

"Nigel, Prim will always hate me because she thinks you loved me before her, every time she sees me it will cause problems, and I really am sorry about that, but I am going to fight her for the Chair. Honestly, it is not personal, I just do not think she is good for this village?" He gave a slight smile.

"Abby, you should run the council, you are the only one who understands what it is like to live here. You will be good for these people, they need a leader with courage, and you have that. Primula just sees it as a chance to make money, she will lose to you." I gave a sigh.

"If she does you will suffer Nigel, and that bothers me a lot." He turned, and looked right at me, as I watched him over my glasses.

"Abby, she is my problem, and even though she scares me, I have to face her. You have really helped me and I will never forget it, just win, I will be fine."

I was not convinced, but he was right, just as Birch had told me, it was his marriage and not my place to interfere. He looked at his watch, and then me.

"I have to go Abby, I promised to meet my mother for coffee, I am glad we talked." I gave him a nod and smiled.

"Me too, thanks for stopping Nigel, take care of yourself."

He gave his usual nerdy little wave and walked off, I watched him cross the road, and head towards the Tea Rooms. In a strange way I wanted him to be happy and succeed. I really had no idea if he would, but I guess my part was played out, and it was up to him now. Only time would tell, and I sat watching him lost in thought. In a way we had gone full circle, and it was time now for him to forge his own path, and I had to step back, and become an observer.

"Hey sexy lady, would you perchance want to date me?"

I smiled, there she was with her amazing long birch bark hair, and insanely beautiful green sparkling eyes, God, she looked good. I looked at her and thought about it.

"So... You wanna be my bird?" I gave a snort.

"I'm banging in bed you know, fancy shagging a sexy bitch do ya?" She gave a squeal, and danced on the spot, and clapped her hands.

"YES... OH GOD, I DO!" I started to laugh.

"So hot totty, where ya taking me?" She squealed with joy, and pulled me into her arms, God, we were so messed up? She pulled me off the wall, and linked my arm, as she giggled.

"The deli is open; do you want to get your lips on a hot kebab?" I giggled.

"Now ya fucking talking, I reckon you are going to be a mint bird you are." She squealed with delight, as we walked slowly up Church Rise, and I couldn't help but smile, she really had no idea how much I loved and adored her.

The greatest saving grace about this year's fete, was when you put the Curio's, G5, and Sweeties Retreat's staff together, you have more stewards than you know what to do with, and my mum was delighted, and so was I, because that meant loads of time for pissing about.

Friday was a day of insanity, but with Petal, Bess, and G5's van, and lots of drivers, getting all our jams, cakes, and flower arrangements, as well as all the promotional posters, and stock to the event was easy. Plus, we had the added benefit of a rat free Bess, with a stove and a small fridge. Bess was parked behind our tent, with the windows open and the curtains closed, so we could slip through the open back flap and make brews or grab cold beers. We were teamed up in groups, Nigel, Sophia, Molly, her husband Kenneth, and a few of her friends did their bit, and we pissed around and did ours.

The D&D Tent had special display boards on stands, and a long table of Curio t shirts, sweat shirts and other merchandise. All my books were on display, as was a large selection of Chloe's merchandise, except for the limited edition books, those had to be bought from the gallery. The tent became our official head quarters, and was filled with laughter and joy, and right next door, care of Anthony's great planning, was Hatty and Clive's art tent, so we could sneak beer and brews her way.

Security was top priority, and so Terry and Chloe stayed overnight and slept in Bess, which Chloe was really excited about, although, we very much doubted there would be much sleeping. We all came home tired and sweaty, and dived into the pool, and just relaxed, it had been a roasting day, and we were cooked. Our meal was a salad made by me, and burgers care of Edwina, who was the only one brave enough to stand dripping and naked in front of the barbeque.

Saturday started as always, sat at the island at six in the morning, wishing I had died in my sleep as I sipped coffee, with Deli, who looked equally as rough. Sophia had stayed over and was wearing her yellow security bib complaining.

"Well, it's not really designer, I am defo not putting this on Insta, yar, I have twelve thousand followers now, yar."

Birch drove to the Fete, we were all too tired to care if we died, so we made it there on time. I yawned as I was handed the clip board, as candidate I got the job of showing my organisational skills. I was happy to hand over at lunch, and take the rest of the day after my break in the D&D tent.

I headed up to the rest tent, it was sort of tradition to eat there, and I knew I would not get that much of a break if I was in the D&D tent, I had already signed a good dozen books just walking around. Birch was happy and held my hand, she was loving the sunshine, we walked in the cooler atmosphere, and as tradition dictates, we checked behind the end of the spare hay bales.

No one was there, and I was a little disappointed, what was wrong with the youth of today? All that was there was an empty space with a long stack of bales in the centre. I had learned a long time ago, never to sit on them, as you had no idea what cold damp substance would stick to your bum. Birch walked into the space, on the far end of the wall of straw, there was a gap, she peered round it.

I watched as she waved for me to come see, I gave a little giggle, was someone doing it in secret? She grabbed my hand and pulled me round, it was just a large dark empty space, I was disappointed, until she pushed me up against the straw.

"You have no idea how much I have yearned to do this Sweetie."

She pulled at my vest and slid it up, I started to giggle and grabbed hers. She lifted her arms, and off it came, but I was not fast enough, she pounced and was on my boobs before I could move, I leaned back into the straw, she was going wild. She was already undoing my shorts, as she kissed and sucked, and I felt my whole body come alive and burn with lust.

"Oh yes Baby."

My shorts hit the floor, and she pushed my leg to move it. Birch was going wild, kissing my tummy as she frantically, undid her shorts, her hand came up and two fingers inserted into me, as she kissed lower and lower, and I moaned and groaned, my whole body alive and tingling.

Her mouth reached me, and I was soaking wet. "OOH!" I grabbed her head, and pulled her into me.

"OOH GOD BABY!"

It was already hot in here, and getting hotter for me by the minute, I could feel the sweat starting to build on me. Birch reached up, as my vagina throbbed, grabbed my hands and dragged me to the floor.

She was so rough, and so wild, oh God, I was going nuts I was so turned on. She pushed me onto my back, yanked open my legs, and swung round, and dropped her sex onto my face, and plunged her mouth back into me. She was soaking as I dived upwards, between her spread thighs and felt the surges of electric as they shot down my quivering legs.

I felt wild, free, and uninhibited, and just lost all control, and ravaged her like an animal. I was so close to exploding, I had not been this turned on in ages, although it had been building, we had been so exhausted it had been well over a week. I felt the pressure build inside me, and just attacked her as hard as I could.

I was not sure how much longer I could last; her tongue was going at high speed, and the ripples of tingles were so fast, I could barely take it. Then suddenly she stiffened and flooded into my mouth, it just exploded out of her and I could not take it all. I thought I was going to drown, but it was so exciting and amazing, and my legs went rigid, and stiffened, and I pulled out of her and dropped my head to the floor as stars exploded in my brain, and my whole body convulsed.

I lay back gasping for air, shaking uncontrollably, I was climaxing out of control, and trying to breathe. Birch rolled off me, and lay back breathing hard.

"It was about time we did that Sweetie."

I gasped out a laugh, trying to catch my breath. I lifted my head and looked at her red face and breasts shining with sweat.

"You washed my hair." She giggled.

"And I think you broke my legs; I have no control at the moment." She turned her head and smiled.

"I love my life with you Deads, I am really happy you know?" I smiled, and tried to breathe.

"I was always yours; it just took me a while to realise it." She stretched out her hand as she smiled, and I reached out and held it.

"AND CUT!" I looked up, as Chloe appeared over the top of the hay and smiled.

"I just made a porno. God, you two are dirty bitches." I sat up.

"Holy shit, do you have built in sexdar, can no one around here screw in peace?" Birch giggled, and Chloe's eyes sparkled.

"I am going to label it D&D the best bits XXXXX." Birch sat up, and grabbed her vest.

"I stink of sex." Chloe smiled.

"All the best people do."

I stood up and grabbed my shorts, vest, and sandwich, and dressed. I was sticky all over, and covered in hay, but felt amazing, and I had a fixed smile on my face, Birch pulled me close and gave me a long passionate kiss. I cannot deny, it was a fantastic moment in my life, I had wondered if we ever would, and I was thrilled we had. We headed back to the tent, and Edwina looked at me, and pulled some straw out of my hair.

"God, you two are slutty bitches, and you stink."

I smiled; I was actually quite proud. Bess had a couple of washing lines attached from Bess's windows to the tent, on which Chloe had hung some old sheets, so we had an enclosed area.

I stripped and grabbed some bottled water, and a cloth, and Birch washed me down. The water was ice cold, and it made me tingle even more. I did the same with Birch and she gasped, it was sort of exciting knowing we were both completely naked in the middle of the fete, I really wanted to stay this way.

We dressed, sprayed ourselves with deodorant, and took front of house, and control of the stand. A lot of people were interested, but confused over our Halloween event, but we had arranged with mum on Monday to give a small presentation, after the guest speaker, so we told everyone to be there, as we would explain everything.

The rest of the day was spent selling items, talking about the event, signing things and also talking to the villagers about their concerns. I had a pad and pen and took notes about everything they mentioned, and Birch did the same.

We crashed into bed early, and slept deep, and woke up Sunday and once again headed for the site. Everyone kept looking at their watches, and then looking at Birch, but I had a plan. She was stood near the gates smiling at the guests as she welcomed them, handing them leaflets, when I walked up wearing my back pack, she turned to me and smiled.

"Isn't it lovely today, I can feel the earth all around me, I love the peace and serenity of mornings." I could see Chloe and Edwina looking nervous, I smiled at Birch.

"Yeah, about that Birch?"

She frowned, I reached up, and stroked her hair back behind her ears, and slipped off my back pack, unzipped it, and pulled out a set of noise cancelling head phones. I had decorated them with flowers, and then stuck bees on springs, so as the head set moved, they bounced up and down, off the flowers, like they were collecting pollen. I slipped them over her ears and smiled, she looked at me strange, and pulled one off her ear.

"Sweetie I cannot hear anything with these on?" I smiled at her.

"Exactly!"

She frowned and then understood, as the first bell struck, she let go of the ear piece and it snapped onto her ear, she smiled, the bells rang out, and she heard nothing. She yelled at the top of her voice.

"SWEETIE, THESE ARE WONDERFUL!"

I guess you cannot win them all, and as the bells rang, Birch smiled, and Chloe and Edwina punched the air.

"SCORE!"

"I LOVE PRETTY FLOWERS AND BEES!" Birch stood at the gates, with her crazy flowery bee infested head phones, and a big bright smile, and yelled at everyone.

"WELCOME, WELCOME, THIS WAY, HAVE FUN, AND THANK YOU FOR VISITING!"

With a happy Bell Twat free Birch, the day shot past, and we wearily headed home feeling baked, and lounged in the pool drinking beer, Deli looked beat but happy, Chloe was riding on a high after selling and signing a lot of merchandise, Edwina was sat with Luke coding on her laptop on loungers, and Deb's soaked in the hot tub, as Anthony and Michael stretched out on the lawn.

Monday was the last day of the event, but not for us, all this stuff has to be taken down and packed away, so we still had a couple of days hard graft to go. Today, we lost Edwina, and some of G5 as they prepared for tonight's presentation.

At four, the loud speakers, announced the guest speaker was to come on stage, and the field started to clear, and we went into packing up mode.

Morty brought the van up to the tent, and we packed and crated everything from the table. The large boards were to be moved to the stage, and were taken through the stage door to the wings, very quietly, as the guest for today was on stage, giving a motivational speech about how to balance your life.

With the van packed, we jumped into Bess and changed clothes, having been thoroughly wiped down by Birch with her baby wipes. It was sort of fun, but Deb's got way too excited when I wiped her down, which worried me. Finally, we all made it into the back stage area and waited silently, the speaker was not that bad. Birch constantly pointed out his weaker points, I was just glad I had taken her head phones off.

Dressed once again in a business suit, and holding my notes, we all got ready for that final moment when the applause started, this speaker was not as long as some, which aided our cause as it gave us extra time. I took a deep breath as he came off stage with a smile, feeling he had done good, and headed for his dressing area, and I watched as mum walked back up to the mic.

"Ladies and gentlemen, as promised, the candidates of Dixon and Dixon, will now provide a presentation of their plans for a new village event. Please welcome to the stage, Abigail and Jemima Dixon and crew."

The applause started, and Birch took a deep breath.

"Here we go again Sweetie."

Together, we walked up the steps through the wings, and onto the stage, and faced three thousand people. Was this my future, it was starting to look like it?

Chapter 17

My Village Home.

With Birch at my side, we walked out onto the stage, and up to the microphone.

People were stood up applauding, and I waited for them to stop and settle, before I smiled, and faced them all.

"Ladies, gentlemen, visitors to Wotton Dursley."

Behind us figures dressed in all black as skeletons with white bones painted on their clothing, came on stage and started to set things up. The back of the stage was dark, so it did look like a lot of skeletons were assembling things, the audience tittered, I ignored it, I hoped Birch would not notice.

"At the last meeting of the Parish Council, a newspaper article questioned the ability of Doctor Dixon and myself to run and organise the council because for want of a better word, we were lesbians, married ones at that. In response to the article that was supplied by my competitor, Primula Wallace, I told all of you that before the vote, I would show you that I was the only person capable out of the two of us. Since that time, others have questioned as to whether or not I have what it takes. There have been a few questions and doubts about our abilities, so tonight, I want to give you all an insight as to who I am, who Doctor Dixon is, and what you get if you elect us."

A skeleton walked up to Birch and tapped her on the shoulder, Birch turned and squealed, and grabbed my arm.

"Sweetie, I don't like skeletons." The audience started to laugh. Deli the skeleton, handed me the control button, as Birch shrank back behind my shoulder.

Deli walked down the steps off the stage, as the audience chuckled, and ran to the back of the hall, I smiled and looked at Birch.

"Call yourself a doctor, and you are afraid of old bones?" The audience all laughed, and I smiled. I looked at the back of the room.

"Deli my dear skeleton, will you lower the lights please?" The lights began to lower, and the large screen behind me came into view, and a film started to play.

"Ladies and gentlemen, last weekend a few members of this village had the privilege, of taking a coach to London, to visit the very first event staged by D&D Events. It was the book launch and exhibition of the artwork of one of this village's resident artists, behind me on the screen, you can see the footage as I talk of how it was organised and set up, and as you can see, it was a lot of hard work and a lot of organising either online, or in person."

The video showed Birch and myself on the phone, on computers, taking deliveries and talking to a wide range of people.

"This event has been planned and organised behind the scenes for a few months now, and what those lucky enough to visit saw, was the result of all that work. If you do not believe me, go to London and look for yourself, it will be there for at least four more weeks. A few months ago, Doctor Dixon and myself with our dedicated team planned and executed the Curio Live event, which was shown on live stream all over the world, and it has to date raised over ninety million pounds for the Curio Life charity, by the end of this year, we expect to see our first centre open."

I turned and looked back at the video of the old building with all the builders working away. I turned back to the audience and stepped back, and Birch took over.

"These were great events that were very successful for us, but they were not in the village where you could see them up close, and so we looked closer to home. This weekend we teamed up with the Parish Council, and put our people to work for your benefit. As you saw, at the fete, there were more stewards, and faster organisation than ever before, and it has run smoother than previous years. The truth is, we are here standing before you, and yes, we are a same sex married couple, but as we have said in the past, there is a way to take the village forward with a modern approach, that will still adhere to the traditions that have been the standard for hundreds of years, and we think we are just the people to do it. Our rival for the vote, has promised discounted tokens, parking meters, pay and display and a new playground on an unsuitable site, which we oppose, she has as yet still not provided details of the Wotton Dursley Woods Project, and it is very clear to us, that whilst loyal members of this community, worked really hard this weekend, she has yet again been conspicuous with her absence. I would like to ask, where is she today?" Birch stepped back, and I took the mic again.

"If truth be told, if you vote for us, you get a whole lot more than just two, what we offer is this." At the back of the stage a row of skeletons walked on, and Birch covered her eyes.

"Sweetie, could you not have picked ghosts or clowns; I don't like skeletons?" The audience laughed like crazy, as Deli came running down to join the line.

"Jemi, they had to be skeletons for the event, I told you this before." She shook her head and everyone laughed, I smiled and faced the audience.

"At the Summer fete D&D had a stand, and for those of you who wandered in you would have seen this." I pressed the button, and on the large screen behind me, a giant poster appeared, for Curio Carnival Wotton.

"At our fingertips and standing behind us, are some of the most creative and skilled members of this community, you see skeletons, I see a future, a future where everything looks as is, but with the right people organising, we can bring something amazing to Wotton."

I stepped back and Birch uncovered her face, and stepped up to the mic.

"I really don't like skeletons... We have spotted something no one ever has. Wotton has a spring fair, a May Day parade, an Easter week, even a harvest market, and the Christmas weekend, and as we have seen, the biggest and the best Summer Fete for over a hundred miles. All the traders rely on them for vital income, and all the residents for education and entertainment, but there is one missing, and as our bone covered helpers have suggested, what about All Hallows Eve, Samhain, or Halloween?"

There was a murmur around the room, the light on Birch narrowed and the place was almost completely black, so just her face was lit up. She smiled.

"It is dark, it is creepy, and there are things that go bump in the night."

"BANG!"

Everyone in the audience jumped in their seats, and then there were gasps, as a pirate ship rose out of the stage, and glowed in a sinister light. Birch lowered her voice.

"There be mischief afoot, and skulduggery, cast out ye lines and see what ye drags into Wotton."

The audience were spell bound, as more skeletons rose out of the floor and walked to the edge of the stage, there were gasps of amazement. Birch gave a wicked grin.

"Watch out for the witches, they fly low tonight."

There was a loud cackle, and from the back, a group of witches on their broomstick flew across the room just above the heads of the audience, from where I stood watching, it was pretty impressive. The audience gasped and looked around, Deli ran back down the steps and up to the back, and suddenly everything disappeared and the lights came back on, and I stood smiling at the mic.

"Ladies and gentlemen, we are delighted to present to you the Curio Carnival Wotton, organised especially for this village on October 27th. There will be a full sized circus on the show field, a giant fair, carnival attractions, a special creation on the Village Green, traders from all over the country, face painting, a scary Wotton fancy dress for both children and adults, and to cap it all off, a very special light show on the streets right in front of, and above you, the only question is, will you be there, or are you too scared?"

I stepped back, and the audience cheered and applauded. Birch moved onto the microphone with a big beaming smile.

"We are happy to take questions, if any of you have some?" Norman put his hand up, and Birch gave a nod, he smiled a huge smile, as he stood up.

"That was bloody fantastic, are you saying you can do that outside?" Birch gave a wide smile.

"I am happy you liked it Mr Merryweather, and yes, we will put on a full display and have witches, flying above the green, and I don't know, possibly skeletons dancing up Church Rise. It will be different, and it will be special, so for those of you who are here tonight, tell everyone, because no Halloween party will match what we have in mind." He looked very chuffed. Henrietta stood up with a smug smile and raised her hand.

"You called Primula for offering a bribe to the voters, but isn't this just the same?" I stepped up to the mic.

"No Mrs Dennison it is not, I know you have no intentions of voting for us, and yet you will still be a welcome guest. This is not a vote purchase, this is us proving we are up to the job, and we like open honest transparency, if we mess this up and fail, people will see it and not vote for us." Mr Harold Brice stood up; he was a critic of just about every event held.

"What I want to know is who is going to pay for all this, we are not rolling in funds, and that ridiculous light effect must cost money?" I whispered to Birch who it was, and she nodded, and smiled at him.

"Mr Brice, firstly this will pay for itself. It is being arranged and financed through D&D Events, it is sort of being sponsored, and so not one penny of Parish Council funds will be going into this. The way we see it, if it works and brings yet more tourist to Wotton just before Christmas starts, that is good for every business and every person, and I am informed, you are a wholesaler of high quality meat, and there will be a huge barbeque on care of Phillip Morrison, who I believe you supply. So if this works, you will also financially benefit" He looked stern, and looked around the room.

"Fair do's then, if it is costing us village folk nothing, I cannot object." I took over the mic.

"Look everyone, you know me, and you know Dr Dixon, you have seen us sweat at the fete, you know we work hard for the village, yes there is gossip, and most of it wrong. All we want is to show you that the fate of the village is safe in our hands, and also show you how much we love this place and want to protect it. This is an experiment, something this village has never done before, if it fails, the village loses nothing, but if it is a success, then we add it to the agenda, and you can vote to continue it. The thing is, let us try, let us show you that we mean business and want to improve and protect Wotton."

Walter Parkinson stood up, smirked an arrogant smile of superiority, as he looked up at me like I was dirt.

"Isn't this all just smoke and mirrors, to bluff your way into the council by pretending you can do it with cheap light shows?

You are fooling no one here, the future of this village lies in more capable hands." Birch moved up, and pushed me to one side and smiled.

"I take it you are Walter Parkinson, our local MP, it is strange I have never seen you considering I own one of five of the largest residential properties in this village?" He shrugged.

"I am a busy man, I hold a surgery, you are welcome to come." Birch smiled.

"When is your next one, I do have a matter to discuss?" He gave a sigh, and his tone changed, as if he was addressing an idiot.

"It is always the first Monday of every month at seven pm." Birch looked at me, and then turned back. Edwina walked up and handed her a large folded piece of paper. Birch smiled.

"Seeing as you are here, and the local MP of these people, and I have your undivided attention, could you explain this to me, because I have been led to believe that this is a conservation project? Actually, I did scan it, so to make it easier, I will put it up on the screen."

Deli ran back up to the back. The lights dimmed a little and the back screen lit up, I lifted my hand and clicked the button, and the plans for a forty house luxury housing estate came into view, showing all of Wotton Dursley Woods completely destroyed and built over. Where there should be a playground, there was a road onto the new estate. There were gasps all around the hall, and he looked panicked.

"Where did you get those from, those are restricted plans?" I leaned into the microphone.

"From who councillor, this is our village, and we all should have been involved in this, and yet we have not, because those plans are only available to people on the top floor of the council offices in Oxendale, and none of the public have access there?"

There was a sudden outcry as people turned, and started to ask some very awkward questions, my mum walked up to the mic and looked at the plans in Birch's hands. She was very angry, I saw Bradley in the audience smile, and nod at me, Ellen gave a sneaky thumbs up. My mum shouted into the mic.

"MR PARKINSON, EXPLAIN WHY I AM NOT AWARE OF THIS?"

Birch and I stepped back as the crowd fell silent and sat down, mum glared at him with very angry eyes.

"Something this big should have been submitted to the council long before it ever went to Oxendale, explain yourself now?"

He looked very angry, and a little terrified, he smoothed back his hair, took a breath, and looked at mum.

"Madam Chair, I am the local MP, and I do not need to explain myself to anyone." Mr Brice stood up.

"Bullshit, you work for us you greasy twat, we voted you in, and I can bloody well tell you now, I for one will be voting you out." Everyone applauded, and he gave a nod and sat down. I leaned into the mic.

"Mr Parkinson, do me a favour, let Primula know that she may not get her pay off, as I personally will move heaven and earth to prevent this, be it as Chair or not."

He scoffed, turned, and stormed out of the hall, I saw Marjorie just below me, and she smiled and gave a nod. My mum stepped back and I stood with Birch.

"Ladies and gentlemen, thank you for your time."

The row of skeletons behind us bowed and then ran off the stage. Marjorie stood up in the shocked room and started to clap, and I smiled, and suddenly everyone was up clapping. I turned and left the stage as the skeletons ran back on, and started to set up for the awards presentations. I had done the best I could, now I had to focus on the event, and make it the best this village had ever seen.

Back stage everyone changed quickly, Luke, Morty and Edwina were still on stage taking apart the gear, Petal was already parked at the stage door, ready to be loaded, and as things came off the stage, we all pitched in and carried our equipment to Petal. Finally, we were packed, Petal was locked next to Bess, and we walked back, into the Hall.

We got mobbed straight away, as Birch and myself talked of our opposition of the housing plan, and explained how we would defend the woods, and leave it untouched, although, we both thought the paths needed to be improved. Around us Chloe, Deb's and Deli did the same. Marjorie came over with Milton, and she looked at me.

"How did you find out? Abigail, even I did not know, and if I had, I would have stopped it straight away." I understood that, we have had our fights, but this was one thing I knew she would back me on.

"To be honest Marjorie, none of us knew anything about it until Prim mentioned it, and when we looked into it to find out, because if it was a conservation project, I would have teamed up with her to support it, there was no trace anywhere of anything. We used our contacts to get the truth, and luckily someone at Oxendale council also disagreed with it, and let me just say, we managed to acquire the plans through that channel, we got them Friday, and here we are today exposing it. Prim knew about this a good few months ago, if you ask me, she was exploited and used. There again, knowing what it was, she still tried to hide the truth, and I had to expose her whilst exposing him." Marjorie understood.

"I would have acted exactly the same as you two did, you have no need to fear, what you did was absolutely right. I am just sorry that yet again my daughter in law, has failed this family. If there is a fight, I will be giving you every available help possible, this has to be stopped." I smiled.

"We completely agree." She nodded.

"Interesting event you have proposed, I must admit, I am very curious, and Milton is quite the fan of the circus, how much will the tickets be?" Birch smiled.

"Everything will be free, as we said, this is a trial, no one will pay anything." She looked at Birch.

"You have too much money, more than sense I fear, but my family will as always support an event for the village." Birch gave a nod of appreciation.

"All we want is to show the village we are up to the job, if they don't think so after that, they can vote against us."

It felt like forever until it was all over, and we had helped pack up all the chairs. We jumped into Petal and Bess, and the van followed us home, and there was our next problem, now we had to unload. Everyone again pitched in, and we carried all the boxes back into the store room, and put everything back in order, and then staggered into the house and collapsed around the island, as Izzy wearing her first prize ribbon for jam, poured us drinks. The booze was obviously appreciated.

I lay face down on the cool marble top of the island, I was overheated, mind fried and ached all over, in short, I was done. Birch rubbed my aching shoulder blades, and it felt wonderful.

"I will run us a bath Sweetie shortly, you can soak your aches away." I groaned with pleasure, at just the thought.

"Oh yes, I need to not feel anything, plunge me in deep hot water Baby please?" She gave a chuckle, and lifted her drink.

It was too hot to eat, even though the sun had finally gone down, I was just too exhausted to bother. As we headed upstairs Deli came to the top of the stairs, and smiled at us.

"I have started running your bath for you, I thought it might help?" Birch appreciated it.

"Are you jumping in with us?" She looked puzzled; I gave a slight chuckle.

"Deli, you only have a shower, honestly, at some point, everyone jumps in our bath, it is yet another of our weird customs, you are quite safe, it is not a gay thing, just hot soak and talk, it is far too late to fire up the hot tub." She gave a nod.

"If it is okay, I would love to soak." Birch smiled.

"The taps are the straight end."

Sliding down into the water was heaven, I leaned back into Birch, as Deli climbed in, and I just closed my eyes and relaxed, my body felt so sore. Deli watched as Birch rubbed my shoulder with the sponge.

"You two are a pretty amazing couple, you know, it does not bother me, I know I am safe with you. If I am honest, I just don't see you as gay or lesbian or whatever the hell people think. I once got kissed by a girl." I opened my eyes.

"Really, what did you do?" She shrugged.

"I kissed her back, I figured if she wanted to kiss me that much, I should at least give her that. I did not do anything else, but to be honest, it was a nice kiss." I smiled at her.

"I think that is sweet, and it was nice of you not to reject her, she must have really felt safe with you?" She gave a smile, and looked down at the water.

"I still think I am straight; I mean kissing is not the same as the rest. I am not sure I could do that, but I do not know, maybe we all change as we age?" Birch gave a sigh.

"I think we do, this is what I mean about Curio, I think sexuality is fluid, hell, life is fluid, as we grow all our tastes change, and we embrace different things. I know people who have started out as teenage lesbians, and through their twenties they were bisexual, and by the time they hit forty, they called themselves straight. I like that, I like that when we understand ourselves, we learn we can change and be whoever we want to be. Why label it, societies labels say one thing about who we are, but we are so much more than our bed partner." I looked at her and smiled, as she looked at me.

"I think we all understand that better than any, I most certainly do, my biggest regret is I never acted sooner with Birch. I was so busy clinging to what I thought society expected me to be, I almost lost sight of who I actually am. Deli, don't label it, just be you." She smiled at me and gave a nod, and lifted the sponge.

"Every day with you guys, I think I become a little more the me I am meant to be." I winked at her.

"That is probably not such a bad thing then."

Up the road, Nigel sat in his living room with his phone on speaker, he had emailed Primula and told her his terms, and she was not happy.

"I will not go to therapy; I cannot believe you want me to sit with her whores and talk about me. There is nothing wrong with me, I am perfectly fine. If you insist on this Nigel, you will be pushing me away. You say you want to sort this out, but how are we going to do that, are you going to start therapy as well?" He gave a long sigh.

"I am having therapy already; I see someone once a week and have for a month. Primula things are not right, this is not like other marriages."

"There is nothing wrong with our marriage, it is perfectly fine." Nigel looked at his phone.

"Primula do you actually love me?" There was a long drawn out silence, and then she spoke.

"What has love got to do with anything, people live together and get along fine without love?"

"So, you don't love me at all?"

"Nigel, where is all this coming from? It does not matter; it does not change anything at all. We had a child, bult a home, and we will become respected in the community, and I would say even revered by everyone. Love plays no part in any of that." He felt a jolt to his system as he listened to her.

"It matters to me Primula; it matters a lot."

"Oh, here you go, you are acting like a child again, Nigel you need to grow up and sort yourself out, I cannot believe we are even talking about this. I have told you again and again, you need to start facing life for what it is, no one loves like that anymore, it is irrelevant today. What matters is that we are seen as a perfect couple, who people look up to." He shook his head and felt he was getting upset.

"I am not a child, I want someone to actually care, why are you not capable of that?" He heard her as she sighed on the other end of the phone.

"You are being ridiculous, when I come back, we will sort all this out, and you do not need her whores to help you. What you need is to stop acting stupid, and let me sort out everything."

Nigel pulled his hands to his face and rubbed it, he was getting upset, and he needed to calm down. His voice got louder, as he looked at the phone.

"I want to be loved, I want someone to care, and I don't want you back." He realised what he had blurted out and froze, the phone was silent, but he could hear her breathing on the other end.

"FINE, GO TO YOUR SLUT, I MEAN, THAT IS WHAT YOU REALLY WANT, ISN'T IT!?"

The phone went dead, and he let out a desperate gasp, and sat back in his seat, and closed his eyes. He had said it, finally, he had said it, and it felt like a huge step and a large pressure had left him.

Having soaked and talked in the bath, until it started to get cold, we got out, wrapped up in towels, and then sat on the bed drying each others hair with the dryer. Deli was really relaxed as she leaned back whilst Birch brushed her hair as she held the dryer, and blew the hot air across it. She looked so happy and gave a happy sigh.

"I love your idea of living, you know, here I have encountered some pretty weird stuff compared to my life before, but to be honest, it all makes a strange sort of sense. You are all so different to everything I know, and yet to be included as I have, I love it, I just love that I can let go and just be me."

That was kind of the point of us, we refused to follow the line of what was said to be normal, and we found a way to live to the ideals of a moral life, but true to ourselves. Are threesomes immoral if everyone is feeling pleasure, does watching your partner be sexually gratified imply abnormality if it actually turns you on? With Birch I have done things that have given me great pleasure, but they were things I never thought I would do. Hell, I was married to a woman, which most definitely went against anything fourteen year old me would have thought.

Birch had always told me at university that every opportunity was a chance to learn who we really are, and therefore should never refuse it. Her philosophy was try it and see, and if you don't like it, and you did not enjoy it, stop and go do something else. I had lived like that for four years, and without looking or trying, I had found a level of happiness I never thought possible.

The strange thing was, I stopped being what was expected, and what I was told was right, and just followed my gut feelings, and out of nowhere happiness came to me. I suppose it fits the old adage, if you want something, stop looking, and if it is meant to be, it will find you.

It was late and we were all tired, Deli yawned, and decided it was time she was in bed. She thanked us and headed to her room, and Birch and I curled up in bed. I was so tired and still ached, but it felt nice to feel her snuggle up and slide her hand onto my boob. I wriggled back into her.

"This is nice, I am so tired, it feels like for weeks we have been full tilt, it will be nice to slow down a little." Birch gave my boob a squeeze.

"Yeah, it will be nice when we take our holiday, I am really looking forward to it." I frowned, and turned to look back at her.

"What holiday?" Birch lifted her head and looked at me.

"You know, our holiday at Sunny Bank next week, I am sure I told you, I have a week off?" I shook my head.

"No Birch, I had no idea, I mean, I am really excited though." She frowned.

"I am sure I said something... So Chloe, Deb's and Deli do not know either. Crap, I was so busy I forgot. Sweetie, I rang Seth and he is stocking up for us, I thought a rest in a quiet place would do all of us good. I did ask Edwina, but she wants to have some time alone with Luke, so she is staying here, and Anthony is going to spend a week in Spain with Michael, so I arranged for all of us to have some time off."

I suddenly felt excited and happy, and as I lay in my pillow with Birch wrapped around me, I smiled until I fell asleep.

Tuesday my mind was preoccupied, as we packed up everything from the fete for another year. Once everything was boxed, we shipped it out to storage and spent a good few hours sweating, as we moved a line of endless heavy boxes.

The news we were going on holiday lifted everyone's spirits. We were tired and worn out, the exhibition and the start of our campaign for chair, with the Summer fete had burned us all out. Birch was smart enough to see we needed rest, and so with higher spirits, we finally returned home, tired and exhausted, but satisfied we had done our best for the summer fete, and not let the village down.

We had done our best, but as I lay on my bed, I did not care, I was going back to that magical place, where I walked, and talked, and saw a completely new side to Birch, and actually, it was the side of her I loved the most. I was going back to Sunny Bank, and it felt epic.

Chapter 18

Holiday Preparations.

The thought of going away from Wotton is uplifting, and I feel a buzz of happiness inside me, and it was infectious. Chloe who has already been sat with Deb's and Deli excitedly telling them all about it, raved as I walked around the house with a fixed smile.

Edwina was excited, because with Anthony and Michael, heading abroad, and the fact that Izzy was at her club most of the time, meant she had the house all to herself, for just her and Luke. I sat at my computer with my calculator going through the stock levels for the gallery, Anita text me to let me know she was heading there, and I ordered more stock to be shipped directly to the gallery. I increased it a little as it was all sale or return, so for us it was not a problem, we would sell it all on at other events.

The Summer Fete had been a massive success, we had sold a lot of books and merchandise, the Curio Live merchandise was almost out of stock, so with a big beaming smile, I worked out where we stood after the event. I sat back with a big gasp and looked at Edwina.

"We just went into profit, it is not much, but in one week all the expenses are covered, we did it, we made Chloe a face to be known, and we have actually managed to do it all within budget and are now earning profits. The exhibition is our first D&D success." She sat back in her chair.

"Did you ever doubt it, I didn't, my sister is brilliant. I never for one second thought it would flop?" I felt a little surprised by that.

"It cost a hell of a lot to set up, I will not deny, my pulse was going a few times. I mean, I know Birch did not care, but I did, this was my first big venture into the world of business, honestly, I was panicking a little bit." She lifted her cup and took a drink.

"You know I find that crazy, Abby you went to Uni and did literature, business, and public relations, and you aced the lot with distinctions all the way. I have thought a lot about it recently, your dad who was an arsehole at the time, drove you hard and put a lot of pressure on, but you also grew up seeing him work at home. I know you; you just absorb everything around you and take it all in, think about it, you more than any of us, were the only one to organise the gallery event, it is why Birch and myself sat back."

I had never really thought about it that way, I had stood at the side of his desk and watched him asking questions, and I had forgotten how he would sit and explain what each column meant, and how the figures told a story of how healthy the business was. I had also sat with him many times, and watched how he meticulously planned the fete, and all the detail of each plan he made, had I really learned from watching, and did I need to thank him? Edwina smiled.

"You did good Abby, and you made my sister very happy, I am never going to forget standing on that carpet, and just watching her, as overwhelmed as she was, react to all the fans that wanted to talk to her. Honestly, once we were all inside, I went into the toilets and bawled like a bitch, it was sick and soppy and messed up, but that alone made me so happy. Although, Abby, promise me you will never ever tell her about that?" I chuckled.

"Your secret is safe, I had tears in my eyes watching her too." She gave a sigh of relief.

"You know I was disappointed when Birch told me you were not coming to Sunny Bank." She gave a dreamy smile.

"Abby, I have given Sam the week off, and I am going to laze around naked and horny, and just lavish adoration and attention on Luke. We will have candle lit dinners, and lots and lots of naughty filthy dirty times together, I am going to show him what being married to a nymphomaniac is really all about." I laughed.

"Okay I cannot argue with that, it is pretty much what I did with Birch at Sunny Bank, I am really looking forward to it, I think I need it." She gave me a nod as she sat in her chair watching me.

"Abby you are burned out, and you have lost weight. It is fun doing all the things we do, but seriously, eat and rest, your ribs are showing, and that is not good. Take care of yourself Abby, Birch needs you."

It is funny isn't it, everyone looks to Birch and me, but the real mother hen in our coup, is Edwina, and actually, she is pretty good at it. I lifted my empty cup and got up and then stopped as a thought occurred to me.

"Have you guys set a date yet, you have been together for two years, so there is no real reason to wait, is there?" Edwina gave a sigh.

"Abby I really loved your wedding, it was stunning and beautiful, but if I am honest, I really do not want that, the problem is my dad. He is really excited about it, I just want something quiet and close, with you guys and G5, I do not want a huge family thing, with aunties and uncles, and all that crap." I could understand that.

"We did what we did, because it was here, I think if it had been anywhere else, it would have been a lot smaller. You know Birch got this place registered, well the arch is, you could do it here on a much smaller scale." She smiled at me.

"You just want another wedding, you are not over yours yet, I can see it when anyone mentions it, you go as hyper as Chloe." I giggled, as I grabbed her cup and walked to the door.

"I loved my wedding, and yes, I will never forget it, she looked the most beautiful I have ever seen her. No, I will never forget how special and precious that was to me. You will see." I walked through the door and headed to the kitchen; Chloe was bouncing on her seat.

"Abby, tell them about the swing and the stream, and how cool the moors are, they have no idea have they?" I smiled.

"Chloe you just did." Deb's and Deli giggled.

I made a coffee and headed up to my room, and logged into the Curio site. It has become something that really gives me joy, as I read all the comments other people put up to show support. I was not disappointed as I saw Deli, had been on and been really busy, and she looked like she was really embracing her role as a new Curio house member.

Her comments were really sweet and supportive, and she had a lot of people comment how nice she was, that is a good thing, the supporters had embraced her fully, and I was glad about that, I really liked her. Being alone and feeling loved up and happy, I hit my photo albums, and put on a slide show of my wedding and honey moon, I sat back in my chair, crossed my legs, and hugged my coffee cup, as I watched the pictures appear on the screen.

There was a soft knock on my door as I sat smiling, I turned my head and looked, and saw Anita, she smiled.

"Am I disturbing you; I can come back another time?" I shook my head and waved her in.

"I am not really doing anything important; I was just reliving a happy memory." She walked in and saw the screen and smiled, as she sat in Birch's chair.

"How many times have you watched those now?" I gave a little giggle.

"Nowhere near enough... It probably sounds soppy, but I love just sitting here and remembering it all again, it was a very happy day for me. Anyhow what can I do for you?" She leaned back in her chair.

"I was in the area, on route back from the gallery and I wanted to drop in and just thank both of you for the bonus. You know you did not need to, you paid me more than enough." I swung in my chair.

"You worked really hard, and you also brought a lot of great publicity, we both appreciated it, to be honest, you earned it. I was completely exhausted after it all." She gave a sigh.

"Seriously, you guys work at a fast pace, I struggled to keep up with you both, I was knackered when I got back home. I think it has taken me a week to just sleep it off, I still feel jaded now, I have no idea how you do it." I nodded; I understood her. Birch walked in unbuttoning her blouse.

"Hi Sweetie, hi Anita." I looked up, and she came over and kissed me softly, I smiled as she pulled away and noticed the pictures.

"Yep... I am at it again... We are just talking about how tired we were, I think we broke Anita." Birch looked at her.

"You do look tired, were we that bad?" She shook her head.

"It is a quicker pace than I am used to, but to be honest, I really enjoyed it, I think it is the first time I have really been tested and stretched. It killed me, but it did me good. I have no idea how you all did the Summer Fete, honestly, I was going to come but I just slept all weekend." Birch understood her, we were both feeling it. She looked at me.

"Have you invited her to join us?" I shook my head.

"I wouldn't before speaking to you." Birch smiled at me.

"Sweetie, it is your house too and we have room." She turned to Anita.

"Why don't you join us at Sunny Bank for the week and just rest, we are going there for that?" Anita looked really surprised.

"I would love to, but third wheel and all that, would I not be in your way?" I shook my head.

"Chloe, Deb's, and Deli are coming too. Come on join us, we are just going to relax and chill out in the sun, and get a lot of rest." She looked at Birch.

"If it is alright, yeah, I would love to join you all."

It was settled, Anita was joining us for a week of doing nothing, and being an all girl party, I was excited all over again.

The best thing about a bank holiday Monday is, it makes the week shorter, as you drop back into routine, but with only four days to wait, we had just about enough time to go from happy to crazy by Friday. The week was spent busy doing everything that was needed to be done, cleaning the house, and best of all, choosing what clothes to take, and pack. We hit the supermarket for beer, more beer, and crisps, and spirits, and some food, and new clothes. It was a crazy week of racing around, and swapping clothing ideas.

On Wednesday afternoon we had a slight break, as Deli's mum Janis arrived with her husband James. We spent the afternoon and evening in the garden, Deli showed her around the house, and James told us how much he appreciated what we had done for her. They were lovely people, and very kind and caring, it was very clear where Deli got it from. They loved the house and once again, were surprised to see how clean and orderly everything was.

You know, I do love that for some bizarre reason people just assume we are all messy, and so it is always nice when they comment. We had a lovely afternoon sat in the sun, Birch, Izzy Anthony and Deb's arrived home at five, and met them, and after a few more coffees, as Deli had to get ready for work, we hugged them goodbye and informed them that they were always welcome, which Janis appeared very happy about. It was clear, that Deli was very close to her mum, and it was yet another sign of how well Deli had fitted in and was relaxed living here.

Thursday was packing day, and I spent the day sorting through my clothes. Birch arrived home and packed shorts, and vests, and one jumper, that was it, I had flares tops and six pairs of shoes, and Birch just laughed at me.

"Sweetie, I want to spend the week naked, why so many clothes?"

Actually, it was a really good point, so I tipped my suitcase all over the floor, and then dug through the pile, and kept the shorts, vests, and one pair of flared pants and a top. I took one pair of plimsoles, and a pair of boots. I ended up packing more towels than clothing.

Chloe wanted to sleep in Bess, which okay I get, but it did appear a little bonkers as well. It did seem odd considering we had an amazing four bedroom house to stay in, but she was really into the idea of camping out. The good news was that Deli was going in the twin room, so if she did get fed up, we still had a bed free for her.

Deli was worried about Sophia, Molly was back, but she reassured her that she was going to be fine, and she was actually going to go and give Prim her letter, so she could quit the position of vice. Izzy and Edwina both promised to keep tabs on her, so by Friday, Deli was a little more relaxed, and she did promise to keep her Insta up to date, so Sophia was happy with that.

Having had a few days of cloudy dull conditions, we all had our fingers crossed for good weather. Birch had to work, she had a late morning therapy session, so I loaded mine and her laptops and bags in the back of Petal ready. She did have a few online sessions she would be doing mid week, one of which was Nigel, Birch was happy with his progress.

Chloe was louder than ever, as she piled art supplies and all Deb's and Deli things into Bess. Anita arrived and parked her car in the garage, and grabbed her case out of it, and loaded it into Petal. We had food, booze, and the will to use them, and our spirits soared as we closed the vehicle doors and locked them, and then headed to the kitchen for coffee, and waited until Birch was free.

At one o'clock the call came, and I let Anita take the driving seat, as she could do the first leg of the drive. I plugged my mobile power lead into the lighter socket, set it in the phone holder, and we were ready. Debs was driving the first leg for Chloe, so Deli sat in the back with the little raisin, strapped into her baby seat. We all hugged Edwina, the gates opened, and we were off towards Wotton, to grab Birch.

Bess was looking wonderful, with big bright flowers on her sides, and the completed artwork done by Chloe, which was delicate and ornate scrolling vines of tiny flowers. On the front she had painted 'Artisan Life', and inside, she had decorated the tops of the windscreen with tiny little multicoloured tassels. Both Petal and Bess had a new flag on the ariels made by Chloe, which were rainbow striped with the words 'Gypsy Life' on them. They flapped away in the soft breeze, but somehow, I thought they would end up like mum's scarf, which was so worn away, it was just long strings of colour now.

Birch came out with an excited squeal and jumped in, Alex and Megan stood smiling and waving, as Anita pulled off. I handed Birch a hanger, shorts and a vest, we hardly made it to Station Road, before she had her pants off, folded and threaded through the hanger with an excited giggle. We zoomed along Pilkington's and headed for the motorway, my phone rang, it was Chloe, I put her on loud speaker.

"Birch, cute ass ha, ha, ha, ha, show us your boobs?"

Birch screeched with laughter, took off her top and pressed them up against the back door window, squeals of laughter came from inside Bess, and Birch sat back giggling and pulled on her vest top. This was going to be a fun week.

Getting around the car park, that is the M25 took time, but once we hit the M4 we whizzed along until suddenly the phone rang, it was Chloe, and she sounded distressed.

"Holy fuck guys, we need a pit stop... Oh fuck, I am going to Yerk!" Birch leaned over from the back.

"Sweetie is everything alright?" Chloe made a strange gurgling sound, and Deli moaned in the back.

"Oh my god, I have every window open and it's not working. ABBY SAVE ME!" I looked at Anita alarmed.

"Christ, what the hell is wrong?" Chloe coughed and retched.

"RAISIN... GUYS WE ARE DYING, IT IS SO TOXIC."

The services were four miles away, so we prepared to leave the road, it came into view and Anita indicated. I looked back to see them right behind us, Birch was sat with her hands on her face, I smiled.

"Remembering something are we?" She violently shuddered, and moved her hands away from her face as I giggled at her.

"Sweetie, make them park as far away as possible, I cannot smell that ever again."

Anita chuckled, as she pulled into our parking spot, Bess came up behind, I got out and stood in front of the empty parking spot. Deb's parked up, and all the doors burst open as Deli and Chloe hurtled out, and got as far away as possible. I could smell it instantly as it wafted out of Bess. Birch sat in the back of Petal, with one hand on her mouth and wafting with the other, as she bounced on her seat.

"Sweetie, Sweetie, close the door I can smell it"

She suddenly violently wretched. I did try not to laugh, but failed. Chloe was ten yards away on her hands and knees, on the grass gasping in clean air, Deli looked green as she stood bent forward with her hands on her knees, breathing in clean air next to Chloe.

Deb's climbed out and rolled her eyes, as Birch fled from the back of Petal, in the opposite direction looking green. Anita walked calmly round chuckling, she stood at my side as Deb's climbed into Bess, and undid little Jenny's seat clips.

"Ooo, did you poo poop?" Jenny gurgled, and shook her wrists.

She laid out her mat, and put it on the floor of Bess, then laid Jenny down and undid her nappy, Anita put her hand to her mouth, and wretched.

"Oh god that is awful."

She turned away and shuddered. Birch, who was a hundred feet away, danced on the spot, when she saw Anita's reaction, and waved her hands in front of her.

"Sweetie, I don't like it."

It took several minutes to change Jenny, and I suggested we take a break, and go grab coffee. We all headed inside to the café, and sat down and relaxed with a drink, allowing our noses to clear and our stomachs to settle before the return. By the time we headed back to the vehicles, and after some shopping, the day was warming up and the sun was coming through the clouds. Chloe bought a dash fan, and plugged it in to her lighter socket, in her mind, it would blow all fumes into the back.

Deli was driving and Deb's was in the back, I gave Anita a break, and she climbed into the back of Petal, as Birch moved up front. Anita bought some shorts, so did a quick change and took her jeans off and lay back on the cushions, and smiled as she relaxed. Once we were set, I turned on the engine, and we set off again, and headed back onto the M4 heading for the south west.

Birch relaxed with the window open, and turned on the music, and we bobbed along at fifty miles per hour, singing to Avril. She slipped off her shoes, and lifted her legs onto the dash, wearing a very happy smile.

As I drove, I talked with Birch of our last visit, and all that had happened, Anita lay in the back as she listened to us and smiled. Birch had been so hurt and so upset last time, and we had spent the whole week talking and recovering from Katie and her malicious trick. Birch gave a sigh, and leaned back in her seat, it was getting hot, as the sun burned down on us through the window.

"Mum said their meeting after the shares thing was pretty icy. Katie is very unhappy her freedom has been greatly restricted. I must admit Deads, I did not like her attitude, if you ask me, she has not changed much."

Anita closed her eyes and let her mind drift, I looked at Birch as she stared out of the window.

"Birch we are married now, and we are both aware of her, honestly, do not worry about it. We have D&D and Anita; we can do anything we want free of her." Birch nodded.

"Unless of course it is something to do with your writing. Deads, she can still make things hard. Look at my graduation, I never realised, honestly, I never did, and yet she managed to book you an event that clashed. That was deliberate, but she made it look like she was doing her job, and doing what was right for you, but now we know different." I shook my head.

"From now on I will check everything, you know Birch, I have never done it, but I can be unavailable if I want to be. I have always carefully chosen what I will and will not do, which is why I do less press at times. If Katie tries to pull anything, and I even get a whiff of it, I will dig my heels in. Birch, I know after the gallery I can do more in your mum's company, and one day maybe I will, but for now, I am happy working with you and Anita." She turned to me and gave me a smile.

"I know Sweetie, I must admit, I think Anita, you, and me, make a great team, I enjoyed the exhibition, I think we did a good job, I want to do more with us three." I smiled at her.

"We will, we have forever to plan and do just what we want, now let's get to Sunny Bank and forget all this and just relax, we have one more service before we leave the motorway, so we should stop and change drivers." Birch tapped my phone and dialled; Chloe answered.

"Are we there yet?" I giggled as Birch leaned into the phone.

"Not yet Sweetie, we are pulling in for another driver change, and I need a pee."

I saw the sign and indicated, I looked in the mirror to see Bess indicate behind us, my vest was sticking to my back, I felt happy knowing I could get out, and into the fresh air.

We headed down the slip road, as I braked and slowed down, one corner of the car park was lined with trees and I headed for them, I knew some shade would be greatly appreciated. I pulled on the handbrake, and turned off the engine, I felt like I was cooking, Bess pulled in at our side, I lifted my legs, and slipped off my pumps as I opened the door, my feet were on fire.

I jumped out, and walked onto the path and across to the grassed area under the tree, and just felt the warm ground under my hot feet, I could feel the heat pulling down my legs and going down into the floor. Birch has often talked of this; she calls it earthing. Chloe looked red faced, as she flopped on the grass under the tree at my side.

"I want so badly to be naked, even these clothes are too much." I looked at her.

"It is not much further; we should be at Seth's in about an hour or so after we leave."

Anita was still asleep in the back, she looked warm but cosy, so I left her and sat under the tree. Birch went in the cooler and handed out cold beers to those who would not be driving, Chloe sulked at her cola.

"Wish I had driven second now."

Deli giggled looking very red in the face. With us sitting right in front of the vehicles, we left all the doors open to let as much cooler air in as possible. It was surprisingly hotter here than it had been in Wotton. I pulled my hair up into a ponytail, I could see a few people looking at us, we had been recognised and they were pointing, and talking. I sat down to hide behind the cars, no doubt, pictures would appear on Insta today?

Deb's sat on the grass with her back to the tree, and fed Jenny, she placed a fine woven cloth over babies head, to hide the fact she was feeding her, I thought it was ridiculous, how could people be offended? I think breast feeding is natural, and honestly, if someone is offended by that, they need to grow the hell up.

I will not deny, I am not planning on kids, but if I did, I would breast feed, it is the most natural thing on the planet. It baffles me how people think these days, they are happy to sit at home and watch an animal suckle off its mother on TV, but one glance of a human doing it, and they are offended, seriously what is wrong with these people?

Deli disappeared and arrived back with a warm cheese and onion pie each, and at that point my stomach gave a loud whine. She woke up Anita, who staggered out of the back of Petal looking groggy, and was handed a pie and a beer. We sat in a large circle munching away, having a little picnic, and it felt quite nice, there was a soft breeze, nothing too much, but I enjoyed the feeling on my bare toes as I wiggled them.

The time came, and Birch gave the word, and we slowly got up, looking a little more our own skin tones, and less red than we had been, and we all trooped back across the grass and climbed in for the last leg to Sunny Bank.

Within minutes we were on the motorway, motoring along, and soon headed onto the slip road. We bobbed along, driving down country lanes, and through small villages and towns, and I started to get excited.

Birch was getting as excited as I was, as she smiled at the wheel, yes, I was looking at her because we were going so fast. I was terrified to look at the road, and what was even scarier, was Chloe was keeping up with us. Birch glanced at me, and smiled.

"Deads, we will be at Seth's in just a few minutes, let Chloe know to slow down, and follow me into the side parking area." I opened my phone and rang Deli, she answered straight away.

"Deli, tell Chloe we will be arriving at Seth's shortly, and we will be pulling in, Birch is going to start slowing down, we will pull into the side of the road and park up, so watch for the signals."

"Okay Abby, I will tell her, who is Seth?" I smiled.

"Seth and his wife Mable are two of the sweetest people you will ever meet, trust me you will love them."

"They sound lovely, Abby, I am feeling really excited, I have not been away for years, thanks for letting me come." I chuckled.

"You are one of us now, it is not a case of us letting you, this is a group activity." I laughed as I ended the call.

"Deli says thanks for letting her come." Birch smiled, and Anita leaned over between us.

"I must admit, I am getting pretty excited about seeing this place." Birch indicated and began to slow down.

"Sweetie, it will be a while before we get there, because there is no way Mable will let us off her property until she knows everything about all of you." I gave a chuckle, as I saw the turn in ahead, she was not wrong, Mable was about to ask a million questions.

We pulled in, and Birch turned off the engine. I opened the door and jumped out onto the grass, I walked around the back, as Chloe pulled up, and I opened Petal's back door to let Anita out, she looked at the old cottage and gave a gasp.

"Oh, wow this place is stunning."

I grabbed the sliding door of Bess as Chloe killed the engine, and opened it up, it smelt of baby talc and a slightly ominous odour, Debs looked relieved to have fresher air blown in as she unstrapped little Jenny.

Once out, and on the grass, with most of us now shoe free, Birch led, but this time she was not fast enough, and Seth, with Mable wiping her hands on her pinny came scuttling out, wearing huge smiles. Birch hugged Seth and Mable dragged me down and into a bear hug.

"Oh Abby, it so lovely to see you again, congratulations, we are so thrilled for you two."

I cannot deny, I think she is adorable, all the others waited as Mable crushed Birch with another hug, and I gave the happy smiling Seth a huge hug, and then together, we introduced the others one by one. Mable had been at the gallery, so she honed in on Chloe, and gave her a hug and told her what a wonderfully, and creative talent she was, she also recognised Anita, she had seen her with us all the time, and had watched the press conference.

Raisin was a big hit and Deb's beamed with delight as Mable made a huge fuss, and then finally she gave a big smile to Deli, and pulled her into a hug.

"You must be the new Curious, welcome to my home, all of you, come on it is a lovely evening, we shall sit around the back and have coffee, have you eaten?"

I still giggle that she calls us the curious and not Curio's. She never surprises me how up to date she is. As always, she wanted pictures, I am sure Cissy Benson would be peeved to see Mable had again beaten her to meeting the Curio's first. We all posed as a group and alone with her, she was really cashing in on our first meeting to get the best pictures possible.

We sat in her lavishly planted garden around her table, on an assortment of garden chairs, and we had coffee and sandwiches and cake. Seth and Mable loved the company, and asked a million questions, and what was meant to be a short stop for supplies, turned into three hours. It was lovely just sitting there watching and listening to the bees, as they jumped from flower to flower. Without knowing, I had slipped into the slower pace of relaxation, lulled by the air and the gentleness of Seth and Mable.

There is a quality to Devon, that I have not encountered anywhere else before. It is impossible to be in this county and not want to just sit back and relax. Life here runs at a different pace, and the people here have a calmness to them, that just radiates out and seeps into you. If this is the effects of south country living, I will be happy to throw off my clothes, and walk in peace through the fields, meadows, and woodland forever, it is I feel, a writer's paradise

Finally, we stood outside next to the cars, having been hugged what felt like a million times, and Birch gave a beaming happy smile as she unlocked Petal.

"Let's go to Sunny Bank."

She gave a cackle of a laugh as we climbed into our vehicles, and two minutes later, she indicated with a little squeal of excitement, and drove away, on the short drive. I felt very excited and happy, and simply could not wait another second.

Chapter 19

Building Bridges.

My heart leapt for joy as we turned off the road, onto the hedgerow lined drive, and drove up it. At the top, we turned right, and swung round to face the house, and I felt a jolt of happiness shoot through me. Birch smiled as she saw I had unclipped my seat belt before she had even pulled up.

"We are back Sweetie."

I turned to her as she applied the hand brake, her eyes were dancing with joy, I had a fixed grin on my face.

"I love this place; it will always be my most special place on earth." Anita leaned over between us and looked at the house.

"Oh wow, guys, this place is beautiful, so this is where you came to hide from the world and fix what Katie did, hell, I don't blame you, I would live here forever?" Birch smiled as she opened her door.

"One day we will."

She climbed out, and I grabbed my door and swung it open. I jumped out, and the others excitedly climbed out of Bess. Deb's and Deli stood side by side and admired the house, I walked with Birch to the front door, she slipped out the key, and stopped as she put it in the lock.

"Deads, there is something I must do first." I frowned at her, not understanding what, I just wanted to get inside. She turned the key and turned to me.

"I love you Mrs Dixon." I frowned.

"I know, I love you too baby... What the... ARRRGH BIRCH WHAT THE FU...!"

She just bent slightly, grabbed me, and before I understood, she swept me up into her arms, and lifted me off the floor, and carried me squealing through the door. She put me down with a big smile, and then kissed me.

"Welcome home my lovely and beautiful wife." I felt my heart flutter, and smiled as she broke apart.

"I have wanted to do that since we were married." I had to smile; she really was so surprising at times.

We were inside, and the first job was open all the windows and doors to air out the house. I ran through to the kitchen and grabbed the key off the hook, and unlocked the door, I just wanted to see all of it.

I pulled the door open, stepped out and just breathed in the air, as I looked at the table, picnic bench, and the barbeque and the swing set. Oh, it felt so nice and so familiar. She came out behind me and slid her hands around me from behind, and put her head on my shoulder. I leaned onto her.

"I am really glad to be back Birch, this place is so special, that week here alone with you, is one of the best times of my life... Hold up, what is with the big shed?"

I looked up the garden towards the moors, and just past the bridge and the big apple tree, there was a brand new wooden cabin, with large smoked glass doors. Birch turned and kissed my neck.

"It is two things in one. In the glass side, there is a bigger hot tub than we have at home, and the other side is a sauna, I thought it would be nice to steam, and then jump into the hot tub. I enjoy sauna's when they are not filled with eucalyptus to the point they almost blind you." I gave a giggle.

"It kills germs you know, because we cannot have bad bacteria on our bodies?" She giggled.

"I frigging hated the twiglet; I am glad we pissed on her." We started to laugh as Chloe came out of the back door.

"Fucking ace, I am sweating my tits off."

She dropped her shorts, stripped off her top, and jumped down into the fast flowing stream, and lay back in the ice cold water panting.

"YIKES! It's freezing, but oh God, this is nice."

I could almost see the steam coming off her hot skin as it cooled, she smiled at me.

"Try it." I shook my head.

"Nope, that is too extreme for me, I will paddle when the cars are unloaded."

The next thirty minutes was the usual arriving madness, as we emptied the cars, and carried in all the food and beer, and allocated rooms. Chloe was still adamant she was sleeping in Bess, so I left it. Deli did not mind the single beds, so took the twin, and Deb's and Anita took the doubles. I helped Deb's set up the travel cot as she changed Jenny on the bed.

"I can see why you love this place, Abby; it is really beautiful." I smiled as I stood up.

"It is, but that is not why I love it... This place is where the truth and the real Birch comes out. It brings out in her another quality, and that is the side of her I love the most. I guess I am the only one who has ever seen that side of her, and I am not sure she will show it with everyone here, but honestly Deb's, the last time we were here, I fell hopelessly in love with her every day." She smiled at me.

"I know what that is like, I felt that when Jimmy and the band took a break, and we lived a normal life. I saw other sides to him which I really loved."

"This is a special place; it does bring out the best in people... Right, that is set up and ready, so it is time for a beer and to soak my feet in the cold stream, come on, put her down for a while, and come join us, bring your monitor."

Ten minutes later, I sat with my feet in the cool stream, holding a beer, as I watched Birch walk slowly around the garden. It was still pretty hot even though it was getting quite late, and the sky was starting to darken. It felt nice to cool my hot feet down.

Deli and Anita sat cooling their feet too, we were all hot and tired after the drive, I slid my feet out, and walked along to the bridge, and crossed over it, and walked towards Birch. She noticed me and smiled, I walked up and slid my arms around her waist.

"Getting reacquainted with the place I see?" She took a deep breath, and smiled.

"Am I that obvious, and there I was thinking I was being elusive?" I giggled and pulled her closer.

"I am sorry Sweetie; I get all nostalgic when I come here." I smiled.

"I know, and don't apologise, I really like this side of you, I find it super attractive." She smiled, and pulled me closer into her.

"I really love this place Deads, it has such a strong place in my heart, I didn't realise it showed so much."

"Only to me, I guess I see the subtle changes in you others do not notice." She leaned in and kissed me softly.

"I am really tired, and you look pale and wiped out, are you ready for bed Deads?"

I slipped back and took her hand, and walked back towards the house, I looked at the others sat with their feet in the water as they talked,

"We are off to bed, leave the back door unlocked for Chloe, sleep well guys, we have food and beer in the fridge, help yourself."

I walked up the stairs as Birch followed holding my hand, and we walked to our room. I closed the door and pulled her close and kissed her softly, she smiled as we broke apart, I lifted her top, and pulled it off, and pushed her back towards the bed, and then pushed her back on to it.

She lay back with a smile, as I pulled down her shorts, and then stripped, and crawled onto the bed, her bright eyes danced with happiness, I crawled over her, and slowly kissed her, she breathed in.

"Oh Deads, I am so happy." I kissed the side of her neck and slid lower, she closed her eyes and took a long hard breath.

"Oh Deads, Sweetie, yes."

Downstairs, Anita walked around the living room and looked at all the pictures on the wall, Deb's sat behind her sipping her drink, Anita turned and smiled.

"I can see why Jemi brought her here, this place is a huge part of her life." Deb's gave a smile.

"Abby told me that she thinks this is the place where Jemi ended and Birch began. She said, this place is the truth of who she really is, and that alone here with Birch, she saw a part of her no one has ever seen, and she fell in love with her all over again." Anita turned and walked over to the double seat and sat opposite her.

"I felt so guilty when I found out what Katie had done, you have no idea how wretched it made me feel inside? I really admire them Deb's, they have something so unique, it should be protected. I was glad when they came back, and things were fixed. I watched them together and it was so clear to me that they were special, I will never understand why Katie even thought she could damage them." Deb's lifted her glass.

"Katie got too big for her boots, she started to believe her own myth. I see it a lot around the band, they get some nice comments and a bit of attention, and they are like junkies on crack. They crave more and more, and will step on anyone, even their loyalist friends to get more. They always end up the same, alone, looking into a glass, or shooting shit into their arms. They walk on too many people, and at some point, even their most ardent admirers see them for what they are, attention whores, and they turn against them. Katie created her own downfall, and in doing so, she lost two of her greatest friends, she is a fool, and if I hadn't been pregnant, I would have beaten the shit out of the bitch." Anita smiled.

"You are a good friend Deb's."

"I am Abby's best friend, I have seen what she has gone through, and I have seen the struggle she had to come to terms with her life. She loves Birch in ways we will never love, and I will always protect and defend her from the likes of Katie, as I would any of the Curio's." Anita gave a soft nod.

"Before I started working with all of you, I was pretty intimidated, you are all so close, it can be off putting. I really wanted to work with Abby, she has such potential, but the crazy thing is, I became the student. I am learning a lot from her, and also all of you, I fccl a little less intimidated now, and a bit more at ease." Deb's gave a chuckle.

"You were seen as the enemy at Curio Live, it was never going to be easy Anita. I just hope you understand now, that in a way it was an initiation to make sure you were on the level? No one really hates you; we were just looking out for those two, and you got through it."

Deb's got up and walked through to the kitchen with her glass, she stopped at the door.

"Anita relax, and just let go a little. Just be yourself, and go with the flow, I think this week may just surprise you." She walked to the sink, placed her glass down, and came back into the room.

"I am off to bed, I will need to feed Jenny and change her, you should get some sleep too, you still look tired." Anita gave a smile.

"Yeah, I will soon, sleep well Deb's, and thanks for talking." Deb's gave a smile, and click the latch on the door to the stairs, and Anita sat back, lifted her wine glass, and sipped as she relaxed lost in her own thoughts.

I woke up, and screwed up my eyes, and rolled over, I forgot to shut the curtains last night, and I was almost blinded. The bed was empty, as I reached out to her. I opened my eyes, I was awake now, so I thought I had better get up. I headed downstairs, and into the kitchen, as I yawned. I grabbed a coffee, the kitchen door was wide open, and it was a bright sunny day.

I stood outside the door holding my mug with two hands as I sipped it, and blinked in the bright light. Anita, Deli and Deb's, were doing Yoga, Anita had on a tiny top and tight yoga pants, she has a great ass. Deli was wearing her usual red knickers, and Deb's like the rest of us was naked. Baby Jenny, was in her carry crib, under the tree in the shade, and Chloe was sat on the garden wall with her pad, sketching, there was no sign of Birch.

I walked slowly along the side of the stream towards the bridge, and suddenly out of the workshop, a long stack of wood appeared, and almost hit me. I jumped back, sloshing my coffee all over the floor, Birch appeared, with her hair in a pony tail, wearing a baseball cap, the wood was on her shoulder.

"Hi Sweetie, did you sleep well?" I watched as she walked down past the bridge, and carefully slipped the wood off her shoulder onto a couple of sawing horses.

"Birch, what the hell are you doing, you almost knocked my head off?"

She turned and smiled, she had a pencil behind her ear, and a leather tool pouch thing round her waist, but apart from that she was naked. Her eyes sparkled as she gave me another big smile, and announced with pride.

"I am making another bridge; I found my granddads plans." I walked closer as she pulled out her tape measure and slipped the pencil out from behind her ear.

"Can you actually do that?"

She turned her head and looked at me, God, she looked

gorgeous, and to be really honest, just seeing her doing this, really turned me on.

"Sweetie, I told you, I am good at woodwork, you can help if you want?"

I shrugged, I had never done woodwork, I looked at the four heavy posts she had already painted in black stuff and had bolted to the sides of the stream walls with metal brackets.

"I am not sure Birch; I have never really done anything like this before." She walked up to me, and her eyes were dazzling, she gave me a quick kiss.

"I will teach you, and it will make you even hornier than you are now. By the way, your vagina is sparkling, wow you get wet really fast." I felt embarrassed as I looked down, crap, she was right, I could see the moisture glistening in the light.

Helping involved more me sitting, fantasising and sipping coffee, whilst Birch used a big round electric saw, which she called a 'Chop Saw' to cut the ends of her wooden lengths, into angles that fitted together. Watching her bend over, to cut wood, was getting a bit much for me, as I tried to puzzle out why the hell I was becoming so turned on?

I finished my coffee, but needed more, so as she walked off for more things, I walked up the path to the kitchen, as I passed the workshop, she leaned round the door.

"Sweetie, could you help me a minute?"

I turned and walked in, as I came through the door, she grabbed me, closed the door and pushed me up against it, and started to kiss me really passionately, I wasted no time, kissing her back, is it insane that I was so turned on?

Anita sat back on the blanket, Deli lay back, and gave a gasp.

"That was really good, I have not done yoga for years, somehow tomorrow I think I am going to ache like hell." Deb's looked at her and smiled.

"At least you have a flat stomach, I need to get rid of this." She grabbed a chunk of flesh and pulled it out, and sighed, Anita gave a chuckle.

"Deb's you just had a kid, give it time, honestly if you keep up with this, it will tighten all your muscles up and tone you out again."

Chloe at some point had moved, and was sat on the deck in front of the new cabin, sketching, opposite where we had been working. Deb's looked at her belly and gave a sigh, she turned, walked over, and peered down at Chloe's pad.

"Holy shit Chloe, you cannot draw that?" Chloe looked up.

"Why not?"

Deb's pointed at the picture of me, sat on a saw horse, with my legs up, and spread, masturbating, as Birch bent over in front of me sawing wood. Deb's shook her head.

"Chloe, Abby was not doing that." She gave a nod, and looked at the picture.

"No... She was thinking it though." She gave a big smile to Deb's, who gave her a strange look.

"Please tell me you have never drawn anything like that about me?" Chloe just smiled, and Deb's stepped back and gave a huge gasp.

"Oh my god, what have you drawn?" Chloe giggled, as she looked at the panic on Deb's face.

"I have only done one, and it was Jimmy, taking you forcefully from behind." She gasped with horror, and went beetroot.

"Chloe, you cannot draw stuff like that." Chloe shrugged.

"Why, has he never done that to you?" She went even redder.

"Well... Yeah, we have done that." Chloe shrugged.

"So, what is the problem, if you want it, I will give it you when we get back, I am sure Jimmy will love it?" Deb's shook her head.

"You scare me at times... Where is Abby anyhow?"

I was lay back on the work bench trying my hardest not to scream out with joy. I could not take any more, Birch was working on me in a way I had never known before, and I could feel myself losing control. My back arched and I started to shake.

"OH MY GOD... OOOOOOOOH BABY!" Chloe smiled.

"It sounds like she will be out in a second, see I told you she was horny." Deb's squirmed, and wiggled her legs.

"I wish Jimmy was here." Chloe giggled.

"Did you bring the Creamy with you, go and use that?" She squirmed a little more.

"Will you keep an eye on Jenny for me?" Chloe laughed.

"Yeah, go do your Creamy." She looked at Chloe and pointed.

"DON'T DRAW ANYTHING, I WILL CHECK!"

Chloe sniggered, as Deb's hurried off to her room, she stood up, folded the sheet over to reveal a new clean piece, and walked over to the crib, leaned on the apple tree, looked down at Jenny, and she started to sketch.

Hot, sweaty and very red in the face, I staggered out of the workshop with Birch, and headed for the kitchen with wobbly legs. Birch tittered as she went back to work, cutting pieces for her bridge. Anita and Deli lay back in the sun on the blanket, Deli turned her head to look at her.

"It is a shame there are no men around here, I fancy a holiday fling, god, it has been ages since I was touched." Anita smiled.

"Yeah, it would be nice, I could use some loving attention, I am sick of doing all the work myself, it would be nice to have someone else do it for a change." Deli looked up at the sky.

"It is a shame there is no pool here. When I get really hot and bothered, I swim it off, it really helps at times." Chloe looked over at them.

"There, is a river down there, just follow the path, it is pretty deep, we swam in it last time, it is a nice spot, there is a big rock you can jump off." Deli sat up, and looked at Anita.

"You up for a swim?" She sat up.

"I have never swum in a river before, is it safe?" Chloe glanced at her.

"We all lived, how dangerous can it be? Grab a couple of towels, Debs went off to wank, but give her a minute and she might join you."

As Birch went back to work, and I made brews, Deli ran up to Deb's room, there was a lot of deep moaning from the other side of the door. Remembering her previous encounter with Abby and Chloe, as they charged into Deb's room, she felt too embarrassed to knock, so she grabbed a towel, and met Anita in the garden. They left together following the path, and soon found the deep spot in the river.

I sat back on the sawing horse and watched Birch, every now and again, she would need help, so I would hold the wood down, whilst she put in the brass screws. It was fun to watch her, she really was very good, and I could see how the bridge was identical to the other one, wow she is clever, and so good with her hands, and not just with tools.

We took a break at lunch time, and sat with Chloe and Deb's, and had cheese on toast, which tasted so much better outdoors. Birch wanted a barbeque at dinner time, so feeling warm and sweaty, once we had eaten and rested, we got stuck in with the bridge. The platform supports, and the hand rails were in place, all it needed was planking over, Birch stood behind me, and showed me how to use the chop saw, and as she screwed the boards down, I cut more.

She would occasionally look up and smile as she saw me measure the plank, mark it and then cut it, and hand it to her. Slowly she crossed the stream to the other side. By four o'clock it was finished, and she did a quick run over it with a belt sander, so it was smooth and splinter free, and then went to get a can of stain to preserve the wood.

I must admit, I loved this, watching her plan and build, and being a part of it was a real thrill. For me, who knows nothing of these things, knowing that I played a role in building it, just like she had on the first bridge with her grandfather, was actually pretty cool.

For years to come, people would cross the stream to the sauna, and it would be partly because of my assistance to Birch, I had been a part of something that would last. I watched as she painted the bridge, starting on the sauna side and moving backwards, she even stood in the stream to make sure every part of it was protected, and it looked beautiful.

I took a picture, I mean, she has a great ass, so why not? When she was done, I helped her pack everything away in the workshop, and we cleaned up. Anita and Deli returned, and Chloe had taken care of the raisin, and changed her bum, but she was close to feeding, so a relaxed looking Deb's sat, and after wiping her breasts down to ensure they were perfectly clean, she fed her.

I loaded up the barbeque, and spent ten minutes getting it going, inside the house Deli and Birch worked on side salad, while Chloe sorted out the meat, and gathered the plates with Anita, and everything we would need outdoors, it was hot and sunny, and perfect for eating outside.

It was nice to see that Deli and Anita, had now made it to full nudity, as I laid out travel rugs to sit on. Chloe added the burgers

to the grill, Birch came out with glasses and Deli grabbed the
ice box with three bottles of white wine in it, and we were pretty
much set for the evening, it was Saturday night, and we aimed to
enjoy it.

Back in Wotton, Nigel sat with a glass of wine, he had drunk
quite a lot of wine on the boat with Moon, and had got into the
habit. Now he was home alone, with Prim away, trying to sort out
his head, he had bought a few bottles. He was sat deciding what
he should eat, he was even considering ordering take out, when
the doorbell rang.

He got up, and put his glass down, and walked through into
the hallway, and opened the door. Sophia stood there holding a
letter, she looked surprised, but smiled.

"Nigel... You are back, I am happy to see you, how are you?" He
smiled, he liked Sophia, she was always nice to him.

"I am alright, would you like to come in?" She looked a little
nervous.

"I have a letter for Prim, she will not like me when she reads it,
yar, and I have a taxi waiting, yar. I need to eat soon." He looked
at her, and gave another smile.

"Primula is not here, she is at her mothers, but I will give it to
her if you want me to?" She shook her head.

"I have to give it to her; will she be back soon, yar?" He
shrugged.

"I do not know, she rang and we had a row again, I am not sure
she will come back. I was going to order food and probably watch
a film, but I do not know what to order, what do you think I
should get?" She gave a sigh, and looked behind her at the taxi.

"I am having chicken, I cook it myself, you can have some if you
want, I always make too much?" He looked a little uncertain, and
dithered a little, Sophia smiled.

"It won't be horrible, Deli showed me how to do it, if that is
what you think, yar?" He shook his head.

"Sophia I cannot cook much, you know what, I would love to eat
chicken with you, give me a minute, and I will grab a coat."

Feeling quite happy and relieved, he went inside and grabbed
his jacket, and emptied his wine glass. He grabbed a fresh
bottle, and slipped it in a bag, then grabbing his wallet and

keys, he came back out, locked the door and walked to the taxi with Sophia. He opened the door for her, and she slipped in, he followed, and she smiled at him.

"I am glad you are back, I missed you, and I am happy your face is better, yar?"

I lay back on the pillow and looked up at the sky.

"I am stuffed, Chloe that was an amazing burger." My stomach was absolutely full, and all I wanted to do was lie back and watch the sky. Birch gave a loud belch and giggled.

"I am going to use the sauna after, and steam all this good food out of me, are you going to join me Sweetie?" I turned my head and looked at her, she was lay on her side watching me, her eyes dancing with devilish delight, I gave a smile.

"I might, although I would rather just chill in the hot tub." She gave a giggle.

"We steam, and then jump in the tub, it will be fun." Her eyes twinkled at me.

"More fun than the workshop?" She gave a little giggle.

"Maybe?" I nodded.

"Okay I am in." God I am so weak and pussy whipped, but how could I say no? She gave a happy little chuckle, and lay down at my side watching me, I turned back and looked at the sky.

"Oh god I am so bloated, I think it is going to take a lot of steam to sweat out Chloe's burgers."

Nigel sat in the chair in Sophia's living room, as she stood at the cooker, and fried chicken basted in herbs and spices. At her side potatoes and vegetables bubbled in the pans. He poured out two glasses of wine, she only had a small low table, and a lot of large scatter cushions. He watched her carefully, and took note of how natural she was, how calm he was sat in another girls flat. If Prim found out she would go insane. He lifted his glass and sipped the wine.

"Thank you for doing this Sophia, it is very kind of you." She glanced back and smiled.

"I like to cook yar, and we are friends, and I missed seeing you when you went away. Prim is mean to you and it is not right, why do you let her?"

She grabbed the pans and drained them, and then lifted two plates off the rack, and tipped out the potatoes and the veg. She placed the pans carefully into the sink, and then dished out the chicken. His stomach whined, it smelt so good, and he was really hungry. Sophia carried the plate over with a knife and fork, and handed it to him, he slipped it onto his knee and started to eat.

Sophia plopped down in front of him on a large cushion, and put her food on the table, she lifted her glass.

"I can only have one glass of wine, otherwise I get carried away, yar." He gave a nod, as he cut into his meat, she smiled.

"Is it good, yar?"

Nigel was loving it, Prim cooked nothing like this, it was so tasty, he nodded as he chewed his chicken.

"It is really nice, I really appreciate it, thank you." She tucked into her own.

"You did not answer yar, why do you let her hurt you, I do not understand why? I think you are a nice person, yar." He sat up and chewed, as he thought about it.

"Sophia, Primula has a very bad temper, you never see it coming, and when it does, she is very strong, and very scary. I hate to admit it, but she frightens me. I am sorry, I am not much of a man really." She chewed, and thought about it, and then looked up at him.

"You are a man; you had a stick when I kissed you, yar." He almost choked, and coughed as a piece of potato stuck in his throat, Sophia smiled.

"I felt it on my leg." He cleared his throat and took a sip of his wine.

"Primula does not approve of that too much." Sophia stopped chewing, and stared at him.

"Does she not have sex, yar?" Nigel shook his head.

"Primula says sex is only for making babies, and she does not want anymore." Sophia stared at him; her eyes were really wide.

"Prim is angry because she has no sex, she should have sex, I love sex yar?" Nigel shrugged.

"Well Primula does not, and trust me, nothing can change her mind. She is always accusing me of wanting to have sex with Abby, but it was not true, I just wanted sex. I wanted her to have it with me, but she went mad and blamed Abby." Sophia nodded and she lifted up more chicken.

"Abby is pretty, she is my friend, she is an influencer, yar? I would have sex with Abby, she has the right proportions to be nude." He smiled.

"So you are like Abby, you have sex with girls?" Sophia shook her head.

"I just like sex, a girl makes me feel safe, and it is as much fun as with boys. I like sex with everyone, it stops the bad dreams, yar." Nigel looked at her, a little concerned.

"I did not know you had bad dreams; do you have a lot?" She nodded.

"It's alright, my brain gets broken if I do not take my tablets, but they make me dream, when I have sex, it makes them go away. Deli is my friend; she helps me to remember my tablets. I kissed her once, but she only likes sex with boys, yar?" He nodded.

"Yeah, she is very pretty." Sophia smiled.

"That is why I kissed her... Am I pretty, I want to be pretty enough to be an influencer, yar?" Nigel swallowed his chicken.

"You are really pretty; did you not know that?" She gave a giggle.

"I have great boobs, I think they are pretty, my Insta friends like them when I wear a bikini, yar?" She lifted her wine with a big smile.

"I got twelve thousand likes, yar?"

I staggered out of the sauna, as red as a lobster, gasping for breathable air, Birch giggled inside.

"Sweetie, we should sit longer."

I inhaled the cooler air and slipped into the hot tub, which was nice and warm, but not the ten thousand degrees Birch was currently sat in. She giggled as she came out and saw me lay back with my head on the side, the sweat pouring down my face.

"Oh Sweetie, was that too hot?" I looked at her, she was red faced too.

"Birch, if I stay in there much longer, I will become so thin, from dehydration, I will be able to slip out under the door." She giggled as she slid in at my side.

"I am not sure Chloe will last, we better watch her, if she falls asleep in there, she will evaporate." Anita staggered out and took a long deep breath.

"Holy shit... I loved it, but I don't think the burgers were as cooked as I feel."

She climbed into the tub, which was big enough to hold eight, and gave a sigh as she leaned back. Chloe burst out of the sauna, looking like a tomato, and just dived head first into the tub, all of us were engulfed, as the water splashed all over us, and we squealed, Chloe surfaced with a smile.

"Oh fuck, this is nice... Phew, I thought I was barbequed."

We sat back, and just relaxed, as our overheated bodies cooled down, Deli staggered out, panting, we giggled and lay back cooling down, and it felt like bliss.

Chapter 20

Seaside.

Nigel sat up in bed really fast.

"Oh dear, I am going to be late for church!" A long slender white arm came out from under the covers, and slipped across his waist.

"Nigel, God wants you to be happy, yar? Stay here longer and be close to me."

I staggered into the kitchen, and flopped down at the table, Deb's smiled as she handed me a coffee. Deli looked a little rough, Birch was again outdoors, and Anita and Chloe had not appeared yet. Even though I had slept long and deeply, I still felt exhausted. I lifted my cup and sipped slowly as I tried to wake up. Jenny was in her little seat making weird noises. Curious as to what my other half was up to, I got up and went in search of Birch.

She was outside sat on the wall looking radiant, her skin was glowing as I walked up to her, she noticed and smiled.

"Hi Sweetie." I leaned on the wall and leaned on her shoulder.

"My head hurts, but I did not drink that much last night." She slipped her arm behind me.

"It is probably just the change of weather, it is a lot hotter here, and you certainly have been, oh you dark sexy little beastie, last night was pretty amazing."

She gave a little giggle, as I put my cup down on the wall, and slipped into her arms, and she pulled me closer, I rested my head on her shoulder.

"I love you Deads, I have been sat here waiting for you to get up, just thinking about us, I feel very happy today."

It is a really wonderful thing, when someone who you care so much for, says all the things you are thinking, I love that she can do that. Deli came out of the back door and held up her phone.

"Guys you will never believe this?" We turned and looked, as she walked over to the bridge, and came across the grass towards us.

"You will never guess what Sophia did last night?"

I turned around, and Birch slipped her arms round to my tummy, and pulled me back, closer to her, then leaned her head on my shoulder. I looked at Deli, her eyes were really big.

"I don't know, photographed the whole village for Insta? What has Sophia got up to, is she alright?" Deli looked a little confused.

"That is a good question, because last night she slept with Nigel."

Is it me or did that make no sense at all? I had to wait a few seconds to fully understand the impact that it was having on my gag reflex, Birch shrugged.

"Well at least that is three, he does appear to be catching up finally." Deli frowned at her.

"Three, I thought that is two?" She looked at me, and her eyes got even wider.

"Holy shit Abby, is that why he is obsessed with you, did you screw him too?" A jolt of horror ran through my system, and I scowled at her.

"NO! screw you Deli, how could you even think that?" She smiled at me.

"Sorry... So, who is the other mystery woman?" Birch gave a chuckle.

"A secret, you know therapy confidence and all that?" She understood.

"Yeah, I get it, you see him in secret, although..." Birch jerked.

"NO! screw you Bitch, my pussy is a Deadly only zone." Birch gave a shudder, and I giggled. Deli started to laugh, as she closed the messages on her phone.

"I am actually a little happy for Sophia, she has always thought he was a kind guy, and to be honest he is, and she likes him far more than she has ever admitted, although I will just add, I have no idea why?" She started to giggle.

"Those teeth have got to be dangerous?" I looked at Deli.

"He is married to Prim, and if she ever finds out, Sophia will get a whole world of hate, are you sure we should all be okay with this?" She nodded, and looked a little bothered.

"I know Abby, but I am telling you, Sophia will not listen when it comes to affairs of the heart, even I will not sway her. I know she is playing with fire, but you know what, while she can get away with it, I am not going to tell her to stop. I will never touch a married guy, but that is not Sophia." I gave a long sigh and nodded.

"I understand Deli, I really do, I would just hate to see her get really hurt, and Prim can be dangerous." She slid her phone into her shorts pocket.

"I know, Abby I really care about her, I do not want her hurt too. Honestly, I am a little envious, it has been forever since I last got laid, a little attention in that department would be nice about now. I don't really blame her for going for what she wants." Birch moved her head on my shoulder.

"Oh Sweetie, are you that desperate for attention, oh dear, we will have to fix that?" I turned my head to look at her big bright green eyes.

"How exactly do we do that, Birch if you haven't noticed, we are in the middle of nowhere?" She slid forward on the wall, and I felt her prickly pussy on my bum.

"You need to shave." She gave a giggle and wiggled her hips.

"Leave it with me, I need to make a couple of calls, tell the others we are off on a short holiday, and pack an overnight bag." I watched as she walked towards the bridge.

"Are we going somewhere, I thought we were already on holiday?" She turned and smiled.

Deads, Sweetie, we are pausing this holiday so we can have another holiday, and when we have had it, we will come back to this holiday, and carry on with our holiday." I blinked.

"Huh?"

"Sweetie, we are going to the sea side... Well, I hope we are, it is late season, but everything should still be lively, I know a great nudist beach." I looked at Deli who was smiling.

"Is it just me...?" I shook my head.

"Forget it, I should know better, it's a Birch thing." She gave a giggle and looked really excited.

Within the hour, Birch had been online, and on the phone, and had acquired five double rooms, at a hotel in Bude. We all piled into Petal, locked the house, and was back on the road skirting

Dartmoor, and headed for sand and surf. Birch filled us in as she drove.

"This place is a very curious sort of place; it has a motorbike, and some very unusual things dotted all over it. It also has an excellent gin bar; it is pretty special and quirky."

Somehow, I got the idea she had always wanted to go to this place, and it did sound exactly like the kind of place Birch would inhabit, you know, eccentric, and quirky?

Is it funny how you are whizzing along country lanes, and you suddenly get that sudden change of air, and you feel happy, as the sea breeze blows across the land? It is like one minute it is all cow shit and hay, and then boom, you get the sea side whiff, and you get all giddy? Well, I do, and looking at the huge happy smile on Birch's face, she does too.

It is crazy, we are all twenty eight or nine years old, and suddenly, we are tearing along, playing who can spot the sea first like a bunch of ten year olds, and everyone is smiling like an idiot? Deb's bobbed around like a crazy person, and finally she screamed right down my ear as she pointed, and woke the baby. The baby did not really affect me while it was crying, because I had been rendered temporarily deaf.

The sea in view, our spirits lifted, and finally, having parked, jumped out and grabbed our bags, of which Birch had her pull along case, we headed inside and looked around in surprise.

Birch did not disappoint, the walls had murals of bright coloured flowers, there were stuffed animals, a motor cycle in a glass case, and strange carvings of animals. There was even a picture of a stag that had real horns poking out of it, and a large picture of Winston Churchill, and a wall of paintings showing Henry the Eighth and his wives. Yep, this was perfectly Birch, colourful and eclectic, it all felt very British. Chloe loved it, and as she pointed out, it was 'very artisan.'

The room was nice, a little more sedate, although it did have a huge union flag bean bag, and stag cushions, and a large bulldog stuffed teddy on the bed. There were two chairs in front of the windows that looked out on the sea, it felt nice to stand and watch as the water rolled up, with rolling froth, onto the sand.

The hotel made its own gin, which I also think played a large role in Birch's choice, and it had a fully stocked gin bar, and tubs of dried ingredients, such as rose buds, cinnamon stick, juniper berries, and strange twigs and leaves, to infuse the gin with.

The hotel staff were lovely and polite, and really helpful, I liked that, we got a free drink because hey, yep, they recognised the Curio's, even here this far south, it appeared we were well known.

The bar had yet another motor cycle in a glass case under it, and the wall to our side had a mural of carrousel horses, and below it there were two, really old actual carrousel horses, it was a stunning place. Wherever you looked, there was something to catch your eye, from one of many eras of British life, I really loved it.

It was mid afternoon, and we had some free time, and Birch wanted to go to the beach. It was really hot, and the pavement bounced the heat back up at us, as we walked towards the sand and sea. Birch disappeared into one of the many little gift shops, and reappeared with two buckets shaped like castles and two spades, I looked at her like she had gone mad.

"What the hell are they for?" She beamed with pride and delight.

"I want to make sandcastles with you."

"Huh?" She held up the pink bucket, and her eyes danced.

"Sweetie, we can make a huge fortress with these." I was not sure I was believing her, until Chloe gave a big grin.

"Fuck yeah, I am making one to." She disappeared into the shop, I looked at Birch as she smiled like a mental patient.

"Birch you are twenty nine, not ten." She pouted.

"But I want to make sandcastles with you, please Deads, I have not made one in years." I nodded.

"Yeah, because you are twenty nine. Jesus Birch, you are a qualified clinical psychologist, or did you just print those certificates out with your Micky Mouse printing press?" She frowned.

"I would never have a Mickey Mouse printing press, if I had to own one, it would be Goofy's, I trust him, he screws like a normal person."

"Huh... What the hell are you talking about?" She gave a smug smile.

"Goofy was the man, he had kids, Donald and Mickey only had nephews and nieces, Goofy knew how to screw and get things done properly. I mean, seriously Deads, could you honestly see Mickey with a voice that high, taking Minnie from behind doggy style?" I looked at Deb's for help, she sort of frowned, chewed on her lip, and then looked at me.

"You know what Abby, as weird and totally messed up as that sounds, she may have a point?" I gasped at her.

"Don't bloody encourage her madness more than you have too, seriously, you are supposed to be the normal and rational one, you are a parent?" Birch gave a sweet smile.

"Ha... I told you Sweetie, you do not stop playing because you grow old, you grow old because you stop playing." She held up both buckets.

"So, what is it going to be, yellow or pink?" I gave a sigh, and grabbed the pink one, I know how much she loves yellow, Anita chuckled at me.

Birch gave a squeal, and Chloe appeared with a blue bucket and spade, so we headed off towards the sea. We arrived at the beach, which was vast, and had huge rocks sticking up out of it. It was really cool, and the sand was soft and white, and I will not deny, within seconds my shoes were off as I walked along feeling it's warmth between my toes.

We walked close to where the sea was rolling in, and the sand was damp and within seconds, Birch was digging like a coal miner, as she created a large mound. Anita walked with her feet in the water and paddled around with Deli, and I sat on the sand and started to fill my bucket. It was actually sort of fun, I patted the sand inside and then tipped it over and, PLOP! Birch stared at me like a psychopath, I shrugged.

"What, it looks good?" She glared at me.

"We don't want one there, we have to plan this properly, we need defences, and a keep at the top." Okay, she is a bloody lunatic, I just wanted to plop them out, she had some crazy design in her bonkers brain. I looked at her.

"Birch Baby, it's just a fun little castle, it does not have to be elaborate." She considered it and gave me a nod.

"Yeah, we don't have time for the big castle, the tide is coming in, we will just build the smaller defensive keep." And suddenly, sandcastle building was really scary.

I filled my bucket and she pointed at the exact placement, and slowly but surely, the castle started to form into a complex design, she even modelled an archway and drawbridge.

It did look good, and Birch fumbled in her bag for her camera, and her psychotic disposition disappeared, and a more Birch like quality appeared as she clapped her hands together.

"Sweetie it is beautiful, I love it... I want pictures of it and us with it." I pointed behind her.

"Birch Baby, you better hurry up, look at the tide." She looked behind her and squealed, and danced on the spot.

"Sweetie stop it, I need pictures, tell it to go away until I am ready."

"Huh!" I pointed.

"It's the bloody sea, it drowns boats, who the frig do you think I am, King bloody Canute?"

She squealed, as she rooted around in her big bag. She found her phone mixed up in between alcohol, weapons, dildos and possibly imported contraband from our honeymoon.

She dragged me down with a squeal, and tried to do a selfie, but her camera was pointing the wrong way, she gave another high pitch squeal to rival all the seagulls, and tapped the screen, to make the front facing camera come on, and CLICK!

I actually think the picture is pretty cool. We sat side by side with the castle at our side, as water hit us at high speed and sprayed up our backs, and came crashing over our heads. The look of surprise, and horror, on our faces, was actually pretty cool.

I mean the castle was lost below the foam, but the sheer bloody surprise was there. I stood up dripping and held out my hand, our buckets were probably on their way to China, swept out by the current. She looked a little down, as she looked at the smooth bumps in the sand that had once been Castle Dixon. I helped pull her up off the soaked sand, and she pulled at her soaking wet shorts.

"Ew, Sweetie, I have sand up my crack, and it's grinding on my bum cheeks."

Yep, me too, walking was weird as hell, it felt like I had a sander down my shorts. I could actually feel it grinding on my labia as

I walked, and all I could think of, was this is probably what oral with Nigel and those teeth would feel like, which thoroughly disgusted me.

Just to rub salt in an open wound, Chloe had built hers further back, and the tide had not reached it yet, and she still had a bucket, and was sat taking selfies and sniggering. I saw that evil look in Birch's eyes as she lifted her foot, and gripped her arm.

"Birch Baby, you are a bigger person than that." She turned to me and her eyes smouldered with hate, I smiled at her.

"I love you Baby; do you know how much?" She softened, and her eyes sparkled.

"Sweetie, I love you too." I leaned in and kissed her softly.

"Leave Chloe to play with her castle in peace." I pulled her gently away; Birch gritted her teeth.

"Okay then, but if a tsunami comes in and washes her and her stupid castle away, I will not cry." I giggled; she was such a big kid.

I held her hand, to be honest, I was not sure she would not run back, and kick the shit out of Chloe's castle. We walked in the soft warm sand, with scratchy female bits to Anita, who was sat with Deb's and Deli eating chips, out of a paper cone, she held it up.

"Want one, seaside chips taste better than anywhere else?"

I took one, and Birch reached out, and took a really long fat chip out, and lifted it up to look at it.

"Wow this is a fat bloody chip... ARGHHHH!"

We all ducked, as five of the biggest freaking white birds I have ever seen, swooped in and attacked Birch, she squealed in terror, and honestly... I did not want to laugh, but...

Birch fled up the beach screaming like a possessed woman, holding half a chip, as three of the overly large gulls tried to peck her hand and head off. I was very busy rolling around on the sand laughing my ass off, as Anita sat with her mouth open staring.

Deb's was leant over the raisin protecting her, just in case they wanted an extra portion of human with their chip for tea, and Deli was stood up staring in horror. She turned and looked down at me, as Birch screamed.

"SWEETIE, SAVE ME, IT'S HITCHCOCK ALL OVER AGAIN... SWEETIE, TELL THEM TO GO HOME!" Deli looked a little rattled.

"Abby, she looks panicked, should we help her?" I watched her run around like a maniac screaming, as the seagulls swooped in on her again.

"She will realise in a minute, if she drops the chip they will leave her, but the greedy bitch wants it for herself." Anita started to giggle; Deli shook her head.

"I am kind of freaking out Abby, I will never eat chips outdoors again." Birch squealed behind her.

"SWEETIE... CALL PEST CONTROL TO COME SHOOT THESE TWATS, THESE VULTURES ARE GOING TO EAT ME!" I gave a sigh, and stood up.

"Birch, just give them the bloody chip." She stared at me in horror, as she batted the air above her frantically.

"BUT SWEETIE, IT IS MY CHIP!"

I shook my head, another three swooped in, and she screamed at the top of her voice, and legged it faster down the beach. I looked at Deli.

"It's okay, I will identify the pecked to death corpse still holding a cold chip, alone, you won't have to see it. Holy shit, some animal lover she turned out to be?" She was running as fast as she could, screaming death to all birds.

It took her what looked like three thousand yards, before she finally admitted defeat, and staggered gasping for breath back towards us, minus her chip, with her hair sticking out in all sorts of pecked up angles. She stood in front of me, and pushed her head into my shoulder.

"Sweetie, tomorrow I am buying a gun, and when we get back, we will be having freshly roasted seagull with chips for dinner. I am going to stare at its freshly baked corpse, and eat all my frigging chips first, and then I am going to feast on its ass." I put my arm round her and smiled.

"Yummy. I will look forward to that." Anita started to laugh; Birch took a deep breath.

"Sweetie, I don't think pterodactyls died out, I think they evolved into seagulls." I nodded, and tried not to laugh.

"Probably Baby, they did look big." I smirked, and bit my lip.

Sandcastles and seagulls, was enough beach excitement for

today, and with wet sandy hooch's, we walked back to the hotel, and got in the shower. I could not believe how much sand washed into the shower pan, does that stuff breed? Hell, I think there was enough for us to build another castle.

With sand free lady parts, dried hair, and clean clothes, I sat and relaxed and watched the sky through the window, I felt really exhausted, although I had not really done much, maybe it was the sea air.

Birch sorted herself out, and we headed downstairs for our evening meal, and some serious gin tasting. I love good food, and went with the vegetarian option, which was a woodland pie, and it was delicious, and once done, and feeling stuffed, we made our way into the bar, and sat together by the long windows looking out across the town and the water.

Needless to say, we drank a lot of gin, and talked to a good few people, there were several parties there, and luckily no shortage of young men, much to the delight of Chloe, Deli and Anita.

We sat together and I snuggled into Birch, and watched the sun go down, and it was really beautiful. Feeling very drunk, absolutely exhausted, and very happy, with Birch's arm round my waist, we staggered to our room, leaving the three girls alone to play. I collapsed on the bed, and Birch crawled onto me, she looked down and smiled at me.

"That guy Mark was all eyes for you tonight." I gave a happy sigh, and smiled as I lifted my hand to her cheek.

"Maybe, but I was all eyes for you." Her green eyes danced, and she gave me a soft smile.

"Deads, if you need some discreet male attention, I will not mind, I understand you, and just so you know, it would be okay." I ran my fingers into her hair, and softly pulled them through her long white strands.

"I don't need it Birch, not at the moment, I am satisfied with you, but again, if you need it, then go back down." She shook her head.

"I don't, I just thought I would check with you." I shook my head.

"No Baby, I am gloriously happy with you, it is enough for me."

She smiled, leaned down and kissed me softly, my head was buzzing with the spirits, and I felt warm and relaxed, and I pulled her close and drowned in her beauty and spirit.

Chloe took Deli by the arm, and pressed three condoms into her hand. Deli looked down at them.

"Chloe I am on the pill." Chloe gave a knowing nod.

"Yeah, me too, but that does not stop other things, Deli we all play smart and safe, you should too. If he won't wear one, boot his ass out." She gave a slight smile.

"Yeah, thanks Chloe, I hear you." Chloe nodded at her.

"Go on, go have fun and get yourself sorted out."

She smiled as she watched Deli walk over towards a tall blonde guy named Greg, he slid his arm round her waist, and they walked off together. Two minutes later, Deli texted her the room number, just so someone else knew where she was. The room number system was something Birch implemented, whenever we were away from home. The idea was you text a number to the group chat, so everyone knew where you were, just in case you get into trouble.

In a way it is sad that the game has become so unpredictable, but safety at all times was a mantra when we partnered up, and it gave all of us a sense of security. If one of us left the room after, we just texted 'My room,' so everyone knew we had returned safely. To date we had never needed help for any of us, but it was good to know, if we did, it would soon arrive. The all girls together code was important, and playing safe and smart was also a part of that.

Anita partnered up with a young female business executive, and Chloe a slightly older guy than she normally slept with named Alan, he was thirty nine, they all headed off to have some fun.

I lay back into my pillows hot and happy, having just had a huge climax, the room was spinning, and I had sexed head, and it was wonderful and trippy, as Birch rested her head on my shoulder, and gave a happy sigh.

I pulled my arm round her and pulled her close, and closed my eyes, with a happy warm feeling filling me up inside, and slowly my mind drifted to the sound of Birch breathing, and the sea outside, as it washed up onto the beach, and my day ended in happiness.

My mind swam with pictures of bowler hat lamp shades, murals of the Beatles, copper brewing pipes, and pictures of Churchill. This really was possibly the most curious place I had ever stayed in, but it felt safe, because Birch was with me, and that was all I had ever really wanted.

Chapter 21

Relaxation.

It was nice to be in Bude. I slept well, and woke early, but still felt tired, so sat in my room with a coffee watching the sea through the window, as it ran up the beach, whilst Birch slept to my side in the bed. I enjoyed yesterday, but to be honest, I was ready to go back to Sunny Bank, for me it is a very special place, and I was glad we were checking out after breakfast.

It was nice of Birch to arrange this, and I hoped the girls got laid last night, but Birch had planned a beach day, and then we would set off back to Sunny Bank, and honestly, that was all I wanted. I sat in my seat watching the sea, and sipping my coffee, and weirdly enough, I had been pretty drunk last night, but this morning I did not have the usual hangover, although, my body felt a lot weaker than normal.

I had a lot of thoughts going through my head, as I looked at my life, my home, and the people around me. I had really enjoyed working on the exhibition, and was looking forward to getting stuck in to the Halloween event. I also had my campaign against Prim, and if needed, fighting the building of houses on Dursley Woods. I had a lot to think about, and getting back to Sunny Bank, to have the space to think was all I wanted.

My biggest want, is simply time alone with Birch, I wanted her at Sunny Bank, alone, where I could see that special side of her that I found the most appealing. I sipped my coffee, as I puzzled everything out in my mind, at Sunny Bank, our conversations feel deeper, and more important to me. My mind drifted back to the week we spent alone, where she was so hurt and wounded, and the moments we spent walking, or curled up in bed talking calmly and quietly, as I lay there drifting in her bright green eyes.

She will never know the joy of just listening to her, staring into her eyes for hours, drifting in her presence. I have never experienced an intimacy so close before, and I guess I want that moment again. My life had changed so much, but so had my tastes and also my desires, I sat sipping my coffee and wondering about it, was this the full power of a deep love?

She had asked if I wanted a man, but I didn't, I honestly really did not want that, if I am honest even though the sex with her was amazing, I got off more on the emotion, the intimacy, and the closeness I had with her during sex. I loved to watch her, and see how her body responded and the joy in her eyes, it had become so powerful for me, my joy these days was from witnessing hers, and knowing that was her response to me. As mad as it sounds, it made me so incredibly happy.

Was this growing up and maturing, or was it simply the importance of her in my life? I did not know for sure, I just knew that when she was next to me, and I was touching her, even if only holding or cuddling her, I felt this huge sense of inner peace and joy. It was sort of surprising to just sit and think about it, I was happy, actually I was beyond happy, more than I had ever been in my life, and she was the reason.

Two long white slender arms slipped over me, and I looked up, she smiled a soft loving smile, she looked dreamy and sleepy, and her hair stuck out all over the place, her voice was soft and gentle.

"Hi Sweetie... I was watching you; I felt a strong desire to just touch you." I smiled.

"I was thinking about you, about us, and just enjoying it all." She leaned down and kissed my forehead.

"I know that look... We are going back today Sweetie." I gave a small chuckle.

"Am I that obvious?" She stood up, and yawned, and then glanced down at me as she turned.

"I need a pee, and yes, I see it in you, just as I did that week alone, and on the honeymoon, I like that side of you Deads. I loved being alone in the Bahamas, I like that I see parts of you that no one else does, it makes us special... Okay, I am really going to pee on the carpet, give me a minute." She hurried into the bathroom as I giggled at her.

It took a while, but we dressed, and headed down to the restaurant for breakfast, I ordered just toast, and Birch dived into a huge full English breakfast. I have no idea how she stays so slender; she should be as big as a house with her appetite. Chloe was all smiles, as was Deli, they had obviously had a good night, especially looking at the way they glanced across the room, to the guys they had slept with, sat with their own parties.

Anita looked insanely happy, she was sat with a short dark haired woman, who to be honest, was quite cute. Chloe and Deli noticed and giggled; Chloe looked at me.

"She is really into her, when Tabby asked her to go to her room with her, she was like a little teenager, all shy and giggles, we laughed our heads off." I chuckled.

In a way it was nice, I knew she had been avoiding relationships, because she was really scared of getting hurt again, Katie did quite the hatchet job on her. I watched her as she listened and smiled to the woman, Chloe had said was called Tabby, I assumed that was short for Tabatha.

Birch sat back with a huge smile, having finished off what looked like several small animals for breakfast, I noted there was no seagull on the menu for her though.

Having eaten, it was time to pack up and prepare to leave the hotel. We all headed up to our rooms, and began the process of picking up all the unused clothes off the floor, I am sure Birch does it just to feel at home, her idea of unpacking is just toss everything in your case around the bed.

Again, it was another really warm day, and the sun was bright, and the sky cloudless, so I put on shorts and a vest, and folded my boot cuts neatly, and packed them in my bag. I sat on the bed as Birch brushed her teeth, and there was a gentle tap on the door, it opened and Anita leaned in.

"Is it okay to come in, are you decent?" I gave a laugh.

"We have never been decent, but you can come in... You look happy?" She walked in, and sat down on the chair and turned to me.

"I had such a great night last night, I talked with Tabby for hours, we really hit it off, and oh God, we had some mind blowing sex. I think I really needed that, I guess I am pretty much walking on air today." I gave her a smile.

"I am really happy for you Anita; I think the time was right for you." She smiled, and looked down at the floor.

"She has a week's holiday planned, she has one more meeting today, and then she is free, she moved it to today so she could have all week off." She looked a little uneasy, I smiled at her, and Birch leaned round the bathroom door.

"Anita, if you are asking is it okay for her to come to Sunny Bank, you know she can, you do have a double bed there, as long as she understands that we are a little screwed up and do lots of silly shit, she is fine." She looked at Birch and gave a big smile.

"I would love that, I am not really the one night stand sort of girl, and I really do like her, we get on so well." I smiled at her.

"And you want to know if you can get on that well for longer?" She nodded at me.

"Abby, she comes from Lingfield, she is less than a forty minute drive from me, although she travels a lot, and is often in Manchester, which I am too, honestly, we have a lot in common, and I want to know if we could have more." Birch smiled with frothy teeth.

"Sweetie."

She covered her mouth as she sprayed toothpaste everywhere, she held up a finger, bobbed into the bathroom, and spat in the sink, she reappeared.

"As I was saying, Sweetie, if you want some extra time with her, then bring her back with us, if she is in a car, she can follow us." Anita looked really relieved.

"What do we have planned for today?" Birch smiled.

"Nude beach, is she coming after her meeting?"

I had to laugh, if she was going to hang out with us, she was going to have a really rude awakening, I just hope she could handle it for Anita's sake.

We checked out, and Birch paid the bill, she refused to let me pay my share, telling me this had been her treat for all of us. We packed up Petal, and drove to the car park at the beach, and placed a day ticket on Petal. We grabbed the cool box, and Birch's backpack, and walked back onto the warm sand.

Birch knew of a part of the beach that allowed naturists, so we turned north, and walked along the beach, she took my hand and held it, as we walked along the water's edge and enjoyed the sunshine.

The land to our right rose up into high cliffs, and soon we found ourselves at a place, where the cliffs drew back into a cove, filled with small jagged lines of rock, that stood proud of the sand. It went back quite far, so we settled high up the beach, and laid out a large tarp, with a couple of blankets to lie on.

Chloe and Birch were naked in seconds, and lay back on the blankets, I pulled off my vest and dropped my shorts, and stood nude on the sand, with the sea breeze touching the whole of my naked skin, and actually, it felt amazing. I sat down next to Birch and pulled out my lotion, it was starting to get really hot. Deli pulled off her clothes to reveal she was wearing a very skimpy bikini, so was Anita, they were still very new to this.

I lay back loving the sensation, and to be honest being out in public like this, felt very new and a little bit exciting. I turned to Birch, as she lay on her stomach, and opened a book.

"Have you been to a naturist beach before?" She turned to me and gave me a smile, and raised her eyebrows.

"Are you feeling naughty for being naked in public?" I smiled.

"A little bit, this is the first time I have done anything like this in a public place."

"Sweetie, I have done this loads of times, mum prefers naturist beaches, she always searches them out, so I have grown up on places like this one. Mum hates tan lines, she likes the feelings of freedom, and warmth on her skin."

I lay back and looked up at the sky, and the cliffs, it felt huge and open, and it was strange, was this the ultimate feeling of being free, as I lay back on the earth as nature intended? On our honeymoon, we had stayed on a private beach in a very sheltered cove, so it was nowhere as open as this, and there was no public allowed. I had no idea, but it just felt really freeing, like I was more alive than I had ever been before, like I was one with everything. Birch's smiling face appeared above me.

"It feels great doesn't it, come in the sea with me, it is the ultimate naked experience."

The great thing about Cornwall on the first week of September, is the sea is a little warmer than normal, unlike my last adventure in the British sea, where I almost froze my tits off. I sat up, and she grabbed my hand. I stood up, and we ran, what was actually quite a long way to the sea. We came hurtling down in nothing, and right across the path of two fully dressed people walking their dog, they smiled as Birch waved.

"Hello!"

We ploughed into the water, it felt odd, they hardly batted an eyelid, although, I figured they were locals and probably quite used to this. The water was warmer, but not warm enough, and I caught my breath, but such was the momentum we had built up, I had no hope of stopping. The waves crashed onto us, as Birch waded out with me till it was right above our waists and just under my boobs.

It felt so amazing, to just be so free and liberated, stood completely naked in the water, feeling the fresh tingle of it all around my body, as I looked back at the land, and saw the whole length of the beach, it felt crazy.

I had been in the sea naked in the Bahamas, but it was really warm, this felt completely different, like I was aware of my whole body and it was invigorating. I felt so wild and free, I wanted to scream, Birch dragged me into her arms and pulled me close. She leaned in and kissed me, as a huge wave crashed over us, and just for a moment, we were naked and kissing under water.

Oh God, I felt so amazingly alive, she broke apart with bright happy eyes, and a huge smile, and flicked her long wet hair back from her face.

"Glorious isn't it Sweetie?" I had to admit, I had never felt anything like it, this was the true meaning of complete freedom?

"Birch, I feel wild, and free and it's crazy, I have swam in the pool at home a million times, but this, this is beyond everything."

She gave a huge cackle of a laugh, and the waves crashed back over us, she pulled me back into her arms, and I wanted to jump and dance, and yell out my freedom to the whole world, I had never felt this alive in my life.

The wild water washed over us and it felt so invigorating, my hair washed across my face and I took a deep breath, and lifted my hands to wipe it from my eyes, and gave out a huge wild laugh.

"Birch this is absolutely wild, Baby, I feel so alive, oh God, I am so happy we did this."

She grabbed my hand and pulled me back a little into shallower water, and shook her long mane of hair out of her face.

"It is wonderful, isn't it Sweetie, can you feel how wild and alive the sea is?"

I nodded back at her with a fixed smile on my face, my heart was pumping like it never had, it was hard to describe the feelings of excitement and joy that were swirling around inside me. I threw my arms round her and gave her a huge hug.

"This is amazing, I thought swimming in the Bahamas was fun, but Birch, this is not a private beach, this is Britain, and everyone can see us, and no one cares, I love it."

She took my hand and we ran out of the sea onto the beach, and grabbed our towels. I felt breathless when we got back to the blanket, and flopped back, and lay in the sun to dry off fully, I got out my sun lotion and rubbed it into my arms and legs, as Birch picked up her book. I felt giddy and happy, it was nuts, all I had done was go into the sea with no clothes on, why did it feel like such an amazing thing? Birch gave a big smile as she sat back on her towel.

"You look happy, I am glad you enjoyed that. You know Deads, the six best doctors, are Sunshine, Exercise, Water, Laughter, Rest and Air, you need this more than you realise." I gave her smile; she was always looking out for me.

"What about happiness, because that is what makes me feel best?" She giggled.

"Sweetie, that is the best psychotherapy, because when people are happy, they do not need me or the Retreat." I giggled as she lay back

I settled back as the hot sun warmed my skin, while we were in the sea, four other people had arrived and were a good thirty yards away, stripped off and relaxing on their towels, I was starting to really like naturist beaches, this felt like my kind of place.

I put on my sun glasses and lay back and felt the heat on my skin, it was like being rolled up in a warm blanket, and it was nice. I needed this, life had been so hectic for most of the year, and I just let go, relaxed, and I closed my eyes and drifted. Chloe and Deli were in the sea, Deb's was paddling holding little Jenny, and Anita was sat a few feet in front of us rubbing sun oil on her legs.

My mind wandered, as I processed the last few weeks, picking up where I left off this morning. One of the greatest advantages to sunbathing, is that I can just lie back, do nothing, and contemplate everything that is happening all around me. It felt quiet and remote, apart from the sound of the page turning, as Birch relaxed and read her book. I breathed in and out slowly, almost like meditating, and just relaxed as my whole body drifted, as the heat radiated through it. I was so tired, and this was the perfect way to relax.

Time slipped past me as I drifted in the sunshine, I think I dozed off a little. I was lost in thoughts when I heard a new voice. I opened my eyes and slid my glasses down, it was Tabatha, she noticed me watching and smiled, I gave her a wave, and she looked at Anita, and then back to me, she walked a little closer, and looked down at me.

"Oh my God, you are Abigail Jennifer Watson?" I smiled at her.

"I could be, when I am working, today I am just Abby, I am on holiday." She smiled.

"Yeah sorry, I am being rude, but when Anita said she worked with writers, I didn't think she meant really famous ones. I have read all of your books, and I am talking way too much because I am just a little bit star struck... Sorry I will shut up now." I giggled.

"It is nice to meet you, chill out and have fun, and just go with the flow, that is pretty much what we do, this lovely lady is my wife, Jemi." She smiled at Birch.

"Wow you are the doctor; it is so nice to meet you." Birch smiled.

"Nice to meet you too Sweetie." Tabby looked at Anita.

"You do know this is a nude beach, yes?" She pulled off her top, and Anita nodded.

"So why are you wearing a bikini, come on, I want another look at that sexy bod."

She dropped her shorts, and underwear, and folded her clothes, and slipped them in her bag, then sat on the towel and lay back. Anita undid her bikini top and took it off, then slid off her bottoms. I smiled as I slipped my glasses back up my nose, and lay back, it looked like Tabby might fit in well, she would certainly be good for Anita.

We sprawled out soaking up the sun, Deb's came and sat with Deli and baby, under an umbrella to keep a little shaded, and hide her from the public whilst she breastfed.

The day was slipping past, and even though I had wanted to go straight to Sunny Bank this morning, I was actually sad when it came time to leave. I had one more swim in the sea, it was really hot and I had been cooking in the sun, and it felt nice to cool down, and wash off the sweat, and then I begrudgingly got dressed, and we started to walk back along the beach. Birch held my hand as we walked.

"You have been quiet today, Sweetie; do you have something on your mind?" I looked down the beach, that stretched out in front of us like a white fine grain highway, I glanced at her at my side.

"I have been thinking about a lot of things, but also about my last talk with Nigel. He has changed a lot, you have done wonders for him, but I wondered if he is playing Sophia, you know, using her for sex?" She understood me.

"Deads, from what Moon told me, I am not sure Nigel is really that confident sexually. I mean, yes, he learned a lot from Moon, but I am not sure he was the lead player when it came to Sophia. If what Deli said was true, this was probably more what she wanted, and be honest, she is probably the best looking girl he will ever sleep with. He would not say no, I doubt many men would?" I could understand that, Sophia was good looking.

"I worry about what will happen if Prim finds out, Sophia will not handle her, she is not strong enough. Even Deli was not tough enough to outsmart her, and what will happen to Nigel, he got black eyes just for getting a tow from us?"

"Sweetie, at the end of the day, the one to nip her in the bud, has to be Nigel. As hard as that is going to be, he married her, and it is his responsibility to deal with her bad behaviour." I scoffed.

"Well, that is Sophia screwed then, Prim will kick the shit out of Nigel, then devour her." Birch gave a sigh.

"Sweetie, Nigel is moving forward, give him time, he will get there."

"I hope you are right Birch, because she is dangerous, and if she gets her own way, a lot of people will get hurt."

We arrived at the car park, and loaded our things, it was two thirty, and I was hungry, so I headed to the food stand, and bought a load of burgers, and some chips, Birch eyed them with a look of alarm. I took them back to Petal and gave everyone their burger, and then sat in the passenger seat to eat. Birch climbed in looking relieved, but she closed the window just in case.

Jenny was changed, and then strapped into her baby seat, and with Anita in Tabby's car following us, we disposed of our food wrappers in the recycle bin, and then headed off back to Sunny Bank.

Birch wanted to drive, which suited me, as I felt really tired, and I still had no idea actually where the house was situated, I really needed to look it up on a map. I closed my eyes, feeling the warmth of the sun on my face, and let my mind wander, and with the hum of the engine, and the gentle motion of Petal, I drifted into sleep.

The next thing I knew, Birch was gently shaking me, and everyone else was in the house.

"Deads Sweetie, we are home... Come on Sweetie, you cannot stay here, if you need to, go to bed and sleep it off." I blinked my eyes, and shook my head as I sat up abruptly.

"I am sorry, I just feel so tired, I didn't mean to sleep." She smiled at me; her green eyes held her concern.

"Deads, you are really pale, and you know you have lost a lot of weight, you need to rest more, and just let things slide for a while and get your strength back." I rubbed my eyes.

"Birch, I am fine, honestly." She gave me a sad smile and sighed.

"But you are not, you have pushed too hard, and you are run down. Deads, please listen to me, I am worried about you, it is why I brought you here, you need to rest and eat more." I sat back in the seat.

"I will be fine."

"Please Deads, go to bed and sleep, you need it." I turned and looked at her, I knew she meant well.

"Birch please, I worked really hard, and it is just because I stopped, that is all, some of it has caught up on me a little, that is all, honestly I am fine." She nodded at me.

"So listen to your body, and sleep, just rest and take things easy and grow stronger for me." I nodded at her.

"Okay mother, I hear you." She smiled, and leaned in and kissed my cheek.

"Good, go on, go and get in bed, and I will bring you a drink up, and cuddle you for a while, you know I am tired too, we both need to rest."

I know when I am beat, and I was not going to win, so I grabbed my bag and took it upstairs, and undressed, and slipped under the cool duvet, it felt nice after the long hot day, so I rolled on my side, and snuggled into my pillow, and closed my eyes. I did feel tired, and had felt weak all day, maybe she was right, a short sleep would do me good.

Downstairs in the garden, everyone sat around, whilst Chloe cooked on the barbeque. She had filled it with coals, and taken off the mesh, and was using a wok, to cook Chinese food. Deb's sat with Deli and Birch on cushions, on a huge blanket that had been spread out, whilst Anita and Tabby lay on the their sides. A large tub of ice was at the side of them stocked with beers. Jenny was in her travel cot in her room, and Deb's had the monitor at her side, she turned to Birch.

"Is Abby alright?" Birch smiled at her.

"She will be, Deads has taken on a lot recently, and it has burnt her out, if you think about all she does, it is a lot more than most of us." Chloe stood at the table chopping and looked at her.

"How so, she has been resting in between things, I always check on her?" Birch lifted her can, and took a long drink.

"Think about what she uses her brain for Chloe. Have you any idea how much power the brain uses just to write a book? It is mentally exhausting, on top of that she arranged every aspect of the art exhibition, it was a mammoth task, which she pretty much did alone. Then throw in all the emotional energy she used to help Deli and Nigel. All of that was done, whilst taking on Prim, and then there is the council preparations, and the Summer Fete, that took a lot of nervous energy for her, and all of that is just the last couple of months, never mind what came before." Deb's gave a nod, Deli looked guilty.

"I didn't want to be a burden to anyone, especially Abby." Birch patted her leg.

"It was nothing to do with you, that is who Deads is, she was really worried about you, and when no one heard from you, she got really upset. Deli the point is, even though you do not realise it, Deads is watching everything and caring about everyone, I think it is a writer thing. They throw themselves into everything and experience it fully, that is where their inspiration comes from. Think about it, as a kid when she was hurt, she hid under her arch, and now that is a best selling book, she makes small insignificant things, bigger and fuller, and filled with mystery and adventure. That takes a huge amount of emotional intelligence, and it is exhausting."

Chloe nodded, as she threw the ingredients in the wok, and they hissed as she stirred them.

"I never thought of that, I know a really good picture tires me completely out. I suppose it is the same thing, you know, I really do appreciate everything she has done, that exhibition was the best part of my life so far?" Birch smiled at her.

"I know Sweetie, we all saw your face on the red carpet. Deads has also put in a huge amount to the Curio Live project, we work in our room a lot at night, and it is normal for us to work until three or four in the morning, we pack a lot in. I was feeling the strain after the art exhibition, but for her it is treble, which is why I wanted her here, I knew that here she would relax and get her mojo back. I hope here, she will quieten the noise in her mind a little." Deb's rolled her can in her hands.

"So she needs to sunbathe and swim in the river, and have picnics, that sort of thing?" Birch gave a nod.

"She needs to have fun and smile, and take things easy, and she will be fine. I know how she takes things to heart; she feels everything for everyone, trust me, I have had years of long talks with her about it all." Chloe started to scoop the food into the bowls, and it steamed as she passed them round.

"When she wakes up, I will cook for her. Edwina is worried she has lost too much weight, leave her to me, I know all her favourite foods."

She lifted her chop sticks off the table, and sat on the floor next to Tabby, she smiled at Chloe, and looked around at everyone as they ate.

"You know, for me this is pretty cool, I mean, I am sitting naked, in a garden, eating Chinese with a group I met less than a day ago, who all happen to be the Curio's, it is pretty surreal, you guys are like legends where I come from." Anita giggled.

"Yeah, but you are having sex with the one person who is not a Curio, I suppose you got the short straw?" Everyone started to giggle, Tabby shrugged.

"Yeah, but the sex is pretty hot, so I think I did okay." Anita smiled, and Birch gave a chuckle, as she lifted her noodles and put them into her mouth.

When the meal was over, Birch gathered the pots and took them into the kitchen, and everyone relaxed as she washed up, dried them, and put them all away, her mind elsewhere. Deb's walked in holding her phone, and she smiled.

"We had a great time on the beach, I dangled Jenny's legs in the sea, and I think she really liked it."

"That is great Goggle Bear... God I wish I was there; this place is doing my head in. I think I fucking hate yanks, honestly, they are sold into rap, they want to funk up everything. I told em, if you fuck with my tapes, I will fucking shred them, I am a bloody rock artist, not some ponced up twat who has no idea of rhythm and melodies." Deb's gave a sigh.

"I miss you too Jimmy Bear, it is so nice here, honestly you would love it. Look if it is too much, come back to London and mix it all there, at least you will be close to home if it gets too much."

"Honestly it is almost finished, I thought it would take forever, and if they give me any more of their shit cream filled crap coffee, I think I am gonna burn the place down... I tell you what though, listen to this... Hang up let me line it up, I think this mix is mad brilliant, tell me what you think."

Deb's put her phone on speaker and rested it on the table, as the mix of I will be sung by Abby began to play, Birch turned and looked at the phone, Deb's smiled at her. It was very different from the wedding version, it felt more intense and soulful, and yet beautiful. Birch stared at the phone on the table as her eyes filled with tears, holding a plate in one hand and a towel in the other, just frozen to the spot.

The band had done a full remix, and a few overdubs to enrich the sound, but it was utterly beautiful and wonderful, the track faded out, and Jimmy gave a cough.

"What do you think Doll?" Deb's smiled at the phone, Birch

gave a sniffle.

"It has Birch in tears, it really is very special and wonderful Jimmy Bear." He gave a little chuckle.

"Tell Birch I am sorry for making her cry, but you know what, it is brilliant, she is fucking good if you get me, we want to put it out as a single. You know, Abby will get paid a proper royalty and all, we would not rip her off, but hell she is good. I am glad she has not heard it; we want to surprise her with it." Birch dried her eyes on the pot towel, and her voice was squeaky.

"Jimmy, it is beautiful, she sung that for me, and it really hits home, I love it, I really do, I want a copy as soon as it comes out." He gave a little giggle.

"We all bawled our fucking brains out too when we first played the final mix, you got it Doll, first one I get is yours." Birch smiled, and wiped her eyes.

"Jimmy, tell the guys, we all love them, and thanks, it is amazing what you have done with it, I absolutely love it."

"No problems Doll, we love you guys to bits too, you know that?" Deb's smiled a huge smile.

"I love you Jimmy Bear, get it done as fast as you can, and get home to me, I really need you in my bed." He gave a loud giggle.

"God girl, I am so fucking ready, I hope you don't want sleep, I am so pent up I will keep you awake for days?" She giggled.

"Oh God, I hope so."

"Okay Goggle Bear, I got to get on with this, I really need it done, the label is pushing our asses hard for it. Kiss my little princess for me, and I hope to see you real soon, because I need some fucking normal life, these yanks have no idea how dull they are. Birch give all your girls a hug from me, and Baz says give Chloe an extra big one, he has been online every night looking at her exhibition. He was really pissed he missed it, but he wants to see it before it closes, although don't tell anyone, but he has bought two of her pictures for his home studio." Jimmy giggled. "He is a soft twat... Right Goggle Bear, I will talk tomorrow yeah?" She gave a happy sigh.

"Yeah, night Jimmy Bear." She looked up as the call ended.

"He really wants to put that out, he did not know you were here, he would not upset you on purpose." Birch smiled and sat down at the table.

"I am not upset, I love it, Deb's that is her singing her heart out to show me how much she really loves me, that is why I cried. It's my Abby, my Deads, the love of my life singing to me. It really hits home at times how much she loves me, and how I almost lost her because of a stupid label I was afraid to wear. I am so glad I came back when I did, you have no idea how many times I have thought of that night she spent alone on her bed, broken hearted because I was not there to hold her."

Deb's gave a nod, she understood better than most, she had talked often to Abby at that time, she reached across the table and took hold of Birch's hands.

"Let it go Birch, instead of remembering all that pain, look at your finger, look at that ring, because that is all that matters, she is right by your side and always will be. That dark time for both of you is gone, look forward. You know, I hate to say this, but there is a reason the rear view mirror is so small, and the windscreen so large, isn't that what you once told me?" Birch gave a giggle and nodded.

"You are far too clever Mrs Battersby, thanks Deb's, I guess I am worried about her, and today I have missed her chatty manner." Deb's smiled.

"Birch she is only upstairs, go to her, just be beside her and watch over her, after all, isn't that what you have done for ten years?" Birch gave a long sigh.

"Okay so now you are just getting cocky, Sweetie." Deb's gave a giggle and squeezed her hand.

"You are a good teacher, and we all love you for it, especially Abby, go on, take your sexy ass up to her, before I misbehave, I find this side of you arousing." She giggled and Birch winked at her, and got up, she walked to the door and turned back.

"Thanks Deb's." Deb's nodded and picked up her monitor, and Birch walked upstairs as Deb's headed outside, where all the others were heading for the sauna and hot tub, she smiled.

"Hot bathe with naked ladies, and then a little creamy action. Hmmm nice!"

Chapter 22

Secret Words.

I woke with a start and opened my eyes, I was facing the window, but it was not as bright as a normal morning. I heard the turn of a page and rolled over. Birch sat with her back against the headboard, reading. I yawned, and she glanced at me and smiled.

"Hi Sweetie, sleep well?"

I sat up feeling groggy, and I ached, I leaned back and turned to her, I kissed her white shoulder and then leaned my head on it, my mouth was dry, and I rolled my tongue around it and smacked my lips.

"What time is it?"

"Five thirty six." It took a minute to sink in, I lifted my head.

"In the morning, why are you sat up, you should be in bed?" She turned, and looked at me with bright green eyes.

"Sweetie, I did go to bed, I held you all night, it is Monday evening, you have slept for a whole day." I blinked at her.

"What... How the hell did that happen?" She put her book down and smiled at me, and lifted her hand to stroke back the hair from my face.

"Sweetie, you were really tired, you have done a lot in the last few months, it has taken its toll, you needed sleep so I let you sleep. The girls are making a meal, they will be happy to see you at the table."

I was trying to get my head around it; I knew I was tired, and I have slept for a day in the past, I just did not think I would sleep away a day of our holiday. I felt disappointed.

"I am sorry, it cannot have been much fun for you, what have you been up to?"

"I sat here reading." I leaned off her shoulder.

"What, all day?" She gave a nod, and then smiled.

"It was fun, I am reading Sherlock again, and you made lots of little yummy sounds in your sleep that made me giggle, I enjoyed it." Okay, so I knew she was bonkers when I married her.

"Birch you should not have wasted a day sat here; it is supposed to be a holiday for you."

"Deads, I have sat and rested, which I needed, I was with you, and you were funny, it has been a lovely day for me." I gave a sigh.

"You are aware you are completely bonkers right?" She giggled and kissed my cheek.

"I will go make you a coffee, I would imagine after a day of starving your caffeine addiction, you will need one?" She jumped off the bed with a happy smile, and walked out of the room, and suddenly I really needed a pee.

I went to the toilet, and then headed downstairs, Chloe and Deli were in the kitchen cooking, I sniffed the air, and my stomach rumbled, Birch handed me a coffee.

"Are we having Mexican?" Deli turned with a smile.

"Tacos and side salads, honestly Chloe is amazing, I am learning so much from her." I sipped my coffee.

"Chloe makes the meanest taco's ever, I love them, why do I feel you are trying to spoil me Chloe?" She turned and smiled.

"I figured if you had slept well, you would be hungry, and honestly, I love how you love my Mexican. If we throw in a beer or two, it will make for a good night for all of us." I smiled, yep, she was pity cooking for me.

It is nice to see that they are behind me, I have felt rough and tired recently, and obviously my stunningly beautiful big mouthed wife, has blabbed again. I wandered out into the garden with Birch at my side, it was warm, but not too warm, Anita was sat with Tabby, she saw me and jumped up.

"Abby… Oh my God, Abby, you will never guess what, oh God, I am so excited."

I was slowly coming round but I was not awake yet, she ran across the grass and over the bridge, her pale green eyes looked huge.

"Abby, you have been nominated for the Jonathon Grahams prize, for your contribution to youth literature."

She was so excited and bubbly, and honestly, I had no idea what she was talking about, I looked at Birch and she shrugged, I turned back to her.

"Is it a big deal?" Her eyes bulged, in disbelief.

"WELL, HELL YEAH, ABBY THIS IS HUGE!" I shrugged at her.

"Anita, to be honest, I have never heard of it, I don't really look at that stuff, how do you get nominated?" She looked absolutely stunned, and then a little nervous.

"I nominated you, Abby you are brilliant, your books have a huge following, so I put your name up, so the fans could vote. Abby, they voted for you in unprecedented numbers, you cruised the preliminary rounds. Oh God was I wrong, please don't be angry with me?" I smiled at her.

"Jesus Anita, chill out… So the fans voted for me, my readers did this, not some stuffy old cave muffins in London?" She shook her head, and gave me a huge smile.

"Abby this is a really big thing, it is like a huge honour to be nominated, I mean, it is like an Oscar for youth writers, and the fans went totally crazy and have been voting like mad, you are in the top five. Abby your readers love you, and they voted for you to get this, please go to the award ceremony, and meet your fans, there is awards for Tv and Film, and literature, you have an amazing chance of winning this." I nodded at her.

"Okay Anita, if this is from the fans, I will go and accept it if I win, just next time, let me know you are putting me up." She gave a huge squeal, and dragged me into her arms and hugged me, and then suddenly stepped back.

"Oh… That was a totally none sexual thing, it was a, I am just so happy I could explode hug, sorry. That is my girlfriend over there." She pointed, and Birch giggled behind me, I got it, she was happy, I smiled at her.

"Have you any idea how terrified and stupid you look? Anita calm down, I am well aware of the young dark haired business executive you dragged from the beach to your bed, calm down." She smiled.

"Sorry, but I am really excited for you, this is so wonderful, and it carries a lot of weight in the book readers world, just being nominated is a huge honour. It will be televised and everything, and there will be thousands of your fans there to cheer you on. Abby, I am so happy for you, after all the struggles and shit the press have thrown at you, this will really shut them up."

We headed onto the grass and I sat at the table, and relaxed as I drank my coffee, Birch sat at my side smiling, I looked at her grinning like an idiot.

"What?" She giggled at me.

"Only you could be so oblivious to the world outside your bubble. Anita told me about it earlier when she got the call, she is right, this is a big award for you Deads. I mean, it's just a hunk of glass, but thousands of people had to tick the box with your name on it to get you that award, it really is something to be proud of, look it up online and you will see." I pulled up my knees and rested my cup on them.

"Birch I could see how happy she is, and yes, I get it, I am not awake properly yet. I just want to sit quietly with you for a while, I am sorry, am I being a grouch?" She smiled and patted my hand.

"No... No, you are not, you are burned out, which is why you are here, give me your cup, and I will go and refill it, relax and enjoy the evening, and watch out for Deb's, she is thrilled, and very loud at the moment." I gave her a nod.

"Yeah, thanks for the heads up."

The tacos were a big hit, I sat outside at the table, and I felt starving, although, I had not really eaten a whole lot in the last few days. Chloe knows my weak spots, and I more than made up for it, as I stuffed them down, and felt absolutely bloated when I had finished. Wow, she is an amazing cook, I turned my chair and put my feet up on the wall, and drank my beer, Birch smiled at me, I knew she was worried about me, I know that look in her eye, but I was fine, full, and happy.

I was not really in a drinking mood, the food had woken me up, and I felt really alert, so I went in and made a coffee. I had that itchy feeling, like my fingers needed to feel a keyboard. As I made coffee, Birch came in and walked behind me, she slipped her arms round me and I leaned back, she held me tight and it felt nice.

"Deads Sweetie, you seem edgy, is there anything I can do?" I held my cup ready for the water.

"I need to write, I feel it Birch, I really need to sit somewhere quiet and just type." She nuzzled into my neck, and softly kissed,

I felt the shiver run down my spine.

"I know the perfect place, go get your laptop." I turned my head to her.

"Really, because if you want some alone time, I can do that as well?" She gave me a soft smile.

"Sweetie, I know you better, go on, get your laptop, and I will meet you here in a moment."

I am so lucky to have someone who understands, she is used to me. I suppose she sees that look in my eye and the way I fidget, and she simply knows, it is time for me. She let me go, and I ran up to my room, and grabbed my computer bag, which had pads and notes and my laptop in it.

When I got back downstairs, she took my hand and led me towards the front door, we walked right past it to another door. I had never been in what Birch called, 'His Room.' It had always been locked, but behind the door was the second downstairs room, which no one used, she took out a key and slipped it into the lock, and then looked at me.

"The last time I was in here, was a year before he died, that was twelve years ago, it is time I opened it up and went inside."

Birch turned the key, and the door clicked, and swung open, she nervously stepped through, and I followed, and closed the door behind me, was it strange I felt no one else should enter here?

The room was as big as the living room, but most of it was book cases filled with books, it caught my breath as I looked round, this was a really cool room. In the centre, at the far end facing the window, was a large mahogany desk, it was beautiful, and the sort of the desk a writer dreams of. There was a brass desk lamp, and an old lap top on it, nothing else, and behind it was a large soft looking, and well worn desk chair.

Is it weird that somehow, I felt a sense of reverence about the room, like it was a sacred space? I walked slowly round the room looking at the old books, all of them early prints of classic stories, God, this place was awesome, in my mind, it was a perfect writer's room, I felt the itch in my fingers grow.

Birch looked round it with great fondness and some sadness. On places where the book cases had empty shelves, there were small picture frames of silver, each and every one of them containing a picture of Birch and her grandfather. It felt a little like a shrine, a frozen memory of a long past era, left only for remembrance, it was clear how important Birch was to her grandfather, and also clear how incredibly close they were.

Birch swallowed hard, it was obviously a very emotional moment for her, and she was clearly remembering some very private, and personal things. I watched her closely as she stroked items, books or pictures, the edge of his desk.

"Birch are you alright coming in here, you know I do not want you to get upset, I can work elsewhere?" She looked at me and shook her head, her eyes sparkled slightly, her voice was quiet and reflective.

"I loved him dearly Deads, this place is very special to me, I have spent many hours in here, sat listening to him tell me of his life. I want you to write in here, this place is special, I want you a part of it too, so write at this desk as he did, write something wonderful."

Wow, talk about pressure, her grandfather was a huge part of her life, I looked at the laptop on the desk, it was closed shut, but there was a piece of paper between the keys and the screen. I moved to the chair, and looked at the laptop, I have no idea why, it looked like it had been here for some time, it was old and thick, and looked heavy. I reached out and lifted up the screen, revealing the piece of paper, I looked at it and swallowed, Birch just stared at it, as it contained just two words, 'For Jemi.' I looked up at her.

"Birch this is for you, it must be important." She blinked and looked at me, she was clearly really surprised.

"Deads, that is his handwriting, I am afraid to touch it, I am afraid of what is on it." I could understand that, I took a deep breath.

"Do you want me to do it?" She looked nervous.

"Birch it was obviously important to him, he left this note inside so you got it, you should look at it." She took a deep breath.

"I am afraid to look Deads, I am not sure I am ready for this."

"No offence Birch, it's been over ten years, when will you be ready?" She looked at me.

"Deads, I loved him, he was so important to me, I am afraid of what I might find on this." I looked at what was a thick brick like laptop.

"Birch this thing is ancient, it cannot have that big a memory, so whatever is on it, will not be that much. Look, how many times have you told me to face things? Honestly, this is something you should look at." I reached over and pressed the start button.

If I am honest, it has been over ten years, so I was not sure it would even start, but the thing came to life and the screen flickered, it took a while, but a load in screen came up, it was a windows XP system.

"Wow this is old, I only remember this operating system because my dad used it before he went up to seven." I looked up at her.

"It needs a password; one I think only you will know." She nodded, and looked at the screen, and swallowed hard. I could sense the emotion rising inside her, she spoke, but it was almost inaudible she whispered so low.

"It can only be, 'little white sapling,' all lowercase, that is what he called me whenever we were alone."

I leaned forward and typed the words into the box, and the laptop came to life and started to load. I got up out of the seat and offered it to her, she looked terrified. I took her hand and pulled her into the seat, and she faced the screen. It booted up, which took a while, and the desktop screen showed three files, 'Pictures, film, Read Me.' I leaned over as she stared at it.

"I say you should read that document first, and then you will know what this is about."

She nodded and clicked the document and it started to load, I saw the first few words and felt I should not look. 'My dearest Jemi, my little white sapling, I have to leave you, time has caught up with me.' I stepped back, and walked away as she stared at the screen.

Birch read each line, and I stood by the window and watched as her eyes moved along the lines, they filled with tears, and she lifted her hand to her mouth, and gave a soft sob. It felt painful to watch, I hate seeing her cry, but somehow, I sensed she needed to do this, so I lifted my bag back on my shoulder, and I left the room, and pulled the door closed quietly behind me, and went up to our room.

I sat on the bed and set up my laptop, the room has changed

little since our first visit, we do want at some point to decorate the place, but for now, little things have appeared, mainly due to Birch. We have a couple of pictures of our parents, and she even framed a picture of Avril for me, which I thought was sweet. Like all the rooms we have shared, the floor is always littered with clothing, Birch is not a tidy person, and so at times, the wardrobe is redundant until I clean up.

I looked at my screen and felt the words coming, and started to type, yet I knew in the back of my mind, Birch was sat alone in tears as her grandfather spoke to her one last time. I am not sure how long she was down there, but when she finally appeared with red puffy eyes, it was dark and late, and I had outlined three chapters of a new story.

Birch climbed into bed as I shut down my laptop, I slipped under the duvet and she cuddled up to me, and cupped my boob as always, her breathing was soft, but she was not asleep. I tried to look back, but it was too dark to see her.

"Are you going to be alright?" She gave my boob a little squeeze.

"You were right Deads, I needed to do that. I am really tired, can I talk in the morning, I want to, but I just need sleep first?" I slid my hand up to hers on my boob and gently held it.

"Okay Baby, talk when you need to, I am here for you."

She gave a sigh and snuggled into me, and I lay in the dark, my thoughts drifting, and slowly her breathing changed, and I knew she was asleep, I closed my eyes and let my thoughts wander.

It was Tuesday, and September the fourth, and the year was whizzing past, and suddenly I wanted to stay twenty eight forever, as my birthday was just five weeks away, and I was approaching that land mark of my final year of twenties. Birch would be thirty next February, and it felt weird, we were becoming grownups, and honestly, I didn't want to.

I loved being the crazy gothic loving teenager, was it at all possible to be a crazy gothic old lady? I knew Birch would say yes, she has every intention of remaining a child all her life. I will not deny, this year more than most, I felt a lot of internal changes, not unlike those I had when I was at Uni. Was this the process of settling down, or was I going to go through yet another stage of change and would emerge an even darker satanic looking butterfly than I had in my youth?

I had no idea, as I woke up the following morning, and all I knew when I walked into the kitchen, was I needed coffee, and it was served the moment I sat by Tabby. I nodded my appreciation, I think she is becoming used to seeing the naked form of the famous writer, that she was so struck by at the beach, and she appears to be settling in, and normalising to our strange life.

The good news is, she has pretty much been naked since she got here, and it has been a very positive influence on Anita, and for that fact Deli, I have not seen her in her red knickers since we got back from the beach. I looked around the kitchen.

"Where is Birch?" Deb's looked at me.

"She is in her private study, she is very quiet this morning, she asked us not to go in there, only you are allowed, is everything alright?" I sipped my coffee and looked over the mug at her.

"There are things in there, private family things, that have been left for only her. Birch has been avoiding them since her grandfather's death, which was twelve years ago, last night she took her first step forward to actually coming to terms with his loss." Deb's nodded.

"You can see by all the pictures on the walls they were very close, will she be alright?" I put my cup down and thought for a few seconds as I remembered last night.

"It was very painful for her last night, she cried a lot, which as you know is not like her, but this is good for her. She now owns his house, and all the memories that come with it, she needs to do this so she can move on."

"Okay Abby, we understand... Did you start writing again last night, I woke up to change Jenny, and thought I heard you tapping?"

I smiled at her, and lifted my cup, I noticed Anita and Tabby had stopped and they were looking at me, I giggled, as I looked at them all staring at me.

"What? I am a writer guys, it is not a big secret, I write, and yes, I started another book, something a bit different, not quite so gothic." Tabby sat down and stared at me across the table, and suddenly she was all fan girl again, although a somewhat naked one.

"Oh wow Abby, I was here when you began, is it rude to ask what it is about?" I had to chuckle, Anita looked equally as excited, Deb's bobbed on her seat, but I was used to that, I gave a sigh, even Chloe had stopped wiping pots.

"Oh God, if you must know?" They all leaned into me, with excited faces.

"I am playing with an idea of a young girl who inherits her grandmother's house, but she has not been there for four years. When she was twenty one, she inherited the house and the lands, and when she finally arrives a few weeks before she is twenty two, she discovers her grandmother had a secret life that no one knew about. The book is the story of that secret combined with her reliving all her memories of her grandmother, and growing up during her summers there. Okay is that enough?"

Tabby looked very excited, her head was resting on her hands, and her elbows were on the table, she wore a silly smile and stared at me with wonder in her eyes.

"So, what was the secret?" I laughed.

"Read the book when it's done." There were groans all around the kitchen, I looked at them in disbelief.

"Seriously guys, I only thought of it yesterday, although I did get three rough chapters out last night." I gave a sigh, as they stared at me.

"Okay the working title will be something like the old wiccan's cottage or something like that, I am not sure yet, as I said, it is a work in progress."

They all smiled, I shook my head, Tabby suddenly looked all dreamy and mushy, which was disturbing.

"The birth of a novel, and I was here when it happened, I think hanging out with all of you is pretty amazing." Chloe sniggered.

"Stick to shagging Anita, and you will get to witness the craziest shit you ever thought possible." I giggled as I got up and winked at Anita, she smiled at me.

"What about the cursed book series Abby, is that going on hold?" I shook my head.

"Three are done, the fourth is half done, and the last one is laid out, I just have to write it, I will write them side by side with this one."

"YOU HAVE FIVE NEW BOOKS, WHY ARE THEY NOT PUBLISHED?" Tabby's eyes had got bigger than even I thought possible, I looked at Anita.

"Sit her in the garden and explain the process to her, I am going to see Birch."

As I walked into the living room, I could hear Tabby interrogating Anita, it was a good dodge, after all she was my publicist, so she could sate her girlfriend's appetite. I clicked the latch and leaned my head in through the door, Birch was sat at the desk with the laptop open, she looked up and smiled, her voice was soft.

"Hi Sweetie." I smiled.

"How are you doing, last night was pretty emotional?"

I walked in and closed the door behind me, and walked over to the desk. I grabbed a wooden table chair, and pulled it across to me, and sat by her side, on the screen was a picture of her with her grandfather, she looked about ten, she was holding a massive hammer. I smiled, she was cute with her big white bunches, and cheeky face. Birch looked at me.

"He wrote me a letter, saying goodbye." She took a deep breath, and her face wrinkled a little, as she fought back the tears.

"Look what he did Deads." Birch reached down to the drawer at her side and pulled it open, tears filled her eyes, as I looked at two thick long rows of disks. Her voice rose a little higher as she fought back her tears.

"He took every picture he has ever taken or collected, and he created a photo diary of my whole life." Tears rolled down her face.

"Deads, there are hundreds of pictures." She wiped her eyes on the back of her hand.

"I have no idea how he did this; I think dad must have helped him, but he spent his last year alive, compiling a library of my life, so he could leave as many memories of him and me as possible." She pushed the draw back in, and reached lower to the bottom drawer, and pulled it open.

"Deads look... He wrote a journal for every day I was here that documented his days with me and how proud he was. The letter told me he paid a writer in London to type them all up and save them to disks, I have my whole life here with him and gran, on at least a hundred documents." I leaned into her and pulled her close, as she started to weep. All I could do was hold her and talk softly.

"He loved you so much, he did not want to leave you alone Birch, I think it is beautiful, he took every thought and every memory, and he stored it for you. Birch, you will always have him here in his words, like you will always have my love for you, in the words in your book at home. I totally get him, I really do, this is exactly what I did for you." She gave a huge sob.

"I KNOW, THAT IS WHY ALL THIS IS TOO BEAUTIFUL FOR ME TO COPE WITH!" She bawled her brains out into my shoulder, and I held her as tight as I could.

"Birch Baby, I am going to continue what he started, I have thousands of pictures of you on a hard drive, and when everything quietens down, I will sort them all out and burn them all to disks. When we next come here, you can add them, and we will document your entire life, and show how much you have been loved." She gave a huge sniffle, and lifted her head up and wiped her eyes on her hand again.

"Really... But why, Deads, I am not that important in the scheme of things?" I smiled and pushed her hair out of her face.

"You were to him, and you are to me, I completely understand him." She smiled.

"You are very like him at times, I think I saw that in you, and maybe that is why I fell so hopelessly in love with you. I really wish you could have met him; he would have loved you too." I smiled and kissed the tip of her nose.

"But I will meet him Baby, I will sit at your side for the rest of my life, and look at all his pictures, and read his journals, and through that, I will learn all about him, and enjoy sharing my love for you with him." She gave a sniffle and smiled at me; her eyes dazzled me with her tears sparkling in their bases.

"I love that idea, I really want to do that with you, I really do. I love you so much Deads, thank you, I would never have had the courage to switch this laptop on. I am so glad you did, his letter to me was lovely, I cried for hours, but it was so sweet and loving, I am so glad I read his last secret words for me." I leaned in and kissed her softly.

"Good, I am no therapist, but I actually think you needed to do that." She nodded and gave another sniffle.

"Yeah, I did." She pointed to the screen.

"Look I had big bunches, that was when we fixed the fence." I gave a grin.

"You were cute, bunches suit you, maybe you should start wearing them again." She giggled, and slipped her arm round me.

"Look at this one, see, I told you I helped build the swing set." I gave a giggle.

"The bolt is bigger than your hand, how the hell did you manage to push them all the way through?"

I sat at her side and looked at each picture, as she slowly clicked through the disk and told me all about her life as a small girl, sharing most of her school holidays with her grandfather. We laughed and joked, and she giggled as she showed me her whole life, even the embarrassing ones, and it felt wonderful and special, and very sacred.

There was that part of her I loved the most, a strange childlike innocence, and her soft reflective tone, as her big bright green eyes sparkled with joy. She had absolutely no idea how beautiful she was, both inside and out, and as I watched, and thought of her password, 'little white sapling,' I knew I was right; this truly was the place Jemi ended, and Birch started.

I had to wonder, if she picked the nick name because of her grandfather, was the name she used her tribute to him, and her way of remembering all the conversations she had growing up with him? In a way I am not sure I will ever find out, I just know that whatever secret words they shared in their many conversations, which I know she still holds dear in her heart, those words led to the person she became, the tall slender white haired, kind and caring Birch.

There really is no other word that would describe her as well, and thinking back, perhaps that is why when she first came back and stood in my mums' kitchen, after four years of being called Jemi, she broke down when mum and me called it her, I looked at her as she clicked on another picture.

"Baby, I just realised something, Birch is not your wiccan name is it, it was his nick name for you, he was the one who named you Birch, wasn't he?" She sat back and gave a soft smile as she looked at me.

"Only someone who truly loved me could work that out. Yes Deads, he called me his little white sapling for years, and then one day he just turned, and looked across the garden, and he said to me. You are too tall to be a sapling, I think you are more of a slender young Birch now. He smiled, walked over, kissed my forehead, handed me the hammer, and we fixed the gate. That was the day I took on that name, and yes when I joined Moon's Wiccan coven, I told her I was already Birch, and she smiled, and just said, 'Good name,' it suits you, and then came the hair."

We sat, and she talked, and she showed me pictures for most of the morning, and she shed a few more tears, and smiled as she held my hand. It felt special, Birch once again was opening up her secret world to me, and sharing her thoughts and feelings, just like I had done so many times, sat on my bed at Uni, or in our bed in the guest house.

I was happy to see her finally overcome her fear of facing the truth, and accepting the passing of her grandfather. I sat there wondering, if I really had left this world, how would she have managed it? Would she have avoided my home, I did not know, and hopefully it was something I wanted to avoid, I could not bear the thought of leaving her alone in this world?

I felt like I had crossed yet another milestone, and our life together would progress beyond this moment, and we would both reveal more to each other, somehow the future looked great, and that was all I wanted, simply for us to be happy sharing our lives with each other.

Chapter 23

Granite and Grime.

For Birch, looking at her pictures, and reading the journals written about her, left her quiet and reflective, which I actually didn't mind. Through Tuesday and Wednesday, we walked in the woodland, swam in the river, and sunbathed in our favourite spot. We tended to separate from the others, as they grouped together to explore and party. Birch and I did a lot of talking about her life as a girl, and in many ways, we picked up where we had left off on our first visit.

For me, this was idyllic, this was the side of her I had wanted to see, a calm quiet serious side, and I just absorbed the joy of my time with her. We walked miles holding hands and talking quietly, and made love many times in the woodlands or the meadows on her land. I was surprised at how much she actually owned, most of this side of the river and the woodland was her property, and it was a vast stretch of land.

Wednesday evening, we discovered that Tabby had a projector that attached to her computer for her business presentations, and so we gathered together all the pillows, laid out blankets and hung a sheet on a line, and watched the Basil Rathbone film of the Hound of The Baskervilles, out in the garden. I curled up with Birch on a blanket, and watched the movie, knowing that on the horizon, across the moors, was the actual moor on which it was filmed.

It felt sort of intimate and exciting, just knowing that Arthur Conan Doyle, had once walked there and written about it, and I found that inspiring. For me, to know such a great mind and writer, took what he saw and what he imagined, and spliced them together into this wonderful story, that had been adapted into the film we were watching, was amazing. Sat in the garden in the dark, looking at a white bed sheet on a washing line, it felt like a magical time, and something I think I will always look back on with great happiness.

Watching the film and talking about the moors, as we drank beer, and relaxed in the cooling night, wrapped in blankets, somehow the decision was made that we would travel the following day, and visit the large stone mass that was the tor on the moors, and so as the night got late, and we packed up, a picnic was planned on the rocks.

I collapsed into bed feeling happy and relaxed, and Birch curled around me, very drunk, and grinning from ear to ear, then she passed out. I woke up feeling groggy, and sweaty, it had been hot in the night, something made worse by Birch wrapping herself around me. She was fast asleep with her head on my chest, her legs and arms wrapped tightly round me holding me fast.

Once again, as I was becoming accustomed to, I wriggled free, in a selection of bends that any advanced yoga teacher would be proud of, and finally I was free to have a pee, and then seek a coffee.

I sat on the toilet and looked at the new bath, we had not used it yet, so I decided before we go out, I would have a bath. I went down and grabbed coffee's, actually I grabbed four, three for me and one for Birch. I put them on a plate and carried them up, much to the amusement of Anita and Tabby.

I set them down on the toilet seat and ran the bath, and added some lemon zesty bath salts to liven me up, and then I headed into the bedroom with my plate of coffee's and sat on the bed.

"Birch Baby, it is time to get up, we are going out today remember?"

She moaned and turned over onto her back, her long white eyelashes rested gently on the top of her cheeks, I leaned over and smiled.

"I am running a nice hot soapy bath, and I want you to wash all my body with hot soapy water." Her eyes popped open.

"I want that... Hi Sweetie." I handed her a coffee, and she sat up and drank it, and smacked her lips, she noticed the other coffee's and smiled, I picked up the plate.

"Your bath awaits you madam."

I turned with a smile and walked to the bathroom. She scuttled behind me looking groggy, and as I put our coffees, back on the toilet seat, she slipped into the hot water and gave a happy moan.

I slid in and sat back against her, her arms came around me as I sat happily sipping my coffee, this is without doubt, the best way to wake up.

It took longer than I thought, but to be honest, I did not want to get out, although the lemon zest salts really worked. I felt refreshed and alive, when we made it to the kitchen, where picnic preparations were in full swing, and the plasticware was out on the table ready. On the floor was a line of rucksacks and back packs, each of us had one to share the load.

At eleven o'clock we jumped into Petal and Bess, and headed off. The tor was not that far, and within thirty minutes, we were parked with our parking ticket, gathered our packs, and walked through the visitor's centre, and towards the trail up to the large granite stones.

Deb's was excited as she strapped Jenny into a carrier, and we shouldered our packs, wearing shorts and vests, and headed onto the trail. It was getting hotter by the minute, and we had quite an uphill hike on our hands. The good news was, our packs would be lighter on the way back, Birch was already lightening her load, as she opened a can of beer.

We set off, along a well worn, mowed path. Birch led the way, across the smooth grass, with mounds of thick purply pink heather, growing up in patches, through sedge grasses, ferns, and thick gorse bushes.

"Stick to the path Sweetie's, it can get boggy, even in Summer, and you really don't want to step in it."

I could see the rock in the distance, as I walked along, it loomed up, grey, cracked, and smooth, almost white in the dazzlingly bright sun. It was hot, and it looked like we were the only people here, which is the good thing about the date, most families were at home as the children had started back at school.

Birch stopped, and slipped her pack off her back, she pulled off her vest, and took off her shorts, and folded them, and pushed them into a pocket on the side of her pack. She then smiled, as she slipped the pack back on.

Needing little encouragement, Chloe did the same, and soon all of us were walking naked towards the rocks, as the sun intensified. I have never walked naked out in the open, and the light breeze on my skin felt so much nicer than my hot sweaty vest. It also felt rebellious and dangerous, which was really fun. Birch reached out, and took my hand.

"Deads we are walking in the footsteps of a great writer, it's crazy to think he came here and as a result, wrote what is the most famous Holmes story, and hey, you are a writer and a Watson, it is almost like fate brought you here." It was an interesting thought.

"I bet he didn't do it naked though?" She giggled.

"Isn't this wonderful, naked and free in the wilderness?"

I could not deny, this is something I have never done before, and with the soft breeze blowing across me, it felt freeing and liberating, and I wanted to just smile all day.

We were all hot, sweating, and panting a little, when we reached the rocky tor. It was a lot higher than I had thought it was, as the huge hunks of grey stone rose up in the air, covered in patches of moss. Just seeing the height of it, kind of put me off wanting to sit on top of it. Chloe and Birch had no fear, and dropped their packs, and headed around to the lower side, and climbed away, my fear of heights kicked in, and I stayed put, at the base on the green grass.

It felt strange that no one else was there, but it also felt special that we had it all to ourselves. I helped Deb's get her back carrier off, and put out the blanket, so she could change, and feed Jenny. I had grown a new respect for Deb's, having a baby is pretty intensive, and she is a really good mum. She appears prepared for everything, and has a bag armed with every essential need she may incur, her whole life is tailored around the routine of caring for Jenny.

I think I am a little too selfish, I like my private time too much, I am not sure Deb's gets that much. Even so, she appears really happy, although I think she has started to note, I have a little bit of baby phobia. I do tend to steer clear of any care duty at the moment, and I am always happy to step back when Deli, who loves babies, jumps in.

All of us sat and unpacked the food, I had worked up quite an appetite, and sat back with a beer and sandwiches, and just enjoyed the scenery, lying naked in the sun and feeling its heat, it felt idyllic as I looked up, and heard Birch shouting from high above me. She leaned right over and waved.

"Hi Sweetie." My stomach churned.

"Birch be careful, please don't fool around, it is dangerous."

She looked so tiny all that way up there, that it freaked me out, and I had to look away. I tried to focus my attention elsewhere, and I took out my camera, and started to shoot the landscape. I could see for miles, and was in awe of the patchwork of fields and forests that spread across the landscape to the horizon.

There were all sizes and shapes of patches in lush deep greens, surrounded by bronze and pinks, and mustard yellows, all fitted together in a random pattern, below the thick bright blue band of the sky, it was breath taking.

The floor all around us was littered with buried boulders of granite, their tops just rising up through the grass a few inches, or a couple of feet, all worn with the wind and the rain, in smooth shapes, like years of smooth huge pebbles crushed together. I could see layers all stacked and smooth, forming patterns, shapes, and lines on their surface. I found it fascinating, as I took picture after picture. Deb's smiled as I took a picture of all of them feasting, sat on the blanket.

"This is a beautiful place, I am so glad we came, the next time I read Hound of the Baskervilles, I will picture it so differently in my mind, as I now have the actual moor firmly in my brain." I nodded as I looked across the moor.

"It is sort of mind blowing isn't it, to think at one time Conan Doyle himself was here, and then a full camera crew came up here to shoot Basil in the movie, it's a book nerds Mecca." She giggled at me.

"It's defo our Mecca."

She was right, we must have seen the movie a million times together in our youth. Birch reappeared, much to my relief, and walked up, then slipped her arm round my waist.

"Shoot the other side, it looks like that is where they did most of the filming, come on and bring your tripod, I want pictures of us here."

Birch took me round to the other side, and she was right, I recognised part of the splintered rock. I noticed that steps had been cut into the stones, although looking up, I still had no wish to climb. I set up the camera, and focused it on her, and hit record, I thought I would shoot some film, and then lift stills from it, she smiled, and pulled me into her arms.

"Is it filming?" I nodded at her, as her eyes danced.

"Yeah why?" She pulled me close and just as she was about to kiss me, she smiled.

"Elementary my dearest Watson."

I giggled just as she kissed me, and I spluttered into the kiss, but it felt wonderful, stood naked, out in the wilds and kissing her. The kiss was long and passionate, and when she broke apart her eyes twinkled.

"I love this Deads, all of us here out in the wilds naked and free, this is how life should be lived, just being one in all of this, we should get a picture of all of us together here."

I agreed, and returned to my camera, and stopped the film, and watched the file save, I was actually thrilled I had got film of us alone kissing. It felt special and wonderful, and I knew I would play this a lot when we were back home.

Ten minutes later we returned to the group, and I set up the camera, and all of us posed naked in front of the rock. I set the timer and hurried to Birch's side, we all raised our arms in the air as the camera flashed its little beeping light, and we screamed at the top of our voices.

"ELEMENTARY CURIO'S!" The picture was taken, and we all fell about laughing.

For the next few hours, we lounged on the grass and had our picnic and drank beer. Deb's and Chloe were driving so they hit the lemonade, as we larked around, and talked about the future, and the fact that Anthony's birthday was at the weekend. It was actually tomorrow, but he would not be back until Sunday, so we planned for a surprise party, as we would have to leave tomorrow evening, something I did not really want to do.

It is funny how much a place can grow on you, and Sunny Bank had. I really felt at home there, and even though I knew we could come anytime we wanted; I hated leaving. Although I knew going back to Wotton would also be a nice homecoming for me, I did miss my room when we were away.

It was really getting warm, even though clouds had rolled in, and I moved to one of the large grey stones that rose about a foot out of the grass. I sat with my camera, feeling the heat of the rock, under my exposed bottom. There were dark hared horses all over the slope, grazing away, with their long manes lifting softly in the breeze, it felt so calm and peaceful, almost like just being here, the earth pulled the weariness from my body.

How many others had stood here feeling the same, almost as if they were connecting to the earth, and feeling it's energy flow all around them? It sounds crazy, but it felt like that this was a sacred space, a place that had meaning going back thousands of years, a place that had been a landmark or gathering spot, and I wondered, what mystical beliefs had been woven around this place in the past?

Birch came over as I sat with my knees up, pointing my camera at the landscape, she slid in behind me, nudged up, and leaned on my shoulder.

"What are you shooting?" I leaned back slightly into her.

"The landscape, it is so beautiful up here, I want to remember it. I love that your grandfather made a photographic record of all of your life, and I want to continue it. I am going to sort through all my pictures and burn them to CD, and add them next time we are here, but I want it to show us, and our life together. Is it strange I want a record of our life together?" She slipped her arms around my waist and snuggled in tighter.

"I think it is a lovely idea, I must admit looking back through some of the pictures has brought back a lot of happy memories for me. I would love to see what you have from Uni and the guest house; I know you took a lot of sneaky pictures." I gave a giggle.

"I have always taken pictures of you, I know now, it was a huge girl crush. Back then I just put it down to you were different, and interesting to me. I am glad I took them; I sat for hours when I had to come home without you from Uni looking at them, they helped me when I missed you. I have had so many happy moments with you, I am really glad they were captured." She kissed my neck and I shivered, she giggled.

"The clouds are building, I think maybe we should consider packing up, the weather around here can change fast."

She was not wrong, as we folded the blankets and packed everything up, the clouds rolled in and the temperature fell. I started to shiver and put my vest and shorts back on, which to be honest did nothing. It started to rain, at first it was just the odd big drops, that hit the grey stone and spread out, and then the pace slowly increased, and by the time everything was packed up, it was pelting it down, and we were getting soaked.

Deb's had little Jenny hanging from her front, Birch yanked a thin clear mac out of her bag, and pulled it over her to keep her protected. I gave her the car keys, and looked at Deli.

"Go ahead with Deb's, and get them both in Petal, stick to the path."

Deli took Deb's by the hand and led her off fast, as we packed the last of the gear, and checked there was no litter left anywhere. The wind was rising as the rain drove down, it was hard to believe just an hour ago we had been naked, and sweating under a baking sun. Once packed, I looked at Birch, she was still naked and her hair hung lank, her large cloth bag was getting soaked.

"Come on Baby, we need to hurry."

She took my hand and together we started down the path, it was almost impossible to see, the rain was hitting my face so hard. I looked back at the others.

"Stick together, and keep close."

The grass was now very slippery, as the water hit the hard earth, and ran off in torrents, and we slipped about all over the place, it was insane. I had never known rain like it, well, apart from the night Rodney struck. Visibility was almost zero, as the rain was so thick, it was like a heavy fog of falling water droplets, I wanted to hurry, but my pumps were sliding about all over the place.

We trudged on slipping and sliding for twenty minutes, I was drenched and shaking so violently with my shivers, it made my legs slide even more, Chloe yelled at us.

"Let's just run for it, at this rate we will never get off here."

I was shivering so violently I could barely focus on her, my teeth started to chatter and I was soaked to the skin. I have heard so many stories of this, sudden downpours, and people getting lost. They never seemed real, but this was a real eyeopener, and I will not deny, I was feeling really frightened by it. Birch moved closer holding my hand tight, and looked back at the others.

"Running will not help, we can barely stand as it is, just lean into it, stay together, and move as fast as you can."

I nodded, and tried to stroke my hair back behind my ears, it was glued to my face. Chloe shook her head and moved quickly in front, she started to move faster, she had a little bit better traction than I did, with her bare feet.

She tried to run, and her feet slid and she staggered, she gave a yell, and went out of control. The hill was steep and incredibly wet. I watched in horror as she went flying down the slope, then slipped sideways, she headed right into the thick fern and sedge, and disappeared with a mighty splash. We hurried the best we could, she was face down in three inches of water, she shook her head, and watched as her hands sunk into the mud below.

Chloe pulled her arm back, and it came out with a squelch, but her other arm sank deeper. As soon as I saw her, I panicked, after all, I had read Baskervilles many times, and the fear of the bogs that swallowed people was now fresh at the front of my mind. Birch yanked me back from running to her, I tried to shake my hand free, she turned to me.

"Slow down, we will help her, just don't rush." I nodded as we hurried forward, Chloe gave a squeal as her arm sank in further.

"Guys I am fucking stuck; it won't come out." Anita and Tabby were at my side, as Birch stepped forward slowly, she pointed behind her.

"Deads, step there only."

She took another step forward, I could see the pool, I had not even noticed it lost in the grass as I walked up earlier. Birch crouched down, and reached out her arm to Chloe. I was still holding Birch's other arm, and tightened my grip. Birch inched forward slowly.

"Chloe, stay perfectly still, and do not struggle, just relax and wait for me."

Birch inched forward slowly, keeping her feet firmly on the thick tufts of sedge grass. Chloe held out her free muddy hand, covered in the thick slimy ooze. Birch touched her fingers, and leaned forward more, I pulled on her arm to balance her. I was terrified Birch would fall in with her, or on top of her. Anita gripped my shorts at the back. Their fingers touched, and Birch smiled as she curled the tips into Chloe's.

"I always said you were a dirty bitch."

Chloe smiled and relaxed, feeling Birch's fingers gripping hers, they locked, and she pulled, Chloe inched forward. I felt the tension from Birch's hand on mine, as she pulled back, my god, she had a grip like a vice, she almost crushed my hand. Chloe tried to lift her legs and push on the watery surface of the mud, and she inched closer.

"Fuck Birch, my hooch is filled with slime." Birch smiled.

"Trust me, you are usually so bloody wet, you probably have a thick layer of protection, and anyhow, mud is good for the skin, maybe it will improve the look of your ugly taco."

Chloe giggled, and came a little further forward, her other arm was coming out, Birch heaved hard, and I took a step back, feeling Anita pull at my shorts. There was another squelch, as the rain pounded us, and Chloe slid faster, it was probably a good thing she was not dressed, although looking at my white vest, which was pretty transparent, I don't suppose it would matter much?

We stepped back again, and Chloe slid onto the grass and pulled herself free under her own steam. Visibility was not easy, but she clearly looked really frightened, Birch gave a gasp and let go of my hand. I wriggled my fingers to bring them back to life, she helped Chloe stand on the sedge, she was covered in thick mud, but it was raining so hard, it was running down her legs, and she was right, her hooch was covered, I shuddered. Chloe gave a giggle.

"I wondered how you kept your hooch so pretty Birch." She giggled. Birch smiled.

"Organic lube, not that you needed any?"

She laughed, and came back over to the path to join me, I felt so relieved. It was crazy, it had all happened so fast, Conan Doyle was not wrong, this place can be murderous. Chloe smiled, and pulled a huge lump of mud off her hair, it slopped to the floor, I gave a giggle.

"If Anthony could see you now, he would freak, hell Chloe, you scared the hell out of me." She threw her head back and let the rain run down her hair.

"I have had worse things stuck in my hair to freak Anthony out." She looked at me and smiled.

"Freaked myself out too Abby, this place is seriously fucked up."

Back on the path and holding hands, we staggered back to the car park, which was slow going, it was deserted apart from our vehicles. Chloe rubbed herself as the rain pounded down, to get off as much mud as possible, Deli opened the back of Petal, and we threw all the packs in, and I grabbed the blanket and gave it Chloe to rub herself down with.

Deb's had the engine running, and the blowers on full with the wipers going at high speed. Deli rooted around in Chloe's pack, found her keys, and unlocked Bess, and Anita and Tabby jumped in. I climbed into the back of Petal with Birch, grabbed another blanket, and wiped Birch down to try and dry her. Both of us were shivering, and she wrapped it around us both, and we huddled under the blanket to try and warm each other, she giggled as her hands wandered under the blanket.

"Ooh Sweetie that is not supposed to be that cold." I jerked in the seat opposite Jenny.

"Pack it in pervert, children are watching." She giggled and snuggled up to me.

The drive back was a lot slower, visibility on the road was not great, and I was greatly relieved to see Sunny Bank, although it was not that sunny at the moment. I jumped out with the keys as Deb's parked, and Birch unstrapped Jenny's seat. Bess drove in and pulled up, as I unlocked the door, and then ran back for our bags. The sliding door opened and Chloe stepped out, she was pale and shivering, I pointed.

"Go straight in and get in the shower, all of us will need one, just to warm up."

Birch ran with Jenny still in her seat, and got her inside as quickly as possible, and placed the seat on the kitchen table, she turned up the heating, and the boiler fired up. The rest of us grabbed our stuff and ran to the house. Ten minutes later, we all stood dripping in the kitchen wrapped in towels, but smiling, it was actually quite the adventure.

Chloe came down with a smile, and was handed a hot mug of coco, all of us had them, as Anita, made herself useful. We took it in turns to shower and warm up, Birch insisted she shower with me, I think the wild moors had unleashed her inner pervert. We came down with large smiles and Deb's rolled her eyes.

"You two are worse than dogs, talk about bitches in heat?" Everyone giggled.

It was our turn to cook, as the rain continued outside, the house was warm and toasty, and Birch and myself set too, and made a huge pan of curry. We broke out the wine, still wrapped in towels and headed into the living room, where Chloe and Tabby had lit the fire, the wood crackled and hissed in the hearth, and we all sat round with big bowls of curry and runny noses, it was far spicier than we intended.

Tomorrow was to be our last day, and in a way, all of us were a little saddened, we had all slept late and relaxed, and we were all feeling very rested. Our week had been spent gathered together, and living in a relaxed atmosphere, not unsimilar to home, but here it felt different. We sat out in the sun and talked, and shared stories of our lives, cooked together, and laughed together, and I felt much closer to all of them.

Tabby had been new to us just five days ago, and yet she now felt like one of us. I had watched her and Anita all week, and they really did hit it off, and I was pleased for both of them. In some of their talk, it had been clear they had both been hurt in the past, and it felt nice to see them being so nice with each other, I hoped they could make something of it, it certainly looked like they had made a good start.

I was sat with Birch curled up in a towel on the cottage suite, and feeling a little tipsy, I had noted Birch was happily filling our glasses with more wine, I somehow suspected the wild country had ignited a few flames within her, her hand was wandering again under the towel, I jerked and giggled, and her eyes sparkled. It was past midnight, and so I got up and took her hand.

"Guys, my wife is demanding, so I am going to say goodnight."

I walked to the door, pulling the drunken giggling Birch behind me. We made it four steps up, and suddenly my towel was gone, she cackled behind me, I pushed my bum back, and wiggled it, and then felt the pain, and squealed, as she sunk her teeth into my soft round cheek. I ran up the stairs, and she came up behind me laughing wildly, yep, the smell of damp earth had set her off.

I stumbled as she caught me, I sprawled forward onto the bed, my bum in the air, and she was on me. I squealed, and pushed my face into the bed, as she dived into me from behind. I was right, she was wild, and she was attacking my button like a ravenous beast.

I bit into the duvet and gave out a long slow moan, and clawed at the bed, she pulled away and started to kiss my buttocks, and then I felt her fingers slip in and explore me, it drove me wild, as I felt her lips moving over my bum, and her fingers began to vibrate as she sped up.

I screwed up my eyes, and my whole body started to burn and shake, it felt like I was being shocked constantly, and the pressure within me just began to build, I did not think I could take any more. I wanted to move and stop her, it was becoming unbearable, I wailed out into the duvet, and suddenly my whole body spasmed, as I felt her tongue roll around my little rose bud.

My eyes flashed, and my legs tensed, and my whole body exploded, Birch gave a squeal of joy, and bit me again, I yelped and fell over, and rubbed my ass.

"Holy shit Birch that hurt." She giggled and crawled onto me.

"You have a bum like a little firm peach, and I have wanted to bite it for ages, and Sweetie, it was lovely."

She leaned over me, and her eyes were big, round, and green, and she looked possessed, yet really sexy. She moved closer and started to kiss me, and I felt special and adored, and it just felt so great.

I lay back calming down, as she smiled, and curled round me, and I stared at the ceiling slowly moderating my breathing, and drifting in my loved up moment. I cannot explain how insanely wonderful it feels, when this person who feels so much love for you, just grabs you, and goes out of her way to make you feel this amazing.

I never for a moment dreamed I could feel this way when I was younger. My view of the world was so different now, well it had to be, I married a woman. Birch moved, and lifted her head off my abdomen.

"Sweetie, let's get in bed and cuddle, I am sleepy now."

It was hard to move, my legs felt so weak, so I crawled slowly up the bed, and Birch dragged the duvet back, and I slid in.

"Oh Baby, I think you broke me, my legs are still shaking." She chuckled, as I lay back, and she slipped in at my side and pulled the duvet over us. She curled around me and snuggled into my shoulder.

"I loved today Deads, I know it rained like mad at the end, but it was fun. I sort of liked running around in the rain, it made me feel really free and sexy, and you looked so sexy, especially when you held my hand and pulled me back to help Chloe."

She was right, it was chaos, but it was pretty wild out there, I never thought I would walk on a moor naked, or walk in rain like that, and it did feel good and exhilarating, and tonight felt really special, as we all sat round the fire talking.

I felt happy and warm and spoiled, as I lay looking out of the window at the moon, as the clouds rolled past it, and with a slight smile on my face, I drifted, and the sound of Birch's soft breathing stroked my senses, and I went into the land of happy dreams, secure in the world that surrounded Sunny Bank.

Chapter 24

Strange Guest.

I am sure I have said it already, but there is something special about coming home. It is crazy, because my room never really changes, the bed, two desks, and the sofa never move, the only thing that does, is the amount of Birch's clothing on the floor. It felt good to sit at my desk and switch on my computer, as I sipped a coffee.

It had been a pretty busy day, we had risen late with hangovers, drank lots of coffee, and then done a huge clean up of the house, sat in the garden for an hour, and then locked up and left, to get ahead of the traffic. I drove all the way home, quietly talking with Birch, enjoying our last few moments together, and unpacked. Tabby drove Anita to our house, had a quick coffee, grabbed her car, then the two of them left for home. I am not sure who's, but that was a good thing.

Deb's headed for her parents, Birch went into the office to catch up with Izzy, and Deli had Sophia arrive, and they went to her room to talk. Luke looked exhausted, and glad to see us, Edwina was all smiles, and Anthony had uploaded a lot of pictures of him having a great time, to our private server. He would be back Sunday, but today was his birthday, and his presents were piled up on the table in the library.

For the next few hours, I was home, which meant emails on my own website, and the Curio site. I have posted all week to Insta, mainly for Sophia as I promised I would, so a lot of fans knew I was taking a break. They also knew I went dark on social media when I was writing, so as expected, there was not that many private emails for me, just a lot of comments to administrate.

Once finished, I gathered together all the washing for Birch and myself, and headed downstairs to the washing machine, and threw it all in. It was nice to see Chloe sat in her studio, surrounded by sketches from the holiday, as she stared at a clean canvass, putting her thoughts together. It is strange, I had seen her sketching all week, yet not really understood at the time, the millions of ideas she had been thinking of, and every thought would eventually become a picture.

In many ways we are very alike, she sees pictures in a situation, I see words, and write them. Chloe will paint something wonderful, because of the week away, I have already started a story, and it is very different from anything I have ever written, because of Sunny Bank. It was a busy afternoon, but it was worth it to be home and back to normal.

Sunny Bank is wonderful, and I love being there, and on those moments I was alone with Birch, it was very special. Saying that, I guess it is nice to come back to normality, whatever that may be, and so I rolled up my sleeves, and got stuck in, so that as of tomorrow, everything would be as it always is. I was busy folding washing when Birch arrived home, she walked in with Izzy talking, and came down towards the kitchen, she saw me folding her clothes and smiled.

"Hi Sweetie, you know I would have done them, you did the last wash?" I folded her jeans, and placed them on the pile.

"You were busy and I had the time, I also wanted to do mine, it would have been stupid to not have done yours." She kissed my cheek.

"Thanks... I will do the next two washes." She turned for the hallway.

"I am just going to get changed, I am expecting a delivery, if it comes shout me."

I nodded and she headed up the hallway, I pulled my vest out of the dryer, and started to fold it. Halfway down the hall, the buzzer buzzed, and Birch yelled out.

"I WILL GET IT."

She headed to the door and pulled it open, and was startled to see a man in a long green anorak, with a stubbly chin, and long greying lank, greasy hair. He had dull hazel looking eyes, and looked very tired and underfed. Birch was taken a little by surprise.

"Hello, can I help you?" He looked past her shoulder, he appeared on edge, then he looked back at Birch.

"I was told Debbie Ford lived here; can I see her?" Birch stared at him, he was dirty and thin, and to be honest, stunk a little, and she was wary.

"I am sorry, no one called Ford lives here." He looked over her shoulder.

"Look love, it has taken me a long time to track her down, so stop pissing around, and tell her I am here."

Birch gripped the door, and leaned back a little, he leaned into her, and his breath was a mix of tooth decay and alcohol.

"There is no one here by that name, I am sorry it has taken so long, but whoever told you to come here was wrong."

I picked up the folded clothes, and placed them into the large laundry basket and lifted them off the unit, Izzy smiled as she added a shot of whiskey to her coffee.

"You can do mine if you want?" I gave her a chuckle.

"What you paying?" She smiled.

"I won't kill you while you sleep." I laughed, as I turned into the hallway.

"Stop pissing me around, I fucking know she is here, so just go and fucking get her."

I stopped as I saw Birch holding the door, her feet rooted to the spot, and saw the face of the man that was looking right over her shoulder at me. I felt my heart lurch in my chest, as I took a large gasp of air.

"Abigail, I fucking knew it, tell this slag to let me in so I can see her?"

I felt a tinge of fear, as I put the basket down, and walked slowly towards the figure stood in front of Birch. He looked even worse than the last time I saw him. I was not sure what I should say, he had always scared the hell out of me, and I knew what he had done to Ellen. Birch was really close to him, and I felt a little panicked, Birch needed to get away from him, she did not understand who he was, and I had to act quickly. I walked slowly up to just behind Birch's side.

"Mr Ford... Debbie is not here." He gave a sigh.

"Don't fuck with me Abigail, if you are here, she will be, my God, you two are joined at the hip. Just tell her all I want is to talk." I shook my head.

"I am not lying Mr Ford, Deb's used to live here, but she moved out when... She does not live here anymore, I am sorry."

Birch glanced at me, and she saw my fear, she was starting to put two and two together, she turned back to him.

"As I said, she is not here, now if you don't mind, I think you need to leave?" He stared at her and smirked.

"Just who the fuck are you anyhow, standing there fucking giving me orders?"

He moved closer, and Birch's hand tensed on the door, I felt a strong tinge of fear, but she did not move. Her eyes locked on his, Izzy appeared at the bottom of the hallway, Edwina stood at the library door and looked at me, Birch stood resolute.

"I own this house, and I get to say who comes in, now I feel I have been patient considering your abusive language, and so I am asking you politely, considering your daughter is not here, that you leave quietly." He smiled.

"Oh yeah... What if I don't believe you, what if I say you are just bullshitting me, and that she is really here hiding behind your skirts, what then bitch?"

I pulled my phone out of my pocket and started to tap on the messages, Birch smiled.

"Oh Sweetie, I am wearing pants, and as much as I hate to admit it, her boobs are just too big to hide behind one of my legs... The gate is there, and it's open, please use it."

Luke appeared at the top of the stairs, and watched, Edwina was tapping on her phone too. Izzy walked slowly up the hallway to my side, she glanced at my phone and saw the message I had sent to Deb's.

Birch looked at him standing, not really sure of what to do, he looked back at the gate, and then back at Birch, and then over her shoulder to me, and he smirked again.

"What did she say, I saw you on your phone Abigail, did you tell her to get her fucking ass here?" I lifted my eyes and looked at him, I have never liked him, I stared at him.

"I told her to tell her dad you were causing trouble for me."

It was probably not my smartest move, he looked really angry and his eyes glared at me. I saw his temple pulse, like it had done so many times, and his temper just boiled up and thundered out.

"I AM HER FUCKING DAD, THAT WANKER HAS NO RIGHT TO HER."

I shook my head as Izzy moved closer to the door. I stared at him, time felt like it had stopped, as I felt my anger, and my fear grow inside me. I swallowed hard, as I looked at his cold eyes, the tension around all of us felt close and claustrophobic. I took in a deep breath, and stared at him, I felt no kindness at all for him.

"You were never a father, a father is someone who is there and shows love, and actually gives a shit, and that just was not you was it; I know, I was there to hold her when she cried. Where the fuck were you?"

Yeah, I probably should not have said that. He went bright red, as his faced screwed up, I could see the anger boiling up inside him. Izzy sensed it, and her arm moved slowly and pushed me back.

He glared at me, and I could almost feel the tension double, and suddenly, he lurched forward into Birch, pushed her heavily, and she came back through the door sprawling onto the floor. She squealed out, as I screamed, and almost dropped my phone.

He moved at a fast pace through the door, heading straight for me, and everything went from bad to worse. Birch kicked out her legs, and Izzy pounced, as Luke came hurtling down the stairs at high speed, I stood frozen, rooted to the spot, and panicked.

"WHY YOU FUCKING LITTLE SLUT, I WILL FUCKING... OMPH!"

He slammed into the floor hard, right in front of me, with Izzy on top of him, and found his arm yanked up his back, as he was pinned to the ground. I blinked as he yelled out in pain, and stepped back, as Izzy looked over him holding him firm. It happened so fast, it did not at first register on me, Edwina looked terrified, and Luke looked down at him with hate, his fists clenched tight. Izzy leaned over him, and spoke through gritted teeth.

"You were asked to leave; your daughter is not here." He squirmed on the floor, trying to move, but Izzy had him pinned down hard, and he was going nowhere.

He stared up at me with eyes of hate, in the kitchen Chloe was on the phone to Bradley, who had her on speaker, wheels outside screeched loud on the road. I heard the crunch of the gravel outside on the drive, a sliding sound, and Deb's appeared at the door with tears in her eyes as he looked up at me and spat.

"Fucking think you are better than me don't you whore, I know all about you Abigail, you slag?"

I stepped back away from him, feeling the fear rise up inside me, and tears filled my eyes. Birch was at my side, and put her arm round me, Deb's screamed from the doorway.

"DAD STOP, YOU HAVE NO RIGHT!"

Izzy held him firm, as he turned his head back, and saw Deb's in the doorway, on the drive, Bradley stood by his car door watching, as he spoke to Chloe. Izzy leaned over him, and pulled on his arm, and he screwed up his face, and cried out in pain. Her teeth were clenched tight, her anger obvious, she looked down at him, and spoke.

"I am going to free your arm, and you are going to be polite to your daughter, and if you are not, trust me, you are no match for me, and I will break both your arms. I have fought way bigger men than you. Do you understand me?"

Birch pulled me back a few more feet, Izzy looked up at me, and gave a nod, she released his arm slowly, and stood back freeing him, he rolled on the floor, and looked at Deb's stood in the doorway crying, she shook her head.

"It is always the same isn't it, you just cannot be polite or nice, you have to hit and hurt, you never learn? I told you didn't I, leave me alone and stay away from me, I am sick of the violence and the hate, when will you stop Dad?"

He sat up, and rubbed his arm, he gave Izzy a filthy look, and then looked at Deb's as she wept, the shadow of Bradley just out of view.

"You are my kid, I wanted to see you, none of this would have happened if these slags had not provoked me." Deb's gave a sniffle.

"Don't call them that, they are good decent people, why do you have call everyone Dad? Why do you want to see me, you left when I was thirteen, so why now Dad, why after fifteen years, you never cared before?"

He stood up and Birch tensed, he had his back to me, but she pulled me back, stepped in front of me, and gently pushed me back more. I could see how alert she was. Luke stepped to one side, between Jonathon Ford and his daughter, Izzy was level with him on the other side of the door, he held out his arms.

"Debbie, Darling, I always wanted to see you, but she would not let me, I hope you know that? It was never me; it was always her, honestly, come on Princess, I am your dad." She wiped her eyes on her sleeve.

"No Dad, you left and you never wanted to see me, I heard your voice that night, you told mum she and me were just sluts and you had better. I heard you Dad, you called me a spoiled little bitch, and said I was dragging you down. I was there Dad at the top of the stairs, and I saw you with that woman you left with, you didn't want us, so you just left."

He took a step forward and Luke tensed, Jonathon looked at him, and then back to Deb's, he shook his head.

"What is past is past, look I am here now, I came looking for you, it took a long time, that's all."

He took another step forward, and Birch reached out to her bag on the hook, I panicked, holy shit, was she going for her knife? Deb's shook her head.

"It is too late, I am sorry, but you hurt me so badly when you said that, because I loved you Dad, and you said that about me. I am done with you, I have a new life, a better life, I have a husband who really cares for me. He is better than you ever were. You left me, and went off with her, I want you to leave and never come back. I am sorry Dad, but I have a better dad now, and he is so kind and loving, he is everything you could never be. I don't want you in my life, just go away and get drunk like you always do. Dad, you have been asked to leave this house, you should leave, you are not welcome here." He took another step forward and his tone changed.

"I not leaving till I am done, you ungrateful bitch…"

Birch pulled a silver pistol out of her bag, and I gasped with horror and shock. She walked up to the back of Jonathan, and tapped his shoulder, he spun around, and she pushed the gun into his forehead, her eyes burned with fire.

"I am done with this shit, I told you, this is my house, you got your visit, now piss off or I will cap your ass, do you understand this better than politeness?"

He looked terrified, and lifted his arms, and took a step back. I felt my brain going into free fall, what the hell was she doing, did she have no idea at all of what this man was like? Birch pushed, and the gun put more pressure on his forehead, I was in total shock and heading to melt down.

"Birch what the hell!?" She stared at Jonathan, and pushed with the gun, he took another terrified step back.

"Deads Sweetie, it is alright, I have used this a few times, don't worry, I won't miss."

Luke grabbed Deb's, and pulled her in through the door, and dragged her over behind him. Deb's pretty much looked as I felt. Izzy was really bloody cool about it, Edwina looked shocked and terrified, as she just stared at Birch who was looking really pissed off, more than any of us had ever seen her. She gritted her teeth as he backed out of the door.

"I told you where the gate is, get the hell through it, and if you ever come within a hundred miles of this place, I will put 22 calibres of sense into that ignorant head of yours, do you understand me?"

His eyes were wide open, and he looked too terrified to nod, he just stared at her in complete fear. I felt my knees shaking, I hate guns, and all this time she has been walking round with a bloody pistol in her bag? My brain was swirling trying to understand what the hell was happening, who was this mad person I was married to?

Birch walked him out of the door, and he turned and ran for the gates, even Bradley looked shocked as he side stepped out of the way. Jonathon did not wait; he flew down the drive screaming.

"You are just slags and psycho's all of you, fucking mad bitches." Birch smirked and shouted back.

"YOU BETTER BLOODY WELL BELIEVE IT!"

I looked at Izzy and Edwina, Deb's was cowering behind Luke who looked as shocked as we did. I swallowed hard, feeling utter disbelief as I looked at everyone.

"Are you guys okay with this, I mean, she has a frigging gun in her bag?" Izzy shrugged.

"I am okay with it, I have owned a few in my time, I used to shoot on a range in Delph." Edwina was just staring at the door, as Birch walked in with Bradley, and closed it behind her with a smile. I looked at the silver pistol in her hand, and just fell apart.

"BIRCH WHAT THE HELL, YOU HAD A GUN IN THERE ALL THIS TIME, AND WHAT THE HELL DO YOU MEAN YOU

HAVE USED IT LOADS OF TIMES, AND NEVER MISS, YOU KNOW I HATE GUNS?" She shrugged, and her eyes twinkled.

"I have used it many times." She lifted it up, and pulled the trigger, and we all tensed, as a flame popped out of the end of it.

"See Sweetie, I like lighting my spliffs with it."

"Huh?" She smiled at me.

"Oh, Sweetie did you think it was real?"

Edwina and Luke looked really relieved, and started to laugh, my heart was close to exploding in my chest, and my pulse rate was doing overtime, as I stared at the flame with utter disbelief, she walked up to me and smiled.

"Sweetie did you think it was real, I am sorry, I thought you knew?"

She pulled her arms round me, and pulled me close, I was lost for words, and just folded into her as I trembled, as Edwina laughed in the library doorway. My head was spinning as she held me tight.

"Sweetie when confronted with a life threatening situation, most people fail to notice the details, it is basic psychology, so I thought I would see if that was true, and hey, guess what... SURPRISE!?"

I married a psychopath, I am sleeping with a mentally unstable woman, she slipped back, and pulled her arm round my waist, and stuck her fake gun into her waist band, and guided me to the kitchen.

"Come on Sweetie, we can have a drink, you are a little shocked, let me pour you a good rum, it will help relax you a little." Bradley pulled Deb's into his arms, and held her close.

"Are you alright... You did good sweetheart, he needed to hear what you think?" She snuggled into him, and he smiled as he held her close.

I felt numb, as Birch sat me down, and walked around the kitchen, and grabbed the bottle of rum and a glass, I couldn't do anything but stare at the gun in her belt. It looked so real, and she noticed and smiled, she pulled it out of her waistband and put it on the island in front of me.

"Look Sweetie it is not real, no one but a really scared person would take it seriously, it is nothing to be scared of."

I stared at it, and to be honest it looked real to me. I had seen her pull it out of her bag, and felt terrified, but there again, I hate guns, and have never been this close to a real one, I looked at her.

"I was really scared Birch, if it had gone off, I would have died." She smiled as she added cola to my rum, and some ice.

"If it had gone off, all he would have lost is his hair and eyebrows. Sweetie, I would never own a real gun, I feel confident with that one because I know it is not real."

I took a deep breath as I looked at it, and she put the glass down in front of me, Edwina and all the others joined me, Bradley patted Birch on the shoulder.

"Thank you, I did not want to hit him, but if he had put so much as a finger on her, I probably would be under arrest now." Deb's sat down and took my hand in hers, she smiled as I turned to her.

"Thanks Abby." I nodded at her, still feeling dazed.

"Are you alright?" She leaned into me and kissed my cheek.

"Yeah, I am with the only family I need, and I am okay, honestly." She reached out and picked the gun up, and looked at it.

"It does look real, doesn't it?" I shook my head.

"I hate it, I hate guns." Birch sat down in front of me, and looked at Deb's.

"Keep it Deb's, put it with your taser, if Deads really hates it that much, then take it out of the house." I looked at her, and her eyes smiled and twinkled.

"Sweetie, it is just a lighter, but I will get something else if I need to, I don't want something that frightens you. I am okay with an ordinary lighter, I mean, I hardly ever have a spliff these days, so it does not really matter that much."

I sipped my drink and watched, as everyone sat around and talked about what happened, and I watched Birch. I am sure she was aware of it, and yet I am also sure she did not understand that I watched her stand in front of me yet again to protect me, she did not understand how much that frightened me.

I know what Deb's real dad is capable of, I have seen the black eyes he gave Ellen many times. I was there with Deb's the night he cracked her cheek bone, and left her on the floor in pain. It was Deb's and me who picked her up, and took her to the surgery to be seen, and I did not want Birch to suffer like that. She has no idea how lucky she was, Jonathan Ford is capable of far more than she realised, he could have easily overpowered her and hit her before Luke or Izzy could have stopped him, I know, I have seen it.

Everyone was laughing and talking about how funny it was, when she pulled a gun out, but not for me, I was so scared and so afraid. She laughed at the comments and turned to me, her face happy and her eyes dancing, I stared at her across the island.

"I am glad you think it was funny, because it frigging terrified me. It was stupid and irresponsible. Even pointing a fake gun at someone in this country is a criminal offence, why risk it for that worthless piece of shit? For a so called therapist, you can be so frigging stupid at times Birch, and it most definitely was not bloody cool." Her face dropped, and she looked instantly upset. I got up and lifted my glass.

"I have work to do."

I turned and walked out leaving the room in complete silence, I was upset and angry, and I had already said too much. I knew I would regret it; I reached the stairs when I heard her, she did sound upset. I just carried on walking and quickened my pace. I walked up to my room, and sat at my computer as the emotions inside me swirled around mixing with my anger. I needed to calm down, it was just fear, a past memory, that was all, it was not long before she walked in and closed the door. Her voice was quiet, hurt, and soft.

"Deads, I am really sorry, you were right, I did not think."

I turned and looked at her, oh God, she had that lost childlike look on her face, and her eyes had lost their sparkle, she looked at the floor. I took a deep breath as I swallowed yet more emotion.

"Have you any idea how terrified I was Birch, I saw you pull a bloody pistol out of your bag, and point it at him, and then tell him you knew how to use it, as if you had many times?" She looked up, as she stood wringing her hands out.

"I told you, I am sorry, Deads it was not a real gun, it was a replica, with a built in lighter." I nodded.

"Yeah, I get that now, but when you pulled it out, I had no idea. I thought it was frigging real, and it terrified me... Birch you have no idea what he is like, he could have easily overpowered you and took it off you, and used it?" She gave a sigh.

"What to light a spliff for me?" I shook my head.

"Oh my God, you still do not frigging get it do you? This is a guy who beat the living shit out of Ellen. I was the one who drove her to the hospital, and again, I did not frigging know it was a fake gun. Have you any idea what it is like, to think someone sick and twisted, has shot you, because I bloody well have, I lived it once, remember?"

And suddenly she completely understood me, she looked shocked, and scared, and her eyes filled with tears.

"Oh God Deads, I am so sorry, I never realised. Oh Sweetie, you have to believe me, if I had thought for a second anything like that, and how you would see it, I would not have." She shook her head.

"Sweetie, I never want you to go through that again. Deads, please, you must know, I would never knowingly put you through that?"

I closed my eyes and gave a long breath out, I could feel all those wretched feelings bubbling inside me, she came over and dropped to her knees, and took my hands in hers.

"Deads honestly, I am so sorry, please, you have to believe me?"

I really wanted to cry; I wanted this fear that was building inside me to stop. I wanted the pain of those thoughts to leave me alone. I opened my eyes and looked down at her, she looked so sad, and that was too much for me, my eyes filled with tears.

"I cannot lose you, not ever Birch. Please, stop putting yourself at risk, you scare me so much, and I cannot go back to feeling those things again, I thought I was through it all, but tonight... Tonight it just..."

She threw herself around me, and dragged me forward, and I was suddenly buried in her cleavage.

"Deads stop, don't say the words, do not let it come back, we are never going back to that place, I promised. Please Sweetie, I cannot handle that, I cannot see you like that again." I slipped my arms round her and pulled her closer, and mumbled into her bosom.

"Birch just stop being the hero and standing in front of me, you are not bullet proof, and I do not want you hurt because of me, I could not live with that."

She held me tightly in her arms, so tight I could hear her heartbeat, and it was beating really fast.

"Deads, you cannot ask me not to protect you, I will always try to stop people hurting you, but I am sorry. I wish I had thought more, I just wanted him out of the house. I wanted him away from you, and I knew that would do it, but honestly, I am so sorry, I just did not think."

"Birch?"

"Yes Sweetie."

"Your tits are suffocating me."

"What... Oh crap!" She loosened her grip, and I took a deep breath of clean air, she looked down and smiled.

"I am sorry Sweetie, I truly am." I took another intake of air.

"I know, I am sorry I lost my shit in the kitchen, I should have waited until later." She smiled and shook her head.

"No Deads, you called me out, and you were right to do so."

She slipped back to her knees, and rested her head on my knees, I stroked her soft long white hair, and gave a sigh, as I felt my inner turmoil lessening.

"I really love you Birch, you are my whole life, you need to understand, I almost lost you once, I cannot even go close to that again." She squeezed my thigh.

"I am sorry, and I know, Deads I feel the same, I could not let him hurt you, he had such hate in his eyes when he looked at you. I just wanted him as far away from you as possible. I love you too Sweetie, I never want to live alone without you, I did that once and it broke me."

I sat back and cast my mind back to that horrible day after the vicar in the cellar, and the conversation Birch had with Izzy, and how Izzy had pointed out that I was Birch's kink, and how she had fallen apart after I left Uni. God what a pair we were, we were both as bad as each other, hell would we ever really understand ourselves enough to puzzle out our need of each other?

If I am honest, I am not sure, maybe in the back of my mind I don't want to, maybe ignorance is bliss in this particular case, I honestly had no idea. I just knew instinctively, I never want to be without her, and I was not about to question that

I sat in my chair, and stroked her hair, and thought back to all the crazy things that had happened to me since I had met her.

It was hard to believe everything we had faced together, and endured side by side. There are times it feels like we are cursed, and then out of nowhere, there are moments when we are lay in bed cuddling, or just walking and talking in the woodland or meadows, and suddenly I understand why I should be with her.

None of it makes complete sense to me, it is just a feeling, like everything around me is right because she is there with me, and I stop worrying about everything. My life is suddenly a lot better, more complete, happier, and I just smile and walk, or close my eyes and sleep, knowing she is there breathing at my side, and all is well in my world. I looked down at her, and smiled as I stroked.

"Birch I am tired, it has been a long day, I might get some sleep... Birch... Birch?" I shook my head; she had bloody fallen asleep again on me.

"Holy shit Birch, do you have a button you just press, and boom you are gone?"

What can I do, this is Birch and it is what she does, it is a Birch thing, there is no doubt, and somehow, I am not sure I will ever get completely used to it?

Downstairs Birch's delivery arrived, and Edwina took care of it with Luke, it was larger than anyone realised and was stored in the garage. I managed to wake drowsy Birch enough to undress her and get her into bed, and then not worrying about meals or the others, I stripped and snuggled into her, it had been a long day that started at Sunny Bank, and ended here in our bed, and I was happy to just relax and sleep, and I closed my eyes and drifted.

Outside, a little way down Waterside Lane, next to the large beech tree that grew up out of the grass verge, Jonathon Ford watched, as Bradley pulled out of our drive, and turned to head back up the lane with Deb's. He sneered as he saw the car, and then slipped out from behind the tree. He pulled a bottle out of his jacket, unscrewed the cap, and took a long swig, and began to walk up the lane towards the Wheeler Estate, as he refitted the cap, and slipped it into his pocket.

Chapter 25

Normality.

The problem with going to bed early, is you wake up early, well you do if you are me, the blonde with birch like hair, that had drooled all over me, was still flat out, and had me in a vice like grip.

I opened my eyes with a sudden need for a pee, coffee, and food, and had to work fast, to uncoil myself from the death grip I was currently being held in, before I wet the bed. It was not easy, and a very close call, I made it to the bathroom just in time, and felt utter relief as I considered my next move of the day.

I slipped on my black jeans, and grabbed a top, and yawned as I headed downstairs, the house was quiet and still, and it felt nice. In the kitchen, I put the kettle on and slipped some bread in the toaster, and looked out of the patio doors at my arch, out in the drizzle. I miss the sun, but as with all things, the year is turning and soon the cold of autumn will blow through those gothic windows, and we will snuggle together in our living room, and talk of the year to come.

The toaster popped, and the kettle clicked, and my thoughts came back to reality. I grabbed the hot toasted bread, and lifted the butter knife, and prepared for breakfast. The milk was low, I gave a sigh, we would probably get about ten more brews out of it, and I would be having eight of them. I made my coffee, and sat at the island and tucked in. There was a shuffling noise behind me, followed by two long warm white arms round me, she leaned her head onto my shoulder, her voice was soft and dreamy.

"Hi Sweetie... I am tired." I turned and looked at her, she had her eyes closed, and a soft smile on her face.

"If you are tired, why did you get up?" She gave a little moan.

"You were not there, and I wanted to wake up and see you." She opened her eyes.

"You were here so I came to you." I frowned.

"What with your eyes closed?" She nodded, and pulled her lip.

"I banged my head on the door frame." I started to chuckle.

"God you are such a kid, you should have looked where you were going... Sit down and I will make you a coffee, we need more milk, I was thinking of going to get some." She slipped back onto the chair at my side and yawned.

"I can drink black if you want?"

I got up and made her a black coffee, and placed it down in front of her, she did look really sleepy. She lifted her cup and took a mouth full and her whole body shuddered.

"Yuk!!" I sniggered at her, as she screwed up her face.

"Sweetie it's bitter." I nodded at her.

"Black coffee usually is." I grabbed the milk carton and poured some into her cup, and stirred it with the spoon, she took another taste, and gave a happy sigh.

"Mmm, yummy."

She smacked her lips, and smiled, I refilled the kettle, and clicked it on. By the time she was fully awake, I had been able to have a few more coffees, and I grabbed my back pack that was still damp from the moors, and my coat, and together we headed out to the village to buy milk, and more bread.

Birch was much livelier, as we walked hand in hand to the village, she was all smiles, and swung her arm holding my hand. I cannot deny, I love it when she is happy and all giggles, it cheers me up and makes me happy. It felt strange walking up the main street of the village, even though I had only been away for a week, it felt like longer.

In the post office, Mary was delighted to see us, the shop was empty, and I grabbed milk and a loaf, and headed to the counter, Mary was all smiles.

"You look better rested, a bit of stress free living has done you good, honestly, Peter and myself have no idea how you cram everything in?" Birch leaned over my shoulder and added three packets of fruit flavoured pastels to our shopping.

"It is easy Mary, we lay back on a nude beach, and soaked in the sun, and let go of everything, it was divine." She gave a happy chuckle; it was rare the shop was empty.

"Good for you, it was over near Bude wasn't it?" I gave a nod, it still felt strange talking about naturism in the Post Office.

"Yes, it was about a mile north up from the main beach." She nodded as she passed me the loaf for my backpack.

"Yes, I know the place, it has been some years since we were last there, nice little sheltered cove. Well, you certainly had the weather, and to be honest, I think you needed the rest, you have a lot to come. Primula was in the village yesterday, she had a few awkward questions, but she bluffed her way out of them. You know, she is saying some pretty nasty things about you two, be careful girls, her back is against the wall, she can be a really vicious one."

I understood that more than most, I had seen the way she handled Deli, and I had Sophia on my mind. Birch took the bag and smiled at Mary.

"We are honest open and transparent, it does not matter what she throws our way, we can back everything we say and do up openly, which is more than she can." Mary gave a nod, as Peter came in from setting up the veg and fruit stand.

"I know girls, but a little caution will not hurt will it now, she is dangerous, so step with care?"

She was right, I would put nothing past Prim, my biggest concern was Nigel and Sophia. I gave Mary a smile.

"Thanks Mary, we will be extra careful." We came out of the shop, and I stood and looked around the green, it was still overcast, but at least it had stopped raining.

"So much has changed Birch, and yet it hasn't." She looked across the village.

"You know, I remember first getting here and thinking how big this place looked, and yet now as I look around, it feels smaller. So much has happened since that day when you fell apart walking down this green, there was so much fear and anguish, and yet look at us now, we have our faces on almost every window, and we are no longer studied by the transient watch."

I had to smile, looking back, I was so scared of coming home, and so aware of all the disapproving stares. In a way I still get them, but Birch is right, we have both come a long way, and even though we still are not completely accepted, it is nowhere near as severe as it was. We walked slowly down the street, and came level with Deb's shop, Louise was setting up inside, she waved. I opened the door and leaned in.

"Is Deb's not here yet, she is alright, isn't she?" Louise smiled at me.

"She is fine, better than fine, Jimmy got back at midnight, so she is coming in later, you know how it is, she has needs." I giggled.

"Oh yeah, we noticed on holiday, she was getting a little feisty, poor sod, he will have jet lag, and then Deb's lag, he will probably sleep for a week." She laughed as she lifted the new books off the counter.

"You still coming to Anthony's party tomorrow?" She turned with the books.

"Party at your place, definitely, you could not stop me, I will see you there."

Holding hands, we walked home quietly talking, I took out my key and opened the door, Edwina was in the hallway.

"Holy shit, are you two up?" I frowned at her.

"Yes... We went to the shop for some milk and bread." Chloe waved from the kitchen.

"See Edwina... I told you it was not me... Ha... Moody fucking cow, Abby, Birch, you are a life saver, I was just going to go out and get some, because bossy knickers big sis was pissed, because I drank the last bit of milk."

I laughed as I looked at Edwina looking guilty, and slipped off my backpack, I opened the flap and pulled out the four pint carton, and handed it to her, she took it silently and walked back to the kitchen.

"For your information smart arse, I did not know Abby and Birch were up, it was a simple mistake." Chloe lifted her milky coffee.

"Apology accepted." Edwina glared at her.

"Smart arsed cow, I hate you when you are smug."

It was good to be back home and back to normality, I grabbed the loaf, hung up my back pack and walked to the kitchen, slipping off my coat, Birch chuckled as she followed me.

With a louder than normal noise level, it was not long before Deli and Sophia appeared, it looked like she had stayed the night again. Sophia sat eating toast, and Deli sipped her coffee, I sat between them.

"Prim is back, she was in the village yesterday." Deli gave a nod.

"Nigel texted Sophia, to warn her, apparently, she is not happy Sophia has pulled out of the council race, and has drafted in Molly. To be honest after the revelation of the building on the woodland, I would have thought she would have pulled out completely, it just goes to show how few scruples she has."

"I am not worried, Birch and I have our plan, and we will stick to it. The way I see it, we have presented our case, so we will follow it through, and see what happens." She gave a sigh.

"I cannot see it Abby, but what if she wins?" Birch turned at the kettle.

"We buy tin hats and go underground, and do everything we can to oppose anything that is bad for the villagers."

I had to smirk, the thought of digging a bunker to hide from the fall out of Prim, and all of us lined up in tin hats with pitch forks, somehow amused me. For the love of life, I simply could not imagine Anthony in a tin hat, he would probably spend all day complaining it was ruining his lush locks. Birch noticed me smirking and smiled at me, as she sat down.

"Deads Sweetie, do not underestimate her, I know the things she has done to Nigel, she can be really cruel and vindictive. I can assure you; I will be keeping a wary eye out around her." Sophia lifted her drink.

"She only has ten followers on Insta, which tells you everything you need to know yar?"

We sat around drinking coffee and talking for a while, but Birch had things to do and got up. I needed to take care of a few things, but as I refilled my cup and my thoughts mingled around, I turned to Sophia.

"Be careful, if Prim finds out you slept with Nigel, she could really hurt you, and I don't want that to happen to you. If you get any trouble, come to me, and I will help you." She smiled at me.

"You are my friend, yar?" I nodded at her.

"I am Sophia, just be careful." She lifted her camera and 'CLICK!' She smiled as she typed with one hand.

"Insta knows we are friends now, I have an influencer as a friend, I will always come to you to help you too, yar?" I nodded; it was a deal.

With a new coffee, I walked down the hall, the front door was open, Birch appeared carrying a stack of long pieces of wood on her shoulder. I looked at her wearing knee pads, and stared at them for a moment, she looked down and smiled, I met her gaze.

"Is there something I should know, I mean, if you need protection on your knees, should I worry?" She gave a giggle.

"Sweetie, it has been a while since my knees were at risk from that, and as for one of those in my mouth, I think I forgotten what it is like, it's been so long." I smirked.

"So, just what are you up to?" She gave a big smile.

"I am building a wall Sweetie."

"Huh... Do we have one missing?" She gave a chuckle.

"Yes Sweetie, I want to put up a wall in the attic, now we have the two single beds up there, I thought I would make another guest room. I ordered the wood, and plaster board, after we built the little bridge at Sunny Bank, whilst you were sleeping. I had lots of fun, and we do own the house so any improvements we make will help." It made sense to me, but I was not completely sure.

"Do you know how to make walls, is it not a hard thing to do?" She gave me a big smile and her eyes sparkled.

"I have been watching online videos to learn, it is my go to these days whenever I want to do something, and to be honest, it is actually easier than I thought it would be." It was hard not to argue, she appeared confident enough.

"Can I help?" She gave me a knowing look.

"Sweetie, I would love you to help, but honestly, I need to do it all this weekend, if you start getting turned on it will distract me." I frowned.

"You look sexy working with tools, I will try not to molest you if I can."

"Okay, give me a hand with this, and then we can get the rest of the lumber."

I put my coffee down on the hall table, and took one end of the wood, and walked behind her, watching her bum wiggle as she walked... Yeah this was going to be harder than it looked, I was already turned on from just seeing her walk in the door.

One hour later, sweating and slowly losing layers of clothing, and having struggled with the huge boards of plaster, we finally negotiated the bend on the attic stairs, and had everything in the attic, including a new electric nail gun. I looked at it suspiciously, I was not convinced my semi psychotic wife should be handling such dangerous weapons.

We wrapped the beds in plastic, and Birch laid out a massive tarp, and with the aid of two stools, and her pad of measurements, she began to cut the wood with a new circular saw. I sat on the plastic covered bed watching and admiring her, she had slowly shed her clothing as it got warmer up here, and trust me, watching a naked girl work with power tools, is simply the best.

Once all the wood was cut to size, Birch handed me an electric screw driver, I suppose it was the one tool I actually knew how to use. I helped, as she laid down the wood, and double checked all her angles were cut correctly. I marvelled as she precisely fitted everything together on the floor, and would smile to herself, knowing she had got everything right.

The frame for the wall came together on the floor, and she showed me where to put screws. I got stuck in, and started to really enjoy myself. Birch used the nail gun, and fired nails into the frame, strengthening it as she went, I cannot deny, I was feeling hot and sweaty, and I was so wet, watching her was turning me on more and more.

What is this weird affliction I have when she picks up tools? I am a highly educated woman, why do I turn to mush and get all excited like a small child, when she does something with wood? Is this how normal women feel when they see workmen, do they get all hot and bothered? I have no idea really, I just was finding it really hard to concentrate, I tried to divert my deviant and perverse brain away from her ass, which swung seductively as she nailed each section.

"Birch how do you know how to do this?" She looked back and her eyes sparkled.

"I told you Sweetie; I love working with wood... I also watched a few online tutorials. You know, it is only a triangular frame, we just put it all together, lift it up, and if I have done the maths right, it will fit the gap."

I could see that, it was clearly outlined on the floor, she bent over to check the joints, exposing herself from behind, and honestly, I have no will power. I crawled forward like a stalking cat, and at the right moment, I pounced, and grabbed her hips, and plunged into her. She gave a squeal of surprise, and pushed back with a long moan, she was already soaking wet.

She pushed her face into the floor and moaned loudly, I moved my tongue faster, feeling equally as excited as she did. I could not help, but feel the heat burning up inside me. Birch moaned into the carpet, and that was too much, and I slipped my hand down and opened my jeans, and slid my hand inside.

As soon as I touched myself, I felt my legs pulsate, and just pushed my face deeper into her, and my hand started to move between my legs, at the same pace as my mouth. I gulped back air, and rubbed myself faster, I was finding it hard to breathe, and gasped into her, she gave a squeal and arched her back.

"Ooooh Deads... Oh my god, Deads, I am going to cum, I cannot hold it in."

Her legs began to spasm, as I rubbed even faster between my thighs, my own little button tingling like it was going to explode. Birch pushed the top of her head into the carpet, and looked between her spread legs, and saw me masturbating.

"Oh god, that is so bloody hot."

I gulped for air swallowing more of her with the air, my legs were starting to shake, my wrist was aching, and I was not sure I could take much more. Birch watched and her insides built up faster and faster, I paused my tongue, and gave a long slow moan, into her, and she felt the vibration and gave a really loud squeal, and pushed back even harder into my face. Her torso stiffened, and she wailed, as her head slipped back, and her arms stretched, her hand clasped tighter to the gun, and suddenly, my mouth was filling at an alarming rate.

"OH DEADS... OH MY GOD YESSSSSSSSSSSSSSSSS!"

She exploded, and I felt the heat surge up from my legs as she flooded my mouth, and suddenly, I was shaking with her, when, BANG!... CRASH... SMASH!

My head popped up behind her, still rubbing myself.

"What the hell was that?"

"I came and broke the window Sweetie."

"Huh!"

The window at the end of the attic had exploded out, as she gave an almighty squeal of happiness. She had pulled the trigger by accident, but I did not care, I was getting closer and needed to orgasm, the need was so strong, Birch was watching a happy look on her face, I stared at her, and she winked.

Birch spun on the floor, her eyes smouldering with lust, she pushed me back as I fingered myself and rubbed my button, and I sprawled backwards, her hands gripped my waist band, as I fell to the floor, and she tore my jeans down my legs to my ankles, I was gasping and moaning and losing myself, my finger still deep inside myself, and then she shocked me.

Birch crawled up and slid her finger in at the side of mine, oh my god I could feel her finger matching mine, and it was weird and strange and yet so incredibly erotic. She leaned forward, as she pounded inside me, the force of her stroke vibrating upwards into my button, and my legs felt like they were starting to fizz, such was the power of the tingles.

She pulled out my hand, and plunged her face into me, and that was it, I stiffened and gave out a loud wail, and my vagina felt like it had exploded out of my stomach, as I flopped back my eyes swirling and my head exploding in unison with the rest of my body. Birch was still there licking and sucking and swallowing, and my whole body was under its own control, I honestly thought I was going to black out, as I lay limp on the floor, twitching and jumping.

Birch collapsed onto my tummy, and just lay smiling looking up at me. I could not really move, and my jeans were wrapped tight round my ankles, and her face was on my tummy, as her bright sparkling eyes looked at me, and she smiled.

"You know Sweetie, my orgasm broke the window?" I gave a giggle still panting for breath.

"I want that on a badge, or a t shirt." She gave a giggle, and kissed my tummy.

"When I asked you for help with the screwing, I did not think I was included in that?" I gave a gasp and my tummy wobbled, and I started to laugh.

"Baby it's called DIY, and so I looked at you bent over, and just thought, why not just do it myself, when I can do you at the same time?" She started to chuckle and sat up.

"Deads, you wore me out, and I need to finish this, but my legs are shaking."

I staggered up to my feet, and offered my hand to her, I was sweating and panting.

"Come on, the frame is built, so let's get it fitted."

She grabbed my hand, and bent over to pull up my jeans, she ran her finger up my still wet vagina, and I gave a startled squeak, she giggled at me, and sucked her finger and raised her eyebrows, I love her naughty dirty girl side.

After a little lining up and adjusting, we lifted the framework, it was actually a lot heavier than I thought it would be, but there again, my legs were still shaking, and my arms were weak. Birch carefully lined it up, with the marks she had made on the wall, and fired the nails through the frame into the roof joists. I was really impressed, suddenly, there was a wall frame with a door space, it was pretty impressive, I stood back and admired it.

"Wow you really did a great job." I looked around what was going to be quite a spacious room, Birch slipped her arm round my waist.

"We did a great job, you helped, and did a lot of screwing." She gave a chuckle, and patted my bum.

"I need a drink, and then I can finish off nailing it in place, and I will need to ring Albert at the hardware store, and see if he has any glass to cut."

I offered to do the coffees, and headed down to the kitchen, whilst she rang the shop, to organise a replacement window. In the kitchen, Chloe had her head outside the door looking round, she turned and asked me what the sudden crash was, and I suddenly felt a little lost for words as I poured the coffee, I looked at her across the kitchen.

"Don't worry about it, Birch orgasmed, and the window blew out." I smirked as Deli and Chloe both stared at me, Deli looked at me in an uncertain way.

"Hell, is that even possible?" I picked up the coffees.

"It is if you are Birch, but don't worry, she is ordering new glass now." I smirked, as Chloe gave me a shrewd look.

"No... Really Abby, how did it happen?"

"I told you, watching her do woodwork was really turning me on, and she bent over in front of me, and what can I say, I jumped her, and she orgasmed like hell, and she came really hard." Deli gave a small gasp.

"Did she scream?" I nodded.

"Well, it was more sort of a very loud wail come moan, but yeah, she was noisy." She looked really shocked.

"Holy shit, I have been known to get carried away, but hell, that beats me completely." Chloe nodded.

"I told you, she is unique, I once asked her if she was some sort of alien lifeform, and I am still not convinced she isn't."

I walked out carrying the coffee, as Chloe and Deli just stared at me speechless, and stunned, as they pondered Birch's orgasms. I thought I would leave them to their own thoughts for a while.

By the time I reached the attic, Birch had cut a large piece of plaster board, and fitted it to the frame, she was busy screwing it into place, as I stood at the top of the stairs. She stood back, and I handed her the coffee, it looked good, I noticed the other board had pencil lines on it ready for cutting.

We sat and had coffee, as she explained how once the board was screwed on, the gaps would be plastered, and then the wall would be papered and decorated, and as soon as we finished coffee, we got stuck back in. Within the hour we had a wall, it was a little weird, and took some getting used to, as this had always been such a wide open space.

Birch told me a new replacement double glazed pane had been ordered, and so I covered the window in plastic, to keep out the wind and rain, whilst Birch fitted the new door, she really was surprising me, but in a way, it was like she had brought a small part of who she had been at Sunny Bank home with her. Honestly, I just enjoyed sitting and watching her, as she smiled to herself and worked everything out.

I knew how to fit locks, I had helped mum fit a new one to the guest house, but I sat on the floor as Birch talked me through it, because I loved how she explained things, and enjoyed showing me another part of who she was. By the time the evening crept round, we had the attic side of the wall complete. On the inside wall, we would have to wait for Michael, who was going to sort out all the wiring for plugs and lights, and then we could finish off.

We cleaned up laughing and joking, and I hoovered up, and helped pack everything away, and put the beds back. Birch had ordered a small heater, and all the light fittings she wanted, and so for this weekend, our task was done.

Birch went downstairs to help out in the kitchen, and then I wandered back to my room, put on my ear phones, grabbed a book, and played Avril, whilst reading about Lyra. It felt nice to be home, and back to normality, the only problem was, it was once again going to get really busy, but before that, I wanted to just chill out, and relax.

Monday was the start of the real campaign for the Parish Council, and also the big push towards the Curio Carnival, and the Curio Centre, and I also had to send Anita, the finished manuscript for the first cursed book, and I had another new book to write, and suddenly my time between now and Christmas, felt full.

My time away had been so relaxing and fun, but being home for a day, and mucking in with Birch, made the reality of being back in Wotton a little more sobering. I had to find my rhythm again, because we had a lot of work to do, and honestly, I was feeling a little bit intimidated by it all.

By the time I slipped into bed, and lay back, with my eyes closed, I felt that the pressure was building once again. I lost track of time, and felt Birch slip into bed behind me, and cuddle into me, and she was warm and snug, and I drifted around inside my head until sleep took me.

At the top of Waterside Lane, outside the Wheeler Estate, a dark figure stood in the trees, and peered through the high chain link fence, at the smaller complex. Through the patio windows, across the large lawn, he watched, as Deb's walked round the room clearing up, and getting things ready for the morning.

High in the trees above, an owl hooted, and the rain started, Jonathon Ford, flipped up his hood, and stepped back onto the pathway, he turned, and walked down the lane, heading back towards the village.

Chapter 26

Surprised Celebration.

BANG! There was a deafening squeal. I sat bolt upright in bed with a start.

"BIRCH?" She appeared rubbing her head looking miserable.

"Sweetie... I ran into the wall." I felt my tummy wobble, and tried not to smile.

"Why?" She gave a sad sigh.

"I was sleepy and confused, Deads, I forgot we only have one room now, and I was late."

I started to giggle. I slipped out from under the duvet, and walked over to her, she rested her head on my shoulder as I giggled into her ear.

"Birch, why don't you set your alarm for earlier, that way you will not have to run around like a maniac?"

She rubbed her head, and leaned back, I took a look at it, she had a red patch right in the centre of her forehead. I was fighting like mad not to laugh, but my fits of giggles kept escaping. I kissed it softly.

"Birch, I hate to point this out, but you are the boss, you know, you can come and go as you please?" She frowned and rubbed her head.

"I don't like that; I like being there to make sure all is fine before the others arrive."

I shook my head, and took her hand and walked over to the wardrobe, where all her clothes hung, I took a look at what she had. I grabbed what she needed.

"Okay, these pants, that blouse, and this jacket, and here are the new socks I bought you, they are pretty." She smiled as she held her clothes.

"Thank you, Sweetie." I gave a sigh.

"Hurry up, you are late."

And just like that, the whirlwind started again, I headed

downstairs for coffee. I flopped down on my seat, as Edwina handed me a coffee. I lifted it up with both hands, and took a sip, as Birch came flying down the stairs, and whizzed around the house, Edwina frowned.

"Is Birch going somewhere today?" I moved my eyes up to her.

"Work." She looked puzzled.

"Is she working Sundays now?"

I frowned, Edwina looked at me as Birch came charging down the hallway and into the kitchen, Edwina looked at her as she snatched her bag, and then kissed me on the cheek. I smiled.

"See you later Sweetie."

"Birch, it's Sunday, you know Bell Twat day?" She skidded to a halt in the doorway.

"What Sweetie?" Edwina started to laugh.

"Did you think it was Monday, what the hell Birch?" She dropped her bag.

"Shit!" I giggled.

Chloe came down the hallway yawning, she looked at Birch and me.

"Why the fuck are you two up, I thought you slept in on Sundays?"

Chloe flopped in the seat opposite me and smiled, Edwina placed a cup in front of her. Birch gave a long sigh, and walked back to the island and flopped down at the side of me.

"Deads, I am tired, and my head hurts." She leaned on my shoulder, and closed her eyes. I sipped my coffee and watched Chloe, she looked at me.

"What?"

"Why are you dressed?" She looked down at her dungarees.

"I am going shopping, it's Anthony's home coming, so I want stuff for his birthday party." Those were the magic words, Birch sat up opened her eyes wide and smiled.

"I love birthday parties."

Suddenly the whole atmosphere in the room changed, and I was going shopping with Birch, nope, scratch that, we were all going shopping with Birch.

Just over an hour later, we were in Oxendale, in the large shopping centre, heading towards the cake shop, and Birch was in shopping mode.

"Right Sweetie's, we need a good size cake, something with flair, and we need party food, we have nowhere near enough time to bake, and streamers, and party poppers, oh, I love party poppers." She stopped to jump on the spot and clapped.

"Chloe, we need a stripper." I looked at Birch.

"His mum is coming; I am not sure she will want some scantily dressed woman slithering all over him?" Birch frowned, then smiled.

"It is alright Sweetie; I wanted a male stripper." I stared at her.

"Birch, that is worse than a woman, his mum will be there, seriously, you cannot see the issue with that?" She shrugged.

"Okay, we will get him a sex toy then." She turned and walked off towards the south wing, I looked at Deli, she looked pale.

"Abby, I have never been in a sex shop before." Birch came to an abrupt halt, spun on her heels and walked back, she smiled at Deli.

"Oh, you poor sweet deprived child." She linked her arm.

"It's alright Sweetie, I will show you all the best stuff."

She walked off, almost dragging Deli off her feet, as she looked back, her face filled with terror, in a look of begging for help. Chloe giggled and followed, and I looked at her.

"No hiding stuff... You hear me?" She gave a sigh.

"Okay, but can I try it out first though?" Edwina shuddered.

"My God, you are a slut, I cannot believe we are related."

Deli looked helpless as Birch informed her of the wonders of sex toys, I did feel a little sorry for her, especially considering that I had never actually been in one either, but I had no intention of telling Birch.

Remember the old saying 'like a kid in a sweet shop,' well actually it should be 'like a Birch in a sex shop.' Deli, poor girl, was beetroot, as Birch wafted ten and twelve inch long, brightly coloured dildos in front of her face. Then she handed her crotchless panties, and edible underwear, and a stainless steel butt plug. I was glad I had kept my mouth shut.

Although Birch did keep yelling, "SWEETIE!" across the shop, and holding things up for me to look at. Chloe was in her element, as she grabbed things off the shelves, and put them in her basket. The fact she needed a basket impressed me. Edwina would randomly walk past her, look in her basket and shake her head, and mutter things like.

"My God, you are a slut." And "Jesus, you are a perverted bitch."

I looked in her basket, where I noted, a lot of sexy underwear, flavoured lubes, and edible underwear for him and her, as well as three vibrating cock rings. Hmm, I think there is a little bit of the pot calling the kettle going on here?

Birch was bright, happy, and extremely giddy, Deli finally broke free, and hid in the underwear section, and got distracted. Birch filled her basket with a BDSM starter kit, cock rings, a double ended dildo, lots of lube, two pairs of leather covered handcuffs, an inflatable man bum, nipple clamps, and she also had ten packets of edible panties, in various flavours, which she assured me, was for us, I turned, and walked away fast.

I found Deli in the underwear section, and hid with her. She looked at me still very red around the cheeks.

"Seriously Abby, do people really use all this stuff?" I shrugged.

"Honestly, I have no idea, Birch knows all about it because of her job, if I am really honest, the only reason I know about dildos, is because her home in Manchester had a cupboard full of them."

Birch looked round from the till, where she handed them a large stack of her business cards, and I ducked behind the nighties. I gave a gasp of relief, she could pay, I was avoiding her until everything was bagged up.

Deli and myself slipped backwards further out of sight. I gave another sigh of relief and turned, an assistant was hanging underwear on the rail and looked at me, and my heart froze.

"Abby?" I spluttered.

"Eric... Er... Hi!" He smiled and came over to me, I felt my cheeks start to burn.

"How the hell are you, it has been ages?"

Well yeah, the last time I saw him, he was putting his pants back on in the tent at the Oxendale Music Festival. I swallowed hard, Deli was staring at me, with a smirk.

"I am fine, you know me, I go with the flow of things?" His smile was really big.

"You got married to the Birch girl, to be honest, it was a bit of a surprise when I read it?" I nodded.

"Long story really... But yeah... Oh by the way, this is Deli." He looked at her, and smiled.

"Hi... I am Eric... I knew Abby at school." He frowned.

"Actually, I know you too don't I... Weren't you something to do with the dance class?" She smiled, and looked embarrassed.

"Yes, I was the lead dancer, we used to practice our flash mob routines on the football pitch before your team practiced." He nodded.

"Yeah... Fidelity, I remember you now, you were a good dancer. I probably should not say it, but we all used to watch you dance, the team were a bunch of perverts." She smiled.

"I know, we used the same place under the stand to watch you all play." He gave a chuckle, and looked at me.

"So, Abby, you came back... And got married, wow, must admit, did not see that one coming. I have often wondered if I should cruise Wotton and see if I could see you again, I thought you would end up in Manchester."

And, I was dying inside of shame, my one night stand, never to be seen again, was in front of me, seeing me. I felt my stomach twist into knots, his eyes were all over me, and I was pretty certain that like me, he was remembering every second of our time alone in the tent. My brain swirled as I tried to find something to say.

"So, what about you, married, kids?" He gave a laugh, and looked a little shaken.

"No... Almost, I was engaged for a while, but..." He looked very uncomfortable.

"The thing is Abby, do you remember James, actually, I think he dated you for a while? Well, to cut a painful story short, Sandy worked with him, and he was sleeping with her. They are married now, have been for just over a year, I have not bothered since, I just focused on my business." I did not know really what I could say, I mean, how do you respond to that? Wow, talk about opening my mouth and putting both feet in it.

"I am really sorry to hear it, he was a shit, my memory of him is not a good one." He looked sad, but tried to smile, I was feeling like I was clutching at straws, and trying to dig my way out of a very deep hole.

"So, is this your business?" He gave a laugh.

"God no, this is my sisters' shop, I am just helping out today, she had a massive shipment of new stock, and was falling behind, so I am mucking in. I run a paint ball arena in the old River Park Mill."

I had heard of it, actually, Luke and Terry had talked about it, they fancied their chances.

"Oh, I love paint ball." Crap, she had found us; her face lit up when she saw who I was talking to.

"Eric Sweetie, long time, how are you, I hope you are not trying to drag my lovely wife in the changing room for some tent action?" I cringed.

God, kill me now, I had successfully avoided the issue, and in she strides, and just lays it all out on the floor in front of us. He shook his head.

"No Birch, I would not do that." She smiled.

"Still the gent Eric, I liked that about you, too polite to ask."

His cheeks started to go red as he looked at me, and smiled, it was obvious he would not say no if I asked. He slipped his hand in his pocket, and pulled out a card, and handed it over.

"We never get girls at the factory, they fear the guys, and the power of the guns, but you have a lot of guts. So, if you can find a team of eight or ten girls who are not afraid of some rough stuff, give me a call. I will throw you a couple of hours of free fun in. Call it for old times' sake." He gave me a really nice smile.

"It has been nice to see you Abby, you too Fidelity, I better get on, we have a lot to get out, take care of yourselves." I smiled.

"Yeah, you too, and Eric... Don't give up, there is a nice girl out there just waiting, you never know?" He gave a chuckle, and his eyes glanced at Birch and then me.

"I wish, from what I have seen, the best ones are taken, but thanks." He walked off and Birch leaned into me.

"See, I told you back then, you should have rung him." I looked at her.

"Birch, I had fallen in love already, it would never have been fair on him." She looked at me and her bright eyes twinkled, as she realised, and she smiled a lovely smile.

"Wow, I only just realised." She kissed my cheek.

"Thank you, Sweetie."

Chloe had two large bags, and I was never going to ask, Edwina had one, Birch had two, I did not want to ask either, as we headed into the frozen food section of the large supermarket.

We arrived home and I was exhausted, I made coffees all around, as Edwina and Chloe sorted out the food, then restocked the fridge with drinks from the cellar. Finally, I headed up to my room, and flopped in my chair, I wanted to move all my pictures from my camera, to the file on my desk top computer, and try to blank today out of my thoughts.

I sat back as the files moved over, I had taken a lot of pictures at Sunny Bank, and it took some time, so as I sat back, I drifted in the memory of the festival. In truth, I had often thought of Eric, especially during that time of separation whilst Birch was still at Uni. Eric was the one I remembered everything from, the others, I had no idea, but Eric had always been different.

That night at the festival, had been wild and daring, he had been a spur of the moment choice, an impulse, and yet if I am honest, he was probably the best male lover I ever had. He knew it was a one time thing with no strings, and yet such was his manner, I had never forgotten him. He stood out, simply because he was so caring, and just so nice with me.

It is funny how the past comes back, and paths cross, today Eric, a couple of months back James, although I think it was clear, James was interested in repeating history, even though as I had now found out, he was married to Eric's fiancée, God the guy was still a shit bag.

There was a soft tap on the door, and I swung round in my seat, it was Deli, she smiled.

"Are you busy?" I shook my head.

"Not really, I am transferring the holiday pictures to my computer." She walked in, and looked a little coy, as she sat down in the free seat.

"Abby, can I ask you something, and if I am being too nosey, you know, you can tell me to mind my own business?" She sat down in Birch's chair, I shrugged.

"Ask away." She looked uncomfortable, and I felt she was picking her words carefully.

"Abby, did you and Eric have something special, you know, was it deep between you?" I gave a chuckle.

"You know today you looked really embarrassed, I was not sure if I should rescue you or do something to help." I gave a long sigh.

"I did feel a little on the spot, but there was no big romance, why?" She flushed a little and I smiled.

"Do you like him that much Deli? You know, every girl at school had a crush on him, it is no big secret he was very popular?" Her cheeks went really red.

"I was pretty crazy about him for a long time. I thought, you know, living here and being the new girl, if there was something big with you two, I would respect it and step back." She is so lovely, so respectful, I shook my head.

"Deli, it is no secret, actually, I would think it is part of Curio history in a way." She looked surprised.

"How so?" I lifted my cup and took a drink.

"Okay, you see that picture of the three of us?" I pointed to the wall above my bed, she looked at it and gave a nod.

"That picture was taken by Hatty a week after I came home from Uni with this hair. It is strange really because it means so much. Just after that was taken, Chloe came up to me and asked for a truce, you know the story of how I hit her at school and defended Deb's, and how Birch decorated her in hot curry, well that was the day, we became mates." She understood.

"How does that involve Eric." I smiled at her.

"That was also the day I first walked into the village, Deb's called me out for hiding, so we planned a trip to the nursery for herb plants. Whilst we were there, Birch saw and bought the junk heap that became Petal. Actually, it was also the day Deb's wore a short skirt and no knickers, and flashed her vagina at Lillian." Deli gave a gasp.

"What the hell, did she?" I giggled, as I remembered the day.

"The thing is, because of that day, Chloe and Edwina, became friends, and a few days later, Anthony joined us. I was living in fear and having a really hard time, when Deb's got tickets for the Oxendale festival, so all of us went as a group with two tents, and it was our first drive out in Petal. Eric got a free ticket from Nigel, who was stalking me at the time, you remember the broadcast?" Deli gave a gasp.

"Who doesn't, I mean that rocked the village?" I nodded at her; it was still a talking point today.

"It was at that festival we really gelled as a group, Birch got laid,

Edwina and Chloe shared Zac, and Debbie lost her virginity to Jimmy, that was where they met for the first time. Well, I was feeling a little left out and lonely, when Eric and Nigel showed up in the dark, as we sat against Petal getting drunk. Nigel finally left, as Birch was pretty in his face and rude, we talked for a while, and I realised Eric was having as disappointing time as I was, so I grabbed his hand, and dragged him to the tent." Suddenly she understood.

"You two had sex?"

"We did... Deli, I told him clearly, it was a one time thing, as I was going back to Manchester. If I am honest, I used him to cater to a need I had. The thing is, he was so nice, so respectful, and really good in the sack, and after we had done, rather than just leave, he stayed and cuddled me and talked. He was so nice and respectful, and he told me, he wanted more, something along the lines of a relationship, I said no, it was a one time deal, and he left disappointed. That is about it."

"But you really looked very uncomfortable today, are you sure you did not have feelings?" I laughed and shook my head.

"Deli, I had feelings today, I was really embarrassed, you know, I had a good few one night stands in the past. Look, the thing was, I always felt guilty for using Eric, none of the others, just him, simply because he is a really decent guy, and I feel shitty about the way I treated him. He deserved much better, so yes, I was really embarrassed, because the truth was, at that time, I was in love with Birch, but too cowardly to admit it." She smiled.

"You know, you are a pretty cool person, most people would never admit that, and to be honest, it was the same for me with the guy on holiday. I had great sex, oh God, I needed it so badly, but I was glad when we left, and I did not have to see him again." I understood that.

"Look Deli, I believe in being up front and honest. Eric wanted more, I didn't, even today looking at him, it did nothing for me. I like him, he is a nice person, which is why I talked to him. Could we be friends, I am not sure, as long as he never asked for sex again, then maybe yes, we could be mates. The simple truth is, he deserves more than a one night stand, and if I ever had one again, it would not be with him, for that very reason." I pointed to the card on my desk.

"His mobile number is there if you want it, I only kept the card because actually, I think we could prove him wrong, and kick his ass at paint ball."

"Sweetie, I love paint ball." She walked in with wide green eyes.

"Can we go shoot stuff, and make it look pretty?" I gave a sigh as Deli giggled.

"Birch, keep your voice down, I was thinking it is not long off Edwina's thirtieth, I thought it might be fun to pull together a Curio army and go take his boys on, and show them we are not as feeble as he thinks." Birch gave a jig, and clapped her hands together.

"Sweetie, that is a great idea... Oh, I am so excited." Yep, I married a crazy person.

Anthony landed at Heathrow, at 17:26 and Edwina went to collect him, for us, it was all hands on deck, as we flew around preparing. Deb's arrived with a smiling Jimmy, and we all got stuck in. The table was pulled out, as Chloe and Deli handled the food. Birch got way too excited hanging streamers and a huge Happy Birthday sign in the living room with Izzy, and I piled all Anthony's Gifts on the low coffee table.

The kitchen island was packed with spirits, and we all jumped in with sandwich making, pizza and sausage roll cooking, and Chloe whipped up a whole range of small eats and treats, there was enough food to feed the village.

People started arriving as we ran around in the madness that was a very hot kitchen. Even though we were all dressed in shorts and vests, we were hot, red, and sweating like mad.

We got the text from Edwina, they were heading to the car, the house was filling up fast, as all the staff from the practice arrived. Lillian and Celia, with their girls were there, with Hatty and Clive, Mum with Patrick, Bradley and Ellen, and a long list of Michael and Anthony's friends, even the band turned up.

G5 arrived, and mucked in with us, and as Anthony's mum arrived with Delphine, with everyone decked out with drinks and party hats, we squeezed them all into the living room, and closed the doors waiting.

Birch stood behind the doors with me, we both had a handle each, and waited for the cue, everyone was excited and happy.

Edwina pulled onto the drive as two very tanned members of our family sat in the back holding hands, Edwina pulled on the hand brake.

"Back to normal guys, council and planning, and the madness of home life." Anthony looked disappointed.

"Oh, Edwina darling, it is so cold and grey here, I cannot deny, I would have loved to have stayed longer. I have had pure sanity; it has been wonderful being back in the normal world." She chuckled as she got out, and headed for the door.

"I am sorry to say, Birch came back looking very rested, and crazier than ever, she has a lot of renewed energy." He gave a sigh as he closed the car door, and looked at Michael.

"Seriously Mikey, the sacrifices we make for the Curio's, we bring reason to the asylum." Michael chuckled as he lifted out their bag from the boot. They both followed Edwina in through the door, Anthony stood in the hall and looked up the stairs.

"It is good to be home, so where are the bonkers people?" Birch and me yanked open the doors at high speed, and Anthony squealed, as everyone screamed.

"SURPRISE!" Birch was definitely the loudest, and a zillion party poppers went off.

Anthony, grabbed his heart, his legs buckled, and he fainted, and crumpled to the floor. Chloe lent round the door and sniggered.

"Wow, milking it much Anthony?"

We all stared as Edwina and Michael patted his cheek, and he moaned, as he came back round. Birch was quite pleased.

"Now that is the meaning of a surprise, I mean, wow, never saw that coming. I mean, look at his pants, that is a good six inch surprised?" Linda was surprisingly calm as she looked at Birch.

"It's not the first time, he does not shock well." Chloe was laughing her ass off, Anthony groaned as he looked up at Birch, she waved.

"Hi Sweetie, Happy Birthday." He nodded, and took a deep breath, I did try not to laugh, but... Well, you know!

A glass of water, some smelling salts, and a few moments of sitting down, and he recovered, and flapped his arms and dabbed his eyes as the emotion of the moment of joy overtook him. We stood back, as he looked around at everyone with tears in his eyes, and waved his hand in front of him.

"I cannot believe you all came to see me; I am just so overwhelmed with the love in this room." Chloe turned to me.

"Abby, it's this house, I mean, if someone farts, we throw a party; how could he not expect one?" Birch leaned forward to look at her.

"I fart a lot." Chloe smirked.

"Why do you think we are always pissed?" I started to laugh.

Once he recovered, the music started and got underway, as Michael dragged him up, and started to hand out his presents, of which there was a hell of a pile. With every present, he got more emotional and louder, I mean it is not like this was not expected, it is Anthony after all.

He got hugs from everyone, and to be honest, it was nice to see everyone making a huge fuss of him, he is at heart a very kind and gentle person, who for so long felt isolated and alone, and today, he was surrounded by genuine love, I was really happy for him.

The living room was loud, and I ended up in the kitchen, sat on the washing machine with a drink, as I watched everyone crowd around the table with plates, and break into smaller groups to talk around the kitchen.

Anita arrived late, and as she walked into the kitchen, I was pleased to see Tabby was still with her, she gave me a big smile as she spotted me and walked over.

"I brought all the VIP passes and details for next weekend over, Edwina has put them on your desk in your room. Anthony looks really happy?" I gave a happy smile, as I watched him smiling and joking with the guests.

"He is, he deserves it, it is nice to see everyone make a fuss of him." Tabby was looking round with wide eyes.

"Wow, this place is Curio Mecca." She was in fan girl mode again, she looked at me.

"You wrote all of them here, it's amazing." I gave a nod as I lifted my drink.

"I finished Seeds of Summer here, I wrote the last three chapters, the day I moved in, but everything since then, yes, this is the home of my work and the arch." She looked blown away.

"I thought the arch was behind your house?" I nodded.

"It used to be, but they condemned it, so Birch bought it, had it restored and then brought here, it is in the garden." Anita gave a chuckle.

"Tabby, if your eyes get any bigger, they will pop." I slipped off the washing machine and took her hand.

"Come see." I walked her up the kitchen, and pointed at the bank of light switches.

"Push that one there, and then look down there."

She lifted a finger, and flicked the switch, and then gasped, even Anita was impressed. Michael had wired up a special light for my arch, a single light shone up from the floor onto it, and bathed it in a soft red light. With the dark cloudy sky behind it, it looked amazing, both Anita and Tabby gasped.

"I love my arch; it has inspired me in so many parts of my life." Tabby stared through the patio doors.

"Abby, it is beautiful, I completely see why, wow, I am blown completely away, it is magnificent." I smiled, I loved that she admired it so much, I noticed Stacy walk to the window and look out at it, she noticed me looking at her.

"Would you like to stand under it?"

She looked terrified and happy at the same time, I reached for the handle and unlocked the door, and stepped out. Tabby and Stacy walked with Anita and me, down the long lawn towards it, they approached it like it was a sacred monument, it was sort of amusing, and yet so respectful. Tabby bubbled over, and grabbed Anita's hand.

"I want a picture." She pulled her onto the stone, I took her phone off her, and they posed, in the red light, and I took it, and Tabby was overjoyed and all smiles, I turned to Stacy.

"Would you like one too, no other fan has ever stood next to it, I would imagine you will be the envy of Insta?" She looked completely at a loss for words, she swallowed hard, and blinked.

"If it is alright, I saw it at your wedding, but I was right at the back. This is amazing, would you stand with me next to it? I mean if not, then that is completely fine Mrs Dixon." I gave a giggle and took her hand.

"Stacy, I have told you before, I am home, call me Abby."

Anita took her phone, and also mine, and she stood next to me under the red lit arched window, and the pictures were taken. She gasped when she looked at her phone and saw it, and her voice was really quiet and soft.

"Oh Abby, this is like the best day ever, you have no idea how much this means to me, I love your books."

In a way, it is crazy, it is just what is left of a once productive mill, the crumbled remnant of a bygone age, something so old and decayed, it had been condemned for demolition. Yet to Birch and myself it was hallowed ground, and it appeared as equally sacred to Tabby and Stacy. I wrote about it, Chloe drew it, and Hatty painted it, and in some strange weird way, it was immortalised, and yet I love that about it.

I had pondered it at Sunny Bank, because I love that house, and yet when I seriously thought about it, I knew in my heart, Waterside Lane is where I will reside for the rest of my life, simply because, my arch was here. I could not possibly leave this behind for someone else to have, as old as it may be, I see it as my arch, and a symbol of who I was, and who I became, and I was never parting from it.

The party went on until two in the morning, I gave Anita the guest room for the night. Most of the guests left by midnight, but there were one or two sprawled out on the sofa. At the top of the stairs, I put my arms around a drunken Anthony and smiled.

"I am glad you had a great party, happy birthday." I kissed his cheek, he smiled at me.

"I love you, Abby." I knew that.

"I love you too, you are one of my closest friends, in my heart, you are my brother, and always will be." He filled up and gave a smile, and squeezed me hard.

"None of you will ever know what it means to me to have you all, honestly Abby, I would die for any of you."

Michael gave a nod as he watched, but I think we both knew that was true, and Anthony knew it was a two way street. I kissed his head and wished him goodnight, and walked exhausted to my room. Birch was flat out in bed, I chuckled as I pulled my vest over my head, and unbuttoned my shorts.

I wearily slipped into bed, and she instinctively rolled to me, and cuddled up, and so I closed my eyes, and drifted into a happy sleep.

Chapter 27

Awards And Deals.

The morning after Anthony's party, I think I was the only one who did not have a hangover. Our first job was cleaning, and there was a lot to do, so I got stuck in, much to the annoyance of the remaining guests, who did not really appreciate the hoover. Deb's and Jimmy stayed over, and Deli mucked in with Chloe in the kitchen, and then it was back to business as normal.

Tabby had to leave, and I smiled as I sat in the kitchen and watched Anita hold her close, and kiss her goodbye for now. I was thrilled for her, and she was really happy. Edwina took control, the house was done, and there were events to plan and organise, and suddenly we were mad busy.

It was decided that because we were planning a big event, we would use the attic space, our kitchen table was nowhere near big enough, so G5 mucked in, and built a large wooden temporary table down the centre of the attic, on to which Edwina rolled out a huge, to scale plan of the village, and I got the job of placements of all the traders and food stands.

At the side of the plan, Terry had created a small model of the village on his 3D printer, and with Luke, they built a tiny scale copy of Wotton. Edwina had spent three hours with a thick pad of measurements, attaching cotton to the tops of the buildings, that showed the triangulation of her equipment placements.

Birch and Edwina had excelled, and the show field had a huge circus tent and a fair, with rides and attractions, and it was equally as big as the summer fete. It is funny, all those years of helping dad suddenly paid off, the event was going to be massive, and a few of the group were intimidated by it, but not me, I just fell right into my role, and got stuck in marking it all out just like dad had shown me.

In the evenings, Michael and Birch, finished off the spare attic room, and got it wired up with lights and plugs, and by the time it was finished, it was actually a quaint little room, with sets of draws, and a wardrobe, and it even had a table with a large plant on in it, next to the newly replaced window.

My week became a blur of phone calls, letter opening, and typing, as Deli jumped in at my side, and we all began the long process of confirming who would go where. Edwina was handling the fair, Birch the circus, Deb's the parade, and Chloe the food vendors, and I was over all site coordinator. Anita took over promotion, and we were all busy, but actually it was fun, with a lot of banter.

On Friday, everything stopped, as we planned for the weekend and my award, which meant another night in a hotel bed. We slept deep and rose early packed our bags, and headed back to London, and yet another hotel.

Like all things with award ceremonies, there is a catch, if I win, I have to go on a stage and speak. Whilst everyone around me was excited and happy, my insides were swirling, it felt like Curio Live all over again. My greatest asset, was Ella, she had been told whilst we were in Sunny Bank, and she was busy on yet another dress, honestly my wardrobe was starting to fill up with her clothing, so much so, we have moved all her designs into the wardrobe in the spare room.

The event was being staged in a large premier luxury ballroom, and large screens had been erected in the huge civic square right outside, as it was televised live, on all the independent TV networks. I arrived at one o'clock in the afternoon, with Anita and Birch dressed in jeans, for a walk through, and was a little bit intimidated.

There was a mass of activity, all over the square, barriers were already up and fans, were already arriving. A huge group of fans, who were held back over a hundred yards away from us, yelled and screamed at me. I stopped with a smile and waved.

It felt a lot of pressure on me, as I was up against Johanna Friel, and Amanda Peacock, two of the largest teen writers alive. Johanna had won it four years running, and I felt my hopes get trashed, because the truth was, I just simply was not in their league when it came to book sales.

Inside was equally as busy, there were crews and wires everywhere, as we were shown in and given instruction of where we would be placed. We had a huge table for our group, in what would be a lavish affair, with the cream of the crop of TV, Film and Literature for young readers. The organisers talked me through the process of what would happen camera wise, and in the event, I won, I was shown how to conduct myself. I felt really nervous, as Birch held my hand, but to be honest, I could not see that happening.

We returned back to our hotel, and headed for the bar, I was unsettled, and needed to calm down. I sat in the bar in the hotel and I gave a sigh, Birch took my hand.

"Sweetie, this is nothing to do with sales, this is fans that vote, you have as good a chance as any." I shook my head.

"Birch, their sales treble mine, and it is fans who buy them. Hell, I have read their books, especially Johanna, her forest of dreams series, is one of the best I have read, even you have read all of Amanda's books. I have to face facts, they are genius writers, they are even my hero's, and what I aspire to."

Ella arrived filled with smiles, and we all headed up to my room, it was a little crowded, so we all sat on the bed as the girls prepared the bags. Anita had brought April back in, she had done my makeup for my wedding, and we all took it in turns having our makeup done. Anthony as always, did my hair, he had touched it up, Wednesday night, and in true Curio fashion, he had given Deli, violet highlights, and it looked amazing.

With my wonderful gothic eyes, done in as April put it, 'completely tear resident makeup,' I finally prepared for my dress. Ella smiled a huge smile as she unzipped the bag, and I gave a gasp. The dress was a rich burgundy with black, and it fitted at the top, and flowed down into a wide circle, it was elegant, feminine, almost vintage, and very gothic, as it was decorated with tiny black glass beads round the bodice, it was also backless. I excitedly slipped it on, and she pulled it tight and fastened it, and Birch gave a gasp.

"Deads, Sweetie, oh God, you look stunning." I smiled as I looked in the mirror, Ella handed me a matching new parasol, I was delighted.

Birch was dressed in a tight backless figure hugging deep green dress, which accentuated her figure beautifully. I cannot deny, as she turned with her white hair and dark green eyes, I felt a lot of tiny tingles run up my legs. Wow, she looked as hot as hell, Ella smiled.

"I want the world to see, that you Abby, have exquisite taste in women." I giggled, she absolutely thought of everything.

Chloe did not want a new dress, she was going with her dress from the gallery, Edwina had a long flowing black gown, and she looked really elegant, Ella turned to Deli.

"Okay, the new Curio. Now, I got your rough measurements, and I was pushed for time, you girls do keep me busy these days. So, I looked through my new line, and I found this, I am so glad you got the violet highlights, although, Anthony did tip me off." Deli looked at me.

"I am getting a dress too?" I smiled and gave her a nod.

"Of course, you are one of us now, Floyd is minus a vicar, so he will be your escort tonight." Ella unzipped the bag, and lifted out a deep rich purple gown, Deli gasped and looked totally shocked, Ella gave a chuckle as she looked at her.

"As I said, I am sure this will look great on you, I really do need her measurements on file Abby. This laces up the back, and she has a similar chest size to you, I did have it on hand for emergencies for you, but with that hair, this is simply perfect for her."

Deli stripped down to her underwear in a flash, Ella and myself giggled. Ella held up the dress.

"No bra with this one, love the red lace thong though, very sexy."

She giggled as Deli excitedly stepped into the dress and Ella slid it up her figure. It was a little lose at the top, but Ella laced it up, and she looked incredible. It is probably a good job we all had water proof makeup, because she took one look at herself in the mirror, and burst into tears. It took a while to calm her down, but eventually, with Birch sliding her hand over my bum, and giggling, we were ready, and I felt a jolt, as my nerves started all over again.

I was really nervous when I arrived in the bar ready. Anita in a long flowing gown of black, and silver, organised the cars, they would collect us at the rear. Deb's had on a Gucci dress, and she looked stunning with her hair up, Jimmy looked pretty cool in his black suit and bow tie, as did Floyd, and Luke. Anthony as always, was immaculate in a deep blue, almost black fitted suit, and honestly, Michael looked really hot. I noted how Chloe was looking him up and down, as she stood with Baz. As always, I got Markus, he gave me a huge smile.

"Mrs and Mrs Dixon, you look stunning together." I gave him an even bigger smile.

"Markus, as always, you look impeccable too, and as you know, you are my most favourite driver, in the whole world." I reached up on my tip toes, and kissed his cheek.

"I know it is not allowed, but hey, I am a rebel."

He chuckled as he closed the door, and we sat back for the drive, Birch took my hand, I was really nervous, and my stomach was churning. She leaned on my shoulder.

"Sweetie, you will be fine." I swallowed hard.

"I really regret that salad; the onions are playing havoc with me." She giggled, and snuggled up to me. The cars drove in a long line, like a presidential parade, and as we approached, Markus dropped the window.

"We are almost there, I know you know the routine, but look happy and attentive with each other, hold hands, and smile."

I love Markus, he is always there on hand at these things, and has some great advice for us. He was also there for me earlier this year, and I will never forget his kindness that night. There was a linc of cars waiting, up ahead, celebrities, industry officials, and billionaires, were getting out onto the red carpet. I looked through the tinted windows, and there were thousands of fans waving and screaming for everyone who stepped out, there were also a lot of tv cameras.

Michael and Anthony were first out, and their car sped off, to be replaced with Anita and Tabby's. It was like strobe lights, there were so many flashes, Chloe jumped out with Baz, and waved with a huge smile as fans screamed for her. Deli was terrified when she got out, this was much bigger than the gallery, and her name was screamed out by a lot of fans. Her and Floyd signed autographs and talked. Sat in the car, I heard the roar of the crowd, as Jimmy and Deb's got out, talk about a number one A list celebrity couple, the press was all over them.

Luke and Edwina were next, and I saw the carpet come into view. I had been spotted in the car, and the press were already trying to take pictures through the window. Markus pulled up and smiled as the door staff grabbed the handle.

"Good luck, and bring home a prize."

I gave a giggle as I lifted my parasol, and got ready as Birch stepped out, and the noise went tenfold, she was as famous as I was, which I loved.

I pushed out the parasol, and flicked the switch, and it shot out, and opened, it was becoming my symbol these days, although there was a little fine drizzle. The noise exploded as I stood up, and Birch linked my arm, and together we walked from the car, stood for the press and faced them. A barrage of flashes went off, and I could barely see, and blinked, and with a huge smile, Birch turned me, and I saw thousands of smiling happy faces, waving books at me.

Up in front, none of the Curio's had made it inside, all of them talked to the fans, and signed autographs. I loved that about them, we had talked so many times of making sure we never neglected a fan, and both Birch and myself, made our way signing everything in front of us. Both of us would be guided to news stations for a few brief words with the press, and then we would go back to talking to fans, and slowly, we zig zagged up the red carpet.

As we reached the half way point, we were guided by the staff back towards the tv cameras, and I saw Amy wave next to the BBC. Jimmy and Deb's were talking to her, I stood with huge smiles in front of Anna Cole, and she held up her mic.

"Mrs Dixon, Abigail, how are you feeling, this is a massive honour to be nominated?"

I gave a big smile to the camera, it was not that hard, because I felt so amazingly happy.

"I am so delighted, I never thought for a second I would make the cut, so just being here is simply wonderful." She nodded at me; it was so loud with all the screaming.

"How is married life, you both look stunning, and very happy indeed." I giggled as Birch squeezed my arm.

"We are, we had such a wonderful wedding, and we are just loving our life, although we are very busy with a lot of projects at the moment, we do make a great team."

"You have a huge fan base here tonight, Abigail, and we wish you the very best of luck." I nodded.

"Johanna and Amanda are amazing writers, as I said, I am just happy my fans voted me this far, after all, they are the most important aspect of my writing." She smiled.

"Good luck, and if you win, please come and talk to us."

"I will, thank you."

Amy grabbed us as always, and she raved about us, we were being encouraged to move on, and it was hard as I wanted to talk more. River TV more than any company had always supported me, and I appreciated it, Amy was all smiles.

"Honestly Abby, I want to hug you I am so happy."

I leaned in, and she leaned over the rail, and I laughed, as we were reminded yet again by an official, we had to move on. I released my hug on Amy, and we were escorted on, and in through the doors, apparently, the Curio's were holding the line up.

The ballroom was huge, with a stage draped in gold and blue, and we were to be seated around a large round table, it seated fifteen, which was good, as there were fourteen of us. The waiter pulled on my chair to seat me, and I felt a tap on my shoulder, I turned and gasped in shock. Johanna Friel smiled.

"Abigail, I just wanted to say, I love your books and good luck." I was stunned and lost for words, I struggled to talk as I went complete nerd fan girl.

"Miss Friel, I am a huge fan of your books, honestly, the Forest of Dreams series is magnificent, you will win hands down." She gave me a smile.

"Abigail, do not underestimate yourself, the Hands of Death series, is wonderful, I loved Resurrection Sword, it was inspiring to read it." I am sure my jaw clicked, as my mouth snapped shut, I felt lost.

"You have read my books?" Birch giggled at my side; Johanna gave a chuckle.

"I have, and I loved them." She gave me a smile.

"Don't look so surprised, they are brilliantly written, you know, I am not that far from Wotton, we should meet for a coffee and talk." I gasped, like a complete nerd, oh God, was I becoming a Tabby?

"I would love that." Birch giggled.

"She is a little awestruck Johanna." She slipped her arm around my waist, and squeezed me, Johanna smiled at me.

"I have to get back to my table, but here." She pulled a card out of her bag.

"Call me soon, and we will talk." I nodded like an idiot.

"I will." Chloe leaned across the table, as I stood staring watching Johanna walk to her seat.

"God Abby, talk about wet knickers, you are such a nerd." Everyone giggled, as I sat down, and felt a little flustered.

"Chloe, that was Johanna Friel, she is like a goddess in the book world." She smirked.

"Abby, she has tits and a hooch, just like the rest of us." Birch giggled, and leaned on me.

"I think that was sweet."

Drinks were served and we all sat back, as the night began, as all the categories came up, we all expressed our preferences, and applauded as the winners took their prizes, and gave their emotional speeches. All of us were happy and really enjoying the night, as we were surrounded by famous celebrities, and were in awe of them.

You see this is why I love this group of people, in many ways, all of us have become well known and famous through our Curio Live work, and Jimmy was an A list celebrity now, and yet there, all of us were exactly the same as we had been back in my guest house all those years ago. We were just simple people, with dreams and fantasies just like every fan outside watching the large screens.

We did not see ourselves as famous or more important than anyone else, if anything we saw ourselves as just ordinary normal people. The real Abby was scruffy, mainly naked and a workaholic, not the glamorous designer dressed up person I was tonight. That was the persona that was the gothic looking Abigail

Jennifer Watson, a well known writer of gothic novels. The real me, loved Birch, sunbathed and swam naked, and sat each morning talking about normal life with Chloe over coffee.

I was miles away enjoying the moment, almost in a state of complete forgetfulness of why I was there. Colette Fanning, who was hosting the event, stood by the microphone, and suddenly I was snapped back to reality with a bang.

"And now for the award, for youth literature, and here to tell us the results, please welcome to the stage, possibly one of TV's most well read presenters, Mr Gordon Stimes." My heart began to beat, and I swallowed hard, as it suddenly dawned on me why I was in this seat.

Everyone applauded, and I noticed the cameras all turn to face me and the other authors, my heart started to race, Deb's gave a little squeak, Chloe's eyes got huge, and Birch gripped my arm like a vice, she was holding her breath.

I felt suddenly really hot and panicked, my knees started to tremble, and my stomach squirmed. I knew I had no hope of winning, but just that little tiny part of me wanted to, and it surprised me knowing that. Anita reached up at my side and took my hand and held it, she looked like she was praying. Gordon walked onto the stage and gave a bow to everyone as the applause continued. He gave a wide smile and looked out at us; he caught my eye, and smiled right at me.

I was suddenly, utterly terrified, I was glued to him, hanging on every word he spoke.

"Ladies and Gentlemen, wow, what an impressive line up. I have had all three of these wonderful guests on my show, and all of them are immensely talented. Alright, the nominees for this year's youth award for literature, are. Amanda Peacock, for her series, 'The Tales of Meg.' Johanna Friel, for the series 'Forest of Dreams, and I am so delighted to see, Abigail Jennifer Watson, for the Hand of Death series." Birch exploded, and gasped out for air, and bounced on her seat.

"Sweetie that is you." Chloe stared at her.

"Birch, where the fuck have you been, that is why we are here?"

I felt Anita squeeze my hand tighter, I was holding my breath, he opened the envelope, slipped out the card and smiled, I was sure I was going to pass out.

"Oh, how absolutely wonderful." I was heading toward cardiac arrest, he looked right at me.

"Such a fitting recipient, and I for one am delighted to say, Abigail Jennifer Watson, for the Hand of Death series."

The table exploded, with wild screams and cheers, it was insane, as I sat stunned, and felt tears in my eyes. Birch was wrapped tightly round me, squeezing the life out of me, as was Anita. I felt numb, shocked, and yet really happy.

Deb's and Jimmy were up on their feet with all the other Curios, clapping and cheering, the whole room was applauding. I was dragged out of my chair, as Birch pulled me into a tight hug, and held me tight.

"Sweetie, you did it." Anita pulled me free with tears in her eyes.

"Go get em Abby, you really earned this."

I smiled and wiped my eyes with my hand, Tabby handed me a lace hankie, and I wiped my eyes again. I felt shocked, stunned, like it was some sort of unreal dream, as the camera's followed me, in what felt like the walk of shame. I made my way to the steps with shaky legs, and a staff member held out their arm to show me the way. It just felt so surreal and overwhelming, I had so many emotions flowing inside me, it was hard to focus. Johanna stood up as I passed her, and she was smiling and clapping really hard, she winked.

"Abby, you deserve that."

I wiped my eyes again, I could hardly see, and headed up the steps, and walked towards Gordon, who was holding a large glass orb, he had the biggest smile I have ever seen. I was shaking, and trembling, as he placed it into my hands, and leaned in and kissed my cheek.

"Well done Abby, you really earned this the hard way, good on you."

He stood back, and held up his arm, and I turned to the lectern, and saw a sea of a thousand happy clapping smiling people, and lots of cameras. Right below me, sat my Curio's, and Birch looked at me with shining tears in her eyes, and wearing the hugest smile.

I took a huge breath, as every emotion I have ever had surged up inside me. I put the award down, it was so heavy, I was afraid I would drop it. I looked down at my friends, and wiped my eyes.

"Guys, I won." The audience laughed as the Curio's cheered, I looked back up and noticed the camera flashing red in front of me.

"I am a little wrong footed tonight, I was just happy to be here, and to be included with Johanna and Amanda, who for me, have been such a great inspiration."

I took a deep breath; my heart was racing. I swallowed hard fighting to compose myself. I let a long slow breath out, and tried to focus, Birch was watching with tears in her eyes, holding her heart as she smiled at me.

"When I first started writing, Katie O'Reilly and the Dixon Group took a huge risk. I was unknown, and writing what was considered a dead genre, and I will be forever grateful to them for that. I honestly was not sure if people would read my words, and I am so glad it paid off eventually for them. My mum and dad really supported me, and what can I say, Chloe, you gave my books the most amazing covers, you have no idea how wonderful it is to have worked at your side on all of them. I owe much to so many, Anita my publicist, and my wonderful Curio family, without your support, I probably would have panicked, and hid in the wardrobe tonight." The audience laughed.

"I mostly want to thank my biggest inspiration, without her I never would have had the guts to write, my wife. Jemi, Birch, I love you, your faith is what brought me through the darkness. You have been my rock, and have supported me in all of this. I love you; I never would have made this far without your utter belief in me." I wiped my eyes as I smiled at her.

"I especially want to thank, all my wonderful fans, they are always there to meet me, and encourage me, and they really have given me so much support and love. This award will always be a little part of all of them, and I thank them from the bottom of my heart." My voice quivered.

"I am probably going to cry now."

Every one applauded, and it was deafening, as my eyes filled with tears, and Gordon took my arm, and helped guide me off the stage, which is good, because I was shell shocked, and struggling on my shaking legs, and blinded by my tears. Birch got up, and dragged me into a hug as I arrived at the table, with my big glass orb.

"Sweetie, I love you, I told you remember? One day people will know your name, well Deads, they do tonight."

I looked up into her bright shining, green, tear filled eyes, and she smiled a huge smile, she leaned in and gave me the softest kiss, and boom, a million flashes went off, but who cares, this time we were dressed.

Sat at the table was so crazy, as my award got passed around, everyone was buzzing, and in party mode. Anita ordered more drinks, and I sat back, still shaking and took a huge breath, my emotions were all over the place, Anita smiled at me.

"God Abby, I am so bloody happy, working with you has become my dream job. Roni is at home screaming and dancing with Will, this is the first real literary award the group has won, she told me to tell you, she is so proud of you."

I was simply lost for words, and grabbed my drink, and took a huge swig. Deb's held my award, and her eyes sparkled as she looked at me.

"I am so proud of you Abby; you have no idea how much it means to see you get this." I shook my head.

"Don't set me off again Deb's, I am barely holding it together." She giggled, and blew me a kiss. Chloe looked at it.

"Where you going to put it Abby?" I smiled at her.

"On the mantle next to the Curio statue, where all of you can share it, you did the artwork, that is also a tribute to you." She gave a big smile as she looked at it, and Edwina winked at me.

The problem with winning, is you have no choice but to talk to the press. As the awards evening ended, Anita guided me through the side doors, to yet another red carpet, only this one was sectioned off, and each section had a different TV company, and they were worldwide.

I was guided along talking, and it felt like forever, and yet again I was in front of the BBC, and Anna welcomed me in, and stood next to me as the camera man stood in front of me, with Birch at my side, holding my award, like it was the crown jewels.

"Abigail, congratulations, you must be delighted?" I gave a huge sigh of relief.

"I am feeling a lot of emotions at the moment, I honestly did not think I would get it. I thought either Johanna or Amanda, my fans are just amazing for voting for me." Anna leaned over.

"If I may Doctor Dixon, how are you feeling?" She gave a huge chuckle.

"I am just so happy and proud of my amazingly talented wife, I knew she would win, but she would not believe me, she has no idea how good she is." Anna gave a chuckle.

"Abigail, you have a huge following, not just from the books, but also the Curio's, and I see once again they are out in force to support you, honestly, did you ever see any of this happening?" I gave a laugh, and shook my head.

"No, I never thought my books would sell, and when we made the Curio Life site, none of us thought it would get as big as it has. I am so glad it has; we have helped a lot of young people out there." Anna nodded at me.

"How is the new site going, we have seen a lot of pictures on the Curio site, and it is starting to really take shape, how much longer will it be?" Birch leaned into the mic.

"Most of the building work is completed, at the moment they are working on wiring and plumbing, and then it will be decoration, and furnishings, we are hoping for mid November, and we are on target, we will be doing a lot of press before it opens." She turned back to me.

"Abigail, I will let you go, as I am hoping we can grab Chloe, but again, congratulations and enjoy your night."

I turned and waved over to Chloe, who was walking with Baz as Jimmy and Deb's talked to the other station at our side, she smiled and walked over, and Anna thanked me as I stepped back. The place was madness as my name was called from every angle, we stood together as cameras flashed, it felt draining. I finally made it to Amy, she was over the moon.

"Oh, Abby, we are all so delighted, we were dancing around the camera when you won."

I giggled, we were being herded by organisers to keep moving on, which was annoying, I saw Amy look at the stewards, and give a frustrated sigh, so I leaned in close.

"Call Anita in the morning, you will have an exclusive, sat at my arch, in my garden, and I will tell you all about it." Her eyes sparkled.

"God Abby, I love you, you are a journalists wet dream." Birch gave a cackle of a laugh, I nodded and smiled and walked on.

Apparently, there was an after party in the hotel next door, and we were taken through a side door, into a fenced off area, that created a walk way full of fans, they all screamed when I walked out, and I was thrilled, these were the people who voted, and they were going to get my time.

It took forever as we posed for photos, talked, and signed pictures and books, and I felt happy and excited, and just as good as a girl can get. Chloe, Deli and Deb's joined us at our side, and it was so exciting as we all laughed and joked with the fans. Birch loved it, and got louder and louder, as she laughed, smiled, and talked, it took forever to get to the party.

We were handed a bag of goodies each, and as we walked towards the door, we placed them in a crate with my parasol, and they were bag checked, and I was given a ticket for collection afterwards. I had to keep the award on me, as everyone wanted to see it.

I walked in to be confronted by Gordon, he smiled a wonderful smile, as he walked over to me.

"Abby, you have no idea how thrilled I was when I opened that envelope, I really think you deserved this." I took a deep breath feeling completely overwhelmed.

"I owe some of this to you Gordon, after the show we did, my books really rocketed. This was not just me, there have been many along the way that helped." He smiled.

"Without the words on your pages, none of us would have noticed, you earned this Abby, enjoy it." I smiled as Birch squeezed my waist, he winked and lifted his arm to guide me to the table.

"Go have fun."

It was nice to finally get off my feet, and I placed the award on the table in front of me, it weighed a tonne, and my arms ached carrying it.

The party was nice, but to be honest, it was a lot of rich people and celebrities, and felt similar to the gala night at the Curio event. We all sat together and laughed and joked, and people would come up and congratulate me, to gasps of appreciation from the others. If I am honest, I hardly knew any of them, and after they left, Chloe or Edwina and Deb's would fill me in on who they were.

I think I found it unsettling, these people would come up and call me Abby, then talk to me like I had known them all my life, and yet this was our first meeting. In true Curio fashion, we had drinks, pissed about, and laughed a lot, Johanna came over and sat at my side, she gave me a big hug.

"I am delighted for you Abby, I really am." Chloe stared at her across the table.

"Are you not disappointed you did not win it?" Johanna gave an almighty laugh.

"Good grief no... If I had won, I would have had to make yet another trophy case, Chloe my dear, these bloody things take up space and need a lot of polishing, I have quite enough to keep me busy."

I giggled at her; Chloe appeared a little lost for words, Johanna turned to me, and looked very serious for a moment.

"Abby, one of the reasons I wanted to meet, is because I have been having a few issues with my publisher, my God, they can be a pain in the ass. I have one book done to finish Forest of Dreams, and to be completely truthful, after that my contract expires, and to be honest, I feel it is time for a change. Now I have a new series, but I was wondering if you could put a good word in for me with the Dixon Group?" I felt shocked.

"You want to come over to us? Johanna, you are like huge, you do not need my word, talk to Anita, she will bite your hand off."

Anita was sat stunned; Tabby was bouncing all over the place. Anita looked at her.

"I would sleep with the Pope to get you in the Dixon Group." Tabby pulled Anita's card out of her bag.

"Here, call her tomorrow." I laughed; Tabby's eyes were huge. Johanna took it with a smirk.

"Wonderful, I will arrange a meeting, I still want coffee Abby." I nodded.

"Yeah, me too, we will set something up for you." She smiled and got up.

"Wonderful, you know, I feel very excited, again, congratulations." I turned, and looked at Anita, she was white in the face.

"Jesus Abby, if I can pull her, Roni will love my ass forever, she is a legend."

It was a long emotional day, and I was so tired. Birch took my arm, and guided me back to the limo, where Markus stood with a beaming smile. I grinned as I climbed in and relaxed, and Birch snuggled into my arm. The drive was not long, but as we approached, Markus dropped the screen.

"Mrs Dixon, the press know where you are, so be prepared, they are camped out waiting for your return, get ready for them." I leaned forward and slid the gift bag through the screen and dropped it on his seat.

"I normally give these to Chloe, but she has one, give it your wife, there is all sorts of things in it I am sure she will love. Tell her, I said thanks for loaning me such a wonderful husband. I keep you out late, so this will compensate her." He gave a chuckle.

"Always the writer using just the right words, to make it impossible to refuse you." I giggled and sat back.

"It is the perk of my lifestyle Markus, but seriously, you work long hours for us, and I for one really appreciate it." He gave a nod as he pulled in.

Markus opened the door and we slipped out, holding the award, the press shouted out, 'Abby how does it feel?' and 'Abby how is married life?" I linked Birch with a smile as we walked up to the doors, I turned and stopped, the flashes exploded as I lifted up the award.

"It is absolutely wonderful."

We walked, giggling like idiots through the door, and into the hotel.

Chapter 28

War and Love.

I woke Sunday to the sounds of my screeching, and insane wife, as she leaned out of the window and shook her fists at London.

"CAN YOU NOT SHUT THE FUCK UP, YOU TWATS, IT'S FUCKING SUNDAY, AND US SINNERS ARE TRYING TO SLEEP!"

Yep, hotels are not sound proof like home is. I pulled the duvet over my head, and closed my eyes, and tried to pretend that I had no idea what a bloody liberty it is, and how we should write to the Church of England, and tell them to shut the fuck up on Sundays. God, I really love her, she is loud, but she is lovely.

Birch made coffee, grumbling about the opening hours of Marks and Sparks, and how all their customers knew the opening hours, so why the fuck after two thousand years had the Christians not learned them yet? It is a hard life for Pagan's apparently.

I sipped my coffee and went through my phone; I had a zillion message's.

"My dad says he is so proud, my mum is raving, and Hatty and Clive got pissed and passed out in the garden naked, and got rained on." Birch smiled.

"You deserved it Sweetie, I did a live broadcast to Facebook, from your page, so all your fans online can watch it over and over. Sophia took pictures of her TV and posted them to Insta to show the power of her friend the influencer. Prim hated it, she slagged you off on Insta, and Chloe gave her a virtual bitch slap." She giggled, I frowned and looked at her.

"How the hell do you do that?"

Birch turned her phone to me, and I read Chloe's post which read 'Shut the fuck up you rancid bitch,' followed by a row of palm emoticons. I giggled, and then stared at the phone. The profile picture was a woman with long red hair, that was vaguely familiar, wearing dark glasses, I frowned.

"Who the hell is Marianne Magdalene?" Birch gave me a big smile.

"It's me Sweetie, it is my Christian Troll profile, I use it to watch all the people who piss me off. I messaged Prim and told her I bloody hated you, and she added me, I am one of her twenty two followers, although her baby pictures give me nightmares, I don't look at them." I frowned.

"Birch, you do know that Mary Magdalene was portrayed as a whore in the bible, don't you?" She gave a sweet smile.

"I know... I love the irony." I leaned over her shoulder.

"Marianne has some weird friends, what the hell, Ivor Biggerone, seriously, is that you as well?"

Birch giggled, and opened the profile, I saw shit loads of dicks, with faces and hats on. It did not take a huge amount to work out who was behind that. Birch sniggered.

"I love Chloe, only she could fool their algorithms, and get away with posting these." Birch turned her phone and I jumped back.

"Whoa... Holy shit!" She smiled.

"Look familiar... Creamy is her greatest like, this has had almost a million views." I sniggered, it had a big happy face, and it was wearing a bowler hat.

Breakfast was very noisy, Chloe looked around.

"Where is your award?" I frowned as I bit my toast.

"It's in my room." She looked stunned.

"Why?" I stared at her.

"Seriously Chloe, I am not bringing it to breakfast, that is seriously messed up you know?" Deb's giggled and Chloe shrugged.

"I would." Edwina gave a sigh.

"Chloe, with that sort of logic, and if they gave out awards for artistic slut of the year, then we would need a much bigger breakfast table." Deli sniggered; Chloe just shrugged.

"I would win it, and show it off wherever I went." Deb's looked at her.

"You pretty much show off everything else you have off, so why not?" Chloe nodded, and pointed her fork to Deb's, as she looked at Edwina.

"See, she understands." I started to laugh, I love her, she is so lovely.

It took some time before I felt awake, but we packed our bags, and headed down to the underground car park, for Petal and Bess, and very soon, we avoided the press, and headed home to Wotton. Bess stopped outside the post office, and we drove past. Chloe had arranged for a copy of every paper with Abby on the front, and sure enough, it was most of them.

The press were once again outside the house, I opened the window and smiled, as question after question bombarded us.

"I am very delighted, and I will treasure this forever, as my fans voted for it." Birch drove through the gates, and I gave a sigh of relief.

It was nice to be home and normal, although, I am not sure what normal is really, for us it is working and organising. My award got pride of place on the mantle next to the Curio statue, and I will not deny, it was nice to see it when I entered the room each day. My fans gave me that, and it means something, I do not need to polish it, as I have found my house mates do it daily, they appear as proud of it as I am.

Three days later, Amy showed up with her crew, and filmed one and a half hours of us sat talking at the arch, as I talked of my feelings of what it was like to win the award. I also talked about being married, getting away, and my thoughts on the end of the Hand of Death series. All in all, she had plenty to work with, and was delighted as she left, having yet again, acquired another exclusive from me.

Back in the village, Prim was out in force, with Molly and her new clean up the canal campaign. To be honest, the canal was beautiful, and I had no idea what else needed doing, although, I publicly agreed with it. Anything that added to the beauty of the village had my support. True to type, she attacked us, and called us sinners, and immoral, untrustworthy due to our deviance, and honestly, I wanted to punch her. Her latest attack was how she felt that the security and harmony of the village could not be trusted to such people of such deviant and corruptive behaviour, she noted the village would be overrun with deviant lesbians if we got in. I seethed with anger.

Birch constantly calmed me down, and told me to just let it go and focus on our plan, and stick to it. It felt really hard, and the injustice of it all really ate away at me. She was such a hypocrite, but as Birch constantly reminded me, the whole village had always been the same, why worry about one more. I cannot deny, it felt grossly unfair.

I made regular trips to the village, always with a pad, and held five focus groups at the retreat after hours, so villagers could meet, and talk about their issues, with Birch and myself. They appeared popular, and were very well attended. In between all that, the carnival was growing, and we were working on a million things. There were props all over the house, and most rooms resembled a workshop. Deli had the amazing idea of a 'Flash Mob of the Dead' and went back to her old school drama teacher, and suddenly Oxendale High School and College were involved.

We had dance troops, and some floats for a parade, organised by Deb's, and all the time Edwina ran small simulations in the garden of her programs to test them.

Behind the scenes we prepared for her birthday, which was basically a war competition at the paint ball factory. Birch was wild about the idea and went on line, and three days before the event, having recruited Anita and Tabs, we had a team of eight ready for war. Birch called us together and handed out our kit, I was a little surprised as I opened my box.

As with all things Birch, she had been online and checked out the factory. Eric had built a full size town inside the huge old factory, there were crumbled buildings, piles of rubble, and it looked very post apocalyptic and dark and dingy. I actually thought it was awesome, and I got a little excited.

I had let Deli do all the organising with the assistance of Birch, and it had been set up as teams of eight, and we were going an all out ladies' team. Much to our delight, Jimmy and Luke decided to form a team each. Eric had the A Team, as in Alpha, we named out team A.G.T the all girls together team, Luke had G8, and Jimmy went with Taco Takers.

It was going to be a competition of four teams, with a draw to see who fought who in the first round, and then the two winners would face each other, and it was a fight to the death. Once everyone was hit, the game ended, and there was no time limit.

We all dressed in our combat coloured tops and pants, which were a blue, grey, black mixed combat, as Birch assured us it was urban warfare in a darkened room, and with our heavy boots on, we looked like a really top notch military unit, with tits.

We stood admiring each other, with our skull shaped black face masks on, we actually looked mean and angry, actually scratch that, we looked like a crack butch lesbian force. With the living room doors closed, and dressed to kill, Birch unveiled our long silver boxes with handles, that housed the guns. Birch opened my case and lifted out mine.

"Sweetie, are you going to be okay with this, I know you hate guns, and I do not want you getting upset?" I nodded.

"Birch, I know it's a toy, I will be fine." Izzy sniffed.

"It is hardly a toy Abby, these things won't kill you, but they do leave a mark if you are hit." Chloe stared at her.

"Where the fuck did you get that?"

We all turned, and stared at her long dull pink camouflaged coloured rifle, with a telescopic sight. Izzy smiled with immense pride, as she held it out in front of her.

"This one is mine; I was well known for a time in Manchester, I prefer a more sniper role, and I don't miss a target ever."

We eyed her rifle with envy, it was pretty awesome. Deb's looked at her, she had been worried all week, she was not good with computer games, and this was the real thing.

"Are you really that good?" Birch chuckled.

"Girls, you have no idea."

We wanted proof, and so headed out into the garden. Izzy lay on the patio, her rifle had little legs to stand on, and she lay down, and pulled it into her shoulder. We were impressed, she looked really cool, so we all walked to the far end of the garden, where Birch balanced a coffee jar top on the branch of a tree, I scoffed, it was so small, there was no way anyone could hit that.

At the top of the garden there was a faint 'Piff!' and the jar top turned pink. and shot off the branch, our jaws hit the floor, as we all stared with shock, and utter respect.

"No fucking way!?" Izzy really was that good, Birch beamed with delight.

"Girls, these boys think we are weak, so let's prove them wrong, and kick their ass." Suddenly, we were all very confident, and rowdy, yeah, we were going to kick ass.

Luke had G5, but needed three more, we were all girls, so he recruited Anthony and Michael, as well as Alex, who was now Morty's permanent girlfriend. Jimmy needed more, the band was not enough, so Jimmy recruited Baz, Gail, who was semi Floyds woman, and Megan was recruited by Alex to help out, so we now had three teams of eight, and we would meet Eric's team when we arrived. G8 wore black boiler suits, and the Taco Takers wore full green combats, I cannot deny, both teams looked pretty sexy in them.

Edwina was thirty on Sunday the 30th of September, and we were booked in at one in the afternoon, so we got up early, and all celebrated giving her gifts, and making her feel special. She was happy and relaxed and loving the attention, and everyone was in very high spirits. We turned up at the arena at twelve thirty, to walk the layout, and do the draw, as to who fought who.

Birch, Luke, Jimmy and Eric, all stood, as a referee held up a black bag with four disks in it, they reached in one at a time, and handed the disk to the referee. Birch reached in, it was black, the referee placed it on the table. Eric reached in, and pulled out a pink, and my heart sunk, G8 faced us in the first fight, Chloe looked down hearted.

"Fuck!" Luke smiled a smug smile.

"Sorry girls, them are the breaks."

He smirked, and had a cocky air to him, and Edwina seethed. Just to make sure, the other two disks were pulled out, the Alpha team, were placed against the Taco Takers. We tossed for the order, and we won, Birch looked at us, and then back at the referee.

"We will go first, no point in hanging around."

Eric smirked, his team were all big guys, especially Barry and Wayne, well they were more fat than toned. Gazza was a cocky ass, but slim. Fred, Peter, Colin and Duke, were tall and well built, and pretty ripped. I knew them, they all played on the football team at school. They were very confident, and overly cocky, they just assumed they had this in the bag, and laughed at us preparing, their whole attitude was Alpha male, and it really pissed me off.

The factory was an enormous old mill, and a whole fake town had been built out of what looked like plaster. It was basically a massive indoor set, but it looked very real, and had the feel of a bombed out town. I kind of liked it, I felt this would be a place vampires would definitely hang out in. We took a lot of pictures as we waited to be organised.

We finally made our way with a watcher, yes, we had guys in bright orange to make sure we did not cheat, ours was called Simon, he was a complete moron. We were led through the town, to a house next to an old town hall, this was our camp, which we had to defend. I felt a little more than nervous, as Birch handed out bag loads of pink round paint balls, and we loaded our weapons.

Birch pulled out a tin of what looked like boot polish, she smiled and her eyes danced, as she stuck her finger in it, and then smeared it on my face, I had two thick lines on my cheeks, she winked.

"Oh God Sweetie, I am so turned on seeing you like that."

To be honest I did not really see the point as we would be wearing face masks, but like all things Birch, she got completely into it and carried away. She passed the tin round, and everyone looked disgusted as they smeared the paste on their cheeks, Deli looked completely appalled, as did Anita, although Tabs was up for it. Edwina just dived in it and put a black hand print on each of her cheeks, she looked mean and scary, but weirdly enough, pretty hot.

Izzy smeared her whole face, and looked like a red haired Creamy like demon, Chloe sniggered, and Deb's looked oddly aroused, and squirmed crossing her legs. Izzy pulled out her bright pink rifle, and shouldered it.

"Abby, give me a lift."

She was on a ladder up to the roof. I am no fan of heights, and nervously followed her carrying her bag for her. It was more out of fear of blacked up Izzy, I found her a tad intimidating. She crawled onto the roof, which had a line of sand bags on the top of it. We had all been given an ear piece by Edwina, Izzy popped hers in and I followed handing her the bag. She loaded her rifle, and then from her bag, she pulled out a knife, and cut into one of the lower sand bags. I was not sure what she was doing, but she looked mean as hell, so I didn't ask. Yep, I really am that big a coward.

From her side pocket she slid out two pieces of plastic card, and wedged them through the hole in the bag to push the sand either side. She was scary, and in full commando mode, which was a little bit terrifying for me.

With the sand separated, and held back by the card, she had a square hole, with just the cloth of the sand bag at the far side. She smiled and slipped her knife into it, and cut through the fabric, she now had a viewing hole, three bags down from the top. She looked back at me and smiled, yep, I was definitely terrified of her.

"They will look at the top of the bags to see if we are up here, but they won't look carefully at the rest of the bags, get back down, and try and distract them. Tell all of them to spot the targets and speak clearly, and I will cover all of you. G8 think they have this in the bag, it is time for some girl power, and some ass kicking."

I actually felt really confident, as I came slowly down the ladder, and turned to Birch.

"Izzy is ready, holy shit girls, she is on a whole other level in this to us, she is really serious, and honestly, I am a little bit terrified of her." Birch turned round, looking intense and official.

"Right guys, Luke is the big problem, he is called leveller for a reason, he is fast and accurate. So, if he appears, make yourselves as small a target as possible, and shoot the shit out of him." We all nodded, and suddenly we were all scared shitless, Deli looked petrified.

I took a doorway, with my legs starting to shake, Birch took the other, so we had full view of the street, Chloe, Tab's and Deli had the downstairs windows, Edwina was just outside behind a wall, Anita was at her side. Deb's was upstairs shaking like a leaf on her own as a spotter. We had a plan that we had rehearsed, and all we could do, was hope to hell it worked. We pulled our masks down, and Birch could be heard in our ear pieces.

"Okay Sweetie's, get ready." I breathed in and smirked, with my mask on, I sounded like Darth Vader.

I stared at all the buildings looking for any sign of movement, my heart thumping in my ears, as I heard myself breathe in my mask. I was absolutely terrified, and felt my legs and arms shaking, why the hell was I even doing this? A really loud air raid siren went off, and I jumped out of my skin. It was game on, and too late to back out, and I was really regretting eating so much toast this morning.

G8 were gathered behind an old broken down wall, at the far end of the town. Luke pulled on his face mask, and laughed.

"Guys, and Girl, today we are going to kick ass, this is in the bag, take no prisoners. Morty, Alex, Creamy, go left. Anthony, Michael, Bosh, go right. Bongo, we go down the centre full tilt, make loads of noise, and scare the shit out of them, they will probably squeal, drop their guns and run, Edwina is mine."

I was terrified and more alert than I had ever been in my life, every slight sound had me scanning the whole town. I saw movement, and panicked.

"Broken wall top of the main street!"

Piff, Piff, Piff!

Morty, Alex, and Creamy stood up, and splat... Splat... Splat, all three of them were hit with pink paint, and fell back with squeal, looking shocked. Chloe spoke.

"Hard right, three of them."

Piff, Piff, Piff!

Anthony squealed like a pig, Michael staggered, and Bosh fell back, Luke looked at Bongo.

"Holy shit, is that Edwina?" Bongo looked worried.

"Where the fuck are they, I saw nothing, I fucking told you she was lethal, she kicked the fuck out of me on WOW?" Luke looked around, as the others lay back, guarded by the Watcher, who had ruled them out.

"Screw this, I am going in, I am not letting a bunch of frigging girls beat us."

As I watched, Luke and Bongo vaulted over the wall at the far end of the long street and began to scream and run, they came fast, like shooting maniacs, I flattened myself against the wall, my legs trembling.

"INCOMING LEVELLER AND BONGO!" Edwina smirked, and got ready.

"LUKE IS MINE!"

Piff!

Bongo took a shot to his face mask, and went staggering off blind, and ran into a wall. Luke screamed his lungs out, as he ran firing towards us, the wall lit up with bright green paint. Deb's squealed and hit the floor, Chloe and Birch were one handed, holding their guns up, and firing, but not really hitting anything. Anita ducked with her hands over her head, and Tab's crouched down laughing. Luke was getting closer, I stared at Edwina, she was ready, I gave a nod as he was in range, and she leapt up and fired a single shot.

Luke staggered as she hit him full in the chest, and flinched, and he fell to his knees with a gasp.

"What the fuck, where did she come from?"

Edwina turned, winked at me, and blew into her barrel, the buzzer sounded it was game over. G8-0 AGT-8. Birch danced and screamed, and fired into the air with happiness, like a wild Mexican, which would have been fine outside, but we were in a house, although, the ceiling did look very pretty painted pink.

"SWEETIE, WE WON, WE WON!"

She was elated, Izzy dropped down the ladder to join us, as we all walked out, and G8 all came onto the street disgraced, and covered in pink paint. We walked with pride towards them, Luke pulled off his mask and threw it on the floor, as Edwina smirked at him.

"Leveller... Ha! You are no match for Banger Bobbles, and her girls." He started to laugh.

"I should have bloody well known. Honestly, you guys' rock." I smirked.

"All girls together, and yes, you should have known better." He gave a nod, he did, but even so, he still got macho, and paid the price.

We happily walked towards the winner's lounge, passing the holding room, where we could hear the guys inside laughing.

"Poor girls, they only lasted five minutes, G8 must have wiped them out without breathing."

It really pissed me off, I felt my insides twist as it boiled up within me. I veered and headed for the door, but Birch grabbed my arm, and shook her head, she pulled me away. Simon led us to the winner's lounge with cold bottled wine and fruit juice, and Birch looked round as we trooped in.

"Girls, no booze, we still need to stay sharp, they think they are up against G8, and we will let them laugh. Trust me, we will have the advantage, and the last laugh, when they see us walk out against them."

It made sense, we flopped down, I unzipped my top, and slipped off my backpack.

"Christ, it is hot in here."

Chloe undid her top, and let it hang open, she fanned herself with her arm, we heard the air raid siren go off, and Birch set her watch, I leaned in.

"Why are you timing them?"

"Jimmy is shrewd, he will put up a defence, I want to know how long it will take them to infiltrate it. Sweetie, these guys know this place backwards, they train here, I want to know how well."

Wow, she was really serious about this, and already she was working out their game on a psychological level. We all sat around, there was a lot of screaming, and yelling outside, and then the loud buzzer sounded, the battle was over, we all waited quietly and fastened our tops, Simon reappeared at the door. Birch looked around, God, she looked hot with her camo on her face. I stared at her smiling like an idiot, she knew that look and winked at me.

"Okay ladies, let's end this."

We all walked out towards the start point, we could hear Gazza mouthing off loudly as the others were sniggering.

"Did you see all the green on the wall, I bet they all looked like Kermit when they left the field." All of the Alpha team laughed loudly.

It really pissed me off to hear it, they really did think all women were weak, I hate the Alpha male type, they are so full of their own bullshit, I walked around the corner first.

"To be honest guys, we all have immaculate clothing, although G8 looked stupid washed in pink."

I smiled, the look on their faces was priceless, I looked at Gazza as he stared at me, with a big patch of blue paint on his shoulder.

"I hope that fresh paint washes out, maybe I will add some pink to it." Eric started to chuckle, he nodded at us, and I think was happy to see we made the cut.

Our new position was a row of bombed out houses, on the east side of the factory, Birch looked around the place, eyeing it up carefully.

"We have been stitched up guys." I looked at her, feeling a sense of dread.

"What do you mean, stitched up?" She turned and looked at us all.

Look at the layout, it is impossible to move from here without being seen, the place is overlooked from those five buildings, if they get a sniper up there, we are done for." Izzy nodded as she stood by the door.

"Keep your head set in, I am going rogue before the sirens, I am useless to you here." She slipped out of the door with her pack, I felt a bit panicked, I looked at Simon.

"Is this how they win, they always rig the starting points?" He held up his hands.

"I am neutral in all this." Chloe gave a snort.

"He is your boss, so that's a yes then. Girls we need to get motivated and fast." Birch slipped her pack off.

"Chloe, do you remember the toilet in Dog Soldiers?" She pulled her big knife out of her back pack, Chloe gave a big smile.

"Do I ever, Spoon and Sarge are my all time favourite characters." Birch handed her the knife.

"Get digging, we have not got long before the siren goes off."

Chloe dropped to her knees on the back wall, and started to dig through the plaster, these were after all just prop houses, and so getting through the plaster was easy. Birch turned to Simon, as she unzipped her top.

"Take your shirt off, and if you try for one second to give our position away, I will paint you pink from close range, and you know that will hurt, don't you?" She handed him her top as he stared at her boobs.

Birch tied back her hair, took off her black neck scarf, and used it as a bandana, she took his orange shirt and put it on. She turned to me, and I shuddered and felt tingles, oh God, I am so weak, and actually, I have a filthy mind, because the fantasy in my mind, was pretty bloody X rated.

"Deads, go along the back of these buildings to the very end, then cut across, and make your way around. By the time they get here, we will be long gone, and we will have them in their own trap. Be as quiet as mice, but hurry, they will come fast. I will be right behind you Sweetie." She kissed me, and my legs trembled, wow, I am so messed up.

Chloe was through, and dragging the others through the gap, I pointed the way to Chloe, and slipped through. We had about three feet of space between us, and the factory wall, we moved swiftly and silently. Tab's was loving the excitement, and was full of smiles, Deli still looked terrified. The air raid siren went off, and I felt the pressure increase, Birch was alone waiting for them, and my heart was pounding in my ears.

It was not long before Gazza appeared, Birch stood back from the window, slightly crouched, and fired, pink splattered on the wall a foot from him, and he dived for cover. Birch moved to the doorway, and leaned out slightly exposing her orange arm.

Wayne and Barry, who were waddling round to the side of the building, saw the orange and sniggered, Birch lifted her gun and fired. Piff! Piff!

She hit them both on the side. Well, it was a wide enough target, it was not like she would miss. High up in the bell tower Duke aimed at inside the window, Birch headed for the hole in the wall at speed. Piff"

Splat!

The red blob smeared up the wall just to her side, she dived and scrambled through, suddenly there was a hail of red blobs, as they rained in on the wall. Birch was running as fast, and as quiet as she could down the back. Izzy lifted her rifle, sat at the back of the room of a three story house.

"I see you, Duke."

Eric whistled, and Duke raised his head, just enough to peep over the ledge. Izzy smiled. Piff!

Splat, she swung the rifle round, and Piff!

Colin who was stood at the side of Eric got a mask full of pink, and Eric dived for the floor.

"Holy shit, where the hell did that come from?"

Chloe was digging away with the help of Anita and Deli, when

Birch arrived, she slipped off her orange jacket, and handed it to Simon.

"Now I know why you wear orange; Eric has this whole place rigged to his benefit." Simon slipped off his top staring at her boobs, she smiled and looked down.

"Do you like them Sweetie, I think they are quite good too. If you stay out of sight and don't give us away, I might let you have a quick play after, would you like that?"

He nodded his head and smiled, and Chloe sniggered. She was through, and we all slipped into a new building, we were now on the other side of the factory, and Izzy was on the move, I could hear her in the ear piece.

"I got their sniper, the two fat ones are out, thanks Jemi, and I took out his second Colin, I would have got Eric, if he had not have dived so fast. Where are you now?" Birch was still breathing hard.

"We are on the west side, we dug our way through the wall, and legged it, Izzy this whole place is rigged in their favour."

"I know kid, I am using the roof tops, it is the only way to move in this place without being seen. Okay, I know where you are so don't fret, I will get you cover." Birch nodded.

"Thanks Sweetie." It had been a fast run and all of us were sweating, and red in the face. Eric discovered the hole in the wall.

"Slimy bitches, they have got out of the box, and doubled back on us. We need to move and move fast, or we will be trapped. I should have known, a psychologist, a gamer and a writer, what a lethal bloody combination."

They scattered out of the building, they knew all the cover and blind spots, Izzy had her sights ready, but they were very elusive, and not easy to hit. Birch was getting ready as Izzy came back on the ear piece.

"Jemi, they have four down, and I only see three, watch your back, one of them has gone rogue, they could be following you."

Anita dropped down to the hole, and listened, she looked back and pointed, Izzy was right. We all moved to the side of the hole, and spread flat along the wall, as we watched through the window. Peter had been sent after us, he had a radio mic, we heard him talk quietly.

"They came out at section three, there is no sound." He slowly knelt down and looked through the hole, I could just make out his shadow as I looked down.

"I cannot see them, they must have moved on, check out section two."

I held my breath, as I saw movement, his arm with his gun came through first, Edwina was on the other side of the hole. He slid his gun through, and then pushed with his feet so his torso came through, it was not that big a hole, but for his bulky body, it was a tight squeeze. Edwina nodded, and I lifted my foot and stood on his back pinning him to the floor, Edwina bent down, and snatched his head set off him, he flattened down to the floor.

"Oh shit!" I fired. Piff! He grunted, I looked at Birch.

"Just Eric, Fred, and Gazza left, what now?"

Piff!

"Fred is out." I giggled; Izzy was amazing. Chloe took off her mask.

"I am cooking alive in this mask." She opened her jacket, her face and even her boobs were red, Anita and Tab's were fanning themselves. Edwina smiled at her.

"Chloe what is your greatest achievement?" She leaned back on the wall as the sweat ran down her face, she shrugged.

"I don't know, I paint and I fuck." Edwina smiled.

"Has any man ever turned you down?" She sniggered.

"Seriously, look at these boobs, have you ever known a man, not look at boobs and...?" She smiled. Edwina hit her ear piece.

"Izzy, where exactly are they, I have an idea?"

Eric was good, he stayed under the radar, but Izzy was tracking him, and firing close by him, and talking to us, as she observed him. He slipped backwards into the room watching outside, he was alert, well almost. I coughed, and he jumped, twisting around, and his eyes opened wide. I waved.

"Hi."

Deli and myself stood stark naked, on either side of the opposite doorway, our guns propped up against the wall, I smiled at Eric.

"One time deal, her or me, pick quickly?" Deli smiled a sweet sexy smile. Eric put his gun against the wall, and started to undo his ammo pack.

"Abby, oh God, Abby I would love to, but you are married, and I am not that guy. Oh fuck Fidelity, I used to watch you dance and dream of this, I would die for a shot with you."

"Granted Sweetie." Piff!

Splat!

"You bitches." Birch stood in the doorway between us smiling, a sweet smile. I sniggered, and walked over to him and picked up his gun.

"Good choice Eric, it was always a one time deal with me, but Deli, if you mean what you said, you potentially have a life time deal with her."

I kissed his cheek, and his pants fell down, I giggled, Deli took a good look and smiled at him, he blushed, and slid his hand over his parts.

Gazza slipped into a three story building tapping his ear, his voice was tense and he sounded very nervous.

"Eric, where the fuck are you, I heard shots?"

"I am the big sister, I should screw him first, it is my birthday Chloe, and then you can have him."

"Okay Edwina, but why don't we tag team, and screw him together?"

"Hmm, Chloe, you might have a point, I mean, after all, Eric is screwing the other two."

Gazza lifted his gun, and Chloe and Edwina walked unarmed, and naked into the room, he stared at them.

"Holy fuck, are you serious, because I will shag you both all night?" Chloe looked at Edwina.

"Do you think he has a long rifle?" Chloe looked at him.

"Well, do you?" He put his gun down and grabbed his pants quickly, Chloe and Edwina separated.

Piff!

Splat! He looked up at Deb's grinning in the doorway.

"All is fair in love and war Gazza." He gave a long sigh. His pants dropped and the three of them all looked.

Aw... Fuck!" Edwina gave a sigh and looked at Chloe.

"You can have him, I needed a howitzer, and all I got was a tiny little hand gun." Chloe sniggered as he looked down, Gazza gasped.

"I am fucking stressed girls, give it a minute." The buzzer sounded; he gave a snort.

"Fucking, sneaky, conniving, bloody, women, I should have known better?" Chloe giggled.

"Just look at us Gazza, you just missed out on both of us, in your bed, all night." Deb's held out their clothes, he looked utterly devastated, Deb's chuckled.

"Girls, we need to regroup."

As we marched them all up the central street, with their hands on their heads, we felt proud, the watchers let out the others from the waiting room, and they all laughed as they watched us march with pride, and started to clap. Luke was all smiles, Jimmy pulled Deb's into his arms.

"That's my Goggle Bear, tough and smart." She gave him a massive snog. Eric finally turned around with a smile, and shrugged.

"You know Abby, we do have a rule about not shooting at bare flesh." I smiled.

"We know, what do you think gave us the idea?" He started to laugh, and shook his head, he knew he was beaten, and it was pointless to argue.

"Okay, so you won, what do you want as a prize?" Birch pointed looking serious, and sexy as hell with her camo face.

"All of you against the wall, we have loads of ammo left, you thought we were soft, so let's see just how tough you all are?"

They had padded jackets, we spared Anthony, and Michael, and Mcg, Alex, and Gail but G5, Battered Taco, and the Alpha's, no, they had been far too cocky for their own good. We lined up and took aim, they looked scared shitless, as Birch looked at us to her left.

"Right girls, all together... Aim... Fire..."

"Ow, ow, ow, ow, ow, ow, ow!"

It was awesome watching them dance, and turn pink, Edwina laughed her ass off, it was the best birthday ever.

Chapter 29

Best Birthday Ever.

We were riding on a high, when we sat in the bar, as the boys bought the drinks, call it the spoils of war. We had a rowdy afternoon, and hugged the guy's, and headed home, as Deb's drove, and I sat in the back curled up with Birch, as I thought of my conversation at the bar.

"Eric, do not give up because one woman treated you bad. Look, Deli really likes you, and she is a good quality traditional girl, just ask her out for God's sake. I actually think you will find you both have a lot in common." He looked at me as he gathered the drinks on the tray.

"Abby, what about you, I hate to point it out, but we do have a past, is that not going to cause problems?" I giggled as I lifted the gins.

"Eric, Deli knows all about it, I told her what happened, and I also told her, I am with Birch. I have no issue with you dating my friend, the question is, do you, because honestly, I never lied, it was a one time deal only?" He understood.

Sat on the floor with my head leaning back on Birch, I closed my eyes, as she stroked my hair, it felt so nice. She was happy, and I felt good. Edwina had a blast and had loved her birthday, although we still had cake and her birthday tea to come, G8, the Taco Takers and the Alpha's, were all invited.

It was a fun night, having been the conquering heroines, our very sore and badly bruised opponents, having learned humility, were administered to, as we all played nurse, although I did feel Gail was getting a little too carried away with the ointment she was rubbing on Floyd.

The week started, and Birch was getting excited, and I was heading towards my 29th birthday, which was October tenth. Before that, there was lots to do, as we had to start doing tests in the village, for the carnival.

In the yard behind Sweetie's Retreat, and Cogs and Wheelers, scaffolding had been erected, and a platform added on top of the roof, we also had one on top of the gallery, and two on the roof of the Church Hall. Edwina and G5 took over, and started to set up their equipment, which comprised of what looked like large glass boxes.

They were actually made of Perspex, and would be used to keep all the expensive electrics, safe and dry, after all, winter was coming, and it was starting to get wet, and cold. Edwina had spent a lot of time with a laser, to get everything set and lined up properly, and we were ready for the final test run.

I will just say, I had no intention of going up there, just the thought terrified me, and I got giddy just looking up at them. It was one in the morning, and I walked with Birch up Church Rise with my radio, and ear piece, everywhere was quiet and still.

"Okay Edwina, we are ready when you are." I stood at the top of Green Street, and looked down the village green, Edwina spoke.

"Guys these are tests, just to make sure everything is lined up, and so I will just be running shapes, get ready."

Birch slipped her arm around my waist as we stood in the darkness, the street lights went out, and suddenly it was almost pitch black, I felt nervous and excited. Birch bit her lip, there was a lot riding on this, I could feel how tense she was. Just above the green, a snowflake appeared, it was about ten feet across, and it shimmered as it hung in the air, Birch gave a gasp.

"Oh Sweetie, it is beautiful, I love snow."

I smiled, as I glanced at her, she held her hands together on her chest, and bounced slightly on her toes. Out of the floor a love heart rose out of the grass, and floated up towards the snowflake, Birch gave an excited squeak.

"It's so pretty."

She slowly walked towards it, and words started to write themselves, inside the love heart. I stared at it in amazement. 'Deadly heart Birch.' She giggled, and bounced on her toes, with a huge happy smile.

"It's true, it's true."

Her eyes were so big, and filled with happiness, as she started to walk closer.

"Deads, it is so beautiful."

She looked up in amazement. I watched as she stood below it, her face so happy, and her eyes so bright and sparkling in the darkness, there was that childlike quality in her I loved so much, I smiled at her. The heart started to stretch out getting bigger and bigger, she giggled.

"Sweetie, I love you this much."

She stood on the grass and leaned back, as she watched it grow. I cannot deny, it was stunning, and I marvelled at Edwina's incredible ability. Birch stared at the huge heart, her white hair hanging down and glowing in the darkness, God, she looked like a lost angel, I felt a tug at my heart. She reached up to try and touch it.

The heart morphed into a hideous face, and fell towards her. Birch gave out a death defying squeal, and ran like hell towards me.

"Sweetie, I don't like it, tell it to go back."

She flew up the green, grabbed me, and swung behind me, hiding her face shaking with terror. I really wanted not to laugh, but you know me... Edwina's giggles came through the ear piece.

"Sorry Birch, I could not resist, that was funny as fuck, Chloe and Luke are pissing their sides laughing up here."

Birch mumbled behind me as she shook. All I could make out was something like 'uckin wats.' I laughed my ass off.

She popped up at my shoulder, where just the snowflake hung slowly turning in the air, the words 'Sorry Sweetie' appeared above it, and she giggled, then gasped as it turned to smaller snowflakes, and they fell to the floor. I stood watching as the snowflakes rained to the ground and sunk into the grass, it was captivating and beautiful.

They went out, and the street lights came on, it had been a very successful first test. Peter Saxon walked across the green towards us, he was smiling.

"Sorry, I heard a scream and came out to check. That was unbelievable, wow, it was mind blowing." I smiled at him.

"Thanks Mr Saxon, it's a start, to be honest, I have no idea how they do it, I just know, they will not let the village down."

He gave a nod as Edwina, and Chloe came walking from the side door of the Church Hall, and walked towards us, Luke was still on the roof closing things down. Peter turned and gave a huge smile.

"Edwina, that was amazing, I stood at my shop door, and I was completely mesmerised." She looked really happy.

"Thanks Pete, we have a lot to do, but everything is lined up, and set, I still have a few more programs to test, but wait until you see what we have in mind, that was nothing compared to the show we have lined up." He was thrilled.

"I must admit, I am really excited about all this, we need something new." Birch gave a nod.

"This will prove without a doubt, that we can use modern tech, and work it into rural life, and keep all the traditions alive. You know Peter, one day, what we are doing now, will be seen as out dated and traditionalist, that is the daft thing about everything. What this village calls tradition, was once new and cutting edge." He gave a nod

"I believe you are right Birch; I take it this is still all hush hush?" She smiled.

"For now, yes, all we want is to provide something breath taking, something to make people remember Wotton, and return for a long time to come." He understood.

"Have no fear, I won't say a word, I have told Mary many times, I love how all of you have embraced this village. It has not gone unnoticed, I know there are some who don't see it, but a majority do, and we appreciate it. There was a time when all of us worried no one would come after us, and I am happy to see that will not be the case, you are all remarkable people." That meant a lot to me.

"Thanks, it means a lot to hear you say that. We love this place just as much as everyone else, and we do want to preserve the culture of this place." He patted my shoulder.

"We see it, anyhow, I have an early start, so goodnight, sleep well all of you." Chloe waved.

"Night Mr S."

We packed up, and walked home together happy, it was getting exciting, and I felt a warm glow inside me, although Birch was rubbing my ass, and perhaps that had something to do with it.

The next few days saw me holed up in the library, with Deli, working. Emails were flowing in to D&D, and we spent most of our days, evenings, and into the night answering messages, giving advice, and sending out itinerary's. between that, Deli was at the high school rehearsing with the students, and I was writing, updating blogs, and managing the Curio, and my own website. Most nights, I would crash into bed, and fall straight to sleep without even moving.

Birch and Edwina were working even longer hours, and in between, Chloe, Anthony, Michael, and even Samantha, were jumping in and helping out, in what had become a massive operation.

I awoke to a squeal, as a happy wide eyed and crazy woman landed on the bed. I opened my eyes feeling exhausted, she sat on me smiling, and bubbling with excitement, she reached out in front of her, holding a wrapped present.

"Happy Birthday, Sweetie."

It was like the fuse was lit and fizzing, and at any moment, a huge explosion was going to go off the moment I took it, and I had not had coffee yet. I sat up, which brought her closer, she was very excited as I took the present, her hand moved, and I pulled it away.

"Birch, this is my present, I unwrap it." She bubbled.

"Sweetie, I am so excited, it's your birthday."

Yep, she was loud, and very overly excitable today. I slowly unwrapped the paper, which I knew was torture for her, she wriggled and twitched, it was driving her insane, as her eyes sparkled, with explosive joy.

There was a long green box inside, and I looked at her as she dithered, her eyes were wild with excitement. I opened it and she twitched, and I looked up at her.

"Birch it's beautiful."

WHOMP!

I was flat on the bed with hair everywhere, and she kissed the living shit out of me. I came up coughing and spluttering, with a mouth full of her hair.

"Sweetie, I love you." She snatched the box out of my hand.

"I am putting it on you."

She lifted out the necklace, and it sparkled. It was a delicate chain, with the carefully crafted word 'Deadly' on it, with tiny little bats on either side, it really was stunning. She undid the clasp, and reached around my neck, her eyes were huge and green, she spoke softly.

"I had it made specially, it is hand made, white gold, and a complete one off, just like you." She sat back, and smiled.

"Perfect, like you are to me."

I smiled and leaned forward to give her a proper kiss, without hair, and it felt so good, it had felt like so long. It took her breath away; she pushed me back on the bed.

"Oh God Deads, I really need you." She leaned down and kissed my neck, and my body responded.

"Oh Birch, it has been too long, this bloody carnival is killing our sex life." She moved lower and I gave a happy moan.

"Oh God yes, I need this." Her hands were all over me exploring.

Downstairs Deb's walked around nervously.

"Where is she, I thought Birch went to get her?" Edwina smirked.

"Deb's think about it. We have worked long hard hours, been late in bed every night exhausted, and this is Birch, and it is Abby's birthday, now what do nymphomaniacs like to do to people on their birthday?" Deb's suddenly realised, and sat down.

"Yeah, I forgot about that, it is those two, they will be at it." Chloe giggled as she lifted her cup.

"Relax, it could be some time." Deb's gave a frustrated sigh.

"I cannot believe an orgasm is more important." Anthony gave a snort, and flicked his fringe out of his eyes.

"Who are you, and what have you done with Debbie darling?" There were sniggers all around the kitchen.

I staggered downstairs with a giggling happy Birch, she was still all over me, but I was enjoying it, I had not orgasmed like that in ages. I headed into the kitchen and WHOMP! I was surrounded in copious amounts of a fox like ponytail, and Deb's squeezed the life out of me.

"Happy Birthday Abby." I hugged her hard.

"Thanks Deb's."

I felt happy, as I sat down, Edwina put a coffee in front of me, and kissed my cheek. Chloe leaned over and kissed my gay cheek, with her oh so straight lips. I giggled; Anthony hugged me from behind.

"Birthday tidings, Abby my darling."

I held his hand and squeezed, it felt wonderful to be surrounded by everyone. Deli staggered into the kitchen, she had worked late last night, she leaned down and kissed my cheek.

First coffee, then presents, I took a sip as gifts arrived on the island. Deb's watched nervously as I unwrapped a Victorian, lace decorated purple parasol, it was beautiful. Anthony gave me an Avril t shirt and hoodie. Edwina a pair of long flared violet coloured pants, Deli gave me a book, the complete guide to vampires, werewolves and the undead, it was brilliant, and Chloe handed me a wrapped picture.

I stood up to open it, it was A2 sized, and I gasped, and laughed when I saw a detailed sketch of me sat on a sawing horse masturbating, as Birch bent over sawing wood, Deb's leaned in to look, and gave a squeak, and went red.

"Oh my God Chloe, you gave it her?"

Birch leaned over my shoulder to get a closer look, I felt her hand slide slowly down my bum crack and go lower, I gave a little squirm, Deb's looked down, and stepped back going purple.

"Holy shit Birch, don't stare at the picture, and start fingering her in front of us." Birch shrugged.

"I like the picture; it is turning me on." Edwina looked at it, and nodded.

"I must admit, it is making me wet." She looked at Deb's.

"Does it not turn you on... You know, just a little bit?" Deb's was going even more scarlet, and her legs closed and started to rub together.

"I don't want to say." Chloe gave a smile.

"So that is a yes then, and I made you want to cum without a sponge." I started to laugh, Deb's was getting redder and redder. Chloe got up and walked to her studio, she came back with a large sketch and handed it Deb's.

"Here, I told you I would let you have it." Deb's looked at it and squealed, she looked at all of us, and pulled it close her chest.

"Chloe, I cannot believe you drew this?" Wow she was as purple as my parasol, I leaned over.

"Let's see it then?" She shook her head rapidly, I frowned.

"That's not fair, I showed you mine." Birch sniggered; Deb's looked panicked as everyone stared at her.

"Please guys, it's embarrassing." Birch grinned.

"Show it."

She looked so terrified, and took a huge gulp of air. Deb's closed her eyes, and turned it around, and wow! Chloe had drawn Deb's bent over, her huge boobs swinging, as Jimmy ploughed her from behind with a huge vein riddled penis, wearing a very big and happy smile. Anthony rolled his eyes.

"Well, I hope he is that big in reality, oh Deb's darling, you must show me pictures." Her eyes snapped open.

"No frigging way, you pervert." I giggled, as Birch turned her head on the side.

"I think it is a very good likeness, what do you think guys?" She turned it around and pulled it back to her chest.

"You are all perverts, I bet if I had a sex tape you would all have pop corn and watch?" We all nodded with big smiles. Chloe lifted her coffee.

"We saw it, and you were actually quite good." She gasped, and looked horrified.

"When... How... You are liars." Chloe shook her head.

"You left your hard drive under the bed, and I found it when we were cleaning. I mean seriously Deb's, who names their sex tape XXX?" She stared at us horrified.

"I cannot believe you did that?" Birch shrugged.

"We made five on our honeymoon, I burned them to DVD, would you like to borrow them?" I smiled as I remembered those nights, and slid my hand down Birch's bum, she gave a little squeak, and glanced at me with a smile. Deb's frowned.

"Don't think about your honeymoon and finger her Abby, Jesus, you two are worse than normal, behave."

"They were good nights, you should watch them, I don't mind, I mean it is not like we have not watched each other before is it now, Deb's at the tree with Edwina, on the lake?" Chloe nodded.

"You should borrow them Deb's, I loved them, and I am straight." Deli sat quietly watching.

"Wow, you guys are that open?" Chloe shrugged.

"I have loads, do you want to watch a few with Eric?" She gasped out loud.

"Seriously?" Chloe nodded.

"I have about thirty doing Percy." We all turned to her in unison, and screamed.

"NO!" I shuddered, just the thought was terrifying, Deli sat back.

"I think I will leave it; I am happy not knowing." We all nodded in agreement.

I ate toast, and drank coffee, and got hugged to death a million times by Birch, Deb's was jumpy, she grabbed her laptop, and opened it up, and typed into it, as she watched me over the top of it. I felt a conspiracy as everyone suddenly got animated and started smiling, I put my cup down.

"Okay, what are you all up to?"

Deb's phone pinged and she opened her messages, she smiled, and everyone appeared to be in the know except me. Deb's dialled and held it to her ear. She smiled, and turned her laptop around, on the screen was a live stream from what looked like a radio station, everyone excitedly gathered around it. Deb's came around the island, and unmuted the speakers, where a DJ was talking.

"Okay folks, we have a huge announcement for all you rock fans out there, because here in the studio with me this very morning on SER Rock 77, I have Battered Taco, who have released their new album, with a new single today. Guys it is great to have you here."

The camera panned out to reveal Jimmy, Floyd and the guys, Jimmy leaned forward.

"Nice to be back, we have had some time off, we bloody needed it, we were knackered, but it has given us some time to regroup, and work in the studio." The DJ smiled.

"So, the new album, a little different, a little more mature I think, and honestly, it is a really good album, and a few ballads, are the Taco's settling down a little?" Floyd gave a smirk.

"We have always mixed things up, but you know, we are growing up a bit, and we had some time off to think about things. We wanted to play around with our sound a bit more." The DJ gave a nod.

"To be honest guys, I love it, I like the softer edges, it is good quality classic rock. As for the new single, which we will be playing in a moment, I got to say, wow, great track, tell me a little about how that came about." Jimmy gave a smile.

"To be honest, I did 'don't look with my wife,' on the solo album, and I never thought it would get as big as it did. We were larking about in the studio one very special evening, and luckily Baz kept the tapes rolling, so you could say it was a happy accident." I felt my heart lurch, and sat back and looked at Deb's.

"Oh God, they haven't?" She smiled at me. Jimmy gave a laugh.

"She did not know we had a camera rolling for a new documentary on the band, and so we thought what the hell, we will put a video out as well." I felt my insides twist as Birch leaned on my shoulder. The DJ leaned into his mic.

"For all of you listeners out there, we have the video set for the live stream, so jump online and watch, but let me first explain. If I am right, this was filmed the night before her wedding, you were trying to calm her nerves, and that really is amazing, because she is fantastic, no one would know she was nervous." Jimmy giggled.

"I should just say at this point, she is actually with my wife watching this live, so sorry Doll, we had to use it, because it is absolutely beautiful, just like you are, and happy birthday, we all love you."

He waved to the camera, and all the guys leaned over and blew kisses, I smiled, and Deb's gave my shoulder a slight squeeze. The DJ faced the mic.

"Okay all you listeners, because this is very special, so pay close attention, because this is the new single by Battered Taco, and it features the vocals of none other, than writer and author, Abigail Jennifer Watson. She is amazing, and it is spell binding." Jimmy leaned in.

"Just to add a little context, she was in the studio, and we told her to think of her beautiful wife to be, and then sing."

"Okay here it is for the first time ever, and don't forget you heard it here on SER Rock 77. Battered Taco, featuring Abigail Jennifer Watson, and a cover of Avril Lavigne's, I will be.

The video came up, and I watched myself stood at the mic in the home studio, those twats filmed me, and I did not even know it. Birch slid her arm around me, and snuggled up, as the pictures changed, and showed me in my dress walking down the stairs. I felt the tears in my eyes, and wiped them, and Birch squeezed me. I watched me walk out from the marquee towards the arch, it was such a special day, and my dad looked so proud.

I wiped my eyes, and gave a sob, as I watched her take my hand and slide my ring on, and all to the sound of me singing. The band had mixed it, and added a longer intro and more background, and it did sound wonderful. The song came to an end, and the picture froze as we kissed, and the words appeared. 'Congratulations, we love you guys.' Birch was in tears, and I sniffled, and wiped my face, with my hand.

"It's beautiful Deb's, I really love it."

Her phone rang, and I could see Jimmy holding his up to his ear as the DJ gave a gasp.

"Wow, Abigail what great vocals, everyone out there, get out there today, and buy this album, it is brilliant. That track, it really touches deep, the video, is just amazing, no one has seen any film of that occasion, just the pictures, and it looked beautiful." Jimmy gave a big smile.

"It was, she is in tears at the moment, I got the missus on the phone."

"Can she talk, Abigail if you can hear me, can we have a quick word?" Jimmy put his phone on speaker, and Deb's handed it to me. I gave a sniffle into the phone.

"Thanks guys, it made me cry, but it was really lovely to watch it."

"No worries Doll, we love you." The DJ leaned over.

"Abigail, I have to say, wow, your voice is beautiful, there is a lot of love in that song, your good lady is pretty lucky." Birch giggled.

"She is amazing, and yes, she is the love of my life." He chuckled.

"She is a very lucky lady, I believe it is your birthday today, so happy birthday from all of us at SER Rock 77, and we hope you have many more. So, will it be a big party, or just a quiet one? I do know that you can be a bit of a hermit, as my wife is a huge fan of yours, and she will be really miffed I spoke to you." I swallowed my tears and gave a giggle.

"I am staying home, with Birch and my Curio family."

"Okay, have a wonderful day, and honestly, you should sing more, we all love the track. Okay folks, that was none other than Abigail Jennifer Watson, Author of Seeds of Summer and the Hand of Death books, and she is the featured guest vocalist on the brand new Battered Taco album, 'Tell it like it is.' Guys it has been great having you in the studio with me, loved being able to get a first look at the new stuff, you are always welcome, and as you know, nobody rocks better than SER Rock 77. Good luck with the single, and give Abby a birthday hug from me."

Deb's leaned over and muted the sound, and everyone went bonkers. Deb's reached into her bag, and then placed a copy of the CD on the island in front of me.

"Happy birthday Abby, from Jimmy and the boys."

I picked it up, and saw them all smiling, actually on the locks of the canal, and Moon's barge was in the background. Birch snuggled into me.

"You sung to me, and I loved it, I am going to go upstairs and bawl my brains out, because it was so beautiful, I will be back in a minute Sweetie."

I giggled, as I saw the look of terror on Chloe's face.

"Holy fuck, you have put it on a CD, what the fuck is wrong with you, are you trying to kill all Jimmy's fans?" Deb's gave a smug smile.

"To be honest Chloe, when Jimmy played it me, I got so turned on, I pushed him on the floor and shagged his ass off." Chloe stood up, and lifted her coffee.

"Holy fuck, next year the world will be swamped in Battered Taco Babies."

It is crazy, all this, and it is still only eight in the morning, I felt exhausted, I gathered my presents together, and headed up to my room. Birch was lay on the bed, I put my things down, and crawled on to her.

"Baby, it is eight, you will have to go to work." Birch slid her arms around me, and smiled, her eyes were red.

"I am not in until after twelve, I told Izzy I needed some time with you on your birthday." I gave her a smile, and kissed her softly.

"Good, get under my duvet, and we will have a little party of our own, I have missed touching you, and I want to thank you for my present." She gave a giggle.

"Sweetie, I so want that."

With laughter and shrieks, we climbed under, and I sat on top of her, as she looked up at me and giggled.

"I have another surprise for you, but wait until Saturday, do you like your necklace?" I smiled, and touched it on my neck.

"I love it, it's perfect." I reached behind me and slid my hand slowly up the inside of her thigh, she gave a little intake of breath.

"I love you so much Deads... Ooh!"

I giggled and slid back, she bit her lip, as I lifted my legs up and parted hers. I slowly went down watching her eyes follow me, she gave a slight gasp.

"Oh God, I really need this." I dropped and pushed my face into her tummy and blew hard, making raspberry noises, and she squealed.

"Deads no that tickles... Deads please, I cannot take it, ha, ha, ha, ha, ha, ha, Deads please!" She screamed at the top of her voice as she thrashed on the bed.

Deb's looked up at the ceiling as she lifted her cup.

"I really love those two." Edwina smiled and placed down a plate of toast.

I sat on the bed, having had a long morning alone with Birch, and a hot bath together, and I dried her hair. She had to go to work for a few hours, and tonight she had a session with Nigel, but I was not going to complain, I had spent a long happy morning with her, and it was a Wednesday, which for her was a normal working day.

I hung from her neck at the door, she looked lovely with her long white and patched hair, all fluffy from being washed, and her eyes sparkling with happiness, as I kissed her passionately.

Life had been hard for a couple of weeks, and we had been so busy or tired, our love making had pretty much fizzled out. It was nice to just take a few hours for us, and it made my birthday feel more special.

I walked happily down to the kitchen, and clicked on the kettle, Deli was sat with Chloe talking in the studio, they looked like they were having a deep private conversation, so I decided to leave them for now, and head to my room. Deb's had headed to her shop.

I wandered back upstairs with my coffee, and Chloe leaned around the door of the studio.

"Fuck that was close."

Deli giggled behind the door, holding a half decorated birthday cake. I sat at my desk, and slid the new CD into my drive, and turned up my speakers, and then opened my website, it was filled with happy birthday messages, the word was out, and my fans were playing the tune, and they really loved it.

I spent the rest of my day smiling, as total strangers wished me happy birthday, I was miles away, playing the new Taco album for about the fourth time, when her slender arms came round me, and she kissed my neck, I gave a shudder and smiled.

"Hi Sweetie." I lifted my arms up to her.

"My fans are wonderful, I have had hundreds of birthday wishes, and they love the Taco tune, and you made love and had a bath with me. I love my birthday." She gave a chuckle and kissed me again.

"I am happy for you Sweetie; your mum told me she would come over with me after I have spoken to Nigel. I have a little free time; and I need coffee, do you want to come downstairs for a bit, and sit with me?"

I slid out of my chair, and she pulled me close and kissed me again, I gave a happy sigh, as I picked up my cup, and hand in hand we headed downstairs.

She walked me into the living room. "SURPRISE!"

Mum, Patrick, Hatty, Clive, Anita, Tabby, Ellen and Bradley, stood with Deb's and Jimmy and the band, and also G5, and all the practice staff, I was completely thrown, I turned to Birch, and she smiled.

"I phoned Nigel and met him in Millington, we did an hour there." I jumped into her arms, and hugged her, and everyone hugged me and kissed me, and gave me gifts, it was magnificent.

I spent an hour, sat down on the sofa, surrounded by everyone, opening my gifts of perfume, and shawls, and clothing and bracelets, and I felt so excited, and so loved, honestly, these people are amazing.

Luke walked in with the karaoke machine, set it down, and pressed play, and suddenly in walked Birch, Chloe, Deli, Deb's, Edwina, and Anthony, and they all had long blonde wigs on, dark eyes, short school skirts and white blouses with a tie. They burst in to Avril's, 'Here's to never growing old.' Anthony looked hysterical, and I fell about laughing so hard with everyone else, that I nearly peed myself.

Although to be honest, long blonde hair suited him. Hatty was in fits as they danced around me, Ellen was holding her sides, Mum was in tears, and Jimmy was filming it. They came to the end and, I screamed with joy, and we all applauded, my God, it was so funny, and the party started.

The girls stood looking like Avril, and started to sing happy birthday, and in walked Michael with a huge cake, decorated with bats, and a small candelabra, with lit candles, and as they finished, I blew them out, as Birch hugged me.

It was a long night, made even happier when the doorbell went, and as I opened the door, I saw Dad and Angela, he pulled me into a hug.

"Happy Birthday Abigail."

I dragged them inside, and they joined the party, I could not have asked for more, it had been an amazing day. The party ended at midnight; everyone was working tomorrow. I pulled Birch, still dressed as Avril into the bedroom, and turned to her.

"Oh God, I am going to live out a fantasy that would make Avril blush tonight."

I spun her round, and pushed her onto the bed, and she lay back looking up at me with those sexy black eyes, and I crawled onto her, and pulled at her tie.

"OMG, I am so turned on right now!"

Chapter 30

Birthday Surprise.

Thursday was not a good day, I woke at eleven, having missed Birch, and had an epic hangover, from a great night and an amazing birthday party, and my day just got busier and busier after that. At seven that night, still feeling rough, I was still sat at my computer, facing Deli, with Birch and Edwina on either side of me.

The carnival was just over two weeks away, and everything was finally coming together, but it was all those little things that needed to be done. The idea had been a simple one, but it had grown into a huge event, bigger than anything the parish had ever done before. Like all things with Birch, her idea expanded over time, and yet we had handled it all, and done what was expected.

In the garage, Chloe and Anthony had been hard at work creating more props, so in between all the chaos of organising, we had taken time out to muck in. It had been fun, but long hours. We had a stack of boxes all containing items that would be needed on the day, and the place was starting to look like a movie set storage hanger.

The coming weekend, was our last, as of the weekend after, we would be on duty full time, as the circus and fair opened for a whole week, ending on the big carnival weekend on Saturday October 27th. I cannot deny, we were all nervous and feeling the strain, this was going to be the most challenging thing we had done to date.

Chloe's exhibition had been a huge success, and another six weeks had been added to the event. We had made a huge profit for our first event by D&D, but that just put even more pressure on us to follow on. I was very aware that Roni was watching closely, as she was looking to see if we really had what it took, to run a large operation.

Friday was spent in the village, I hung out with Deb's in the shop, and spent some time with mum at the gallery. Prim was on the prowl, strutting around with Molly, she was now going to repaint the station car park lines, and was campaigning for better road signs from Oxendale to Wotton, as she felt there were not enough. She also wanted a large piece of granite put on the borders of the village, with a coat of arms, and the village name on it. Her jibes about Birch and myself were again evident, as she slandered and insulted us, and all with a smug smile.

It was hard to not lose my temper, as her comments about me were passed back to me through the gossip channels. On the occasions I saw her across the village, I had to dig deep, and control my feelings, as I really wanted to slap her smug face. Birch did not really appear that concerned, but I was worried. Prim was taking the line that we could not be trusted, she was questioning our honesty and implying we would over spend and bankrupt the village, and there were some who were agreeing. Once again, I could see how people's priorities worked, and money was top of their agenda, and Primula was starting to gain ground using it.

Did no one understand me at all? I could not understand how anyone could believe her, my mum was as honest as they come, and actually, so was my father, surely people knew that, and I had been raised decent? Deep down inside, I felt a deep concern building, and my mind was preoccupied with how I could show my honesty and try to show Prim was nothing but a lying scheming bitch. It felt so unfair, she did not have to prove I was guilty, and yet I had to find some way to prove I was innocent, and nothing like she was describing me.

I campaigned hard, and talked preservation, youth employment, better services for the elderly at the surgery, and something Deli had come up with, which was some benches for Dursley Woods, and country park status, to preserve its natural beauty. At one o'clock I met with a journalist, in the back room of Sweetie's Retreat with Birch, to do a special interview, and give our view of the future for Wotton, and we both talked in depth about our plans and policies.

When asked about my views on Primula, as much as I wanted to trash the cow, I simply stated she was my opposing candidate, and she was doing her best to win, as were we. He did not appear happy that he got no dirt on her, and we took the chance to give a little more information of what we billed as the spectacular Curio Carnival Wotton, where the proceeds would be split between the village and the Curio Life Project.

I was tired when I got in, and I sat in my room with Birch, we ran a bath, and slipped in together, and I closed my eyes and relaxed.

"Oh God, I need this, I ache all over, and I have wanted some more alone time with you." She slipped her arms round me, and kissed the top of my head.

"I know Sweetie, it will not be long, and we will have lots more time together. I would like to get up and see mum, and spend some time at her place." I turned.

"Birch I would love that, oh God, can we please?" She smiled.

"If you really want to, we will Sweetie, I must admit, it has been nice seeing her at events, but it is not the same as living there, I miss it a little." I felt the excitement rise inside me.

"Can we go and see a band, and walk on the moors?" She giggled.

"Sweetie you are getting me excited, oh God, I want to do that now, I really want to hold your hand and walk around the dam, and on the hills." I leaned in to her and kissed her, with a happy smile.

"Can we see Bev as well?"

"GUARD YOUR VAGINA!" Birch giggled at the sound of Chloe's voice in the hallway. I snuggled into her.

"I love our life, I love being married, I love living with you Birch." She just smiled at me and her eyes twinkled.

"I do too, I love this, just this Deads, just us two... Sweetie, the water is getting cold, we will need to get dry soon."

I gave a happy sigh and climbed out and wrapped a towel around me, and handed her one, and we walked back into the bedroom, to dry ourselves, and blow dry our hair.

Ten minutes later, we walked into the kitchen, and I was surprised to see Anita, she was stood smiling next to a box on the island.

"Anita, why didn't you text me, and let me know you were

coming?" She gave a smile.

"Chloe told me you would not be much longer, I have been here about fifteen minutes talking with the girls, we have a little surprise for you." I frowned, and Birch took my hand with a giggle.

"Sweetie, tomorrow, Gordon, should have been interviewing Tony Peterson, but he has been in a road accident, and he rang Anita, and asked if you could fill in? You know, he has been trying to get you on his show for a while, so we agreed."

"But Birch, you had a surprise planned for me, what about that?" She gave a giggle. Anita opened the box on the island.

"These are advanced prints, the official release date is November tenth, but I thought it would be nice to make the announcement with Gordon."

She lifted out a thick hard backed book, and handed it to me, I looked down and felt my heart jump, as I looked at, 'The Circle of White,' which was the first in the series of the 'The Cursed Books of Krisandra series.' I smiled as I looked up, I could see Chloe fidgeting, she was dying to see her art, I handed her the book.

"You get the first one, you are the artist." She took it, her eyes were huge.

"Oh, wow Abby, thanks."

She held it like it was gold, and looked at the figure with long flowing hair, holding a sword in her right hand, and a large book under her left, as she stood in a circle of white flowers. I gave her a smile.

"That is my favourite picture yet." Anita and Birch were all smiles, I love the reverence Chloe shows my books, she opened the cover, and read the dedication.

'For Chloe, The inspiration for the series, and a magical artist.' She looked up with tears in her eyes.

"God Abby, I have no words left." Edwina smirked.

"That's a first, you soppy bitch." Chloe giggled and gave a snort, Birch got giddy, and jumped up and down on the spot.

"I want one, I want to know what happens to Karen."

I pulled out a book and Anita handed me a pen, and I signed the book for Birch, she squealed with delight.

"I love that I sleep with my favourite author." She hugged the book tight.

I took the next one out and signed it, and handed it to Anita, and signed the next one to Tabby, and handed it to her.

"You know she will want a copy?" Anita smiled.

"She will, she has been driving me mad knowing I had the new manuscript. Honestly, it is probably good that you put another book out so fast, ever since Sunny Bank, she has been itching for this."

I handed a copy to Edwina, and signed one for Anthony and Debs, and signed another one for Deli. As promised, and as I had done with the last book, I signed one for Stacy, which I would drop in tomorrow.

We headed into the living room, and suddenly as we sat down Birch looked at me with an odd expression, I frowned at her.

"What?"

"Sweetie, how did Chloe know what to draw?" I gave her a huge smile.

"I gave her a manuscript, why?" Her eyes went huge.

"She knew... You mean Chloe kept a secret?" I giggled at her.

"She certainly did, possibly for the first time ever, but she held it inside all this time." Birch looked shocked, and disappointed.

"Crap, I could have interrogated her, and I missed my chance." I patted her leg.

"You have a copy now, so you can read away." She hugged the book harder.

"Can I borrow your copy; I don't want to spoil mine?" Anita started to laugh, Birch smiled, and her eyes danced with delight.

I sat with Anita and went through all the plans for tomorrow, and the Gordon Stimes interview. She left around eight, as she was meeting Tabby for a meal in Millington, I walked down the drive with her.

"How are things with you two, it looks like it is working out pretty well?" She turned and gave me a big smile.

"Oh Abby, I adore her, I am having such a wonderful time with her. She really gets me, and she is so loving, honestly, don't laugh, but last Friday when she left for work after spending three days at my place, I cried, I was so happy." I understood that feeling.

"I cried twice on my honeymoon, just because I could not contain my happiness, so I know how that feels. I am really happy for you Anita; I think you deserve it." She nodded.

"It is all down to you two, do you know that? You two set such a great example of how things should be, Tabby and me have learned from it. My life has changed so much since I started working for you, I have got to tell you Abby, I find you inspiring." I shrugged.

"I am just me; I am just doing me; it is all I can do."

"Yeah, but Abby, you really are worth knowing, I love Birch and you, both of you mean the world to me, and both of you have taught me so much, I will always be grateful."

"Likewise, Anita, now go on or you will be late, you have a book to deliver, give her our love, and we will see you both tomorrow."

I watched as she jumped in her car, and drove off with a wave and smile, I turned and walked back to the door, and gave a happy sigh as I locked it, although, her car is a trash heap, she really needs to buy a new one.

I made a drink and headed upstairs, Birch was nowhere to be seen, and it did not take a lot of working out where she would be. I arrived in the bedroom to see I was right. Birch lay on the bed, on her tummy reading her book, she looked up and smiled as I walked in.

"Oh Deads, this is so good, I love the transformation from Karen to Krisandra, her uncle is a total shit, this is powerful writing."

I climbed on the bed and sat back against the pillows and sipped my drink, as I watched her focus, and turn the page, whenever she got excited, she would wiggle her bum, which made me laugh.

It is strange even now, to see someone so engrossed in what I write, I lay back and closed my eyes, and just drifted, listening to the sound of the pages turn, as Birch read on, and every now and again, the bed would move as she got excited. I felt tired and worn out, it had been a long week, and as I drifted, sleep took me.

I woke up under the duvet, with Birch curled round me, and Edwina sat on the bed. She smiled and put a coffee down on the unit.

"Abby, you have a busy day, you need to wake up." I yawned as I sat up.

"What time is it?"

"It is just gone nine. I am making some bacon for breakfast."
Birch sat bolt upright with her eyes still closed.

"I love bacon!" I giggled, she turned and opened her eyes, and
smiled.

"Hi Sweetie." She leaned on my shoulder.

"I love your book, but I am tired."

It took a while to wake up, especially for Birch. I sat her down
in front of a large plate of bacon, and slowly she came to life,
as I got myself ready. Today, I was going to wear my new dark
purple pants, a new black top, which did show a small amount of
my little round boobs, and a silk purple scarf, with a black lace
sleeveless duster jacket.

I laid out a pair of boot cuts, and a long black top for Birch, and
grabbed my three inch wedged heeled boots, and did my makeup,
and I was pretty much done, which is the best thing about long
straight hair with a fringe, a quick brush, and I am ready. I
grabbed my shoulder purse, and purple parasol, and headed back
downstairs to the library, for everything Anita had left us.

Birch arrived dressed, still looking a little tired, I giggled at her
as she tried to brush her hair, and got her parting all wrong, I
took the brush off her. She parted her hair to the left, so it swept
across her face and over her shoulder. I had always liked it, and
had at one time thought of doing it myself, until she suggested a
fringe. I looked at her as she sat in the chair and smiled.

"I have no sympathy for you, that is what happens when you
read for most of the night." She looked up at me.

"Sweetie, it is really gripping, honestly, I could not put it down,
I am loving it." I smiled; it was in a way really nice to see how
much she loved my work.

"Okay you are done, come on, we need to get ready."

She stood up and gave me a quick kiss, and went to grab her
bag, and her long black shawl, and ten minutes later, there was a
knock on the door. Markus had arrived with the limo. We jumped
in with a smile, I dropped the partition, as he got in, and asked if
we could stop at the Tea Rooms.

Henrietta Cole Dennison, and Bethany Goodwaters, were sat
at their usual table in the Tea Rooms, when the long black limo
pulled up outside, Markus got out, walked around and opened

the door for me, and I winked as I got out. The Tea Rooms went silent as I walked in, and Lillian gave a gasp.

"Oh Abigail, you look stunning." I gave her a smile, winked, and she blushed.

"Why thank you Lilly, you as always, look very lovely."

I turned to see Stacy looking at me, I walked over to her, and opened my bag.

"Stacy, this is an advanced copy, as I promised." I lifted out the book and put it in her hands, she looked like she was going to explode.

"Abby, it is not out till next month, oh God, I am so excited." She looked at me with a huge smile. "Thank you."

"My pleasure, and thanks for all the lovely comments on your Insta, and for loving my books so much. Okay, the car is waiting, so I better go."

I turned and waved to Lillian and Celia, and headed back out to the car and jumped in, Markus closed the door and walked back around to his door, the whole street had come to a standstill watching, it was actually rather fun to see it.

Stacy beamed with delight, as Celia and Lillian came out from behind the counter to look at her book, Henrietta gave a snort.

"I have no idea what this village is coming to, she swans around like Lady Muck. When Primula wins the vote, that will knock her down a peg or two, she is like her mother and needs putting in her place. I will not even speak about her criminal father, all I can say is he was lucky to get away with his crimes, and that Abigail is like him, she wriggles off the hook too easily. I trust Primula, she speaks the truth, this village will suffer with those two sinners in charge. From what I have heard, her books are not even that good, they are filled with her sacrilegious filth, but there again, what do you expect, when she lives a life of sin in that hovel of a tasteless whore house?" Stacy spun round, hugging her book.

"I am sorry Mrs Denison, but you are wrong, her house is beautiful. It is immaculate and tasteful, and Abby and Birch are the kindest sweetest most caring people I know, and as for her writing, she is brilliant, and adored by all her fans." Henrietta gave a huff, and stared at her.

"You are supposed to be working are you not? I need more milk, get me some." Stacy walked to the other side of the room.

"You can wait your turn, I am busy." Louise turned her back to them, and started to clear another table. Celia gave a smile as she walked back behind the counter.

We slowed at the rear of a large conference hall, and I looked out of the window, at the tall sterile looking grey building.

"Are we not going to the theatre, I thought I was seeing Gordon?" Birch snuggled up and chuckled in my ear.

"Sweetie, he is doing something different this time, I am sure you will love it." I looked at her suspiciously, and felt a jolt to my system.

"Oh Christ, what have you done?" She giggled.

"Sweetie, it will be you and Gordon, you know, you are way to suspicious these days, not everything is a plot to get at you?" I narrowed my eyes. The car entered the rear into a large covered area and pulled up.

"I live with you; I need to be."

She gave a loud laugh, as Markus opened the door, and she slid across the seat and climbed out, I slid over not trusting her one bit. Security met us, and within seconds, we were ushered into the back of the arena, and into a side room, where Monica stood smiling. It was really nice to see her again, she gave me a big smile.

"Come on you two, it is good to have you back, I hope you are going to stay dressed Doctor Dixon?"

I giggled, as she fed the wire through my top, and attached the receiver to my waist, then started fitting Birch with one, I looked at her.

"Why are you being fitted with a mic?" She gave me that smile that meant mischief.

"Sweetie, I am joining you on stage." I scowled.

"I knew it, you have set me up?" Monica chuckled.

"Now girls, that is the kind of natural spirit we want to see today." She turned to me.

"Abby, go up there to Gordon, and be yourself... Okay you are up in ten." I frowned, and felt panicked.

"What... I only just got here?" She winked.

"I will be waiting stage side to switch you on, grab a drink and take it with you if you want." She left the room, I looked at Birch, feeling a little panicked.

"Birch, what is happening?" She leaned in and gave me a soft kiss.

"It's a surprise." I frowned.

"I hate surprises."

She giggled and took my hand, and led me to the table and poured two large gins. Five minutes later I was stood at the bottom of the stairs leading up to the stage, and could hear an audience, and then sudden applause, and swallowed hard, as my stomach churned. Inside the arena, Anita walked on stage, wearing a head mic.

"Ladies and gentlemen, today we have a very special show for you, which is a little different from the normal format Gordon does. But I will let him tell you about that."

She lifted her hand, and Gordon walked on stage from the opposite side to me, I could not see him, but heard the applause, I felt my legs tremble, Birch took my hand and squeezed it.

On stage, Gordon was stood in front of a chair, and two large sofas', behind him was a large white screen.

"Good afternoon, ladies and gentlemen. Today is very special, because we are here to pay tribute to an extraordinary person, but rather than stand here and tell you about her, let's get her up here. Winner of the Jonathon Graham Prize for youth Literature, and youngest ever recipient of it, Abigail Jennifer Watson."

The audience went crazy, and Birch grabbed my ass and gave it a squeeze, and I jumped, she giggled.

"Go meet your fans."

She gave me a push and I giggled, and stepped onto the steps, and nervously walked up to the stage, I had no idea what was going on, but walked on to cheers, as Gordon smiled at me.

The place was huge and packed, there were film cameras everywhere, as I crossed the stage, and he took my hands in his, and guided me to one of the sofa's. I turned as the audience applauded and smiled, but I was shitting myself. Gordon sat down, and made himself comfy, I noted the two tall glasses of pale liquid, on the table in front of me. He smiled as the audience quietened down.

"Abby... So lovely having you here, which I know is a bit of a surprise for you, do you know why you are here?" I gave a nervous giggle.

"I started to feel a set up a little earlier, I think my wife has conspired against me." He chuckled.

"I am afraid to say she has. Abby, today we are filming what will be the very first of a new series of specials for television, and you will be the feature of the real Abigail Jennifer Watson." I felt a nervous jolt.

"Oh Dear." The audience laughed; he pointed out into the audience.

"Abby every person here today, has read your books, these are your fans." I looked out into the huge arena, and smiled, it was a little surprising, and a bit mind blowing, there were so many, I looked back at him.

"Really?"

He gave me a nod and smiled, I waved and a thousand fans all lifted their hands and waved back, it really hit me, and I felt a strong surge of emotion rise up inside me. Gordon looked at me and smiled.

"Abby, there is something they want to say to you, are you ready to hear it?"

I felt a little nervous, he looked at the audience, and my eye caught another slightly smaller stage to the side of the one I was on. A spotlight lit up, and Floyd walked out from behind a black curtain with his guitar, and started to play a squealing solo, and then suddenly all the audience started to sing happy birthday to me.

It caught me completely off guard, and I lifted my hand to my mouth, and smothered a sob. Gordon just smiled, as thousands of people sang their heart out, and I felt the tears in my eyes. It was amazing, there were so many smiling faces, and they were all looking at me singing. I did not know what to do, as a huge wave of emotion swept over me. I gave another huge sob, as they finished, and then applauded. I wiped my eyes on my hand and to the left, the cheers erupted, as Birch walked on with tissues. Gordon lifted his arm.

"Doctor Jemima Dixon."

They all cheered and screamed, as Birch slid down at my side, and handed me a tissue, she put the box on the table, and snuggled up to me with a huge smile. Gordon looked at her.

"That was very special, she had no idea, did she?" Birch held my hand and giggled, as I wiped my eyes.

"None at all, but I think it has done her good, Abby loves her fans, and now she can see they love her too." I dabbed my eyes dry, and took a deep breath.

"I knew you were up to no good." The audience giggled, I looked at them.

"Honestly, she is a nightmare, I never know what to expect." Gordon sat back in his seat with a chuckle.

"Jemima, you are married to the youngest ever recipient of the Jonathon Graham Prize, she is one of the driving forces behind Curio Life, and a very successful author, who has single handily revived a whole genre of books, and brought back gothic horror. I also believe, with your new company D&D, she has proven to be a very successful business woman, you must be really proud of her?" Birch was all smiles as she squeezed my hand.

"She is an inspiration, not just to me, but to everyone around her, it is why I fell so hopelessly in love with her. You know, she has no idea at all how talented she is?" She leaned in and kissed my cheek, I giggled at her as her eyes danced.

"Don't try buttering me up now Doctor."

Gordon gave a mighty laugh, as the audience laughed with him. Birch was loving this; she had completely thrown me again. Gordon nodded at me.

"You know, you do inspire a lot of people with your words, especially this guy."

He pointed as Jimmy walked onto the side stage with a stool, and a guitar, he smiled at me as he sat down and leaned into the microphone.

"I told my missus, if she cries, it is not my fault."

The video screen above me came to life and the audience roared, as he started to play, above me pictures from the Curio website came to life.

'Hi I am Chloe, Hi I am Anthony. Hello, my name is Birch, you know, it's the hair thing. Hey everyone, I am Edwina, Hi I am Debbie, and I am a Curio.' The pictures showed me, I turned and laughed. 'Guys I messed up again, I keep hitting the wrong buttons, oops, shit! Hi all, my name is Abigail, I am twenty four, my life is shit, and I am most definitely a Curio, actually I am very curious as to how the hell this camera works.'

The audience laughed, as Jimmy played on, as the pictures turned to all the outtakes, we had with us hugging and crying and just giving long sighs. I felt the emotional surge, as he leaned into the mic and looked at me, and started to sing.

"Don't look at me that way. Don't say the things you say." I felt the thump in my chest, as Birch slipped her arm around me, and Jimmy sang the song from the Curio Live event, and more tears rolled down my cheeks.

The audience joined in and sang it with him, and I dabbed my eyes as they all looked at me and sang their hearts out. He came to the end, and I was almost at breakdown. I wiped my eyes as everyone applauded, Gordon reached over and patted my hand, I leaned forward and lifted my glass of water, it was gin and strong, I took a huge gulp, and sat back.

"Christ guys, I thought this was going to be a happy thing, you guys are killing me." Gordon sat back with a chuckle.

"Abby, I am led to believe that all those lyrics, were actually lifted from letters you wrote to your friend. They are very powerful, and they have raised very important funds for the Curio project." I wiped my eyes and gave a nod.

"Yes, it was not an easy time in my life, I was in a very dark patch, and trying so hard to write, and I was not really succeeding."

Deb's walked on the side of the stage, she waved to the audience as they went wild, as she beamed a huge smile. She sat down on the opposite sofa with a huge happy smiling face, Gordon turned to her.

"Debbie, you are Abby's oldest friend, tell me, why you decided to use her letters to write a song?" She looked a little saddened.

"All the Curio's had a great summer together, but we all started another year at Uni, and college, and when Abby came home at the end of it, most of us had left the village to find work. Sadly, she was alone, and there were some who would not accept her, and they said some horrible things to her. It was a really dark time in her life, and watching her suffer was a terrible thing to witness. We talked by email a lot, and when it came to Curio Live, and Jimmy really wanted to help, I told him about the letters, and we just got really inspired by her words. I ended up sat on the floor, and highlighted them with a marker, and sorted them into what are now the lyrics. I felt then, and still do now, those words needed to be heard, although, I am sorry it upsets Abby to hear them." He nodded and looked at me.

"I must admit Abby, I felt a little twinge of guilt, when I saw your reaction, I hope it did not bring back too painful a memory? They say every writer needs some darkness; do you think it helped with your writing?" I smiled.

"Gordon, I am married to a therapist." I chuckled as Birch leaned into me.

"It was a very dark place for me, and became the motivation for me behind the Curio's, but I am fine today. If I am honest, Jimmy sings it with such heart and belief, it really touches me deeply. I think you can feel the darkness in the first two hands of death books, and it certainly influenced Sanctuary Arch, especially the separation." Deb's smiled at me.

"He loves you Abby, and really believes in what we are all doing."

"Christ Deb's, stop... I have already cried twice today." The audience laughed. Gordon gave a giggle.

"You are a real inspiration Abby, and you work really hard behind the scenes, I spoke with Edwina a few days ago, and she sent me this, take a look at this everyone."

The video screens came to life, and it was footage of me during the set up of the Art Gallery event, sat at my computer, or lifting boxes, and walking around the gallery with Chloe as we sorted out her pictures. You know, Edwina is such a sneaky bitch, I never saw her with a camera once? One small film clip, showed me lost in thought, as I wrote part of my book, the montage played on, and on the small side stage, the small happy figure of Chloe walked onto the stage, in new black dungarees and a vest. The spotlight hit her, and the audience erupted.

She waved with her bright smile, and there were screams and whistles, as she stood there happily waving back. The audience quietened down, and she turned and looked at me, and pointed.

"Hi guys, I am Chloe, and I am a friend of that amazing lady there." The audience erupted again, and she laughed. God, I love her bright happiness, and I gave her a big smile.

"I had an exhibition, well actually I still am, I just came from there, because I love the pictures I drew for Abby. I love them because firstly, her stories captivate me, and secondly, because without her and Birch, my life would be pretty bleak, their kindness changed my life." She turned and started to walk slowly towards me.

"Every day, I sit with Abby, and every day we talk, I tell her my secrets, and get her advice, and honestly, I think I would be really messed up if she was not in my life. I think Abby understands people in ways no other will, she certainly understands me that way. I love her deeply, in a totally straight way of course." Birch and I both laughed, God, she is so lovely.

"The real Abby, is quiet, reflective, and yet actually more confident than she realises. I love that she does not judge, and worries about us all, and she is always there to help people in trouble. You guys have all seen our new Curio housemates' video, she masterminded all of that to help Deli. You know, the press are horrible, because they have no idea who she is, so they slander her, I hate them for that." She turned and looked at the audience.

"You guys know her though, you know who she is, don't you?" The audience screamed into life, and she giggled.

"I knew it." There were laughs all around.

"I just did her new book cover, it is my best one yet, I am sure you will all see it soon. I never told her, but I drew her, I just gave her blonde hair, because if you look real hard, you will see, it is everything she is." She walked right up to me, leaned over, and kissed my check.

"You are an amazing writer, and friend, thanks for all you have done."

She sat down next to Birch. Oh God, I felt my eyes welling up again, and took a deep breath, and tried to compose myself, Chloe giggled and waved to everyone. Gordon turned to me.

"So, Abby, Resurrection Sword, what an amazing book, I cannot deny it is my favourite so far, but the series is over, and yet, there is another book out soon, but no one really knows anything about it, will you give us an idea, we all want to know?" Birch blurted.

"It's brilliant, I am half way through, and oh my God, it is her best ever." I looked at her.

"Birch... Shush, it is supposed to be a secret." She suddenly realised, and covered her mouth, the audience started to laugh, I turned to Gordon.

"You will have to ask my publicist." I giggled at him, as he looked crushed.

The Audience started to applaud, as Anita walked onto the stage carrying a book in one hand, she stood by the microphone, and waited for quiet, she gave a really big smile and took a breath.

"Ladies and gentlemen, fans of Abby. On November tenth, the Dixon Group are proud to present the start of a brand new series of gothic stories, written by Abigail Jennifer Watson, entitled, 'The Cursed Books of Krisandra."

The audience went mental, and their screams were deafening, I sat there watching all the bright happy faces, and I felt so happy, I giggled at the reaction, Gordon looked elated. Anita waited, which took a while, and she gave a chuckle.

"The first book in the series, will be entitled, The Circle of White, and it is available to pre order as of today."

She turned and walked over, and as she did, on the large screen the cover came into view, the audience saw it and went bonkers. I looked back, and Chloe's cover looked fantastic that size, I smiled, and looked at Gordon, as Anita handed me the book and then sat next to Deb's.

I held the book on my knee, and could see him eyeing it, he was clearly really excited. The audience quietened down, and I looked at them.

"Look at him, he is almost foaming at the mouth." They all giggled, as I handed it over to him, he took it with joy.

"I signed you a copy, this is one of fifty pre-printed copies." He took the book and smiled, and opened the cover, and read the inscription.

"Oh wow, Abby, I am lost for words, thank you so much." He turned it over and read the back of the jacket.

"Finally, having saved Willis and Gabrielle, Karen leaves them behind, as she fears the growing power of her uncle Abraham. Because of her late father's work, she is aware that he intends to seek out the forbidden books of curses, and bring them together, in order to wipe out the vampire race forever. In a bid to travel unrestricted, she changes her name and identity to Krisandra, and sets off in hot pursuit, to discover the whereabouts, and obtain the books before him, all of which lie hidden in circles of white." He took a deep breath and looked at the audience.

"Oh wow, are you all ready for this?" The audience exploded, and he laughed, it was so nice to see, Birch was bouncing on the sofa at the side of me.

"Sweeties, it is so exciting, I have read twelve chapters, and I want to get home to read more, oh, I am so loving it."

There were murmurs of excitement all around the area, I smiled, it was so nice to see, and it made me feel really happy, and more excited than I normally am at a book release. Gordon looked thrilled; Anita shifted in her seat.

"We have two spare copies, and if you look under your seats, you will find an envelope, all of which have a post card of one of Abby's books printed on it. Only two have the cover of the new book, and if you have it, then please make your way to the stage, and Abby will hand you a signed copy."

There was suddenly mass excitement, as everyone bent down, and excitedly opened their envelopes, a wild scream announced the first winner, as a young teenager waved the postcard, and everyone stood up as she moved along the line to get to the aisle. Monica walked on stage with two copies of the book and a pen, she winked as she handed them to me. I took them with a smile as she walked off.

Anita walked back to the mic as another person screamed at the back, announcing a second winner, she waited patiently. Security guided the first winner up the steps to the stage, and she came gasping up to Anita, who lowered the mic stand slightly.

"Hi, what is your name and how old are you?"

She patted her chest as she got her breath back, her eyes fixed on me, as I lifted the pen and opened the cover.

"My name is Anabel, and I am fourteen years old."

I wrote her name, and signed the book, and then stood up, and walked towards her, she looked terrified, as her eyes opened wider, I handed her the book.

"Thank you for being here, and reading my books Anabel." She looked star struck, and gasped in air.

"Miss Watson, you are a wonderful writer, I love your stories so much... I know it is cheeky to ask, but could I give you a birthday hug?" Her eyes were so huge, I smiled and opened my arms, and she gently put her arms around me.

"Happy Birthday, I am so happy right now, I think I will cry soon." She released me and I smiled.

"Cry away, I will probably join in."

She giggled, and took her book back off Anita, and hugged it tight, the security guy took her down off the stage. Birch came up with the second book and my pen, and held it open, as the second winner came up, she was a little older than me, she gave me a huge smile.

"I am Saffron Waters, and I am a little bit older than you are." I giggled.

"I am so thrilled to meet you Miss Watson, and belated happy birthday wishes to you."

She held out her hand, and I shook it. She was quite calm, but I could see the excitement in her eyes. I turned and signed the book to her, and Birch closed it, and handed it to me, I turned back and handed her the copy.

"I hope you enjoy it." She smiled a sweet smile.

"If this was the worse book you wrote, it would still mean more to me than anything, because you handed it to me personally, honestly, I am so thrilled, I think I am going to explode, but I am holding it in." Birch leaned in at my side.

"I know that feeling Sweetie, I struggle containing it too."

"WHEN?" I turned back with a giggle.

Deb's and Chloe both looked at each other and laughed, Birch smiled, and Saffron walked from the stage looking happy and proud, Birch slid her arm round my waist and we walked back to our seats.

Gordon was sneaking a look at the first chapter; I smiled as I sat back down and he looked up. He was so excited, and he rambled a little, and then we talked about the awards ceremony, and Deb's, Chloe, Anita and Birch chipped in about how amazing it was, and how terrified I was. I talked to the audience and thanked them for such loving support. The subject changed to Curio Life, and we all chipped in as we talked of what it was like to arrange the live show, and how excited we were to see the first of the new centres getting ready. Then we talked about the Hands of Death series, and all of us added to the conversation, as over an hour passed by, and finally, Gordon gave a sigh.

"Abby we never have long enough, sadly, again the show is almost over, but for you, I have one last surprise." He pointed across to the other stage, and a black curtain rose up, and Battered Taco were set up and ready to play.

Jimmy stepped up front as the new extended intro began to their new single, he lifted his guitar and started to play, as he leaned into the mic, and began to sing, suddenly the drums crashed to a halt, and the guitars went all over the place, he stopped and looked back.

"What?" Floyd leaned into the mic.

"Jim mate, sorry, but your shit at this." Jimmy gave a loud laugh, and turned back to the mic.

"You know what's missing, don't you guys?" I felt utter panic flood into me and slid back in my seat, and gripped Birch's hand like a vice, he looked right at me.

"Guys, we are missing a vocalist and a backing singer."

I shook my head, Deb's blanched white, and looked at me with a terrified stare. Birch pulled my hand.

"Sweetie, you are needed." I swallowed hard, and felt ice cold terror run through me.

"Birch, I cannot sing in front of all these people." She leaned in, and covered her mic.

"Sweetie, do you love me?" I stared at her in terror.

"That's a daft question, you know I do." She whispered very quietly.

"Then sing to me, look at me, and let me see how you felt when you recorded it, come on, because I really want to see that."

I gasped for air, Chloe was pushing Deb's, and she looked like a rabbit caught in the headlights. Birch took my hand and stood up, she looked back at me and smiled, and just for a second, I hated her. I was caught between a rock and a hard place, I had no choice, and I knew it, sometimes it really sucks to know the Curio's

As I got up the audience went wild, and Birch holding my hand walked me over to the second stage, and Jimmy gave a huge smile. I glared at him with hate, he leaned round sniggering and switched off my mic pack so there was no interference, and handed me a set of ear plugs. He wired me up, and led me to the mic, my heart was thundering in my chest. He spoke quietly in my ear.

"You love her Abby, just think back to that night, and let it show." I nodded, and took a deep breath; I was crapping myself.

Birch turned me round slightly, and smiled, she was really close, and her eyes looked huge, behind me the music started, and I swallowed hard as Deb's stood next to Jimmy on the second mic, I could feel my legs shaking. Birch took my hands in hers.

I started to sing, and Birch squeezed my hand, as we locked eyes, and I just focused on her. Jimmy smiled, as he watched, and I sang my heart out, as Birch's eyes filled with tears, and she smiled away.

Holding her hand, I sung loud and from my heart, and the guys in the band all smiled happily away. My nerves faded in her gaze, and all the love and joy I felt floated up inside me, stood singing and looking at those gorgeous green eyes, I felt complete. Birch wiped her eyes on her sleeve, and as I reached the end of the song, she pulled me into a hug, and squeezed the life out of me.

"I love you so much Deads."

The band stood smiling, as the audience roared, and I held her tight, and felt really emotional, Gordon, Anita and Chloe walked onto the stage at the side of us, he smiled at me with a huge happy smile.

"Ladies and Gentlemen... The inspirational, Miss Abigail Jennifer Watson."

The applause was deafening, as Birch slipped her arm around me, and wiped her eyes, and I waved to all the audience. Monica walked on with a huge bunch of flowers, and handed them to me, and Gordon held up his arm.

"Happy Birthday Abby, from everyone here." Birch turned and kissed my cheek.

"No one will ever beat that for a birthday surprise Sweetie." I had to laugh, it was pretty impressive, I could not deny it, although my legs were still shaking like tuning forks.

Chapter 31

Dark Dealings.

Birch was right, my birthday week ended on a high, we left the stage and attended the back stage party, which was pretty wild and fun. Gordon left early, it was obvious he wanted to read his book, which he clung to all the time he was there. Feeling more than a little tipsy, and joined by Chloe, and a lighting guy called Tom, we jumped into the limo, and Markus drove us home, where I dragged Birch to bed, and ravished her. I felt I needed to show her my appreciation.

Sunday was a slow day, we all had banging headaches, I finally dragged myself out of bed, and staggered around, with coffee, and then sat in my desk seat in the library, to discover hundreds of tags on Insta, from the arena, including my two winners, who proudly held their books up. I wrote little happy comments to all of them, thanking them for making my birthday so special for me.

My life feels so crazy at times, people see me so different than I actually am, it is almost like being two people, and the one I like most, is the naked, hot bathing, Birch cuddling coffee addict, who lounges around and writes stuff. The public figure who watches her words, gets emotional and shy, is like an alien version of me.

The me I am today is also another part of me, as I walk up and down the show field, with Edwina and G5, marking out the placement of everything, with orange string and tent pegs.

It is Monday, and on Saturday, the circus and the fair, start their weeklong run, which will end in a carnival, and so I am out in the drizzle, in boots and a yellow D&D Marshal vest, coordinating with the group, and preparing the spaces for each stand, and living in hope, everything runs smoothly. Primula is again in the village handing new leaflets detailing my immorality and slagging me off.

In the Church Hall, Chloe and Deli, are stood at a long table, preparing all the passes, and doing last minute checks on everyone taking part. Birch had got consent for, ordered, and had delivered a garden shed, that was twelve feet by eight feet, and that was being erected just to one side of the show gate.

We intend to use it as a base camp, from which all the arriving traders and staff, would check in, and this would be donated to the parish after the event was over, so they could use it. I was looking forward to it being finished, just so I could get out of the drizzle, and make a coffee on the portable gas stove that was going to be installed.

At ten minutes past two, a huge truck arrived on the field, the circus crew were here, and I walked up the site with Edwina, and showed them the huge marked out area, for them to set up on, and within minutes, the support trucks arrived at the field, and the men got straight to work.

It is fascinating to watch a big top tent go up, I saw it on TV as a child, but watching the speed and precision these people worked at was mind blowing. Within an hour, the roof of the tent was being lifted up the central pole, and suddenly, our carnival was becoming a reality.

Once the shed at the gate was up, the propane gas tanks were installed at the back, as we put together a flat pack work bench, for the cooking hobs to sit on. The engineer fitted all the lines and tested them, and then walked us through the procedure for using them safely.

When he had finished and left, we put the kettle on, pulled two sets of garden furniture out of Petal, put them together, and placed them in the shed. Luke fitted coat hooks to the wall, and a long row of hooks down the wall, on which were hung clip boards, with all the details of who would be arriving, and where their pitch would be. The final job was to add the huge water container, battery powered lights, and all the cups and plates, and two bowls for washing up in, and the shed was ready for action.

Outside, Luke helped attach an office sign, and two large poles with signs on, requesting trucks and traders check in at the office to be given their placement details, it was all starting to look very official, and very orderly. I stood back and admired our work, as the little kettle inside the shed started to whistle, it was time for coffee.

The good news was, we had a hangout, for over the coming week, with chairs and a kettle. With no power, there was no fridge, but we did have an ice box for keeping the milk and beer cool in. This was Chloe's idea, and she placed boxes of spare marshal vests, and other little odds and bods, we would need over the week on the bottom of the work bench.

My day was over, and Chloe and Deli would be taking over from here, most of the big tent was up, and the generators and lighting was going up. We did have flood lights arranged, but Michael would be supervising all that tomorrow. At the far end of the huge field, the caravans and animal trucks arrived and parked up, as the light faded into a cool autumnal evening.

The village was buzzing with excitement as we walked back down, and onto the green, the sight of circus trucks, had everyone very excited, Edwina chuckled at my side.

"Crazy isn't it, not that long ago they hated us, and now look at them. I want to hug Prim, because through their fear of her, they found a love and respect for us. The fact we have all killed ourselves for years at every event, has meant little to them, my God, they are hypocrites."

I had reached that point of no longer caring. Birch and I had talked for a long time about it, and her words of 'it does not matter, Sweetie, this is no longer about you and me, or even them, this is about protecting the village, our home.' It made sense to me, I did not care that the Shrew Crew would never accept me, or that Prim would slander me, I knew my value, and I knew what those who cared for me thought, and in a way, I had simply let go of it all.

"Screw them Edwina, if this goes to plan, it will raise a lot of money for the village, and Curio Live, and both will continue. I honestly no longer care what the likes of Agnes, Primula, Henrietta, or Bethany think, they were never going to accept any of us, simply because we make them look bad. Think about it, how much have they done over the years to help the village. Marjorie has at least tried?" She gave a snort and patted my shoulder.

"Hell Abby, when did you suddenly grow into an adult?" I

chuckled and looked at her.

"I know right, I married a crazy childish woman, and it still happened, hell, life is weird." We both laughed as we crossed the road, and headed into Deb's shop, we were in dire need of another coffee, and a warm heater.

Birch came home after work, and had a meal, and then headed out for the site to meet Deb's. Chloe was staying on the site in Bess for the night, and had a small portable generator, for two halogen lamps on large tripods, and to run some heating in her van. Baz had volunteered to stay with her, so we knew she would not sleep much.

The house felt quiet, as Birch grabbed some hot food for them, and shot off in Petal, and so I headed upstairs and sat at my desk. With a new book coming out, I had time to update my website, and add some of the pictures Anita had arranged to be taken at my afternoon with Gordon, which would air on TV this coming Thursday night.

The web site and the Curio Site had pictures on, and announcements for the carnival, as did the D&D site. Edwina had planned a live stream of the light show, which would go out on the website with a five minute delay, and as I sat at my desk, and darkness had descended, she was out in the village again with G5, running tests and checking all the equipment was fine. She had many thousands of pounds of tech, locked in the glass boxes, and she had to make sure every night, all of it was working well.

I felt tired, and collapsed on the bed, it had been a long day, and tomorrow would be just as long, as the fair ground people arrived to set up, it was not long before my eyes closed.

Chloe and Deb's sat with Birch and Baz, on the chairs in the shed, they had the burners on the small hob running to keep the place warm, as they each had a beer, Birch was going over everything on a long list of things to be done, when Deb's turned to Chloe.

"What was that?" Chloe instantly stood up.

"Fuck off Deb's, don't start that shit here, I have to sleep with a graveyard across the way." The room fell silent, Birch leaned back in her chair.

"I don't hear any…" There was a faint rustling sound. Chloe gave a sigh.

"Oh fuck, I heard it that time, I fucking hate your bat ears Deb's."

Birch stood up and grabbed a torch, she opened the door, and looked out. The nearest street light was just outside Anthony's shop, so it was pretty dark, there was some light at the far end of the field from the circus people. Down this end, it was pitch black, Birch clicked on her torch, and slowly moved it across the site, there was nothing there. She leaned back in.

"I cannot see anything, maybe we should take a walk round, just to be safe." Chloe looked at her.

"From what?" Birch smirked.

"You do know Gwenda is buried in that church, they put her under the day I arrived back, it was her funeral I held up?" Chloe shook her head, and swallowed hard.

"Why the fuck did you have to tell me that, Moon fucking thinks she is following me, Jesus Birch, what if she knows we are close, and she wants to come meet us?" Birch giggled and Deb's looked at her.

"She won't do that, the dead stay dead, Birch tell her, Gwenda won't come here."

Birch turned and looked back at both of them with white faces.

"You know I was born with brown hair, and then Moon told me the truth of the spirit realm. It turned snow white overnight, seriously, she told me some freaky messed up stuff." Deb's swallowed hard.

"Like what?" Birch looked really serious, and lowered her voice.

"Like when the spirits walk, they sound like rustling leaves." Chloe jerked and shuddered.

"Okay, you can just shut the fuck up, I have heard enough, so stop it."

The rustling sound came again, and Deb's jumped up off her seat, and grabbed Chloe by the arm.

"Okay, I am really freaked out, I don't want ghosts that rustle." Birch sniggered.

"I am having a walk around the site, who is coming with me?" Deb's clung to Chloe.

"I will go if you will." Chloe shook her head.

"I am getting in the van and locking the doors." Birch gave a low chuckle.

"Chloe, ghosts can pass through all solids, unless of course you bless Bess with holy water. The church is that way, it is right past Gwenda's grave." She walked out onto the site, and Baz got up, Deb's panicked.

"Where the hell are you going?" He looked back, and smirked.

"With Birch, the way I see it, she is getting further away from the grave yard, that leaves you two closest. I am frigging staying with her, she is a witch, she has protections." Chloe looked at Deb's.

"He just made a bloody good point; I am fucking catching her up." Deb's nodded rapidly.

"Good point... BIRCH, WAIT UP!"

They ran outside, and saw her light flashing across the field, then ran towards it, and it suddenly went out. Deb's panicked, as she stopped and looked around in the darkness.

"Where did she go?" Chloe shook her head.

"Oh fuck, Gwenda got her." Deb's spun round.

"Just shut the hell up Chloe, I don't want Gwenda anywhere near us."

Deb's eyes opened really wide, as a large dark shape appeared behind Chloe, she felt the fear rising up inside her as Chloe stared at her, Chloe swallowed hard, her face was white.

"Oh fuck, Deb's, she is behind me isn't she, I fucking knew it, it always gets you from behind." Chloe turned quickly, and... SMACK!

Chloe hit the ground, as Deb's screamed, something reached out in the darkness, and grabbed at her coat. Chloe felt dazed, and looked up shocked and disorientated, as she watched, and from nowhere, a white glowing apparition appeared, and suddenly, there were lights spinning round, and then with a loud CRUNCH!

The dark figure went backwards and hit Chloe's legs, and fell backwards over her, Chloe squealed out in utter terror, and pulled her legs up fast.

Deb's rolled on the floor, and then felt a yank on her arm, as she was lifted into the air breathing hard, and felt her feet on the floor. She looked around, and there on the floor next to Chloe, was a dark figure, with Birch standing over it, holding a length of timber.

"I told you to stay the hell away, why did you come back?"

Chloe swallowed hard, as she pushed on the ground, and moved back quickly, getting away from the dark shape.

"Holy fuck Birch, you caught a ghost." Birch turned to look at Chloe, her hair looked as white as a ghosts, giving her an ethereal appearance.

"Huh?" Chloe pointed, and moved back more.

"What the fuck is that dark mass?" Birch stared at her.

"Chloe, this is past history, but it is not passed on, or dead, it's Deb's dad. He has been hanging around for a few days, we have seen him on the Retreat CCTV, and have been waiting for this."

"Huh?"

Birch gave a sigh, and lowered down, and leaned over him, then yanked down his hood. His face was cut, and bleeding. Baz turned on the torch, and illuminated his face, Deb's looked down at him from the side of Baz, as her father tried to shield his eyes from the bright light.

"What the hell Dad, why are you here, I told you to leave?"

Birch was knelt on his chest; she moved back and released the pressure. He looked up at her with hate in his eyes, as he shielded them from the light, then turned to Deb's.

"I told you, I wanted to see you, but this slag just fucking hit me." Birch gave a snort, and looked at him.

"How much are you after, because let's be honest, it is the only reason you arc here? I have looked you up, drunk and disorderly, minor drug arrests, violence to women, I know your sort, and I am warning you, hurt her, and there is nowhere you can hide that I won't find you."

Birch stood up, and he sat up, and held his hand to his face, he looked at Deb's.

"It has been hard of late, I just needed a few things to get me straight, you know, you are my kid, I am family whether you like it or not? I just wanted to see if I could lend a few quid." Birch stood back, and shook her head.

"Christ you are so predictable, you abandon her, and as soon as it looks like she has a few quid coming in, up you pop like the bad frigging smell you are." Deb's looked really angry.

"Is that true, is that all I am, a revenue source, to keep you pissed or high?" He looked at the floor.

"I have been through hell, I lost everything, you don't understand." Birch gave a sigh.

"Drink does that." She looked at Deb's.

"I can help him Deb's, but not with cash, I won't spend a penny to go into his arm or down his throat."

"What do you mean Birch?" Birch looked at Jonathon Ford.

"If you want help to be a half decent father, I am your only hope. I can have you in rehab, in less than an hour, and then you may have the slightest chance of seeing your kid again. If you say no, the gate is there, get through it, and if I see you in Wotton again, I will keep my previous promise. It's up to you?" Deb's nodded her head.

"Dad, listen to her; she can really help you." He got up off the floor, stood rather unsteadily, and looked at Birch with hate.

"I don't need help from a slag like you, fuck you, fuck all of you slags." He turned, and staggered off towards the gate, Birch watched him with cold eyes.

"Just stay away from her, if I see you in Wotton again, you will regret it." He turned as he disappeared into the darkness.

"Fucking whores, screw fucking all of you, I know how to get by." Chloe pulled Deb's close.

"Are you alright?" She nodded.

"To be honest Chloe yes, I am actually. He was never a dad, I don't feel anything for him, all he ever did was hurt mum and me. My real dad is at home, waiting for me, to hug me and love me, because he loves me Chloe, and he loves my mum, and he is good to her." Chloe gave a nod.

"Yeah, he is pretty fit too for his age." Birch giggled. Chloe looked at her and frowned.

"Don't look at me like that, there is not one of us who would not fuck his brains out." Baz gave a cough.

"Actually, I wouldn't." Birch gave a cackle of a laugh, and Deb's giggled. Birch looked at her.

"Will you guys be alright, I am going to take Deb's home, and then go and cuddle Deads." Chloe sniggered.

"You are so totally wet thinking about Bradley." Birch gave a chuckle.

"Says the girl who has been waiting all night for us to leave, so she can screw Baz in her van." Deb's started to laugh, as Birch slipped her arm around her shoulder, Chloe stared at them.

"SO?" They chuckled as they headed towards Petal, Chloe looked at Baz and smiled.

"So, how about it then?" He gave a smile.

"I have been waiting all night, come on girl, let's test the springs on that van." Chloe slid her arm round his waist.

"I love it when you talk my language."

Birch drove Deb's home, and sat with Bradley and explained what had happened, and how Izzy had picked him up on the CCTV a few times around the village. Jimmy was angry, he obviously knew the full story of Deb's. Bradley contacted his security, and told them to be extra vigilant, and finally Birch headed home, and found me sleeping on the bed.

She turned on the bath, and it started to fill, and she quietly got her things ready. I jerked awake, and saw her undressing by the wardrobe, she turned and noticed me watching her.

"Hi Sweetie, I am going to have a bath, are you joining me?"

I sat up, and stretched, and slid off the bed, and pulled my clothes off, and followed her into the bathroom. I slid down into the hot water and leaned back onto her, it felt so nice. Her arms came around me, and she leaned on my shoulder.

"Hmm, I needed this, I have missed you today, Sweetie." She kissed my shoulder softly.

Birch sat in the bath, and told me about Deb's dad, and how he had reacted, none of it surprised me at all. I had seen him in the past, I lifted her leg and washed it.

"Birch, sobering him up won't change anything, you miss the point, he has always been like that. It is not booze or drugs, he was that violent long before he started drinking."

"I don't like him Deads, you know, it might not show it, but he scares me a little." I leaned back, and looked up at her.

"That is a good instinct with him. I always stay out of arms reach with him. I once saw him just lash out, and he sent Deb's flying, just because she asked him to stop hitting her mum. Birch, he really terrifies me." She gave me a soft squeeze.

"It's okay Sweetie, Bradley is on to him, and if Jimmy and his boys get hold of him, he will need all the gods to help him. Jimmy was really angry tonight, it was so sweet the way he pulled her close, and she snuggled into him, and felt safe." I gave a slight smile.

"I do love that about him, he really does look out for her and protects her. You know, all the band can be a bit wild at times, but I do think they are really nice people. I like the way Baz quietly looks out for Chloe, I think he has really fallen for her, but understands her lifestyle." Birch chuckled.

"He is a brave man, Chloe is a really beautiful free spirit, but she will be hard to pin down. If I am honest, I admire how she has a vision of her life, and lives it thoroughly." I sat up and turned and looked at her.

"Birch, marrying me did not take your freedom away... Did it?" She smiled and her eyes twinkled.

"Sweetie, marrying you gave me my freedom back, I absolutely love being married to you." I did not really understand her.

"How so?" I slid around in the bath to face her; she gave a lovely smile.

"Deads, when you left, and I was alone, like you, I stopped living, and if I am honest, I woke up one day, and I was living at home, commuting to Manchester, and stuck in one place. I had lost all my spontaneity, lost my joy of being me, I was no longer Birch, I was Jemi. To be honest I was becoming a bit dull, my colour faded from my hair, I wore suits all day, and deep inside, I had an uncontrollable ache."

I really understood that, I had done pretty much the same, I nodded as I looked at her.

"I was blonde and boring, in sweats and dirty jeans, sad and lonely, hiding in the guest house, so I really understand that." She reached up and cupped my cheek.

"I came home to my heart, I blocked the street with Petal, and as soon as I put my arms around you, I felt the real me come rushing back. When I stood in your mums' kitchen, and she called me Birch, I wanted to cry for days, because that was when I truly knew I was me again. Just like at Sunny Bank, it was a place the real me belonged. Deads, this, us, this is our wild true selves, why do you think I asked you to marry me, this is supposed to be who we are?" I lifted my hand to hers.

"Good, you scared me then, I thought I was holding you back. Birch, I love my life with you, I really do, I know it does not always show, but honestly, I don't want to be anywhere else." She gave me a lovely smile, and her eyes twinkled.

"I know Sweetie, and I am really happy to hear it, oh Deads, we have so much living to do, and we will pack in a lot of crazy, but I promise, it won't be boring." I giggled.

"Oh God, it has never been boring." I started to laugh.

"Hell, we have had crazy after crazy." She sniggered, and suddenly, we were sat in the bath laughing like mental patients, and had no idea really why?

We headed into our room and dried our hair, and then got a drink and just chilled out on the bed talking, these were my absolute favourite times with Birch, this was when her quiet reflective side came out, and I found it so alluring.

I fancied toast, so we wandered down to the kitchen, and I grabbed the bread, as the toast popped, the front door banged.

"I AM HOME!"

"IN THE KITCHEN!" Deli came in looking exhausted, she dropped her bag, and flopped on the stool, and unbuttoned her blouse.

"God what a night." I put a coffee down in front of her, as Birch grabbed a slice of toast.

"Was it that busy, Monday is normally usually a pretty quiet one?" Deli shook her head.

"Some idiot broke into the Charity Shop, and triggered the alarm, we had police everywhere. They were all up the backs checking out the yards, in the restaurant, he legged it, and they chased him. They finally got him down near the nursery and arrested him, and dragged him up the road, honestly, it was mad for a while. I was going to check on Chloe, but then I remembered she was with Baz, I thought it was safer not to go looking." Birch gave a giggle.

"Yeah, the van will be rocking tonight. So, who did it?" She gave a shrug.

"Some guy from out of town, he was yelling and shouting all kinds of vile things, and then he just lost his shit, and tried beating the crap out of a couple of officers. They gave him a real pasting, and handcuffed him."

It was not a huge stretch to work out who, Birch was already there as I looked at her, she gave a nod.

"It is for the best Deads, he is better locked up, maybe they will put him in the program and clean him up?" Deli looked at us.

"Okay, so I am missing something, do either of you want to elaborate?" I picked up another slice of toast.

"There was a run in earlier with Deb's and her dad, he wanted money." She gave a nod, and lifted her cup.

"Well, if that was him, she won't be seeing him for a while, Sergeant Mondale, pasted the hell out of him, there was blood all over the path. To be honest, it turned my stomach, I do not like that level of violence, it sickens me." I lifted my phone.

"I best let Deb's know it could be her dad." I typed a message and hit send. Her response came back pretty quickly, I read the message.

"It is him, he gave her details, he is in Oxendale hospital, and is under arrest, apparently they really beat the hell out of him, but that is Mondale for you, he has always been a bully." Birch sipped her coffee.

"I will sleep better knowing he is not in the village, we have a big event to do, the last thing we need is a violent drunk causing Deb's pain."

I switched out the light, and the three of us headed upstairs, we said our goodnights to Deli, and headed into our room. I was tired, and I slid into bed, I lay back as Birch slipped under the duvet, she snuggled up with a sly grin on her face, I looked at her.

"What?"

She giggled, and I felt her warm hand move south, I smiled, and she gave a little squeal, and slid under the duvet to play, God I loved my life.

Tuesday was no better than Monday, Anthony had the morning off, and we all headed up to the show ground. Anthony and Michael were handling the floodlights, Chloe who looked tired, joined Deli, hanging orange bunting along the village street which had little Halloween pumpkins on, Henrietta scowled as she walked up the street.

"I never thought we would see the day when we would openly worship Satan and Witchcraft in this village, it's disgraceful." Chloe leaned off her ladder.

"It's alright Mrs D, you can still do it in secret, we won't tell."

Peter Saxon gave a snort and turned abruptly, and walked into the shop, Hatty who was leaning on the paper stand watching sniggered, Henrietta gave a loud 'Tut!' and stormed off to the Tea Rooms.

Down Oxendale Road came a long line of big trucks, Deli sent the text, and I hurried down from the gate and across the green. The first huge truck was filled with large metal frames, and covered in bright light bulbs as it came into the village. I waved from the green and he pulled up, his loud air brakes hissing. He wound down his window and leaned out, I gave him a big smile and pointed up towards the field.

"You need to go around the green, and up that street, then through the big gates onto the field. Marshals will be there to show you where you will be setting up." He leaned right out, and looked down.

"Okay miss nice tits." He gave a roaring laugh, I looked down, he could see right down my top, I looked up and smiled.

"Thanks, they are small, but they have all the right bits." He gave another laugh.

"They are pretty sexy, well, I like em." I giggled, as he leaned back into his cab, and the huge truck roared forward.

I stood back on the green, as truck after truck arrived, and followed the road round and up to the field. I ran across the road when I saw a gap, and walked up the pavement, people were stood watching and looking excited, even Mary was out viewing the scene, she gave me a smile as I walked up.

"I have to say Abby, you do not do things by halves, all this looks pretty impressive, we have never seen so many trucks." I watched as a folded up roundabout drove by.

"We want to show everyone what can be done with a little hard work, we are really hoping this benefits everyone in the village. It has been a lot of work, but if we pull it off, it will be the biggest thing this village has ever seen." She lifted her arm, and patted my shoulder.

"You are so like your mum, Abby, you worry too much. If what people are saying behind closed doors is right, Primula has not got a chance of winning; you were pretty much in the lead, the day you announced you were going to run." I gave a sigh.

"Prim has lied about us, and she has powerful friends Mary; I will not underestimate her." She chuckled.

"She does, there is no doubt, but you are forgetting Abby, they do not live in the village. Honestly, do you think people are so stupid they cannot see through her?"

Peter came out with a stand filled with horror masks and smiled.

"We have costumes and plastic pumpkins in the back, we will put on a good show for you Abby, we always support a good village event." It really made me smile.

"Thanks Mr Saxon, it means a lot to us." He walked over and stood at my side.

"Abby, we are all behind you, just look at the village, you are so busy, you have missed how excited everyone is." I followed his hand, and looked round.

Outside the Tea Rooms, Stacy and Louise were hanging ghostly bunting, and had large pumpkins on the window. The craft shop had a window filled with make your own Halloween mask kits, Amanda the florist, had little ghosts and pumpkins in all her flower arrangements, and a sign selling large pumpkins. The gallery had a haunted house window display, the salon had adverts for temporary orange and green hair, the deli had a huge inflatable ghost hanging above it, and even the dress shop, was offering high class Halloween costumes.

Deb's as always had gone mental, her shop looked like a horror palace, as Jimmy and Floyd worked up ladders attaching large spider webs, even the butcher had dressed his window in orange and green. Peter patted my shoulder.

"It took a few quiet words, and they all jumped at the chance to muck in and support you. Abby, it has not gone unnoticed how much you and Birch have done for this village, there are a lot of happy parents living here." It felt nice, and I felt a little emotional.

"I have only ever wanted to protect this place, I always wanted to be a council member that made a difference and kept this place beautiful. It's crazy, I was born here, but I feel like I have had to fight so hard just to be seen as one of you." Mary leaned in and gave me a slight hug.

"Abby, you are, and they all know it deep down, even Henrietta and her group know deep down, you have been raised right, and will always do everything you can to protect this place. You have a bright future here Abby, and I have to say, I really admire you." That surprised me, I looked at her.

"You do?" She gave a hearty chuckle.

"Oh Abby, you honestly have no idea, I mean, look at you. Abby, you are a young beautiful woman, who is a successful author, you are kind and caring and generous, you have a gorgeous wife, and you love your home, you are everything and more I expected of you, and a credit to your parents." I felt a tear well up in my eye.

"Mary, that really means so much to hear it." She smiled.

"Abby, I have watched you and your mother grow up, and honestly, you are the woman she should have been. Don't get me wrong, your dad is an honest man, but let's be honest, he ruined your mum and tamed her, but not you. Even you were too strong for him to break, that takes courage and stamina, and folk's notice."

I smiled, I always thought people could not see it. It never surprises me living here, there is always some revelation that just makes you sit up and take notice. All these years I felt isolated and hid from the village, and all along they knew. That is the problem with villages, there are no secrets, and the gossip network, is the one thing faster than email. Village life is not for the faint of heart, no matter what you do or how hard you try, you can never really hide.

Chapter 32

Fears and Frights.

It was a long week of organisation, and we still had a week to go. It was Friday night, and the fairground was set up and was doing tests, as we all gathered for the big village meeting in the Church Hall. This was to be the big pre vote evening before everyone submitted their postal votes for leaders of the council. Around all of the walls were parts of a new display to be built once we left, and even the hall would host it's own special Halloween feature.

We all sat at the back, in a long line, even Mark and Sally, who now worked at the Post Office joined us full of smiles, oh how our little rebellious band has grown. As we were surrounded by the youth of Wotton, even members of Deli's dance troop who lived in the village sat with us, and what was once a row of just the five of us, was now a full seven rows from the back.

Prim was wearing a huge rosette, and surrounded by a group of about twenty, all wearing smaller rosettes, and she was still handing out leaflets and hunting last minute votes. The place was packed as the Committee walked up to their seats on the stage, and the meeting began. Primula walked up first to give her speech; Birch giggled.

"Christ she is ugly, she should wear that rosette on her face and spare us all." We all started to giggle.

She began with her pitch on how parts of the village were looking shabby, and needed to be upgraded, and how the canal although pleasant was in need of some tidying up. Her list was growing longer, from painting lamp posts, new road signs, new markings on the station carpark, better paper bins, and a new contract with the Oxendale Horticultural and Parks department to supply good quality plants. She then began the bit I wanted to know about, she looked out at everyone, God, she had a face like a smacked baby. Molly stood at her side looking useless, like she had no chance of speaking.

"After recent events, the developers involved with the Dursley Woods Project have pulled out, and it has been suggested that the woods are to be given a park status, and so I intend to pursue that avenue as Chair of this council. I feel improvements need to be made, that will enhance the beauty of the woodland, and I hope the village will support such a motion when presented." Deb's gave a nod.

"Excellent dodge, I have to admit, that was a smooth about turn." I smirked; I was aware there were eyes on me. Chloe looked at her.

"Smoother than your vagina?" Deb's giggled.

"Hell, not that smooth, I would let you stroke it, but you are oh so straight." Birch and myself started to giggle, Chloe shrugged.

"Fuck, that is smooth." Deli burst into fits of giggles. Primula finally brought her speech to an end.

"I look forward to the vote, and just know you will all see sense and vote in a traditional member with a traditional and trustworthy lifestyle." She just could not resist that last dig, she looked at me and smirked, I smiled back. My mum walked up to the mic as villagers gave a weak applause to Prim leaving the stage.

"Would the candidates Mrs and Mrs Dixon, please present their final comments to the village residents."

Dressed in suits with pony tails, and looking as business like as possible we got up and walked towards the stage, Primula scowled at us, Birch gave a sweet smile as she passed, Nigel smirked. We walked onto the stage, up to the mic, and faced the audience. I smiled at the side of Birch, and took a deep breath.

"Ladies and gentlemen of the village, may we begin tonight by recognising two of the most dedicated members of our council's history, because it should be recognised. Would Mrs Marjorie Wallace, and Mrs Felicity Watson, like to come up and stand with us?"

Marjorie and Mum looked completely surprised; Marjorie got out of her seat as there was utter silence in the room, she walked up to the stage, looking very wary, mum got up, looking as equally wrong footed. They both came to the front; I looked out and smiled.

"Ladies and Gentleman, I am twenty nine years old, and for my entire life, these two amazing woman have served this community with a level of dedication, I would hope I can emulate. They are the unsung heroes of this village who have dedicated endless amounts of their time to all of us, and served us in a faultless manner."

Amanda the florist walked onto the side of the stage with her assistant, and handed them two large bunches of flowers, both of them looked so surprised, and shocked, I leaned into the mic.

"Tonight ladies, as a village, we would like to show our appreciation and heartfelt thanks."

I stood back and started to clap with Birch, and the whole village stood on their feet, and gave a deafening applause. It was sort of funny, I completely turned the tables on them, as they both stood looking overwhelmed holding their flowers, and smiling, as the villagers showed them the upmost gratitude. It was actually really nice to see.

All the rest of the committee stood smiling behind the table, at the back there were whistles and screams, it was really lovely to see it, as both of them wiped their eyes, and nodded accepting the thanks of the community they had served.

They returned to their seats after a very long applause, and I smiled at the village.

"Thank you, all of you for that, they truly deserve such a wonderful show of gratitude." Prim had a really angry look on her face. I looked back out into the mass gathering.

"We have stated our case twice now, and you all know where we stand on our views. We have stood with most of you in the last month, and taken note of everything you have said to us. We would like to add, that we personally agree with the new direction that Mrs Primula Wallace has offered, although it is shame this village had to deal with such a despicable business proposal to begin with. If we do get elected, we will take on board her suggestion, and invite her and Molly, to join in and campaign to make Dursley Woodland a designated parkland. We would also add, that we will ensure that every tree, also has a full preservation status, to ensure no developer ever try to use a backdoor tactic again, to overrule this village, and destroy the woodland for real estate." Birch stepped up to the mic.

"We are still available for discussions, should any of you be unsure as to how to vote, and as untraditional as we are, we do recognise long standing traditions, and aim to uphold those of this village, although some traditions, such as domestic abuse, should not be tolerated. Thank you all for your time."

The applause was deafening, and there was some sniggering, as we turned and walked from the stage, we came down the steps, and Prim looked purple she was so angry, Hatty watched with a smile, as people shook our hands.

"You know Flick, I am going to love working with those two." Flick looked at her with a worried look.

"You have no idea how much it terrifies me that you three will be together in the heart of village life." Edwina gave a snort, and put her head down.

The meeting continued with all committee business, and finally towards the end Mum stood up and announced a final presentation, by the representatives of Curio Carnival Wotton, to a resounding applause. Birch and myself stood up, and were joined by Deb's and Anita who had arrived a little late, and walked back to the stage, the four of us gathered as a group, and once again I smiled, I was actually very excited. I took a deep breath.

"Residents of Wotton, I am sure all of you have seen the many preparations going on in the village. I must admit tonight, as we hear the thump, thump, of the music in the background, you are all aware the fairground is doing all its safety checks in preparations for tomorrow. We have a lot to get through tonight, so firstly, I would love to tell you all of how proud we are to see the village embracing this event. To every shop owner, we take our hats off to you all, and thank you warmly, the shops are looking fantastically ghoulish and delightful, and we are so happy to see it. So, what is going to happen, we will start firstly with publicity, and Miss Anita Dickinson." I stepped back and Anita stepped forward, she smiled.

"We have done a lot of publicity for this event, and even though this is technically a Curio Live event, this village is already seeing the benefit. There is a massive amount of publicity on the websites of Curio Life, Abigail's author site, Sweeties Retreat, Waterside Galleries, Wheeler and Cogs, D&D, and also the village website. Local press has ads, and we have ten thousand posters all over the place. We have saturated the coverage for it, and we are hoping the next week is going to be a very busy one, especially for our village traders. Please help, if you are on social media, share the hell out of it and keep the word going, because there are already benefits, as we look into new more modern approaches for promoting this village." There were some impressed and happy faces, as Birch stepped up to the mic.

"Ladies and gentlemen, we have had a lot of questions about costs, and I will not deny, they are high, but this is a D&D event, designed to promote this village, so rest assured, no cost will fall on this council, or this village. I would like to start by firstly thanking the sponsors, because we have had some people approach us to aide funding, which again is a more modern way of raising capital. So, we would like to publicly thank Oxendale High and Arts college, who did a crowd funding online, and raised an amazing twenty five thousand pounds to contribute to this event. They have also given up their weekends to distribute posters to all of the shops across the whole of the Oxendale region." There were gasps all around the hall, Birch smiled.

"The event has also received sponsorship, of one hundred thousand pounds in a joint donation from Wheeler Developments and the Dixon Group, to cover the costs of free entry into the circus, and the fair rides, no one will pay a penny for this entertainment. I would like to also publicly thank, Wotton Drama Group, who have sponsored us by donating their time and energy to the final night, as they will be involved in the final presentation. Local support has been outstanding, and we are so proud to be part of this village tonight." She took a breath.

"So, as we currently stand, before our weeklong entertainment begins, I am so relieved to say, that currently, this village, which will earn a percentage of the profits, as the rest will go towards Curio Live. Currently this village has a donation of eight thousand pounds due to its coffers after the event finishes. Please help promote it all week, and hope we can grow that donation even larger. Thank you, all of you for standing with us with your support."

It was funny to see how the mention of money coming in started an onslaught of quiet conversations. Debbie stepped up to the mic, and gave her usual big bright smile.

"I am really happy to be organising the carnival parade, which will start at 4pm, on Waterside Lane, and move slowly into the village, travel up Church Rise, down Green Street, on to the high street, and then go back up Church Rise, past the church and complete the circuit on the show field. We have had a lot of people approach us, and so we will feature the lead Curio Live Float, The Oxendale Junior school, Oxendale High School, and the Art College. We also have floats from the Army cadets and Air Cadets, as well as a Sweeties Retreat float. The Scouts, Girl Guides, and Brownies, and I am really happy to see that there will also be a Taco treat float, provided by the rock band Battered Taco, so get all your kids up front, because there will be lots of treats, and knowing them, a few tricks." The audience giggled; Deb's smiled at Jimmy sat at the back.

"The parade will also include, Brass bands, Morris Dancers, Oxendale Line Dancers, Majorettes and a few others, it should be bright, happy, and a lot of fun, so please, get all the kids out front and line the pavement along the route. Cheer and take pictures, and have a really fun time, because at the end of the day, that is what this is all about, having a wonderful traditional family village day." I stepped up and smiled.

"It is a packed program. Okay, the circus and fair will open tomorrow at one o'clock, and run every day until the following Saturday, which will be the final day. We have traders arriving all week, and there will be a lot of fun stuff on the show field, but remember our shops and stores. This is an event for their benefit, and it is vastly important revenue for them. As you know, the carnival parade will begin at four pm on October 27th, so mark it down on your diaries, and invite everyone you know, especially for the finale, which will take place at seven pm on Saturday October 27th, and trust me, it will be out of this world. We have an amazing show for you, so wrap up warm, and surround the green, and enjoy what should be one of the most spectacular nights of entertainment this village has ever seen. We will be recording and live streaming it from the D&D and Curio website, so if you have friends who live too far away, let them know." Birch stepped back up.

"Don't forget, during the parade on Saturday, we will also be having a fancy dress competition, so get your kids dressed up, as there will be cash prizes, and adults, act like kids and get dressed up too, because there will be a cash prize of one hundred pounds to the best male and female costume. And finally, Miss Chloe Pemberton and Mrs Daisy Merryweather will be running a pumpkin carving workshop, on Wednesday and Thursday, at eleven in the morning on the village green, which has been sponsored by Merryweather Organics. We want to thank them for providing another free event, so bring down the kids and let them make your pumpkins to light us through the darker hours. Don't forget the circus and fair are free, so go see them as many times as you want. Thank you once again for supporting us, and enjoy this wonderful week to come."

She stepped back and suddenly everyone was on their feet applauding, it was so nice to see, as all of us stood smiling, we were almost there, I looked at Birch, as she giggled, her eyes bright and happy.

"Whose idea was this?" Deb's sniggered.

"Massive event, impossible odds of pulling it off, in a village that hates us, there is only one person I know barmy enough to even suggest that." Anita laughed, as Birch smiled.

"I love Halloween Sweetie, I wanted to do it for some fun."

We left the stage, and suddenly people were thanking us, I don't think I have ever spoken to half of them, we all smiled and told people to have fun and enjoy themselves, and it was nice to see it. I was glad it was just a week away, I was feeling the strain a little, but with a vote just two weeks away, I felt I had done everything I could, and I was fine with that, if I lost, it would not be from lack of effort.

It took forever for the hall to empty, I was pleased to see Tabby and Eric were waiting, as we walked out onto the cool street, it was Friday night which meant only one thing, Birch turned and looked at the group surrounding us.

"It's Friday night, Uni rules apply, so let's head home, and party like we have never partied before." It was greeted with delight, and wild cheers, and a convoy of cars.

I woke Saturday, face down between Birch's legs, I blinked and looked up, and stared right into her freshly shaved lady parts, and smiled, God, what a night, although, I did feel like death.

"Birch, we have to get up."

She groaned lay flat on her back, her legs wide open, she tried to move, and gave a sigh and flopped back.

"Birch, Baby I am dying, but we have to be up and on the field today." She groaned again but did not move, I gave a wicked grin, and inched forward.

"Hmm breakfast." I started to softly kiss her; she gave another little moan.

"Sweetie, I am tired." I pushed out my tongue and wiggled it, she giggled.

"Oh Sweetie, you dark little beastie, you almost broke me last night." I ran my tongue up her to her little button, and gave it a wiggle, she giggled.

"Oh God Sweetie, I am a slave to my lust of you." I love making her happy, and I started to move all around her, she gave a long happy moan.

"Oh God Deads, YES!"

Floyd sat up at the side of the bed and made me jump.

"What the hell Floyd, you scared the shit out of me." He blinked.

"Sorry... Fuck, yeah carry on, I am good." He pointed, and I leaned over the side of the bed, to see Gail's head bobbing, he smiled and lay back down. I giggled.

"There is nothing like a good session or oral, to wake up by." Birch looked up and frowned.

"Sweetie, don't stop now."

I flopped down between her legs, and she gave another happy moan. Is it weird that watching our local vicar give a rock musician a blow job, turned me on a little? I slid up my hand, and as I worked Birch's little happily growing button, I slid in a finger, and she gave a wild gasp.

"OH GOD YES!"

Little moans and slurps came from below the bed. It was weird, but holy hell I was so turned on, and sped up, and Birch groaned, and her back arched, Gail suddenly appeared, Floyd was obviously ready, I watched as she slid on, and started to writhe on top of him, Birch turned and watched and gave a wail of pleasure. I was getting really excited, and worked even faster, Gail was really riding Floyd hard, and I cannot deny, I never noticed before, but she had great boobs.

I worked faster on Birch keeping pace with Gail, Floyd started to moan, and Birch joined in, and I felt a huge jolt of excitement inside of me, as I got faster with my fingers and tongue.

Eric sat with Deli, Chloe, and Deb's, she had stayed over, and Jimmy and Jenny were still sleeping. They all sat having coffee, and breakfast, there was a squealing wail through the floor, Deb's looked up.

"Who was that?" Chloe looked up, and frowned.

"It sounds like Gail; you know how noisy she is when she shags." Deb's gasped.

"Are Birch and Abby having sex with the vicar?" Edwina laughed.

"Wow, disappointed much Deb's? It's not what you think, Gail and Floyd crashed in their room last night." Deb's looked relieved, and Chloe sniggered.

"Wow, you are screwed up Deb's, for a moment I could almost smell your disappointment." Birch gave a howling orgasmic wail, everyone looked up, Edwina shook her head.

"She spent thousands sound proofing the house, and never once thought of sound proofing the fucking floor."

Birch lay back and gasped for breath, Floyd moaned and then gave a loud grunt.

"Oh Fuck Gail, I think I love you."

I froze, and stared at Gail, Birch was having trouble lifting her head, she glanced down at me, Gail smiled a happy smile.

"Floyd darling, you will never find another vicar who screws like me."

I cannot deny watching her got me really hot and bothered, I had to agree, she was bloody good at her administering of her flock. Birch sniggered and lay back.

"Oh Christ, a guitarist and a Bell Twat, Sundays are just going to get louder and bloody louder." Gail giggled, and she rolled off and collapsed on the floor.

"We were loud when we did it on the altar." I sat up.

"Holy frig Gail." Birch giggled.

"Pretty much." Gail lay back on the floor red in the face, and panting.

"Why not, the lord created us all to have joy?" I stared at her.

"But it was the altar, I mean, holy shit, it's sacred." Floyd lay back and breathed hard.

"It bloody is now, I have never known a woman cum so hard." Birch sat up looking excited.

"I want to do it on an altar, I have done it on a grave, and in my own church, but oh God, a church, oh Sweetie, take me to church. Bend me over the pulpit, and let me preach." Gail laughed.

"Not sure the parishioners would appreciate that on Sunday, although we have not done that either, it does sound fun." Birch nodded.

"I suppose if you are going to shout oh God during a climax, that would be the best place?"

Gail laughed. "Trust you to think of that."

Having had copious amounts of coffee, we made our way on site, to check all was well. It was dry and crisp, and everything appeared fine, the gates were open, and locked back, and we unlocked the shed, and prepared for the day, taking it in shifts. All of us wore Marshal jackets.

This was the first official day of a week of festivities, traders arrived and set up, my head was still banging, even though I had taken pain killers, and we walked around throughout the whole day smiling and welcoming people, and handing them flyers for the big event next Saturday. Mum and Hatty joined in, and I noticed Milton arrive with Nigel for the circus, he appeared very excited, I mean, his teeth were moving, so I presumed so.

The shed was a great idea, and in between shifts, we messed about outside the shed, and had access to plenty of hot coffee, yeah, there were a lot of trips to the porta loos too. The biggest advantage we had, was due to a deal Birch did for Deb's wedding, the field had been expertly levelled and land drains fitted, so even if it did rain, the water drained away pretty fast. Every year gravel had been added, and the car parking area was now almost pure gravel. The funniest thing by far was the announcements over the personal address system, as Birch loved it, and would grab the mic and it would buzz then announce.

"Sweeties, the circus will be starting soon, I love the circus, so come on, and enjoy it." Or "Please be Sweeties, and use the gravelled area for car parking, and be nice to each other, and space your cars appropriately."

I giggled every time I heard her, but the crazy thing was, the visitors loved it. She would stand at the gates, with her big bright happy eyes, in her yellow neon vest, with her long white hair lifting in the breeze, and wave to all the kids, and lead them to the circus tent, like the pied piper of Wotton.

The nicest thing of all, is how many happy smiling faces you see doing events like this. Children get excited, and point with wonder at the bright lights, and the many rides of excitement. Parents light up when they see the joy in their children, and I recognise this in my own life with Birch.

The crazy thing about Birch, is she is super intelligent, and a multi millionaire, and she is highly educated. All these things tick all the boxes of society, but the real Birch, the Birch I live with is so different from those first perceptions. The truth is, she has no interest in money or status, she is happy with the simplest of things, such as four years ago, I stitched her a bookmark, and it is one of her most treasured possessions.

She can talk on any level, and she can be loud and filled with excitement and happy, to the point where it is so infectious, you become as happy as her for no reason. She also has a quiet, deep reflective side, where her conversations are well thought out and rational. But the side I love the most, is when the simplest of things, be it a gift or a gesture, or an old memory, bring out a strong childlike quality in her, and she sees the wonder of something as simple and as beautiful as a flower.

Throw a circus and a fairground on a field, and she is as bad as all the small kids, she is wild about carousels and candy floss, and loves toffee apples, and will squeal with delight if she sees a big slide. She will grab a rug and hurry to the top, and slide down squealing with joy. Birch will take the most joy in everything she can, she lives for the moments, and regrets nothing, and always has a bright happy smile and sparkling eyes. Walking around the field with her, has been one of the most enjoyable days of my life.

I was happy to head home for a good meal, and a bath, and I did feel a little tired, it had been a long day, but there were donations in the money buckets, and that was all that really mattered, making those extra funds for Curio Life.

Anita and Tabby, arrived with cases, they would be staying with us for the whole week to muck in, and they were added to the rota of staff on hand. The kitchen was noisy as we all mucked in and made a meal, Jimmy and some of G5 were on security detail on site, as the fair ran until ten at night. The guys decided it was safer to have men on view, as it acted as a deterrent to anyone who could cause a problem.

We sat in the living room, and all ate together with plates on our knees, and then as a group, we mucked in, and washed everything up. The greatest thing about Tabby, is because she came to Sunny Bank, she knows our routine, and so just joins in with us all, and by seven I was feeling exhausted. I ran a hot bath, and slid in with Birch, as we quietly talked, and then once we had dried our hair, we slid into bed and she curled into me, and before I knew it, I was flat out in a deep sleep.

Sunday was pretty much the same, apart from the fact that firstly, Birch had her noise cancelling ear phones with bees and flowers, to avoid the Bell Twats, and we also left Edwina and Luke to sleep in. Not only had they covered their shifts, they had also been up late every night in the village, running simulations and tests on all the equipment. After all, Edwina had the biggest pressure on her shoulders, as she was the one running the light show.

The day ran smooth, there were a few hitches, but we problem solved as we went. The biggest of which was Birch, who kept sloping off to the carousel, where she would go round on a unicorn with a huge smile, throwing her legs in the air, and shouting 'WHEEE! at the top of her voice, which meant every kid copied her. It was really funny to see, and honestly, with her long white hair with black patches, flowing behind her, and those green eyes sparkling like emeralds, all I could do was giggle as I watched her.

The day felt longer, and as we moved into Monday, it all began to blur, as traders packed up and moved on to other events, and new traders arrived, and we all lived on our phones.

Two years ago, when Edwina took on her role with the Parish

Council, one of her first jobs was to introduce free Wi-Fi in the village, most of the shops had a password displayed in their windows for it. In order to do it well, G5 installed a mast on the Church Hall roof, and because this was Edwina, she also added a secure private network as well, which meant we all had internet capabilities no matter where we were in the main village area, including the show field.

Most of us spent our week sat at the table in between security shifts, either talking on phones, or answering emails, and doing live updates to the Curio social media. We did a couple of live streams to Curio Life, and talked about the event and answered questions, and in doing so, Edwina got to test out the stream to ensure all was well for the big night. Deli went off for her last major rehearsals with the dancers, and I worked with Birch and Luke, on the last part of the set up. On the night, we needed the green to be hidden from sight as we set up, and so, we attached two tall four by four beams, to the posts of the Wotton notice board at the bottom of the green using steel straps.

On the top we mounted large metal brackets, on which we fitted a steel wire, that ran all the way back up the green, to two other posts, steel strapped to the lampposts on the top ends of the green. Using shower curtain rings, we managed to hang large black cloths, which hung down to the floor, creating the longest, tallest curtains I have ever sown. With a winch in the marquee, we had set up for the pumpkin carving, we could hit a button, and finer steel wires running through pullies, would pull open the curtains to reveal the green.

Creating the hidden space, gave us a little more time on the night to set up as soon as the carnival parade had passed by. The detail and lengths we were going to, was insane, but we all knew, it had to be perfect on the night.

Wednesday and Thursday, were bonkers, Chloe and Daisy aided by Hatty, mum, Bradly and Jimmy, were chaos. We had the make and carve your own pumpkin workshops, and they were packed. Chloe being Chloe got all the parents involved as well, and there was laughter and screams, and over two hundred pumpkins were created. We all dived in at some point, Bradley was excellent at cleaning them out, and even Tom Jessop from the Craft shop appeared to help, he had not been seen that much since his conviction for weed growing.

All spare carved pumpkins, were distributed around the village green edge, or left lit outside the shops in the darkness, to be honest it looked great after dark walking through the village. Friday arrived and we were all in high gear running on nervous energy. Oxendale High and Arts College, had spent the week working on a haunted maze in the church hall, and it opened to the public, as students ran around the village encouraging people to come and try it. I could not resist, and grabbed Birch.

"Come on we have to support them." She shook her head and bit her lip.

"Sweetie, I don't like it." I shrugged.

"How do you know, have you been in it?" She looked freaked out.

"I saw them take skeletons in." I giggled.

"Birch, they were plastic; they are not real." She looked scared, so I took her arm, she panicked, and I laughed.

"Birch my books are filled with devils and ghosts and skeletons, but you love them, this is no different." She shook her head.

"I close the book, and have a lie down when I get to those bits." Chloe sniggered.

"Some fucking doctor you turned out to be." We walked slowly towards the door; Deb's came out at a fast pace.

"Nope, nope, nope, nope." She saw us and pointed behind her.

"There is a frigging huge spider in there." Chloe gripped her arm.

"Deb's, this is a Curio sponsored event, as Curio's we are obligated to visit every attraction, look at Birch, she is terrified of skeletons, but she is going in." Deb's nodded and gave a sigh.

"You are right Chloe, when eight Skeletons ran out of the wall and grabbed me, I must admit, I shit myself." Birch's head snapped around.

"WHAT?" She turned to me, and gripped my arm, looking utterly terrified.

"Sweetie, go tell them to hide until I am through, I don't want skeletons running out of walls."

She tried to pull free, but I was hanging on to her arm at all costs, she started to whimper as I dragged her inside, and she clamped onto my arm with both hands, and I swear I could hear her teeth chattering in the dark.

Young children were not allowed, and I realised very soon why, it was really dark. Small dim lights lit up what looked like old mansion walls. There were pictures of hideous looking people, and as we walked past, their eyes followed us, it was very creepy, but realistic, and my stomach gave a slight churn.

At the bottom of the first corridor, was a small round gothic mirror, we stood and looked at it, Deb's turned and frowned.

"What was that?" Chloe snapped round on her.

"Shut the fuck up Deb's, it's creepy enough without your bat hearing."

"Oh... Chl... oe?" She froze and looked at me, her face was going white.

"Oh Fuck, I heard it too... I fucking hate you Deb's." A distant ethereal voice whispered.

"Chloe?"

I must admit, even I was a little freaked out. In the mirror right in front of us, a white misty face appeared, Chloe froze on the spot, it spoke.

"Chloe, I am here with you, come to me." Birch was shaking and her teeth were getting louder. Chloe swallowed hard, as she leaned forward, her voice trembled.

"Who are you, this is just a trick, right?"

"I have been waiting Chloe, you owe me a picture."

Okay so now even I was starting to freak out, Birch was shaking like hell, and Deb's had taken three steps back, Chloe swallowed hard.

"Who are you, and why do I owe you a picture?" The face in the mirror faded, and then came rapidly back into focus.

"Chloe, why do you not recognise me? I am... GWENDA!"

Chloe screamed, Deb's screamed, Birch screamed, as the picture shouted, I jumped out of my skin, and Chloe crashed back on the floor, in terror. The mirror opened out and Edwina's head came through the hole in the wall, and she was pissing her sides laughing, she held up the microphone.

"Chloe, you pussy."

Chloe lay back gasping for air, I tried not to, honestly, but I was laughing my ass off, Chloe looked up.

"I fucking hate you Edwina, I shit myself then, I thought she had escaped from the house."

Edwina grabbed the latch laughing her ass off, and pulled the mirror shut, and we were back in the darkness.

I could not help it, I had fits of giggles, as we walked around a corner and passed more creepy pictures, and walked further down, when Deb's suddenly stopped.

"I don't like this bit." Birch looked around with big eyes. I looked at her.

"Birch, can you not just clench your teeth tight, you sound like a group of drunken tap dancers?" She shook her head.

"Sweetie, I am frightened." I patted her arm.

"You are safe with me baby, so don't worry."

A hand came out of the wall, and touched my face, and it was cold and very clammy. I shit you not, my scream was the freaking loudest Wotton has ever heard, it was so loud, it would rival the shredders laugh, and crack concrete.

Birch was hysterical as she laughed her ass off, Chloe looked shocked, and Deb's stuck her finger in her ear and wiggled it.

"Holy shit Abby, I am deaf in one ear."

My heart was pounding, three steps shy of cardiac arrest, and I was breathing very rapidly, and faster than Chloe approaching Birch's vagina. I walked away from that spot as quickly as I could, and turned the next corner, with my heart hammering in my chest. I walked right into a huge spider web, which stuck to my face. Deb's realising we were moving, hurried round the corner, into the web and squealed with terror.

I pointed up, and she lifted her head, and saw the ceiling was covered in spiders running all over the place.

Honestly, I thought she was going to faint, her scream almost rivalled mine... The web swung back, and we moved through. Deb's legged it, and shot around the next corner, so we hurried to catch her. We came around the corner and Deb's was stood still, we were in a corridor of wardrobes, and it appeared to be a dead end, just a dozen wardrobes, she looked at us.

"How do we get out?" Birch gave a sigh.

"Sweetie, I thought you had read Narnia?"

She opened a door, and a skeleton lifted its hand and touched her, she screamed the wildest, most blood curdling scream I have ever heard, I am sure her hair went rigid and horizontal. She slammed the door, and moved to the next one, and screamed again as she opened it, she turned and opened the next one, and gave another loud scream.

I was on my knees laughing so hard, I thought I would yerk. She screamed again, I shook my head, Chloe was pissing her sides laughing, so was Deb's. I took a breath.

"Birch, stop opening the bloody doors, you daft bitch."

She disappeared, as I looked up, I staggered to my feet still laughing and wiped my eyes. I walked towards the door she had gone through, and opened it, on the other side was a long courtyard, Birch was on her knees shaking, I crouched at her side.

"Are you alright?" She had tears in her eyes, and I felt a little guilty.

"Sweetie, I don't like this; I want to get out." I helped her up, and pulled her into a hug.

"Okay, come on, it cannot be much bigger, we must be almost out."

At the end of the court yard a young student in a big baggy hoody, was working on a mannequin, which was lay under a guillotine, he looked at us as we walked up.

"I won't be a second, we are having a slight technical difficulty." I gave a nod as he lifted the head under the line of the blade.

The blade dropped, he pulled his head back, and I saw his hands come clean off, he screamed and stood up with two bloody stumps, and honestly, how I did not piss on the spot amazed me. We all screamed in complete terror, my legs went weak, and I honestly thought I was going to faint. All of us shook from head to foot.

He started to laugh, and his hands popped out of his sleeves, to show us two fake bloody stumps. I gripped my heart, Christ, that was scary. Birch danced on the spot and clapped, her eyes big and bright.

"That was wonderful Sweetie." Deb's looked at her with a white face.

"Hell, you are seriously messed up, and weird as hell."

Behind him was a gate, that led through the side door, we

staggered through, our hearts still racing, and we were back in the light. I breathed in the fresh air, Birch, snuggled into my arm.

"Sweetie, that was fun."

I stared at her big bright eyes, set in her happy face, at an absolute loss for words. You know, I am convinced she is not quite right in the head.

Chapter 33

Carnival Parade.

The big day finally arrived, and all of us were nervous. We got up early, and as we had breakfast, Chloe face painted us with day of the dead faces, and we all were dressed in black skeleton suits, which thankfully were two pieces. The thought of going to the loo, and having to strip out of a one piece in the cold porta loos, was just too much, so we had gone for a top and bottoms.

It was going to be cold, so we slipped our pants and thick tops over them. The tops had been specially printed, and had the Curio Live logo on the front, and the Carnival on the back of them. Birch was a little freaked out, and refused to kiss me, but with her long black patched snow white hair, she looked amazing, but refused to look at anything reflective, for fear of seeing herself as a skeleton. Edwina took our picture as we were done, against a black sheet in Chloe's studio, these would be added to the Curio Live float.

We had black lipstick, which I hated, as it made everything taste funny. Once we were finished with our faces, we set off into the village, and slipped on our marshal jackets, and began the day of ensuring everything was running smoothly. In the village, it was still early, but everyone was out setting up, and restocking all their stands. I walked up Church Rise, Gail was on the gate with Floyd, she smiled at me.

"Abby, you look amazing." I gave a giggle.

"Tell that to Birch, she is terrified of skeletons, and has refused to kiss me." She looked down the village.

"You guys have done something wonderful. You all look exhausted." I shrugged.

"We have done the best we can, it has been hard work, but if we pull off today, it will be worth it." She nodded at me, and smiled.

"You are a special group, and the future, I knew that when I first came here. Without your support Abby, I never would have survived here, and if they do not vote you in, it will be the biggest mistake this village has ever made." It was nice to hear it.

"Thanks Gail, that actually means a lot." She patted my shoulder.

"I am with you all the way, if you need help at any point today, shout out."

The gates to the field were open, and the shed was unlocked, G5 were placing orange cones all along the streets to stop cars parking and to keep the pavements clear. Today we had a lot of extra marshals, which would really help. The Marquee was open, and face painters were getting ready. Some areas had black cloths draped over them to hide props, the front flaps were opened, and we were ready for action.

The Wotton Drama Society, were getting ready as they dressed in costumes, and gathered the collection buckets. I was happy, and returned to the shed, where on the table, a line of radios were ready and charged. Michael had rigged us a temporary power line from the Church Hall. Being us, we took advantage, and brought the toaster we had gotten as a wedding present, it was spare, so was donated to the cause.

On the green, there was now a grave yard, with headstones sticking up out of the grass, it actually looked really creepy, even in the day light. Each grave had a stone surround, and a printed cloth to create soil, it looked really cool, and it had been a lot of fun carving strange names into them, before Chloe and Hatty, used their paints to age them. The Dramatic society loved them, so we told them they could have them after the event.

Today the Curio's would be high profile, as Alex, Meg and Eric and his Alpha team helped marshal the show field, for which they all got a free Curio Live sweat shirt, which they were thrilled about, because these also had, the Curio Carnival logo on the back, and were very limited edition.

Around ten o'clock, we were ready, and walked down Church Rise, in our Curio live tops, and carried large black bags on our shoulders, and we began our day, as we walked around the green, handing out sweets to all the arriving children. It was actually loads of fun, and the kids at first would jump back, and then we would open our bags, and pull out hands full of sweets, and they would smile, and hold up their bags or buckets, for us to drop them in.

Peter Saxon was very grateful, he had hundreds of pumpkin shaped buckets, and he was selling them fast, as the kids needed more carrying capacity. Curio fans appeared dressed up, which we loved, and we posed for pictures with them, and signed autographs, and the village was packed to capacity.

Tabby joined Hatty, with instant shot cameras, and they took pictures of the kids and their parents for the Halloween competition, they were going to judge it later with mum and Ellen.

Phillip Morrison had his huge burger stand in the gap between the Hunters and the houses, which Prim had wanted for a playground. The Deli had a marquee up, and were making salad and fresh hot meat sandwiches, as well as kebabs, and the Tea Rooms had extra tables, although the road had to stay open for the parade, but we helped set up extra tables along both sides of the pavement, that ran right up the front of the Church Hall. They had extra capacity, and a ring side seat for the parade, and Lillian and Celia looked great dressed as witches. Wotton was looking magnificent, and better than anything. Roni and Will had come down and brought Bev, she bounced up to me, and gave me a huge hug. She stood back.

"What do you think, it's mint in it? I am quashed his mojo."

I giggled, she had drawn an extra eye above her left one, and was trying to keep her left eye shut, she gave me a twirl.

"Me tits are bigger than me hump, I think I am more of a hunched front." She gave a loud laugh; she really was adorable. Roni and Will hugged us.

"The village looks amazing, I cannot wait for the finale, just from the little I have heard, it will be spectacular." Birch looked anxious.

"I hope so mum, just for Edwina's sake, she has killed herself for this." Roni smiled.

"I think you all have, and I must say, it was a huge feat, but you appear to have pulled it off. I mean, honestly Jemi, who has a circus and a fair?" I chuckled.

"Apparently, we do." Will gave a laugh.

I suppose we are completely bonkers, I mean, talk about setting impossible goals, but looking at the village, there were ghosts, ghouls, monsters, super heroes, witches and wizards walking around, all smiling and having fun, and a constant stream of cars up to the field. It was a lot busier than the Summer Fete, and it was good to see all the shops were full, at a time of year when they usually had few customers.

The Drama Society looked great, and all of them were filling up their donation buckets, and that really was all that mattered to us, funding other centres and organisations.

The day moved on, and we were at full tilt running around making people laugh, directing visitors to all the traders and attractions, never in my life had I walked or talked so much in one day.

I took a break as the afternoon wore on, and I stood at the top of the green next to the marquee filled with happy adults and kids, all getting face painted, just watching my home filled with happy people, when Marjorie walked up to my side and stood next to me.

"This is impressive Abigail, I have watched you all, and you have worked very hard indeed, and I am very impressed. This is the most tourists I have ever seen in this village. I commend you and your doctor." I turned to her.

"Coming from you, that is the greatest compliment I have ever had, thank you." She gave a grisly smile.

"Your campaign, commitment, and endurance have impressed me a great deal. Personally, I feel you should be the next chair, you have fought hard to prove your worth. You don't just deserve it, you have earned it, and my respect." Okay, so I was completely mind blown.

"We have always wanted to protect this village and keep it as it is, we never wanted to spoil or damage it, we love this place as much as you do, and I mean what I say. I will keep your traditions alive, I love my home village Madge, we all do." She gave a nod.

"I see that now, you know the thing I admire the most, is neither of you can be bought off, unlike certain young ladies I know. It is a fine quality, your mother raised you to be a formidable and determined woman. Good luck in the vote."

"Thank you, she has taught me a great deal over the years, I was lucky to have her to guide me." She smiled another grisly smile.

"I am off to find Milton, no doubt he is at the circus, he has been every day, it has really made his week." I chuckled.

"I have had to keep dragging Birch off the carousel, I think she has been on it more than anyone else."

"It is the price we pay my dear." My radio bleeped; it was Deli.

"Abby I am at the shed, we have a problem, can you come up please?" I smiled at Marjorie and lifted my radio.

"On my way." I jogged up to the field, and walked into the shed, Chloe was stood with her legs spread.

"They split Abby, and my lips are hanging out." Birch stood in the doorway panting.

"Well, it's not the first time Sweetie, I mean, most people recognise you these days by that." Deli gave a smirk and bit her lip, Chloe looked up.

"What should I do, I need this costume for the big ending?" Edwina leaned in through the door.

"Looks you have had way too many big endings. My God, you are a slut, which fair ground guy did it, what did you do, tell him you were a virgin and leave them on?" I gave a snort; she handed me a roll of black heavy duty tape. I looked at her.

"What the hell do I do with this?" She smirked.

"Tape it up and give the men a break." Birch gave a cackle of a laugh, Chloe looked down between her legs.

"It won't heal up, will it?" I could not help laughing, Edwina shook her head.

"Hell, that is all she cares about, losing her ability to shag, God, I cannot believe she is my sister." I pulled out a large piece of tape.

"Inside or outside?" Chloe stared at me.

"What the fuck Abby, I don't want it in there, and you can keep your soft fucking hands away from there, I have heard all about you?"

"It's not my fault, no one had ever touched me that way." I closed my eyes. God, I will never live that down. Deb's arrived and stood watching, which was unnerving, I looked at Chloe.

"Pull your pants down and lie on the table." Chloe looked at me suspiciously.

"Yeah, I heard that story too, I know she is around."

I shook my head as I smirked, giggles broke out all around me. She slid onto the table, and pulled her tights down, and opened her legs, and suddenly I was nervous.

"See I told you hers was bigger than mine." I gave a snort.

"Deb's please, I am trying to focus." I lined up the tape to get a size, I measured it, and then tore the tape off.

"Bev Sweetie, you made it." Chloe's legs snapped shut fast.

"Guard your vaginas!"

Deb's shot inside the shed, as Birch laughed her ass off. I lifted the tape, Chloe stared at me, and suddenly snapped her legs open wide, I blinked. I slowly lowered the wide tape to her hooch, and stretched it over, and then pressed it down, and gave it a soft pat.

"Oh oooh." I jumped back.

"Stop that, it is unsettling, be straight, this is freaking me out." She gave a little breath out.

"Sorry, she is tender, and it made me tingle." I took another step back.

"Tingles are not allowed, rub it on yourself, I am done." Deb's leaned over the table.

"I can do it if you want?" Chloe's leg snapped shut.

"Fuck that, I don't trust you, even when you have no sponge." She slid her hand between her own legs and started to rub the tape, and yep, that was disturbing. Edwina gave a sigh.

"Oh wow, you are such a perverted tramp, don't play with it, just put your tights back on." I handed the giggling Deli tape.

"Don't laugh too much, you might have to do it next time."

I smiled as she looked freaked out, Chloe winked at her, and she went pale. I laughed, as I came out of the shed and looked at my watch.

"Deb's you will need to get over to the parade, we will be going into phase two shortly, come on this is the last leg, let's get ready."

The time moved on, and we all headed into our positions, and as the last hour ticked away, I felt nervous. Our big finale was almost ready to start, and I knew, this had to be a big success, every part of our reputation was riding on it. In the village, the face painting was finished, and they were cleaning up. Up on the roof of the Church Hall, on the scaffold, under a temporary wooden enclosure, Edwina was sat in her seat with two laptops set up. Behind her, Morty and Bongo, were preparing their drones, as Luke sat down in his seat next to Edwina, and prepared the live stream. A count down appeared on the stream.

Below them on the green, I handed Birch a roll of yellow tape, and we separated, and I walked to the top of Green Street, and tied the tape to the lamppost. I walked down the street slowly, wrapping the tape round each lamppost and tree, creating a barrier, it was starting to darken as the sun slipped down in the sky, and lights were coming on.

I reached the bottom of Church Rise, and tied the tape off, then walked back up the street, making sure everyone was behind the line. Crowds were starting to gather, and line the curbs, kids were sat down on the curb, and there was a hum of excitement. Birch was on the other side, as the pavement filled with excited faces, it was a great atmosphere, and it felt really good.

In the marquee, Deli had taken control, as all the students from Oxendale High School gathered, and started their process of transformation. I clipped my radio to my pants, and pushed in my ear piece and slipped my head set mic on.

"Edwina, we are going to phase two." The line crackled, and then she came in loud and clear.

"We are ready, the live stream is on count down, and the drones are about to lift off. Creamy is ready with the roof cameras, and Deb's is in position."

I took a deep breath, and walked out onto the green, Anthony stood waiting, with a mic, he was dressed as a ringmaster, with a day of the dead face, he looked brilliant. I walked up and stood by his side, and he smiled, he was nervous, but not the only one. I was waiting for the all clear.

"This is it Anthony, it is make or bust time." He smiled.

"Abby Darling, no matter what happens, all of us will remember this as one of our happiest times together, I for one will never forget it."

I smiled and nodded, he was right, it was hard work, but it had also been great fun being together and doing all of this. I stood nervously waiting for Edwina to give the signal, it came through my head set, and I took a very long deep breath.

"Abby, Deb's is ready, you are good to go, Anthony's mic is live, and the drones are air born. The live stream is ready and going live in Five... Four... Three... Two... One, GO!"

I patted Anthony on the shoulder, as the drones hovered above us, he stepped up on the short ladder, and moved up onto his high podium. Standing high up level with my head in full view, he lifted the mic. His voice rang out loud from all the speakers situated around the village.

"Ladies and Gentlemen, Children, welcome to the Curio Carnival Wotton." His voice boomed out of the speaker system, and everyone suddenly turned to look at him, as a flood light below him lit up.

All round the village there was sudden applause, and excited laughter and squeals, from the children. Anthony stood on his podium, and turned slowly, as he addressed the crowds.

"The parade is about to start, so please consider your safety, and stay behind the yellow tape at all times. Tonight, for your entertainment, we will present you with a parade of floats, dancers and musicians. We will also announce the prize winners of the fancy dress competitions, and for the first time ever in Wotton, a light show, like you have never seen before, can I have the lights please?"

All the strings of lights from Christmas suddenly came on, and the whole village was lit with different colours. In the background, from Waterside Lane, a drum beat sounded. Boom... Boom... Boom, and the tension in the village started to rise, I walked back up the grass to Birch as she stood outside the marquee, and she did a little dance.

"Sweetie, I am so excited."

Deb's stood with Samantha at the bottom of Waterside Lane. She got the signal from the police, Station Road was closed to traffic, as was Oxendale Road at both ends. Deb's blew her whistle, and all the trucks started their engines. She felt giddy and excited, and her face was a permanent fixed smile. At the end of Waterside Lane, a police car blocked the road with its lights flashing blue, and the parade was ready to go.

The New Orleans band took their position at the front of the parade, and burst into a tune. Along the line of trucks decorated with flashing and twinkling lights, groups of dancers prepared, all of them dressed for the occasion in Halloween dress. Deb's waved her hand held yellow glowing batons, and the band began to march, the drummer beat the pace of their feet, as they walked onto Manor Road at a slow pace, and headed for the village.

The drones hovered above filming the progress, as it streamed live from the Curio Life, and D&D web sites. Luke monitored the stream, and watched both cameras, as he flicked from one to the other. Behind him, Morty and Bongo, sat with their digital face displays watching the live feed from their drones, and everything was flowing smoothly.

At the main control, Edwina monitored everything. This had been meticulously planned, and we all had our fingers crossed, the big question was, would we pull it all off?

Birch and myself, lifted yet more bags on to our shoulder, over the other side of the green, Anita with Tabby did the same. I reached into my bag, and pulled out a hand full of glowsticks, and snapped them, and they began to glow in many colours, Birch squealed with delight, and started snapping hers, and yep, suddenly she had them around her head, and round her wrists and neck.

"Sweetie, look, they are so pretty."

I shook my head, and we began yet another long walk around, handing out glow sticks to all the children. They had the same magic in their eyes as Birch, she is such a kid, as she danced and skipped along, handing them out to bright happy faces, she was like the crazy illuminated death fairy.

The music got louder, as the parade, moved from Manor Road onto the high street, the band dressed up as witches and wizards, played a mournful tune, as they walked slowly towards the bottom of the green. Deb's was up front, with her bright yellow light batons, guiding them, as she stood at the end of the green, and waved them onto Church Rise, as darkness fell.

All the floats flashed and twinkled with their lights, it was spectacular, as the long line of trucks lit up all the street around them. The band hit the bottom of the green, and burst into 'When the saints' and suddenly the whole atmosphere exploded with an air of excitement.

I handed out glow sticks by the handful, and could not help smiling, the children were bouncing up and down, and pulling their parents hands as they pointed, the whole of the village was packed out, with not an inch of space free.

People at the back, stood on the low walls of the Hunters, as they filmed, excited parents pointed things out to their children, and it was so loud, and yet exhilarating. Birch was dancing along, laughing like a crazy woman, covered in glow sticks, making everyone laugh, as the huge Curio Live float, came up the centre of the road, on Church Rise.

The Curio float had been designed by Edwina, and built by G5. It had two huge screens on the back, that had a split screen, one half of the screen had a slide show of each Curio, in their day of the dead makeup, with our names, and the other had the live feed from the D&D website. People waved at it, as they saw themselves on the camera from the trucks side, and people were cheering and waving, honestly, it was deafening, and yet so wonderful. I just could not help getting carried away, and was laughing and smiling.

The sky was getting really dark, as the Oxendale Morris Dancers danced behind the Curio float, with their pom poms lit up with glow sticks. Anthony stood on his black platform at the end of the green with his microphone.

"Let's hear a scream for the Oxendale Morris Dancing troop." The audience went wild, the next float had a dungeon on it, with zombies in cages, Anthony lifted his arm.

"Scream for the Oxendale Arts College, Zombie Dungeon float."

Birch was dancing up and down screaming like a maniac, and all the kids were copying her. I saw Anita shake her head and laugh. Behind them came the line dancers.

"Wail for the Oxendale Line Dancing mummies."

I had to laugh, they were all bandages, cowboy boots and hats, but I loved it. Anthony was loving his role.

"Scream for the Oxendale Junior School, little shop of horror float."

All the kids were dressed as scary flowers and danced on the back; to be honest, it was more cute than scary.

"The Millington Sea Cadets, marching band." They all walked dressed like Frankenstein, with green faces, playing their instruments.

"The Wheeler Development Corporation, Dracula's Castle." Wow it was mind blowing, with its black walls and bats, and vampires hanging and waving from the windows

"Give a wail, for the Girl Guides and Brownies, dance group of horror." They were all dressed as zombies and mummies and vampires, they looked brilliant.

Deb's reached the top of the rise and stood waving them round the green, and down Green Street, she had somehow acquired a witches hat, and Birch had decorated her in glow sticks.

"The Oxendale Army Cadets, Grave yard of death." It looked amazing, they had really worked hard, and had grey cracked stones, and dead trees, filled with cobwebs and hanging moss. Anthony was having a ball, as he waved his arms in grand gestures.

"The Oxendale day of the Dead Dance School."

They were all dressed as day of the dead characters, and had light up tops and shorts, as they did calypso dances up the street. They were brilliant, and everything was so bright and lit with millions of lights, it was mind blowing.

I walked up and down shouting 'scream for Halloween,' and the kids danced and yelled, and all their parents watched on happy and laughing. Wotton was filled with such joy, and so much excitement, most of it encouraged and led by Birch.

"Scream for Wotton's very own Brass Band."

The crowd roared, and I screamed my lungs out, as they all marched in step, playing the theme to Harry Potter, dressed in long black robes.

"Ladies and Gentlemen, Children, get your sweetie bags ready, for the Sweeties Retreat Beetlejuice Sweet Shop."

Colin had to be the gayest Beetlejuice I had ever seen, but I loved it. The float had a large staircase on it, where Pat stood dancing dressed as Lydia, as she threw sweets into the air. The huge float was lined with bags, filled with gifts and sweets, as Gill, Alex, Izzy, Susana and Megan, dressed as lady Beetlejuice, grabbed the bags from the side, and handed them out to the excited children. Birch joined in, with screams of laughter, Colin gave a skip as he saw me.

"Oh Abby, go on say it, say it three times." I looked at the kids, and they all jumped for joy.

"BETTLEJUICE!" He laughed wildly, and slid his hands up his sleeve, I stamped as the kids dared me.

"BEETLEJUICE!"

I looked at the kids, and they were dancing, with their parents laughing, they egged me on. I stared at Colin with his happy round face, I glanced at the kids, they screamed at me with their parents.

"SAY IT!" I looked at Colin and stamped on the ground as hard as I could.

"BEETLEJUICE!"

The kids screamed wildly, as suddenly, his long sleeves unrolled, and Colin stood laughing his ass off, with really long stripy arms. He ran up to me, and flung his arms around me and kissed me on the cheek, I was laughing so hard, I had not expected it, and the kids were all laughing like crazy, as were their parents. Anthony threw his arms in the air.

"The Wotton Dursley Majorettes."

They marched along twirling their glow stick batons, dressed like zombies, God, I was loving every minute of this. There was a wail of a guitar, and that could only mean one thing, Anthony wailed as the last float made it onto Church Rise.

"Ladies and gentlemen, The Battered Bones Taco float."

Floyd had put a rib cage on his guitar, and it looked like he was playing a dead human, as the rest of the band played, dressed as skeletons, and yep, there was a blood curdling wail, as Birch ran screaming from the float, and loads of kids suddenly ducked under the yellow ribbon, and huddled around her to protect her. It was the sweetest thing I have ever seen, as Birch crouched down with her eyes covered wailing.

"SWEETIE'S SAVE ME!" The kids all stood in a circle with their arms outstretched, protecting her, God, I love her, she is the most amazing human I know.

The parade was a huge hit, and the Curio Live float headed around the village and was back on Church Rise, and heading for the show field. I walked slowly back towards the marquee, happily watching. It really was mind blowing, I pulled my hair back into a pony tail, the big finale was next, and we needed to hurry. Deb's with Anita and Tabby, took control, as in my ear piece, Edwina spoke.

"Guys, the footage we have is brilliant, get ready for phase three, and hurry."

Birch waved to all the children as she ran up the road, and I slipped into the marquee, Deli looked amazing, Eric, with Denise and John were stood ready, Birch slipped in as she looked at all the Oxendale High dance students.

"Wow, you all look amazing."

I grabbed a sponge and slapped it into her face, and she spluttered, and I started to wash off her face paint. Birch undid her pants ready. Her face was clean, she kicked off her shoes and down came her pants, revealing her skeleton leggings. She pulled her Curio sweat shirt off, and was almost ready. Deli back brushed her hair ready.

Chloe sat her down, as I slid on her red shoes, and grabbed her long black wiccan robe. Chloe painted fast, as her face turned green, and then she gave a sinister under tone to her eyes, she was almost ready, and I helped her slip on her robe. Chloe stood back as I fluffed her white hair up. Her head mic was fitted, she smiled, I grinned at her.

"Fuck, you are an ugly bitch." She gave a cackle., I gave a nod. "Done."

I pulled my sweatshirt over my head and threw it in the basket, and undid my jeans, and then threw them in the basket, and slipped my black pumps back on. Birch pulled my hair back, and lifted my tight hood up, and suddenly, I was a full skeleton, she gave a shudder.

"Sweetie, you to eat more, I can your ribs."

Chuckles broke out all around the marquee, Chloe pulled up her hood and nodded. Outside the wailing guitars of Floyd, were loud, they were the last float, and were passing to great applause, I gave a nod to Chloe, as I adjusted my face mic.

"Okay, last leg, get ready everyone, he we go." I switched my mic pack back on.

I stepped out of the tent at the side of Chloe, gave a nod, and ran over to the post office side of the green, and grabbed the black curtain, I was breathing hard, and very nervous. At the bottom of the green Anthony stood on his podium, with a huge smile, as two drones hovered in front of him.

"Ladies and gentlemen, and Children, Welcome to this beautiful village, we are very grateful that you took the time to join us tonight. Would you please give a big round of applause, for everyone who has worked so hard to create some amazing floats, for our first ever carnival?"

I smiled, as everyone clapped and cheered, there was not an inch of space in the village, I had never seen so many, and it felt so wonderful. Anthony waited for what was a loud and very long applause to die down. Edwina spoke in my ear.

"Okay go with the curtains." I gripped hard and ran down the green, dragging the curtain with me, Chloe was doing the same on the other side, Anthony looked round.

"In just a few short moments we will move on to our grand finale, and we hope it will be something like you have never seen before, but as you watch this, please remember, tonight we are here for two reasons. Behind the scenes the Curio team have slaved away. The poor darlings look exhausted from some very long days, and long nights." He looked down as Chloe and I arrived dragging the sheets.

"I mean look at them, Oh Abby, and Chloe darlings, you have lost weight, eat more dears, we can see your bones."

The audience burst into laughter, I smiled and waved to the audience and then slipped in behind the black sheet, Anthony, took a breath.

"It has taken a lot of work, but it is all for a good cause. Shortly we will be announcing the very first Curio Centre, and as we move closer to opening, there is a lot of young people out there tonight, who really need help. If you enjoy tonight's show, then please show your appreciation with a donation, members of the Wotton Dramatic Society, have donation buckets, and are moving around all of you, it is such a worthy cause, and we really want to build more centres."

I slipped inside the hidden green, I moved fast, and Chloe and myself grabbed a metal frame with a fake fire on it, and carried it to the centre of the green in the heart of all the grave stones. Eric and John carried a huge wooden and fabric cauldron, and I knelt down, and flicked the buttons as a fan started and blew torn red, orange and yellow fabric into the air, I flicked the second switch, and an orange and red light came on. I stood back and John and Eric lowered the cauldron into place.

Anthony was announcing the fancy dress competition winners, aided by Anita, and we had to move fast. Birch climbed up and lay on top of the cauldron, and adjusted her head mic, she gave the nod, and we pulled a large black sheet over her. Eric grabbed the dark fine line, and walked backwards to the Marque, and waited. I tapped my ear piece.

"Edwina, the crazy is in place."

Outside, Anthony was talking about the preservation of Wotton, Chloe and myself ran down and slipped out of the curtain, as students inside ran down the grass, and Deli got them into position. I waited for the signal, feeling out of breath, as Anthony came towards the end of his piece.

"So, in order to keep Wotton thriving and providing high quality events for all our visitors, a percentage of tonight's fundraising will go to the Wotton Village fund." Edwina spoke in my ear.

"Okay, we are good to go, everyone is in place, give Anthony the nod." I reached up and tapped his leg. He turned with a big smile.

"So, are we all ready to be blown away, and feel a little bit scared, as the afterlife awakens in Wotton?" The audience yelled a big yes at him. He gave a giggle.

"Oh darlings, you have no idea what you just asked for." The audience giggled.

"Ladies and gentlemen, here in the heart beat of Wotton Dursley, I am so proud to be a part of this, and present to you, Curio Lights."

Edwina yelled in my ear. "GO…. GO…. Go." The drones rose into the air, and through the speakers came the sound of a heartbeat.

'Bump, bump…. Bump, bump… Bump, bump…'

Suddenly across the sky right above the village, a green line shot across then spiked 'BLEEP!' The audience gasped, as the line faded, and a rough voice spoke with insane amazement into the speaker.

"It's alive!"

The curtains started to open, as another green line crossed the sky. BLEEP! It moved a little further, BLEEP! I watched as the curtains drew back, no one had noticed, as I walked slowly up the green, they were too busy looking up at the sky, as the line traced across it, I cannot deny, it was really incredible, suddenly it flatlined.

'BLEEEEEEEEEEEEEEEEEEEEEPPPPPPPPPPP!" And everyone gasped, the speakers wailed.

"NOOOOOOOOOO!" We had everyone in the village, captivated. Anthony gave a sigh.

"It died, we wanted it to live so badly, but there is no coming back from the dead... Or is there?"

The audience gasped, as they suddenly saw the grave yard on the green, as a mist from the smoke machines billowed across it, illuminated by eerie green spot lights on the grass, and it looked as creepy as hell.

Chapter 34

Carnival Lights.

The green line faded away, as everyone looked at the graveyard on the Village Green. The cauldron looked strange, lit by the fire light. Through the speakers, came the sound of bubbling, and there was a sudden very loud crazy cackle, and everyone jumped.

In the air, green lightening streaked across the sky, and again everyone jumped. The rumble of the thunder came through the speakers, and shook the night air. It was amazing, there was a low murmur all around the village, as the mist thickened, then suddenly, light flashed from each corner of the village, and the black cloth on Birch shot off her, under the smoke, and she jumped up on top of the cauldron with a deafening cackle.

"HELLO MY SWEET PRETTIES?"

It scared the shit out of everyone, and then they giggled. With her hood up over her green face, and all that white hair hanging down, she looked amazing. She turned slowly round, and then spotted Anthony, and pointed at him.

"YOU!" Everyone jumped.

She pulled up her robe, and showed off her red shoes, her voice was creepy and broken.

"Anthony, tell me honestly, do these make my bum look bigger?" She wiggled her ankles. Everyone giggled, Anthony flicked back his hair.

"Oh, honestly Green Witchy, they are so you, they are simply divine, they are as red as your bloodshot eyes." The audience gave another chuckle. She pointed at him, and stared a creepy stare, her voice lowered.

"I hope you are telling the truth, because I have been invited to the dance of the dead, and if you are wrong, you know what I will do?" He clasped his hands to his face in horror.

"NO, ANYTHING, BUT NOT THAT!" She threw up her arms, and cackled a wild insane laugh, as she looked around the village.

"Yes, I will turn you into a journalist, and melt down your scissors." The audience roared with laughter. Anthony screamed and fell to his knees.

"I would rather be dead." Birch looked around the green, the place was absolutely silent, her voice was really creepy.

"Well, that can be arranged, death is but a doorway, and all you need is to reopen the door... Watch my sweet pretties."

Birch threw back her hood, lifted her arms, and a flash of bright green lightening streaked across the sky, she threw back her head and cackled. She was brilliant.

"COME TO ME, MY NOT SO SWEET PRETTIES!"

Another flash of light streaked through the sky; the audience was spell bound. Birch's hair fluttered above her shoulders, she was loving every moment of this, and so was I, it was brilliant.

"Curse the Bell Twits." Yep, I made her clean that up, there are kids here you know?

"With hubble and bubbles, and a little bit of cinnamon, and just a touch of mint, and boil the bones, and add the sin, and let them below, rise from within." Lightning flashed from the sky, as she threw back her head and reached up with a deafening cackle.

All the lights in the village went out, and there were some startled screams, as Birch gave another loud terrifying cackle of a laugh

Through the speakers' moans started, and creepy groans, and the green lights on the village green faded low, casting all the smoke across the graves, with an eerie glow, it looked really sinister. The fabric soil in the graves began to move, and there were gasps from the audience as they spotted it, and the creepy moans grew louder, Birch looked down and smiled, and opened her arms.

"Come to mamma, my babies." I could hear Edwina chuckling in my ear piece.

The ground moved, and arms suddenly appeared, clawing at the sky. Even I stepped back, with surprise. Thunder rumbled, and more lightening streaked overhead, and slowly, the twisted creepy figures, pulled themselves out of the floor of each grave. Birch gave a sinister soft laugh; her voice was low and pretty terrifying.

"Oh, look at you, rising from the dead, to make Wotton your own, come my babies, rise up to me, for tonight, we will dance the dance of DEATH!" I shuddered.

As the figures rose up, all stiff and jerky, everyone was transfixed, as the creepy moans and wails echoed round the village. They stepped out of their graves, and staggered towards the road, on either side of the green, the kids who were sat down, pulled their feet up off the road, and slid back towards their parents.

I was really impressed, we had not been sure this would work, but Deli had put hours of work into it. As the zombies staggered onto the road, Birch gave a sinister laugh.

"Oh, what have we here? Do I spy a dead Deli Curio?" Anthony looked up.

"You see, partying all day and night, that is what you get. God, she has let herself go... Oh my god, have you seen her hair, oh Deli Darling, if I live through this night, you just have to let me put some life back into that thatch." Giggles broke out in the crowd, I was so impressed, and the crowd were loving every second.

Deli and her walking dead, staggered onto the road on each side of the green, and the music started, and from the Hunters and Deb's shop, zombies flooded out onto the road, Anthony looked round.

"Oh, Abby dear, did you order a trash mob?"

The music erupted, and it was obviously thriller. The audience erupted with applause, as the dancers came together, and did the thriller dance up the street. The green floodlights brightened, and it looked pretty spectacular, the audience started to clap. Birch boogied on her cauldron.

"YES, DANCE, MY NOT SO PRETTIES!" I had to laugh, she looked like a raving lunatic, flapping out her arms and kicking up her legs.

I slipped up my head mic and got ready, as Deli danced up the street, and as the music came to an end, everyone applauded, Anthony lifted his Mic.

"Ladies and gentlemen, The Oxendale High School Dance Group, led by our new Curio Deli, give them a massive round of applause, that was sensational."

They all stood panting in the street, and gave a bow, as all the visitors clapped, and whistled, it was so nice to see, they were all under sixteen, and had worked really hard. They were brilliant, and I felt so happy for them, Birch spun on her cauldron.

"WHAT ABOUT ME, MY DANCING WAS DIVINE?" I walked out of the marquee towards her, she looked down.

"SWEETIE, YOU LOST WEIGHT?" As the audience chuckled, I climbed up beside her.

"Have you been causing mischief?" She put her hands behind her back and swung her hips from side to side, as she tried to act coy.

"No, I have been a good girl, honestly Sweetie, I just danced with some friends." The audience laughed, I fought back the smirk, as I looked around at all the children.

"Children, did she cause mischief?" All the kids screamed at the top of their voices.

"YESSS!" I laughed, as I looked at her.

"Did you, be honest now?" She lifted her hand, and used her thumb and finger to make a tiny little gap.

"Well maybe just a little bit Sweetie." The audience giggled.

"Okay then, if you have been almost a good girl, maybe I will give you just a tiny little kiss for behaving."

I leaned in, and gave her a soft peck on the lips, and as I did, I slid off her robe, and it fell to the floor, revealing her skeleton costume. I stepped back, and looked at her.

"How was that?" I fought back the laughter; her eyes were dancing with delight.

"Wow Sweetie, that was a good kiss... OH MY GOD, IT SUCKED MY SKIN OFF!"

Even I laughed, it was hard not to, she was so good at this, the audience thought it was hilarious, Birch turned around and looked at everyone.

"Don't laugh, I hate skeletons, ask my Sweetie, she will tell you?" The speakers boomed in a sinister voice.

"So, you don't like Skeletons, well we shall see about that."

The audience gasped with amazement, as skeletons of green light, rose up from the floor. Birch squealed, and grabbed my hand.

"SWEETIE RUN, WE ARE BEING INVADED, I DON'T LIKE THEM, SWEETIE TELL THEM TO GO HOME!"

We jumped off the cauldron, and ran to the marquee, and the green lights went out, as the skeletons started to dance, and the music came on, the audience was completely sold on the show, and we all took a breather, as Edwina and Luke took over.

As the skeletons danced along the road, Chloe, Deli, Birch and myself, lifted a wooden black box and moved it down the green, as Eric and John switched out the lights, and carried the cauldron and the fire back to the marquee. We set the box down, and then ran back, and grabbed another, and set it at the side of it, creating a long low stage.

In the skies of Wotton, bats swooped, and witches flew, and even a dark wizard appeared in a dark symbol. Ghosts floated, and a huge galleon sailed up the high street, and pirates jumped off scaring the audience.

Vampires appeared, and werewolves howled. Frankenstein's monster, rose up in the grave yard, and wandered about howling with hate, it was mind blowing, and I realised how far Edwina had come with her technical abilities. I stood with Birch, and watched at the marquee doorway, as she slipped her arm around my waist.

"Wow, if I am honest Birch, I doubted her at first, but hell, this is magnificent, I have never seen anything like it." She leaned onto my shoulder.

"Nothing is impossible Sweetie, I mean, miracles take a little longer, it took us five years to realise, but a miracle still happened." I turned and looked at her with her green face, she smiled a sweet smile.

"Fuck you are an ugly bitch, I preferred Gloria." She gave a giggle.

The light show lasted for over forty minutes, and was a massive success, as it ended the words Thank You lit up in the sky, and Anthony lifted his mic.

"Ladies and Gentlemen, and children, the time is moving on towards bedtime for the little people, and so we must prepare."

There were actually moans and groans, in the audience, as we all gathered together in the marquee.

"We hope you enjoyed your night with us, and there is still hot food available at the Hunters Hotel side, brought to you by Phillip Morrison the butcher. The Deli is still open, serving kebabs and hot meat sandwiches, and the Tea Rooms are open for hot drinks. Before you all leave, please welcome back, those responsible for tonight, ladies and gentlemen, the Curio's and their talented team." The audience burst into applause, as Anthony announced us.

"Chloe Pemberton, Debbie Battersby, Fidelity Hannigan, Abigail Jennifer Dixon, Jemima Dixon, and I am Anthony, your Ring Master for the night."

The applause was deafening, as we walked down the green, and stepped up on to the black boxes as the village lights came back on, and we pulled back our hoods and let our hair fall down to our shoulders. We stood waving as Anthony continued.

"Please also thank Anita Dickinson, and the real star of tonight for her amazing light show, she has been on the cold Church Hall roof all night coordinating the light show, ladies and gentlemen, the inspiring, Miss Edwina Pemberton."

She ran down the green panting in her skeleton costume, as the drones hovered above us, and jumped on the small black stage. It was amazing, and such a great feeling, we had done it, Anthony walked up and joined us, and handed the mic to Birch, it took a long time for it to quieten down, and Birch smiled as she looked around. She was so happy, it killed us to put this on, but yet again, another one of her crazy ideas, had been a resounding success, she looked around with big bright tear filled eyes.

"Thank you, all of you, this village lives on visitors coming and joining in with all we do, it is a place very dear to our hearts, and the money donated at all our events allows us to keep doing more. Tonight, was a huge risk, and yet I don't know why, because look at this, I have never seen so much support, and we are so grateful to all of you." She handed the mic to Debbie, and she giggled.

"We would like to thank everyone who has taken part, and given one thousand percent of effort, the local schools, the local residents and traders, my hubbies band, G5, the local drama group, dance groups, the circus and the fair. They have given their all for you, to make this such a wonderful night, please thank them."

There was another round of applause, and Deb's handed me the mic, I smiled and felt so giddy inside.

"Ladies and gentlemen, Curio Life is such an important site, it has done so much good for our young adults. They are the future, just as all these adorable children here tonight will be their future. There are lot of young people out there who need our help, too many are ending their lives, and we want desperately to help them. If you have donated tonight, we are so grateful, because those funds will make a huge difference, and all of us Curio's want to thank you for that. Please do not forget, the fair is still open until ten, so go enjoy yourselves. We hope you enjoyed the night; I have no idea what we will do next, but we will be back. Thank you from everyone in Wotton Dursley for such wonderful support."

There was a roaring applause and we stood smiling and waved as cameras flashed everywhere, and all I could see was happy smiling faces, it warmed us all to see it. We jumped off stage, and ran to the marquee, where I dragged Edwina into the biggest hug ever.

"It was insane, and amazing, and honestly, it blew me away." We all hugged, and Chloe, opened a cool box, and handed out cans, we stood in a circle and chinked cans.

"CHEERS!"

Hot water was provided in plastic bowls, and we washed off the face paint, and put on our clothing over our costumes. It was getting really chilly, but it was not over yet, like all things, there is always the clean up.

We spent the next hour moving everything off the green, a task hampered as people came over to thank us, and we all signed autographs, and had yet more pictures taken. Edwina went back up to Luke, where G5 were removing the projection equipment. The live stream had ended, and a copy had been saved, which would be put on the Curio Life web site, to watch again.

We lifted fake graves, took down the curtains, and put everything in the marquee for tonight, tomorrow it would all be stored away. The steel lines came down, and the poles were detached, and within the hour, the green was empty. It was just gone ten, and the village was starting to empty, as I took down the yellow tape. The trucks with the floats on, were taken back to their locations, to be stripped down, and I walked around winding up the tape, as the last rides of the fair boomed out their music for the last time in Wotton. Mum came out of nowhere with Hatty, they were so excited, Mum dragged me into a big hug.

"I am so proud of you tonight, all of you, that is the best event this village has ever seen. My god Abby, it was mind blowing."

It felt nice to hear her say that, I guess even now after years of patching things up between us, I still love it when she says it, and it is so nice to hear it. She pulled out of our hug, and just looked at me with a huge smile on her face.

"Abby your dad has left, it is getting late, he was so proud of you tonight."

"He came to see it?" She smiled, and Hatty leaned in.

"That alone shows you how good it was, it even warmed his clockwork cold heart." I sniggered, and she dragged me into a hug.

"You did good kid, it had everything, good humour, some jumps, and Edwina has pretty much blown all of us away, that light show was spectacular. People in the village will talk about this for a long time."

It was good to hear it, after all, we had now proven our worth, and just the reaction of the audience alone, showed everyone how successful it was. I rolled up the tape with the help of Hatty, Birch was across the green doing the same, talking to her mum. I smiled as I saw Roni hug her, I know how important it was to her, and yet in a way, it was daft, Birch had surpassed her mother when it came to producing a stage show.

It made me wonder, just how good was Katie? When you think about it, she uses everything supplied by others. Birch was different, she could match Katie stroke for stroke, because she did have superior organisational skills, but for this event, not only had she brought things in, we had also built most of it ourselves, it made me really wonder, as I thought about our weeks of work sat in the garage creating the props.

We packed everything into the marquee, and then all walked up to the field to grab Petal, the fair was over, and the circus had been paid and was done, we locked the shed, and made our weary way home.

We were tired, but it was still rowdy, Bev, Roni and Will sat with us, Bev made me giggle, as she bobbed on her seat, and went on and on.

"I am telling you, when that fucking skeleton come up out of the floor right in front of me eyes, I crapped myself. I thought, fuck that is creepy, but also it was blinding, the whole thing was mint, and when you sucked her skin off Deadly, I thought aye, aye, been there, done that."

We all shuddered, Deb's looked horrified, and that was the freakiest thing I had heard all day. The laughter continued, but I was so tired, and I made my way along the hall, and wandered into the library, there was a line of forty large white beer brewing buckets, all filled with cash. They all weighed a tonne, and Luke was wiped out and sweating.

"How are you, Abby?" I flopped in my chair.

"I am done Luke, I am so tired, and my body is aching all over." He smiled at me.

"You know what, you and Birch are a phenomenal team, G5 are good, but working with you guys, hell, we struggled to stay up with you. No one can criticise tonight, and as for Weena, she has left all of us in her wake." He gave a small chuckle.

"You know, when we were at school, I gave her some simple coding lessons, she really did learn fast, but writing that program for those lights, even I struggled to understand her. She is a genius you know; I don't even think she understands how good she is?" I leaned back, and closed my eyes.

"Luke, she does not care, all she has ever wanted was to be with you. I really don't think you understand how deeply she has loved you, since those coding lessons. Proposing to her, is the greatest thing in her life, no code or computer can do that for her. So, you tell me, who is the genius now?" I opened my eyes, and he was smiling.

"Abby, I love her equally as much, I have for a long time, I honestly thought I had blown it with her, I am really glad I haven't." I was too tired, I got up out of my chair, and walked past him, and patted his shoulder.

"You did good Luke, you two are meant for each other, don't screw it up."

I came out of the library, and headed up to my room, the kitchen was still full of giggles. I walked in and Birch was stripping.

"Hi Sweetie, there you are, I wondered where you had gone. I've run us a bath." I pulled at my top.

"Birch, you are a goddess." She pulled me into her arms.

"I am going to wash and bathe you, then lie you on the bed, and massage you with warm fragrant oils, and then Sweetie, I am going to slide between your fragrant legs." Her eyes danced with devilish delight, there was no doubt, she had my full attention.

"And then, I am going... To suck your skin off."

I went completely cold, and shuddered violently, and she giggled. I looked at her big bright green eyes.

"How the hell does someone even do that, and what did she mean... Actually, don't tell me, I have seen her at work twice, and I have way too many messed up pictures in my brain?"

She took my hand with a giggle, and led me into the bathroom, and she slipped into the water, and I slipped in, and leaned back into her, the heat from the water radiated all through my tired aching body, and it felt so nice.

When we had finished, true to her word, she lay me face down, and oiled my skin, and gave me a massage, and I moaned into the pillows, it felt so nice. She rubbed me up my back, and it felt wonderful, I lay relaxing, just enjoying the sensation.

"Sweetie, you know the other morning, when Floyd was here?"

"Hmm." She ran her hand up my spine.

"I saw the way you admired his manhood; did you want it?" I gave a low moan.

"He is with Gail, but I won't deny, I would have probably slipped on if he asked me, why?"

"I just wondered, I thought you maybe wanted some man pleasure, you know, I cannot touch those spots like a penis can." I gave another moan, as she rubbed my shoulder blades.

"Birch, I love sex with you, and yes for a moment I sort of wished you had one, I would totally screw you with a dick." She giggled.

"What like this?" I felt something slide inside me, and I gave a gasp, it went right in deep, I pushed my face in the pillow.

"Oh God, what the hell is that, it feels wonderful?"

"My dick."

"Huh?" I lifted my head and tried to look back, she was sliding in and out of me, she smiled.

"I have one in me too; it is double ended." I looked at the strap on her hips, she was wearing the strap on Bev had bought us for our wedding.

"Although Sweetie, I don't seem to have the hip movements men do."

I flopped in the pillow, and gave a moan, oh God there was that need, one I have not felt for a long time.

"Don't stop, it is perfect, oh Birch, I have missed this."

Sunday morning, the talk of Wotton, was the carnival. We were all extremely tired, I was brain dead, and I had shaky legs. Birch had pounded me quite hard last night, and wailed out her loudest climax ever, but today, I was walking like I had ridden a horse a hundred miles none stop. She was tired, but as with all things Birch, happy and giddy, and so it is a good thing I remembered her ear muffs, and slipped them on as the church bells rang.

We had a long row of black bags on the green, all ready to be taken to the tip. We had walked the whole village, with litter pickers, and made sure it was clean, and as spotless as it has always been. Marjorie appeared pleased, as she commented to the others gathering in front of the church. I leaned on a brush, as Celia and Lillian walked towards me, with huge smiles.

"Oh Abigail, you all look so tired, are you alright?" I smiled.

"I am fine ladies, between you and me, Birch got a little excited last night, and she has worn me out, she pleasured me so hard. Honestly, I thought I would faint." Lillian gave a gasp and fanned herself.

"Oh my, oh to be young, wild, and free." Celia gave a reassured nod.

"I like a woman with stamina." I gave a gasp.

"Celia, I can barely walk my legs are so shaky, and as for other parts, I am afraid to bend down, I am so sensitive." Lillian gasped.

"Oh, you poor, but very lucky dear." I chuckled; they were the oldest perverts I knew. Celia gave me a serious look.

"How do you feel about the vote, because from where I am stood, it is looking pretty dammed good for you two?" I looked around the village.

"We still have a lot to do, I am aware that criticism now could derail us, so we are going all out to make sure everything is as it should be. By tonight, everything will be gone, I am just waiting for the marquee to go. The circus is already out, and the fair just has a few more trucks left, and they will be leaving shortly, and then I am going home and sleep to catch up." Celia gripped my shoulder.

"What you all did, was impressive, and don't you worry, we have been singing your praises everywhere." I smiled.

"Thanks ladies, that means a lot to all of us."

By two o'clock, I had shaken hands with many visitors, picked up way too many bags of litter. Loaded up three van loads of equipment, to be taken to storage, and filled Petal with everything going home, and I was done.

Birch held my hand as we walked back to the field for Petal, the fair was gone, and the field was litter free, and empty. Bess had gone back already with a load of stuff, and we were the only two left. She turned to me and pulled me close.

"It is our time now Sweetie, we can rest and relax." I leaned on her shoulder.

"Can we though? it is the vote in seven days, and we will then have all the committee business if we win. Oh God Birch, I am so tired, I can hardly stand." She held me close.

"It is alright Sweetie; you can rest up now, and catch up all the sleep you missed. You know, you are not taking supplements, or eating enough, I think from now on, I am going to be watching you better, and I am going to get you back to full health." She twisted, and opened the door.

"And that starts now."

I climbed in, and she walked smiling around to the driver's door, and climbed in. Birch drove through the gates, jumped out, and locked the gates, we were finally done. I sat back with my eyes closed, as she drove like a maniac, but I was too tired to care.

We arrived home to be met by Anita and Tabby. Anita looked at me.

"You look worn out, Deb's went home, Chloe and Anthony are in bed already. Edwina is in her office going through the money raised, I am going to join her soon. Izzy is out with her friends, and we are going to bed ourselves soon, and as much as I would love epic sex, Abby, I am so bloody tired." I smiled as I sat down, and Tabby put a coffee in front of me, my throat was so dry.

I felt a little better after a coffee, and refilled my cup, then we headed into the office of Edwina. Her metal security door was down outside the glass wall of her office, and she was sat on the floor, leaning against the glass window, at the side of Luke. The whole floor was filled with plastic bank money bags, and piles of notes wrapped with paper bands. I stared at all the cash covering the whole floor.

"Holy shit Edwina, have you had to count all this?" She pointed to the desk, and the electric money counter.

"Even using that, I thought we would never finish, and I am so tired guys, I am utterly done." Birch looked impressed, as she sat on a desk chair.

"How have we done?" Edwina lifted her pad.

"Looking at all the income from traders, and the sponsorship, less what it has cost us, and then all the donations from online, less the D&D expenses, we have a total of one hundred and fifty two thousand, and some change. Less the twenty five percent cut for the village fund, it leaves one hundred and fourteen thousand for Curio Life." I gave a gasp.

"I was hoping for ten grand, guys that is brilliant." Edwina smiled.

"To be honest Abby, that is pretty unbelievable, it is far more than even I thought possible. All I know is, taking all this cash to the bank in Oxendale, is going to be a huge pain in the ass, I am not even strong enough to lift all the pound coins." Birch gave a cackle.

"Sweetie, have a good sleep, and then use the gym in the attic to build up your muscles, you will need to." Luke started to giggle; he got up off his feet.

"Oh, crap, we emptied the buckets, and now we have to put all this shit back again."

We all mucked in, and Edwina made note of what money went in what bucket, and finally after an hour, we had a row of tall white buckets, filled with cash. Edwina set the alarm, and we made our way back into the kitchen, we were exhausted, and just headed upstairs, and climbed into bed.

Birch slid in at the side of me, and snuggled up. The bed was soft, cool, and the pillow felt so soft and fluffy, she gave a happy little giggle.

"Did you enjoy this morning Sweetie... Sweetie.... Sweetie?"

I was out cold, and not intending to wake up anytime soon.

In the Hunters Arms Hotel and Bar, Derek and Margret Pemberton, were surrounded by residents, who shook their hands warmly, and told them of how amazed they were by the work of their daughters and friends.

All of them talked excitedly of how wonderful it was, and how they had seen the group working hard all week in the village. Margret smiled and nodded politely, and told all of them, that a vote for Abby and Birch, was a sure bet now they had proven their value.

It was so nice for them, there had been too many occasions where they had heard snide comments about Chloe or Edwina, most of which ended up with Margret in tears. Today it was completely different, and it was a pleasant change.

They sat down, and Margaret smiled as she opened the menu, and saw the top line. 'The Hunters Arms, supporting Dixon and Dixon for Council Chair and Vice Chair.'

She showed her husband.

"Oh, how the times have changed Derek, common sense has finally arrived in the village, bless them, they have worked harder than anyone, and deserve it." Andrew walked over with big smiles, and a bottle of wine, he placed it on the table.

"Today, everything for you is free, any parent of a Curio here, will get the red carpet, enjoy your meal."

As we all know, Derek Pemberton loves to save money, and he was not going to argue, he gave him a huge smile and held out his hand.

"Thanks for supporting the girls, Andrew, we all appreciate it." Andrew shook it with a smile. The waitress walked up and poured the wine, Derek sat back in his chair, his chest out, and a look of complete delight on his face.

"I could get used to this Maggie, I told you, we raised great girls, even if they do hardly visit these days."

Chapter 35

Election and Hospital.

I did not wake up until seven in the evening the following day. Birch had slept in until twelve, and then left me, as she had a two pm session with a client. I felt bad when I woke up, as she had been to work, and returned home when I got up. I was relieved to find; Chloe had not got up until two hours before me.

We had a meal together around the table that night, and Birch placed four supplements next to my plate, with a glass of water. She was watching me like a hawk, but I sort of liked that.

Prim had been out in force with yet more flyers trying to point out aspects of the event that were dangerous or lacking, as she trashed the whole event as a propaganda stunt to buy votes. Once again, she laboured the point of how we could not be trusted, and it concerned her that the event had raised a lot of money, and could we be trusted to make sure the village got its fair share. Chloe was really angry, and wanted to find her and as she put it.

"Knock her the fuck out!"

As the days passed, I felt much better, although I did sleep a lot, and had a daily walk into the village with Chloe. Wherever we went, we were stopped and complimented, it was so nice, but honestly, I was getting a little bit fed up with it, everything took me four times longer to do.

I went to bed earlier, and had not drunk since that can of celebration in the marquee, and I was feeling stronger and happier, and amazingly hornier. On the following Wednesday, Birch had her regular meeting with Nigel, and he had black eyes, Prim had found out he visited the circus, and watched the light show, and she had lost her temper again.

Nothing changes behind closed doors in this village. On the bright side, Tom Jessop had been very reclusive since the whole growing weed in his back yard incident, but being involved with the pumpkin competition, had really helped, and he was back in the shop with his daughter serving.

Chloe's Gallery run ended, and we travelled to London, and cleared out what stock was left, which was not that much. Accounts were settled, and Birch was delighted to see, we made three times the cost of the event, which was a huge deal for our tiny little company, and Chloe got a great share of the cash. I was happy to have the picture of my arch, finally hung in the living room, above my award.

Anita stayed for five more days resting, then went home, she was needed in Manchester. After a lot of heated debate, Edwina planned her wedding for April next year, and she got her own way. Her dad was so happy with a free meal, and all the praise, he caved in, and allowed a low key wedding, after all, it would cost him a lot less.

Birch and myself, gave one more open house meeting, which to be honest had proved to be very popular, and once again laid out our plans for the village, and listened carefully to their concerns. As we walked home hand in hand we talked.

"Deads Sweetie, we will win this." I was not convinced.

"I am not sure Birch, she is throwing money around all over the place, her advertisements are everywhere, and we have not been painted in a very good light at all." Birch just smiled.

"Deads, freedom of thought and freedom of speech are a universal right in a democracy. Look at how things were when you first came back from Uni, Marjorie ruled over everything, she controlled speech, and people hid their thoughts. The villagers have seen you are open to listen, just like tonight at the meeting, by removing the fear to speak, you gave them something they have not had for a long time." I smiled as I understood her.

"Yeah, I suppose so, mum made things easier, but even she held back because of Marjorie, with us, we have been seen to be open and honest and paying attention, I suppose it counts?" She squeezed my hand.

"It does Deads, they already see Prim is oppressive, and you are open to views, trust me Sweetie, that will swing the vote."

As the days ticked by, I started to feel nervous, even Birch had moments of apprehension. It is the not knowing that rattles you, when Sunday the fourth arrived, and all the votes were in, Brimley, Douglas, and Banks solicitors, oversaw the vote count, but we would not know until Wednesday the seventh, at the final announcement of the vote, and it felt intense.

There were five thousand, six hundred, and seventy eight, possible votes, and we needed two thousand, eight hundred, and forty, to have a majority. That is a lot of votes. If you look at it, I do not even know that many people, and I have lived here all my life.

The night arrived, and we both wore suits, and nervously sat at the back, we had a lot of thumbs up, from people passing by. Primula was strutting around like she had already won, which made me ten times more nervous. I was trembling sat with a much larger group, I noticed Walter Parkinson was on the same row as Primula, he had not shown his face for a while, but that did not bode well, as he wore a smug smile. Birch took my hand.

"Relax Sweetie, worrying will not change the result, be calm, and be ready." I took deep breaths, as Vanessa Douglas walked up to the stage, towards the microphone, she cleared her throat.

"Good evening, all." I could feel my heart rate increase, Birch squeezed my hand.

"As a neutral party in all this, and to ensure complete transparency, every voting slip has been counted and checked twice. The voting slips will be available for open examination at our office on Station Road for the next ten days." She looked down the hall.

"Could I please have the candidates on the stage please?" Birch stood up, and held my hand tight, Chloe smiled.

"Relax Abby, it's in the bag."

The village applauded as Prim and Molly made the stage before us, Primula stood there as if it was all for her. I swallowed hard, and tried to smile to all the people who looked at me and gave a nod, my stomach was twisting and squirming.

We walked up the steps, and walked to the opposite side of Vanessa, and I looked out, and spotted my dad, I was not even aware he was here. He smiled and gave a nod, and lifted his camera, I smiled back to him, in a way seeing him here was nice.

Vanessa unfolded her sheet of paper, she looked from side to side, and nodded to us, and then she faced the front. I could see my mum at the council table, I think she was holding her breath. Vanessa coughed.

"Ladies and gentlemen, in this vote, there was a possible 5678 votes available, of which, 108, were either spoiled, or not returned. The vote was cast as follows. Primula Wallace for Chair, and Molly St Vincent for Vice Chair, one hundred, and ninety two votes."

There was clapping, not a lot of it, and Primula scowled, Birch dithered, and got really excited, she grabbed my arm and squeezed it.

"Abigail Jennifer Dixon for Chair, and Jemima Dixon for Vice Chair, five thousand, three hundred, and seventy eight votes." The roar was deafening, as Birch pulled me into her arms, and jumped on the spot.

"Sweetie, you won."

I was in shock, as she squeezed me to death, and in the hall, people were on their feet whistling and clapping, and I just felt the tears in my eyes, as Birch let go and grabbed my face, her eyes were exploding with joy and so bright, she put her hands to my cheeks.

"Sweetie, you finally did it, you earned their acceptance, I am so proud of you, and I love you so much."

My mum was in tears, my dad was in tears, now Birch was in tears, and I was in tears, I felt stunned, as yells of: "SPEECH!" Rose up from the back, Vanessa turned and shook my hand with a smile.

"Congratulations Mrs Dixon, that was a resounding endorsement if ever I have seen one." I felt numb as I nodded and smiled, Molly came up offered her hand, and I took it.

"Congratulations Abigail, and you too Dr Dixon." Birch smiled.

"Thank you, Sweetie."

I looked around, as I wiped my eyes, people were still clapping and cheering, Prim was not on stage. My mum walked up and wiped her eyes, and shook the hand of Vanessa, she stood in front of the microphone, and the room started to settle down, she was wearing a huge smile.

"Ladies and gentlemen, it is customary for the defeated candidate to offer their thanks."

Prim was at her seat grabbing her coat and things together, Molly looked nervous, my mum smiled at her, and she came to the microphone, I could see her legs shaking.

"Ladies and gentlemen, I would like to say, on the behalf of Primula and myself, a big thank you for everyone who voted for us, and also congratulations to Abigail and Dr Dixon, they fought a good clean campaign, and we wish them every success." Primula spun at her seat.

"DO NOT SAY THAT FOR ME, I WILL NOT WISH THOSE WHORES GOOD LUCK!"

Primula, snatched up her things, and stormed up the centre of the hall, as the villagers gasped in shock.

"NIGEL, GET HERE NOW!" Molly watched panicked, as Marjorie stood up, her face dark as thunder.

"PRIMULA WALLACE, YOU WILL APOLOGISE!" She spun on her heels.

"NO, THEY ARE WHORES, AND GOD WILL PUNISH THEM!"

She turned, and walked right into Chloe, and BUMP! She fell back on the floor looking shocked. She scrambled back to her feet, and stared at Chloe with hate, her eyes filled with rage, and her face wrinkled with anger and hate.

"GET OUT OF MY WAY, YOU SLUT, OR I WILL... I WILL!" Chloe stared defiantly at her.

"What, hit me... Go for it, bitch?"

She stared at Chloe, her eyes narrowed, filled with hatred of all of us, her fist was clenched. Chloe leaned into her.

"Apologise." I looked at Birch feeling utterly panicked.

"Oh shit, Chloe is really pissed off." I walked up to the front of the stage.

"Chloe, just let her go, it is fine." Chloe looked up at me and her eyes glared, she was really angry.

"NO, SHE WILL APOLOGISE BEFORE SHE LEAVES!" Prim screamed into Chloe's face.

"NEVER!" She lifted her arm, and took a swing at Chloe, and WACK!

Everyone gasped, as Primula hit the floor, her nose flowing with blood, she screamed at the top of her voice, holding her nose.

"NIGEL GET HER, STICK UP FOR ME." I watched, as Nigel stood up, and turned, he was red faced and clearly very embarrassed.

"NO… APOLOGISE FOR YOUR DISRESPECT."

I was, as they say up north, gob smacked. I heard Birch give a small titter behind me. Primula screamed on the floor, got up, rammed her way past Chloe, and ran screaming from the hall, Nigel turned around and looked at the stage.

"I am very sorry Abigail and Doctor Dixon for my wife's disgraceful behaviour, you both deserve better than that." I felt flustered and did not know what to say, a voice shouted out across the hall, it was Andrew.

"Well said young man." A murmur rose up as people looked to Nigel, and gave a nod of agreement. Mum took her chance, and leaned into the microphone.

"Marion dear, would you bring the mop, I would not like anyone to slip." Chloe looked up at her with a smirk.

"I will do it, I made the mess, I will enjoy cleaning it up." Birch leaned into my shoulder and whispered.

"I bet you ten quid she bottles it, and sells it online." I sniggered, and gave her a dig in the ribs. My mum smiled at me, turned and calmly addressed the audience, wow she was pretty cool.

"Now order is restored, I give you, the new Chair and Vice Chair of the Parish Council, as they prepare to take over as of December first. Ladies and gentlemen, Dixon and Dixon."

We stood next to the mic as the applause continued, and we both smiled, and nodded our appreciation. Once everyone settled down, Birch leaned forward.

"Oh, you are all such Sweetie's, and we are so honoured you voted for us, and we want to thank you so much for your confidence in us, and I promise, we will not let you down."

I smiled, as she held my hand tight. She stepped back, and I stood there in front of everyone from my home village, I felt the tears in my eyes.

"Ladies and gentlemen, you have no idea how much this means to me, I have dreamed of this for a very long time, as I watched my parents plan for village events. I cannot express my gratitude and my thanks to all of you." I wiped my eyes.

"I would very much like, whilst she is still chair, to make her last task on this stage, a really lovely one, because under her chair ship, she took a huge risk, and allowed an untested event to happen, which was a roaring success. So tonight, I would like to present Mrs Felicity Watson, a cheque, from D&D Events, for funds raised at the Curio Carnival Wotton. After all costs were deducted and paid, the twenty five percent of the profits as negotiated by her, came to a grand total of thirty eight thousand pounds for the Village Fund."

She looked astounded, as she walked up, and Birch held up the cheque, with a bright beaming smile, and handed it to her, the applause was deafening.

"Well done, Mum, you went out on a huge high."

Marjorie smiled and nodded at me. Birch stood by my side, and leaned into the mic.

"Ladies and gentlemen, thank you for supporting us and the village, it truly humbled us to see all of you give us so much support, and we know it was a good boost for the local economy. Thank you on behalf of all the Curio family."

We left the stage, and my dad dragged me into his arms, and almost squeezed me to death, and then he grabbed Birch.

"You two are magnificent, what you have done, is beyond comprehension, I am so proud of both of you."

All I could do was smile, and shake hands, and say thanks. It took forever for everyone to finally leave, and even as the new chair of the council, there is no escaping putting away chairs and tables. Marjorie walked up and looked at me.

"Good luck Abigail, and thank you, this village I feel has been saved a fate worse than death." I took her hand and shook it.

"Thanks Marjorie, you know, you have been a great example of how a chair should conduct themselves, and I aim to emulate it." She gave a smile.

"Some traditions should never die." I nodded, and she walked towards the door.

"Miss Pemberton, I do not agree with violence in parish meetings." Chloe looked scared to death, and turned white as she froze on the spot, Madge smiled.

"However, self defence, is an understandable, and justifiable situation, do not do it again." Chloe shook her head, looking terrified.

"I won't Mrs W, I promise." Madge nodded, smirked, and walked out; Edwina giggled.

"Ha, ha, you got busted." We all started to laugh, as we stacked the chairs, Chloe just shrugged and gave a smile.

"Guys, that felt so fucking good, I have wanted to smack that bitch for ages."

Mum and Hatty laughed, as they walked up the hall towards us, Celia approached Birch and me, with a very happy Lillian on her arm. She looked at us both.

"Girls, I cannot tell you how happy I am for you both, you two have been a tonic for this village since you first came home from university. I was dammed proud tonight when I saw this village, finally pull its head out of its ass, and see the potential in both of you, and so..."

She leaned forward, and gave Birch a soft peck on the lips, Birch blinked, and she turned to me with a smile, and did the same, I caught my breath, and blinked. Celia stood back with a very happy smile.

"Oh girls, you have no idea, how wonderful that was."

I looked at Birch, she looked completely blown away, and her cheeks were pink, Lillian gave a little titter.

"Oh my, Celia, you naughty girl." She wafted herself with her hand. Celia gave a giggle.

"Mischief is my middle name Lilly dearest."

They both giggled, and walked off. I noted Celia slid her hand on Lillian's ass, and she gave a happy giggle. Birch was stood frozen, I leaned in and looked at her.

"Are you alright?" She blinked, and her eyes sparkled.

"Sweetie, I wonder what tooth paste she uses, her lips tasted..." She smacked her lips, and ran her tongue across them, I gave a grin.

"Sort of naughty and deviant?" She gave a beautiful smile, and took my hands in hers.

"We won Deads, we actually won... Oh shit, what have we done?" I smiled, and winked.

"I think we just untied the house boat?" She swallowed hard.

"Oh crap!" I gave her a pull, and she took a step forward.

"Come on it's Wednesday night, let's go home, celebrate and get naked." She frowned at me.

"Sweetie, that is Friday, it's Uni rules." I pulled her round, and lifted my arm in the air, as I looked at the happy smiling group.

"Curio rules, it's Wednesday, so we go home, get naked, and drunk, and then we have sex, lots of shameless sex." Birch jumped up and down on the spot.

"Sweetie, I want to do that." I gave a loud laugh.

"Baby, let's go get our kit off and bang like bitches, wow you are a really mint bird, you, so, you want a kebab?"

Birch squealed with delight, and with happy smiles, and mad conversation about tonight, we walked out of the Hall, and down the green. It was a cold chilly night, but it was beautiful, and I felt unbelievably happy.

The house was full, and people were celebrating, Edwina stood on the coffee table, and called for silence, she was a little tipsy to say the least, she had snuck a bottle of vodka into the meeting, and put it in her drink bottle, and started early when the count was made. She swayed with a huge smile on her face.

"Abby... Birch... Four years ago, we all had shit lives." Hatty looked up.

"Mine was fine." I giggled; Edwina looked at her.

"Bollocks!" She smiled, and blew a kiss.

"Hatty you have always been our symbol of hope, but face it, you're a genius artist, but you were a miserable bitch, who needed a shag?" Hatty gave a snort of a laugh, and lifted her glass.

"Guilty." My mum leaned in and hugged her, Edwina swayed, with a smile.

"We love you Hatty... But be honest guys, life was shit, and we were not coping at all well, and Abby was falling apart, and that is because we fucking missed our glue." Chloe frowned.

"Shut the fuck up you mad bitch, it was in the glove box." Birch sniggered, as she snuggled into me, Edwina swayed, and looked down at Chloe.

"Fuck, Chloe, I have told you a thousand times, put it back in the kitchen drawer... Hold up, where was I?" We all yelled.

"GLUE!"

She smiled, and waved her glass, and her eyes saw it, so she took a drink, and smacked her lips.

"Glue... Yes... We missed it... BIRCH! We missed you Birch, we needed you, and oh god, Abby needed you so badly. Without you, she forgot who she was, and it was horrible, she had shit hair, and no dress sense." Anthony raised his glass.

"Oh God, it was frightful, I used to have nightmares her thatch would never condition again." I started to laugh, he looked so terrified, Edwina waved her glass, and gin splashed everywhere, we all ducked.

"Birch, we needed you, oh God, we were all so lonely and afraid, and we really needed you to come home, because we loved you so much, and it hurt not seeing you. I got to see you in Uppermill, but it made me cry when I drove home, because I wanted to see you every day, and Abby did, and Debs did, and..." Anthony rolled his eyes.

"Seriously girl, abbreviate or we will be here all night, a simple 'we needed you' will suffice." We all tittered, Edwina pointed at Anthony, and swayed.

"That too... Birch, when you came back, Abby was so happy. You know, I am not sure you know this, but Abby had stopped living, she was dead inside?" She gave a hiccup, Anthony sighed.

"No that was not at all obvious to the therapist." Birch sniggered. Edwina swayed.

"I was dead inside too, I was so lonely, and so afraid, and my sister was hurting so much, and I could not save her, and I was falling apart." Tears rolled onto her cheeks, Anthony put his glass down and stood up with a sigh. He pulled his hankie out of his pocket, and handed it to Edwina.

"Darling, we all know this, we all hurt, and we all missed her, none more so than Abby. Edwina my darling sister, that is old news, and life is better now, come on, dry your eyes, Chloe is safe now." She took his hankie and wiped her eyes.

"I love you Anthony, I really do, you are like a brother to me." He smiled.

"I know darling, all of you are my sisters, now please darling, get to the point, or we will all be sober by the time you are done." She stood up straight, and burped, and then giggled.

"Birch, you brought us back from the brink, and we love you for it, and we love that you love Abby and she loves you, because we all knew she loved you. But you did not know you loved her, and she did not know she loved you, and so we all needed you to love her as much as we loved her."

"Good God Girl, get to the point darling." Anthony was looking confused. Birch and I giggled as she swayed on the table, she looked at Anthony.

"Will you shut the fuck up, I lost my place now?" Hatty laughed, Edwina suddenly looked serious, and held up a finger, none of us knew why, but it was up there waving at us.

"The point is." Oh right, that's why, good, I understand now.

"The point guys is... Fuck I forgot." We all groaned. She suddenly remembered and jerked.

"THE POINT." All of us were laughing.

"Yes... The point... Birch without you, Abby did not know who she was, and when she... nope... when you came back, she did, you see she remembered?"

"I wish you would darling, by the time this is done, I will have to cut everyone's hair." Edwina looked at him and gave a huff.

"BY REMEMBERING!" We all jumped.

"Abby learned who she truly was, and that gave her space to grow as a person, and understand, she could do so much more than she thought possible. Hell, we all did, I mean, who would of thought I would ever do anal?" My mum and Deb's gasped, Deb's looked at me with her eyes wide open, Hatty squealed with laughter.

"Did you know about that?" Birch laughed so hard; she nearly fell off the seat. Edwina lifter her finger again.

"Birch, you gave us our life back, and showed us the joy, and because of that Abby stood for council, so I want to raise a glass and make a toast." She lifted her glass and yelled.

"CHAIRS!"

"HUH?" We all looked at her, Anthony flicked his hair back.

"Seriously what's next, the fucking table?"

Edwina swayed, and gave a satisfied nod, Luke stood behind her, and yep, he knew her so well. She flopped back, and he caught her, and she hung limp as he lifted her into his arms, Chloe gave a sigh.

"What a lightweight." She stood up.

"What she was trying to say to you guys, is we love you, and we are happy for you, and we will be with you in the council all the way. Guys... Birch and Abby." She winked, as she lifted her glass, and they all toasted us.

"BIRCH AND ABBY." I smiled at them.

"Thanks guys, and we are behind you all the way too." I lifted my drink, and took a sip.

It is funny really, four years ago this would have been a huge explosive party, but apart from Edwina, who was drunker than I have ever seen her, we all wandered around downstairs, drinking and laughing as we talked, and just being happy.

Birch was really happy, but not loud, she was soft and loving and filled with joy, her arm never left my waist, as we talked, and she leaned on my shoulder, and by midnight, as we hugged mum and Hatty, she was quiet and thoughtful.

She took my hand and led me upstairs, and we slipped into bed, and cuddled up, it was nice. I lay back looking at her, with her white, black patched hair, and I lifted my hand and stroked it back. Her eyes sparkled bright green with life and happiness, I spoke softly, more in a reflective tone, as I voice my thoughts.

"As funny as her speech was, Edwina was right, I was lost and in pain, and had no idea who I was anymore, you saved my life Birch, you gave me back to me. I needed you so badly, without you, I am not sure I would have made it this far." She smiled.

"Sweetie, I was always going to come back, how could I not, you were my Lillian, I needed you too?" She leaned over and softly kissed me, and I slid my arms around her, and pulled her tightly to me. The kiss was long, soft, and caring, and I drowned in her love.

The door banged open, and we jumped, Deli stood in the doorway holding her phone, Birch rolled back off me.

"Sweetie, is everything alright?" Deli looked at her phone.

"Sophia is at the hospital." I sat up.

"Is she alright, what happened to her?" She nodded, as she stared at her phone.

"Sorry, it's not Sophia, who is hurt, it's Nigel, Prim threw him down the stairs, he has a broken leg and is unconscious." I gave a gasp and turned to Birch.

"Oh God, she is really pissed off." Birch gave a nod, and slipped out of bed.

"Is Sophia with him?" Deli looked at her.

"She is in the waiting room with Madge and Milton, they are looking him over and fixing his leg, apparently it is a really bad break." Birch nodded, and lifted her jeans.

"We should be there." I felt panicked and shocked, and drunk.

"Birch, we have drunk too much, we cannot drive." Deli shook her head.

"I am not, I only had one glass of wine, it's my time of the month, I feel really bloated."

I slipped out of bed and grabbed my pants, and threw on my Curio sweatshirt. Ten minutes later we had run down the stairs, flew round the kitchen, and made quick coffees in our travel mugs, and I had texted mum, to let her know. We jumped in Petal, and Deli sped to the hospital.

We ran into the waiting room, and Madge sat looking worried holding her hankie to her mouth, she had been crying. Milton looked tense and worried, it reminded me very much of the night I sat waiting for Birch, he had come to my aide that night, and I felt it was right I came to his. I looked down at them both, as I stood in front of them. Molly, with baby Rupert, and Sophia sat at their side.

"Madge are you alright, we came as soon as we heard?" Tears welled in her eyes, and I crouched down.

"Abigail, he is my son, and she has really hurt him, we do not know how bad yet." Milton squeezed her hand, and she gave a sniffle and wiped her eyes. Birch looked around, and slipped her ID badge out of her pocket.

"I will find out how he is." She walked over to the reception desk.

"Hi Sweetie, I am Doctor Jemima Dixon, I believe you have a client of mine here, a Nigel Wallace, is it alright to go through, and speak to the attending?" She tapped on her computer.

"He is in bay nine, and attended by Doctor Smithers." Birch smiled.

"Thank you." The door buzzed, and Birch walked through, I crouched and looked at Milton he looked very worried.

"How did this happen?" He gave a long sigh.

"I am sure you understand the situation Abigail, how have any of his injuries happened?" Sophia leaned forward.

"He called me yar, I am not allowed to drive anymore because I crashed a lot, so Molly gave me a lift yar." I nodded and looked at Molly, she looked really nervous.

"Tell me what happened." Molly nodded, little Rupert was asleep, Deli leaned in, and lifted him out of her arms.

"Have a break Mol, I will look after this little chap for a bit."

Molly got up, and nodded to me to follow her, she walked over to the coffee machine, and put some money in.

"Abigail, I really wish I had listened to Fidelity and Sophia, I feel awful." I understood that.

"Have you spoken to Prim?" She nodded.

"I rang her right after the ambulance, Sophia went to get his parents. Abigail, I never believed you were having an affair with him, I remember school, it was a local joke how he kept asking, and you kept saying no."

"But?" She lifted her coffee out of the machine.

"I should have known it would be Sophia, she has been mad about him for years. Prim was convinced it was you, she found out he was going to your mums, so after she lost, she went insane, and she accused him of sleeping with you at your mums' house. He denied it, but he told her he was in love with Sophia, and had been seeing her." I gave a sigh.

"Shit!" She nodded.

"She ran upstairs screaming, and started smashing everything up, apparently, she has smashed all the furniture in the bedroom. He texted Sophia, and she freaked out, and came to me, she wanted Fidelity, so I told her to text her, and tell her what was happening, and then she insisted I drove her to Nigel." I nodded.

"Okay, but that does not explain how he got hurt?" She shook her head.

"Sorry, I am so scared Abigail. Prim told me, he came upstairs as she was coming out of the room, and they had an argument on the landing. She told him she wanted a divorce, and he agreed, he told her he hated her, and she told him she would take his house and all his money for shaming her. Nigel told her he did not own the house, his father did, and she completely lost it, and punched him. He went backwards down the stairs, and she grabbed her bags, kicked him as she passed, and left in his car." I gave a sigh.

"Poor bastard, God, has he not suffered enough?" She looked back at his parents.

"Abigail, she did not even take the baby, I mean, who does that?" I looked at her, and shook my head.

"Apparently, Prim does." She looked wretched.

"I have been cruel to you, and I regret that." I lifted my coffee, and thought to myself, oh how the mighty fall.

"That was then Molly, this is now. Nigel will need help; we all have to be there for him." She nodded.

As I talked to Molly, Deli sat opposite Madge, with little baby Rupert, Madge gave a smile.

"You have a natural way with children." Deli looked up and smiled.

"I love kids, I take little Jenny out at times to help Deb's, it is why I trained in child care, I want loads of my own one day." Milton looked at Marjorie, it appeared they both had the same thought, Milton looked at her.

"You know Fidelity, Nigel will need help, he has said in the past he would raise his son alone if he had to, and to be quite frank, I am not sure a young child should be around someone as volatile as Primula. If you have some time, we would appreciate the help... We would pay you the full rate of course?" Deli smiled.

"I would love that, and I could sure use the extra money." He gave a smile, well, his teeth moved, so she assumed he did.

"Call me tomorrow, and we will talk." She gave a huge smile.

"I do have all my qualifications and references, for you to inspect, I am fully licensed." He appeared very pleased.

"Yes, yes, you must come for coffee, and bring them, we will talk."

Birch came back through the doors and smiled at me, she walked over to Madge, and Molly and I followed. Birch crouched down, and took Madge's hand in hers.

"Okay, I have seen him, he is conscious, but in a lot of pain, he has really damaged his leg. I spoke with his doctor, and he has three breaks, one on the left Femur, and one to the left Tibia, and one to his left Fibula, and he is pretty bruised all over. They are arranging for surgery; he will have his leg set, and a couple of temporary plates fitted to help him heal and strengthen the leg faster. He is going to struggle for a while."

"I will help him yar, I can be a nurse, I have a costume, I put it on Insta, and got eight thousand likes, yar." Birch smiled.

"Sophia will help, and so will all of us. Madge, he is going to be fine, a little inconvenienced, but he will recover." She started to cry, and Birch squeezed her hand.

"His doctor will be out soon to take you to him." Madge nodded.

"I am so grateful, I am glad you came, I was worried sick." Birch patted her hand. I smiled as I watched, Birch has such kindness, she even melted the heart of Madge.

"Relax Madge, and find some of that warrior spirit, Nigel will need it." She gave a nod and sniffled.

"Yes... My son needs me." Birch winked.

"That's the spirit." Birch stood up and walked over to me, she slipped her arm round me.

"It is going to be hard on them Deads, but with help from the village, they will be fine." She turned and kissed my cheek. Molly stared at us.

"You two are really in love, I mean, this is not a phase, it is real deep love isn't it?" Birch gave a smile.

"Mol Sweetie, we are the real deal, Deads is my Super Sweetie, everyone knows that." Molly frowned, for her, this was confusing, she lowered her voice and leaned into me.

"But how does that work, actually?" I gave a giggle.

"Ask her, she is the doctor."

I walked off towards Madge and Milton, Birch did a double take, and looked at Molly. She smiled.

"Hi Sweetie... Mol, it is like this..."

I sniggered, as I watched Birch talk quietly to Molly, she went purple and jumped, yep, that was Birch, she did not hold back, I heard Molly suddenly blurt out.

"Really... Oh my God, I never knew?" She was bright purple, but weirdly interested.

Chapter 36

The Curious Thing.

Nigel came out of hospital a week later, having had plates put in his leg. He was plastered up, and on crutches, which was not easy for him. Sophia never left his side, and Deli attended an interview, and was given the job, of taking care of Baby Rupert.

Once home, Nigel rang Prim, and told her he had spoken to the family solicitor, and he was applying for custody, he offered her a cash sum, she took it, and surrendered her rights to full time child care, but had visitation rights. He did not press charges for assault, personally, I think he should have.

The nice thing in all of this, was Nigel was calmer, and more relaxed. Sophia was practically living with him. With the aid of Luke, and some of the G5 guys, we cleared up the bedroom, Prim had literally smashed up everything, and I mean, crushed to splinters. Sophia took Nigel shopping, and handled his interior design, I cannot deny, she did a great job, and had a really good eye for décor.

It is strange, they really worked as a couple, he clearly was very into her, and she him. Sophia even taught him how to cook, there were a few occasions as we helped out, that she stood at his side, and showed him, exactly as Deli had showed her, it was really sweet.

Work on the Curio Centre was finally completed, well phase one was, there was still a lot to do. We had bought a run down, old stately home just outside Tethering Dibley, it had been converted to a care home for the elderly, but had become so run down, the private company that owned it, had put it on the market.

Bradley negotiated the deal, and got it at a really great price, and then moved in a double crew to completely rebuild, repair, and modernise it at a discount. I had seen it when we all first looked at it, and honestly, it was a shit hole, but Birch could see it's potential, and we knew from experience, if she could see it, we could do it.

It had been planned in stages. Stage one was the home itself, stage two, would be the new building put up behind it, and it would be a modern, top rated facility. The grounds looked rough, and the old gardener, Walter, was a little too long in the tooth to really stay on top of things. We kept him on, because he had first hand knowledge of the property. When we found out Bev had been on a ground keeping course, we gave her the job as his assistant, and she promised, she would keep up her online courses and do horticulture as well.

Bev took the flat above the workshop, that housed all the mowing equipment, and moved down from Manchester straight away, and decorated it, it was bright, and garish, but she loved it. Bless her, she is so lovely. Don't tell anyone, but we have bought her a motor bike for Christmas, hers is still in bits in her mum's garage.

Tethering Dibley, is only forty minutes away by car, and so Bev was a lot closer, which thrilled Birch, as she would see her more. Birch would visit the centre twice a week, once it opened. Aden would also be a regular visitor, as he was their IT guy.

With our bags packed, we all made the journey for a couple of nights stay to help with the preparations for opening, even Roni and Will came down to join us, which was wonderful, because now we were on the council, there was no hope of Christmas in Uppermill, as we had to run all the events.

The facility had forty rooms for patients, and staff quarters for ten resident therapists, as well as six double rooms for visiting practitioners, so we had a place to crash whilst we helped prepare. It did not take Chloe long to find a new young therapist, and drag him into her room, for pictures and fun. No doubt we will see it with a face and a hat on Insta at some point, I have started following Ivor myself.

We decided to rename the place to 'Curio Clinic for Mental Wellbeing,' and we made sure everything was spic and span, and looking its best as we prepared to open. I was really impressed, it was clean, warm, and very homely, Bradley had done an amazing job of keeping the character of the place. From outside it looked beautiful, but inside, it was modern and high tech.

The first choice for practice manager decided to go to Africa, shortly before opening, and in a panic, Izzy stepped in and called one of her friends, and after a brief interview, where she had amazing credentials, Juliet Hopkins was given the post, and she moved from Manchester, to the clinic, much to our relief.

November 29th arrived, and we all got ready for the big opening and the press, we had a long table set up in the dining room, and put up a backdrop of Curio Live logos. The placed was filled with TV cameras, and journalists, yeah, I know, I hate them. We all dressed to impress, I wore my suit from the gallery, with the white lace blouse. With the new management team, we all sat behind the table, with microphones in front of us, as Anita conducted proceedings.

There was an army of press, and TV, and as always, Amy from River TV was there, she had filmed a behind the scenes exclusive with us, and Aden was right in front with his equipment, as he live streamed the event to the Curio website, with the aid of Luke.

Anita stood in the centre, I was on one side, and Birch, her other side, as she began, she talked of the centre, and all of its facilities, and how it was a modern high tech unit, with some of the best therapists around. She finally came down to questions.

"Ladies and gentlemen of the media, we are delighted to be finally here, it has taken a huge amount of effort, but as you can see, it was all worth the work. Please address your questions to each panel member, and name them, and also name yourself, and I do not think I need to remind you, please keep all your questions related to this clinic." We sat answering endless questions, she pointed for the fortieth time. The journalist smiled and sat forward.

"Jessie Everet, US Daily. Abigail, if I may, you really were the start of all of this, how does it feel to be sat here, in this modern medical practice, that will help so many? And if I may, will you guys be considering a practice in the US at some point?" I smiled; she popped up everywhere I went.

"Hi Jessie, it is lovely seeing you again. To be honest, we have worked so hard for so long, no one will know the hours and late nights, that have gone into the Curio cause, since we began it four years ago. I will not deny, there were a few times I thought we would never get here, but today, I am so happy I want to explode. I mean, look at this place, it is amazing. As for the states, I would love to come over and raise awareness, we watch suicide numbers all over the globe. It is on our to do list, but I will warn you, it is a very long list." She smiled.

"You will always be welcome state side." Anita pointed.

"Ben Shepperton, Oxendale Mail. Doctor Dixon. This has been quite a year for all the Curio's, what with marriage, the art show, the amazing carnival, and now congratulations I believe are in order, as you and Miss Watson have become Chairs for your local community Parish Council, and now you have this. Could you tell me, what toll has this taken on both of you, especially Miss Watson?" Birch leaned forward and glanced at me, she smiled, and turned to Ben.

"It is Dixon, Mrs Dixon, Watson is now her pen name, please get it right Ben, in your last four articles you have not." The other journalists laughed.

"Ben, despite rumours and untruths, we live a very healthy life, we take supplements, work out and we eat healthy, and we even have a drink at times. All of us wanted to do the things we have, we believed in each project we did, was it hard work and do we get tired? Yes, of course we do, but we also have a little private get away, where we relax and recuperate. We also, as you can see are a group, and we all share the load. Each of us plays to our strengths, and so we all just fall into our natural places, when we choose to do something. The Curio's are not just good mates, we are a close nit family, and that applies to everything we do as a unit. I would also like to add, we have highly trained expert staff behind us, such as Juliet, who will manage this operation for the charity."

Anita pointed. "Deborah Mace, Mail Today. Miss Dickinson, you spend a lot of time at events with the group, are you a Curio too, and if I may. Fidelity, you are a new Curio, what is it like, were you intimidated when you became one?" Anita looked a little surprised, she smiled.

"I am the press girl, I suppose I am like extended family, but no, a true Curio, is part of the household, and I live in my own home." Deli leaned forward.

"I have known Abby, Deb's and Chloe since school, although

they became really famous, so moving into the house took some adjustment, but that was mainly because it is so big, and beautiful, and I was used to a small one bedroom flat. These guys were really friendly and down to earth, and actually, being around them is the easiest thing to do, you simply be yourself, and they accept you. I love my life as a Curio, and really have been shown a lot of love on the site, I am a very blessed person, and there is not a day goes by, I do not think that." I leaned in.

"She was terrified really." She giggled, and the press laughed.

"Look, we were the ones that invited her to join us, we knew she would fit, and understand our lifestyle around the site and the work we do, and to be honest, I feel, she has fitted in really well, and found her place. The dance routine at Curio Carnival was all her idea, and her work, and it was a brilliant addition to a great night." I looked right at the live stream camera.

"And to all you Curio's out there, who go on the website, we all want to thank you for embracing Deli with such warmth and love, trust me guys, it made her week." I smiled, as the other Curio's all nodded in agreement, and Deli blushed.

Anita pointed. "Devon Atkins. Daily Times. To all of you. This is a grade two listed building, and you have certainly raised a lot of capital, with the Curio Live thing, the carnival and art show, how much is your cut?" Anita moved, and Birch grabbed her arm.

"It is alright Anita, as Peter Ford's old writing colleague I expected this. Mr Atkins, I love your trash pieces, they make me laugh, they are so ridiculous they are funnier than the comic strips at the back." The journalists laughed.

"What is my cut you ask, well let me tell you, let's see now. The gallery that would be one hundred and twenty five thousand, the carnival, five hundred thousand, and Curio live, all in all, about one hundred and fifty thousand invested by me personally, as to my cut, it was zero. Print that in your rag of a paper, and finally for once, you will print the truth." Birch sat back, he frowned at her.

"Are you honestly going to sit there, and tell me you have not had one penny?" I shrugged.

"I got a free sweatshirt; I was stoked about that." Chloe sniggered.

"I wanted Curio g strings, but they wouldn't make them, so I got a sweat shirt too." The journalists laughed; Edwina leaned forward.

"Mr Atkins, try doing some homework, instead of making things up. Curio Life is hosted for free by Sweeties Retreat, and all the accounts are administered by EFG, the Ethical Finance Group. Now I can understand why you would not want to look it up, because it does have the word 'Ethical' in the title, but go on, be daring, you might learn what journalism is really about." We all laughed, as did the other journalists, we sat back and he shut up.

Anita smirked, and pointed. "Amy Walker, River Cable TV. Guys, yesterday we did a filmed walk through of this facility, and it is outstanding. Having followed you all the way through this project, guys come on, for the hundredth time, will all of you sit down at home with me, and do a full length feature of life with the Curio's, have you any idea how much people want to see that?" Deb's looked at me.

"Hell, I would watch that." Chloe smirked.

"You would watch a plant grow if they filmed it." We all sniggered like school girls, Birch looked at Amy.

"Wow you know, for a tiny woman, you are persuasive, and never give up. Amy, we have been a tad busy, what with books, live appearances, the carnival, and just being us, it is exhausting. Come and spend a day with us at Christmas, and we will let you see, just stay out of our bedrooms, that is where we hide all our deviant and lustful items, I would hate for Devon to see them." Amy gave a laugh.

"This is a live stream Birch; I will hold you to it." I leaned forward.

"Birch what the hell have you done; I will have to dust now?" Everyone giggled, and Anita stood up.

"Okay ladies and gentlemen, we will be moving outside shortly, to take a look at the building, and you will be free to ask more questions out there. Thank you for your time."

We all got up, and headed to the break room, to grab quick coffees, before trouping outside, where we posed for endless pictures. We made sure Juliet got dragged up front, and pushed in front of all the cameras, after all, she would be running the place, and so needed to be ready for what was to come.

For the rest of the afternoon, we did interviews, together and apart. I have no idea how many TV cameras I spoke to, it all became a blur. We all ate together with the staff in the cafeteria, and as she ate, Roni looked at Birch.

"You got NHS referral status, that was a smart move Jemi." She looked across the table.

"This may be a charity, but it is also a fully registered private mental health facility attached to Sweetie's Retreat. I figured why not, this place has overheads, and the NHS will pay us for taking their referrals. It is a none profit organisation, but I am not going to refuse cash." Roni sat back and wiped her mouth on her napkin, she lifted her glass and took a sip.

"Jemi, you don't have to be defensive, I am not knocking this place, I am highly impressed." I looked at her.

"You are?" She nodded.

"Abby, I have sat back and watched you two, but I am not looking to fault you, actually, you would be surprised to know, I am learning from you." Birch looked really surprised, and I will not deny, I was too. Birch stared at her mum.

"What are you up to?" Roni gave a giggle.

"For the love of God Jemi, I am up to nothing, well actually…" Birch sat back in her seat.

"I bloody knew it!" Roni chuckled.

"Jemi… Darling… All I was going to say is, I would appreciate you looking over my practice, and see if you can find anything that could be improved or modernised, that is all." Birch stared at her.

"You want me to do that, but Mum, you are the best there is, I doubt I will find anything?" She gave a soft smile.

"Jemi, I am set in my ways, and you have a whole new more modern approach to things, be a consultant, take a look, and give me a report. Sweetheart, if I can improve things, I will, that is all I am simply saying." Birch gave a nod.

"Wow, you want me home that bad?" She shook her head.

"You are such a suspicious little beastie." She nodded.

"With you, yep… Mum we were going to ask if we could come up for new year, we miss you both, and want some quality time, but with the council, we will be busy all Christmas." She gave a big smile.

"I would love you two to come and stay, oh that would make New Year such fun." Chloe leaned over the table.

"Can I come to; I will bring my pads?" Roni gave a chuckle.

"All of you are always welcome, we have two spare rooms, and the attic room, with a sofa bed." Chloe smiled.

"Hey guys, we are getting pissed with Roni at new year, everyone is invited." She turned to Roni.

"I have Bess, so I don't need a room." Roni frowned.

"Chloe, it gets really cold up north at new year, you may freeze to death." She shook her head and gave a big smile.

"I got a Baz heater; he is toasty, and does dirty things with me." Roni gave a howling laugh.

"You should study her Birch, there is probably another book in it." Edwina sniggered.

"A guide to slutology, ha!" We all started to laugh, and suddenly Birch stopped, and looked at her mum.

"What do you mean, another book?" Roni gave a knowing smile.

"Seriously, did you and Anita honestly think you could just slip a book through unnoticed, come on Jemi, I am not that stupid? I have had the printing staff on alert for anything with your name on for two years." Birch looked crushed, as I sniggered.

"Jemi sweetheart, I only read the draft, when do I get to hold it? I know it was printed, and by the way, it's brilliant, and a fantastic first book."

It was so lovely to watch Birch, she smiled, and small tears appeared in her eyes.

"Honestly, you would not lie to me would you, if it is bad, please say so?" Will looked down the table.

"Jemi, I loved it." Tears ran down her cheeks, and she smiled.

"Thanks Dad, thanks Mum, honestly, hearing you two say that, is a dream come true for me, I would hate to let you down." Roni smiled at her.

"Jemi, you haven't, and you never could, we love you so much." I felt a lump in my throat, as she smiled such a beautiful smile.

Once the meal was over with, we had a big meeting with all the staff, where Birch took control as the senior consultant for the whole centre. We all talked informally about what we wanted for the centre, and what our vision was, and the staff asked lots of questions. Edwina had built a website for the centre which had a private forum attached for staff to talk to all of us, she briefed them on that.

Once the meeting was over, Birch, Anita, Deb's and myself, jumped into Petal, and Roni and Will followed, as we made the forty minute drive home again. We had to be back, as tomorrow was the last day of November, and we took over the Council on the first of December, and we had all the Christmas events to run, it was going to be busy, and Anthony was alone, and he needed to be supported.

Chloe, Edwina and Deli, stayed behind, as the very first patients would be arriving the following day, and Chloe especially wanted to meet them all at the door, and welcome them in person, she is so lovely.

At home, Anita unloaded her car of boxes of books, and Birch handed her mum and dad signed copies, and honestly, they were delighted. The book was officially being released on December third, her grandmother's birthday.

Deb's had one hundred ordered for the shop. Roni and Will had the guest room, and after a lot of talk and a few drinks, I took our bags up, and flopped on the bed, it had felt like the busiest year of my life, but it also felt amazing.

I lay back on my bed, and stared at the ceiling as my mind wandered. A good few years ago, my mum told me, that life has many bumps in the road, and Birch and myself, have spent a few years encountering them. This year, our road had been a little less bumpy, and honestly, I was glad of it.

It is strange how just one person can have a huge impact on your life, take Marjorie for instance. Marjorie ruled this village for seventeen years as a council chair, she intimidated everyone to such a degree, it forced everyone to hide who they really were. I have never forgotten that speech of Roni's from the talk at the fete, when she told everyone, 'Grownup's bully too.' It had a profound effect on me, and I think it was from that moment onwards, I truly began to understand where I lived.

Coming home and being shamed, and hiding away, I was as bad as all the other villagers, and it gave Marjorie even more power. Birch was different, with her bright smile and her go with the flow ways, she changed not only my life, but everybody else's, and strangely enough, even the life of Marjorie. We have faced so much together, it is hard to believe we made it through, and yet we did. Because of Birch, I managed to make a stand against my father, something I would never have done alone, and because of it, I finally got him to see me as worthy.

It is funny what things you remember when you think back, painting Petal, and how mum and Hatty took over, because we had become such a fun group, they even saw the joy and love between us and they wanted to join in. I laugh often, as I think of Ellen, Roni, Hatty and mum schooling us at our hen party, and teaching us true rebellion, as they escaped the health farm, and came back with chips and booze.

All those years ago Deb's bless her, arrived on my first day back from Uni, to let me know she was proud of me for being shameful in the eyes of the village, and as Bradley dropped us off, he leaned over his seat and told me, 'Stay your course.' It was such good advice. I do not think I realised at the time how good, but it was right, no matter what they threw at us all, we stuck to our guns, and eventually we won over.

I could easily look back at my last ten years and complain, it has been rough at times, and yet look at my life today. I have the wonder of Edwina, a calm mind to guide me at times, or Anthony and his reassuring hugs, he has changed so much from that young boy who twitched and jerked. I love and adore Chloe, who would ever have seen that coming, she is such a beautiful person, I mean, yes, she is a sexually deviant pervert, who swears like a sailor, but I love her so much, and she too has changed.

She does not plaster her face with makeup, or have long nails and weird eyebrows, she is actually quite plain and ordinary these days, but she is so pretty, and so amazingly talented. Deb's is my oldest friend, and I cannot deny, I have no idea what I would have done without her in my life. She has grown up so much, and she is so different from that shy terrified girl I protected at school. Wow, she is a mum, and a great wife, and she is even seen now as a major celebrity, it just goes to show, how much a person can change, and also how much impact they can have on you.

One person can change your life, and each of the Curio's has, all of them have added a little bit to the puzzle that was broken me, and through them I found all the pieces to put me back together and make me whole again. Of course, driving all that from behind the scenes, was my Birch, my wonderful crazy, massively clever, adorable and fun room mate from Uni. How different my life would have been, if I had not been allotted to share with her. Birch has been my biggest influence, and yet she never showed me the way, she simply sat back and told me, 'Be You', and whatever that was she accepted, and it changed me forever.

Back in June this year we were married; I know crazy right? If you had asked me the day I sat on the train, as I travelled with my trunk to Uni, where will you be in ten years, I would never have seen this. My life is nothing like I planned, every concept I had as a young seventeen year old, planning my future was wrong, and maybe that was because I had not really sat and thought about who I was deep down inside.

They say sexuality is fluid, but to be honest, I think every aspect of people is. We need to understand that we will change as people as we grow and our tastes will change. Maybe being so rigid in our thinking is the problem, and I have begun to wonder if that is what has plagued this village.

Marjorie had a vision for who she would be, and it was unbreakable, and in a strange way, I think that it became a cage, and maybe two transients needed to walk into her life. Maybe Primula needed to enter the frame, so that even she could be broken free from her strict iron clad cage, because ultimately at the end of the day, it took two transient whores, to open her eyes and make her see the real value of those around her.

The problem with people is that they fear change, and yet as I discovered, life only begins fully, once you step outside your comfort zone, and for me that started with Birch. I love her so deeply, she truly has been my rock, she has always told me, she did not like the road of life, she always saw it more as a river, and she had dropped the sail and was drifting along, going with the flow. Well now, I am in her boat with her, yeah, I know, I got the crazy captain of the vessel, but you know what?

Life is a curious thing. There is always going to be wind and rain, and at times there will be snow, and the river may freeze. But at some point, the ice will melt, the rain will dry, and the water will warm up as the sun shines.

When that happens, I will tie up the boat, take her hand, and we will swim naked in the warm river, and bask on the bank in the sunlight, and I cannot deny, I absolutely love it. You should try it for a while.

It's a Curio thing, and you know what? You will get used to it.

Be You… Appreciate each other.

"Whoa… hold on… Birch, I just realised something… Oh my God, how the hell have you got away with calling my dad Ed, for ten years?"

"Sweetie, he loves me really, I mean, I do have great tits and a sexy ass."

"Well yeah, I get that, but he hates anyone shortening names."

"Sweetie, I told you, I know people."

"Yeah… I know… It's a Birch thing, and I will get used to it."

"See?" Sighs.

More Author's
From
Violet Circle Publishing

Mike Beale. (Children's Book)
Crumble's Adventures.
ISBN: 978-1-910299-06-7
Digital ISBN: 978-1-910299-08-1

Colin Smith (Play)
Heaven knows I'm Miserable Now
ISBN: 978-1-910299-16-6
Digital ISBN: 978-1-910299-23-4

Ted Morgan. (Poetry and verse)
Wordsmith's Wanderings.
ISBN: 978-1-910299-04-3
Digital ISBN: 978-1-910299-09-8
Peregrinations of the Wordsmith
ISBN: 978-1-910299-18-0
Digital ISBN: 978-1-910299-21-0
Silhouette Soldiers
ISBN: 978-1-910299-19-7
Digital ISBN: 978-1-910299-22-7
A Menu of Memories
Digital ISBN: 978-1-910299-32-6
Digital ISBN: 978-1-910299-33-3

Robin John Morgan. (Fiction/Fantasy/Slice of Life)
Heirs to the Kingdom.
Book One, The Bowman of Loxley.
ISBN: 978-1-910299-00-5
Digital ISBN: 978-1-910299-10-4
Book Two, The Lost Sword of Carnac.
ISBN: 978-1-910299-01-2
Digital ISBN: 978-1-910299-11-1

Book Three, The Darkness of Dunnottar.
ISBN: 978-1-910299-02-9
Digital ISBN: 978-1-910299-12-8
Book Four, Queen of the Violet Isle.
ISBN: 978-1-910299-03-6
Digital ISBN: 978-1-910299-13-5
Book Five, Crystals of the Mirrored Waters.
ISBN: 978-1-910299-05-0
Digital ISBN: 978-1-910299-14-2
Book Six, Last Arrow of the Woodland Realm.
ISBN: 978-1-910299-07-4
Digital ISBN: 978-1-910299-15-9
Book Seven, Bridge Of Sequana.
ISBN: 978-1-910299-17-3
Digital ISBN: 978-1-910299-20-3
Book Eight, The Circle of Darkness.
ISBN: 978-1-910299-26-5
Digital ISBN: 978-1-910299-29-6

The Curio Chronicles.
Part One, Abigail's Summer.
ISBN: 978-1-910299-27-2
Digital ISBN: 978-1-910299-28-9
Part Two, Curio's Summer.
ISBN: 978-1-910299-34-0
Digital ISBN: 978-1-910299-35-7
Part Three, Curio's Christmas.
ISBN: 978-1-910299-38-8
Digital ISBN: 978-1-910299-39-5
Part Four, Abigail's Wedding
ISBN: 978-1-910299-42-5
Digital ISBN: 978-1-910299-43-2
Part Four, Curio's Carnival
ISBN: 978-1-910299-46-3
Digital ISBN: 978-1-910299-47-0

Of The Ravens of Berengar Trilogy.
Rise Of The Raven
ISBN: 978-1-910299-30-2
Digital ISBN: 978-1-910299-31-9
The Countess Of Darkness
ISBN: 978-1-910299-40-1
Digital ISBN: 978-1-910299-41-8

Violet Stone
ISBN: 978-1-910299-44-9
Digital ISBN: 978-1-910299-45-6

Other Works.

Han's Cottage.
ISBN: 978-1-910299-36-4
Digital ISBN: 978-1-910299-37-1

Find out more about our authors and their books at
www.violetcirclepublishing.co.uk